THE DISGRACE TRILOGY

DISGRACE

DISGRACEFUL

GRACE

DEE PALMER

THE DISGRACE TRILOGY

DISGRACE

DISGRACEFUL

GRACE

DEE PALMER

Warning: ADULT CONTENT 18* This story is on the filthy side of smut and isn't suitable for those who don't enjoy graphic descriptions that are erotic in nature, but for those that do, enjoy ;)

For free stories, sign up to my Newsletter on the contact page at deepalmerwriter.com
(Promise No Spam)
or click here

FREE BOOK
First In the Choices Trilogy (But no cliffy ..So can be read as a standalone:))

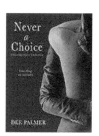

Never
a
Choice

DEE PALMER

Table of Contents

DISGRACE

A Choices Novel

DEE PALMER

DEDICATION

The Chosen Ones
"Find your Tribe and Love them Hard"
I Love my Tribe

PROLOGUE

Sixteen Months Ago

Sam

"You still there, Sam?" I can hear the concern in his voice, but it fades into the mix of nerves and sickness threatening to escape my mouth. Saliva pools at the back of my throat and I swallow, the slight metallic taste an indication that I have scraped my teeth against some soft tissue. My jaw is clenched so tight I didn't even feel the bite. "Sam!" His tone is urgent almost panicked.

"I'm here…sorry. This is harder than I thought it would be that's all." I grip the phone a little tighter, angry that my hand is actually trembling.

"Look, wait there. I can be there in an hour. You shouldn't do this on your own. I told you this but you never bloody listen." He lets out an angry breath, which makes me smile. All my life I never had someone care about me the way he does. I am so very grateful. I tell him often enough, but it's never enough. He saved me.

"No…no don't come, Leon. I will be fine. It's just a house." I swallow that pooling water again. So loud this time I can hear him let out a sigh filled with only a fraction of the sadness welling in me.

"Yeah…just a house. Like Manson was just a guy. Sam you don't have to do this in person. The solicitor can deal with this shit. Come home. You can beat the crap out of me and make us both feel better."

I bark out a dirty laugh. I love that he can turn my mood on a dime. "God, I love you." I feel some tension leave my frame when I push out a fortifying breath. "I will be fine. I am made of much stronger stuff…now." I add before he reminds me of the empty, broken girl he slowly helped transform ten years ago.

"Call me when you're done…and the offer still stands." His silence is filled with hope.

"Leon, I found you an excellent replacement and you need to start using her." My tone is resolute if a little sharp.

"I know…I know…It's just when you've had the best—" His flattery will get him nowhere…absolutely nowhere.

"You're my best friend, Leon." I add softly.

"Which might be an issue if we were fucking." He is pushing me and I feel all that tension back.

"Leon!" I snap. "Enough…You can be such an arsehole!"

"But you love me?" I can almost see the devilish grin creeping across his dark features. We share similar colouring, rich coffee skin, deep brown eyes and impossibly dark brown hair that falls just shy of jet black.

"I do." My tone is clipped.

"Did it work?" He asks after a short silence and before I get to ask what, he adds. "Are you feeling all angry and distracted now?" I sniff out a laugh and shake my head though he can't see that part.

"Yes, Leon…Thank you." A tentative smile tips the corners of my lips, sleek and shiny with my trademark red.

"My work here is done. Now go and sort the house of horrors…and come home. Where you belong." He hangs up and I chuckle. He never says goodbye.

I straighten my shoulders and hold on to the false bravado trickling through my veins hoping it's enough to get me through this next hour.

It's a beautiful cottage. The perfect picture of an idyllic Home County village dwelling. Honey coloured, washed out stone, four tiny windows under a mottled, red slate roof and an old oak front door with polished wrought iron fixings that wouldn't look out of place on a church. The Old Rectory, my family home. The garden is bare now, cut back and pruned to within an inch of its life. My mother would spend hours—days—tending the flower beds. She craved the attention it brought from passersby, strangers, people who meant nothing.

The bones of the wisteria cling to the front of the house like some distorted exoskeleton, the branches so thick the blooms would block the sunlight from the windows in the spring. I slide my key into the lock. She didn't change the lock when I left. Why would she? There was no need, I was the one who left, and I promised I'd never return as long as she lived.

The door opens to a shrill discord of creaking hinges loudly objecting my presence. I push the heavy door wide with a firm shove. The stale, dry air hits me with an aroma brimming with memories. I puff the air from my nose. I have no desire to reminisce; memory lane is for masochists. There is only one room I want to see.

It's been so long, but I need to remember so I don't let it happen again. I walk through the dim hall, lit only by the soft winter sun spilling in from the open front door. Everything is neat and tidy with a fine layer of dust that only now dares to settle. Now she's dead that is. I drag my finger along the welcome table, swirling patterns, irregular and petty. Her coat is still hanging from the gnarled hatstand, and I wipe the dust from my finger on the thick woollen sleeve.

The stairs exhale a painful groan with each step, and I find myself hovering on the final tread. This was the only step that made a sound when I'd lived here. This was my warning. I place my foot down and feel my tummy tighten as the unique sound makes my foot start to shake. I stamp it down heavily. The sound is different this time, and I stamp my other foot, too. *No need to fucking tremble, Sam. She's not here,* I reprimand myself. I stride the remainder of the corridor and don't hesitate when I reach for the door handle of my old room. I step inside.

I'm surprised. I don't know why I'm surprised, but I thought she would've changed it. The small metal framed bed with the pink floral covers and a rickety bedside table with no lamp. The walls are plain light grey, as are the curtains cinched back with a thick rope tie. Above the bed and on each wall hang several embroidered pictures. A different prayer for each of my sins. My lips thin with bittersweet amusement. The walls would collapse under the weight of prayers needed for my sins now. I look to my feet just inside the threshold.

"There...something that has changed. That is new," I say to myself. The point on my toe all shiny, in patent black knee high lace up boot, flips the corner of the new rug which is awkwardly placed at an angle by the door. "And that is why." My voice catches, my eyes clamp tight and my hand flies to my mouth, an attempt to stop the sob that's being wrenched from my chest. *Don't you fucking cry one more fucking tear in this house.* I dig my long acrylic nails into my palms with such force the pain is exactly enough to stop my tears. I turn and walk to the window. I need some air. I lift the window catch from its cradle and push the small lead-encased pane, but the window is jammed. I roll my eyes. It's not jammed; it's nailed shut.

I let out a sharp laugh that bounces uncomfortably around the still silent room. It's funny how, with time, your memory tries to trick you. You rewrite your own history. Some memories are exaggerated to make them a little more intense or a little more amusing. Others are suppressed, and some you think couldn't possibly be as bad as you remember, so you do yourself a favour and forget. I shouldn't have come.

"Hello!" A gruff voice calls from inside the house. "Hello, Ms Cartwright! Is that you?"

"Upstairs," I reply and take a steadying breath. I hear Mr Brown, the solicitor in charge of my mother's estate, climb the stairs and I watch him stumble and trip into the room. Flustered he tries to compose himself. He kicks the badly placed rug exposing more of the bare floorboards.

"Who places a rug there, like that?" He pulls the cuffs of his jacket one at a time to straighten the bunched up material. "Oh…Look at that." He muses and leans to take a closer look. "I can see why now but still…it seems a stupid place." He mutters, "What do you suppose that stain is?" He tips his head at the mark but my eyes are already fixed in the shadow on the wood…my mind unfortunately is hurtling into my past.

"Blood…lots and lots of blood." I don't recognise the chill in my own voice, and Mr Brown turns to look at me as if for the first time. He doesn't respond to my macabre declaration. Well, he might have, but I don't hear him. As much as I fight it, the flashback hits me like the first strike of a palm across my cheek, and I recoil as I stand just as I did back then.

Sam aged seventeen

"You filthy little slut!" His voice is menacingly low and he draws his hand back to strike me again.

"Richard, please!" I cry holding the heat in my cheek from his hand. It doesn't hurt. I've had worse from him. Even his words don't slice me like they used to, but the fury today distorts his face. Harsh lines twisted into an ugly scowl, thin lips pursed and pulled tight into a hate-filled grimace. He doesn't look like my boyfriend. He looks like a monster. Clenching his fist this time, he swings and cracks my jaw so hard I feel it like a blade behind my eyes. An unbelievable pain that knocks me to my knees.

"You spread your legs for me quick enough. How do I know the little bastard is mine, hmm?" He sneers at me, down his too straight nose, his blue eyes wild with anger, spit now dripping from his lips.

"Richard, please. I'm sorry. It's was an accident. That one time maybe, when you…you didn't wear the condom." His eyes widen, and I shrink rushing quickly to rectify my mistake. It's too late he hauls me up by grabbing a fistful of my hair and throws me against the wall like a rag doll. Strange, I never thought him to be that strong, with his slight build. But he is taller than me, and obviously, with the pure hatred running through his veins, his strength is no match for me. "Richard, I didn't mean it was your fault. You know my mother…I can't risk taking birth control. She would kill me if she knew what we'd done." I plead into vacant eyes.

He strides over to me and again grabs my hair, my scalp tender from hairs being torn from their roots. I grab his forearms to try and support my weight.

"Yes…let's not forget your social-climbing mother in all this. She really

believed me when I said I was going to marry you. Christ! To think I would have someone like her in **my** family…someone like **you**. A half-bred slut, who's probably fucked every boy in the village while I was at boarding school," he mocks.

"Richard, don't…that's not true. I love you." My voice is horse from crying, and I choke back the words when his large hand reaches around my neck.

"Say that again… whore!" He squeezes and I gasp for air. His eyes darken, and I feel him harden against my stomach. Jesus, how can he get off on my terror? The thin cotton dress is no barrier at all. I panic because this doesn't feel like the times he has abused me in the past. Something has changed in him. He looks unhinged. He needs to calm down or he's going to really hurt me. I soften my voice.

"Richard, my love, of course I love you. There is only you…you **know** that." I struggle to swallow against his grip. He loosens a little, and I let out a breath and try to smile. It catches when I realise, too late and with utter horror, his intention. He pulls his arm right back and levels a punch directly into my stomach. I collapse gasping for air that won't come, winded and in agony I roll onto the floor. My arms wrap tight across my tummy trying to protect what's inside.

I flash a glance at the monster before me just in time to see him let his heavily weighted boot swing forward. Easily crashing through my arms, again and again. Pounding his full force and weight into my abdomen. I try to curl in on myself tighter, but he grabs my head and stretches me out. I limply take punch after punch to my face. The pain is everywhere but the only noise I can distinguish is his heavy breathing and the sound of softly crunching tissue and sometimes bone. I can't seem to scream…cry…I can't find my voice at all.

"Who makes you happy, sweetheart?" His demonic chant rings in my ears. He always asks the same damn question, every time he hurts me the most. He repeats but emphasises each word this time with a carefully placed brutal kick to my stomach. "Who. Makes. You. Happy. Sweetheart."

I try to answer because I know from experience he won't stop until I do. But large floaty black spots seep across my glazed vision, tempting me into the darkness when an almighty cramp shocks me enough to sit bolt upright. Richard steps back and we both look at the large dark mass of liquid running between my legs. My white dress quickly unable to absorb any more of the blood as it drips, drips onto the floor.

"Richard, please." I cry and hold my hand for him to help. The confusion in his face must mirror mine. Why won't he help me? Can't he see what's happening? Can't he see I need help?Can't he see I'm going to lose the baby?

"It looks like we're about done here, don't you think?" He pulls his cuffs down and brushes at the specks of my blood that now pepper his sleeves. Little streaks and smears cover the pristine white material. "What's good for getting blood out of cotton?" He inspects the material like it is the only thing remotely significant. I'm haemorrhaging badly, and the agony is barely masking my utter devastation. I drag myself toward the door just as it opens. My mother steps into the room and gasps. Not because she has seen me or the blood, but because having Richard in my room is strictly forbidden.

"Mr Brookes-Hamilton, I know you intend to marry my daughter, but please do not take liberties with my kind nature." She gushes with her false reprimand, but her colour drains when he pushes the door a little wider to reveal me in a crumbled heap, losing more blood than I can spare.

"Mother…please." I manage to cry before I sink back into myself.

"Oh, Grace, what have you done?" Her grave words are laced with accusation and venom. "Mr Brookes—"she pleads as Richard moves to her side. "—Richard please don't go. I am sure there is a very good explanation." She reaches for his arm to stop him from leaving but his thunderous scowl prevents her actually making contact.

"Oh, there is, Mrs Cartwright, there is…Your daughter is a whore." I hear her suck in a sharp breath as his footsteps recede quickly or maybe my level of consciousness fails to distinguish the sound of him walking away and he is still there. I don't care anymore, I just need help.

"Mother, please, you need to call an ambulance." I reach for a hand that isn't offered and freeze when I recognise that expression of stone and hatred settle on her implacable face. Her beady blue eyes narrow and her cheeks burn with anger. She looks like she is desperate to once more spew all her hatred and bile. But not today it seems. I know that everything bad that has ever happened in her life is **my** fault. She's drilled it into me since I could talk, and now I have just ruined her chance at a life she believes she deserves.

My hand falls to the floor, skidding in the sticky mess and I slump down, flat on the boards. I manage to turn my head and meet her gaze…She could freeze ice with the warmth of her compassion for me. She's not going to help my baby…she's not going to help me. She steps back through the door and leaves me in an ever-increasing circle of my own blood. She leaves my baby to die and I don't doubt for a moment she hopes I will too. I pass out to the sound of a solid click of the door closing and the turn of the iron lock.

"Miss, are you all right? You don't seem to have heard what I just said." I feel the cold chill as the sweat from the flashback that instantly coated my skin, just as quickly dries. I shake my head even if the residual image is too fresh to ignore. My heart is still racing, but I hold my arm out as steadily as I can.

Mr Brown is a portly man, and that is being kind. He is most likely in his early sixties with thinning grey hair and tiny, wire-rimmed glasses. His beady eyes comically widen when he really sees me for the first time. I get this a lot. Even living in a cosmopolitan, vibrant city like London I know I stand out, but in a sleepy village such as this, I must look like an extra from Underworld in a Miss Marple Sunday afternoon special. My choice of wardrobe was very deliberate today, though. It's my armour. I offer my hand, and I swear he bends as if to kiss the back of it. I raise a brow and he stiffens with embarrassment. He shouldn't be embarrassed; under any other circumstance it would be charming. In certain situations it would be expected. He opts now for a light shake and I offer him a warm smile.

"Grace Cartwright, I presume." He is slightly breathless and I think there might be a little drool on his chin. I pull my hand sharply from his hold and straighten my back. His expression flashes from gentil to guarded.

"I legally changed my name when I was eighteen, Mr Brown. I'm Sam Bonfleur. I took my grandfather's surname." I correct.

"And Sam?" He nods but starts leafing through the pages of papers he has clutched to his chest.

"After a drink." I gave it no more thought at the time other than I didn't want to be called Grace ever again.

He chuckles as if I were joking. I wasn't.

His sudden frown causes more deep-set wrinkles to form. "I'm glad you could come today. Your mother had many antique pieces I am sure you will—"

"Sell everything. I want nothing. Honestly, I didn't think she would've kept me in her will at all." I keep my tone level and, with considerable effort, maintain a much softer timbre than I feel. Rage and sorrow blend and course through me; my nerves are raw and knots the size of footballs roll in my stomach. Mr Brown shifts uncomfortably and won't meet my eye.

"Um yes…you are right. Sadly, I believe that was her intention." He clears his throat. "There was some irregularity in the documentation and essential forms weren't completed correctly. In such cases the will is nullified and by default the estate would be bequeathed to the *closest* living relative." I scoff derisively at his misplaced assumption and inwardly smile that my mother would be turning in her grave at this outcome.

"Only *living* relative." I correct and draw in a steadying breath. Did I honestly think she would've softened over time and this be her final gesture of forgiveness? Of course not, she was evil, and evil is timeless. I shake myself free of the useless thoughts. "Regardless, it is what it is. You have my instructions. I just came today…" My voice catches, he doesn't need to know why I came. He doesn't need to know my gory past. "Sell it all." I repeat.

He looks a little shocked but nods. "I know it's of little comfort, but you will be a very rich woman, Ms Bonfleur." His smile falters on his pallid face, and there is sweat beading on his top lip. I make him uncomfortable. I smile. I like making men uncomfortable.

"I am a very rich woman already. I don't want a penny from the sale. I don't want to take anything for a keepsake. It is all to go to the charity I listed. You have something for me to sign?" I hold my hand out expectantly.

"Why did you come then? We could've done this over the phone or at my offices." His tone is a little irritated when he hands me a small stack of papers with little markers. I quickly work my way through signing my childhood away.

"I needed to remind myself. I needed this fresh in my mind so I won't do it again." I curse myself that I mutter this out loud enough for him to hear. I return his pen and he nods with kind eyes of understanding.

"Fall in love." He offers with a knowing look but my bitter laugh cuts him dead and now I do feel like I have to clarify…He does need to know.

"Not fall no, sometimes that sadly can't be helped. But I needed to remind myself why I will never again tell someone I love them. All men lie, Mr Brown, but once you tell a man you love him, he seems to think it gives him certain rights, rights to hurt and control you." I take my time to look him up and down, my glare accusatory. I feel only a tinge of shame that I judge all men by the one very bad apple, especially when I know it isn't true. Leon isn't like that, but it is better to be safe, to live by this rule than die being sorry. "Never again will I let someone control me." I step past him but turn when he coughs for my attention.

"Sorry, Ms Bonfleur, but I need a forwarding address. I can't use the PO Box I'm afraid, but perhaps I could send it to your office," he stutters.

"My office?" I hold back a smile.

"I noticed you had passed the bar. I assumed you were practising law somewhere?" He is checking his notes again, and I let out a light laugh.

"You have been busy." I turn to face him, drawing up to my full five foot ten height, six foot in my heels. His cheeks pink and he drags a finger across his shirt collar. He has the decency to look a little sheepish.

"You took some finding." He shrugs and I bite my lip. He obviously didn't look hard enough or he wouldn't be asking this question. Or maybe he did.

"I qualified but I don't practice, Mr Brown." I raise my brow and fix him with a glare to see if he withers…To see if he is hiding my secrets and trying to play me but he doesn't flinch. Satisfied he knows no more than he has alluded to already, I hand him my card, my smile widening with the stretch of his upturned brow. "Send whatever you need here. This is where I work."

"What do you do?" He flips the black card over. There is nothing on the back and just my signature on the front and the club address.

"I'm a whore." I smile sweetly at his sudden dropped jaw.

It's not until the houses start to crowd together, vying for prime location space that I start to relax. The endless expanse of lush green fields diminish to tiny pockets of manufactured parks and protected communal areas as the train speeds closer into the heart of the city, toward my home. My *real* home. Leon was right. I didn't have to be there in person to sort the sale. Documents could easily be signed and witnessed elsewhere but something made me want to remember. No, not something...*someone*. Jason Sinclair.

Despite what *I* call myself, I don't fuck for money. I fuck because I want to fuck, and I wanted to fuck Jason...very much. A hook-up with a hot guy at Bethany and Daniel's wedding. That was *all* it was supposed to be. I knew his reputation for absolute dominance. He's a silent partner in the club I work for, for Chrissakes, but I felt safe to cross the line in a civilian setting. I could blame the whole 'weddings make people crazy' notion but... well, I might've mentioned Jason Sinclair is fucking hot! Taller than me by several inches but eye level when I'm sporting my six-inch killer heels, broad, built shoulders that narrow to perfection in his immaculate three piece navy suit. Light brown hair with natural flecks of gold that just beg to be gripped and tousled. But his eyes, oh God, his eyes. As if the rich honey with the same golden highlights hypnotically swirling wouldn't captivate a mere mortal. The intensity with which he wields his most potent weapon, well I was a fool to think hooking up was anything but his decision.

A one-time thing, I could handle a one-time thing. It is all I have ever done since leaving home. Not so many as to warrant my moniker but always just a one-time thing. I can feel the hairs on my neck dance as a delicious chill sweeps my body when I recall the moment when he put his strong palm around my neck and squeezed a little too tight. I came so hard I couldn't breathe. I wanted it...I wanted more, but more shocking still, I realised I wanted him, and that thought terrified me.

That is why I didn't return his calls and that is why I came today. I needed to remind myself why I won't let another man control me...ever.

Today

Sam

"You know I can't eat any of those." Leon stretches his over-sized frame on my couch. The muscles in his torso flex and contract with the effort he is putting into his waking yawn. His hand automatically dipping into his lounge pants… checking. I snicker. He lifts his head to see me peering over hob on the kitchen bar.

"Is it still there? I raise a brow and point my palette knife directly at his crotch. His hand unashamedly massaging himself. He winks but doesn't remove his hand.

"You know it." He lets out a satisfied sigh. "But I am worried the little fella might not be working properly, and as my best friend, I feel it is your duty to help me out." It never gets old. Almost ten years of trying to get in my pants, and he is as fresh as the day he found me in that club. Saving me from making the biggest mistake of my life.

I left home on my eighteenth birthday, took the train to London and checked into a hotel. I was on a mission. A new life, with no rules, no boundaries and no limits. After all, I was a whore. I may as well live up to the name. I had no family and no friends thanks to my strict upbringing, but I was determined to change all that. I found myself in a sleazy nightclub slowly getting drunk with the nastiest guy I could find. Shaved head, thick neck with bulging muscles so large they distorted the ink on his skin to unrecognisable markings. I don't remember his name, but I do remember the second he was called away an arm swept around my waist, the briefest of conversations, and the next moment, my feet barely touched the ground as I was whisked away from the danger zone and out of the club. I remember at the time I didn't feel scared. I should've been scared, but I was either numb or stupid; Leon told me I was stupid. The guy at the bar I later found out was Eastern European mob, had just slipped something in my drink and was just checking if the van out the back could take one more. I pinch myself every day at my lucky escape thanks to my Knight in Giorgio Armani.

"But not today." The stock response I fire at him with a smile and a kiss. He rolls himself up to a sitting position and drags his hand through his shoulder length glossy dark hair. "Today, I am making Danish pancakes...*a lot* of Danish pancakes so you have to eat them." I flip the tiny delicate circles in the pan and whisk some more mixture for my next batch. It's a ready mix packet that all I have to do is add milk and even then, with my innate skill in the kitchen there is no guarantee they will be edible.

"I'm leaving for my flight in an hour, and I don't want the plane to have trouble taking off because I have a shit tonne of your 'coping strategy' setting like concrete in my gut." He slaps his toned, flat stomach with a loud tummy clenching sound. "What's got you in such a state anyway?" He saunters over to the kitchen completely at ease with his near-naked appearance. Sliding onto the high stool, he picks up a handful of the pancakes and slowly munches them despite his protestations. He closes his eyes and moans, an overly sexual sound, savouring his enjoyment. I roll my eyes and throw the oven gloves I'm holding at his bare chest. He catches them and holds them hostage in his lap.

"Behave." I warn, and he hands them back looking a little sheepish.

"Sorry, Sam...I can't help myself sometimes." He grins.

"Try harder. You're living here now, and I don't need—"

"Actually, from what I can see, that is exactly what you need...unless you are really trying to give Mary Berry a run for her money?" He takes another two pancakes. I turn the heat off and start to tidy away. "Come on Sam talk to me, baby girl. I won't leave until you do. Then I'll miss my flight. Then my mum will be mad at you because I will blame you, and she is mean when she's mad."

"Your mum doesn't have a mean bone in her body, Leon. It's why you are the way you are...adorable." I scruff his shaggy hair, but he growls and straightens out of my reach.

"So what's your excuse?"

I know he's joking but it still stings. I hate that I didn't just appear from thin air, anything would be preferable than a connection to a woman more concerned with social status and reputation than whether her daughter lived or died.

"Skipped a generation. You should've met my grandfather." I smile softly and he takes a moment to pull me into a hug. Tight, secure and filled with love. He kisses my head and whispers.

"Yeah, I would've liked that." Leon lifts me back onto the stool. "So?" His head tips to the mountain of carbohydrates I have diligently crafted into little Danish treats. Enough to feed an army.

"Jason." I exhale, and he waits for me to continue. "I had a cryptic and very personal message on my voicemail this morning. It's kind of shaken me up a bit. I mean, I know I see him around the club. It's not like I've avoided him since the wedding. I really couldn't, but he hasn't tried to make contact in over a year. Why would he pick now?" I nibble distractedly at the tip of my fingernail. Not really biting, they are acrylic, and I would probably lose a tooth before the nail gave way.

"Ah, well that might have something to do with me." His finger starts to draw nervous patterns in the sugar that is covering the marble top.

"Leon…what did you do?" I try to keep my voice level but I can feel my heart begin to race.

"Nothing…nothing bad." He briskly rubs his hands clean and rubs them on his pants. He then places them on my thighs and leans forward with his most sincere expression. His dark, dark eyes crinkle with concern and warmth. "I saw *your* Jason—" I scoff an interruption, but he's not put off and repeats, "I saw *your* Jason last night at a party. We got to chatting. He's actually a really nice guy…anyway I may have let it slip that I am not…in fact…your boyfriend." My bones cease to function and I collapse into myself letting out a frustrated groan.

"Oh, gahhhhhhd." I start to rub the instant pressure in my brow. Flour falls from my fingertips down my face, settling on my lips, under my nose, and I sneeze, sending a plume of flour from the kitchen surface into a billowing cloud that completely hides a very sorry looking Leon. Good, he should be sorry. He has just made my life so much more complicated. The powder settles, and I change my mind. He doesn't look sorry at all, he looks self-satisfied and smug. I could kill him right now. I have the tools, but he smiles and shrugs and I remind myself once more that he saved me.

With Leon out of town until the New Year, Christmas Eve is eerily quiet, too quiet. As much I would like to continue to ignore Jason—actually a huge part of me wants to hide completely—I won't. That is not my style. I don't hide. I meet head-on.

I pull the belt at my waist tight enough to pinch in an attempt to block the icy wind from reaching my scantily clad body. The thick cashmere full-length coat is doing an admirable job against the subzero Christmas weather. Even so, the short distance from the cab to the club door is enough to have my teeth clicking together, the sound drowned only by my heels on the steps to the basement destination. I swipe my card and wait. The new owners installed state of the art security. The front door won't open unless they know exactly who is outside. Not just a visual through a peep hole, but name, date of birth, blood type, and most importantly, bank details. Despite this intrusive level of information exchange, members hand it over without question. This is *the* exclusive club in London for the *scene,* with a wait list so long, if you don't have a personal recommendation would-be members would probably die by the time a space opened up.

The door opens and a giant beast of a man steps aside to let me in. He is the most intimating man I know. I offer my brightest smile even though I know Gus' stony façade will not crack.

"Hey Gus," I give my body an exaggerated shudder to try and get some heat into my bones. I check my coat and am acutely aware of the loss of its protective warmth. I rub my hands vigorously up and down my bare arms. The chill of the evening clings to the sexy slick PVC halter neck cat suit, but it will quickly warm once I get inside.

"Hey." Gus's gruff response makes the corners of my mouth curl with pleasure. He is a fierce looking mountain of a man, and I don't doubt he rattles a few of the most hardened alphas who strut in here, but he is just a big bear, especially to me. I lean up even in my heels and my natural height to plant a colourful kiss on his cheek.

"Merry Christmas, Gus." I wait with my hands on my hips, one dipped, and narrow my eyes. Gus looks over my shoulder. There is just me and him, and no one is going to call him out for cracking a bit of Christmas cheer.

"Merry Christmas, darling." His deep voice rumbles with an echo through the empty corridor.

"Is it busy?" I tip my head toward the heavy, rich, red velvet curtain separating the entrance door from the stage. Every time I step through that curtain, I am here to perform, I have my costume, I have my act, and the main reception room of the club I like to refer to as my stage.

"Not exactly." Gus replies.

"How come you're working tonight?" I'm curious because, although they always have someone on the door, Gus is a senior someone, and this is Christmas, after all.

"I could ask you the same thing." He raises a teasing brow.

"Oh, no rest for the wicked, Gus. You know that." I wiggle my brows. He grunts out a deep laugh and rolls his eyes.

"You're not as wicked as you pretend to be, darling, and I'm not wicked at all. Working tonight means I get until New Year to spend with the family." He puffs out his chest with unabashed pride. Gus has a large brood, six children, and has been happily married to his childhood sweetheart for twenty-three years. He is the poster boy for getting it right.

"Oh, wow, that is great…I mean I'll miss you and all…" I give a playful wink.

"Yeah, yeah, go on now…time is money," he quips.

"Ain't that the truth." Although in my case, I think my issue has more to do with idle hands. I have been smart with my money. The necklace I got on my eighteenth birthday pretty much secured my future, if not the husband, as my mother had hoped. After my rocky start, and with some guidance from Leon, I found a job I love and I am extremely good at. I rarely have to spend my own money, so I save. My nest egg is such that I really don't have to work, but I hate having down time. I despise having time to think…time to remember. I turn and slip through the gap in the curtain. *Show time.*

I can't help the shocked laugh that escapes my mouth when I freeze just inside the entrance. It's like a surprise party, and someone forgot to send out the invitations. The opulently decorated room has been transformed into Santa's sinful grotto, with a thousand sparkly handcuffs, extra-large diamante nipple clamps and tinsel covered cat o' nine tail whips hanging from the ceiling and light fittings. With the subdued lighting and featured spotlights, the whole room sparkles magically but it is empty, well almost empty. The striking distinctive outline of the not so silent partner sits at the bar nursing a glass of his favourite single malt.

I draw in a deep breath and make my way to take the seat beside him. It's not like I haven't seen him, spoken to him, tried desperately hard to ignore the spark of feeling I get whenever our paths have crossed these past sixteen months. I have. I have tried and failed. I confess I panicked when I started to feel my control slip because, despite my visit home, I am drawn to him. So like a coward that is most unbecoming of a Domme, let alone a notorious one such as Mistress Selina, I called in one massive favour. Leon became my boyfriend. The ultimate barrier and cock blocker *extraordinaire*. It would appear that favour expired last night and now it is time for me to face the music, pay the piper and swallow what Jason chooses to shove down my throat. He is a Dom and he is not a fan of liars.

I slip silently onto the high bar stool, but he knows I am there. His head tilts almost imperceptibly before he turns to face me. His deliberate slow movements increase my anxiety, a foreign feeling and one that sits uncomfortably, competing for attention with my racing heart. His predatory look takes in every inch of my body, I can almost feel it leaving a scorched path across my skin. My full-length one-piece cat suit barely leaves any skin on display but his gaze leaves me feeling naked, exposed and vulnerable. I pull my shoulders back and straighten my back because I am none of those things…I am London's best Dominatrix.

"Samantha." The timbre of his voice is deep and gravelly and my name sounds like sin on his lips. I know those lips.

"Jason." I manage to say his name without inflection despite my heart rate spiking and that familiar ache that begins to build.

"You know I prefer Sir." He fixes me with a stare that would make any submissive quake, and therein lies the problem.

"Ah, we both know that is not going to happen." I accept the drink Jason has managed to magically order without me noticing. "And I am Mistress Selina here as you well know, Jason." I bite my lip to stop from smirking with satisfaction at the sudden narrow stare flashed my way.

"Since I am your boss, what if I insist on Sir?" He sips his drink, and his lips tip with pleasure.

"Jason," I take pleasure in the way his name rolls deliciously around my mouth. I emphasise each syllable with a sensual tone that makes his jaw clench. "You're not *my* boss. You just happen to own the place where I choose to work."

"Keep telling yourself that, *Selina.*" His low grumble makes the hairs on my neck stand as though little shots of electricity have been fired through them. "And I'm not your boss…yet." My body gives an involuntary shudder and I internally berate myself. His expression is utter wickedness and evidence enough that he noticed the shiver he'd clearly caused.

He lets out a breath and I find I'm holding mine. "It's been a long time since it's just been the two of us. If I didn't know better I might think you were scared to be alone with me. Are you scared to be alone with me, *Selina*?" His sensual tone curls around my stage name like pure sin. His soft volume drops a level and I find my body leaning in. No. I'm being drawn to him. I have to fight to release my breath in anything remotely level. I grip my glass and choose to down the liquid to give me a moment of respite from his scorching intensity.

"Hardly, Jason." My voice is surprisingly calm even as I can feel my cheeks begin to heat with the lie. "We've seen each other plenty of times." I let out a light laugh, and his mouth may quirk with pleasure but I get the feeling it has very little to do with my comment.

"True but we have not been alone since…" He pauses and stares deeper into my eyes. I can see the exact memory dance in his lust filled eyes. No doubt a mirror of my own. "…the wedding." I interrupt but barely suppress the sexual tension sizzling like a live current between us. I am grateful for the dimly lit room when I feel my face burn with the memory. He lets out a deep and dirty laugh.

"The wedding," he repeats slowly.

Eighteen Months Ago

I had found myself squeezed against Jason in the tiny chapel at the hospital for Daniel and Bethany's surprise wedding. Surprise for Bethany that is. It was standing room only as the few seats available were taken up by family, but I didn't mind. I was happy to be a part of their day, but as the temperature in the room rose, so did my own body heat. Every furtive glance from Jason, every intentional brush of his hand against my thigh or hand elevated my pulse. I knew exactly what he was doing. There wasn't much space, but he really didn't need to be that close. I thought I tipped the balance of where this was going when I stepped to angle myself against his body and reached up high on my toes to whisper in his ear. The words were irrelevant, but I took a deliberate moment to breathe his clean woodsy scent deep into my lungs and exhale just as slowly. His eyes dipped to meet my gaze, nothing hidden in the stare we shared, dark with desire and pent with lust.

When I stepped back, the draw was still there. Like a tangible field of sexual tension radiating around our bodies. The ceremony finished, and the guests were being ushered along the corridor into a makeshift reception room, and that's when, as the last to leave, Jason dragged me into a room I hadn't even noticed. That would be because it wasn't a room as such, it was a large storage cupboard…with a lockable door. I didn't get a moment to protest, not that I would have, but instantly, his mouth was on mine, his hands frantic at the tiny buttons on my blouse. My palms first flat on the firm curve of his chest muscles, swept down to his belt, and with deft fingers, I quickly had his trousers dropped to his thick, taut thighs. Frustrated with his slow progress, he growled and tugged at the bottom of the material, lifting the blouse over my head. He froze for a moment at the sight of my frantic attempts to draw in more air. I don't ever remember feeling so out of control, so wild and needy. My breasts rose and shook with the effort, smooth mounds barely contained by the delicate ivory lace balcony bra. My nipples were taut peaks, aching for his touch, and my skin glowed with the sheen of perspiration.

"Are you a screamer?" Jason's deep tone was hoarse and breathy.

"I'm not usually the one who screams...no." I exhaled and Jason's lips tip into a wicked understanding.

"So I don't need to gag you?" He raised a brow and my eyes dropped to the slow draw of his tongue across his soft, full lips.

"I'd like to see you try." I slapped his chest forcefully.

"That makes two of us." He growled and pushed roughly against me. Hard enough that he was flush against me grinding his solid length against my soft centre.

"In your dreams, Jason," I scoffed with arrogance and understanding. He knew what I was and he knew this would be different, but it was still on my terms. At least I thought it was. I pushed back and ground against him. We both drew in ragged breaths. "No gag." I confirmed and moaned as Jason grabbed my breasts, cupped and squeezed them with his large hands, his fingers finding the hardened peaks and pinching to the point of and just beyond pain.

"Ah!" I gasped.

"No gag...are you quite sure?" His wolfish grin and arrogant tone set the challenge.

"You wish!" I bit back with confidence. I promised myself I was not going to make a sound. Dominant Jason Sinclair...King of the club had met his match.

"That I do." He pinched my nipples to punctuate his declaration and I blinked rapidly in lieu of the cry at the back of my throat. My lips spread into a salacious smile once the pain ebbed and I pulled him by the tie and crushed my lips to his. The moan that escaped his chest was almost as loud as the cry I suppressed.

Now

"Yes...the wedding. What is it about weddings?" he muses.

"I'm not sure it had anything to do with it being a wedding." I laugh lightly.

"No...You might be right. It had much more to do with you looking hot as hell, a convenient storage cupboard and a lockable door." He tips his glass and nods for a refill. I do the same, suddenly feeling like I need the liquid courage to play with the inferno sitting next to me. "After though...You didn't return my call." His gaze darkens.

"That would be because there would have been no point." I quickly down the sweet coffee liqueur and mouth a large ice cube. I take my time playing with it in my mouth, relishing the effect I am now having on the implacable Mr Sinclair. He swallows thickly, his eyes never leaving my mouth. I know I am playing with fire, but it feels so good.

"And why is that?" His casual tone betrays the heat in his eyes and the intensity of his glare. "Did you not have fun? Because I seem to recall you had a great deal of it." He leans forward and pushes his hands between my legs and grabs the edge of the bar stool. My legs spread of their own volition just enough before I try to rectify the error. Clamping tight against his wrist, he pulls my seat closer to him. His muscular thighs trap me, his hand wedged between my legs. Heavy lidded eyes bore into me with a fierceness that burns through my veins like wildfire, his thumb languidly stroking my inner thigh.

I take a moment and relish the utter pleasure these strange erotic feelings coursing through me evoke. My heart is beating a hypnotic pattern in my chest, hard and fierce. I am acutely aware as the precarious balance of control I hold so dear begins to slip. I feel the shift like a physical change and it is alarmingly seductive how natural it feels to give over to someone as absolutely dominant as Jason. It's too seductive. I raise a brow, my calm façade a mask to my traitorous emotions. I use the tips of my fingers to remove the remaining ice cube from my glass, quickly palm it, and stretch out to hold it flat and hard against Jason's rock solid erection. The ice water soaks his trousers but doesn't diminish the heat in my palm one bit.

"Fuck, Sam!" he barks out but doesn't move. If anything he grinds into my hand and releases a deep moan. I can't help laughing; that was not the reaction I was anticipating but then I should've known he wasn't likely to run. He was much more likely to rise to the challenge he obviously thinks I am.

"Jason." I sigh reluctantly removing my hand. "Two Doms don't make a right. We would not play well together. The wedding was an exception. I will give you that it was an amazing exception but—"

"But nothing." He growls his interruption.

"See, that's exactly why I didn't return your call. I'm not one of your little submissives, and you sure as shit aren't going to kneel for me anytime soon… although…" My index finger lightly taps my lips, which carve a wicked grin at the very notion.

"Yeah, keep dreaming beautiful, because that is all that's *ever* going to be." He sniffs derisively, but his eyes narrow while he slowly sips his drink. "But you weren't always a Domme Selina?" His serious tone and leading question instantly kills my flirtatious mood.

"Oh, you have been busy." I straighten myself creating a cool, noticeable distance.

"Daniel was just as much my wingman as I was his before he met Bethany, and you know that. I'm not being intrusive; I am stating a fact. You weren't always a Domme." His dismissive tone is doing little to calm my irritation.

"I doubt Daniel would've disclosed any details, but if he did, he would've informed you it was one time and it was the very last part of my training. My instructor insisted I understand both ends of the whip as it were." I clarify stiffly.

"Quite right, too." He nods in agreement.

"But that doesn't make me a sub, Jason."

"No, Samantha, it doesn't, but you enjoyed it, so that does, in fact, make you a switch." His gaze seems to sear right through me with fire and so much desire I'm starting to melt. What exactly I am struggling with? Is it that I actually *like* the turn this conversation has taken? No…I can't… I won't let it go there.

"Not necessarily but your point is what exactly?" My attempt at annoyance seems to amuse him. He moves his hand from his drink to lightly pinch my chin making sure he holds my full attention. Not that I could look anywhere else…not that I'd *want* to.

"My point, Selina, is that I want you to *switch* for me." His lethal glare scorches my breath from my lungs as I let out an inaudible gasp. "So tell me, Selina, what is it going to take?" His assured cockiness is interrupted by my incredulous laugh.

"Oh, Jason, that is sweet, and I'm flattered, really I am." His instant scowl darkens at my flippancy and condescending tone.

"What is it about me that you think is sweet exactly? Do I look like a man who doesn't get everything he wants?" He slips his hand around the back of my head and grabs a tight hold of my long, sleek ponytail. I don't flinch but my heart does feel like it is trying to beat its way through my chest.

"Do I?" I retort and hold his fiery gaze.

"Damn-it, Selina, you most definitely do *not* look like a man." He laughs out, then his lips quickly bite back a grin. "Give me one day." He pauses to let the words sink in but the evident confusion must be etched on my face because it makes him clarify further. "Give me one day to change your mind. Spend the whole day with me and if I can't convince you to submit to me…then…"

"Then?" I tip my chin for his answer but my movement is still restricted by his hold.

"Then it will be the first time I do *not* get what I want." He grumbles, and I laugh loudly shaking free from his grip.

"And if I do agree to submit… it will be a miracle." I taunt.

He stands, stepping into my personal space, putting pressure enough to widen my legs to accommodate him just that little bit closer. "I'll pick you up first thing in the morning." He leans down, his words kiss my neck like a tempting promise.

"Tomorrow? It's Christmas Day." I sag a little when he moves away, fighting the moan at the sudden loss of heat.

"Perfect day for a miracle." He pauses at the doorway, holding my gaze for long seconds before stepping through the curtain leaving me a mess of heat and confusion.

Jason

"What the fuck! You scared the crap out of me, Daniel! What are you doing here?" The door to my office swings open, and apart from the night security guard, I thought the whole office block was empty. As it should be this late on Christmas Eve.

"I am going to ask you the very same question. You are going to make me feel like Ebenezer if you tell me you are working." He flicks the main light on because I have been hunched over my laptop with just the glow of the screen to illuminate my office. I blink and rub my eyes at the instant bright light.

"No, not working, just trying to find *unobtainium*. It's proving a little tricky." I slap the lid of my laptop shut and stretch my spine out with my knuckles, cracking a few pockets of air as I do. I feel the late hour now, and I am suddenly tired. Daniel strides into the room and walks straight to the shelf where I keep my best whiskey. He pours two fingers in each glass and hands me one. Taking the chair opposite, his face is impossible to read even after all these years of working as his number two. But his raised brow is indication enough that he is listening.

"I got a second chance with Sam. Just one day…tomorrow. I don't want to blow it but I have sort of left myself no time to actually sort anything special." Daniel lets out a clipped laugh and sips his drink.

"I wouldn't waste your time." He notices my back straighten, but waves his hand to stop my misunderstanding. "Back down, I didn't mean it like that. I meant Sam, or more likely Selina, will have been to every fancy restaurant, gallery, concert…whatever in the city. You name it, she will have seen it all on the arm of one of her clients. I doubt she would consider anything like that *special*. What else have you got?" He swirls the amber liquid and fixes me with his intense boardroom stare. Usually I don't have a problem with that particular look because, in a business setting, I am never without answers and solutions. In this instance, however, I have left myself absolutely no time. I have no solutions to my own problem. I hold both my hands up in surrender.

"I've got nothing. I was planning to spend the morning at the Mission, Skype the family in the afternoon and then watch all the versions of *A Christmas Carol* on Netflix…Hardly earth shattering, heart stealing activities." I take a large gulp and wince at the hit of alcohol. I let out a heavy sigh.

"Is that your plan? You want to steal her heart?" His voice is level, and his face is again implacable. I'd hate him for that if I didn't consider him one of my best friends.

"She may have kicked me to the curb after the wedding, even when I knew there was something more. I felt it, and she sure as shit did, too. Maybe that's why she ended it before…I don't know. Whatever the reason, she shut me down. I've given her time, but it's enough now. I know she still feels the same. You can cut the fucking sexual tension with a chainsaw when we're in the same room and up until tonight we've never actually been alone. Tonight, I made my play. Had the whole Christmas miracle thing as my backdrop. She didn't stand a chance. Anyway, it's Christmas, and I promised to change her mind about us… if she'd give me one day." His lips curl with a knowing smile, and I feel tension build at the bridge of my nose. "I know…I know…I may not have been thinking with my head…not entirely anyway…It's Christmas Eve…everything is shut… I'm totally screwed." I take another long draw of my drink.

"You do know what she does for a living?" His tone almost sounds like a warning. I fire my own judgmental scowl at him. "Look, I'm not saying that to be an arsehole. I just want you to go into this with your eyes wide open." He shrugs lightly, and I relax because any hint of judgment was clearly on my end.

"I'm no fucking saint, Daniel. I own a sex club, and I didn't buy *any* club, I bought the club where she works exclusively. So yes, I know what she does, and it doesn't make the slightest difference to me." I focus on the swirling liquid, a mix of gold and lightning bouncing off the cut crystal. I murmur more to myself. "There is something about her—"

"Does she know you're the sole owner of the club? Does she know why you bought it I mean?" He interrupts my musing.

"She thinks I'm a part owner, and no…that might creep her out." I have the decency to look a little sheepish. I definitely had my own selfish reasons for buying the club. For one, I could be there on a regular basis without looking like a manwhore. But, more importantly, as the owner, I was able to censor the membership list and, subsequently, Sam's pool of potential clients. I also told myself at the time I just wanted to be close in case she needed my help. It took no time at all to realise that Selina could more than take care of herself, and I was kidding myself that she was any type of damsel in distress.

"You want my advice? Be honest the first chance you get. One thing I do remember about Sam is she doesn't like lies. In fact, from memory, she thinks all men are liars so you, my friend, are not off to a stellar start." He grins.

"Maybe not, but that makes two of us, and I am not technically lying" I sniff at the hypocrisy of my statement. "What else do you remember?" I pause, hoping my loaded question is heard loud and clear.

"Hmm." His brows knit together with unease. "You put me in rather an awkward position, Jason." He narrows his eyes, but I hold his stare.

"I know." I raise my brow for him to continue. For him to answer my question.

"Only because you are pursuing this as a relationship I will answer as my conscience allows. I was asked to complete Sam's training. Her mentor believed in order to give pain one must understand pain." He repeats what Sam had told him earlier. "I didn't fuck her. That wasn't the point of the session."

"What was the point? Or was it just about the pain?" I find myself leaning forward eager for the insight.

"It was about pleasure," he replies without inflection.

"Did she enjoy it?" My jaw tenses at this, and I feel an angry heat burn in my chest. Stupid I know; it was a long time ago. Before I'd even moved to London, but the thought that someone else gave her pleasure through pain drives me a little crazy. That's what I want...me and only me.

"You would have to ask her that. I don't believe she was disappointed with the outcome..." He pauses, but my stomach is already churning with distaste. "Honestly, I don't think pleasure is what she took from it. She has too many barriers for one session, but then, the purpose wasn't to train a sub. The purpose was for her to understand her role as a Domme, and that was an unmitigated success." He switches back to my more urgent concern, effectively halting any further questions I might have that he is clearly not going to answer. "If you ask me you have solved your own problem. Take her with you tomorrow...be with *her*. Be with Sam not Selina. You want to be with her. She is never going to believe that if all your interactions are at the club. Show her you understand the difference." He knocks back the remaining whiskey and places the glass on my desk. His words sink in with the same warmth the liquor is causing in my bloodstream. He is right. That's perfect. I leave my glass with the remaining finger of whiskey untouched.

"When did you get so smart about women?" I stand and grab my jacket from the back of my chair.

"Since I married an exceptional one." His retort is deadpan, like I have asked the most ridiculous question.

"Too bad it hasn't rubbed off on you then…coming to work at eleven thirty on Christmas Eve—" I quip and switch the lights off as we both leave my office.

"I dropped Bethany at Sofia's family for midnight mass. I may have left her gift in my office safe." He smiles and holds his hand out.

"Fuck! That is a first. Good to see you're just as fallible as the rest of us mortals." I laugh and shake his hand before I turn to leave. "Merry Christmas. Send my love to Bethany," I call to his retreating back.

"Good luck tomorrow, Jason…you're going to need it!" I almost miss the last part as the lift arrives with a loud ping, but I heard it…loud and clear.

I arrive just before seven in the morning, and Sam instantly buzzes me up. I don't generally get overly excited. I keep control of all things including my emotions but I would be lying if I didn't acknowledge the anticipation I feel is causing a nice little buzz. I can't believe I didn't see the solution sooner. I think it was a case of forest for the trees, but once Daniel pointed it out, everything just fell into place, and I am more than happy to take it from here. She doesn't stand a chance. My lips carve a wicked smile just as she opens her front door.

She dressed in a loose fitted cashmere, long, scooped neck sweater with long sleeves. The sweater rests just mid-thigh. Her skinny leatherette leggings hug her curves and leave little to the imagination. She is holding a black leather jacket and is standing almost eye level with me in black ankle boots with killer heels. She is tall, five foot ten maybe, but she still has to lift her chin to meet my eyes. She looks a little flustered, her chest rises with little rapid breaths, and she has a flush to her flawless cheeks that just makes my balls ache. Her hair is long and loose, and falls in soft waves around her face. Her eyes are so dark they look almost black but are soft too, and are framed with the longest lashes I have ever seen. She doesn't have a scrap of makeup on, and she is flawless.

"Fuck, you are beautiful!" She looks a little shocked at my words or maybe the ferocity with which I delivered them but gives me a tentative smile all the same. Daniel said to be honest. I may as well start as I mean to go on. She steps forward but I carefully guide her back into her hallway. "But you may have to reconsider the foot wear." I can't believe I am saying that. Those heels look amazing, my cock twitches at the thought of her legs spread wide wearing nothing but those very boots. Nevertheless, they are wholly wrong for this morning.

"One doesn't *reconsider* Louboutins, Jason," she quips. "Unless you are planning to take me on a hike around the streets of London?" She lightly laughs at what she believes to be a rhetorical question.

"That's exactly what I have planned." My tone is as serious as my expression.

"You're kidding." Her laugh is a bit incredulous but falls flat when I remain silent with only an impatient rise of my brow. "Um…okay." She steps back into her flat. "Come in while I find something suitable." I smirk at her confusion and follow her inside. My large frame fills her small entrance corridor. Looking flustered, she quickly disappears into what I assume is her bedroom. I get a tingle of satisfaction that I have evoked this reaction when she is always so collected. I move closer to her door, which she left slightly ajar. I can hear her swipe through hanging clothes in her wardrobe letting out an exaggerated breath as she does. She sighs and there is the sound of her slumping to the floor.

"Problem?" I lean on the frame, and the door drags on the carpet when I push it wide open. I casually cross my arms. She looks my way. Her eyes crawl up my body at a glacial pace, greedily taking in every inch of my body, hovering at my thighs, crotch, torso, biceps, and back to my crotch. She quickly flicks her gaze up to my eyes with a shake of her head. I try to contain my shit-eating grin.

"Hmm?" I've distracted her, and I get that warm buzz again.

"Is there a problem? You seem to be huffing." I bite my lip to keep from laughing at the irritation dancing in her eyes. I am glad I don't laugh because in the next instant, she shoots to her feet and strides toward me pushing me hard in the chest. She manoeuvres me back out of her bedroom and into the hall.

"Other than you being in my bedroom you mean? Yes, I have a bloody problem…these"—she waves some worn, pale pink bunny slippers in my face like a furry weapon—"are the only bloody things I have that don't have a heel. So, sorry, but this date…this day…is now cancelled." She throws the bunnies down to emphasise her anger.

"I can only assume you don't lose you temper that quickly in the club or you would have to be the worst Dominatrix in history." I chuckle and step up to her, placing my finger on her lips silencing her anticipated come back. "And I happen to know you're the best." Sam flips from instant rage to pliant at my touch. "Nothing is going to stop this day from happening. So step away from the bunny slippers and let's go. Don't want to be late." I flash my best smile, which she can't help but reciprocate, and I take her hand. She kicks the offending slippers back into her bedroom, grabs her bag, and lets me lead her out of the flat.

I park my Audi R8 at the back of a large warehouse on the outskirts of the East End of London. The sign above the side entrance gives nothing away: The Mission.

"Wait here, I won't be a moment." Sam nods, her face the perfect picture of confusion. I return moments later, open her door and proudly hand her a pair of combat boots and a thick pair of socks, both items in her size. She takes the boots and, without question, swaps her designer heels for the replacements from the army surplus. I reach for her hand again, and my chest squeezes when her lips spread into a shy smile just as her fingers tighten around mine. She trusts me, there is no reservation in her eyes, no uncertainty, and I fucking love that. This is what I felt sixteen months ago, and it makes today more perfect. I just need to make sure she won't shut down again.

I confidently lead her into the building, my eyes never leaving her face. However, practised she is at maintaining her other persona, her calm, her mask, the part of her that performs so well as Selina, she could not have prepared herself for what was going on inside the large building. Her face lit with understanding when she stopped just inside the door.

An organised army of maybe fifty people stacking blankets, loading waiting vans with boxes of food, drinks and kindness. Two larger mobile kitchens were already pulling out of the building when Sam turns to me, her jaw dropped, but she doesn't make a sound. I've made her a little speechless. I slip a thick fleece lined hi-vis jacket over her slender shoulders and turn her to face me. I bite my lips together, unable to fully suppress my smile. I tug and shuffle the jacket closed and zip it up to her neck. Tipping her chin, I cover her lips with mine, the tenderness makes her gasp with shock, and my grin widens with pleasure. That is twice I've surprised her in the space of five minutes, impressive even by my standards.

"Shall we?" I wait for her to slowly open her eyes. She nods shyly and squeezes my hand.

"Okay, we're going out with this team here for the breakfast run but we have to finish stocking the van. All this needs to be in there." I point to neatly stacked supplies, which are already being loaded into the waiting van. "This is Rita and Ray." I introduce Sam to the two helpers at the table of supplies. Rita and Ray smile, and Rita gives a little wave before grabbing an armful of blankets.

"Hi." Sam gives a tentative smile and starts to help with the loading. I keep to her side. The loading takes no time at all, and every second of it I spend with a closely guarded eye on Sam. Despite my initial confidence, I am still taking a risk bringing her here; I know that. But I also know Daniel was right. I had to do something exceptional. I know her clients are rich and probably lavish her with expensive gifts. I know her independent nature is not to be underestimated, and I know money is not going to impress her. I needed to find the chink in her kinky armour. At the very least, I had to challenge her preconception of me enough to push her to reconsider what *we* could be.

I pull her into the back of the van, and she giggles when she loses her footing and lands in my lap. It's such an honest sound, light and innocent. I could listen to that all day...well, that and her gasps. I'd quite like to hear those an entire day, too. I take the opportunity of her fall to wrap my arms tight around her, keeping a firm hold in place as the van pulls out of the Mission.

"You can let me go, you know. I won't fall." She tips her head to meet my gaze but doesn't pull away.

"And that is why I am not going to let go. I have waited far too long, and I want you to fall." My voice rumbles with a deep, earnest tone that makes her shiver. Her eyes hold the intensity of my gaze and reflect it back tenfold.

We spend the morning handing out blankets along the embankment, under the arches and in shop doorways. Anywhere people with nowhere to go find it secure enough or sheltered enough to rest. I carry the blankets, and Sam carries trays of warm soup, returning to the van for refills.

"You're very quiet," I remark on our last return journey to the van. Sam has been warm and friendly, taking extra time with those wanting to chat, and respectful of those who don't, but she has been silent for a little while, and that troubles me.

"Just...." She hesitates, and before we reach the others I turn her to face me, lifting her chin with a single finger.

"Just?" I hold her gaze, deep eyes filled with so much turmoil.

"It feels wrong that I have enjoyed this. I mean it's awful and tragic that in a city with so much wealth there are so many people like this, but I've..." She shifts uncomfortably.

"It's not wrong. How about you try not to feel uncomfortable about helping and look at it like this... that you have rightly enjoyed spending time with me." I tilt my head and wiggle my brows, which just makes her laugh out. I place my hand over my heart, and my mock wound. "That was supposed to be my most seductive look." She laughs louder and slaps her hand to her mouth to quiet the noise.

"Oh, I'm sorry, but that was not seductive. Remember, I have seen you being seductive. I have been a victim of your seduction." She waves a warning finger, which I eagerly grab. My eyes focus and narrow on her fingertip. I take it into my mouth and grip it with my teeth. She freezes, but a burst of sudden heat flashes adorably across her cheeks. I can't hold in the deep groan that escapes from the back of my throat. I suddenly wish we were anywhere but a grimy back street in the heart of the city, and I seriously over-estimated my control if I think we can spend the rest of the day chilling to various versions of a festive Dickens classic.

We arrive back at the warehouse and join the other volunteers for a cup of tea and a mince pie. Sam blows the steam off the nuclear hot liquid. "So Jason?" Her perfectly arched brow is full of curiosity and something else, maybe confusion.

"So Sam?" I slowly sip my own drink. I share and hold the intensity of her gaze but wait for her to actually ask what is clearly concerning her if the tiny lines that now furrow her smooth forehead are any indication. I sit back and silently observe her. She is so beautiful, breathtaking really, but today, I witnessed much more. Today, I saw behind her mask. Her heart is filled with kindness and empathy, freely given without reservation or judgment. Her true nature unwittingly exposed couldn't possibly be part of a performance when it so clearly came from her soul. She continues to hold my gaze. Her lips curl in a tender smile.

"So Jason…You do this a lot?" She leans forward and rests her chin on her steepled fingertips.

"Take a stunningly beautiful Dominatrix to a soup kitchen on a date? No, never. You are my first." I mirror her image and lean so we are now inches from each other across the table. I notice her breath hitch a little when my arm brushes hers. Her eyes darken, and she is just about to sweep her tongue over her lips. I know this because my mouth is equally dry. Her tongue darts out, and it takes all my restraint not to grab the back of her neck and chase her tongue back into her sweet mouth with my own. I do lean in closer though, so my breath is now skimming her neck as I whisper. "I want you to be my first, Sam."

I clear my throat the same time a tiny gasp leaves her lips. Those fucking lips. Her eyes widen when the meaning of my words settle. I am no more a virgin than she is, but if she were to switch for me, she would be the very first Domme to submit to me. It's a heady thought, and my cock is forcing its own painful opinion on the subject, uncomfortably large in the confines of my jeans. I can see the lure of this idea is just as intoxicating to her. Desire is blazing like a raw fire in her eyes. She physically tries to check herself, straightens her back and drags her body away from my trawl. But I can sense her wavering resolve. My eyes narrow and hold her gaze. I draw in my bottom lip and drag my teeth across the flesh. Her eyes are drawn to the sensual movement only to close tight at my knowing grin.

Filled with a surge of confidence and sense of inevitability, I suck in a deep breath and choose to break the tension. "Actually, I don't do this very often but I do volunteer at the advice centre, mostly helping with sourcing apprenticeships and some basic IT training. The Stone Foundation donates funds to several outreach projects in London, but the company encourages actual volunteering, too. This project is special…to me." I cough to cover my error. Today is not the day for full disclosure, I doubt any day will be. She noticed my hesitation; it was hardly subtle, but I am grateful she doesn't pry. "Volunteering's not just for Christmas, Sam," I tease and flash another bright smile, dispelling the momentary darkness just as quickly as it appeared.

"Oh, no, I know." Sam flushes, strangely embarrassed. "I think this is great —" she starts to mumble.

"You could always volunteer," I interrupt, and Sam scoffs.

"Because what these people really need are tips on being a whore." She laughs off her joke that not only flatlines but fucking pisses me off. I snap, my volume tempered because of the surroundings, but my fury is evident in my tone.

"Don't do that…ever!" Sam's eyes widen with genuine shock. "Don't disparage who you are, Sam. You would be valued, however you chose to help." She struggles to swallow and pinches her eyes tight. When she blinks, I can see the wetness on her lashes. Fuck! I lean over and take one of her hands in both of mine. "Besides that's not what I meant. I meant your legal knowledge would always be welcome." Sam pushes back from the table, standing abruptly, her chair skidding loudly across the floor.

"What?" she whispers.

"Sam, I'm sorry I didn't mean to upset you. Your flatmate was quite chatty, and he may have mentioned you passed the bar together." I step quickly around the table and close the distance until there is none. I cup her face. She places her hand over mine.

"*May have mentioned*? Or did you interrogate him, Jason? Did you deliberately get him drunk? Tell me the truth, or this date ends right now." Her soft tone couldn't sound more serious.

"We had some drinks together, but it wasn't my intention to get him drunk. He wasn't drunk when I left. But I won't lie, when he started talking about you, I did ask more questions than may have been appropriate for a casual conversation. I want this, Sam; I wouldn't have asked it if I didn't." My knuckles stroke the incredible softness of her cheek. "I am in no position to judge the choices you make with your life, and I don't. But I did want a little more information, and Leon was like a fucking gift horse."

"Leon…always thinking he knows best. I don't blame you. He probably targeted you." She shakes her head and lets out a resigned puff of air. We are standing in a strangely intimate hold oblivious to our surroundings. It is only the noise of old metal shutters being pulled closed that breaks this trance. I take her hand in mine, grab our coats from the back of the chairs, and lead her outside. We leave the building, I swing her into my body, and she hits me hard, the impact is enough to wind her. She gasps, and I take that moment to seal my mouth over hers and claim that very breath as my own.

My tongue dives and dances with hers, hot, urgent, possessive. She fights and parries my every move. Her hand grabs my jacket, pulling me tighter to her soft pliant body. A deep groan vibrates through me, causing her to shudder. She sucks in deep steadying breaths. "How would this even work, Jason?" She tries to ask calmly but her panting betrays her riotous emotions.

"Say yes, Sam. The rest is just details." My hand slips to her neck, my thumb tracing the rapid pulse at her jaw. The pressure is firm, and Sam's eyes widen with the sinful intent this simple grip holds. She hesitates, and the pressure on my grip increases, so subtle, barely at all, but the heat from my hand mainlines like a shot of pure, erotic fire straight to her eyes. I sense the exact moment she decides. I am instantly rock hard. She hasn't said the word, and she really doesn't need to. It is like an unveiling of some great treasure. She is alight with acceptance and understanding. Her body thrums under my fingertips.

"Yes." Her voice is barely audible, her affirmation is consumed by my passion, so raw it bruises her swollen lips and robs what was left of her resolve.

THREE

Sam

This is new territory for me, and my body fails miserably to hide its strange mix of excitement and sudden surge of nerves. I don't get nervous...ever, but my fingers tremble, shaking the keys in my hand as I fumble with the lock on my apartment door. He threw me a complete curve ball by taking me to the Mission this morning. I did not see that coming from the enigmatic co-owner of London's elite sex club. *I can't believe I said yes.* I'm not surprised my body is super eager to reconnect with all his hotness. I pinch my legs tight and my mouth actually waters with the erotic recall of what that man is capable of making me feel. That one time, I could barely handle. I mean the sex was phenomenal; we were explosive, but the draw I felt toward him had me running for the hills. What he is asking for now I know is more than sex, but how much more terrifies me.

I'm relieved Jason agreed to come back to my place and didn't insist we go straight to the club or his flat. I need to regain my balance. I feel the subtle shift in power like a physical presence. My heart is pounding, and I am very much outside of my element. At least here I have the comfort of being on my home ground.

Maybe that is why Jason agreed so readily, happy to make this concession because he sensed I was already struggling with the choice I'd made. Intuition is a very seductive quality that I can now add to his ever-growing list of positives. But I am under no illusion about what I'm giving up so he *needs* that very long list. He covers my fingers and holds them still enough to help twist the key in the lock. I drop my head and exhale a deep sigh.

"Sam we don't have to rush this. I want to do this right. I want this more than anything, so I will take it slow with you." His tender words are going to end me, I just know it. A tentative smile creeps across my lips as a warm feeling begins to spread deep inside, a soothing sense of calm. I feel reassured by his softly dominant tone. I nod and push the door open. The door clicks shut behind him, and there is a moment of strange, awkward silence. Other than Leon, I have never actually invited a man back before, but then I have never agreed to switch, either.

Before I get another second to hesitate Jason spins me into his arms fast and slams me with shocking force against the wall in the narrow hallway. I gasp out in surprise only to have the sound swallowed but his passionately demanding kiss. His tongue dives desperately between my lips, tasting, swirling with mine, eliciting unbidden moans from deep inside both our bodies. His hands are pressed on either side of my head, caging me with his large frame. I fist his sweater, curling my fingers and pulling the thin material from his body. My fingertips graze his skin, so warm and tempting, I fight the desire to venture further underneath. I fully admit I am a mixed up mess of confusion. I would normally take exactly what I want for the win, demand to be given what I need to satisfy my own lust. But this isn't *that* game, and we haven't exactly taken the time to set out the rules of play. I forcibly rest my hands against his trim waist and draw in a deep, steadying breath when Jason breaks the kiss.

"So much for taking it slow." My voice is breathless, ragged pants of air.

"There is much to be discussed." His gaze holds me captive. His voice is soft and mesmerising. "How we proceed with this relationship, Sam…with me as your Dominant… I intend to take slow. But how I feel right now has nothing to do with that and has fuck all to do with being slow. I need to be inside you… now." The sexual tension radiates off him like a palpable force, permeating my every nerve ending with wanton desire and rendering me almost speechless… almost.

"Oh." One breathy exhale is all I can manage.

"Oh," he repeats. His lips curl with a knowing, nefarious smile that makes my tummy tighten with anticipation. In one swift sequence of smooth manoeuvres, Jason grabs my hand, strides purposefully straight into my bedroom and dramatically swings me into the centre of the room. He steps me flush to the bed, pushing me back. He follows my reclining body with his; only millimetres separate our combustive heat. He lifts and pulls my sweater over my head and pushes me flat, his fingertips splayed on my chest. He must be able to feel my heart thumping from the inside. "Don't move." His deep voice is gravelly with lust. He crawls back down the bed, hooking his fingers in my waistband and dragging my leggings and panties all the way down my legs. He takes his time, and I squirm with the build-up of delicious pressure at the apex of my legs.

He kneels on the floor and cups his large palms around the back of my knees, pulling me toward the edge of the bed. Scooping my legs over his shoulders, he clamps his hands around my hips and lifts me so my centre is within kissing distance of his lips. "Fuck, I could die right now, because this is heaven." His words blur with the cry that escapes from deep inside me, the moment his tongue touches my core. Soft, then firm, the pressure is perfect as he works his mouth from my tender folds to my needy nub of nerves. His lips cover me, and he sucks for what feels like a lifetime. His hands grip hard because my whole body is thrown into a wild display of spasms and convulsions. If it wasn't for my cries of *'don't stop'* I'm pretty sure he would think I was having a seizure. *God, this feels so good.* I thread my fingers into his short but surprisingly soft hair, making my need to grip a challenge. It's a futile attempt to control him though, because my hand is just pulled along any which way his head chooses to go. He inserts a finger, maybe two, and curls them around, swirling and teasing my most sensitive tissue inside.

I push my head back into the mattress, and my back strikes the perfect arc as every muscle in my body tenses; not even a breath escapes me when I freeze. He holds me there on the crest for days. Christ it feels like days because I sag with utter exhaustion by the time my muscles relax and I am cognisant again.

He looks at me through his dark lashes and sensually drags his bottom lip through his teeth groaning with pleasure as he scrapes the taste of me from his mouth. "You look sleepy." He lets my floppy legs slide off his broad shoulders, and I don't have the strength but to let them slide off the side of the bed, too. I hear a buckle chink and some clothes rustle and drop to the floor. I can't move. He chuckles as he stalks up my body, slowly rousing it with gentle kisses. "You can't be sleepy." His tongue flicks my perky nipple through the delicate lace of my bra. He nips the end through the material, holding it hostage in his teeth. I sigh and stretch, sinking my body away from his bite, just enough that I test his hold and up to the point where it hurts. I whimper and can feel his lips carve a smile against my breast. I lift my head just as he releases me from his teeth but grabs and moulds me in his hand. "I'm still hungry." He sucks my whole nipple into his mouth, hard. I feel the draw from my toes. The lace of my bra is now wet and feels rough against my soft skin, the suction is incredible. If I didn't know better, I would swear he's trying to mark me. His large hands sweep under the edge of my bra, around and under my back. He releases the clip and pulls away, triumphantly swinging my bra like a trophy.

I laugh at his goofy grin, but the heat in his glare evaporates any humour from the room. This man is lethal. He wedges his knees between my thighs and slides onto his side, half on me, half supporting his full weight. One arm is draped across his muscled, cut torso, his hand fisting his impressive cock. I still haven't had the chance to take him in. In the cupboard at the wedding, I could feel his body was toned, felt his muscled back and chest but he kept his suit on the entire time. Even now we are a tangle of limbs, I can't really see his body, but I can see his cock. Large doesn't do him justice. I thought his hands were big but they look more like a child's as he languidly strokes himself up and down. His grin widens when he catches my stare, he chuckles when I snap my jaw shut. How did I not remember *that*, and why the fuck did I not return his call!

Oh yes, because this isn't just sex; this isn't the thrill of a casual hook-up and this isn't me in charge. This is much, much more dangerous.

He leans over my body and pushes the velvet head between my folds, and it feels surreal, delicious and erotic, and wrong. I clamp my legs together but he is firmly wedging them wide.

"Condom!" I cry, but it sounds more like a screech because he physically recoils at the volume.

"Sorry?" He looks down to where we are almost joined. He nudges a little further, and I curve my spine sharply, ensuring minimum safe distance.

"Condom, Jason," I repeat, but his eyes narrow, and he breathes in deeply through his nose like I have said something irritating.

"You're clean…I'm clean. You told me last time you were on birth control. I don't want to wear a condom with you, Sam." He grates out the words slowly with a touch of menace.

"You can't be serious, Jason. I'm a whore!" That made him flinch, his jaw clenches, and his eyes look like they could burn my soul right out of me. He is furious.

"I don't give a shit what *you* call yourself, Sam. Give me one damn reason why I can't fuck you bareback. One reason relating to health that is, because I won't accept any other reason." His tone softens. I can't believe he doesn't care that I'm a whore.

I mean I can't believe that he obviously cares but not about that, and he doesn't even know the truth.

I am in so much trouble.

I shake my head, and with agility and precision, he rolls me onto my back, sinking balls deep in one violent thrust. We both let out a groan filled with angst and ecstasy. He drives deep and deeper still with every pump of his hips, and I meet him stroke for stroke. Fire and lust course through my veins, my fingers grab and claw at his body. His shoulders are solid under my fingertips, and taut muscles flex and move with each undulation. His hands sweep every part of my body, light and searching, coveting. His whole body covers mine. His body leads and mine follows. We move together as one, in tune, in sync…in lov—

"Arhhhhh" I scream when he pulls me tight, angles his hips and sucks hard on my neck. Overwhelmed, out of control and out of nowhere I come…hard. Tiny white stars streak my vision, I can't breathe, and that sound I made is probably the last noise I will ever make. The power of speech has left me.

Relentless, and giving me only the briefest moment of respite, he pulls me up into his lap. We are almost nose to nose. He takes over and lifts my hips, making the necessary movement for me. I am incapable; only his strong arms are holding this limp body rigid. His lips cover mine, his mumbled words wash over me, but I can't understand what he's saying. I am floating somewhere near, held in his arms and just on the edge of heaven.

A deep groan leaves his throat, and I feel it rumble into my mouth as he continues to consume me with reverent kisses. He stops, and I swear time stands still. Our bodies are slick, our collective breath held. I can see the vein in his neck pulsing wildly, an indication that the only sound to be heard would be the synchronised beating of our hearts. Long seconds pass, and the silence is broken by a soft exhale. I watch as the corners of his lips turn up into the most amazing smile.

"Hey," I say. He laughs and slides onto his side. I am still on his lap, albeit on our sides, and he is still buried inside me. He tugs the cover over our bodies and pulls me a little tighter against his chest, even if there really was no space at all to begin with. God, this feels good.

His hand traces my hairline, his finger gathering the stray hairs that are now stuck to my forehead. He carefully tucks them away and just stares at me. His soft brown eyes glow golden and shine bright. His dark brow and strong jaw are relaxed and those lips...smiling. "Hey." He tucks my head under his chin and kisses my hair. I don't think I have ever felt this cherished.

I get a sinking feeling all too soon because I know this isn't real. This isn't what he wants, and I am not going to ruin this and pretend that it is. I am not that naïve...not anymore. I hate that I am doing this, because what we have right now feels kind of perfect. But there is no point if we are not going to be honest. Whatever this is, it has no future if we can't be honest.

"So Jason, now that you have that urge out of the way. When do we start?" I try to keep my tone light, but even I can hear the curt edge. His eyes narrow, and he purses his lips like he has some nasty taste in his mouth. I instantly feel bad and try to rectify my mistake. I soften my question. "Sorry, I didn't mean it to come out like that but this"—I wiggle my finger between us because there is no distance at all due to the way he is still holding me—"this isn't what you want is it?"

"Actually Sam, this is exactly what I want." He tips my chin, closing my mouth because yet again he has rendered me speechless. "I want a relationship. Granted, we—and I mean both of us—it won't ever be a conventional relationship, but I want this. I want your body; I want your time, and I want your submission. But there is no rush. We can sort all the details later. The important thing is you said yes." He kisses the tip of my nose. "I got exactly what I wanted for Christmas. I got you." He holds my stunned gaze with utter sincerity.

"I…I don't know what to say." I manage and he barks out a laugh.

"Did you get what you wanted?" he teases, and I can feel him swell inside me. I sigh.

"Hmm, well, I don't remember asking Santa for several mind-blowing orgasms, but then he is magical, so maybe he just knew," I mock.

"Several you say…I only counted two. But the night is young, and I do have another present I wanted to give you." He flings the covers back and leaps from the bed, his semihard erection bobbing under its own weight, tempting me. I crawl over to the edge and stretch my hand out to try and grab me some.

He steps away. "Nah-ah, naughty girls have to wait for their treats." He bites his bottom lip, and his eyes drag salaciously over my nakedness. I am pretty sure I could tempt him back, but he obviously has plans.

"You going somewhere?" I tuck the loose sheet around me and watch him step into his clothes.

"*We* are going to the club." He wiggles his brow, his face alight with mischief and wickedness. I roll my eyes.

"This is you not rushing. I'd hate to see you in a hurry. You must be like Wylie Coyote on speed." I shuffle to the end of the bed with a little sadness swirling in my tummy. It's going to be hard to believe he wants more when the first thing we do is head for the club. But if I don't trust him, I should just back out now and I don't want to, not really. I have reservations, huge reservations, but trust isn't one of them.

"We don't have to go. But I thought as it is closed to the public…"

"No, no, it's perfect. The sooner the better. The anticipation is killing me." I stand with the sheet wrapped like a toga, loose and dipping low. He steps up to me and lifts me into his arms. There is safety in these arms; I feel it in my bones.

"I want this more than you know, but we really don't have to start today." The concern etched on his handsome face combined with his tender words is my undoing.

"I want to." I don't need to tell him twice. I wouldn't get the chance. His lips consume me, his embrace surrounds but in-spite of his secure hold, I fall.

I have been silent since Jason pulled his car into the reserved parking space at the rear of the club. I know the club is closed, but I also know why we're here. Besides, Jason is one of the owners, so hours of business don't really apply to him. Honestly, my heart hasn't really recovered a normal beat pattern since we finished in my bedroom a short time ago, but I try to take some calming breaths nonetheless. I take enormous comfort from Jason's protective arm around my waist and then his tender hold of my hand as he leads me through the back office. He leaves me for a moment—to get a key, I presume—then he leads me along the corridor and stops just outside one of the private rooms. The only sound is the blood rushing with the fierce pumping of my heart, but I doubt he can hear that. He swings the door wide open and motions for me to step inside. The lion's den, where, up until this moment, I have always been the lion tamer: strong, in control and with wicked whipping skills. Not for the first time since agreeing I question my sanity.

Jason makes me crazy, causes me do crazy things at the very least. Why on earth would I relinquish control like this? But Jason steps up behind me, and all I feel is burning heat and desire for him, to please him. He wraps his strong arms around my waist, holding me tight against his frame; his embrace is so secure it steals my breath. My body is alive with tiny electrical currents dancing over my skin. I tingle from head to toe with longing, lust, and a need so raw I am helpless to do anything but listen to it. Listen to my body and trust that Jason is the right man to relinquish everything I hold dear.

His soft lips caress my neck, and I move to give him all the access possible. He takes his time breathing me in, peppering my skin with a million light kisses, down my neck, along my collarbone and settling on my desperate lips. Gentle and reverent attention morphs into urgent and needy, and an uncontrolled moan escapes the back of my throat. My twitchy fingers ache to hold him. His hands are intertwined with mine, and he is holding them firmly at my side. His deep chuckle and smile against my lips is evidence enough that he knows exactly the effect he has on me. He pulls back and drops all contact, smiling wider at the instant result of his absence and my involuntary deflated posture.

"Hold out your hand." His deep tone drops a little lower, I recognise the authority in the timbre of his voice. I get a flash of a thousand prickles on my skin. The sensual lighting reflects the glow of instant perspiration. I am surprised with my own innate response to his unmistakable switch from affable to dominant, a testament to his natural commanding aura. The ease with which he wears his cloak of Dominance is unmistakable, and I find I am intoxicated. I immediately offer my hand in supplication. His eyes shine dark and crinkle with pleasure. He reaches into his back pocket and slowly releases a long strand of diamonds; they must be almost a metre long. I struggle to swallow the thick, dry lump in my throat. The cool weight sparkles in my palm. I know from the clarity of the crystal shine, that these are the real deal.

"I want you to wear this," Jason states without inflection, "and nothing else." He pauses but remains impassive despite my sudden sharp intake of breath. I am a little stunned and hesitate a moment too long and in a much sterner tone he adds. "Strip…now."

I jump a little but check myself. I am by no stretch a newbie here, yet you wouldn't know it today, since I'm very much acting like one. I straighten my shoulders and step back. I tug at my sweater pulling it over my head, one hand clasped tightly around the diamonds.

Jason turns his back and takes a seat in the winged back chair in the corner of the room, shadowed slightly in the darkened room but no doubt with an unobstructed view of me. I kick off my shoes and pull my leggings down my legs. My confidence in undressing is completely at odds with my riotous nerves, which are alive with anxiety. My legs start to judder when I rest on each one in turn to remove my panties, shaking uncontrollably. I quickly slam each foot flat to stop the visual verification of my uncertainty. I unclip my bra and stand for a moment staring at the darkness in the corner, only Jason's suede walking boots visible.

I let the chain drop to its full length and put my head through the large loop. The diamonds glint and sparkle even in the dimly lit room. The chain falls over the curve of my breast, my light coffee-coloured skin a stark contrast to the pure crystal shards of light reflecting across the room. The necklace hangs low and skims just below my belly button. It is cold on my skin, but that isn't the reason my nipples are hardened peaks or why my breathing is now shallow, rapid pants. Jason makes an exaggerated, disgruntled sounding cough, an 'ahem' noise. I pull my brows together for a moment of thought. What could I have done to cause his displeasure? It takes effort to think this way. I am not used to putting myself on the other end of the whip…so to speak. I shake my head and sniff at my own 'special' moment. I drop to my knees. I lower my head and place my hands on my thighs palms up, my knees spread but not wide, first position.

We haven't discussed boundaries or limits, and I am really not prepared to give up too much too soon, not when we have yet to start our proper negotiation.

The chair scrapes with the sudden movement of Jason standing, he takes three large strides and is directly in front of me. His foot taps the inside of one of my knees. I resist the pressure, my jaw clenching tight enough to make my head pulse with the pressure. The thought that this is never going to work flashes across my mind and I exhale in a loud puff through my nose. Jason drops to his haunches and lifts my chin so I am staring directly into his golden brown eyes. The look of adoration goes some way to appease my anxiety. His dark, lust-filled stare is deeply erotic and calms me enough that the slightest pressure from his other hand has my thighs spreading wider under his fingertips. He groans with satisfaction and draws in a deep breath.

"Hmm, fuck, Sam…You have no idea what you do to me like this. I am one lucky man." His smile is so genuine it steals my breath like a hit to the chest. My own timorous pleasure at his words tips my lips into a reciprocal smile. He stands up, keeping his hand under my chin forcing me to arch and stretch my neck to keep eye contact.

"Tell me what you are, Sam." His deeply possessive tone sends an erotic chill up my spine and settles in a swirl in my tummy. I struggle to swallow the lump the word I know he is waiting to hear are creating in my throat. "Sam," he repeats with more force, "tell me what you are." His grip tightens. His eyes darken with resolve and unmistakeable possession.

"Yours." I barely get the word out. My voice is croaky, but I feel the truth of my declaration like it is carved into the ancient oak of the St Andrew's Cross he is no doubt going to tie me to. As if reading my mind, he scoops me up, with no effort at all, into his arms and carefully places me on the plinth that holds that very cross. He methodically straps my ankles and my wrists and only pauses once he is finished. I don't bother testing the restraints. I know he is more than proficient at his job; I am just struggling with mine. I haven't ever been a willing submissive for my own pleasure, and this new role is testing me on every level.

"What are you, Sam?" His throat obviously constricts, and he slowly swallows. The gravely words escape on a whisper.

"Yours." I raise my chin and meet his gaze. I feel a fire burn inside me, a scorching flame, fuelling the sort of strength I know I am going to need… if I am, in fact… his.

"Mine." He cups my neck and swoops in to steal a kiss that takes us both by surprise with its intensity and urgency. He rests his forehead against mine while we both regain our breath. He runs his hands down the length of the necklace then twists and loops it until it is wrapped several times around my neck. He unclips it to make the last few loops. The single strand is now a tight choker, holding my neck straight and high. "Safe word, Sam, what's your safe word?" His lips are at my ear, and his cool breath chills my skin, goosebumps dance on the surface like little beacons of panic.

"You said we'd go slow, Jason." My voice is pitched with worry, and his hand instantly soothes with a gentle stroke down my cheek. He plants a tender kiss on my lips.

"We will go slow but I want you to be able to stop this if it even gets to be a little too much. I am not going to ruin this opportunity with my impatience…" I nod with relief and understanding. "So a safe word?" he repeats.

"Switch," I say after a moment of thought. I struggle to swallow, my throat is so dry. Honestly, I can't remember a time when I've felt so conflicted, so turned on, so alive. I have been numb for so long I no longer have the strength or will to fight this pure desire saturating my soul.

He gives a curt nod and flashes a wicked smile. He slips two fingers through the choker tightening it and restricting my breath in one move. I gasp, my body tenses, and my muscles flex against the restraints. I feel the intensity of my desire like a molten pool of liquid building in my core. My eyes widen when the next whispered words cut the sexual tension with a precision scalpel.

"Not anymore, Sub."

Jason

Jesus, I am a lucky man. I'd pinch myself right now if I thought she wouldn't notice. She notices everything; her eyes are bright and curious, scrutinising my every move. Dark pools of desire blend with a mixture of wide-eyed innocence and trust. That fucking trust is what makes me the luckiest man alive. She may have reservations about the role I want her to play but she trusts me enough to try, and that is such a fucking turn-on. She's not just a Domme; she the best damn Domme in the city, and I have her tied up and trembling.

Luckiest. Fucking. Man Alive.

I stand inches from her naked body, naked save for the diamond choker I bought with her delicate neck in mind. My jeans hang loose, and I ditched my shirt the moment I sat down to watch her strip. The heat between us is charged, and tiny sparks like a live current jump the sliver of distance between our bodies. I draw in a deep breath. I can smell her arousal, and she is intoxicating, sweet, and sinful. My hand is still twisted into her collar, and with the smallest clench of my fist, I can restrict her airway, but my hand is relaxed…for now.

I place my finger on her mouth and push between her soft, full lips. Her sweet little tongue eagerly wraps around my digit, and she sucks me in on a moan. My cock hardens, uncomfortably restricted in my jeans, but this feels so good. I pull from her mouth and draw the wet tip of my finger along her collarbone and slowly down between her breasts. Her gaze never leaves mine but her lids flutter closed when I reach the tiny landing strip of hair pointing directly to her centre. I sink my hand between her legs and swirl my thumb in a steady pattern around her clit. Her breath hitches, and she bites back a whimper that lurks at the back of her throat. I bite my own lips to keep from smiling but flash a wicked grin when I sink two fingers into her fresh wetness. That whimper she tried to hold back escapes, and her hips sink on my hand, greedy for a little more. She sighs with a grumble of frustration, tugging against her restraints even as her lips curl with a knowing smile. This is a game she is familiar with, I am sure. She sucks her lips into her mouth, and I can see she is struggling to hold her tongue. I help her out and cover her mouth with mine. My smile spreads wide as I try to crush that grin off her lips. My tongue dives and plunges, tasting her and swirling in a delicious dance with hers. I pull away, and she wraps her lips tight around my retreating tongue, sucking it back into her mouth. I can feel the erotic pull of her sucking me like that deep in my balls.

A low groan rumbles from my chest, and she giggles. This may be a challenge for her, but I can see she is fully prepared to test my own skill set every step of the way. I relax with a deep sense of calm because this is no challenge at all. I believe we are made for this, made for each other, and her breathtaking smile and soaking wetness clenching around my fingers are all the evidence I need.

"Do I make you happy, sweetheart?" My breath whispers across her skin, but she is instant ice in my hand. Her eyes glaze and all colour drains from her flawless skin.

"Switch." She mouths the word but there is no sound. I only see it because I am staring with utter confusion at her face. She's like a statue, a shell, no little tells from her sweet body silently begging me for more, no sighs or cries… nothing. One second she is warm and sentient to my touch; the next she is frozen.

I have so many questions, but I don't voice them now. I lean up to unstrap her wrist, my hand stretching across her face. She flinches away from my reach, and her body begins to shake. She's sucking in large gulps of air, but she seems to be struggling to breathe. Her chest rises with building panic, and her lips are tinged with blue. *Shit.*

"Sam, look at me." I keep my voice calm but stern. I don't know where the fuck she has gone but I need her back with me. Just me. "Look at me, Sam." I repeat just as firmly. Her eyelids flutter, and her brows knit like she is trying to concentrate, but she doesn't seem to be able to focus. Her eyes fix on mine, but they are vacant pools of sadness. I manage to unclip her arms and hold her steady, afraid she will fall if I release her. Her arms fall lifelessly to her sides and she sways unsteadily. I deftly unclip her ankle straps and sweep her into my arms before she falls. I step quickly over to the bed and grab the loose silk sheet at the end. It's large enough to wrap around both our bodies, but it's thin, and the room is air conditioned to a cool temperature. It won't afford much warmth, but my body heat will. I cocoon her in my arms and wait. I slide us up the bed and lean against the headboard. Her body still trembles, but her rapid deep breathing has calmed.

I rest my lips on her hair and lay kiss after kiss, gently rocking and squeezing what comfort I can. I am good at what I do. My role as a Dominant is as natural to me as breathing. Although one can learn how to be a good Dom, to be the best, I believe, has more to do with natural inclination than anything that can be taught. I know how to read people. I see them in their masks, and I see them at their most raw, but it doesn't take a rocket scientist to see that, for Sam, I just triggered something bad.

I'm not sure how long I've been asleep, but I wake when I feel her wriggle in my arms. They protectively lock on instinct in a frame around her. I look down and see her big soulful eyes looking at me with such sadness it cleaves my chest apart. I bury it, though. She doesn't need my worries piling on top of whatever shit-storm she is currently processing.

"Well, that was new." I exhale a light laugh because I can see her face is a picture of turmoil and devastation. I can deal with sadness. What I don't want is regret, and she needs to know nothing has changed. Her lips falter with her first attempt to smile at my comment. She swallows thickly and draws in a deep, slow breath.

"I need to leave." She drops her head and averts her eyes. I try for calm, but it comes out as a frustrated, loud exhale. She shifts to move but I just grip a little tighter.

"You need to talk to me." She shakes her head.

"Jason, you don't want this…trust me. This is all wrong." Her voice catches, and I don't know whether to shake her or just hold her some more. I hold her. I lift her chin up so she can see my eyes. I have to credit her strength because she doesn't shy from the contact. "I can't give you what you want."

"I want you, so I think you can." I know she feels unbearable sadness for whatever reason, but I won't let her give up on this. I flash my most confident smile, which causes her brows to wrinkle with suspicion. Suspicion is better than sadness. "You would feel more comfortable at home?"

"I would." Her voice is filled with resignation. She closes her eyes this time, but not before I see the hurt settle in deep. She drops her head, again.

"Okay." I lift us both from the bed and place her carefully on her feet. Her hands reach for my hips to steady herself, but she quickly lets go. I don't say a word when she turns and walks away. I don't speak as we both quietly put our clothes back on, and I remain silent until she is sitting in the passenger seat of my car.

"I won't be a moment. I have to lock up." She doesn't even look up just nods and stares at her cupped hands. Now I happen to fucking love submissive gestures like this, but this is fucking killing me. I slam the door, making her jump. It takes me less than five minutes to pack my duffle bag with enough clothes to last the week. I throw the bag over my shoulder into the back seat when I slide into the front.

"Home?" I check one more time.

"Please." Her voice is such a sad whisper I want to reach over and pull her into my arms all over again, and I will…soon. "I'm sorry Jason," she adds. Her eyes shine with moisture, and I have to grip the wheel to prevent myself from tearing her from her seat. She needs to be home…where she feels safe.

"I know." I rev the engine to a loud roar so I'm not sure she heard me, but she has already retreated in on herself, so it doesn't matter. The only thing that matters is getting her to talk to me, and she won't do that unless she feels safe.

The streets are empty, dark and rightly deserted. I keep casting my eyes her way and notice she has dipped her head and tilted to see the Christmas lights that hang across some of the main London roads. She's smiling, so I decide to take the long way home, weaving my way down every festively lit street I know. She turns her head to me when she realises what I'm doing, her smile is brighter than a million Christmas lights. No one in their right mind would actually chose to drive around London, deliberately picking longer routes. But it's Christmas Day, and I wouldn't be surprised to see a lonesome bushel sweeping down Bond Street.

This year, the most expensive shopping destination in town has large white peacock feathers spanning the width and running the entire length of the road. A canopy of mock diamonds sparkle overhead, a poor cousin to those on display in the Graff or Cartier windows or the ones that still lie flush against Sam's neck.

We drive slowly along Piccadilly. The arcades on either side tend to go all out with the decorations, and this year is no exception. But the window displays are always worth checking out. I pull up and park outside Harrods, something that would have you clamped and fined within five minutes on any other day. Each window has a fairy tale theme, and the one we are looking at is *Cinderella*. I don't think they could've fit anymore sparkle in that tiny space.

"Beautiful," I say but I don't mean the display because that pales in comparison to what I have sitting beside me.

"Cinder-fucking-ella," she sniffs out and looks over to me because I am silent and clearly waiting for her to clarify. "I can relate to the evil stepmother, but honestly, there is no such thing as Prince Charming."

I grin and her eyes drop to my lips when I drag my tongue slowly, deliberately along the seam.

"I agree. I personally prefer the big bad wolf. You know exactly what he wants, he can see you better, hear you better and—" I wink when her laugh finishes my dirty train of thought. *Yeah I can definitely eat you better.*

I pull the car into a space a few houses down from Sam's place and switch the engine off. She turns to me with a brave face and a tentative smile.

"Thank you, Jason, and I'm—" I don't hear the rest of whatever excuse and brush off she had prepared. I reach over into the back seat to grab my bag. I open my door, and I take my time stepping around the front of the car. I keep my eyes fixed on her, and she closely watches my face, but I'm giving nothing away. I open her door and wait, smiling to myself at the look of complete surprise painting her face. "Um…" She takes my offered hand, and once the car is locked, I pull her into my arms. My hand threads into her hair, skimming the choker and cupping her head.

"Sam, you're an intelligent woman. You didn't really think that was the end, did you?" I raise my brow and keep my smile wide.

"I…Jason…" She stiffens and her brows furrow. She's working up to making some sort of objection I just don't care to hear. I cover her mouth with mine. We have plenty of time to talk. Right now, she needs to remember just how good we taste together. She instantly relaxes in my arms. My tongue sweeps across her sweet lips, and she breathes out a light moan that mainlines straight to my cock. I walk her back and press her against the hood of my car, her back curves with the pressure I'm putting on her small frame. Sprawled and pressed together our bodies collide. We lay with heat matching that rising from the engine underneath, zero to full throttle in no time at all. Fuck, she feels so good. I use one hand to protect her head, her thick dark hair falls in a halo pattern, glossy and rich and a sharp contrast to the matte black paintwork of my car. Her dark eyes shine, and although I am pressing her body flush to mine, she is somehow able to make tiny undulations beneath me. The sexiest fucking movements ever. They are driving me insane. I hold her fixed against my mouth. My other hand drifts down her side. I grip around the back of her thigh and pull her leg around my hip. She doesn't hesitate, her demand for me equals my own for her. Urgent, breathless kisses, swiping her tongue around in a delicious duel with mine, her hands fist and pull me hard against her. We could go right here. I know it. I stand back, leaving her heaving in much needed oxygen. I drag my hand slowly down her body, between her breasts, resting in the centre where I can feel the power of her heartbeat in my palm. Just where I want her.

"Still think you can't give me what I want?" My voice sounds gravelly and heavy with lust. "Still think this is wrong?"

Her lips spread wide into a wicked smile. "Well, we are in the middle of the street."

"And fucking outdoors is wrong?" I quip and nudge my straining hard-on against her centre. She laughs out but covers her mouth to hide the sound. I hate when she does that, I love that sound. I pull her hand free.

"Not at all, but curtains are twitching and public fucking isn't my thing." I pull her up from the car and push her hair out of her eyes, which are now smiling.

"Good to know. See? Now I know one of your limits." I pause a moment before I go on. "This was my fault, Sam. I was too eager and I should've known better. I do know better. Let me make this right." I keep my light tone but shift it mid-sentence to soft and sincere. "I know you want this, Sam…as much as I do." I kiss her lips; I can't stop myself. "Do you trust me?" As much as I want this, as much as I can't keep my hands off her, this is the clincher or deal breaker. Because in any relationship, but more so with BDSM, if we don't have trust… we have nothing.

"I do."

My smile is so wide my cheeks ache. I really like the sound of that. "Good." I thread my fingers through hers and relish the instant grip she gives in return.

Sam ran herself a bath and I have been searching in her kitchen for something to cook. I wasn't necessarily expecting there to be all the ingredients for a full-on Christmas dinner, but I did expect a little more than this. The refrigerator is almost as empty as the day it stood in the showroom save six bottles of Bollinger and a litre of milk. The cupboards are filled with cans, ready pancake mix and tubs of weird protein powders for gaining bulk, some cereals, and very little else. I am using what she did have. A small tub of cream, some dried pasta, overripe tomatoes, and a sorry looking basil plant from her window ledge. The sauce takes less time to cook than the pasta, which is simmering nicely, and she did have a packet of those part-baked baguettes, so I am just waiting for them to turn golden. Then we are good to go.

The aroma fills the small apartment. It's a cosy space considering the extra height of the ceilings and large windows. A converted first floor apartment of a much larger Victorian terrace house in the fashionable and expensive West End of London. The living space is open plan. Just off to the left of the kitchen is a small dining table with four chairs and a low hanging chrome light in the centre. It is laid out with fresh flowers and now holds two place settings. The seating area has two small sofas, not matching but with various cushions and throws rugs. There is one leather armchair, and I am pretty sure that is a sex lounger disguised as a chaise-lounge tucked against the far wall. There is a massive television with a stack of controls for both an Xbox and PlayStation. I know the apartment has three bedrooms. I have only seen one, but I get the feeling Sam is sharing her home with a guy.

Sam enters the room in the cutest pyjama set I have ever seen on a Dominatrix. White with a million pink frolicking bunnies, but on closer inspection, they aren't frolicking, they are fucking. I laugh, and her cheeks colour and she giggles. She raises her perfectly shaped brow to challenge me to say something, but I just smile and pour the pasta to drain. She slides on the stool opposite and leans on the kitchen island. I have set the plates ready for food.

"That smells good." She sniffs in a deep, satisfied breath. "Can I do anything to help? Actually, don't ask. I didn't even know I had pans." Looking more than a little sheepish, she points to the pan with the simmering sauce.

"You don't say." I mock and start plating up. I'm no gourmet chef in the kitchen, but I can cook. Surely it's an essential life skill. "Do you mind telling me what you *were* planning on eating today?"

"Apart from you…" She drops her voice low and sultry, and I nearly drop both plates. Fuck, I'm instantly hard, but I'm happier she is back to her confident self. She jumps down from the stool and follows me to the table. "I would've ordered take-out." She shrugs and shakes her head like I have asked the dumbest question.

"It's Christmas Day…nothing's open."

"It's London, and I think you'll find everything is open if you know the right people." She dips her finger in the sauce and sucks it clean. That would've been boiling hot, and she didn't flinch. So, high threshold for pain. Not helping the hard-on but good to know. I drop the napkin in my lap to hide my tenting jeans.

"Oh, I can do drinks!" She leaps from the table with excitement. Pulling a chilled bottle of Bollinger from the fridge and grabbing two glasses from a high shelf, she sashays back to the table. "My oven is hot." She twists the cork with the bottle supported between her thighs, and I am all kinds of distracted. Was that a euphemism? Because if it was then *mine* is hard…fucking hard. "Is there something in the oven Jason?" Her knowing smile has me adjusting my pants. Shit! The bread! I jump from the table and run the short distance to the kitchen. I open the oven to a billow of steam, which fortunately, is still white. The ends of the bread had started to turn and catch but the rest is fine. I bring it over to the table pulling chunks apart and handing Sam a piece. I'm all about the presentation.

I raise my glass for a toast and she eyes me with suspicion but tips her glass to meet mine all the same. "What shall we toast, Sam?" The glasses hover millimetres from each other.

"To wishful thinking." Her smile falls flat, and I shake my head.

"Oh, I think we can do better than that. How about to truth and trust. I already have one and I'm getting the other tonight." Her eyes narrow but she chinks her glass against mine and takes a small sip of the bubbly.

"You are awfully confident about that, Jason." She eyes me over the lip of her glass, her expression a mix of I'm not sure because she has regained some of her former sass but there is a tinge of sadness, too. I don't answer but take a big gulp of Champagne. We eat the meal in comfortable silence, and when she places her cutlery together on her clean plate, I take one of her hands and hold it between mine. I lean toward her and smile when she mirrors my move.

"Tell me, Sam, did me tying you up turn you on?" Her breath catches as my words float on a soft exhale toward her lips. She tips her tongue out to wet the sudden dryness before she answers.

"You know it did." She exhales softly.

"I did know, but I wanted you to acknowledge the truth." She tries to slip her hand free, but I hold it firm and kiss the individual fingertips. Her breath catches on her reply.

"The truth doesn't really matter does it?" She sighs, stretching out some tension in her neck by rolling her head from side to side. Her hair falling in the loose ponytail as she moves. She straightens her shoulders and flashes me her most seductive smile. Her sinfully breathy voice washes over me. Her words are like audible Viagra. "Of course you turn me on. Look at you. Even if you didn't look like Apollo, you fuck like a porn star. I'd have to be in a coma not to get wet around you."

"Hmm, flattery will get you fucked, Sam, but it won't stop this conversation from happening," I reply deadpan, but laugh when her shoulders sink. I wonder if she has ever had someone read her like this.

"I wonder if you are so used to getting your own way that you even realise when you are in manipulation mode." She flutters her eyelashes with mock innocence and finally pulls her hand free only to place it on her mock wounded heart. I chuckle and push back from the table. I take her hand and lead her to the softest looking of the sofas, the one near the sex lounger. "Don't insult me trying to deny it. Just know it won't work on me. I won't let you top from the bottom so we better just get that straight right now." I roughly pull her to sit between my legs, my arms around her, my thighs encasing her, and her back to my chest. As much as I mean those words, when her eyes well with sadness it will take a much stronger man than I to deny her a single thing.

"It turned you on when I restrained you, so that wasn't an issue for you?" I rephrase my question, and although I feel her initially tense, she also relaxes back against my chest. I languidly stroke the length of her arm and across her tummy. "Just the truth baby, nothing more." I kiss her hair.

"It did. I was nervous, but yes, it turned me on…a lot." I smile into her hair. This is progress.

"That pleases me." I pause to let that sink in. "How does that make you feel?"

"I…I…That turns me on, too. I like to please you." My thumb rests on her wrist, and I can feel her little pulse beating double time.

"And you do—"

"But—" I silence her interruption by cupping my large hand over her mouth, which makes her giggle.

"Shush…we're making progress." I laugh, too.

"I have to ask, Sam. You flinched from me after you safeworded out. Did you really think I would harm you?" The fact that I have to ask this cuts me to the core, but after her meltdown, I really can't take anything for granted. She twists in my arms and tucks her knees up under herself, so she is kneeling in between my legs. She strokes my cheek, and her eyes are filled with remorse.

"Not ever. Not you." She drops her head, unable to keep eye contact, but I won't let her avoid me like that. "I'm so sorry, Jason."

"Don't…You have nothing to be sorry for. You did *nothing* wrong." My thumb catches the stray tear poised to tumble down her cheek. "I want you to tell me who did?"

FIVE

Sam

This is a clusterfuck. The last time I felt this vulnerable was the day Richard destroyed me and my mother abandoned me, that day, over ten years ago. I may have felt a little lost when I left home, when Leon took me in, but I haven't felt this raw since the day I was left to bleed. I don't want to relive any part of my childhood, I don't want to remember *that* day or my relationship with Richard. But I know if I want to have more than a one-night-stand with Jason, it's exactly what I will have to do. I let my head sink back against his hard chest and feel the strong thump-thump of his heart. I savour the quiet, gentle breaths he takes that make both of our bodies rise and fall. The calm before the storm. This is my choice, I know. I could shut him down. Tell him it's none of his damn business and hide, like I have done every time anyone has dared to get close. Everyone except Leon and now Jason.

His hands are large and strong. So much power and control at his fingertips. I don't doubt for a moment he could easily crush me with his physical strength, but there is more to control than overpowering someone. I am five foot ten, slender build, and I have men twice my size quake when I enter a room. No, it's not about brute strength; it's about trust. Do I trust Jason enough? Not just to give up control, but do I trust him enough to let him in?

He delicately traces his finger the length of my arm, circling my palm and dipping across my tummy. Feather-light and hypnotic, I fall a little more under his spell.

"Sam?" His voice is level, but I can feel the heavy weight of the unanswered question. I draw in a breath, and he slips his fingers between mine, entwined and secure, and he grips my hand.

"My mother." I am surprised how emotionless my voice sounds. She only died recently, but still I feel nothing but bitterness and bile for that woman. My only living relative, the one person who was supposed to love me and protect me, but instead, she gift wrapped me and gave me to a monster. I hate them both.

Richard's abuse was mostly physical, but the mental abuse I lay firmly at my mother's feet. The guilt, the shame, the hypocrisy and hell I lived, every day was her poisoned gift to me, her only child.

"My mother pimped me out to the son of the wealthiest family in the village. Insisted I date him, ignored the bruises and cuts even when I told her exactly who had done them. When I dared to break up with him because I wouldn't let him fuck me, she locked me naked in the coal shed for a week with no food, my penance for sinning. I wasn't allowed to *say* the word fuck, there was no way she wouldn't kill me if I actually *did* fuck. She made me beg him to take me back, promise him anything. To *her* anything meant my heart and hand or some misplaced romantic notion. But to *him* it meant I was going to become his personal fuck toy."

"Why didn't you leave?" Jason's words startled me. I had started to drift to a much darker place. His rough, sexy timbre grounded me back to now.

"I was sixteen, Jason. I had no other family, and because my mother was so strict, I had no friends, either. I didn't have a mobile phone until I left home at eighteen. We had a television, but only for the news, and I had to use the computer at school for any homework. I was *very* sheltered," I pause, "but not at all protected." He hums in understanding. Solutions always seem so simple from a distance. "I left the first chance I got but it was too late, the damage was done."

Sam aged sixteen

I pull my bedcovers over my head shutting out the first light peeking through the gaps in the curtains. I don't have to fake illness to try and avoid the day. I feel like shit. My stomach is in knots and I am consumed with an overwhelming sense of dread. I hate that she made me call him. I hate that she made me beg him to take me back when I finally had the strength to break it off. I knew what he wanted. I knew what he was going to take regardless, and I knew she'd kill me if I let him. Either way I was fucked.

I don't remember her being this twisted, this deranged when I was little, but as soon as I started to grow into a woman, I was apparently destined for hell. I wasn't allowed friends let alone boyfriends. She would walk me to school and pick me up. I did my chores and homework, and as slight as she was, she was

quick with a belt and fierce, with a volatile temper. It didn't take me long to step into line and accept this was my life.

That all changed when I was fifteen and the Brookes-Hamilton family moved into the Loughborough Estate. Their land stretched the length of the small county and surrounded the village where I lived.

I was waiting for my mother after school, like I always did, when he walked over to me. He stood so close and bold as anything, he stroked my face. He twirled a long strand of my hair around his finger before tucking it behind my ear. My mouth must have fallen open because he chuckled and I quickly snapped it shut. I remember the heat in my face and the strange feeling in my tummy. He was handsome, taller than me with white blonde hair and piercing blue eyes. He had a light tan and smooth skin. I wasn't sure how old he was, and even though he wasn't in school, he was still school age, maybe a few years older than me.

I felt excited at the time to receive his undivided attention. I thought I was mostly invisible to everyone, but he'd noticed me. I shrank back from his touch though, when I saw my mother approach.

I shouldn't have worried about her wrath; she knew exactly who he was, and in turn, he charmed her with his perfect enunciation and immaculate manners.

It wasn't the prospect of his family's money that flashed in her eyes. We weren't rich, but we were doing okay, and we had my inheritance. No, money wasn't her obsession. She was driven by a misplaced sense of injustice that she was born into the wrong class of people. She was corrupted with her need to be better than anyone else. Evil intent lit her dull grey eyes with the understanding that before her in the form of Richard was her golden opportunity.

*For the first few months it was like living in a Jane Austin novel. I was chaperoned on my dates with Richard, and she dangled my inheritance before him like an archaic dowry. He was the perfect gentleman, and any reservations my mother had about his intentions evaporated when, one afternoon, he declared he would make me his wife as soon as I turned eighteen. She couldn't have been happier, and I felt like I had died before my life had even begun. I liked him. At the time, he was sweet and kind, a little obnoxious at times, but I didn't love him. I hadn't lived any part of my life as my own, how could I possibly just become someone's wife? I didn't know who I was or what I wanted. How could I know if he would make **me** happy? How could I know if I could make **him** happy? It was a joke, a horrible, twisted joke. But once he made this announcement, I no longer required the chaperone, and I was no longer safe.*

My mother strides into my room and briskly pulls the curtains wide. I pinch my eyes shut. Even with my head under the covers, the glare from the sun is too much.

"Why aren't you up?" she snaps and starts to pull at my blankets. "He'll be here in no time at all. You have to look your best." She has this sing-song voice when she's happy that is just on the nausea-inducing side of being too sweet. It makes my stomach roll and my toes curl. I don't want to look my best. I don't want to see him again, but as with so many things, I don't get what I want. I pull myself up and scowl at her back as she picks her way through my limited wardrobe. I am probably the only girl in school that loves her uniform because it's the most fashionable thing I get to wear.

"He doesn't just want to hold my hand, Mum. What am I supposed to do?" My voice is soft but I hope she can hear the desperation I feel because it fell on deaf ears the last time I tried to reason with her. She spins round and launches herself across the room, slapping me hard across my cheek. Raising her hand to strike again, I know better than to try and protect myself. I just close my eyes and take another hit. She grabs my hair and yanks me from the bed. I crumple to the floor and my scalp screams as she tears the loose hairs on the edge of her grip. I cry out and try to stand to stop the pull.

"You listen to me, Grace Cartwright. I did not raise you to be a whore. No man will ever want a whore as their wife, and make no mistake, you **will** be his wife." She releases her grip and I slump to the floor rubbing my tender scalp. Her eyes are wild, her nostrils flare, and for a moment, she looks more demon than human. She certainly doesn't look like a mother. "You will not ruin this chance we have to become the family we always should have been." She straightens her shoulders and lifts her chin high, looking down her haughty nose at me. I want to scream, 'I'd rather be an honest whore than a pretentious snob', but I bite my tongue because she honestly scares the life out of me. The last time I answered back, I starved and nearly froze to death.

"What if he doesn't really want to marry me, Mother?" I plead, my cheeks still blazing. She waves her hand dismissively.

"Don't be ridiculous. He knows about the necklace." She shakes her head at my silly suggestion. Christ that fucking necklace! More like a millstone. My grandfather bequeathed it to me, some family heirloom that is supposed to be oh so valuable but it just makes me feel so utterly worthless. Like no one could possibly want me for *me*. I am not enough, I will have to buy my way into someone's heart. A position reinforced on an almost daily basis by my mother. "Richard will marry you, I made sure to show him…he understands." She snickers and taps her nose like it's a sweet little secret. I hate her so much. I don't care whether his proposal was genuine. He told my mother a formal announcement would be made on my eighteenth birthday. But that is three years away, and I know with absolute certainty that there is no way he would be happy just holding my hand for that length of time.

"He's strong, Mother." I swallow the lump in my throat. At this moment, I fear her temper more than I fear him and the scowl that distorts her face makes me recoil further back against my bed. She steps up to me and pinches my chin between her bony fingers; her nails are like blades against my skin. The pressure increases with each hate-filled word she utters.

"You listen to me, Grace. God may have given you the body to sin, but it is on your head if you chose that **short** path. I will not tolerate it. You will be no one's whore, Grace. I'll see you in a coffin before I let that happen. Do I make myself clear?" Her calm tone is as eerie as it is cold. I can feel the trickle of blood down my chin where her fingernails finally broke the skin. I nod silently and feel her hand relax. "Now, let's get you ready!" She claps her hands together. The blood on her fingers also drips down my face onto my nightdress. Her brow furrows with darkness and a challenge that I am not equipped to accept. I won't defy her. She terrifies me. She may be deranged but that doesn't make her any less capable of carrying out her threat. I flash a quick and insincere smile, silently praying that my crushed spirit, which she would interpret as insolence, is hidden beneath my cheery exterior.

"What shall I wear?" Every muscle in my body works to make my voice sound bright and excited when all I want to do is cry.

"Do you always have to dress like Mary Fucking Poppins?" Richard sneers and pulls the top buttons of my blouse loose. He pulls his car out of our drive and revs the engine loud and unnecessarily. I close the buttons back up to my breasts as he managed to undo them to my waist.

"It's not my fault, Richard. You know my mother." I let out a resigned sigh when he sniffs with derision.

"Ah, yes, your mother. I guess I have **her** to thank for our little reunion. I should perhaps send some flowers. Nothing says 'thank you for pussy' quite like flowers." He grunts out a sleazy laugh. His hand drifts to my knees and he pushes his fingers roughly between my legs. I clamp them tight. "Come now, sweetheart, you know I'm gonna make you happy." Sickness crawls in my stomach, and I shudder. He laughs loudly but returns his hand to the steering wheel.

The private drive to Richard's house is about a mile and winds through dense woodland, and this time of year, the ground is covered with a thick blanket of bluebells. Shards of sunlight filter through the heavy spring canopy, dropping spotlights of sunshine on the beautiful flowers. It's magical. I can't hide my smile at the view, but it freezes on my face when I look at Richard regarding me with no warmth in his eyes. His car churns the gravel driveway as he speeds past the front of the house and fails to slow down. He continues down an unmade part of the drive that is more overgrown. I rub my arms at the sudden chill I feel, despite now being out of the shade of the woods and in the open, heading toward the lake.

"Where are we going?" I shift, ill at ease, and hold my arms across my waist, a useless barrier, I know. Richard drops his hand to my knee once more and slides it roughly up my leg to the very top of my thigh. I clamp my legs to stop him hitting his target. He howls out a sickening laugh.

"The lake house...thought we shouldn't have your first time in the house. My parents are home, and you might be a screamer." He spreads his lips wide with pleasure.

"Richard I...I don't think I'm ready. I don't want—"

"Sweetheart—" His interruption is sharp and his tone is clipped. "This isn't about what you want though is it? This is about what your mother wants and what I want. I thought we understood each other, Grace. If that isn't the case, I can take you home." He tilts his head with mock compassion, but his smile is more sinister than sincere.

"No," I shake my head. I can feel my eyes tingle with imminent tears. My nails pierce hard into my palms and I blink rapidly to stop the flow. I swallow the lump and try to force a smile that barely curves my lips. "I'm just nervous."

"Stage fright." He squeezes his hand at the top of my thigh so hard I know it will bruise. "I have something for that." His eyes glaze with a dark vacant glare that freezes my heart. He screeches the car to stop in front of the wooden steps leading to the weathered lake house. Several cars are parked on either side.

His friend's cars.

"Are you having a party?" I can't help my naive hopefulness filling my voice. Richard regards me carefully and then sniffs out a bitter laugh.

"Not a party no, more like a show and not tell." He snickers and leaps from the car. Every part of me wants to run. I slam the lock down on my side of the car. He drops down to meet my eyes. He raises a brow, shaking his head at my pathetic display of defiance. He clicks the door open with his remote and pulls is open before I can hold it shut. Gripping my arm he yanks me from my seat and throws me against the bonnet of the car. His large body quickly pinning me immobile.

"Richard, you're scaring me." I cry out, my body is shaking and I hope he can hear the fear that is surging through my veins and turning my stomach. He wedges his body between my thighs, pushing my legs wide, one hand on my hip and one gripping my jaw.

"Do you love me, sweetheart?" He says through angry gritted teeth.

"What?" I choke out my surprise.

"It's a simple question, Grace. Do. You. Love. Me?" With each word he increases the pressure of his grip until tears spring to my eyes from the pain. I try to nod but his scowl looks more demonic than human, and I give him his answer, fearing for my life if I didn't.

"Of course," I whisper.

"Of course what, sweetheart?" he growls.

"Of course, I love you." I can't swallow the lump in my throat, my mouth is so dry.

"Good. Then you will do everything I demand without question or hesitation understand?"

I nod but quickly reply, "Yes."

He drops his head to my forehead and lets out a heavy breath. His body is a dead weight on mine and making it difficult to breathe. I start to panic as I struggle to draw in another breath. His eyes cloud and I fail to see any life in the dull blue colour.

"Now is your time to prove just how much you love me, sweetheart. I told my friends that I am your Master and you will do anything for me. But they obviously didn't take my word for it." He pushes up and I draw in a gasp of air and cough in an effort to get more oxygen. He pulls me hard against his body. His hand pinches a clump of my hair and he yanks it sharply. "You will obey me, Grace, because you love me and want to make me happy." He taps my nose playfully, and I am speechless as I look at the devil himself straighten his clothes and drag his hand through his floppy hair. He takes my hand and leads me numbly up the steps. "The best way to get rid of stage fright is to have a very appreciative audience." He swings the double doors wide, and I recoil at the stale, dusty smell, and ominous tension that hits me like a brick wall. I don't move. I can't. I am terrified. Twenty of Richard's buddies line the outside of the room, beer, cigarettes or both in their hands. Smoke swirls like a toxic gas. I just pray it is poison enough to knock me out. I don't want any part of this nightmare. The room is hazy, dirt curtained windows hindering the natural light *of the midday sun. My stomach drops when all eyes turn toward me.*

I squeeze Richard's hand noticing the small sofa dressed like an altar in the middle of the room. My eyes are wide with panic, Richard peers down his nose, eyes cold and a sneer distorting his lips.

"Please don't do this, Richard. I beg you."

"That's a start at least. On your knees, bitch," he snarls and I drop to my knees and hope to die.

I shudder now at the memory and at the retelling.

Jason shifts to the side and slips around so he is on his side and I am lying flat with him staring down at me. His finger traces my hairline, along my jaw and over my lips. A soft pattern he follows with his dark eyes, his gaze is deep and intense. It causes an equally deep furrow on his brow and mars his perfect face with obvious concern.

"What are you thinking?" The silence is understandable. I laid some unpleasant baggage to process at his feet, but he did ask, and the longer he just watches me, the more unsettled I feel.

"The trigger wasn't anything I did. It was what I said." I nod even though it wasn't a question. "It's very likely there will be others." Again a statement, but I stiffen because this feels like a brush off. I laid myself out there or at least started to and he sounds like he is starting to make a list of reasons. But, as if reading my mind he takes the hand I had started to wrap protectively around my waist. "Hey, Sam, look at me." His fingers lock with mine as do his eyes. "I'm just letting you know I know *that* trigger; it won't happen again, but given what you've told me, others might surface." His tender voice and confident smile warm me. "We will deal with them exactly like this. We will talk. You know how much shit gets fucked up because people don't just talk. That won't happen with us." My lips smile wide when he says that and he chuckles. "Oh, you like that, huh? Yeah baby, we're an *us*, and I want full disclosure. Half of the shit Daniel and Bethany went through wouldn't have happened if they'd just fucking sat down and talked. I don't play games like that." His voice drops with a husky whisper. "There are much better games to play."

"Full disclosure? I'm not sure you can handle that, Jason." I sigh as his fingers sensuously walk down my tummy and dip under the edge of my panties. But I slap his hand hard to prevent any further exploration. "Besides I don't hear any of your deep, dark secrets."

"Hmm…That might be because I don't have any." He wiggles his fingers, but I keep my grip firm.

I scoff. "Now I find that very hard to believe."

"Oh, please, don't tell me you're one of those who believe anyone that is involved in kink has to be fucked-up or damaged?" His eyes shoot to mine with instant worry. "Fuck, I didn't mean to be dismissive. Shit, I'm sorry, Sam—"

"Don't. Stop that shit. You do not have to wrap me in cotton wool, Jason. I deal with my damage, and no, I'm not one of those people. Assumption is the mother of all fuck-ups in my profession. What I mean is *everyone* has baggage. Mine, I know, thanks to a few enlightening years of therapy, but not surprisingly, is a result of my mother and Richard. But even 'normal' people have hang-ups, quirks, kinks." I offer up my explanation.

"Oh, baby, I am the King of Kink." This time, with his abrupt movement, he manages to slip his whole hand right between my legs, his fingers just hovering at my entrance and coated in a slick wetness because…because he has been stroking my skin for the last half an hour.

My back arches a little to press into his contact, but I keep my voice level, impassive. "What I mean is, you're a successful businessman, single, and hot as hell, why are you *not* someone's Mr Happy Ever After?"

His gaze lingers on mine, heat seeping into the dark swirls of chocolate and gold flecks that make his eyes shine. "Simple. I'm not *normal*. I own a sex club, I like to tie up and beat naughty girls until they howl my name and come apart in my hands. There is nothing I haven't tried and will *always* want to try. I think I mentioned I'm a kinky son of a bitch." His finger sinks inside me then two and three. My eyelids flutter closed so he doesn't see my eyes roll with the delicious sensation he is just beginning to stir. "I'm not looking for Happy Ever After, Sam. I'm looking for Extraordinary Ever After, and that level of *normal* is hard to find." His mouth captures mine when I exhale a deep sigh. His thumb is slowly circling my clit, and I begin to rock into his palm in earnest. His tongue is deep and swirls in a sweet fight for dominance with mine.

God, I love the way he kisses. I don't kiss very often. Even with my one-night-stands I just want to get off. I don't like the intimacy that comes from a really good kiss. This isn't a good kiss. This is a life-affirming, heart-stopping, soul-stealing kiss. Around and around sweeping, diving, consuming me with just his tongue, his soft, full lips and all that passion focused on that one simple act. It's not foreplay it's the *only* play. Sweet and soft, demanding and possessive, scorching hot and not too wet… making me soaking wet. He owns me with this kiss and from the smug spread of his lips when he breaks the contact, he knows it, too.

"Blindfold?" His words take a moment to sink in, and my tummy tightens with the possibilities.

"I would love to." My words falter with understanding and his comically raised brow. "Sorry, you mean me." I bite my lip to hide my smirk.

"You have no idea how much that look and your sassy mouth makes my palm twitch." His grumbled words are heavy with desire and light with the sensual threat. I grind myself harder on his hand, but he moves away to reduce the contact. "Ah ah. My way, baby, we do this *my* way." His tone is a mix of playful and stern. I know he is being cautious, and I love that he seems to be adapting his role as much as I am switching mine. "You have been blindfolded before, I assume?'

"Richard was the only relationship I have ever had and he was a Dominant, so yes, I have been blindfolded before." I state and I swallow the pooling saliva in my mouth at the flash of images bombarding me of the times he did. My stomach turns, and Jason must feel my reaction because his hand freezes with his fingers still deep inside me.

"Sam…" His voice is strained, and I can see the muscles in his jaw dancing with fury, and I can hear his teeth crunch together with the force of his clenched jaw. "I think we need to be clear. He may have been your boyfriend through no choice of your own but he was no Dominant. He was an abusive fucking arsehole and a coward. He was given you. A beautiful, bright and sexy as all fuck woman—just a girl then—who he had the chance to cherish, but he chose abuse. You of all people should know the difference." He brushes my cheek with light tender kisses, and I pinch my eyes shut tight to stop the tingle of tears.

"I know the difference now…I didn't know there was any difference then. He told me what he was and showed me what that meant for me." I suck in a stuttered breath. I hate that I am still affected like this. This is why I don't talk about it. This is why I hide this shit away. I try to sit, but he positions his weight just a little further onto mine, effectively pinning me to the sofa.

"Sam, I don't mean to upset you. I just want you to know that I am likely to lose my shit…badly, if I have to think about what that dick-head did. So we need to find a way where we can discuss this without causing a meltdown for either one of us. He deserves not a second of your time, not a single thought. Any pain you experienced by his hand I will erase. Your pain and your pleasure belong to me now…it belongs to us…Understand?

"And, the only time I will give him will be if we ever meet because then I can teach him how *bad* I am with a Bullwhip." His voice drops lower when he continues. "I'm not a religious man, but I will pray every fucking day that I get the chance to do just that." The menace and certainty in his words should chill me, but I glow from the warmth spreading through my veins.

His mouth covers mine, and he captures my bottom lip between his teeth. He bites enough to make my eyes widen and his to crinkle with pleasure. I feel it like a jolt of high voltage electricity firing though my body...*our pleasure.*

"Ready?" Although, both his hand between my legs and his fingers inside me have barely moved since I mentioned Richard's name, when he smoothly removes them I whimper with the loss of contact. At the same time, he slides right on top of me, and I am momentarily breathless with his full weight before he kneels upright.

"Yes." I don't hesitate. I have no idea what I'm doing and I have no idea if this thing between us really stands a chance but for the first time...ever, I feel alive.

His eyes narrow but the stern expression is softened by his pursed lips. "I am happy to re-educate you, Sam, but please, do I really have to start from scratch?" I feel like an idiot but I am going to chalk that one up to being an *idiot.*

"Sir...sorry, I meant to say, yes Sir, or would you prefer Master?" I can't help myself. I have been in charge for so long. This may feel right but I just can't make it that easy. He barks out a laugh and his face lights up.

"Oh, baby girl, and there was me thinking we'd have to work up to using the gag." He pulls a slim, dark silk tie from his back pocket. He's like fucking a Boy Scout. I don't get the chance to voice a word only a disgruntled squeak escapes when he takes advantage of the gap my dropped jaw has created from sheer surprise. Forget Boy Scout; he is more like a bondage ninja, quickly securing the tie, without pulling a single hair. He also rolls my tank top up and fashions a make shift blindfold now that the tie was needed elsewhere. Satisfied and smug don't come close to describing the expression fixed across his handsome face just before my eyes are covered. A tiny piece of me wants to feel pissed at the speed with which he has secured me helpless, but a much larger part is comforted with the knowledge that, regardless of our relationship, he is a good Dom and knows exactly what he's doing.

This feels right. No, this feels perfect. I trusted him with my truth, I trust him with my body, and that is enough. It has to be, because whores don't get the happy ever after.

His weight shifts, and his breath kisses my cheek. "I prefer Sir, as you well know."

SIX

Jason

I never feel I have to prove myself. I never have to go searching for someone to play with. I am damn good at what I do, and I get a good deal of my pleasure from just knowing that there is always someone kneeling and waiting.

Until now.

Just looking at her drawing in slow, steady breaths and watching her pulse jump in her neck with excitement, maybe nerves, it's like the ultimate high. I can't explain it better than that. Nirvana. This stunning woman owns every room she chooses to enter, has more people than I care to think of wanting to serve her. To submit, worship and treat her like the queen she is and yet, here she is, trusting me, *submitting* to me. The pleasure I feel coursing through me is potent. I can't help an underlying feeling starting to form and gain purchase deep inside me. If she is brave enough to switch, she *will* own me.

Her hands grip my thighs, and her white knuckles are evidence that she is feeling more nervous than excited. I know this isn't going to be easy, but I want this so fucking much I'm willing to adapt and give her just what she needs. And right now, she needs to relax, have a little fun and enjoy the ride. I loosen the tie and remove the gag, but place it close by on the nightstand just in case.

"Put your hands above your head and hold the edge of the sofa." She obeys me instantly, stretching her toned arms over her head. Her rib cage pushes her tits high like an offering. Her shallow pants make the soft flesh bounce, her hard, peaked nipples just begging for my mouth. I swallow the instant dryness and fight the urge to mould her in my eager hands. Instead, I adjust the painful erection that is causing absolute agony in my jeans. "I don't want you to move. Do I make myself clear?" I expect her to hesitate, simply because taking orders is a new concept for her. She takes in every word. She gives a vigorous nod. Her skin flushes with desire, and her breathing becomes a little deeper. I place my hands on either side of her waist, and she sucks in a sharp breath but doesn't otherwise move. God, she's amazing…she feels alive under my fingertips, raw energy pulsing through my fingertips, contained and explosive at the same time.

I drag my hands down her body peeling her pyjama bottoms all the way down her long, slender legs. I work my way off the end of the sofa and just gaze at my prize.

Fucking jackpot.

The room is warm, but her body is peppered with gooseflesh, and she begins to tremble. I don't move. The only sound is my steady breathing and her rapid pants. Time slows, and I watch for the moment when her lips tip at the corners, her face softens, and her frame relaxes.

I'm impressed. Her understanding of my intention took barely ten minutes. "Good girl." I encourage. Her smile widens as does mine. Success, her first real test was for her to simply relax and accept. Her second was to take pleasure from my pleasure which, by the spread of her smile, I would say is another win. I walk around and loosen the tie and remove the gag. She turns her head toward me but immediately rectifies her error, snapping quickly back into place. I stroke her cheek with my finger and playfully tap her nose. "Present yourself," I command but keep my tone soft. She hesitates again, and I know it's not because she is unclear about what I am asking. "Tell me, *Selina*, when you give a command how long do you expect to wait before you are obeyed?" She lets out a light laugh and starts to draw her knees to her chest. I tap her knee and push her leg flat. "Nah ah. And tell me, *Selina*, when you ask a question does it amuse you to be ignored?" My voice is thick and gravely, the humour and playfulness dwindling with each passing second. She answers instantly this time.

"I'm sorry, Sir. I expect them to answer immediately; I demand they obey instantly." Her left cheek has a slight dip where she is either sucking it in or chewing on the inside.

"And do you think I deserve any less respect than you?" My tone is softer to compensate for her obvious agitation.

"No, Sir, not at all, I just—" Her voice catches and I stroke her cheek to soothe her concern.

"I know…shhh…I know, beautiful. Let's try that again, shall we?" I stretch my neck to release the tension, but it doesn't pop. All my tension is further south. "Present yourself." I choke back a cough when she pulls her knees to her chest, spreads and holds them wide with her fingertips. My 'good girl' praise comes out more like a strained groan. She bites back a smile but sucks in a sharp breath when she feels the sofa dip and I take up the best position in the world. Inches away from her… wide, wet and open. "Pick a number between one and twenty."

"Three." She shouts out instantly but drags her top teeth over her bottom lip to suppress her smile.

"Chicken." I rumble out a deep laugh. Whether it's too much pleasure or too much pain she's clearly not feeling *that* brave. "Very well. I will bring you to three orgasms." She opens her mouth to speak but wisely thinks better of it. But I am intrigued enough to ask her thoughts. Normally, I wouldn't tolerate chitchat or questions that weren't solicited or at least about safety. But nothing about this...us, is *normal*. "You wish to say something, beautiful?" Her smile spreads so wide when I call her that, I intend to use the moniker often. She shakes her head in denial, but I know she does. "You can speak. In fact, your reticence just means I want you to tell me now."

"You're being sweet." Her response is brief but instant.

"Hmm, I said I would bring you three orgasms. I never said I would let you *have* three orgasms." I cover her body with my frame holding myself above, just an inch or two. Heat and fire jumps between our bodies, and I lean down to whisper across her lips. "Will you still think I'm sweet when I deny you all three?"

"No, Sir." She exhales a shaky breath as I pull back onto my haunches. Her mouth parts, and I place my two middle fingers on her lips. Her tongue darts out, a quick inspection before retreating.

"Open your mouth. Make my fingers wet." I slip them inside, and can't help the groan that escapes the back of my throat when she wraps her hot tongue around my digits, twisting and pulling them deeper into her mouth. When I pull them free, my cock twitches painfully like a fucking jealous bitch, and all I can do is endure. Agony and blue balls will have to wait. My focus is her...re-educating Selina and seducing Sam. I drag my wet fingers lightly down the centre of her body. Skimming the indent in her collarbone and the swell and dip between her breasts. I lightly touch her belly button, which makes her catch her breath but she lets out a much deeper exhale when I slide once more inside her heat. I waste no time following my fingers with my mouth. My tongue swirls her clit, flicking lightly, at the same time, curling my fingers deep and stroking the soft flesh inside. She instantly tenses, but then she's already soaking from having my fingers inside her before so I'm not really surprised she's taut and just about ready to explode. I soften the movement of my fingers. I don't want her climbing too quickly, but I don't want her crashing over the edge, either. It's all about balance.

She holds remarkably still because I know from the short, panting breaths and her little angry sighs she is frustrated as hell. I sweep my tongue flat with firm pressure from the tip of her nub of nerves to where my fingers sink into her soft centre. She's so damn wet, and I can't get enough of her taste. My lips cover her, and I suck and mouth, pulling her folds gently between my lips, grazing her clit with my teeth and pump harder with my fingers, building her pleasure, teasing her higher and higher. Her muscles twitch against my fingers, her tummy clenches with the need to roll her hips against my hand. At the first tilt of her pelvis, I relax and pull away.

The little heartfelt cry that escapes the back of her throat almost has me helping her out, but I wouldn't want her thinking I'm *sweet*. Her jaw is clenched and her fists, resting on her knees are curled, white-knuckle tight. Her sweet little body is resisting the inevitable loss of her climax with tiny judders and spasms. I blow cool air on her core and she nearly kicks me in the head with her convulsion, throwing her bent legs out straight. I duck quickly enough but pull them flat to either side of me for safety.

I scooch down for round two. I deliberately take a little longer this time, pausing almost every minute because I can feel her instant response to every touch, every swirl of my tongue, even the warm air I puff from my nose has her climbing. She fails to hold back her cry this time, and I am glad she can't see my shit-eating grin because that would probably make her mad.

She's strong and sassy, bright and resourceful, every inch a first class Domme, and the last thing I want is to make her mad. I want her pliant, agreeable, but more than my next breath, I want her as my sub.

She attempts to control her breathing, and I give her a little time to recover. My hands sweep up her legs, along her sides, over the perfect swell of her breasts, skimming her skin with feather-light touches, trying to cool the searing heat that is colouring her flawless skin. She's on fire, and her body continues to tremble with pent up pleasure.

"How you doing, beautiful?" I watch her nod her head but squeeze her lips flat, biting back any chance of sound. "I asked you a question, Sam." My tone has a bite, which instantly grounds her and reminds her of her job.

"I'm good, thank you, Sir." She swallows thickly and once more bites her flat lips flat.

"Only good?" I strum my fingers idly on the inside of her thigh.

"I'm very…frustrated, Sir."

"I'll bet. Still think I'm sweet?" She snorts out an uncontrollable laugh, and it's my turn to bite my lips to stop myself from laughing. She is trying so hard, and her lapses, instead of requiring a punishable intervention for breaking protocol, I find adorable.

"Sorry Sir, forgive me. I don't find you sweet…well, I do, but not right now." She rushes to make amends and clarify.

"Is that so?" I trace my tongue up her inner thigh along the crease where the top of her leg meets her apex. I sweep my tongue up her centre and swirl in little circles over her clit. The tiny patch of hair, waxed with precision into a narrow landing strip hides a puzzle piece tattoo. I hadn't noticed before but I am guessing that is the point. *Interesting.* I pause for a moment tracing my finger over the ink, not much bigger than my thumb and almost entirely covered by the hair. I'm distracted enough to realise she hasn't answered my question. She's holding her breath, feeling my gaze and the weight of my own unasked question. But it would be unfair to ask her now. Now she *has* to answer me. She's trusted me enough to open up about her past; I want to give her the choice to open up some more.

"Sam?" My tone a reminder to us both.

"Yes…sorry, yes Sir. I don't think you're sweet. Would you like me to tell you what I *do* think you are?" I close my eyes. That mouth will be the death of me…death by blue balls.

"That depends. How long would you like me to continue?" She shudders and gasps when I sink my tongue deep and clamp my lips tight around her clit.

"Ah…ah…I-I don't want you to continue any longer than you said please, Sir." She puffs out sharp, steadying breaths when I pull back. "Sorry, Sir," she adds, but it sounds more like a plea. I push my fingers inside. Her folds are swollen, and her needy nub pulses with the rush of blood surging through her veins. She is so ready to fall with maybe one, two thrusts of my fingers. My thumb applies a little pressure below her clit and rocks up in a gentle motion but it's enough. Her muscles clamp around my fingers, her thighs twitch and I pull right back. Her whole body sags on a whimper.

"Apology accepted."

"You're very good at this aftercare thing." She sighs heavily and sinks back against my chest. The warm, bubbly water swishes around her breasts. Soft peaks of foam dot the other exposed parts of her body and mine. I may have rubbed and massaged every inch of her body, but this isn't my standard aftercare routine. I just can't keep my hands off her.

"I'm glad you think so." I scoop a handful of ginger scented water high and dribble small amounts like a waterfall, trying to hit one of her perfectly perky nipples. I repeat and try the other side, too. I'm all about balance.

"Is this official downtime?" She tilts her head to the side and lifts her chin. I know she's asked a good question, but I cover her mouth with mine, pulling her hair gently. She tries to slip onto her front, but my solid thighs clamp tight to prevent her—a tricky task given how slippery she is. She groans with frustration.

"I think until we establish some rules and protocols outside of a scene, I believe it's safe to assume all our time is downtime. What with your sassy mouth and all." I tease and tweak her nipple at the same time.

"Ha! Sassy mouth. You really have no idea." She scoffs her interruption.

"Exactly my point." I pinch the other nipple for emphasis. She falls quiet with my sterner observation. "I want to go easy, so we will need some guidelines or your arse is going to be red and raw," I add for clarification but press a kiss into her hair to soften my previous statement. This is new for both of us and doubly difficult for her, I believe, so I need to take it slow. She tilts her pelvis and slides her smooth arse the length of my ever present, rock-hard cock.

"And who says that's not exactly *my* point?" she purrs, and I growl, my fingers flying to her hips to stop the torture.

"Sam," I warn, and she stills in my hands.

"Sorry," she breathes out, but is suddenly too quiet.

"Sam?"

"You did go easy on me. Thank you, and I did love it but…"

"But?"

"This might prove harder than you think, Jason. This might not be worth the trouble." She lets out a solemn sigh.

"If the trouble you are referring to is you, I would respectfully ask that you let me decide that. And I didn't go *that* easy on you. I kept you begging a long time, *and* I didn't allow you to come."

"Oh, please," she teases. "I would've had a cock ring wrapped around you so tight Satan himself couldn't have caused you more pain. And then I would have made you wait while I watched a whole episode of Buffy *if* I was going to let you get off…maybe two if it was a cliffhanger episode." She smirks, her eyes gleam with wickedness.

"Ah now that would make *you* a sadist, but thank you, because it also gives *me* a benchmark. Every day's a learning day." I wink at her grumble and laugh at her loud exhale of frustration when I won't release her hips to continue her grind and tease. "Besides, that would only torture me, and this week isn't about torture. This week is about us."

"Week?" She squeaks out in shock and manages to slip right round this time. But the bath isn't really that big, so she tucks her knees under her and wedges them tight between my thighs. My erection bobs, eager and ready. She only flashes a quick glance, but is more distracted by what I have just said.

"Yes, week. A crash course as it were. Cancel your appointments." I keep my voice level because I try not to think too hard about what that means. "We can play here, at my place, or the club. We will still take it slow. It will just be intense."

"I think you'll find that is a contradiction right there." She just stares at me, wide-eyed and gorgeous. Soft, tiny bubbles cling and slide down her silky body, assimilating with much larger shapes once they hit the surface of the bathwater.

"I think it's perfect. I think you're perfect. It can be like a baptism of fire. If, after the week, you are uncomfortable, or we decide this can't possibly work, then…" I shrug. She furrows her shapely brow, causing a cute crinkle above her nose. "But you know we *do* work. We are perfect together, and it's just one week." I am confident I can make her happy, but I need her concentrated time. The timing couldn't be better with everything being quiet because it's the silly season. "I'll close the club so we can use the facilities without interruption. Our own private playground." I wiggle my brows playfully.

"You'd do that? You'll lose thousands. Jason, that's crazy." She shakes her head.

"It's not crazy, Sam. That's not what I'm afraid of losing." Her eyes light with hope and pool with tears.

"Jason, I'm a whore." She drops her gaze. I take a huge scoop of water and dump it on her head. She sucks a breath in surprise and starts to choke. She splutters but recovers quickly and splashes me back. I grab her hand before she drowns us both.

"Sam. There may be more infractions that deserve punishment, but for me, this is the biggest. I will punish you if you *ever* call yourself that again. I know what you do, but the way you say that, you insult yourself. It's not who you are. Understand?" Her lips tip in a tentative smile, and her cheeks flash with colour. Her eyes blink rapidly, but her hair is drenched, and she uses the dripping bathwater to disguise the tears in her eyes. She nods, and I raise my brow impatiently. She grins and flutters her lashes in all innocence.

"I understand." I point my finger to my lips, and she leans in and pecks my pout.

"Good girl." She flashes her beautiful smile and slides back around, her back to my front or more specifically her backside to my cockside. She slinks her body up and down, up and…down. I think she is about to stretch her legs out and lie back flush on top of me but she keeps her crouched position. "Or maybe you're not such a *good* girl."

"Oh, I'm the *best* girl." Her words escape on a sexy-as-hell exhale, which mainlines like a shock of pure electricity to my impossibly hard shaft.

She raises her hips, wraps her hand tightly around my straining erection and slips the head of my cock between her molten folds. She sinks down hard, and a wave of water drenches the sides of the bath and floods the floor. She groans the most erotic sound out and throws her head back on a sigh. Twisting her head round, she flashes me a cheeky wink and starts to pump her tight little backside up and down my cock. Her back dips in to a sensual curve as she leans forward on her hands, resting on my legs above my knees. The water glistens, and soap slides down her skin, tracking its way to the crease of her arse. I could stare at this view forever. Soft, round flesh, bouncing and rippling with each impact drop against me, an erotic little grind against the base of my cock before she lifts herself almost free. It's my turn to come undone.

She hovers for perilous seconds, which feel like agonising hours because I know just how good it feels to be buried inside. But lucky for me, my previous intimate ministrations mean she is in no hurry to deny herself. She drops down and repeats, increasing the pressure each time at the base of the journey and steadily increasing her pace.

I sit up so I am flush to her back, and her sweet little body glides against my chest as she moves. One of my hand slides around and grabs her breast, while the other cups her neck and twists her head around to meet my eager mouth. She moans when my tongue dives to taste and take, each swipe and dance is reciprocated with equal passion and desire. "Oh, fuck!" I moan out into her mouth, her lips curl with pleasure, and her eyes shine with pure lust and fire. Her hand is wrapped around my balls, and her grip and tug has me thinking of football results and nasty diseases, anything or this is going to end right now.

As fucking turned on as I am, as close as I am, she is not controlling when *I* get to come...ever. I jerk my hips, roughly breaking her rhythm and making her grasp the sides of the bath to keep her balance.

"You don't like that?" She drops her chin onto her chest, catching her breath but looks nervously over her shoulder.

"I like it very much." I watch her eyes, so dark and guarded, almost black and inscrutable. But her face is an unfathomable mix of nefarious confidence and vulnerability. "As *you* well know." My tone is a warning. I am under no illusion that she isn't fully aware of what she is doing. I understand her default setting is to take control, but as I had mentioned to her before: I won't be topped from the bottom. Even if her bottom is delicious. I push my hand flat between her shoulder blades forcing her to move forward further and onto her hands. I slap her wet arse cheek with a playful strike, and I dig my fingers into her hips. I take control.

Loud, slick sounds of skin colliding, water splashing and desperate gasps of air fill the room. Her muscles grip me like a vise, scorching hot, coating my cock with her arousal. She feels like molten silk and takes me so fucking deep I want to die right here because here is heaven.

"Stick your thumb in my arse." Her breathy request does two things. First, it makes me instantly want to blow my load and, second, gets my back up that she can't seem to help herself.

"Sam." I growl her name in frustration.

"Sorry…please…please," she pants, and I can hear her desperation. In this instance, I don't think she's playing me. I hope for her sake she isn't. "Sorry, Jason…I …just really…please will you stick…ahhh! Oh, God yes! Thank you… tha…" Her mouth might be working. I can't see from here, but there is definitely no sound.

I barely get my thumb inside her tight hole when her muscles start to clamp down. I curl it round and stroke the thin layer between my thumb and my cock, which causes me to swell inside her just that little bit more. I didn't think that was possible. She crashes over the edge. No more breaths, no more movement, well, no external movement. Her body is taut and tense, silently riding wave after wave of euphoria. I feel each crest because her body saturates and spasms around my shaft. Shuddering, she draws in ragged breaths, coming down from her high as the pleasure ebbs. I pull her back onto me, hitting her deep inside and doing exactly what I had hoped.

"Oh, God!" She moans out an erotic sigh. An audible cue but her sweet little centre had already begun to grip, ripple and contract around me. Fuck, she feels so good. My hips jerk, and my jaw is clenched so tight I could crack a tooth. I thrust hard, hold tight, and chase my own release.

I'm on fire…she's on fire and with hot soapy water swirling around us, I feel like I am going to melt. I can't breathe. I slam the tap on and push the dial to blue. Ice-cold water spurts and splutters, spraying our joined bodies, instantly cooling our fever. I lift us from the bath, still balls deep, but she stretches on her tiptoes when her feet reach the floor and I slip from her body. She turns and steps back, grabbing a couple of towels from the rail. She holds them out for me to choose, and she looks shy, her arms now crossing her body. What the fuck? I take the bigger looking towel with one hand and pull her into my arms with the other. I scoop her up my body and wrap the soft sheet around us both. She drops hers on the soaking floor, we didn't need two.

I hand her a hot chocolate. She has her knees pulled tight to her chest and is leaning against her headboard, defensive and protective. I am lying across the end of her bed. I reach up and grab one of her feet. I pull it to my chest and start to rub. She lets out a sigh and wriggles a little lower so her leg is comfortable.

"I get that you don't like the way I refer to my job but that doesn't negate the fact that I am a"—I flash a glare that makes her freeze—"that I am a Dominatrix." She breathes out when I return to my foot rubbing.

"I understand that. I have given it some thought actually, and I would like you to consider something." I look over to her and she is peeping over the rim of her cup all wide-eyed and curious.

"I'm all ears"—she wiggles her toes in my hand—"and toes." I suck her big toes into my mouth, and her jaw drops. Her fingers grip her cup like a vice and her whole leg trembles. I release her toe with a loud plop.

"Oh, my god, that went straight to my clit! Do it again." She pushes her toes to my mouth, and I laugh.

"We can't keep using sex to avoid this conversations, Sam." I hold her foot inches from my face, her big toe wriggling as she tries to get closer.

"I think you'll find we can." Her breathy tease falls flat. I scowl, and she relaxes with a resigned huff. "Fine."

"You have your job, and I respect that, but I would prefer if you didn't fuck guys. Your male clients who require only pain as their sexual preference, that's fine, but I don't want you fucking them. Women you can fuck and do the pain thing. I'm cool with that." I state as a matter of fact.

"Wow, you have given this some thought." She purses her lips and blows the steam from her drink. I wonder if she is aware that almost everything she does looks sexual to me…gets me hard. I catch her glint and raised brow. Oh, yes, she's aware. My loose pants do nothing to hide my growing hard-on.

"Is that a yes?" I push.

"Why women?" She takes a sip, and her lips shine with moisture.

"Honestly, I can get off on that idea. Other guys fucking you when I'm not present? Not so much." I shrug lightly.

"But if you were there?" She's playing with me. Her sensual, breathy voice is low and alluring, but this game still needs some rules.

"If I was there, it would be *my* decision and under my direction," I clarify.

She sniffs out a laugh. "Sadly, that is one fantasy I'm never likely to have."

"Why? That's a fantasy of yours?" I shift and drop my hand down my pants to make a quick adjustment. "I don't mean why is that a fantasy, but why would that never happen?" I massage the intense pressure that has quickly accumulated at the turn of this conversation. I am now uncomfortably hard.

"I know the fantasy itself shouldn't be a shocker; it's most women's fantasy if they are honest. But as a Dominatrix, it would mean giving over too much power. I would fear losing control. No matter how well trained my clients may be. I don't have that level of trust to give myself over to two men." She wipes a mock tear. "Alas, poor me…but women you say?" She waggles her perfect brows mischievously. "Interesting that you are okay with me fucking a woman. I get that you would get off on it; don't get me wrong…" She pauses at my sudden shift in position.

I let her foot go and stalk up the bed crowding her, my arms on either side of her body, pinning her in place.

"I don't want some other man giving you pleasure." I growl.

"I think your concern is misplaced then, because if anyone knows how to really give a woman an orgasm, it's another woman," she quips confidently.

"You did not just say you get better orgasms from a woman that you do from me," I warn with a low, disapproving grumble.

"Oh, no, not me *personally*. I love cock too much for that, but you know, as a guide." She snickers wide-eyed and shrinking away from me with every taunting word. I take the drink from her hand and crush the grin from her lips, only coming up for air when she is a soft, pliant mess in my hands.

"What about you?" She exhales a sexy, satisfied breath as I roll to her side.

"What about me?" My head rests in my hand, while my other snaked around her waist, always touching.

"If I agree, I am effectively becoming a nun, and you? What are you abstaining from?" she challenges.

"I promise not to fuck men, either." I reply dead-pan.

"Oh, my god, you're a comedian, too! Mad skills in the sack *and* a comedian. I've hit the jackpot!" I grab her roughly and pull her onto me.

"And don't you forget it," I growl against her lips, which smile against mine. "I'm never going to be vanilla, Sam, but I won't fuck anyone else unless you agree. Unless we are together, both fucking that someone else." I hold her gaze to see how she reacts to my stark but honest declaration. I think I hold my breath.

"You say the sweetest things…my very own Prince Charming." She sighs and fans herself. I snatch her arse in both my fists and squeeze her. She rubs her sweet little self against me. Her eyes are on fire with lust and desire. I needn't have worried. I roll her onto her back.

"There's only one way to find out, baby. Let me get my glass butt plug and see if it fits."

"I think you'll find one size fits all, Jason." She chokes out a dirty laugh.

I may not be Prince Charming but I'm pretty fucking sure she's the fucking *one*.

SEVEN

Sam

I really need to pee but this feels so unbelievably good, I don't want to move. Jason slid his glorious thick cock into me in the early hours, sweet, sleepy sex that felt more like a dream. I floated on the very edge of consciousness where ecstasy became my reality. The light filtering through the gaps in the blinds is unseasonably bright for this time of the year. It can only mean it's either very late in the morning or early afternoon. I think it's early afternoon because I really, really need to pee. I am acutely aware we must have fallen straight back to sleep, maybe not during but certainly immediately after. He is no longer inside me, but I can feel his cock twitch nestled as it is, between my cheeks. And his large body feels welded to mine, hot, firm and immovable. His arm is a dead weight across my body as I try to prise myself free, wriggling over to the far side of the bed. I manage to roll myself so his meaty hand is the only body part left resting on my hip.

With speed that belies his sleepy state, his hand glides fully around my body, and he picks me up with one arm and pulls me back into his hold.

"I need to pee," I whisper, which is stupid. He's obviously awake.

"Ten more minutes," he grumbles and nestles his nose into my hair, inhaling deeply.

"Ten more minutes and I will pee all over you, and I charge extra for that." I snort out a harmless laugh, but Jason is on me in an instant with a fierce scowl etched on his handsome features.

"It was joke, Jason. I don't actually do wet play…not my particular kink." I try and give him a tentative smile to lighten the dark cloud that hangs heavy between us.

"Not mine either but that is beside the point." His stiff tone is clipped, his jaw is clenched and his eyes darken with barely contained anger. "Sam, I think it's safe to assume certain references to your work are going to piss me off." I stiffen beneath him, and he releases his hostility and frustration in one slow breath. "Look, I know what you do, and honestly, I don't care. I want you period, no caveats, no if onlys…I want you as you are. But I am also not going to pretend that, when you refer to yourself in a derogatory manner, or reference the work you do in a way that I can't help but picture someone else touching what I consider mine…that is going to piss…me…off." His kisses soften the blow of his statement, although I shouldn't be surprised. Jason may not be a typical submissive-owning Dominant but he is *all* alpha male—controlling, demanding and possessive, I just wasn't anticipating adding sensitive to that list.

"Sorry," I hold his gaze and witness the rage dissipate just as quickly as it came. His lips spread wide into his megawatt smile before he rolls off and releases me. I swiftly slide to the edge of the bed before he changes his mind. "It wasn't even my joke," I mumble as I slip his t-shirt over my head. It hangs very loose and falls to my knees. I look over and watch him watching me. He is resting now with his back against the headboard and one arm stretched up and round the back of his head. The sheet has pooled at his waist, and his muscles are taut and flexed from the pull on his arm. He has a light dusting of hair on his sculpted chest, which thickens as is progresses down his body. Not too much but enough to scrape my fingers through and just the right amount to make him look a little wild…untamed. His eyes are stormy with desire and a deep rumble vibrates in his chest but is barely audible. I back away with my hands up in surrender.

"Okay, okay, take it out on Leon when he gets back. It's his joke." I back away, because he is lightning fast if he decides he wants me back in his arms, and I'm about to burst.

I return to the bedroom, but the bed is empty and there is the smell of melted butter coming from the kitchen. Jason has his naked back to me, his fitted boxer shorts hugging the perfect round muscle of his arse. *I know what I want for breakfast.* I slide onto the kitchen stool, and he turns when he hears the squeak of the leather announcing my arrival. He is vigorously mixing something making the muscles in his biceps jump and flex enticingly. Yup, that's breakfast sorted. I slide back off the stool and stalk around the island. He eyes me warily, his own devilish grin warming his features. I swipe a tea towel hanging on a cupboard handle and fold, deliberately slowly into a neat, thick square. I drop it to the floor and watch his eyes light with desire. He raises a knowing brow, and his mixing slows down but still continues, stopping when I sink to my knees. I hear him switch the heat off the stove, but instead of holding my head, cupping gently or gripping with intent, he simply resumes his mixing, slow and steady.

I rake my nails up the thick, defined muscle of his thighs and slip my fingers up the legs of his boxer briefs. I grab the waistband from the inside and pull them down his legs. His solid erection springs free; it barely bobs at all, despite its considerable weight. It is rock-hard and straining to reach his own belly button. I cup his heavy sac and squeeze. He grunts out a deep moan, and I waste no time wrapping my fist and lips around his shaft. My tongue swirls and wipes the pre-cum that is already wetting the tip. I hum my appreciation and notice the muscles in his thighs flex. I can still hear the whisk lap the sides of the bowl, but the rhythm is more erratic. I smile briefly to myself before I pull and suck him to the back of my throat. My fingers tighten at the base, synchronising the pump and gentle twist of my grip with my mouth. I use my other hand to tug and massage his balls, which tighten in my palm. He whispers out a stuttered curse when I try to take as much of his length as possible. A challenge, he is fucking built, thick and long. My lips feel the angry, pulsing vein, and I take a moment to guide my tongue along its length, teasing light flicks that make him catch his breath.

I swirl my tongue, dipping the tip into the slit. He groans and gently rocks his hips. I graze lightly with my bottom teeth, but even that is a little too much judging by the hiss he sucks through his teeth. I pull my lips to offer more protection to his sensitive tip and suck him deep into the back of my throat. He holds still, letting me set the pace, but I can see the tension in his thighs and hear the rumble of pleasure vibrating from deep in his chest. He hits the back of my throat, and I relax and swallow him down, then swallow some more and press firmly with my middle finger directly on the pressure point between his arsehole and his balls.

"Jesus fucking Christ!!" He slams his hand on the counter. The bowl misses me altogether, and the whisk hits my shoulder before hitting the floor. But the cool, thick liquid contents fall with a slick splat down my back, his cock emptying his own essence down my throat. I lap and lick him clean as he pulls from my lips, but I remain kneeling because I am dipping with egg, and moving is going to make this mess so much worse. He takes a moment to compose himself, and looking up, I can see his head is bent, and his eyes are scrunched shut. He mutters something I can't quite make out, but I think it's maybe something like praising the Lord. He seems to focus and take me in with wide eyes and a huge smile.

"Fuck, Sam, that was…shit…" He runs a hand through his short hair, the slightly longer top forming adorable spikes. He grabs the other kitchen towels and scoops the mess from my back, although gravity had done an admirable job, and most of the sticky mess is on the floor behind me. Nevertheless, now relatively clean, Jason helps me to my feet and lifts me to sit on the counter.

"You've left me a little speechless." His lips quirk. He looks a little shy, and that has left *me* a little speechless.

"Ah, Jason, did I break your blowjob cherry?" I twirl a long strand of my hair around my finger, and he chuckles, a deep, hearty sound.

"Cute…It fucking felt like it. Everything about you feels like the first time." He threads his hand around the back of my neck and tilts my head back to meet his intense stare. His words were said with humour and affection, but his gaze is laden with something more serious, something I find disconcerting for someone like me. "And now there is officially nothing to eat in your flat." He shakes his head with amusement. "Right, shower, then my place." He bends down and, with sudden force, pushes his shoulder into my waist, effectively doubling me over and scoops me onto his broad shoulder. I squeal and grab his arse for support. I might start to massage as well when he strides from the room in search of my shower. It is a mighty fine arse.

The journey to Jason's apartment takes less than fifteen minutes. I thought for a moment he was going to take me to the club. I know he has a flat on the top floor of the building, but we drove past that, turned, and headed towards London Bridge. His house is nothing like I'd imagined. It's a house for a start. I assumed he would have some swanky penthouse fuck pad with sleek chrome, glass and leather furniture and fittings, stylishly minimalist and clinically cold. His home is a narrow, four-story, mid terrace, Georgian town house, set one street back from the river. But even from the first floor it has an amazing view of the South Bank. He swipes his finger to unlock the front door. The building may be over two hundred years old, but the facilities are very much twenty-first century. He carries both our bags over his shoulder and continues to hold my hand. He really hasn't let go for a moment.

At my apartment, from the kitchen, he'd carried me into the shower and washed every inch of my body. No, that's not right; he cherished every inch of my body. His touch had been constant with intermittent squeezes and random strokes of his thumb on the back of my hand, my palm, my cheek. He was very good at making me feel…*unsettled*.

The entrance hall is light with white and black tiled floor and an archway leading to the rear of the house, possibly the kitchen. The walls are duck egg blue, and there is a large gilt mirror dominating the half-landing, adding much light to the space. The cream stair runner is held in place by beautiful golden claws on each tread. I smile to myself but the bitter edges barely curl my lips.

"Sam, is something wrong?" Jason breaks my unpleasant daydream with his equally unsettling insightfulness.

"Sorry. It's nothing…just the carpet. My mother would approve." His brow furrows, and his features darken at the mention of my mother. The thought that we have that in common warms me, and I swallow the unpleasant taste her memory invokes. "She thought you could tell a lot about a person's breeding by their home. You have a posh person's carpet on your stairs, very thick, top quality, and doesn't reach the edges. See?" He glances over his shoulder, and his face registers the stairs as if seeing them for the first time. "If she hadn't already pimped me out, that would probably have earned you a date." I sniff derisively. Honestly, I barely think of her, but sometimes the ridiculousness of her life lessons hits me hard. Jason steps in front, towering over me, his face is etched with concern.

"I paid an interior designer, Sam, and you know your mother was fucking insane, right?" His voice is so serious, I snort out a laugh.

"Yes, Jason, besides," I drop my voice a little lower, and he leans down to catch my words, "it's not about the quality; it's about the length." I laugh and scream when he lunges to grab me as I dart around him and make a break for the very stairs. I take them two at a time, but my speed is no match for his long gait and powerful stride. He catches me two from the top, breathless, panting, and in a fit of uncontrollable giggles.

"You're so funny, Sam. Tell me again, because I am pretty sure you just insulted my manhood's quality."

"No…no, stop!" I squeal and wriggle uselessly against his relentless tickling fingers and his dead weight pinning me beneath him. I gasp and struggle to get my words out between the panic and laughter. "The stairs…I meant the stairs!" I cry out.

He pulls back, his finger hovering at my side. "What's wrong with my stairs?" His face softens, and his lips turn downward with a sad little expression.

I lean up and cover his adorable pout with my eager lips. He takes a moment to engage, only a moment, before his tongue is pushing and demanding entrance. I catch my breath and grin. "There is nothing wrong with your stairs. They are very long, beautifully crafted, very, very big, top quality stairs. I think they are perfect." He runs his tongue sensually along his bottom lip, and I mirror his action. His eyes widen, and the heat between our bodies has gone from scorching to inferno in a blink of his lust-filled eyes.

"Good." He growls and captures my mouth and my breath in one determined move. Hours pass, it maybe minutes but it feels never ending. I love that feeling. Kisses with him, I never want to end. He pulls back and a wicked grin spreads slowly across his flawless face. "Just so we're clear, you meant my cock right?" I collapse with the most unladylike snort-laugh. "Just checking. I don't know you that well. Who knows, you might be really into interior design. That might be your kink?" His smile widens, flashing straight, white teeth, and he lets out a deep laugh. The sound is relaxed and sexy, curling my toes and warming my heart. He sweeps loose hair away from my eyes and holds my gaze. Intense scrutiny with a mix of lust and fire but also happy. He looks really happy, and I think my eyes must look exactly the same.

I let out as deep a breath as I can manage, given his full weight is still on me. "I definitely meant your cock. Besides, I told you my kink." I push his chest lightly, and he pulls himself upright, lifting me straight into his arms. I wrap my legs tight around his narrow waist and grip harder than is necessary. The apex of my legs melds against his tummy. He should be able to feel the heat, I wonder if he can feel the wetness. He lets out a deep groan and fists the cheeks of my arse, grinding me tighter to his body. That will be a yes.

"Your kink?" His voice is strained and hoarse.

"Double penetration with the threesome sex I'm never going to have." I sigh and mockingly fan myself.

"Oh, fuck, Sam. Can you feel how fucking hard I am now?" He drops me a little lower so I am nudging his hard-on with my own heat.

"I can now." I giggle.

"You said that *was* a fantasy. You've never done DP?" He clears his throat with a deep cough and proceeds to climb the stairs only stopping at the very top. His breath is a little ragged, but I think it's due to this conversation rather than the exertion of the climb and my extra weight.

"I guess it's not a kink because it is just a fantasy. And yes, of course, I have done double penetration but only with toys…not how I'd like to in my *kinky* fantasy." I smile sweetly but my innocence is lost when I grind my core over the tip of his rock-hard cock. Not that there is much innocence to loose.

He kicks the door to his bedroom wide open.

The room is dark with the curtains drawn. The only light filters in from the hallway behind. He strides in and unceremoniously dumps me in the middle of his bed. I gasp and no longer feel like laughing. The room isn't the only darkness in here. I swallow the dry lump and bite down on my bottom lip. He towers and I tremble.

"I consider it my job to fulfil all your fantasies, *beautiful*." The words rumble with delicious intent, drifting over my body like liquid lust and purest desire. I drop my head back and moan. "Your desire is my pleasure, your pleasure is my goal. I only want to make you happy…That's not entirely true, I want to make you scream. I live to make you tremble, and I need to make you fall so fucking hard that I *own* every part of you." His eyes pierce right through me.

"I'm already trembling, and I think you're just about to make me scream, so two out of three isn't bad going for a first date." I point out.

"Maybe I need to work on that fantasy then, too, if I am to make you fall. If I find another guy I can trust to fuck you with me, Sam, would you like that?" His gravelly voice has my skin tingling. His words are scorching a trail straight to my core.

"Two guys fucking me? Why Jason, you say the sweetest things." I let out a puff of air and smile, my attempt to lighten the searing intensity of what he is suggesting. His assertion is causing a riot of emotions in my head and combustible heat between my legs. He grabs me behind my knees, roughly pulling me to the edge of the bed. He holds my knees together, his large hands poised to prise them apart. His face is in shadow, but the desire is palpable and radiates between us like a physical entity. Inky black eyes penetrate me.

"Tell me Sam, when I'm buried deep in your arse with someone else in front, fucking you raw…when I fulfil your fantasy, will you fall? Will you be mine? Will I own you then?" He groans.

My head is dizzy. I can't breathe. *Don't say it, Sam. Don't you fucking say it!* I draw in a desperate breath. I feel the fateful words dance on the very tip of my tongue as my unsettled mind loses its battle with my eager heart and declares that it might be too damn late for that. I think I may have fallen…he already ow—

Oh, thank God! Hard, urgent lips silence me, and I couldn't be more grateful. This is too damn close. I can't let myself be this way, vulnerable, naïve, stupid. I may be a lot of things but I don't repeat my mistakes…I learn from them.

Sam aged eighteen

*Despite my mother's desperate attempt to lure Richard back into my life, her efforts were entirely wasted. Six months after **that** day, his family emigrated to the States, and although my life didn't really change for the better, I felt happier* for his departure. I would no longer fear running into him in the village or... well, I only ever left the house to go to school or the store, but in my mind, there was always that chance. I kept my head down, took my exams and waited for day I turned eighteen. My suitcase was packed and I had placed it just inside the front door. She sat at the table with a small flat present neatly wrapped with a pale blue ribbon. She grimaced when I entered, her attempt at a smile but she still wouldn't meet my eyes. I don't care. I hate her with every fibre of my being. Why would I want to look into those soulless, hate filled eyes?

"This is yours now, Grace. You are to date Gordon St John-Smythe. Your first date is this evening, and he will make an excellent husband. I have told him you are sullied, but he was kind enough to overlook all that when I showed him this." She places her pallid hand on the parcel and pushes it toward me. My blood boils, and my stomach burns with acid. I clench my jaw, swallowing back the venom for a few moments longer. I unwrap the gift, knowing what it is but needing to make sure it is actually mine.

"This is mine now? Really mine?" I whisper running my finger along the string of natural pearls, looped and nestled in the silk folds of the Cartier box. It is a beautiful piece but I doubted it was genuine. My mother was delusional and all too desperate to believe the romantic ramblings of my grandfather. Regardless, it was important to her, more so than I ever was and now it is mine.

"Yes, it is. Your grandfather was explicit in his will. This belongs to you now." She goes to place her hand over mine, but I snap the lid shut and pull it out of her reach. Her eyes widen with shock then narrow with the all too familiar hatred.

"Good." I stand so abruptly the kitchen chair topples over, the loud crash makes her jump. I turn. I don't rush but stride purposefully toward the front door, pausing to grab the suitcase on the way, clutching the necklace with a vise-like grip in my other hand. I drop the case, open the dark oak door for the last time, and step outside, inhaling a deep lungful of air like it's my first breath. Her bony hand grabs a fistful of my hair and spins me round. I lose my grip on my case, and it drops by my feet. Her face is thunderous, her eyes cruel, lifeless beads, piercing me but not penetrating. I twist out of her grip and straighten my shoulders, returning her glare.

"Where do you think you are going?" she snarls, but her voice is a tempered whisper, mindful of being overheard. I can see from her ticking jaw she wants to howl.

"I'm leaving, but don't worry; I'm sure with this"—I wave the Cartier box but not too close—"I'll find someone willing to trade a warm bed. If not, I'll always have this." I sweep my hand up and down my body. Her eyes widen so large, and her face is mottled bright red, she looks like she is about to explode.

"You are not some common whore, Grace," she snaps.

"Really? Because that is exactly what you made me when you forced me to fuck Richard! When you let him rape me!" I bite out the words quietly, but I might as well have used a bullhorn. She reels back and falters. I have never spoken to her like this…never.

"I did no such thing…You…" She points her finger, her hand shaking with rage. "You did this…you chose that path. You became his whore, and he threw you away, and I don't blame him." Spits flies with each angry word fired at me, but after two years of hearing the same tune, I am immune.

"You made me mother; aren't you proud?" I pick up my suitcase. My tone holds no emotion, my expression impassive. "I'd rather be a whore than your puppet." Her eyes narrow at me but flit between me and the box I am clutching to my chest. "I'll give you a choice: Take me back and let me live my life how I want to and I keep the necklace, or never see me again but you keep the necklace. Me or the necklace?"

She didn't hesitate. "I don't want a filthy whore living in my house. I'll take the necklace."

I turn and walk down the path.

"You said I could choose…you said I could have the necklace," she screeches after me.

"Don't you know, Mother? You should never trust a whore." Her expression is one of utter rage and shock. It should make me smile, but over my eighteen years, she has managed to suck every human emotion from me. I am a shell, but at least now I am free.

"You are no daughter of mine. You're a disgrace."

"That I am." Perhaps I can smile. My lips begin to twitch.

This bar looked as good as any, sleazier than most. The dimly lit basement club is filling with a cosmopolitan mix of people, but then it is in the heart of the city. The booths around the edge are only barely visible. A single flame encased in red glass casts a sensual glow, but is too weak to cast anything but shadow on the patrons seated there. The bar itself is at the far end of the room, away from the speakers, which are pumping out indiscriminate beats, loud and constant. People gather in the ever-decreasing space on the dance floor, a writhing mass of sweaty bodies. I try to slide onto the empty stool, but the surface is suspiciously sticky so I just perch on the edge. I am surprised I am not more nervous. I have never been out on my own, never to a bar and never somewhere like this. This morning, my mother called me a whore; tonight I'm going to prove her right.

"Can I buy you a drink, gorgeous?" The deep voice at my ear makes me jump. I was miles away. My little flashback was only this morning but it already feels like a nasty, distant memory. Maybe not distant enough. I think a drink would be perfect.

"Thank you...double vodka...straight." I swallow thickly at his sudden raised brow. Is that okay? Isn't that what women drink? Richard never allowed me alcohol, always wanted me sentient, and never permitted me the luxury of numbing the pain. The man steps up to the bar, dipping his head, but he flashes me a wide, friendly grin, which makes me relax a little. I steal furtive glances at his profile, up and down his body. I wonder if this is my first client. He is tall, slim, liquid dark eyes that shimmer when he looks back at me and holds my gaze. His hair hangs in long, inky strands that flop and fall into his eyes. A similar length all round that reaches past his neck and has slight waves. It looks thick and soft. I clasp my hands to stop my itchy fingers from embarrassing me. He hands me my drink, stepping a little too close and brushing my fingertips with his when I take the glass.

My hands aren't shaking, but I can feel my tummy start to turn. Okay, this is it. I knock the drink back and nearly spit it all back out. Fighting my body's natural reaction just makes me cough and splutter and I make a complete mess of the front of my dress. The man hands me a handful of napkins, and I can feel the burn in my cheeks worsen by his wry smile and low level chuckle.

"Maybe vodka's not your drink?" He teases.

"No...It is...just went down the wrong way." I tip the remainder of the liquid, thankful it is only a small amount, and I manage to swallow it down without further drama.

"So?" He pauses waiting for me to fill the gap. So...so what? So...ah, my name. I don't want to be Grace here. I don't want to be Grace ever again, but I hadn't given it any thought. In that instant the bottles on the shelf behind the bar grab my attention. Tia Maria... Gordon's... Bombay Sapphire... Sambuca.

"Sam...My name is Sam." His eyes follow mine to the shelf. He regards me carefully, his lips pursed and dark, thick brows pinched together. He is quite handsome. He is smartly dressed in a white button down shirt that fits his broad shoulders and wide chest. His sleeves are rolled up, and his arms are muscular with ink patterns covering all his skin to his wrists. He is slim but fit. Clearly defined muscles are evident with his well fitted clothes. His waist is narrow and the stretch in his jeans fails to hide his muscular thighs and bulge in his...Jesus, stop looking at his...

"So what do you do, Sam?" He smirks when my eyes meet his. They must be the size of saucers, and I cringe that I was caught red-handed staring at his crotch.

"I'm a whore," I blurt and it's his turn to almost choke on his beer.

"Excuse me?" he coughs.

"I'm a whore." I arch my back and lean into him. I can do this. Richard had me flirt with his friends all the time. He got off on it. He never let me be with them but had no problem fucking me in front of them. I shouldn't be embarrassed at staring at a stranger's cock when I have had much worse.

"You're one of Roman's girls?" His voice is sharp with surprise.

"Um...no." The man is looking directly over my shoulder, and I follow his gaze to a group of men gathered around one of the booths. I use the term 'men' loosely. They are massive mountains, almost as wide as they are tall. Dark, angry scowls fix their faces, and I shudder when they look my way. One of them was just at the bar beside me knocking drinks back until he was called away.

"Well, you're brave working here right in front of them." His voice is low and serious.

"Night off," I add with a tight smile, wishing I had more vodka to quell my rising fear. What the fuck am I doing?

"No such thing, sweetheart." He grabs my hand and roughly pulls me from the stool. He drags me from the club with no effort at all. I struggle against his grip pinching his hand that is clamped around my wrist, but the minute I start to shout, he has me muffled against his chest. Someone stops us, but before I can call for help, he easily dismisses their concern.

"My girlfriend, she's had a little too much to drink." I squeal and wriggle against his iron hold but quickly lose my fight when I hear a low grumble that chills me.

"You can leave her here, Leon. Roman noticed her at the bar. He'd be happy to help you out."

I suck in a breath and go limp in his arms.

"Tell Roman thanks, but she's mine. He'll understand." The other man chuckles, and the next thing I feel is the warm evening air hitting my bare arms. We walk for a short distance before he pulls me into a deserted alleyway. Shit, this is it...I am such a fucking idiot. All that rage and hurt I felt when I left home, did I really think it would change me? Did I really think just because my mother *called me a whore, it would actually make me that person? Shit.*

"You are a fucking idiot!" *The man shouts at me, and I step back in shock. I was expecting him to pounce, maybe hit me but not this. His eyes are filled with concern. Worry and anger crinkle his brow, and he drags his hand through his thick hair with obvious frustration.*

"I'm sorry." *My voice catches and I can feel my eyes prickle. What the fuck? I am a mess, but I don't need to break. I just need to get back to my hotel and figure out what to do with my life...alone.*

I turn to walk away but stop when his hand cups my elbow and pulls me back to face him. His lips creep wide into a warm smile, and I let out a sob. Don't be kind, please don't be kind. *My hand slaps my mouth to stop the cry, but it's too late. I can't hold it in. My shoulders start to shake, and he pulls me into his chest. His strong arms embrace me, and I feel all his warmth seep into my sad self. Everything that happened leading up to this day, this morning with my mother and what could've happened just now, completely overwhelm me and I collapse into this beautiful stranger's hold. Long minutes pass but I eventually pull back, the tears are still trickling down my cheeks but I have stopped the heart-wrenching sobs.*

"Where do you live?" *he coaxes, his voice gentle and soothing.*

"I...I am staying at a hotel." *I exhale with a loud hiccup. Could I possibly look anymore pathetic?*

"Okay, but where do you live?" *he presses, but I fall silent. Regardless of my fuck-up, I am not going back 'home'.* "Fine, but you're not staying in a hotel. Roman might have us followed, so you are coming with me. You'll be safe with me." *He holds his jacket up and slips it over my shoulders, drowning my shaking frame.*

"I don't know that...you're a stranger," *I state as I start to regain some common sense.*

"A stranger you were going to let pay you for a fuck not five minutes ago. Where do you think we would've gone to do the deed, hmm?" *His tone is mocking but his face is filled with kindness and compassion, and he's right.*

"Maybe I fucked up   " *I straighten myself, but he interrupts.*

"No maybe about it, sweetheart." *He openly laughs, and as shitty as I feel, the humiliation is now clawing inside and morphing into anger.*

"Look, you're right. I did fuck up, but tell me why going with you now isn't just another fuck-up. It's not like math...two fuck-ups don't make a positive," *I snap, but my indignation is short-lived because a surge of sadness consumes me. I have no one. I have no clue what to do now. I am so lost. I look up, and his features soften with the glaze of my tears, but even I can see the genuine concern etched on his face.*

"Here, have my phone. The police are on speed dial, number nine. If at any time you feel unsafe, press it, but trust me, you will be safer with me than alone." *His words are softly spoken. He presses his phone into my hand.*

"Why? Why are you doing this?" *I'm falling apart and filled with confusion.*

"Because I am a really nice guy." *He squeezes my shoulders, pulling me into his solid frame, and he walks us slowly out of the alley.*

"Are you going to…um…" *I pause my words and stop us both walking.*

"No, sweetheart, I'm not. You're not my type…yet." *I stopped walking, but he chuckles, a deep, friendly laugh, and pulls me back alongside him.*

"Please don't call me sweetheart," *I whisper.*

"Okay, Sam. Is that your real name?" *He looks down into my eyes. I can still feel the sting of tears behind my lids, but looking into his kind face I don't feel remotely sad. I've got this.*

"It is now." *I say with more confidence than I have felt in a really long time.*

"Okay, Sam, well, I'm Leon."

EIGHT

Jason

I had every intention of taking her to my flat at the club. Even as I started the car I thought about which playroom we could use. But catching her delicate profile and soft smile when she notices me looking her way just made that impossible. I know so little about her, but what I do know is a paradox to the image she portrays. I get the feeling her image is a comfortable costume she is too quick to hide behind, and if I want her to open up to me, to really be mine, I have to take her out of her comfort zone. I smile to myself. The irony is not lost that she finds comfort in a dark place with whips and chains and things that go more than bump in the night. She undulates with the touch of my fingers down her side; she shivers and her skin prickles with gooseflesh. Her skin is so damn soft, and her delicate little sighs make me so damn hard. She is lying with her back to my chest, tucked right in, but I am almost bent double from my hips, trying to keep my erection from digging into her arse. She is obviously tired to have fallen asleep so quickly after we made love earlier. Made love…Jesus, when did I grow a vagina? I don't make love; I fuck. She sighs again, and I lose my tentative hold on being a gentleman and roll my hips against the ripe, round curve of her butt. I freeze when she starts to mumble, her body is instantly rigid in my arms and she is trembling.

"You killed her!" She sobs. "Grace….no….no …please." Her skin is instantly clammy and she sits up with a cry, gasping for air. Her head drops to her chest as she draws in deep, calming breaths. I place my hand on her back, and she spins in shock, eyes wide with fear but flash only for a moment then soften with recognition.

"Sam?" I sit up and place my arm around her, pulling her still trembling body against mine. She feels so cold, I lay us back down and pull the covers up to her chin. I make a big deal of tucking her in, and she giggles. It's what I was hoping for because she feels ten times more relaxed in my arms than just a few seconds ago. Long minutes pass and I begin to wonder if she has fallen back to sleep, but she tilts her head up to me. The sadness she holds in her dark brown eyes makes my chest hurt.

"Bad dream?" I ask softly.

"Bad reality." Her lips pinch to one side, and she gives a light shrug but I turn her chin as she tries to retreat from me.

"Sam, I want to know. If you want to tell me," I urge. I wait and don't realise I'm holding my breath until she starts to speak, and I exhale loudly.

"I miscarried when I was young…and…it still haunts me. *He* still haunts me." She adds with bitterness.

"He?"

"Richard…my boyfriend. He was angry, and let's just say I didn't stand much of a chance. I lost the baby, actually I nearly died but it obviously wasn't my time." She gives a tentative smile, which doesn't reach her eyes.

"What do you mean you didn't stand a chance? He forced you to have an abortion?" My tone pitched with disbelief.

"No…no he forced me to miscarry. He beat me so badly I lost the baby." Her voice is barely audible, and her face is wet with silent tears. I use my palm to wipe them dry.

"Jesus, Sam. This is the same guy that—" The words and anger clog my throat, and I have to fight to contain the rage. "Richard…is the one who abused you." She nods into my chest. I kiss her hair, and for a long time, I am utterly speechless.

"Where is he now?" I am surprised how calm my voice is when I want to tear the bastard limb from limb.

"He lives in the States. He comes to the club sometimes. He claims to be the ultimate Master or some shit. He has a big following, which is utterly terrifying. That people think he is some sort of BDSM guru makes me sick." She physically shivers and I have to agree.

"My club? He's been to my club?" I am shocked.

"Yep."

"Have you ever seen him there?" I can feel my anger start to boil. This is exactly why I bought the club.

"No, thank God. I get the heads up from the admin team if he is signing in. It's not that I don't think I could handle it. On my home turf, with my armour, as Mistress Selena I mean, I'm sure I could, but *if* I couldn't. If he somehow made me break, I would lose too much, and he is not worth it." Her tone is resolute but tinged with an unbidden vulnerability.

"I checked all the members when I bought Angus out. We only have two Richards from memory…" I mumble absently.

"He calls himself Master Alpha, but he uses the Greek symbol. Can you believe it? Pretentious arsehole…wait…what? You bought Angus out? So you're the sole owner?" She sits up and far out of my arms. *Shit.*

"It doesn't make any difference." I add quickly and try to brush the comment off and add with a light laugh. "It doesn't make me your boss or anything." I reach for her, but her face darkens with anger, and her eyes flash with hurt.

"You're damn right it doesn't!" she bites. "What it does mean is all this truth bullshit is one-sided. I have told you nothing but the truth and you…you…" She points her finger but her hand shakes, a sarcastic laugh spilling from her tight lips. She snatches the sheet from the bed as she stands, angrily wrapping it around her sweet body. She looks furious. She looks sexy but mostly furious.

"I didn't lie. It never came up." I find my hands instinctively shield myself between my legs; she looks really mad, and I am very naked.

"Oh!" She laughs bitterly. "Oh, really? Lying by omission defence. That's what you're saying? Well, Angus has been absent for the last eight months, and in that time, we've seen each other at the club what? Maybe two or three times a week? When did you buy him out exactly?"

"Eight months ago." I admit reluctantly.

"And why might no one have told me in all that time?" She narrows her eyes with justified suspicion.

"Because only a few people knew, and I said their jobs depended on keeping it confidential." No point lying now. Her brows rise, then pinch when her eyes narrow once more. If looks could maim, I would be in agony.

"Sam—" I rise from the bed but halt at her hand.

"Don't you fucking move. If you value what you hold in your hands, don't move a fucking muscle." She drops her sheet, and I stand impotent while she hurriedly dresses, murmuring curses under her breath.

"Sam…" I step, but my foot doesn't reach the carpet just hovers midair before retreating back to its original position.

"You're such a fucking idiot, Sam…Idiot and I'm gonna kill Leon for setting this up!" She practically screams. She shakes her head and tears fall onto her cheek. *Shit no.* Her voice is soft and catches. "You know Jason, I don't give a fuck whether you own the club, but lying…I thought you were different."

She grabs her bag and is out the door and down the stairs before I can grasp what just happened. I hear the front door slam and panic. This is not happening. I snatch the sheet from the floor and gather it round my waist. I race out the bedroom door, leap down the stairs and run barefoot out into the street. It's midafternoon but Boxing Day and, thankfully, not a soul around. Not that I would care. I would run bollock naked after her if I had to. A frantic search up and down my narrow street before I see a flick of dark hair disappear around the corner onto the river walkway. I don't hesitate, my bare feet pound the cobblestone and I skid around the corner to see her stomping away. Her hands clearly wiping her face. I run to catch up; it only takes a few on my long strides.

"Enough!" I shout loud and gruff and a little bit pissed off.

She halts and spins, shock and amusement fight for precedence on her flawless face. I drop the sheet and step up to her and hold her shoulders stiffly. Wide eyes and amusement win.

"I'm sorry I didn't say something sooner. I should have. But then you might've asked why, and I wasn't ready to answer that, not without sounding like a creeper at least." I draw in a breath and shiver, the wintery chill in the air hitting all those usually hard-to-reach places. Her gaze is a mix of vulnerable confusion and utter shock, but my eyes are just as intense and filled with the passion I feel for her. "I bought it so I could veto the membership…so I could keep you safe. I really like you, Sam. I have *liked* you for a long time." I draw out the emphasis on the word 'like' very deliberately. She has to know I feel more. I just don't want to freak her out any more than I already have. "There didn't seem any point telling you about the club while you were 'dating' Leon. And, it didn't seem like a first date type of conversation, but I never lied to you. I would never lie to you. I am different. Let me prove it. I have nothing to hide from you, Sam." I hold my arms out, my nipples could cut glass, and I am literally freezing my bollocks off. She rushes forward and wraps her arms around me, barely covering my naked body with her small frame, but I appreciate the sentiment and relish the warmth. She rubs her hands up my back vigorously.

"You fucking idiot! You'll catch pneumonia." She drops to pick up the sheet just as some squeals of laughter erupt from a group of girls on the bridge ahead crossing the Thames. Sam laughs shaking her head. "Fuck, Jason, what we're you thinking?" She pulls the sheet closed around my body and lays her hand on my chest, over my heart. I move my hand to cover hers.

"I was thinking I would be a fucking idiot to let you go." Her smile lights her eyes and warms me though to my bones.

"You're naked on the South Bank. I think you have established a new benchmark for the idiot title." She snickers. I swiftly bend and scoop her into my arms. Dipping down to retrieve the bag she had dropped. I silence her laughter with my mouth, desperate to taste what I so nearly lost. I slowly step toward home, reluctant to relinquish her lips. I reach my front door. Leaving the house in haste like I did, I am thankful I have a fingerprint entry system. I drop her bag and carry her back up to my room.

"I need to tie you up." My voice is gravely and hoarse with urgency. It's more than desire; it's a primal need I feel in my veins like liquid fire, raw and relentless. I need to reclaim what is mine.

"I know." Her voice is tentative but her body is awake to my demand. Her eyes darken with pent up arousal swirling seductively in dark chocolate pools. Her chest rises and falls in rapid, sexy breaths, and her tongue traces some moisture onto her dry lips. She needs this as much as I do, she just doesn't know it…yet.

"Comfortable?" I tighten the last restraint on her wrist and slip my finger under the tie to check for circulation. I don't actually keep toys and kit at my home, kind of redundant when you own a sex club, but that doesn't mean I don't know how to improvise.

"Yes, Sir." Her breathy voice is pure sin. Her eyes meet mine with a mix of fire and nervous hunger.

"Good." I won't be long. I walk to the door.

"Jason?" she calls, her tone incredulous. I bite back a smirk and fix her with an impassive expression. "Sir?" she amends, but it sounds dangerously like a snarl. I step back and trace my finger down her cheek, all the way to her collarbone and toward her breasts. I hold her nipple between my middle finger and thumb and begin to squeeze. Her eyes widen, her breath catches, and her legs flex against their hold.

"That tone, sweet girl, now means I will take as long as I damn well please." Her back arches with the final pressure and sags when I release. I don't turn back for fear I'll never get to leave, if her face is anything like the fiery expression in her eyes.

It takes me five minutes to gather the bits I will need but I decided to wait it out for another twenty. I am tempted to sort myself out, I am so fucking hard just thinking about how Sam is waiting upstairs but decide against it. I know exactly where I want to come. I push the bedroom door, her head snaps to face me then just as quickly returns back to the centre. Her breasts rise and fall with her rapid breathing. Perfect swells of soft round flesh, peaked with pert, hard nubs. She swallows thickly and lets out a long, deep sigh.

"How are you feeling, beautiful?" I walk to the side and put the items on the small table. Her head twitches with the noise, but she remains still.

"I'm good, Sir. I missed you." Her genuine smile is warm and breathtaking.

"I'm glad." A deep groan rumbles in my chest when she whimpers at my soft touch, cupping and squeezing her breast. "Don't close your eyes." I reach back to the table for the ice. She jumps at the first drop of freezing water that lands in her stomach. Her eyes are wide but the effort to keep them like that is clear from the clench in her jaw and her thin lips. I trace the cube swiftly and lightly across her skin, leaving a thin trail of liquid along the edge of her hip bone, up her side, touching the curve of her collar bone and down the valley between her breasts. Her skin prickles with the chill, and she trembles and gasps when I circle her nipples. I drop the cube in her belly button, and she bites back a squeal, her back arching slightly. The muscles in her legs flex and tense against her restraints.

I pick up another cube and palm it, sliding it down her tummy and in between her legs. She jerks and cries out, her eyes scrunched tight.

"Open your eyes, beautiful." She tilts her head to scowl at me. I am now perched in between her legs with a raised brow. She huffs out but calms her riotous body with some steady breaths. She meets my imperious gaze with her steely one. "Cold?" I blow on her folds with warm breath but slide the cube over her glistening entrance. I drag my bottom lip in at the memory of her taste. Her eyes follow my tongue and but narrow at my deviant grin.

"Sir, a little yes." She shivers, a visual confirmation of her plight.

"Would you like me to warm you up a little?" My warm breath kisses her core and her hips tilt fruitlessly to try and edge closer to my mouth.

"Yes, please, Sir." Her eager, exasperated plea makes me smile, and I swipe my very warm tongue along the length of her silken, soaking folds. Her legs wrench and try uselessly to clamp around my head, a futile attempt to prevent the onslaught of pleasure or maintain it. Either way, she growls out in frustration when I evidently, and too quickly, pull back.

"Something you want to say, Sam?" I coax.

"No, Sir," she grits out and maintains may gaze. I stand and walk over to the candle that has been slowly burning into a nice pool of liquid wax. I pick it up and hold it high.

"Good. How are you doing, Sam? I'd like you to answer honestly without fear of consequence," I explain.

"Oh, good, well, in that case, *Sir,* I am fucking off the charts horny and really, really want you and your massive cock fucking me until I can't breathe." She rushes her words, breathless and urgent.

"I meant with the restraints, but I think your answer has pretty much covered that." She giggles, and her cheeks flush to an adorable pink.

"Oh, sorry, yes, they are fine. Everything is good…*really* good." She smiles, and her mouth forms a silent 'O' when I let the first drop of wax fall from the jar. Her eyes are like saucers and her little chest is frantic with rapid pants. I continue to dribble the almost too hot liquid over her torso. Hitting her breasts, her nipples, around her belly button and the top of her landing strip. The crease where her thigh meets her apex is particularly sensitive, and she bucks wildly when I hit very close to her clit. Her whole body is a trembling erotic display of submission, her wetness is dripping onto the bed sheets, and I can't wait to bury myself inside her.

Just one more thing. I pick up the large blade from the table. Her eyes are half dreamy, half glazed but snap open with the glint of the knife. Her gaze flicks from my eyes to the right side of my stomach where the skin puckers with some poor stitching and an angry scar.

"War wound from a family altercation," I clarify, but she doesn't look remotely convinced. "Do you trust me, Sam?"

"Yes," she answers immediately despite the reservation in her eyes.

"Then I suggest you hold very, very still." I lie on the bed next to her and spend the next twenty minutes carving the dried wax from her skin. The blade is smooth against her skin. The wax comes away in satisfying ribbons, curling away from her body like butter on a warm knife. Only a sudden movement would cause any blood to flow, and Sam is perfectly still. I can feel her heart beat a strong staccato under my fingertips as I follow the blade with my hand and sweep the wax from her skin. I have traced, touched, and teased every inch of her skin. She is alive and trembling, and I can't wait a second longer.

I stand, slide my lounge pants to the floor and crawl between her spread and tethered legs. I swipe my cock from her entrance to her clit, up and down several times. Her eyes fix on mine, pleading and fierce with lust. I sink inside in one thrust, and she cries out. Her muscles contract like crazy and take me completely by surprise. Her thighs flex and clench, her back curves in a perfect arch, and her hands grip the ties like they are her lifeline. She comes hard around my cock. It takes all my resolve not to follow her release, but this one was for her. I pump gently inside, easing her down. Her gasps for breath turn to whimpers and sighs, her body limp and sated.

My hips continue to move, my thrusts becoming more urgent. I love the way she feels around me. I love it when I'm really deep. I shift up the bed and rest my hands on either side of her shoulders. Her body undulates beneath mine, grinding with me, meeting each thrust with irresistible fervour. I stop before it's too late and pull out. I fist my cock and continue to pump hard. Both our eyes train on the thick ribbon of come that shoots from me onto her tummy, the force splashing the edge of her breasts. I pitch onto one arm, and with my free hand, I smear my essence all over her skin. And that one, was for me.

"Are you sure you can eat all that?" She smiles shyly as she folds her menu and hands it to the waiter.

"I worked up quite an appetite." Her sensual tone is low and sexy, leaving very little to misinterpretation. My cock twitches, and I wince when it rubs a little too close to my zip. The waiter loses all his composure and fails to clasp his hand around the proffered menus, letting them spill across the floor. Sam snickers when he scrambles to the ground to pick them up. He apologises and swiftly departs. She wriggles her brows, full of mischievousness.

"You get that reaction a lot, I assume." I adjust myself and sit back, my finger lazily tracing the rim of my water glass. Her eyes flick to my adjustment then to the waiter making a hasty retreat.

"I don't know what you mean." She flutters her lethally long lashes.

"Hmm." I pour some of the champagne, happy to watch her shine. She is still wearing my diamond necklace and the tiny rocks pale in contrast to her luminescent skin. She is stunning and that necklace looks fucking perfect just where it is. She notices my eyes settle at her neck and her fingers reach to touch. Her tender smile hits me hard and warms my soul.

"Will you wear it?" I ask, and for a moment, her smile widens so much I think she might be about to agree.

"You know I can't." She shakes her head lightly.

"I'd like you to wear my collar, Sam." I lean forward, rest my elbows on the table and fix her with my most serious gaze. She mirrors my image in every way, a challenge.

"And I'd like to tie you up and torture you, but from what I do know about you, that is *never* going to happen, *Sir.*" Her voice drops to a whisper with the last word.

The waiter arrives with the drinks, and a second follows with the first of our many dishes. She sits back and takes a big sniff of the delicious Asian fragrances drifting up in billows of scented steam from the little baskets placed before us. She has eagerly opened each one and rearranged the baskets in what looks like order of preference. I chuckle when she wastes no time with her chopsticks. I feel bad that we haven't eaten today, but then, she is very distracting.

We pretty much inhale the Dim Sum starter and comfortably wait for the next course. When I remember one of the many things I want to discuss.

My brows must furrow, because before I say a single word, Sam speaks.

"Uh oh, this looks serious. Let me guess, I should be eating my meal off the floor," she quips, but her eyes flash with something quite dark. I get an unpleasant twist in my gut at the notion.

"Um no. Humiliation isn't my kink." I sip my drink. All the same, my mouth is dry. I have no idea how she is going to take this. "Sam, I have asked you to stop seeing certain clients, and I need to know you will be all right for money...I mean, I would like to make sure you don't need money."

"Are you offering to pay me, Jason, because wouldn't that just make *you* a client?" Her voice is flat but she's bitten her lips flat, and I don't know if she's holding back hurt, rage or laughter.

"Fuck, no!" I snap, but lean in, adjusting my speech to a more tempered volume. "That's not what I meant at all."

"Relax, Jason. I was teasing." She fails to suppress her smile this time. I scowl because it seems not telling the truth causes her to run out but insinuating I am going to pay her for sex is a laughing matter. This is fucked up. "Sorry... sorry, my bad. Not something to joke about. I get that." She purses her lips in mock seriousness. "It is very thoughtful of you but, really, I am fine for money."

"Really?" Not that I doubt her ability to charge a premium price, but she lives in one of the most expensive parts of London. She left home at eighteen, and I struggle to see how she manages to maintain the lifestyle she does.

"Leon's rent covers my living costs—"

"Leon lives with you?" I interrupt.

"Yes. My best friend shares my flat," she clarifies with a touch of attitude in her tone. "As I was saying, his rent covers most my expenses. I have no mortgage, and if I get to keep my other clients, I can still make my other investment commitments. It's all good." She cups my cheek, but I'm still reeling from her sharing a flat with Leon. He is a player at the club, very attractive, and until two days ago, I thought he was her boyfriend.

"Leon?" I repeat.

"Leon saved me. I owe him everything. I trust him with my life...just in case I am not being understood." She arches her perfect brow but then hums out her musing. "Hmm although, he does have an annoying habit of thinking he knows what's right for me."

"You regret him talking to me?" My voice is soft. I can't help the stabbing pain just below my collarbone, maybe a little lower.

"Oh, no, not at all." She pushes herself out of her chair and slides onto my lap. With the fixed table and wall seat there is no room, but we manage to meld together. Her slim arms wrap around my neck, and my arms slip around her waist. "Like I said, he saved me, and not for the first time." Her lips cover mine for long, sensual minutes; only an embarrassed cough interrupts our intimate embrace. The waiters layer several dishes on the table, with a glossy colourful feast on each individual plate.

"Oh, yum!" She slides back off my lap and settles in her seat for round two.

"So how did you two meet?" I take the bowl of sticky rice she offers me and start to load my plate.

"In a bar…a sleazy bar. I had left home, checked into a hotel, and went to the first bar I could find. Not my proudest moment. He spotted me and saved me from making the biggest mistake of my life. I had no idea what I was doing, or what I was going to do with my life. He sorted me out, helped me find my way."

"Excuse me if I don't champion him as a true friend, because he sounds more like your pimp," I scoff. Her shoulders lift in a dismissive shrug.

"Anti-pimp more like. No, no, you don't understand. I know how lucky I am to have him in my life. I know exactly where I would be if he hadn't dragged me out of that bar."

I raise my hands up in surrender. I know a futile conversation when I hear one. Despite his initial help, he is high on my 'jury's out' list.

"All I had when I left home was the damn necklace my mother had used all my life as a type of dowry to try and get some rich titled guy to marry me." She lets out a resigned breath, but I can see the pain still evident in her eyes. She shakes herself and stabs at some crispy chilli beef, scooping it into her mouth. She chews slowly, collecting herself. "Leon took me to Sotheby's to get it valued. It had once belonged to Queen Mary. I couldn't believe it was genuine. I was expecting them to laugh me out of their offices and tell me it was from *Accessorize* or some chain store. They took a week or so to establish provenance but gave me a valuation at the time of around a million pounds. When it went to auction, it sold for over double that." She shrugs nonchalantly. My chopsticks are hovering about an inch from my mouth. I drop the sticks. "It was my grandfather's. Part of me wished I could've kept it. It was the only thing I had, other than a few clothes, when I left home but he wanted me to have it, and I needed to sell it to live."

"Two million?" I repeat.

"About that…so really, you don't need to worry. I bought the house I live in and converted the four other floors into flats. I still have to work; the money is all tied up in property, and this is not a cheap city to live in, but I can cut back on clients without it hurting. Without it hurting me, I mean. The clients wanting pain pay more." I open my mouth as she has her own chopsticks at my lips with something; I have no idea what, but I chew and swallow. She is just full of surprises.

"And who's Grace?" I take a sip of my water.

"Grace?" Her back straightens, and she looks confused.

"Your nightmare, you called out Grace. Was Grace the name you gave your baby?" I ask softly but she shakes her head.

"No…no, I'm Grace…that was my name but I legally changed it." She draws in a deep breath and flashes a smile clearing any sadness with her own radiance. "I think I've done my bit…How about you?" She sips her champagne, there is still a mountain of food, but she doesn't look nearly finished. I like that. I hate it when women don't eat; it's like air and sex…natural.

I run my hand through my hair. "Not much to tell. Normal family, met Daniel at Oxford, but he dropped out, and I stayed. I helped him regroup when his company was in trouble. He had the financial backing from Jack Wilson but needed someone he could trust as his right hand." I pause, and the silence swells between us like an ominous tide.

"You're right; that was not much to tell." She sits back and eyes me carefully. I hold her gaze because she knows there's more.

There is always more. The choice is mine. I teeter. If I am open, we will have a chance to continue down this path. However precarious and fragile our relationship may be, we will at least have a chance. If I bluff and hide, this ends right now. I can feel it.

"I have a twin brother." She takes another sip of her drink but says nothing. "He got mixed up with the wrong people. I'm not making excuses. He knew what he was doing, he just didn't care. He was a drug addict, stole from his friends and family, lied every time we tried to help him get clean. One night, when he was high, he came home. Our mum tried to help him, and he lashed out, knocked her to the ground. I came in just too late. She was unconscious. I flew at him, but he had the kitchen knife my mother had been using. He turned just at the right moment. The knife entered under my ribs, sliced up a few organs. I was bleeding out, and my mum was…she could've been dead for all he cared. He ran and I was glad." Sam reaches across the table and takes my clenched fist, peeling the digits open from the white knuckle grip.

"Your scar?" Her eyes dip to my left side from earlier. I nod.

"I was in Intensive Care for a few weeks but made a full recovery. My mum has no recollection of anything that happened that night. A blessing, but she was broken when Will never returned."

"Do you know where he is now?" She squeezes my hand, and I welcome the warmth.

"Florida…He's a marine biologist." I sniff out a laugh at her obvious confusion. "He went missing for two years but surfaced. He was clean and studying for a degree funded by an outreach programme where he volunteered. He was too ashamed to come home, but his counselor convinced him it was the right thing."

"The Mission…That's why it's special?" she asks remembering my words from yesterday. *Jesus, was it just yesterday?* I nod.

"They saved him when we couldn't. He'd be dead if it wasn't for that programme. I don't doubt that for a moment." I can feel a pinch and tingle behind my nose. He's my brother, and I could've lost him all too easily.

"You forgave him?" Her tone is a little sharp but brings me back from my own nightmare.

"It wasn't him, Sam. Again, I'm not making excuses. I think he was weak to take that path, especially when he could see the damage he was doing. But once he was on that path, he was no longer my brother, he was a different person. When he came back to us, he was Will again. I had to forgive him. My mother was broken, and he healed her. He healed the family."

"I never forgave." Her tone is bitter.

"And I wouldn't if I were you, but this was different, don't you think?"

"Yes. Sorry, I didn't mean anything by that. I just think some things are unforgivable." She shakes away the dark cloud. "So, twin brother, hmm?" She gives an impish grin.

"Jesus Christ, Sam." She winks, and I laugh and pat my lap for her to join me. She shakes her head still picking at the food. "Do you have hollow legs?"

"I'm stocking up .Who knows how long until you feed me next?"

NINE

Sam

"I'm not going." I tuck my legs beneath me on the sofa and push the mass of shiny red material Leon has just dumped in my lap on to the floor. He huffs and picks it up, swirling my six-foot, handmade, bright red bullwhip in his hand. "And I am definitely not using that." I snort.

"You owe me," he goads with a challenging peak of his brow. He lets out a frustrated puff when I remain unmoved. "I'm happy the *Beauty and the Beast* Disney romance thing seems to be working for you, Sam. Honestly I am…I even cleared the way for it to happen, hence I'm calling in the favour. But it's been four weeks of vomit-inducing weeks with all the gooey, lovey dovey eye contact and marathon fuck sessions. Which, don't get me wrong, I did fear you had healed up in that department. So I'm pleased you're getting some." He barely draws breath before continuing his friendly diatribe. "Four weeks, Sam! I need more than what my right hand and a passing pussy are currently providing." He grumbles and shoves his hand roughly down the front of his jeans emphasising his crude dilemma. "Please, Sam." He pouts and drops to his knees in front of me.

"You know this is weird right?" He rests his head on my lap, his dark eyes pleading and mischievous at the same time. "You know Charlie is more than capable of helping you out."

"True, but when you've had the best…" He slowly blinks his indecently long lashes before he goes in for the kill. He's a lawyer by trade and ruthless by nature. "At the risk of repeating myself. You. Owe. Me." He pitches up on his knees and lightly pokes my nose with each word. A self-satisfied smile spreads wide across his handsome face.

"The reason I'm reluctant is the same reason you think I owe you." I wrinkle my nose and roll my eyes at his impassive face.

"Jason?"

"Jason," I confirm. Just his name is enough to make my lips morph into a sappy wide grin.

"Correct me if I'm wrong…but I am never wrong, so just shh." He pushes his fingers firmly against my lips. "This is the first night in four weeks he isn't hanging off you like some love-struck teenager. He's not the only starving man in your life, Sam," he practically growls but then softens his tone. "I consider it your duty to make the most of this impromptu time out from lovers' cloud nine where you have been hibernating and spend the evening with me." He picks up my cat suit from the floor and pushes it into my hands. "I have been very accommodating and have yet to mention the wanton neglect of your best friend duties." He sits up and leans his frame over me.

"You're pulling the best friend card?" I quip.

"You bet your arse I am. It has to be good for something other than having live porn in full surround sound streaming through the bedroom walls all night." I snicker and can feel my cheeks flare with heat.

"I don't ask often, not nearly as much as I want to." His jokey tone is softer now, tender with a touch of desperation, and my heart squeezes for my best friend when he adds his closing argument. "I trust you, Sam, like no other."

"I don't understand." I shake my head with resignation. I bet he wins all his cases.

"Ours is not to question why…" he recites in a light triumphant voice.

"Our is just to whip and cry." I sigh at his triumphant wicked grin.

"You remembered." He leans in and kisses my nose.

"Every lesson." I nod and smile with fondness at our unconventional shared history.

"So do I," he whispers with a flash of his best winning smile. "Shall we?" He springs to standing and holds out his hand, helping me up, his sheer delight and pleasure is plastered across his face with the widest smile. It is enough to cloud my reticence with guilt and rightly make my reluctance misplaced. He is a good friend; he's my best friend. In all other aspects of his life, he is just as dominant and demanding as any other alpha I know. Equally, in his position, it's not like he can ask just anyone to beat the crap out of him, or more specifically, whip him raw. A great deal of what we do and who we are is built on reputation and trust. I know he fears he would lose his standing if people knew. This may be true in the vanilla world, but in the safety of the club, I happen to think he has more to lose by hiding who he really is, but it's his life. And he is not the only one hiding.

The night of the day I left home. I found myself in a stranger's flat, having the weirdest birthday I can ever recall. Leon lived on his own in a dank basement flat in a grimy part of Camden. I clutch that phone like my life depended on it and to be fair, alone in a basement with a stranger, my life could've depended on it. But this was Leon. He pulls out the sofa bed and set about fixing the sheets. I just stand there watching, awkward and nervous, and wondering every second when he is going to pounce. He pulls back the comforter and I crawl in fully clothed. He tucks me in and goes to the kitchen. He returns with two steaming cups of hot chocolate but after the first searing sip I can feel the burn of something more potent lurking.

"Rum," he says. "It warms the soul and loosens lips." He gives a playful wink and sits down beside me, and long minutes pass in comfortable silence. I sip the drink and begin to relax. Leon drags his long legs onto the bed but stays on top of the covers and like me, is fully clothed. He starts talking. I start talking. At some point I drop the phone and lean against his strong chest. He wraps his arm around my shoulders and I relax. No, it was more than that, and it sounds trite, but after just a few hours, I felt like I was home.

That long soul-searching night spent talking with Leon turned into a month sleeping on his sofa couch. He was right; he was one of the good guys.

Newly qualified Leon works as a junior in a law firm. He works long, irregular hours and seems to like coming home after a hard day to a clean flat and a badly cooked meal. My mother had insisted when the time came for me to marry that I would have staff and would never need to so much as heat toast, leaving me with life skills of a preschooler. Still, I could pierce a film and press a microwave button like a pro.

He never once tried for something **more** despite the obvious attraction. Obvious on my part at least. He is fit and extremely confident in his skin. He rarely wears more than boxer shorts round the flat. His torso is lean and ripped with tight muscles. His smooth, dark, tanned skin stretches over strong, muscular thighs and broad shoulders. On more than one occasion he makes my mouth water. He is kind and beautiful, inside and out. I am definitely attracted to him, but I desperately value our friendship and need that so much more than I need to quell my burgeoning desire. I am grateful for the friendship, but I'm thrilled to be able feel something other than dread when I think about sex.

One evening, Leon returns and drops a pile of University prospectuses in my lap.

"With your results, you could pretty much pick any course you want, but if you pick a London university you are welcome to stay with me. I'll look for a bigger place, and if you pick law, I'll be your private tutor." He slides his long legs over the back of the sofa and sits heavily at my side. He chuckles and tips my mouth shut. I shake my head, I didn't realise my jaw had dropped open, but I am speechless.

"What are you talking about? I can't go to University, Leon, that's crazy." I shift so I am facing him. It's his turn to look confused.

"Why not?" His face is etched with concern, his tone very serious. I don't know what to say. I never gave it any thought. I never really believed my life was mine to make any choices. The silence stretches. He lets out and soft breath and reaches for my hand. He pulls it into his lap and twists to face me.

"Don't get me wrong I kinda like having you here for me every night, but you are more than this, Sam. You can do anything. You're free to be anyone you want to be." His smile falters when he sees my frown deepen.

"I'm…that's not what I'm supposed to do with my life. Thank you, but I can't." I try to pull my hand back, but he clutches tighter, and I shift, uncomfortable with his scrutiny.

"Can't what?" His tone is sharp.

"I look this way because I am only meant for one thing. I'm not going to University, Leon, it's not right for me." I can't hide my agitation.

"Really? And tell me what is right for you?" His voice is thick with sarcasm.

"My mother thought—" I snap my mouth shut at his bitter interruption.

"Jesus fucking Christ, Sam! Do not finish that sentence! Your mother was insane, and she whored you out to a monster for a shot at jumping up a social class or two. So please, spare me all her parental guidance. The last thing I expected to hear from you was confirmation that she was right." His anger is palpable. He fires his fury with each word. When I say nothing, he loses it. "Maybe she was right, maybe you are just a whore."

A silent cry escapes my shocked open mouth, but an instant surge of rage races through me. I pull my hand from his grasp and slap him hard across his face, the force snapping his head to the right. He slowly turns his head to face me, his face impassive, but his eyes darken, and his lips start to tighten into a smug smirk. I slap him again. There is a sharp sting in my palm, but I don't feel the pain; I just feel warm. I do it again, and his breath hitches. I drop my hand, but he shakes his head.

"Again please, Mistress."

I did my law degree and even qualified as a solicitor but my true talent was exposed that night. Leon saw it, claims he knew the very first night we met, said that's why he let me stay. I don't know if that's really true but we both received what we needed from the partnership. I gained a willing Guinea Pig and he was able to keep his secret. I don't agree that he would suffer if he exposed his 'switch' tendencies but that is his decision. I spent the next four years training before I accepted my first paying client. Although training never really ends and practice not only makes perfect it's also lots of fun.

The cab jerks to a stop, abruptly breaking my little reminiscence. Our driver uses some extremely colourful language to critique the other person's driving skills. Leon's mouth drops open in mock horror, not remotely offended. His own language is no better than that of a well-seasoned sailor.

"Not that I give a shit, but do you want to tell me why Jason gives me the stink eye every time I come home. I thought we got on before Christmas. He seemed kind of cool and now he, my dear"—he takes my gloved hand in his and pats the tight leather—"is rapidly approaching douche territory. He does know there's nothing between us right?" He continues to hold my hand but threads his fingers through and squeezes.

I chuckle. "Yeah, he knows. I think it might have more to do with him thinking you're my pimp," I add and squeeze one eye shut and peeking to see his incredulity and irritation flare.

"What? You told him I was your pimp?" He pinches the bridge of his nose and puffs out his anger. He doesn't let me answer but continues to muse. "No, that's ridiculous, but if he doesn't think there's anything going on then…" He draws his bottom lip in, chewing softly, a habit when he is concentrating. "Hmm and he is okay with the Dominatrix gig." I can almost hear the cogs turning.

"He still thinks I'm a whore," I blurt but in a hushed tone.

"Why? Why wouldn't you tell him the truth? He cares about you, Sam, anyone can see that." His thick, dark brows knit together to form one intimidating scowl.

"I know." I sigh and shift uncomfortably under his intense glare. "And he doesn't even care that I am…or that I said I was…you know." I shrug because I am struggling to defend my position.

"Look Sam, I know why you tell people *that*. I mean fuck 'em, right? The ones who judge don't deserve your time. Sure, I get it but I know you use it as a barrier, too. Not just a barrier, you weld it like a weapon. No danger of anything more than a one nighter. No one's taking a whore home to meet mummy, right?" he adds more softly.

"Yeah," I exhale.

"But Jason would?" he nudges.

"Yeah." My voice catches.

"And that's a problem because?"

"It can't go anywhere, Leon. We can't be more than this, so what's the point?" I can feel a tight pinch behind my nose and I blink the first sign of tears away.

"And why is that?" He won't give up. He's relentless.

"Um, he owns a sex club, Leon. How long do you think he will be happy with one woman?" I snap.

"He bought the club for you remember? To keep you safe. Sounds like *more* to me."

"He was a *regular* long before that, Leon," I add like that is its own justification.

"And you're a professional Domme. You're hardly the poster child for vanilla," he counters.

"My job, my fantasies, are very different from my reality, Leon. I want a normal relationship." My exasperation is wasted on him.

"Normal?"

"Well, no, not *that* normal." I grin and he chuckles before his expression is again all serious.

"You could have that with Jason, but you need to tell him the truth." His tone is stern, his argument compelling. "You threw a shit fit when he lied to you. Look, I know fuck all about relationships, and he doesn't even like me, but doesn't he deserve the same courtesy?" He sits back and crosses his arms, resting his defence.

"I guess." I won't meet his gaze. I hate that he's always right.

"No Sam, you don't guess. You fucking know! Now stop being such a pussy." His eyes narrow, but they gleam and spark with a thrill that is indisputable.

"Oh, you did *not* just call me that." The cab pulls to a smooth halt in front of the canopied entrance to the club. He remains definitely tight lipped. "You will so pay for that," I murmur. He pushes a twenty through the Plexiglas and opens the door for me.

"I was counting on it."

"I think you like this bit more than the bullwhip." I finish smoothing the arnica cream along his broad shoulders and help him slip his t-shirt back over his head. His eyes are soft and dreamy. His body moves with the slightest touch from me, and his lazy smile is adorable. I take his hand and lead him to the sofa in the corner of my favourite playroom. The dark walls are covered in a rich red velour paper, which is enticingly tactile. The wall lights are soft flames, and there is a very comfortable chaise for some relaxing aftercare. The St Andrew's Cross dominates the room, but most of the playrooms have one. This room, however, has no peephole, no windows, and no way of gaining entry once inside. It is completely private and only available to very few members. Leon lays his head in my lap, and I stroke his long hair, threading it through my fingers, my nails lightly scraping his scalp. He shivers with pleasure and sighs. His eyelids drift closed, and his weight noticeably increases as he falls into a deep sleep.

We never enter the room or leave together. Afterward, we meet at the bar, and Leon has my drink waiting. He still has this gorgeous afterglow, which warms me. Even if I do wish he could find someone else to trust enough, I am happy that I can help him in this way.

"So where's lover boy tonight?" he teases.

"He had some international conference call or something, but my phone's been playing up, so I actually have no idea what time he's finishing. He always texts or calls, but I haven't been able to switch the damn thing on all day. I left it at the flat. Useless piece of crap," I moan.

"Tell me about it." Marco appears at the end of the bar where Leon and I are perched. Sofia's twin brother took over as assistant manager only a few months back. He fancied a break from the family restaurant business and jumped at the chance when I mentioned the vacancy at the summer barbecue at Daniel and Bethany's family home. "The refurbishment next door cut through our data cables. Our computers have been down all day. It's like living in the Stone Age having to take down everything manually. Luckily Gus pretty much knows everyone so the door hasn't been too much of an issue. But checking guest applications has been a nightmare." He drags his hand through his elegant, styled, short hair and flopping fringe.

Leon's phone buzzes in his back pocket and he grimaces when Marco scowls. Its club policy that all phones are surrendered at the check-in.

"Sorry Marco, I didn't realise I still had it. I must have been distracted when we came in." He winks at me and steps around the back of the bar into the darkness to answer the call. But I can still hear the one sided conversation.

"Jason?" he queries and now I pay a little more attention.

"It's busted, not worked all day. She's with me though so if…At the club why? Who?"

I have just held my drink up toward a frazzled looking Marco. "I think you need this."

"Richard who?" I hear Leon's concern as the drink I am offering up slips from my fingers and crashes onto the glass top surface of the bar. Smashing spectacularly into a million pieces. Despite the mess and noise I freeze, my eyes are as wide as Leon's, who still has his phone at his ear.

"Not that I can see but…Look, we'll leave now." He swipes to end the call and steps back to me.

"Sam, are you okay?" He cups my cheek, but I barely feel his touch, I just feel icy cold. I have avoided him for years when I learned who Master Alpha really was, because I honestly had no idea how I would react. I know now. Why wasn't I told? The admin team here are excellent. Why wouldn't they let me know? Oh, the computers. I nod numbly at my own answered question but reach for the whip I had placed on the stool beside me. I need to leave before—

"Grace?"

The voice isn't as deep as I remember, but still, the timbre turns my stomach. I fix my smile, fix my mask. I'm not Grace. I'm not Sam. Here I am Mistress Selina. I turn and straighten my shoulders. I stand, my five foot ten, and in six-inch heels, ensuring we are eye level. His eyes flash with uncertainty but only for an instant. His thin lips sneer, distorting his face into something less than human, something evil. That look I do remember.

"Not for a *very* long time." My icy demeanour is reflected in my tone.

He thinks I am pausing to maybe remember what to call him but I am quiet because I notice for the first time the woman on her knees bent over by his feet. A long chain fixed around a cheap dog collar one end and the other gripped in his fist.

"You may call me Master Alpha," he sneers and tugs at the chain. The woman whimpers, and I get a sharp burn of acid in my chest.

"Hmm, not in here, *Dick*," I muse. He flinches at the abbreviation of his name. He always hated it, not that I ever dared to call him that in the past, but some of his friends would, just to rile him. I draw on every ounce of strength my costume and alter ego affords and hold my coiled whip under his chin. He tips his head a little, and I fix him with my most hate-filled stare. His eyes widen, and he stiffens at the contact. "You're in my playground now, *Dick*, and you get to call me Mistress." I turn toward the bar. Leon is still at my side and Marco pales significantly at the volatile situation unfolding. I smile at him and wink to try and reassure him. I have no intention of creating more of a scene; we already have enough curious eyes focused on us. I just won't allow him to affect me. He is nothing to me, and I bask in this revelation. "Marco, make sure *Dick* gets a glass of champagne on me, and that his companion gets the whole bottle. I'd like to make sure she has at least one pleasurable experience this evening." My smile is sweet with the perfect mix of saccharin and vitriol.

Richard purses his lips, the muscles in his jaw bubble under his *manscaped* blond stubble. His pale blue eyes darken with fury, but he accepts the offered flute. I step up to him, and he pauses for a moment but steps aside. I wouldn't be surprised if he couldn't see the fierce beat of my heart pounding against the skin-tight cat suit. The platform walkway from the bar is clear and I slowly walk toward the exit, Leon is at my side, his fingers twitch to reach for mine but he doesn't. I can feel the eyes of the room. I almost make it to the curtained doorway…almost. Richard's voice booms across the room.

"Do you still blush when you are fucked in front of an audience?" I freeze. "Do you still scream for mercy when you take it in the arse?" I turn slowly. He raises his glass and tips to take a sip, his expression full of malice. I shouldn't be surprised. He was never going to make it easy for me. He never had the whole time we were together. Why would he change that now just because I have?

And I have changed.

I sigh and drop my hip in amused annoyance. I tap my lip as if wondering how to respond. My right hand gips my six-foot bull whip. I know exactly how I'm going to respond. I slowly sashay back along the walkway. I stop when he speaks again.

"You may think you are some sort of big deal, *Selena*, but face it…you're just a whore." This last word is drowned by the sonic crack from the tail end of my whip. Followed almost instantly by his curse and the shattering of his glass. His shocked eyes focus on the large bubble of blood coming from the knuckles on this hand where my aim has sliced his skin. It was a stupid move in such a confined space but I was confident in my skill and the area was clear. It had to be done. I'll gladly take the consequence for breaking this club rule. Just looking at the surprise on Richard's face is reward enough but I get a real surge of warmth that comes from retribution. It might not be much, but I made that bastard bleed.

I crack the whip once more with a showy Tasmanian cut back, which loops and cracks loud just behind me. It is perfect for garnering the attention of my target and the entire room. I stride right up to him, he takes a step back, and I snicker and raise a brow. He steps forward but too late for his error to go unnoticed. Perfect. We are nose-to-nose, I grab his chin and crush my mouth to his. His lips soften, and he groans, leaning into me, but I hold his distance with my grip. His urgent tongue is hungry for more, and when I pull back he almost falls forward chasing my lips. His eyes are liquid fire, his need and desire as transparent as the glass I have crushed beneath my boots. His chest heaves to calm his breathless state.

"I may be a whore...but I will never be *your* whore." I pat his cheek, my tone is laced with condescension. "But you, *Dick*...you will always be my bitch." He stumbles back, his eyes narrow, but he is silent. He looks around, noticing for the first time the enraptured audience. He roughly pulls his companion to her feet and marches away, through the curtained entryway and hopefully out of my life. Around us, the room resumes its normal level of noise and activity, but I remain transfixed on the doorway. Leon sweeps me into his arms and hugs me tight.

"Holy. Fucking. Shit. Sam, that was...shit, I am so fucking hard." He slides me down his body to let me feel the evidence of his statement. His mischievous grin eases the weight of the tension coursing through my veins. I slap him on his chest but wince when he flinches. He will be raw under his shirt, and I didn't mean to hurt him...not this time at least. I mouth 'sorry' but he shrugs it off.

"You are so not the only one, Leon." Marco lets out an exaggerated groan and visibly adjusts himself.

"Because that was my main objective, to give you two hard-ons." I sniff and stretch my neck, the last bit of tension leaving my body with a pop. I slide back on to my stool and lay the whip on the bar. "I'll have a glass of that, Marco... now the bottle's open," I smirk.

"I would say, hard-ons aside, you more than fulfilled your objective." Leon wraps a protective arm around me, as he was unable to do so earlier for fear of highlighting any vulnerability I was absolutely feeling. "Proud of you, babe." He kisses my hair, and I can feel his wide smile against my head. It must mirror mine.

"I'm proud of me." I reach for the glass; all eyes take in my shaking fingers. I let out a deep breath, the adrenaline still making my poor heart race and causing havoc with my nerves, now that I don't have to hold my emotions in check. I tip the flute back and down the entire glass. Fuck sipping, I'd be mainlining this if I could. Leon and Marco chuckle, and a calm settles over me as the liquid works its magic. "I doubt he'll come back, but I'm happy I can deal if he does. No more hiding."

Leon raises his glass, and with a pointed stare, he raises a toast.

"I'll drink to that, no more hiding." I close my eyes, acknowledging the portent of his words. No more hiding from Jason. He deserves to know the truth.

TEN

Jason

"Fuck! Fuck!" I end my call to Leon. I know it's nobody's fault. The computers are down, but I had banned that fucker the day after Sam told me who he really was. And now he is there…with her. I need to leave.

"Problem?" Daniel raises his brow. Our meeting had just started, but I slip my phone in my pocket and grab my suit jacket from the back of my chair, eager to leave.

"The club," I reply. He stands as I head to the door. "Sam's ex just showed up, and because the computers are down, he got in. I've only just found out, because I set up an independent alert direct with the server, but Sam wouldn't have got her normal notification, and she's there now. I have to go."

"Of course." Daniel gives a tight nod and follows me through the door. "I'm sure Sam can handle herself." His tone is calm, and I can only hope his confident assertion is correct. I am well aware of the image she portrays, but I also know the fragile foundation it is built on. I shake my head.

"I'm not so sure. You have no idea what he did to her." My voice trails, and I can feel anger heat my veins.

"Go, we'll sort the rest tomorrow." We walk along the corridor, but it takes a moment to register what he said.

"The rest?" My mind is very much elsewhere.

"The meeting?" he clarifies with a curious raised brow.

"Oh yes, sorry, Daniel. My head isn't here." I shrug, but I am more worried about getting to Sam than discussing tomorrow's agenda.

"Obviously. Do I need to be concerned, Jason? You know our baby is due any day now, so I won't be around." If he is really concerned it is far from evident in his tone, and his face is ever impassive.

"You don't need to be concerned, Daniel. You have been a little distracted yourself since the wedding, and the company is still standing," I challenge, only mildly affronted at his remark. "If I'm honest, I could do without hand-holding the intern you dumped on me."

"Ah, Peitra, yes, my apologies. You have to admire her tenacity. I am not one for nepotism, but she was very quick to highlight her business achievements and that she isn't, in fact, related to me." He presses the lift button. He shrugs lightly.

"Tenacious is one word. She may not be related to you, but being your wife's best friend's cousin meant she got close enough to ask for the placement *personally*. Something no other candidate was ever likely to do." My irritation is evident but not entirely related to the topic. I re-press the button. Is it stopping at every damn floor on the way here?

"True, but she's very bright I thought she would help." Daniel offers and I raise my brow when I face him.

"If it's help I need, then let me have Colin, your PA, and not some love struck graduate." He grins at my comment. I may have only met her one time, but I would have to be numb from the neck up to not know her interest was more than business related.

"Don't tell me a beautiful woman makes you uncomfortable. That's a first." Daniel chuckles.

"Beauty I can handle—"

"Jason, if she's a problem, reassign her to another department. I only put her with you because I will most likely be on paternity leave and, sitting in an empty office, she is not likely to learn much." He reaches for his phone, which started to buzz. He nods to indicate he is going to take the call.

"She won't be a problem." He acknowledges my comment with a silent grin. The lift doors open to the soft ping indicating its arrival. "We will resume this meeting first thing tomorrow." I drag my hand through my hair and punch the ground floor button aggressively.

"Make it mid-morning, Jason. Don't rush in if Sam needs you, okay?" The doors close before I can respond but I'm grateful. He doesn't need to see that it might not be a case of what Sam needs.

It's late, but on Friday night in central London, it may as well be rush hour. It is taking forever to get across town. I've never had a full-time submissive, never committed to more than play sessions, and the crushing pain in my chest makes me realise exactly why. I have let her down, and if she breaks tonight, I will never forgive myself. If that bastard lays a single finger on what I consider mine, the murky waters of the Thames will have one more body to take out with the morning tide. I blast my horn at a group of drunks spilling onto the road, clearly scaring the shit out of at least one. The others I see flipping me off in my rear view mirror. Why is every fucking idiot out tonight? I swear the next time I'll just mow them down. I slam my brakes as I hit a solid line of stationary taillights. *Fuck!*

The glow of the lights casts a demonic filter over my reflection. All I can see in my red haze of rage is the vision of my girl. I'm too far gone for her image to calm me. I'm too far gone when it comes to Sam, period. As much as she could belong to anyone, I consider her *mine* because she willingly surrenders to me. It's the most beautiful thing when she submits to me, open, vulnerable, and that trust just fucking blows me away. But, even at that moment, when her life is truly in my hands, she is never completely vulnerable. That has only ever happened when she is reliving her time with *him.* She is a remarkable woman, sexy and strong, but the second her memories of the horror she endured at his hands invades her thoughts she is shattered, rendered broken and so fragile I barely recognise her.

Having witnessed this firsthand makes my stomach churn, and I struggle to see how any interaction will not end in disaster. I let out a frustrated howl, slamming the wheel at the impotence of my situation. I'd abandon my car if I thought I could get there on foot any quicker. *Wait.* I check the map, a mile, maybe two on foot. I swerve my car as close to the curb as I can get, grab my phone from the dash and leap from the car. The driver behind me leans out of his window and screams something. I shrug. It's an arsehole move to dump and run, but the other cars behind can still get around.

I turn and hit the pavement, strong strides quickly covering the distance I need to get to my beautiful girl.

I round the corner to the square. The club is in the middle of a row of Georgian terrace houses, which are mostly offices; very few are family homes. Some, like the building I own with the club have a private residence at the top, but this is mostly a commercial area of the city. This time of night, parking shouldn't be a problem, but I notice every bay is filled, so either way, I would be blocking a road with my car. Least of my worries. I am just about to swing around the railing and descend into the basement entrance when I pull myself to an abrupt stop. Very nearly too late, which would've sent me, Leon and Sam tumbling down the concrete stairs.

I draw in a deep, steadying breath. I grab her shoulders and my fingers eagerly sweep and investigate her coat covered body. Unsatisfied that I am learning anything, I roughly push the garment from her shoulders. I take another sharp breath but not from the exertion of the run. Fuck, she looks smoking hot. Skin-tight, halter neck, bright red, PVC cat suit shines and teases in the light of the streetlamp. I only pause for a moment then continue to cover every inch of her skin, exposed and undercover, I check for anything amiss. She giggles and jumps when I touch her waist at the side and groans once I thread my fingers into her messy bun. I tug and she arches her neck exposing her delicate throat. She hums out a sweet moan, heavy lids with luscious long lashes frame eyes dark with wanton desire, but I haven't finished. I release her and cup her cheeks.

"Sam are you…? Did he…? I banned that fucker, you have to know that." My words are a garbled rush, but I have too many erratic, volatile thoughts to make a coherent sentence.

"You did?" Her voice is just as breathless, but she sounds surprised.

"Of course." I fix her with an incredulous look. How could she think I wouldn't? "Sam you…I…" I hesitate, unsure what I want to say with my emotions all over the fucking place and adrenaline coursing through me like cocaine. I opt for something safe. "Are you okay?" I search her face for any sign of trauma although it's difficult to see past her perfection, her natural glow and fire.

"I'm fine." She offers a wide smile and my whole body sags with relief.

"You didn't see him? Is he still in there?" I trace my finger down the side of her cheek, and my chest clenches when she leans into my touch.

"Oh, man you missed the show!" Leon shouts out. His face looks fit to burst with laughter. "Sam was fucking awesome! Not that I had a doubt, but I still have a boner from that whip display." He crudely grabs his crotch, and Sam winces in my hold. I raise my brow in silent query and wait for an explanation. She scrunches her face and peeks sheepishly through her lashes. She bites her lips nervously, and Leon continues to chuckle. She elbows him in the ribs but he just holds his side at the impact and carries on grinning. "Hey, don't shoot the messenger." He winks but takes a cautionary step back when Sam scowls.

"Please don't tell me you used your bullwhip in the main room?" I tip her chin to meet my glare. That would garner a lifetime ban for showboating at best, and a serious health and safety issue at worst. Those things are lethal.

"The area was clear, and he had it coming. I didn't have a choice. It was him or me, and it was never going to be me, not again." Her tone is resolute and she tries to step out of my hold. Her brows knit together with anger.

"Did you hurt him?"

She scowls at me this time, and I know she is upset by my response. Her dark eyes flash with sadness.

"Just his ego," she mutters. "He backed down in front of an audience, something I don't think he meant to do…and I may have sliced his hand."

I draw in a deep breath and run my hand through my hair. "Fuck!" I squeeze the back of my neck where an instant knot of tension has formed like iron. She takes advantage of my one handed hold to step further away.

"Well fuck you very much, Jason," she snaps, eyes glassy, tempering the edge of her hostility with obvious hurt. "Sorry I broke one of your precious rules, but that arsehole had it coming and more." I pull her roughly back into my hold.

"I don't give a fuck about that, Sam!" I growl but softly place both of my warm hands on her cheeks, her impossibly soft skin cool from the evening air. "Honestly, I don't." My gaze captures hers, and I sense she sees the truth and my concern when she softens in my arms. "You did what you had to do." My thumb brushes the fat tear that plops onto her cheek. "But you have just publicly humiliated a very dangerous man, and *that* I do give a fuck about. Your safety Sam, I give lots of fucks about." I kiss the tip of her nose.

"He's not dangerous, he's just a—"Sam begins to retort but Leon interrupts with perfect timing.

"A cunt!"

Sam giggles.

"Agreed, but he has progressed or rather digressed since you knew him." Sam and Leon exchange curious looks before Sam shrugs lightly.

"I know about his arrests, Jason." Her tiny palm rests on my chest, my heart still pounding. Her voice is clipped with sarcasm. "And I'm sure it wasn't sexual assault, either, but Leon said the actual convictions can't have been that serious or he wouldn't be allowed to travel." She looks toward Leon who nods, but he is looking intently at me, my gaze is unwavering from Sam.

"He has some very powerful friends, because those two cases were dropped for lack of evidence even though there was plenty at the time. But it's not just sexual assault, Sam." I swallow the sick churning in my stomach. My skin chills, thinking that she ever had anything to do with someone like Richard. "Have you heard of Caligula?" She laughs and points to herself.

"Lyrics in a Smiths song." She gives a sassy little wiggle, which under any other circumstance I would find adorable.

"Not *that* Caligula." My voice is low but deadly serious. Leon steps closer his expression devoid of any humour.

"The underground party organisation?" Sam looks between me and Leon with utter confusion. Leon's face visibly pales and I nod, sharing his disquiet.

My arms instinctively tighten around Sam's waist. "Shit! I thought it was urban myth." Leon's eyes widen with worry but Sam lets out a light laugh.

"Um boys, not to dampen this caveman thing you have going on here, but it's not like I haven't been to an illegal party."

"But you came back alive," I remark coldly. Her breath catches, and I hate that I sound dramatic but this is not a game. "It's not myth, these parties actually happen. No one knows how they are arranged, and my brother says they most likely happen in international waters. They keep mobile, which makes it difficult to locate and that's a big ass ocean, which helps with the bodies."

"What? What bodies? Jason, what are you talking about, and what has it got to do with my douchebag ex?" Sam snaps and pulls her coat back onto her shoulders, wrapping it tightly around her body.

"When I investigated him, Richard's name came up in connection with Caligula. He is based in New York, but he has a place in Miami. I contacted my brother because he shares his apartment in Florida with a couple of CIA agents, and I passed on what I knew. They didn't come back with much more, but Caligula is real and Richard is involved. The CIA believes he *is* the organisation." I reach for her hand, and am happy when she lets me take it in both of mine.

"Organisation for what?" Her voice is soft, and the streetlight casts a pallid glow.

"Very illegal, no limits party. For high-end clients only. They get the ultimate hedonist experience. For the sex slaves, they get no choice, no safe words and no chance of getting out alive."

"Jason?" Sam's voice breaks, and it crushes me.

"I'm sorry, baby. I won't let anything happen to you, I promise, but just…if you see him anywhere, just leave. Call me and leave. I don't want you anywhere near him, okay?" She nods but she looks rightly shaken.

"Hey, babe." Leon drapes a protective arm over her shoulder even as I have her in my arms. "There is no way he will come back for more. Unless he's a masochist, which he isn't, only the best people are." He winks at her, and she smiles though it doesn't quite reach her eyes. "Come on let's go home. I'm sure we can think of something to do to lift the gloom." Sam may roll her eyes at his suggestive flirtation, but her eyes still spark and darken all the same.

Sam was actually fine after her initial shock. The likelihood of her ever running into Richard socially is pretty slim. In ten years she never has, and I have set some new security measures in place that will ensure that piece of shit doesn't step foot inside my building. She also agreed that I could install the same at her home, which makes leaving her this morning or any morning a little more bearable. She asked more questions about my brother than Richard in the end, and that's why I am confident she isn't really concerned. Her eyes twinkled with mischief, and she came like a fucking train when I told her all the things I'd let him do to her before I would join in. I have never had a problem sharing, but then I have never had someone like Sam, so *if*, and I mean *if* I was to share it would have to be with someone I trust with my life. Ah shit, I really should not be thinking about any sort of fucking with Sam when I have a meeting with Daniel and my new intern in thirty minutes.

My phones buzzes in my suit pocket as I reach my office door. I see Sam's red lips on my screen and smile. I didn't notice when she set that picture as her profile, but my cock twitches at my memory of that colour wrapped around my shaft. Her breathy voice invades my senses.

"Jason, tell me what you will let your brother do to me; I really need to come," she sighs and my balls tighten. I hold the phone to my chest.

"Sandy, will you hold my calls and move my meeting into the boardroom. I will be along shortly, but I have to deal with this matter." My personal assistant smiles as she jots down my request.

"Of course, Mr Sinclair. I'll let Mr Stone know. Peitra is already with him. Is there anything I can help with?" She smiles and looks with unnecessary concern at my clutched hand. I glance down at the phone but shake my head.

"No, thank you, Sandy. I am going to have to deal with this." I push the door closed and turn the lock. This is a first for me. I never mix business with pleasure, and although I am not exactly fucking Sam across my desk, I am about to do the next best thing under the circumstances.

"You have my attention, Sam." My voice is hoarse and deep. I hear her exhale a deep breath, a little moan escaping with the air. I can almost see her writhing with each draw of oxygen. Almost isn't good enough. "Switch to video, beautiful. I want to see you when I make you come." She gasps, and a moment later, her face appears. She is holding the phone above her, and her hair is fanned out in a mass of dark waves on the crisp cream pillow. Her lips curve into a sensual smile, and her tongue darts along her soft full lips. That action alone has me adjusting the very painful budge in my pants. I loosed my belt and flip the button, easing the zipper down. The pain is a distraction, and it's her I want to focus on. I cup and squeeze to alleviate some of the pressure.

"Oh fuck, Jason, are you touching yourself?" She bites her bottom lip, and her eyes widen with obvious desire.

"You called me, Sam. I think this is about what you need, don't you?" My voice deepens, and her eyes darken with the commanding tone.

"Yes, Sir," she sighs, and hiding my movement from her with the angle of the phone, I start to stroke my length. It seems I now have the restraint of a horny teenager rather than a seasoned Dom.

"Kick the covers back. I want to watch you touch yourself." I swallow thickly. Without hesitation, she does exactly as I say. She is wearing a pale pink cami-top with spaghetti straps and boxer shorts that are scrunched up high between her thighs and the crease at her apex. "Lose the shorts, and pull your top down so I can see your tits." She keeps the phone high as she wriggles and kicks her shorts free. With her free hand, she pulls her top down and scoops her perfect breasts out one at a time and puts them on display. Her hard dusty pink nipples are pert little pebbles that make my mouth water and my balls ache.

"Spread for me beautiful. I want to see how wet you are." I hardly recognise my gravely tone.

"Jason…" I cut her breathy plea short with a gruff cough. Her eyes widen, and she flashes a wicked smile that stretches her lips wide. Ah fuck, my balls feels like they are going to explode. I grip a little tighter and can't help the groan that hits the back of my throat. Her eyes shine with mischief and understanding. "Sorry…*Sir*." She drawls my moniker sensually from her mouth.

"You want me to tell you what I would let Will do to you? What I want to do you? And …" I pause to watch her body undulate with each slowly spoken word. Her hips tilt, and she grinds her arse into the mattress and pushes two fingers into her glistening core. "What we will *both* do to you." She pulls her fingers out and sinks them back in slowly, swirling and twisting. She curls them at the knuckle and drags the wet tips back out and up, around her clit. I can see her thighs tense, and I watch enraptured as she sweeps small circles before sinking once more inside. I can feel my own cock wet with pre-cum, though not for long if my balls have any say in the matter.

"I want you to suck Will's cock while I have my tongue buried inside you. I want to taste how wet that makes you." I hum my own arousal, the sound gently rumbling from my chest. "I think that will make you drip down my chin don't you, Sam? I think that would make you drip down to your tight little hole." Her mouth drops as she sucks in a deep breath, her hand briefly leaving her core to squeeze and pump one of her breasts. She pinches her nipple and sighs, quickly replacing her fingers, which slide smoothly back inside. Her hips give a little jerk. She is holding her phone remarkably still considering the rapid beat of the pulse I can see jumping in her neck. Her body, unable to hold still for a moment more, begins to shake and her mouth parts to allow for little pants.

"Sir…please." Her fingers pump wildly, the heel of her hand massaging her clit and her eyes are pinched shut.

"You need to be wet for us Sam," I groan.

"Yes," She's breathless.

"Why Sam? Why do you need to be so wet?"

"Ah…Sir…please…" She shakes her head with frustration.

"Answer the question Sam," I growl, low and demanding.

"So you can fuck me," she gasps.

"Where?" I urge. She is so desperate, I can almost taste it.

"Everywhere." She chokes out the almost silent words. Her face is flushed this gorgeous pink, and her chest rises and falls with rapid, shallow breaths. She looks stunning, so fucking hot.

"You want us both to fuck you, Sam?"

"Yes." She nods, sucking in her bottom lip.

"You want my brother in your arse while I fuck you, Sam?" My cock swells in my fist when she screams my name.

"Oh, God…ah…Jason…ah!"

The screen blurs then goes black. All I can hear is muffled sounds indistinguishable from my own ragged breaths. I didn't come, but fuck, I want to. That was the fucking sexiest thing. I may have to put some serious thought into that fantasy of hers. A few moments pass, and I am able to somewhat uncomfortably zip and button my trousers closed.

"Jason?" Her breathless voice and gorgeous face fills my screen. She bites her lip to suppress her grin, her pink cheeks glow and she looks a little shy.

"I'm here, beautiful." Just me and my massive hard-on. "Feel better?"

"I do…much, thank you." She sucks on the tip of her finger and it takes a second to register that *that* finger has just been knuckle deep inside her. I twist as fresh blood surges back to my painful erection. I try to ignore the very erotic visual or I will never get to my meeting.

"You are most welcome. I consider it my most important job, to make you happy."

"You do make me happy," she whispers, her smile is bright but her eyes flash with something, not sure what though since it was too brief. Not sadness, but something.

"Ditto." I search her expression, but whatever it was is gone and is replaced by genuine shock.

"Do I?"

"Really, you doubt it?" I shake my head, but her silence unnerves me. "Sam, you make me incredibly happy." My tone is soft and serious.

"You didn't come." I must look both surprised and confused, but either way, I'm stuck for how to respond. She clarifies. "You have a look...after... and you... you don't have that look." She has pulled the covers to tuck around her, and I hate that I am not there to ease her insecurities.

"Not because I'm not happy. That's crazy." I tease lightly. "I didn't finish because I'm at work and I don't mix business with pleasure. Until just now, I haven't so much as Googled the word porn while I'm at work." I joke.

"So I'm a bad influence?" Her own laugh brightens her spirits.

"That you are, but you're *my* bad influence." I add softly, "If I'm honest I'd much rather wait. When I come, I want to be inside you. It's all I can think about. You are all I can think about." Surely she knows this? Her underlying insecurities shock me more than any fantasy she could conjure up. She is the bravest, most honest and sexiest woman I know, how could she ever doubt that? Her lips curl into a shy smile at my words, and I get a warm hit to my chest at her evident joy. "You know there is nothing remotely satisfying about jerking off in an empty office," I point out in all seriousness. She giggles.

"In that case I'll make sure I'm hungry." She exaggerates a long, slow, wet lick of her soft pull lips.

"Now that will make me *very* happy." I half sigh, half groan at the ever-present ache deep in my groin.

The meeting with Daniel was brief. Peitra graduated last year from LSE with a first class honours degree in Economics. She didn't take to banking, which was her first career choice and was looking to do something in business. I love how that covers a multitude of sins and half-arsed choices. I personally don't believe she would've made it past the interview process with a vague answer like that. But, as Daniel said, she is tenacious and has circumvented the interview process by going straight to the top. However, the top is now about to take paternity leave and I am left with more than just an intern. I'm left with a siren.

Peitra follows me back to my office and sits quietly in the chair opposite my desk while I sit back into my own chair and take a call. She has the same strong gene that runs in Sofia and Marco's family, dark brown hair, chocolate coloured eyes, and a strong, distinctive curve to the brow line. She is attractive, but unlike her cousin, who is all friendly smiles and comfortable company, Peitra is a femme fatale. I know women, and even if she hadn't been crossing her legs slowly for the last fifteen minutes or leaning down to fix nothing on her killer heels, she screams trouble. It is more than appearance though, and before Sam, I probably would not have even seen a distinction, but with Sam, the mask, the armour are all appearance. I'm not saying she isn't seductive, because I doubt there's a man on the planet who would deny her but there is nothing underhanded or deceitful. However, looking at Peitra I am not convinced I could say the same. I am more likely to believe she doesn't have a sincere bone in her body.

"Jason…" She smiles and flips her long hair over her shoulder. She dips her chin and looks up through her false lashes. "I know you weren't expecting to have me shadow you, but I promise I won't disappoint you. I am very accommodating." And there it is, capital T for trouble. Her expression fixes in a too-sweet grin. I respond with an impassive look. She isn't the first woman to try this. It's comical to think she is that naïve. I don't believe that for a moment. She visibly stiffens as the silence rests awkwardly. "Daniel has been very sweet, just last week at Sofia's he was—"

"Let me stop you there Peitra—" I interrupt.

"Call me Pip, everyone calls me Pip." She gives a girlish laugh, but falters when I repeat with considerably more hostility.

"As I said, *Peitra*, let me stop you there before I have to endure your entire repertoire to establish some sort of connection. I don't agree with how you gained this position, but you are here. Your academic qualifications aren't enough to keep you here, neither is your tentative link to Daniel. As for me personally, I have a girlfriend, Sam—"

"Sofia's friend, Sam?" Her shock is apparent, and her brows knit with confusion. I know that look. She is really starting to piss me off. She flinches at my sudden scowl. "Sorry." She swallows thickly. I repeat to prevent any misunderstanding.

"Yes, Sofia's friend, Sam, is my girlfriend. And if you flick your hair one more time in my direction, you will have a sexual harassment complaint in your file quicker than you can bat your lashes."

"I'm sorry, Jason—" she stutters.

"Mr Sinclair, and Daniel is Mr Stone. This isn't family. This is business, and I don't mix business with anything but business." I draw in a breath because my tone is harsh, and she has visibly shrunk in her seat. "Look, Peitra, you should know I own the establishment where Sam works." From her initial shock I can only assume she knows of Sam. I doubt she knows much, just enough to pass judgment. "I am more than proficient at reading women. Please don't pretend to look affronted. That insults me and you for that matter." Her face flushes pink.

"Sorry, Mr Sinclair, I really didn't mean anything by it."

"Yes, you did. But you should also know you are doing yourself a great disservice if you think that is all you have to offer." She holds my gaze but shifts uncomfortably before she lightly shakes her head.

"I know. I mean this isn't me." She shakes her head. "I did ask Dan-Mr Stone, but the other stuff…that was just for you." She dips her head, and her face is so red I am tempted to believe she is being genuine. But equally, that could be my male ego wanting it to be true. "I am sorry. I just don't want you to think I am like this, or that I would use…Um, you're really attractive yourself." She slaps her hand to her mouth, and I have to bite back a laugh at her obvious mortification. "Can we just forget this, Mr Sinclair? Rewind and pretend none of this, and I mean *none* of it, happened. I will work my arse off and prove that I am good enough to be here on my own merit. If that's okay?" Her voice is sincere and eyes are pleading.

"I think that is an excellent idea." I watch her body relax. She draws in a deep breath and straightens in her seat. Sitting tall with a fresh, bright smile.

"Thank you."

I am not entirely satisfied about her motives, but I have, at least, made my position clear. "Right, okay, you are to shadow me, but you're not my PA so don't behave like one. If you have a question ask, and Peitra…treat yourself the way you would like to be treated." She nods and flashes a tentative smile, which is the first natural expression to flit across her face. It looked good.

ELEVEN

Sam

Leon slumps on the sofa next to me and picks up the tiny baby blue bunny between his fingers like it was carrying some hideous disease. His hand is stretched as far from his body as possible, and his brow is comically piqued with curiosity.

"Something you want to tell me, babe?" He wrinkles his nose with distaste, and I snatch the bunny from his fingers, but my face must display something other than irritation. I feel the unbidden sadness silently prickle behind my eyes. His arm is instantly around me, and my face is warmed against the strong curve of muscle on his chest. The steady thump, thump of his heart is an instant comfort. It's silly. It's not like I can't think about babies without breaking, but his disdain, even as a joke, was too close to home to be remotely funny. "I'm sorry, Sam. I didn't mean anything. I would be happy for you, you know that. I'd be sad for selfish reasons, but you know I…" He kisses my hair but doesn't finish his unnecessary apology.

"I know, Leon. Honestly, I think I'm going a little crazy. You didn't even say anything, you just had that same look as…" I shake my head. I'm being ridiculous. When I meet his stare, his eyes are filled with kind understanding. "I'm sorry. I've been on edge since my run-in with Richard last week. I can't believe I acted out like that."

He snickers. "Oh, babe, I can *so* believe you did, but you weren't to know he was some sleazy psycho. And you can relax, Jason called to say Richard left for the States this morning, and I'm working on making sure he can't come back." He ruffles my hair, and I feel all warm and tingly that I have two wonderful men in my life.

"Jason called you, why didn't he call me?" I reach for my phone, which is perched on the arm of the sofa. My screen is blank. I grimace when I meet Leon's smug expression. My phone is still playing up, and I haven't gotten around to replacing it. "That might be why." I press the start button to try and wake the sleeping device, exhausted by its rapid burst of flashing screens it quickly flatlines. "Can I use your phone?" I wiggle my fingers and he rolls his eyes. I scroll through his call log expecting to have to recognise Jason's number but I am shocked to see his name as a full on contact with picture and everything. "You added him as a proper contact?" I drop my jaw to exaggerate my surprise. He reaches for his phone, but I pull it back.

"He is important to you," he states flatly.

"Aw, Leon, that's so sweet. You're letting him into our little family," I coo, but he smirks and raises a brow.

"You didn't look at the picture, did you?" He grins.

"It's a bell. It's not a wedding bell, is it?" I splutter.

"Not exactly, to be very specific it's the end of a bell." He looks fit to burst with his own mirth.

"Mature, very mature." He fails to hold it in and snickers out a light laugh, but rolls off the sofa and out of my slapping range. "Make me a hot chocolate by way of apology for calling my boyfriend a bell-end." I call after him as he strides toward his room. He makes a swift U-turn and detours to the kitchen instead.

"Leon, is Sam all right?" Jason snaps.

"It's me." I can't hide the smile that erupts across my face. "You were worried?"

"I'm always worried when it comes to you, beautiful." His voice is softer, almost a whisper. "But maybe we can both relax a little now. Did Leon tell you?"

"Yes. How did you know?"

"I have my ways, and I know you. Your very responsive body has been all tied up in knots, and I should be the only reason that ever happens," he drawls seductively, then his tone abruptly changes. "Richard left through a major airport. I had asked our security team to keep an eye on him. Is there anything else you wanted to know?" I pull the phone away from my ear to check that I am still talking to Jason.

"Excuse me?" I stutter. I think for a moment then realise someone must have walked in on him for his manner to change like that. I know he likes to keep his private life private, and maybe he doesn't want whoever came in to know he is talking to me.

"If there is nothing specific, my intern is here Sam." He clips. "I will see you later, much later, though, so no need to wait up." His cold dismissal is a stark contrast to his sensual greeting.

"Oh, no danger of that, dickhead!" I snap the phone shut and throw it onto the pile of cushions on the floor.

"Hey, hey don't go breaking the only phone we have between us that's still working." Leon approaches with two mugs and a bottle of something tucked under his arm.

"Sorry," I mutter and take the piping hot drink from him. Before I take a sip he drops a large slug of rum by the smell of it into my cup.

"Trouble in paradise?" he teases.

"Did Jason strike you as bipolar?" I sniff only half serious.

"Um, no." He chuckles.

"No, me either, so he's just being an arse then?" I grumble.

"Oh, he definitely strikes me as being an arsehole."

"I said arse not arsehole," I correct.

"To-may-to….to-mah-to." He shrugs dismissing my concern and changes the subject. "So what's with the baby clothes?"

"Sofia's best friend, Bethany. Her baby is due any day now. It's why I am not going to cut Jason's bollocks off when he gets here," I mutter begrudgingly.

"Jason's the father?" Leon chokes back his drink, just avoiding spluttering over us both with his shocking question.

"He wouldn't be alive if he was." I quip. "No, Jason's boss, Daniel Stone, is the father. He's on paternity leave so Jason is working *all* the hours. I told you about them." I roll my eyes at his blank expression.

"Probably…doesn't mean I actually listened." He nudges me and gives me a cheeky smile.

"Don't be mad, beautiful." Jason's warm breath kisses my neck; his strong arms wrap around my waist. Even sleeping, my tension is evidence that I am still angry enough to resist his embrace. Not too much and not for long, because ultimately, I relax into his hold, and he softens to allow me to twist around. I hitch my leg over his hip, and my hand snakes down between our bodies. He groans with satisfaction but chokes back a yelp and freezes, and I grab hold of his balls, my long finger nails exerting enough force to make their presence abundantly apparent.

"Sam," he growls out a warning, even rolling his hips into my grasp. His cock swells from semi to rock hard. "I am sorry if I upset you, but I didn't think it was professional to carry on talking to you like that. I was at work."

"I am aware of where you were, Jason, but that doesn't mean you have to be a full-blown arsehole to me. Wait…why would it be unprofessional to talk to your girlfriend in front of your intern?" His eyes widen because my grip just tightened.

"Do you want to let go of my nuts so I can answer that question?" His voice is level, but there is underlying stress in his delivery.

"Actually, no. I want to hold them right here." I tug a little, closing my fingers around his most precious sac. A deep groan escapes his chest, and he rocks his hips and his hard-on against my tummy. I can feel my own heat melt, but I won't be distracted. "Jason?"

"She's been invaluable this week. With Daniel MIA I have welcomed the help, and she's worked every extra hour I have." His explanation sounds remarkably like an excuse.

"As she should…she's an intern, but why would it matter how you spoke to me?" His evasive answer has my hackles rising, and the flash of worry in his eyes is justified. I am holding his life in my twitchy hand.

"I have just been impressed with her hard work. Surprised actually. She's been very focused and hard working." His iteration is fuelling my fire. My grip tightens, and he puffs out a sharp breath with the truth. "She has a crush on me, that's all, and as much as I have made my position clear, I'm still not that much of an arsehole to rub you in her face. I didn't want to hurt her feelings."

"But being an arsehole to me is perfectly acceptable?" I let go of my hold because this is no longer a cheeky bit of fun. I leap from the bed. He sits abruptly and reaches out, trying to prevent me escaping. I stand away from the bed and roughly pull on my yoga pants and t-shirt, which were lying in a wrinkled heap on the floor. I glance at him sitting bolt upright and naked, his face hidden in the shadow of the room. Only his cut chest is illuminated by the light from the door when I open it to storm out. He is hot on my heels as I reach Leon's door.

"Where the fuck do you think you're going?" He grabs my hand as I reach for the handle. His fingers wrap mine, and he crushes me against the smooth metal. I don't cry out but turn my head to scowl at him. His face is impassive but his eyes darken with rage.

"I'm going to bed. It's all right, Jason; I've made my position with Leon *perfectly clear*." I repeat his ridiculous sentiment back at him. He breathes heavily through his nose, and I can see his temper start to fray. Good, fucking arsehole.

"You're being childish, Sam." His voice is low and menacing, but I still try and open Leon's door. It swings wide but not from any effort on my part. Leon stands completely naked, with floppy bed hair falling in his sleepy eyes. I barely notice because he rarely wears much more, but I can feel Jason stiffen behind me. I straighten in surprise, but my shock isn't at his appearance, it's the fact he's awake. He usually sleeps like the dead.

"Children, children, can you please keep it down." He absently grabs his cock, although not to cover himself, more to massage the semi hard-on he is sporting. "Unless you are planning on joining me, why don't you both go and settle this…whatever this is…like adults…naked with tongues." He grins at me, and with his free hand, tips my open mouth shut just before he slams his door. Jason chuckles behind me, and I swing round but collapse against the rock hard impact of his shoulder in my tummy. He scoops me high, and slaps my bottom hard before striding back to my bed.

Dropping me from a great height into the centre of the bed, I squeal and shuffle back away from his encroaching frame. I have to bite back my smile, because as sexy as he looks—and he looks fucking delicious—I am still mad.

"Stop!" I slap my hand on his naked chest as he hovers over me, all hard and hot.

"No, you're jealous, and I love that, but you have nothing to be jealous of, and I'm going to prove it." He takes the wrist of the hand holding his chest and the other too, and holds them high above my head.

"Awesome sex doesn't prove shit." I fight him and the desperate moan at the back of my throat as he pushes his strong legs between mine and works me wider. I am so damn wet, and I bet he knows it. He draws in a deep breath and purses his lips as his eyes darken with undiluted desire.

"You're right. Actions speak louder than words, though. Sam, I promise I will never give you another reason to be jealous." I sniff out a sharp, derisive snort. "You doubt me?" His brows pitch together, and he looks utterly sincere.

"Men lie." I try to shrug, but my arms are taut, making the action difficult.

"Everyone lies, but I'm telling the truth, and with my actions, I will prove that over time." His lips cover mine with a sweetly possessive kiss that steals my breath. "You trust me, and I won't betray that. I know what it means, beautiful." I sink and sigh when he calls me that. He looks at me like I'm the only girl in the world and so precious because of it.

"Trust me?" His deep stare pierces right through me. I am exposed and vulnerable, and I couldn't be any happier.

"I do."

"Good…now for those actions." He grunts and thrusts so deep I gasp out a silent cry. I am not silent for long.

"That's so fricking hot." Lili giggles.

"I love it when they do that." Bethany grins and winks at me nudging Sofia at her side. I am having a great night. Sofia arranged an anti-Valentine girls' night out for Lili, a waitress from her family's restaurant and a really close friend. She's a single mum, and since we are all a little 'loved-up', we collectively decided to have a night off.

"When they do what? Slap your arse or carry you away caveman style?" Sofia snickers when Bethany and I answer together.

"Both." We all collapse into giggles.

"I don't get it." Sofia frowns in all seriousness.

"What don't you get, sweetie?" I try not to laugh as her face turns a glorious shade of red.

"I'm not a prude or anything, but spanking hurts. Paul did it once, and I nearly punched his lights out. I think he only got one slap in before I stormed out. It was humiliating." Her brows are bunched tight.

"It can be, and personally, I'm not into that, but spanking doesn't have to be humiliating. It can be very arousing." I notice Bethany shift and I give her a pointed stare. "Want to help me out here?"

"Oh, no, I plead the fifth." She holds her hands up in surrender. "I am heavily pregnant, and horny as hell. If I start talking about Daniel and sex, I will not last the evening."

I chuckle and turn back to Sofia. "All I'm saying is it's very much 'for each to their own'. Like any relationship, everything is very personal. The point is, you don't know until you try, and as long as you trust your partner and can happily communicate your wishes, then it can be lots and lots of fun."

"And being tied up…that's fun for you?" Sofia asks. I smile when Bethany snaps her lips shut tight and shakes her head, leaving me to fill in the blanks. "Yes, sweetie, that is lots of fun."

"But you can't, you know, move? I mean you can't grind or grab where you need them to be with your thighs. You can't touch them. It's so frustrating." She puffs out a breath to try and expel some of the heat she is holding in her cheeks. She snaps up the shot glass of champagne that comes with the cocktails and downs it in one swallow. I am silent, with a subtle grin while I watch her think about what she just said.

"Is that the point?" Her voice is excited with her self-revelation.

I offer an encouraging smile, and her face lights up, but just as quickly, she frowns again. "But you would have no control over…you know…coming." She whispers the last word, and we all bust out laughing. "Oh…that would *also* be the point." She nods slowly at her enlightenment. "Well, there is no fucking way I am giving Paul that kind of power," she states and fixes us with a stern glare and serious tone. "And I'll thank you to keep all this to yourselves. I don't want him getting ideas above occasionally sticking his dick in my—"

"More drinks I think?" Bethany blurts out. Sofia slaps her hand over her mouth, covering her loose, over-sharing lips and cursing her alcohol addled brain. I get the next round, and we settle back to more mundane conversations and catching up.

I have known Sofia for a few years. We instantly hit it off. She is fun, but more than that, she is a good friend. She works at an exclusive private club, and when I first went there with a client, she cornered me in the ladies. She knew him as a member and had heard rumours. Her face filled with concern, she asked if I was okay, if I needed any help, did I need money, *anything*. I think she was prepared to call the police and have my 'date' arrested. I probably should've told her the truth then, but I didn't, and now it just doesn't matter. She didn't judge me then, and these girls don't judge me now.

It feels really good to relax. I didn't realise how on edge I was until Jason told me that Richard had left the country, and I physically felt the tension seep from my body. A respite that was short-lived. Since our fight, I can't hide the fact that I find myself in brand new and totally unfamiliar territory: that of jealous girlfriend. It is like a clawing sickness that clouds my rational brain. I can't help it; all I can do is acknowledge and try to deal with any fallout.

"So what happened?" Lili asks. "Actually, you know, I don't think I can handle any more details. This night was supposed to cheer me up. Tales of your hot-as-hell guys is not helping," she teases and fans herself.

"No details then. We talked…after we'd settled things like adults, that is." I wiggle my brows. "He apologised and said it wouldn't happen again. I explained that, despite all evidence to the contrary, I am, in fact, a very jealous person, and if he were serious, he needs to be mindful. I honestly didn't think I was but—"

Sofia scoffs her interruption. "I'd like to say you have nothing to worry about, but as far as Peitra is concerned, she is very ambitious, and she's had her sight set on Jason for a while." She takes a slow sip of her Porn Star cocktail, and I meet her serious gaze. My stomach knots, and I feel a little sick. The super sweet drinks swirling on my empty stomach aren't helping.

"I have to trust him, Sofs. If I don't, we have nothing." My voice catches, and she leans across to squeeze my hand as I anxiously tear my napkin to shreds.

"Sam," Bethany's voice is full of concern. "I promise you can trust Jason.

He's a good guy, and he is smitten with you. Not that anyone would blame him. Daniel told me just last week, he had never seen Jason act like he does when he is with you, and he has known him a long time." Her smile is wide and warm.

"Oh, God, I don't mean anything like that. Jason loves you." Sofia gushes. I roll my eyes at her sweet but overly simplistic and deeply romantic filter on all things. I let her nonsense slide. She continues, but her tone is more serious. "Peitra on the other hand, well every family has a 'Peitra', I suppose." She air-quotes the name, highlighting my concern here and gives an apologetic shrug. A sombre blanket cloaks our booth. We all reach for our glasses, and I decide to raise a toast.

"Here's to fucked up family and fabulous friends!" The mood lightens when we all clink glasses. Sofia and Lili disappear to fetch fresh drinks and Bethany slides round to my side.

"I'm glad you came, Bets, but I am a little surprised Daniel let you out on Valentine's Day." I nod to her fit-to-burst round tummy.

"Oh, don't worry, he'll be here shortly. I pulled the 'I'm going crazy and I'll take you with me' pregnant wife card. I am hoping he'll chill a little when the baby is born." She snickers at my incredulous expression. "Yeah, maybe not." She notices my hand fiddling with the platinum cuff Jason gave me this morning. "Jason?" she queries and I follow her gaze to my wrist.

"Oh, yes," I self-consciously place my hands flat on the table, and Bethany reaches for my hand. "Valentine gift. I thought because we were out tonight we weren't *doing* Valentine's Day but apparently…" My voice drifts.

"He must like you very much, Sam." She waggles her own wrist, her cuff glinting in the spotlight above our table. "I got mine last Valentine. They have to be specially made." Her eyes sparkle with the reflection.

"I really like him, too." My chest aches and I get a surge of nervous knots.

"Hey don't sound so sad. Surely that's a good thing?" She covers my hand with hers and grasps it tight. My lips try to smile.

"I feel exposed. I don't do vulnerable, Bets…not anymore." I lean forward so I don't have to shout. The background noise has increased with the number of bodies now filling the room.

"You're only vulnerable if the person you're with can't be trusted. Do you trust Jason?" Bethany questions my reservations.

"I do." I reply without hesitation.

"That's a good start." She laughs lightly, squeezing my hand tightly before releasing it.

"Marriage certainly suits you." Her smile is impossibly wide and infectious. She happily rubs the swell of her tummy, and I get a warm burst of something intense inside. I had always shied away from the notion that a happily ever after was anything but a myth. But when the evidence is sitting beside me I can't help but bask in the glow and hope some of that fairy tale might filter my way.

Daniel appears at our booth just as Sofia and Lili return with an ice bucket of champagne for us and a soft drink for Bets. Sofia hands Bets' drink over.

"There you go, sweetie, double vodka and cranberry…you're drinking for two remember." Sofia tries in vain to hide her mischievous grin, and Bets drops her head in her hands as Daniel swipes the drink from Sofia's grasp.

"Hello, Daniel, I didn't see you there." She smiles sweetly. He narrows his eyes. His lips are thin and pinched as he carefully places the now tasted drink in front of his wife.

"Good evening, Sofia," He almost growls her name before addressing the rest of us more smoothly. "Good evening ladies, are you having a good time?" He perches beside his wife, his long arm draped protectively across her shoulders. She leans against his shoulder as we all chat comfortably. The music has started to get loud and people are starting to emerge from the private booths and join the growing number of dancers on the floor. My feet start to twitch and I have enough alcohol in me to throw some serious shapes. I nod at the girls and point toward the floor. Sofia and Lili grab their bags but Bets yawns and slaps her hand over her mouth as her cheeks flush with embarrassment.

"Come on, baby, let's go home." Daniel lifts her from the seat and sweeps her straight into his arms. Lili rushes over to hug her. "Thank you for coming, Bets. I think we should do this every Valentine." Bethany grins at a scowling Daniel, and I laugh.

"I'm sort of with Daniel on that one Lili." I nudge her. "I'm not sure if Jason wasn't working whether I would be here at all…no offence."

Lili shrugs and mock swoons. "Yeah, I don't think I would be either if I was dating Jason."

My own laugh falters when I catch the deep frown on Daniel's face and the brief look that passes between him and a confused looking Bethany. A shared silent moment, I am positive had nothing to do with Lili's proposition and everything to do with my comment.

I suddenly don't feel like hitting the dance floor, my stomach churns and I turn to race for the ladies. I bolt the door just in time, as every drink I have consumed in the last few hours hits the toilet bowl.

My knees are numb from the hard marble ground, my knuckles ache from clinging to the rim of the toilet like it's my only anchor to the world which is spinning wildly around me. I didn't think I had drunk that much. I know I didn't, but I feel sick in my soul. I hear the door swing several times as women come and go, but after a while, it goes quiet. There is a tentative knock on my cubicle door.

"Sam…are you in there?" Lili knocks again.

"I think I had a bit too much. I don't usually drink and those cocktails were lethal." I offer a laugh, but it falls flat. Lili doesn't seem to notice.

"Oh, sweetie, I'm sorry. I'll get you some water; you stay here with Sofs." I hear the door close once more.

"Hey Sam, are you okay? Did something happen? You were fine one minute." She mutters, "Bets had to leave, but she looked worried are you—" The noise from the club drowns out her concern as the door lets another someone in.

"I thought that was you. Sofia, what are you doing here? Is Paul with you?" I hear Sofia suck in a sharp breath, but my stomach retches so my focus is elsewhere, besides, I don't recognise the voice. I just concentrate on keeping my hair from either falling into the bowl or draping along the equally disgusting floor. I freeze at the next word.

"Peitra." Sofia's voice is pitched with surprise.

I bite back the liquid that is pooling in my mouth and hug my knees to my chest. My whole body is chilled and trembling.

"What are you doing here?"

"Date," she gushes.

"I didn't know you were seeing anyone." Sofia's tone drops, and I find I am holding my breath and more.

"Oh, it's only been a few weeks, and it's very hush-hush. It's against company policy, and he's a bit of a stickler for rules." She sighs. "Doesn't stop him fucking me rigid on his desk after hours, mind." Her high-pitched giggle is enough to induce a fresh bout of vomiting, but I am just dry heaving myself raw. I am empty, fitting really. I grab a fistful of tissue and wipe my lips. I close my eyes and let the pain wash over me, my chest heaves, and I feel like a blade is slicing my heart into slivers, slow and agonising.

"Who Peitra…who are you dating?" Sofia's tone is sharp but the reply is sing song sweet and unaffected by Sofia open hostility.

"Ah ah…hush-hush for the time being. I'll introduce you soon enough." I hear her air kiss and leave. I pull the handle and flush the toilet. Sofia is standing against the sink, her hands are clasped tight and her face is etched with sadness.

"It might not be Jason." She steps toward me, but I halt her with my hand and a silent shake of my head. I gaze at the mirror and hang my head to my chest because I don't recognise that shell staring back at me.

I whisper. "But we both know it is."

"I'm so—"

"Don't Sofs…please don't. I'll be fine. Just give me a minute to get cleaned up, and I'll be right out." I flash a bright smile that doesn't even remotely conceal my devastation. Sofia tries again to comfort me, but I shake my head and pinch my eyes tight. The unstoppable tingles threaten to break. I don't want to break, not here.

"I don't believe it. I'm going to check." She turns and leaves before I can stop her. I glance at my reflection. My face is puffy with blotchy red eyes from the violent heaving. My hair is a straggly mess and looking down, my bare legs are mottled with whatever was on the floor. I dread to think of what it was. I start cleaning myself and make a pretty good effort by the time Sofia has returned with Lili just behind. Sofia doesn't need to say a single word her face is a reflection but a fraction of my own heartbreak. I take the water Lili is holding and drink it down. I flash a quick smile, which is plastered over gritted teeth. My makeshift mask.

"I don't know what to say Sam." She looks nervously between me and Lili. "What are you going to do?"

I twist my bright red lipstick up and carefully apply to my slightly swollen lips. Pressing them together, I turn and straighten myself. My skin-tight black leather vest dress hugs my curves; my cleavage is not to be missed, and I now have my red lipstick armour.

"I'm going to rip his bollocks off."

I approach the private area and face the booth Sofia had indicated, but I can't move forward. Even from this distance I can see Peitra is pressed against him, her hand grabbing him beneath the table. His face registers surprise or shock, his brows furrow, but he doesn't make another move. His eyes meet mine. Now that expression is definitely shock.

"Sam!" Jason calls, pushing Peitra's hand from his lap. He makes to stand but freezes at my deathly glare and sinister smile. I will my feet to move and stop just before the unhappy couple. My pulse is racing, and my mouth is suddenly dry.

"Sam, this is Peitra, my intern." Jason attempts to make introductions, I can see by the slow movement in his throat that he is struggling to swallow. Palpable tension lies thick between us.

"Oh, I know who she is, Jason." I snarl his name. He recoils and takes a moment to recover.

"Right, and Peitra, this is Sam, my girlfriend." His voice is calm but his face is etched with uncertainty. I raise my brow high but snap to look at Peitra when she speaks.

"The whore," Peitra offers her hand with a sardonic smile.

"Peitra, fuck!" Jason shouts out, his mortification matching his fury. "You apologise right now!" She withers at his furious glare, visibly shrinking in her seat. I stretch and lean over, my face only inches from hers. Her eyes are wide with panic.

"It's all right, *sweetheart.*" I glance back at Jason keeping my tone cold and laying a heavy emphasis on my most hated choice of nickname. I turn back to address Peitra pinching her chin between my fingers. We glare at one another.

"But you should know this, little girl…I'm not just *any* whore. I'm the *best.* So when he fucks you, remember that it isn't your nails he will feel dragging down his back, it isn't your taste he craves on his tongue, *Peitra.*" I release her chin and pat her cheek with as much condescension as I can place in a palm. "It isn't your submission that brings him to his knees, and it never will be." I hold her stunned gaze for a moment longer before Peitra pulls away. Jason tries to grab my arm as I brush lightly past him. I fight to hold the anger, the hurt, any emotion that would reveal my utter devastation inside. I want to run, push and fight my way out, away from them, but I don't. I float with an eerie air of calm and disquiet.

"This isn't what it looks like Sam." My glare at his touch fails to have the desired effect when Jason tightens his grip.

"It never is, Jason." I spit his name, my voice catches as I try to break free of his hold. "Let me go, or you'll be wearing your bollocks as earrings for the rest of your life." My words are filled with vitriol but my eyes glaze all the same. I hate that he has done this. I abhor that it hurts so much, and I hate that I am going to break in front of him and her. I take a stuttered breath, squeezing my eyes tight to stop the tears falling.

"Oh, my God, she's going to cry!" Peitra cackles out a bitter laugh that is like a sharp slap to my face. I am strangely grateful, because the sadness instantly disintegrates. Jason releases me, his expression a mix of anger at Peitra and—What is that look? Despair, confusion, guilt?—I'm going to go with guilt. I step back, my head high and not a tear in sight.

"Where are you going?" He steps forward as I step away, maintaining the same distance.

"Oh, you know, places to be, people to screw. Time is money and all that." I retort with a tight, bitter smile.

"Oh, very mature, Sam. You misunderstand what's going on here, and your first reaction is to go fuck a client," he growls. I halt my retreat, and he steps forward, towering over me, but I won't back down.

"At least I'm honest about it." I snarl.

"Fuck, Sam, jealousy goes both ways. You think I'm not jealous when you work, when you fuck your clients? You think that doesn't fucking tear me up?" His anger is tempered with a break in his voice that catches me off guard. He doesn't mean it. He's deflecting because he was caught with someone's hand in his cookie jar.

"I don't fuck my clients." I lift my chin to meet his fierce, dark eyes, scowling with hurt and anger.

"Whatever you do then. You think it's any different to know that they are getting off with you, touching you, touching what's mine?" He reaches to touch my face but I flinch. "Sam?" I can hear his plea in his voice, his eyes look so sad as his hand drops.

"I'm no one's, Jason. I'm just a whore." I close my eyes before I turn and walk away.

TWELVE

Jason

"Fuck!" I yell to myself and turn sharply to the table where Peitra is sitting quietly, eyes wide but her lips are pinched tight in a self-satisfied smile that makes my blood boil. I want to tear something apart, I am so fucking angry with myself. Sam must know how I feel about her. She can't have believed there was really anything going on. God, she looked so hurt, she braved out a good show, but her mask slipped, and I could see her break in front of me, just in her eyes but it was enough. *Fuck!* I pick my jacket off the seat and slip my wallet out of the pocket. I screw up a fifty pound note and throw it on the table in front of Peitra.

"Jason you don't need to pay *me*." Her saccharin voice resembles nails on a chalkboard. I flinch at her tone and the implication. *Fuck her.*

"That's a fifty not loose change." I snap, and her brows shoot up in shock. "For my glass of champagne." I slip my jacket on.

"But, Jason, we've ordered over a thousand pounds worth of Crystal!" she protests.

"*You* ordered Peitra." I flash a tight-lipped smile that doesn't reach past my mouth.

"How am I supposed to pay, Jason?" Panic and embarrassment colour her face, a mix of pale and pink.

"I'm sure you'll think of something." I start to walk past, but she grabs my arm and snarls, all white teeth and pink gums.

"I'm not the *whore*, Jason!" Spittle flies from her lips, her eyes are narrow with pure venom.

"No, you're not; my whore has way more class. *You* are just a fucking bitch!" Her expression is one of utter shock, but I doubt that is the first time she's been called that. She jumps back in her seat as if I have slapped her. *If only.* I shake my head as I push through the crowded club, eager to get out. I need to get some air. I need to clear my head, and then I need to make this fucking mess right.

I waited in my club for two hours before I checked on the room Sam had booked directly after storming out. The room was empty and no one had seen her enter or leave, but that's not especially unusual. My momentary irritation at wasting my time is quickly replaced with relief that she wasn't at the club fucking someone else. Her throw away threat was aimed with precision, hitting me hard, but that appears to be all it was, a threat. I know she hides behind her Domme mask and wears her title of *whore* like a shield, but I don't believe she would use sex between *us* as a weapon. Nevertheless, I hurt her and I don't feel nearly as confident that there isn't someone else capable of comforting her right now, and I hate that, because that is my job. The taxi pulls up outside Sam's silent home and idles noisily at the curb at this late hour.

"Do you want me to wait for you, mate?" The driver calls out as I bound up the steps. I shake my head and wave him off. I start to pound on the door and ring her flat number, pressing the button repeatedly. The windows are all dark, but light flickers above the main door before it creaks open. Leon, is wearing at least a towel around his waist, this time.

"What the fuck, man?" He yawns loudly. I ignore his groggy grumble and push past him. His sleepy state is a little unstable and he stumbles after me as I make my way through Sam's flat. Her bedroom door is wide open but her bed is empty. I switch her light on as if suddenly illuminating the room will reveal her, but there is nothing. I hear the front door slam and turn thinking Sam has escaped past me but I am faced with a dark scowl and her furious flatmate.

"What the fuck are you doing, Jason?" He blocks my way as I head for his room. It wouldn't be the first time she sought solace in his room. My muscles clench, hands curl into tight fists, and I square up to him. He is almost as tall as me; we are nearly eye to eye. He is radiating anger in waves, but they simply butt against my own.

"Back off, Leon, I need to talk to her." He places his hand on my chest to stop me from moving forward. I instantly grab and twist his wrist, slamming him hard against the wall. He turned his head just in time to prevent a broken nose but grunts as I lean my full force and weight against his back. "I'm not in the mood for a pissing contest, Leon. I want to see my girl. She's upset and I won't let a fucking stupid misunderstanding end this," I growl in his ear. His initial resistance stops, and when I am sure he is not going to retaliate, I let go. He turns slowly, tightening his towel and eyeing me warily. I hold his gaze because I have nothing to hide and everything to lose.

"What did you do?" His glare hardens, and his eyes narrow.

"Let me see her." I can feel the tension in my jaw. I don't have time for this. "I need to sort this out, Leon. It's important we talk," I grit out with as much restraint as my frayed temper will allow.

"She's not here. Honestly, I thought she was staying with you for a few days." His brows furrow. His expression might be confused, but he is not lying.

"A few days?"

"Her case is gone from the hall. I assumed she was staying at your place." He steps around me and walks into the kitchen. The light from the refrigerator casts a sickly glow over his tanned body, and I wait patiently for him to consume almost an entire litre of milk.

"Where would she go?" I ask.

His brows knit together in thought. "Tell me what happened, and I might help." His tone is both cautious and a warning. I step angrily around the kitchen island. He slams the fridge door and we are again nose to nose. "Or don't and good luck scouring the globe to find her. I'm just looking out for her, Jason. Something I didn't think I had to do since she got with you. But hey, we all make mistakes." His snide comment knocks the wind from my lungs. I slide back onto the kitchen stool and drop my head in my hands, feeling like a complete shit. He's right; she shouldn't need protecting from me. She shouldn't ever hurt because of me.

"I fucked up." I exhale the pain with a deep, steady breath and recall the events of the evening, cringing with every expression of disgust that flashes on his face.

"You did fuck up." Leon leans on his elbows. His tone isn't remotely teasing, and my heart sinks, heavy in my chest.

"I didn't *do* anything, Leon." I sigh because it's a pathetic denial at best. "I did know how Peitra felt about me, and I knew how Sam felt. I thought I could handle some silly crush." I laugh without humour and heavy with remorse. "It just took me too long to notice what was happening tonight. I should've left the minute the champagne turned up. I should've cancelled when the venue for the meeting changed. Fuck! I've never had to deal with jealousy before."

"Neither has Sam." His tone is reprimanding, and I nod, taking his disapproval on the chin.

"I know."

The ensuing silence stretches between us until and Leon sniffs out a tight, sharp laugh. "What she said to Peitra was pretty fucking hot though!" He grins, and I can't help a short laugh escape.

"God, it was." I sniff but shake the memory. "But when I tried to stop her from leaving she threw that 'time is money' and she has 'people to screw' in my face. That fucking kicked me in the nuts as hard as any steel toe." I shift, uncomfortable at the memory.

"She was lashing out."

"Maybe, but that is going to be a deal breaker if every time we argue, she threatens to go on some revenge 'fuckfest'. I know she doesn't need the money, and I respect the shit out of her for doing what she wants with her body. She's the sexiest woman I know, and I know I'm no saint—"

"Jason, you're a slut. Trust me, you have had way more partners than Sam ever has." He sniffs out his derisive comment.

"Cheers Leon, but I doubt that." I pinch out a tight-lipped grimace and narrow my glare, but his face is impassive. "Look, her past doesn't matter; it's irrelevant. And I don't care about her being a Domme, but if she is going to fuck someone else it's because we *both* want that, not because she's out to hurt me."

"You hurt her." His reminder is unnecessary and hurts like fuck, but I won't give up.

"I know. It won't happen again." I meet his sceptical glare and hold it. I mean what I say, if I get the chance, that is.

"Good, but I mean it. She has probably slept with half a dozen men in the ten years I've known her." His tone is serious but he can't be.

"Actual boyfriends I can believe that." I nod in agreement, because I understand his comment; it just needed my own clarification. "She told me as much. She had never been serious with anyone, not until me, but you can't expect me to believe she's had just six clients in that time." I raise my brow, but his face hasn't changed, still serious and intently holding my glare.

"She has many clients as a Dominatrix but she's never fucked anyone for money. Never has, never will," he reiterates.

"Why does she call herself a *whore*? I don't understand." I shake my head. I'm a fucking idiot. I completely understand. She uses it to keep her distance, to stop herself getting close to anyone. It's her barrier and her armour. "I mean I do understand, but why didn't she tell me." I can hear my voice catch, and his expression softens slightly.

"Self-preservation, Jason." He places his hand on my dropped shoulder. "I'm only telling you because you didn't care before. The label didn't keep you away." He removes his hand, folds his arms across his chest, and shakes his head. A bitter, knowing laugh escapes him. "I know her, she will be happy now because she didn't tell you. She'll retreat into her shell, believing she deserves no more than a desolate, lonely future." He drags his hand through his long hair and fixes me with a dark scowl. "She will justify the end because *you* were stupid enough to believe she is capable of—what did you call it?"

"A revenge fuckfest," I reply, quietly ashamed that I even for a moment believed that was the case.

"Yeah, and if I hadn't told you, you might've gone on believing it, and that path leads to relationship destruction. She deserves more." He stares at me and smiles.

"I agree." I get a chill in my bones thinking how that reality nearly came to be. "So where do you think she is?" He shrugs. I curse and almost slap my head. *Fucking idiot.* I take my phone from my back pocket and swipe the screen. It takes a moment to locate her and filter in some other information that is also very useful. "Okay, well, she's travelling at the moment. Quite fast and"—I pause while I read the flight details that have just appeared with her boarding information—"she's heading for Rome. Why is she heading to Rome?"

Leon has a knowing grin spreading wide across his face. "I'm not going to ask how you know where she is." He leaves his unasked question hanging, clearly expecting an answer.

"After Richard showed up, I put some extra security in place. It's just for emergencies." I clarify at his doubtful expression. "So Rome?" I repeat.

"Sanctuary."

"Hmm?"

"I have a flat there. It's called Sanctuary, an apartment just by the Spanish steps. When the going gets tough, the tough go shoe shopping." Leon smirks.

"Fine, put some clothes on, Leon, you're taking me to Heathrow… now." He raises a brow at my curt tone, and I draw in a slow, steadying breath. I am grateful he seems inclined to help, at least a little. I need to curb my temper. He is Sam's best friend, and he is just protecting her too. "Sorry, I don't have my car back, and you will be quicker than hailing a cab this time of night." I plead.

"Where's your car?" he calls over his shoulder as he goes to his bedroom and pulls on some clothes.

"That night I ran to the club, I dumped it at the side of the road, and it got towed. It's still impounded."

"Why haven't you picked it up? That was over three weeks ago." He looks at me like I am all kinds of special. I shrug lightly.

"I live in the city, and I've barely noticed it's not there." Leon scoffs and grabs his keys. I follow him out of the door. "We need to detour to my place so I can get my passport."

"And some clothes," he remarks.

"Hopefully not." He tips his finger, a small salute in understanding. At the bottom of the stairs, Leon opens a cupboard and hands me a helmet. He grins and knocks the two hats together. I didn't even notice the bike parked out the front when I arrived, but I do now. It's a beast, bright red even in the dim street light, a 1000cc Ducati 916. He slides on and hovers his helmet above his head.

"Does Sam ride on this?"

"Oh, yeah," he groans.

"Do you mind not making that noise when you're talking about my girlfriend?" I grumble.

"Hey you're the one talking about fucking her with others. Just know I want first refusal if that ever happens. Not that I'd fucking refuse." He slams the helmet down and muffles more groans and curses. Fortunately, I am too focused on getting to Sam to think much about his comment. The last thing I need is a raging hard-on riding shotgun right behind Leon.

I never give my money much thought, probably because I am nowhere near Daniel's league of wealth, but having access to the company jet anytime I know puts me in a very privileged position. A position I am more than grateful for tonight as my last minute flight has me only, just over three hours behind Sam. Leon promised me he wouldn't call to warn her, and even gave me his key to the apartment. I am relieved at least that her best friend is giving me the chance to make this right. I grip the key hard enough to leave an indentation in my palm. My nerves are frayed with the uncertain hope that Sam will do the same and give me a chance. The taxi driver clearly gets bonus pay for the speed of each fare, whether we survive seems to be incidental. The traffic is surprisingly heavy for this time in the early morning and he weaves perilously close to the other vehicles, barely raising a curse when he clips and nudges a few.

The rain is torrential when the driver drops me at the far end of the street near the Steps. I challenge the wisdom that I didn't take the opportunity to change when I stopped to pick up my passport. But my urgency to get to Sam outweighed any rational or practical thought. My suit darkens as it quickly absorbs the downpour. I am soaked to my skin when I reach the apartment building. There are no names assigned to the apartment numbers but Leon told me it's at the top. Next to the buzzer is a little icon depicting unlocked handcuffs. I sniff out a laugh at the fitting representation and wonder which one of them considers that to be Sanctuary, Leon or Sam.

It's still dark, and with the heavy rain, the early morning sun is struggling to cast any light on the street. The buildings are tightly packed together, sandstone coloured, six and seven stories high. This building has typical architecture of the fifteenth century Renaissance period, which is stunning and prevalent throughout the ancient city. The elaborate wrought iron gate guards the more modern glass doors to the apartment block, but it is unlocked. I open the main doors with Leon's key and enter a spacious marble vestibule. The staircase winds around the square room, and rather than waking the entire building by using the antique looking open lift, I take the stairs. My wet shoes skid, failing to gain any traction on the smooth floor, but the stairs have a thick, green carpet and I am able to take them two at a time.

I take a deep breath when the key sides into the lock. I am soaked to my skin. My heart is pounding like it is desperate to escape my chest. Painful, hard beats thump so loud it's distracting. My mouth is dry, and I realise I am a mix of nerves and desperation. I have to make this right. The hallway is an extension of the stairway, light marble floor and intricate mouldings that edge the walls and decorate the five metre high ceilings. The narrow strip of carpet silences my footsteps and leads a natural path into the apartment. The living room is empty but that isn't a surprise. Sam isn't a morning person. I turn back and walk along the other part of the corridor to the only door that isn't open. I nudge it open. A large four poster bed dominates the room. Elegant and gaudy gold gilt carved wood columns with heavy red velvet drapes on each of the posts almost hide the sumptuous empty bed. My heart drops at the sight.

I feel a chill of a breeze and see the movement as the wind catches the light chiffon curtain and billows it into the room. My heart stops. The image is breath taking. Sam is half leaning, half embracing the stone column that frames the open window. The curtain lifts and sighs with the natural breeze, dancing and teasing her nakedness. Her hair falls straight and almost kisses the base of her spine, the soft curve of her hip and smooth round of her bottom, flawless. Her long, slim legs cross one behind the other and—*fuck me*—she's wearing heels! Six inch, white satin with thin straps, crisscrossed at the back of her ankle. Delicate white feathers dance in the breeze. Fuck, they are sexy. But it's the middle of the night, or early morning, why the fuck is she wearing heels?

"Fuck," I breathe and snap my mouth shut, too late to not be heard. She jumps and turns grabbing the sheer curtain to cover herself. Her face is shocked then instantly broken. *Shit.* I step forward. I can't stand it. Her eyes are glossy with tears, red and ugly with the pain I've caused. She's so fucking beautiful. I hate that I have marred her perfection. I step forward and she shakes her head. "Sam…" My voice is stern, it's the only way I can keep it from breaking at her sorrow-filled expression.

Her eyes darken, and she goes to speak, but I worry I won't like what she is about to say. I need to show her what she means to me first. I need to make her *feel* me. Then we can talk. I swoop and crush my body against hers. She gasps at the impact against the marble column. My mouth crushes hers and her fists hit my shoulders, thump and pinch and pull and embrace. Grabbing and tearing at my wet clothes with a wildness akin to something feral. My jacket hits the floor. My shirt is ripped in two, quickly joining the ever-increasing heap of my clothes on the floor. Trousers, pants, socks, everything is soaked and resisting its necessary removal but I am on fire. I suck in my first real breath once I am free and naked. She sucks my lips and bites down, sucking again to taste the blood she's just drawn. I growl into her mouth, and she moans. Her hands thread through my hair and grip and secure me against her. At this moment, I am not sure who is leading this dance, but I am at least glad we are on the *floor*.

We spin and tumble into the room. Her eyes meet mine, the fire and desire has burned away the moisture, but deep down, I can still see the hurt. I clearly need to delve a little deeper. My tongue pushes into her sweet mouth, fighting and taking, desperate movements to consume and be consumed. Breathless and aching, I pull back, turn her in my arms and press her flat against the full length gilt mirror on the wall. Her breasts are pushed flat, her forehead resting lightly, and my arms cage her. She looks up through her long lashes, her breath deep and ragged. Her eyes shine with lust and passion.

"I want you, Sam." I grit out angrily through clenched teeth.

"Yes. I get that." She tilts her hips back to rubs her sweet arse against my painfully hard cock. I hold my position but don't push back.

"No," I pause and draw in a steady breath. "I want *you*." I repeat and she narrows her eyes, her jaw tightening.

"Yes, Jason, I get that. I'm hardly saying no, am I?" She pinches out a tight smile, but her brows flicker with a flash of doubt.

"Sam, I want you." My voice softens and she closes her eyes. When they open the lashes are again heavy with tears.

"Don't." She closes her lids tight and bites her lips.

"I want *you*, Sam." I wait for her to open her eyes. I need for her to see me but she is stubbornly keeping them closed. I lean closer to her ear. My breath makes her tremble. "I love *you*, Sam." Her eyes fly open, fat tears burst onto her cheek.

"You can't love me, Jason." She shakes her head and searches my eyes for the trick.

"Why?" I hold her gaze with utter honesty. This is no trick.

"People like me—" Her voice waivers but I snap my interruption.

"I'm more a whore than you ever were, Sam. We both know that." My voice drops at the end of my declaration and a moment passes before her faces dawns with understanding.

"Fucking Leon." She rolls her eyes then shakes her head with resignation. "It doesn't change anything, Jason."

"No, it doesn't. I want you, Sam." She shifts uncomfortably under my gaze caged within my arms.

"Jason—" her plea is halfhearted but I need to make things clear before we can hope to get past this.

"Do you believe I fucked Peitra?" I relax with her instant answer.

"No, but you lied to me." She levels a scowl that could leave scorch marks if I wasn't already burning.

"And you lied to me." I parry my defence. She releases a sigh. Her eyes well, and tears stream down her face. She's killing me with her tears, but I can still feel her barriers holding firm. She needs to let me in. "Sam, I just want you. Do you trust me?" One barrier at a time, her reply is all I need.

"I do but—"

"There are no buts after that, Sam. Trust is the only thing that matters, and I am more than happy to show you how much I *trust* you." I watch her throat work to swallow. She holds my gaze, searching. I just hope she finds what's she's looking for, because more than anything, I want to give her my all, my *everything*. "Put your hands above your head." Her eyes widen with surprise and darken with desire. My voice is hoarse, but my demand is non-negotiable. She slides her hands above her head stretching them high along the mirror. I smile when I see the bracelet I gave her yesterday still on her wrist. *Perfect.* I unclip the double cuff and slip one off and place it on her other wrist. Her eyes never leave my face but I have to flick my gaze to what my hands are doing. I clip the two cuffs together securing them and her in one of my hands.

"Who do you belong to?" I whisper against her ear, and she tilts away exposing her neck to my lips. I am more than happy with the invitation, but I want her answer. The heat from her skin is like a sensual force field I want to envelop us both. I hover, lips just waiting to take what's mine. I meet her hesitancy with a growl that rumbles from deep in my chest.

"Jason, I—" She gasps out a strangled cry and moan when I sink my teeth into her neck and suck hard, grazing the softest skin and drawing her flesh into my mouth. Her head drops back, her body trembles, and her hands struggle against my hold. My lips pull and suck her skin dry when I release it slowly and repeat my question.

"Who do you belong to?" She's breathless, and I can smell her arousal. She is intoxicating, so potent I don't think my cock has ever felt this big or this painful. She closes her lids and opens them slowly, her eyes are like liquid fire which sears through me, a mainline hit direct to my chest when she exhales the word.

"You."

I kick her legs wide. Her heels make her just the wrong angle so I need her wider or a little lower. I pull her hips back with one gentle tug of my free hand. Her back dips, and her arse raises. My cock bobs heavy and rests at that perfect crease, sliding against her exquisite softness. I nudge forward and can feel her instant searing heat and wetness, slick and molten against the tip of my cock. Adding to my own arousal, I slide inside, and we both groan with pleasure and mutual ecstasy. I push in deep, and she clenches around me. Tight, hot muscles squeeze, massage and steal my fucking mind she feels so good. I start to pump my hips, and her little sighs and gasps encourage me to push a little deeper. She fights against my hold, her arms stretched high. Her back is curved and her arse is arched and meeting my every push, thrust for thrust.

My free hand dips to her hip and pulls her back hard against my forward push, and she cries out in a gasp. I almost stop, but then she pants out the most erotic moan.

"Please, Jason, harder! Fuck me harder, make me yours." She cries out again when I slap her arse cheek. Her muscles clench hard on my cock with each slap. "Oh, God, Jason." Sam's body starts to tremble, and I snake my hand around her hip and dip my fingers between her legs. I barely stroke her clit when she drops her head with a thud to the mirror and her whole body tenses. Every muscle inside clamps down like a vise. Her back arches, and her hands slap flat against the glass. The sweat from her palms causes our joined hands to slip down the mirror until they are resting on her head.

I let her take a moment, but my hips twitch. Her eyes meet mine but they are not sleepy or stated, they are burning for more. Oh good. I unclip the cuffs and watch her expression fill with confusion. She's going to need her hands to steady herself.

"Put your hands flat and don't move them. Understand?" She nods, but I raise my brow. Her lips curl in a tentative smile. We're getting to where I want us to be, but it's still going to be a long morning.

"Yes, Jason."

"Good girl."

I push into her and grin at her sudden gasp when I step forward and push a little too deep. I pull completely out, and she grunts with surprise and scowls with frustration. I hold my cock and slide along her slit. She is dripping wet, which is such a turn-on and completely perfect. I rest my cock just below her very tight hole, applying enough pressure to make my intention known. She draws in a breath and sinks back onto me, wriggling to get the position just right. Her gaze meets mine, her lips part as she pushes back onto me, inch by slow inch. Her brows register some pain, but her eyes are alight with fire, and she holds my gaze like she holds my heart… by the balls.

I run my hands up her back and grab her shoulders for leverage. She likes it hard. She wants me to make her mine. I am happy to oblige. A sharp, breathless gasp escapes her as I start to pound into her arse. She is so fucking tight and every pump and grind against her round cheeks is ecstasy. Every murmur and cry for more is driving me insane. My hands move around her neck, light at first then gripping more tightly. Her muscles contract tight around my cock. Her eyes widen and register a healthy degree of worry as I slowly restrict her airway. But they darken equally with hidden erotic desire that swirls together, a perfect mix of purity and wickedness.

"Who do you belong to?" I growl out through gritted teeth, using every ounce of self-control to not explode.

"You Jason…I'm yours." Her face is flushed, and her tiny panting breaths mist the mirror. She groans and tries to manoeuvre her legs together to gain some relief.

She starts to drop one hand but my growl has her holding position once more. I drop my hands from her shoulders and squeeze her bottom cheeks, pink with my handprints and so fucking sexy I can't stand it. Her reflection is the most beautiful image I've ever seen, dark eyes filled with desire, full breasts peaked with hard nipples swaying with each jut of my body against hers and her body *full* of me.

"Jason, I need to come." Her voice is strained, desperate and breathless.

"Then come, beautiful." I kiss her spine between her shoulder blades.

"I can't…not like this." She gives a little apologetic shrug that almost makes me laugh. I slip one hand around her front and palm her clit and stick my two middle fingers inside her. The tips brushing the thin membrane and touching my cock as I continue to pump into her arse.

"Really?" I curl gently and apply a little pressure to a soft secret spot. It's enough, and she screams so loud I'm sure she doesn't hear me say, "Is that so?"

"Ah…ah! Oh, God, my legs." Her body is shaking, and I can feel her dip as her legs start to give way. I pull out of her tight heaven, even as I am fit to explode. She lowers her eyes when I turn her in my arms. She looks up with a flash of worry.

"That looks painful."

"You have no idea." She goes to wrap her tiny hand around my aching cock but I grab her wrist.

"Let me help you." Her tone is almost begging. She tries to retrieve her hand, and in failing to do that, she starts to sink to her knees. I tip her chin so she can't lower herself, her eyes meet mine, my mouth beams into a warm smile that originates deep in my soul.

"I'm not finished with you yet." My voice is deep, gravelly, full of sensual threat.

"Oh," She breathes out, a knowing smile illuminates her face.

"Oh, indeed." I drop to my knees and lift one leg up and press it back against the mirror so she is wide and open for me. I sweep my tongue along her folds, tasting and licking all the wetness. She is divine. Here between her legs, I am in heaven. Those cries of pleasure are my choir of angels, and when she falls I will die because I have already been to heaven. Her fingers thread through my hair, and she pinches tight. My scalp tingles and her hips roll against my mouth. I lap up her enthusiasm as I lap the liquid dripping from her body. She starts to pant loudly but tries to tilt her body away. I growl and cup her arse cheeks, pressing her firmer against my mouth.

"Oh, oh, fuck, Jason…No…no, I can't." I purse my lips and suck gently on her clit. I know she must be a little oversensitive by now, but I also know it won't stop her from coming on my lips like I want. "Oh, Jesus, ahhhh!" She stops making actual noises and forms cute, muffled whimpers as I lick and stroke her back down from her climax. I stand and watch with amusement as she sways, glassy eyed and smiling. I sweep her into my arms and carry her to the bed. She stares up at me with a smile so heart-stealingly beautiful, I can't help but return it.

I roll her onto her back.

"Don't move." Her eyelids are at half-mast as she offers me a satisfied sigh and nods her head. I leap from the bed with two things pressing on my mind; get clean and get back inside. I return from the bathroom having sorted the former and stalk up the bed and between her legs to make good on the latter. She spreads wide for me with minimal pressure and I slip into her heat. As I start to move, her legs hook around my back and the heel points dig into my arse and make me that little bit harder. Fuck, I need to come. She tilts her hips and pulls me tighter, deeper, we both groan. I support my weight and look down into her eyes. They swirl with depths I can only hope she'll let me explore. I'm under no illusion that winning her heart will be as easy as winning her body, but I can only pray it's a fraction of the fun.

"Who do you belong to?" I whisper against her soft lips. Her tongue flicks out and traces the seam.

"You." Her smile is tentative, but I can see it comes from her soul.

"I own you, Sam." I cover her lips with mine only breaking when we both need air.

"Yes…yes, you do." She sucks in deep, life affirming breath. Her eyes pool with tears, but her smile is so brilliant I get the feeling they are happy tears. Fuck, I hope they are happy tears. I surge forward, and she meets my powerful drive with equal passion. I feel the tingle explode at the base of my spine and an ache that's so intense, the pleasure pain line blurs. I thrust relentlessly, chasing my release. One, two, each thrust pushing me closer…so close. She screams as her body takes over, sending us both spiralling and ascending high out of this world and into a blissful state of utter euphoria that lasts an eternity. In her arms, it feels like eternity.

She shivers. We have been lying naked for several hours. It seems as if the sun has slowly risen. I pull the covers over our joined bodies and kiss her hair, her forehead, and her nose. She smiles, sleep creeping across her tired face, sedating her features one by one.

"Death by orgasms," she sighs. "I thought you liked me?" She fails to fight off a yawn and giggles when it finishes.

"Sam, I love you." She sleeps as my words drift and float waiting to settle more comfortably on her when she wakes.

THIRTEEN

Sam

Oh, ow! That first stretch of the morning shouldn't hurt like this. My muscles scream in agony with the smallest movement. I feel sore in places I didn't realise could ache and I'm burning up. I feel trapped and a sudden flash of panic engulfs me, only to dissipate like a cool breath in a warm room when I remember why I feel all these things. *Jason.* His heavy arm drapes my waist, my back to his front, his large frame cloaking me like a shield. The heat between us is searing but rapidly rising to inferno. I try to move, but he grumbles and pulls me tighter. His deep, steady breathing is evidence that he is still very much asleep, and despite my initial discomfort, I am still bone tired and very quickly sink back in to a blissful sleep.

When I wake again, I am alone. The bed is empty and the pillow next to mine has no dip to indicate I recently shared this space with anyone. *Did I dream last night?* It felt like a dream, unreal and heavenly. I have never felt the way he made me feel last night. The way he touched me, cherished me, and brought me to heights of pleasure that made me dizzy again and again. He told me he loved me. It had to be a dream. Why would he come after me? How would he even know where I'd gone? I let out a heavy sigh, but it felt so wonderful, it felt so real. I can feel the tickle of sadness behind my nose but shake it away and focus my mind on much more pleasant thoughts. I think about the dream, squeeze my eyes tight and attempt to rekindle the embers of the passion that, only a short time ago, lit my blood alive. I need to lose myself again before I have to bear the burden of the harsh reality of truth. No one is ever going to love a whore.

I shake the self-pity away and push my mind to remember. His eyes are staring at me, piercing right through to my soul and warming my heart. The force of feeling is like a shot of pure energy, and I can feel my pulse beat a strong staccato. It's just a dream but it has such power, I sigh out a shaky breath. My fingers lightly trace down my chest, soft, teasing strokes across my nipples that are instantly hard. I know I am wet just from the thought of my dream, but I don't want a quick release. I want to savour. My middle finger rests lightly just touching the soft skin around my clit.

"I could help with that…" His deep voice is hoarse, and he coughs to cover the catch at the end. My eyes snap open wide, and my legs slam shut trapping my hand. I grab the sheet to cover my wanton display. I shuffle up the bed, pulling my knees in tight, strangely nervous. He sits beside me and places an offering of delicious smelling pastries and, hopefully, coffee on a tray before me. His sheepish smile is adorable. He lifts the lid from the takeaway cup and hands me what looks like a cappuccino and smells like heaven. I hesitate.

"Unless you really would like me to help?" His grin is pure wickedness "You know you don't need to ask twice. I just thought you would like some breakfast. Although it's really nearer to lunchtime. Either way, I thought food would be good." He is rushing his words, almost like he is nervous. Why the fuck would he be nervous?

"Food is good." I take the cup and sip while he unpacks a paper-wrapped breakfast feast.

"I didn't know what you liked. You probably have favourites. Leon said you come here often when you need to get away." He holds my gaze then closes his eyes for a moment but too late for me to miss the sadness. God this is a mess. He waves his hand invitingly across the selection and I pick the *saccottino al cioccolato,* which is my favourite. It is literally a pastry sack filled with chocolate. Jason takes a plain *cornetto.*

The silence is comfortable but brief when I take in what he's wearing and snicker. He looks down and shrugs with a laugh. He is wearing Leon's clothes, which are at least one size too small, and Leon likes fitted. The t-shirt Jason has on looks like it's been shrunk to fit and highlights every curve of muscle on his torso. Not a bad look for muscle beach maybe or a float at gay pride in Amsterdam. His sweat pants are slightly better but are clinging to his calf muscles like they are allergic to his feet.

"You don't have any clothes?"

"Only what I was wearing last night. I kind of left in a hurry." I nod and fall silent, nibbling on the pastry and sipping my coffee. "Why did you run, Sam?" His voice is tentative, almost like he fears I will run again. I won't.

"Why did you follow?"

"Why wouldn't I? You're my girlfriend." He sounds incredulous, his tone pitched with genuine surprise.

"Jason, I don't think this is a good idea. I'm not the girl you think I am." I avoid his eyes and pick at the flaky pastry crumbs in my lap.

"Bullshit! " His tone is gruff and stern. "You're exactly the girl I think you are. I told you last night I love you, Sam. Nothing's changed. We just have to talk when we have a problem like a normal relationship." He reaches for my free hand and entwines his fingers, his thumbs softly stroking my wrist.

"But this isn't a normal relationship," I whisper.

"Really? And why is that?" I meet his eyes, which are so dark they look like inky black pools, the flecks of gold invisible.

"Because I'm—" His whole frame tenses, and he sits about a foot taller on the bed, intimidating and radiating instant anger.

"If you call yourself a whore just one more time, I'll tan your arse so hard the neighbours will feel the burn. You're not a whore, Sam, and from what Leon told me you never were." He draws in a deep breath, and his body relaxes with the slow escape of air. "But that doesn't matter. I want *you*."

"Why? No, wait, I'll answer that. You want me because you think you know me." I keep my voice quiet, but I can feel my frustration and temper rise together. "You see me at work and think that's who I am. I know you've seen more than that, I do. But ultimately you are attracted to the no-holds barred, sexually adventurous Selina part of me. I think we can both confidently say the crazy jealous part of Sam outweighs my alter ego by some considerable margin." I tip my chin, but I can feel the pinch of pressure behind my eyes. I hate that I feel so desperate for this not to be true.

"Thanks for giving me so much credit, Sam." Sarcasm and disdain drip from his words. "You must really think highly of me if you think I can't see past your killer body and whip skills." He throws his food down but takes a deep, steadying breath. "I fucked up yesterday but please don't assume I can't acknowledge how I really feel about you. This may be new territory for me but that doesn't make it any less real." He takes my coffee and the tray and places everything on the floor, returning to face me. His deep eyes hold so much love I just want to dive in and never come up for air.

"Jason." My voice breaks, he interrupts but I don't know what I was going to say. That I'm so happy he feels that way? That I'm scared shitless he does or that I feel the same? I'm grateful for his impatience.

"You don't need that barrier with me, angel. I see you, and I want *you*." His lips cover mine, and he steals my breath along with my fragile heart. Long moments later, he pulls back.

"What now?" I compose myself as I internally try to process the magnitude of what he's just declared and how that changes everything.

"I need to get some clothes so you can show me the city. I take it you have all you need?" His eyes sparkle with mischief and his grin is relaxed and so wide, his perfect white teeth just dazzle.

"I do now." Barely a whisper but my words seem to make his smile that bit brighter.

"Why were you naked but for your heels last night? My heart actually stopped at the sight but—"

I laugh with an unladylike snort but can't help myself. I fall back, shaking my head. His brows furrow with curiosity. He waits for my explanation for what it's worth.

"My happy shoes." I declare, but his expression looks none the wiser. "It sounds silly to say it out loud, shallow maybe, but they are so beautiful they always make me smile. The most expensive pair I ever bought, but they never fail to make me happy." I add with a light shrug.

"They work." His voice dips to a low gravelly sound that has the hairs on my neck alert and prickling. "They make me *very* happy."

I am officially the worst guide in the history of this beautiful, ancient city. After we did a speedy shop for essentials so Jason didn't have to spend the rest of the weekend looking like the sixth member of the Village People, I take the lead and Jason happily follows. I know where to go, but other than stating the bloody obvious…this is the Trevi Fountain or this is the Pantheon, I am shamefully ignorant of the actual history. I just fell in love with the place the first time Leon brought me here. I am happy to wander in a daze absorbing the culture if only on a visual level. But Jason doesn't seem to be bothered. He holds my hand the entire time we walk from one tourist trap to another. Many of the streets are too narrow for cars but the plethora of mopeds keep them from being quiet or any safer than the main roads.

Midafternoon we find a small restaurant, and I am grateful to rest my aching feet, but more thankful I had some sandals in lieu of my happy heels. I would be crippled from the miles we have covered this afternoon. As it is, I just have frozen toes. In February, this part of Europe may be blessed with clear skies but this city is not far enough south to stave off the chill of winter. It is not really open toe weather.

We are seated by the window, but it is just one small room with maybe twenty-five covers in all. It is cosy, and the smells from the kitchen cause my tummy to rumble before the waiter even hands me the menu. I feel my cheeks heat because there is no way every patron in the place didn't hear that noise.

My mouth drops open with complete surprise as Jason speaks rapidly and fluently to the waiter, who grins and a playful expression lights his face before he hurries away.

"What?" Jason's nonchalant air is tainted by his smug grin.

"You speak Italian?" I have excelled at stating the obvious all afternoon. No need to stop now.

"*Sì.*" He grins.

"You speak it really well." I frown at my own redundant remarks.

"*Grazie, bella signorina.*" He leans forward, closing the distance from friendly to intimate. His words sound extremely sensual as they fall from his utterly enticing, soft, full lips.

"How come?" I am still in shock. He sounded like a local.

"Every summer while at University I stayed here with friends." He shrugs it off, like speaking one of the sexiest languages on the planet is nothing.

"All summer…What did you do?"

He has the decency to look sheepish. "I was a guide…for the English speaking tourists mainly."

"And you let me make an embarrassing hash of showing you the city, and you didn't think to mention this at any time." I scrunch up my napkin and throw it playfully at his face.

"What? And miss the most enlightening tour of all?" His voice drops, and I scowl. "I'm serious; your reactions to the sights told me more than any guidebook. Your face holds all the information and so much more. There is no way I was going to interrupt." He holds his hands up in all honesty, but I eye him suspiciously nonetheless.

"Hmm, but the waiter, what did you say to him? He smirked at me, so you must have said something." I sit back because the heat we are generating is causing some serious discomfort between my legs. I shift, but it does little to alleviate the needy ache.

"I asked if he could bring some bread and olives or turn the music up because my beautiful girlfriend is embarrassing me." His replies deadpan and serious.

"Oh, my god! You didn't?" I slap my hand over my mouth and look over to where the waiter is speaking to another man. They both glance my way. Their warm smiles turn to chuckles. I want to die or maybe kill.

"Call you my beautiful girlfriend? Of course I did." I narrow my eyes and purse my lips. The waiter returns with a basket of fresh, warm bread and some plump, green olives. I bite back my retort but can't hide my bright, pink cheeks. "You know you look stunning with that colour on your *cheeks.*" He holds my gaze, and he effectively makes my face burn a little brighter from his salacious reference. Ground, swallow me now.

I devour the bread because it melts in my mouth, and I don't want my tummy to register any further complaints. The meal that followed was unbelievably good, simple and delicious. I have the fettuccine with a lemon and parmesan cream sauce and Jason has a pizza. *When in Rome.*

Every minute I spend with Jason feels right. I feel a treasured and special. The only way I can describe it that makes sense to me is that he feels like home. The irony isn't lost on me, because I hated my home growing up, but that didn't stop me from dreaming of the ideal of a loving home. Somewhere to feel safe, somewhere to feel loved. I don't think I allowed myself the luxury of believing I would ever have something like this. I'm nervous about labels but being Jason's girlfriend feels uncommonly good. Leon is the closest thing I have come to someone loving me and me actually believing them, and that hasn't been easy.

Richard walked away years ago, leaving me to die. But that final act of cruelty was just one of a hundred I'd endured while we were 'together'. Sadly, the effects of a toxic relationship will always cause unbidden issues. The damage is done. As an adult, I can acknowledge that and the abuse by my mother for what it was. I can tell myself it wasn't my fault. I *know* it was not my fault. But that rot runs very deep and is very quick to erode the edges of hard-earned positive self-esteem, at any opportunity. It's much easier to believe the bad stuff.

"Hey, where did you go?" His kind smile and softly spoken words continue to chip at my crumbling shield.

"This is new territory for me, too." I meet his gaze, kind eyes and an honest soul.

"I know, baby. But if one thing your background as a Domme does provide, it's the importance of communication." He flashes his killer smile. "I won't know your limits unless you tell me." The sincerity and significance of his words lie heavy. But he is right.

"I think I did tell you the other night," I remind him. He instantly shifts in his seat. His face is impassive, but his eyes flash with a much more devious memory. I raise my brow at his flush of colour. "You're hard?" My eyes dip to the significant bulge in his jeans. I lean over to close the distance, but my breathy whisper just causes him to narrow his eyes.

"And *that* isn't helping." His tone is a stern warning, but his light kiss on my nose softens the sting. "You didn't tell me exactly, but you did show me. And that was the fucking hottest thing ever. I have never had someone go all *alpha chick*." He shifts again and I swear his bulge gets bigger in its confined denim prison. "I know as Selina you *own* the club, but this was real life and wow, Peitra looked like she was going to shit herself." I giggle. He joins with a much deeper belly laugh. "I left immediately, but my departure didn't improve her mood. I may have called her a fucking bitch." I splutter the water I was just sipping.

"Really?" I can't hide my shock. He is fiery, I know, but always professional.

"She *is* a fucking bitch." He casually repeats his character assessment of the delightful Peitra.

"Oh, I know she is, but you're her boss. Isn't it frowned upon to call employees names?" I admonish lightly.

"She's an intern, and I am sure she manipulated that meeting—the venue at least." He scratches his day old stubble pensively. I like the slightly rougher look. He wears the bad boy look almost as well as he wears the sexy business owner. "She probably cancelled the client attending, too." He comments derisively. "I don't think there will be a complaint." He sips his water before continuing. "But she is loosely part of Daniel's family, so that does make it tricky. Not that he would disagree if I sacked her for gross misconduct," he points out ruefully.

"That might make family get-togethers interesting. She's only just graduated; that will kill her career." I may not like the girl, but her actions have far reaching implications I doubt she considered

"Something she might've thought about before she insulted my girlfriend." He dismisses my concern.

"Maybe you could just put her somewhere else?" I offer with a sly smile. His expression is more one of shock than surprise.

"You're defending her?" He sits back and stares at me.

"Not at all, but everyone makes mistakes." I shrug. I'm not a fan but I am also not that vindictive.

"You are too sweet." He sweeps his knuckles softly across my cheek.

"Don't go crazy now. I didn't say *where* you should transfer her. I was thinking maybe janitorial detail?" He barks out a laugh.

We share a delicious creamy coffee desert and sip on the complimentary Limoncello and watch the world go by.

"Do we need some new rules?" I ask after a while.

"I don't think we do." The confidence in his reply is clear in his tone. "As long as we talk first, to avoid any misunderstandings. However hard, it's better to be honest."

"Are you being honest?" I challenge his naïveté.

"Hmm?" His brow is furrowed with confusion.

"You said you got jealous of me, my work."

His brows knit tighter together. "I did say that." He draws in a breath. "But I am not going to stop you working, Sam. I will deal."

His tone is sincere, but I am uncomfortable, knowing that the underlying feeling is still there. If it is a fraction of what I felt seeing him with Peitra, then it's too much.

"I could maybe cut right back," I muse out loud. His gaze is fixed on me, but his face is implacable. I trace the rim of the glass absently with my finger before sucking the remnant of the sticky liqueur into my mouth. "There is really only one client I would have a problem letting go." He doesn't hesitate to fill in the blanks.

"Leon."

"How did you—" I start but he interrupts.

"It's pretty obvious he needs you for something, and I know it's not sex," he teases.

"Oh…wait, why not sex?" I challenge his assumption. His correct assumption.

"I mentioned something about your fantasy, and he asked for first refusal. He wouldn't ask if he was already fucking you, now would he?" He counters my challenge with a knowing arched brow.

"I guess not."

"So you've never had sex with him?" His hesitant tone belies his earlier certainty.

"No. I decided early on that I needed a friend so much more than I needed to get laid. I had nothing, no one, and I couldn't risk losing him. Sex complicates things." I sip the too sweet liqueur, Jason's gaze is intense, but I don't feel his questions are intrusive. I hate secrets, and I have nothing to hide when it comes to Leon. He's my best friend.

"You never considered him boyfriend material?" His tone is sceptical, and I smile because I understand why.

"He's very attractive, yes, and I adore him, but no. I love him as a friend. I know if it was a choice between sex and the other for him, there would be no contest." I sniff out a laugh.

"The other?" He frowns.

"His sexual preference is for me to beat the shit out of him." The need to sugar-coat is completely obsolete with Jason. I like that; it's sort of refreshing.

"He's a Dom!" His shock is a little surprising. Perhaps I did need to soften the truth with some obscure, flowery prose.

"Ninety nine percent of the time, yes."

"He won't go to anyone else?" His jaw tenses with the question.

"We're working on that, but he's very stubborn."

Jason rolls his eyes. His response is curt, emphatic, irritation fixed in his narrow eyes. "No, he is smart. I wouldn't want to give you up, either."

"Care to find out what you're missing out on?" I tease.

He laughs loudly. "Ah, I think we've established when that will happen, beautiful." He takes my fingertips into his mouth and nips the tips. The waiter comes and refills out liqueur glasses.

"We did." I smile at our impossible pact. "Jealousy hurts, and I don't like the idea that I…" I stifle a laugh at the irony.

Jason finishes my sentence. "…that you are causing me pain?" He raises his brow but smiles. His hand cups my face, and I lean into his warm palm. "The only pain I can't handle is the thought of losing you."

"Wake up," His deep sexy voice filters into my subconscious, but my body is too weary to respond. He seems determined to rouse me from my blissful sleep. We rested after our walking tour, then Jason took me to the most amazing restaurant high on the hill overlooking the city. Countless courses of exquisite food and too much wine left me almost fit to burst when we came home. Making love until the early hours did me in, and I am pretty sure I passed out with the last earth shattering orgasm Jason drew from my helpless body. I groan and resist my senses' return to the land of the living.

"Wake up, beautiful." His soft lips cover mine when I mumble my objection. He continues to pepper my face with a hundred kisses, and I finally giggle when I realise this is a battle I will not win. I like the fight all the same.

"If you want to fuck me, you didn't have to wake me for that," I grumble.

"Somnophilia is not my style." He chuckles and I blink my eyes trying to focus on his face. It's still dark outside, and I feel like I have been asleep for five minutes. I can't focus to see the hands on my watch, and squinting at the clock on the bedside table hasn't helped, because that is obviously wrong. It reads two thirty, which would mean I have been asleep for just twenty-five minutes. "You need to get dressed. Something black and wear the flat pumps you bought today. We need to be quiet." He rolls off the bed, taking my covers with him. I squeal and try to grab the sheet before it completely vanishes, but I am nowhere near alert enough, since my reflexes are still napping.

"What time is it?" I close my eyes and instantly feel the pull of exhaustion. I start to curl onto my side when I am lifted with no effort at all and unceremoniously dumped onto my feet.

"It's just after two thirty, and we don't have much time." His face is alight with mischievousness, but it's too early to share his enthusiasm. I am not a morning person even if, technically, this feels like the middle of the night.

"Jason, I am tired; please let me sleep," I whine.

"Sleep when you're dead, beautiful. I want to show you something very special." His smile is a delicious mix of seductive and excited. He looks like a kid in a toyshop, and that in itself makes me a little giddy, too. He is dressed in black jeans, a long, slim fitted, black, roll neck sweater and black trainers. He helps me into a similar outfit, his large hands pulling and tugging me into my clothes. His urgency makes me laugh.

"Where are we going?" I giggle when, from nowhere, he snaps a black beanie on my head. My hair hangs loose around my face, which causes a deep frown.

"Can you tuck your hair inside the hat?"

"Are we doing a bank job?" I snicker but start to tuck and fold my long hair into the hat.

"Maybe." He winks and nods with satisfaction at my now tamed mane. "Let's go." He grabs my hand and practically drags me out of the apartment and down the stairs.

The night air is crisp and cool against my face. My breath forms light clouds with every exhale. I am grateful for the warmth of the hat, although I suspect that isn't the reason I'm wearing it.

It's a thirty-minute walk from my apartment to the Coliseum, but at the pace Jason sets, we make it in fifteen. I'm a little out of breath but completely exhilarated by our clandestine adventure through the deserted city streets. The ancient monument looks magnificent at night. Spotlights illuminate the structure from the ground and cast a bright light over the hundreds of arches. Each archway in the bottom two tiers has its own light, almost golden in appearance. But by the time the light reaches the third and what's left of the fourth tier, the shadows cast an eerie glow, and the arches feel more like the empty eyes gazing out from a different world.

Jason pulls me tight to his side, and we walk from the main entrance around until we pass a second main entrance. Jason stops at the front of one of the access arches that are now gated. He wriggles his brow conspiratorially and pushes the emergency access gate. I hold my breath, wide-eyed, and just waiting for the silence to be broken with the howl of sirens. But the only sound I can hear is the thump, thump of my heart pumping an overdose of adrenaline around my body. I chance a nervous glance around but quickly follow him inside. He leads me down corridors, tunnels and stairs until we are below the arena floor level. The wooden floor has long since rotted away. The crumbling stone dungeons for the slaves and the remainder of rooms that housed the animals are all that is recognisable in the decay of this mini underground city.

The quiet is strangely peaceful, especially when I stop to gaze and take it all in, this moment and this feeling of being in a place so ancient. The sense of what happened here all those years ago causes my blood to chill. I shiver and Jason wraps his arms around me, his warm breath kissing my neck as I continue to look up and around at columns, archways, statues, and row upon row of stone seating, reaching to the gods. It's darker inside, but the light from the exterior is enough to see everything, but even if I couldn't, I appear to have an excellent guide.

Jason starts to speak the minute we stop, telling me everything from the different materials used in construction to where the noblemen and Emperor would sit. He leads me through the building, talking so animatedly about what would happen here, holding my hand in this moment and conjuring images that transport me back to a more brutal era.

"Jason, this is amazing." I am totally blown away, my vocabulary not nearly extensive enough to do my feelings justice. His smile widens with my praise.

"You like?" His smile is tentative, but his voice is filled with justified confidence.

"Very much." I rise up on my toes to kiss him lightly. His arms pull me tighter, and his mouth crushes against mine. His tongue sweeps in, dives and entwines with mine. His attempt to steal my breath is successful. When he releases me, I nearly collapse, grabbing his forearms to prevent my fall.

"I want to fuck you, Sam." His gravelly tone and the heat in his eyes are like a mainline shock to my core.

"Here?" I can't help the little moan that escapes my throat at the idea.

"Yes."

"Won't we get caught?" I try to look around, but his hand cups my face, and his eyes scorch a direct hit to my clit.

"There is always that possibility. You said you didn't do public sex, but I really want to fuck you now…right now." His voice is hoarse, and he steps against me, pushing me flush against the rough wall.

"I was forced to have sex in front of Richard's friends. I don't consider this the same thing at all." Jason stiffens, and his dark eyes darken with anger. I place my hand on his firm chest, pleased his heartbeat is just as frantic as mine. He relaxes under my touch. "And there is *nothing* I wouldn't do with you." I hold his gaze for an eternity before he smiles a wicked grin.

"I'm very glad to hear it." He growls and crushes my lips once more. One hand slips behind my head to protect me from the hard rock and rough, unbelievably erotic invasion of his tongue. His other hand is quick to release the buttons on my pants. I help him push my jeans to my knees. I work his belt loose and do the same to his jeans. His cock springs free, and I quickly take its heavy weight in my hand, wrapping my fingers and moving firmly up and down. I sweep the pre-cum with my finger and quickly suck it clean before I resume stroking his rock-hard length—silk over steel, heavenly. His hips rock forward into my grip and his hand dips between my legs. I sigh when his fingers slide easily between my soaking folds and sink inside. He languidly drags his middle finger along my centre from entrance to clit. I tremble with each pass and whimper, eager for more.

Agonised by his teasing touch, I sag with relief when he removes his hand and places his cock at my entrance. But I am trapped at the knees by my jeans, and I know I am going to die if I can't have him deep and hard. Oh, God, I want him fucking me hard.

"Jason, from behind, please," I beg.

"Really?" He voice sounds as ragged as I feel.

"I need you hard and deep, and that's not gonna happen with my legs trapped." My voice holds all the desperation I feel between my legs.

"As you wish, beautiful." He spins me round and roughly grabs my hips. I barely get the chance to steady myself when he thrusts inside. So. Fucking. Deep. My body starts to shake, and I can't draw in any air. He has pushed it all from my body with each hard pump of his hips. It feels so good, I can't take another breath; all I can do is take him. I feel lightheaded and dizzy. He grinds his hips, and a squeak escapes from the back of my throat. He pulls back and surges forward. This time, I suck in a deep breath, preparing my body for the intense pleasure and borderline pain that thrills me with every pump. I throw my head back and cry out. The sound echoes in the night and bounces off the silent stone surrounding us. His drive is relentless and punishing, and I love every single bit of it. I push back to meet each thrust. Our bodies collide with a wild passion I have never felt before. He pulls my hat from my head and fists a handful of hair, pulling it and arching my neck back.

"So fucking beautiful." He growls and roars as my body takes over. Every muscle clenches and crashes with the first wave of orgasm that hits us both like tsunami. His hips move faster, skin slapping loudly, his fingernails hard against my soft flesh and the pull on my hair just keeps me soaring until another climax takes hold. Bright white lights flash behind my eyes, and the sounds of our panting are drowned out by the blood pumping and rushing in my ears. My legs give way, but I don't fall. Jason has me supported in his arms. I am aware he is quickly pulling my jeans up and speaking, but I haven't come back down to earth yet; I am still floating, but my lazy smile vanishes when I recognise the word his lips is forming.

"Guard!" The next thing I feel is his strong hand dragging me at a flat-out pace as we run for the gate we had entered through an hour ago. Our feet pound the pavement once we reach the street, and we don't stop until we reach the bottom of the Spanish steps. I fall into his arms, I throw my head back and I laugh out loud. I feel so alive, so unbelievably happy. I sigh when I finally stop laughing. His smile would shame the sun as his dark brown eyes search my face. They hold so much love. Can I tell him I feel the same? What would it mean if I did? I think I do; I've never felt like this. But if I tell him, will everything change? I told Richard I loved him and he used it like a tool for torture. It changed everything. I don't want anything to change. I like this, what we have, I like it just the way it is. But if I don't, when his eyes are begging for the words, will he be upset? Will he still want me?

"Jason, I—" I hate the waiver in my voice. I hate that I am not brave.

"I know you do, Sam." His knuckles brush my cheek as his other hand slowly supports my slide down his body to the ground. "You'll tell me when you're ready." He kisses the tip of my nose.

"This has been the best night of my life." I am embarrassed as my eyes instantly pool with tears. I didn't think I was an emotional wreck as well as a crazy jealous person, but this weekend has been an education on many levels. I blink back the tears. Jason beams at me and in one final, grand romantic gesture, he sweeps me into his arms and carries me up the steps and all the way to bed.

FOURTEEN

Jason

"You know I'm a sure thing, right? You don't need to impress me with the fancy dinners, gifts and the private jet." Sam is sitting beside me, seductively stroking the plush leather sofa as we taxi to take off in Daniel's plane, heading home. Her smile is shy and I cover her hand with mine and squeeze. Her words might be all confident bravado, but the uncertainty in her eyes belies the insecurities that consume her. She needs time. I get that, but at least I am happy that I told her how I feel. However, actions speak louder and all that…

"You're not *a* sure thing beautiful, you are *my* sure thing." I try to lift her hands free to kiss her fingers, but they have this death-grip going on, white knuckles and fingernails that look like they are going to pierce the leather on the armrest. "You don't like to fly?"

She swallows and shakes her head. A nervous smiles flits across her lips. "Necessary evil, but I fucking hate it." She grimaces and clenches her jaw tight.

"Would you like me to take your mind off it?" I drop my tone and whisper the words close to her ear. She briefly giggles out a relaxing breath but almost instantly stiffens again.

"What do you propose?" She arches her brow, and despite her obvious fear, her pupils dilate. I chuckle.

"Nothing like that until we've reached altitude, but if you are a brave girl, I'll reward you." I drag my tongue slowly over my lips, my intention perfectly clear by the distracted grin spreading wide across her face. "How about a game? Random rapid-fire questions? The winner gets to come on my tongue." She squeals out a sexy little laugh.

"You're either very confident or very flexible." She teases.

"I'm very confident." I wiggle my brow and flash my widest smile. I love the way her breath catches when I do that, every… single… time. The impact is the same for me, but I feel it like a direct hit to the chest, completely fucking winded. "So, any questions at all, but you have to answer truthfully."

"Sounds dangerous." Her sceptical tone is accompanied by a wary expression.

"Sounds like fun. You start." I wink.

"Wait, are there rules?"

"Oh, beautiful, there are *always* rules." I smirk, and she rolls her eyes playfully. This is already working. Her knuckles are now a pale pink colour. "If you hesitate, you get a forfeit of *my* choosing." My voice drops an octave with the salacious warning.

"Are you always this arrogant?" she quips.

"Yes. Now stop stalling. We reach cruising altitude in about fifteen minutes, and I'm hungry." I turn to face her, and she shifts in her seat, her cheeks colour with a deep blush, but she has actually released her death-grip.

"Bring it on, big boy." She cups her fingers as a challenge. "But if I win, I get to pick my own forfeit, right?"

"Agreed." I slowly draw in my bottom lip, and she stifles a moan. The delicate sound goes straight to my balls.

"Okay. What's the capital city of Uzbekistan?" She smirks, and I purse my lips. She plays dirty.

"You get a double forfeit if you don't know the answer to the question you pose. Just thought I should warn you." I hold her gaze and try to read her tells.

"Changing the rules already?" she challenges, her face implacable.

"Clarifying the rules, and the answer is Tashkent." Her eyes widen, and I close her mouth with my finger.

"Favourite colour?" I don't pause.

"Red. Is that really the capital?" She bites her lips too late to stop and hide her mistake.

"Oh, Sam, tsk tsk." I shake my head, and she shrugs sheepishly. "Honest answers remember, and yes, it is. Next question." She taps her lips with one finger, her brow lightly furrowed in thought.

"Who's the eldest Marx brother?" She smiles, happy with her random question.

"Chico. Who's your favourite band?" I reply without hesitation, keeping the pressure on.

"Pink," she calls out, almost a yell.

"Not a band but I'll let you have that."

I raise my brow for her next question. She looks flustered then shouts, "Who painted The Water Lily Pool?"

"Monet. I'm surprised you're not taking the same opportunity as I am, Sam. It hasn't gone unnoticed that none of your questions are personal." I tap her nose when she scrunches it. "Trying to trip me up or afraid to get a little personal?" I tease.

"Is that your question?" She arches her brow, but tenses at my observation.

"No. What's your favourite desert?" I continue without much of a pause.

"Pavolva, any flavour. I love meringue. How did you find me?" I raise my brow at her first personal question.

"Your bracelet is tracked." Her jaw drops again, but I continue to elaborate. "I knew the direction you were travelling, but Leon filled in the important blanks, or it would've taken me a little longer to get to you. I was *always* going to find you, Sam." My tone is completely serious, and her lips curve into a tender smile before her mouth changes shape.

"Oh." She exhales.

"Oh. I actually understand where Daniel is coming from for the first time." Her perfect brows furrow, confused at my statement. "He is very protective of Bethany. I understand why given what they went through, but still, I thought at times it was a little over the top."

"And now?"

"And now, I completely understand." I hold her gaze, and she blinks at the intensity then peers sheepishly through her long thick lashes when she speaks.

"I'm glad you came."

I swear my heart misses a beat. "I'm glad I came, too." I brush her cheek, and she flashes the sweetest smile. I hold her hand, and her cuff slides down her arm. I frown at the loose fit.

"What's the matter?" Her expression flashes with concern, and she fiddles with her cuff nervously.

"It's loose. It could come off and then…" I draw in a deep breath but don't follow through the unpleasant line of thinking. It's not like I can lock her away, but dammit, sometimes it would make everything so much easier. The need to protect what's mine almost outweighs the need to be a rational human being. "Tracking only works if you're wearing whatever has the tracker and this"—I hold her wrist and shake her arm; the cuff almost slips off her wrist, perfectly proving my point—"is a problem." She worries her bottom lip, and I pick it from her teeth. "*If*, for example, someone were kidnapped, it's likely the first thing that would happen is that person would be stripped. We have come up with something but it still relies on access to a smart phone." I mutter still looking at her cuff.

"What do you mean?" Her face brightens, and she turns fully to face me, keen to learn more. Whether for her own safety or not, I'm not sure, but she knew enough about Bethany's kidnapping to know this isn't a topic Stone

Enterprises R & D department takes lightly.

"In the unlikely event I ever let you out of my sight and someone took you, if you could get to a phone, all you would have to do is punch in my code, and a secret signal would start transmitting GPS co-ordinates to my head office security and my phone." She nods. "But what's really clever is it also sends details of other GPS equipment nearby that I can then tap into. So if you are on a plane or in a car, I can alter the information, slow you down or change the destination undetected. It gives me an unseen advantage and time to rescue you."

"Oh, that is clever," she coos with genuine wonder. I grin.

"It's still a prototype, and it *still* needs the initial phone to activate the signal, but we're working on that. It would be much easier if I could just implant a tracker under your skin." Her eyes widen, and I realise I said that out loud.

"You are not implanting a tracker on me like some dog!" Her tone is indignant, and I hold up my hands in surrender. Not a battle for now; she won't even wear my collar. I don't fancy my chances of her ever agreeing to a permanent tracker.

"Just a thought." I chuckle.

"Well, keep thinking, buddy," she warns. Her eyes narrow, but she fails to hold her outrage, and her features starts to soften. "You *can* tell me the pin number though." She runs her fingernail along my cheek and down my jaw, scratching the two-day-old stubble.

"It's the day you stole my heart." I laugh when she frowns deeply.

"Care to give me a clue?" she coaxes. I slap my hand to my heart with mock hurt.

"If you don't know, I don't think you deserve to be rescued," I quip.

"Fine, forget it." She waves off my wound with a light shake of her head. "I believe it's your question." She sniffs, her remark has an indignant air, no doubt a result of my thigh-lipped response to her plea for a clue.

"What's your biggest fear?" I fire off without drawing breath.

"Telling someone I love them."

Her answer makes me stop. I hold her gaze. Her eyes glaze with vulnerability, and despite the illuminated seatbelt sign, I unclip her and lift her into my lap. She curls around my body as best she can. Her arms thread around my neck, her knees tucked tight against my chest.

"Why?" I sweep her sable-soft hair behind her ear and lift her chin. She is silent for long moments, but I just wait. A little time is nothing if she will open up a little more.

"I thought I loved Richard." She swallows thickly, and her lashes are instantly heavy with tears. "I had to tell him I loved him *all* the time, and he would use it against me. He insisted if I really loved him, then I should do anything he asked. Who am I kidding? He didn't ask, he demanded. Anyway, whatever he did was always worse after he made me tell him I loved him." She actually starts to tremble, and I can feel an angry fire burn in my belly. I wish I had taken that fucker out when I had the chance. I take small comfort in knowing Leon will make sure he legally can't enter the country, and I know from my brother that the CIA is keeping closer tabs on him. I hope he fucks up. I hope he rots in jail and more. But I'd still like my time with him now that I know the damage he caused this precious creature in my arms. I'd like my five minutes for retribution. I wouldn't need more time than that to sever his dick, slice his balls from his body with my own whipping skills. She settles and lets out a sigh so sad my heart aches. "I'm sorry, Jason. I really care for you but…"

"Yeah, you do beautiful." I cover her lips to stop her pointless apology. She may not be able to tell me, but I feel it in my soul, as real as her flesh and bones in my arms. Her words aren't necessary, and if one day she decides they are, she'll tell me. "No more talking. I'm hungry." Her eyes flare with understanding.

"Did you win?" she asks

"I have you. Of course I won." I swoop to steal the breath just poised to escape her sweet mouth.

"Mr Sinclair, you have a delivery." I frown at the intercom.

"And you are telling me because?" I am pretty sure Sandy is more than capable of signing a proof of receipt docket.

"Sorry, Mr Sinclair, but you have to sign." I look out my opened office door and see Sandy peer around the corner and shrug her apology. I push back from my desk and walk over to the courier. The box is heavy but not big. I sign and head back into my office, closing the door tight behind me. I recognise the handwritten label. My cock twitches, like it does every damn time I think of Sam, even after four months together. But then it's not really been four months. Before our first real date on Christmas Day, it had been a very long eighteen months since our initial hook-up at Daniel's wedding, but the last four months made that wait worthwhile. Now, I can't imagine spending a single night apart.

I am so close to asking her to move in with me, but I don't want to frighten her. Her reticence to tell me she loves me when it's so fucking obvious, makes me think she is still skittish about the whole relationship thing. As impatient as I am to take the next step, I will wait for her, for a sign or for the words themselves. She'll let me know when she's ready.

I slide the letter opener along the tape to slice the package open. A neatly wrapped bundle of rope spills to the floor, along with a card and a retro Polaroid picture. I pick up the rope; it isn't new. It is well seasoned, oiled, perfectly softened and fit for purpose. Shit, no more twitching, I am fucking rock-hard, my cock tenting my suit trousers uncomfortably. I lean down and pick up the card and photograph.

I groan out. I am going to get no work done for the rest of the day. Not now. The photograph is the fucking sexiest snap shot of my naked girlfriend's perfect body lying on her bed. One knee is bent and the other is dropped to the side. Oh, shit, she is completely bare. That is new. That is fucking hot. I grab my cock and squeeze to relieve some of the pressure, but I am painfully hard and there is only one way this is going down. I quickly read the card as I fumble in my back pocket for my phone. The card reads *'Happy Anniversary'- I believe four months is rope!* Damn! I press her speed dial number and she picks up instantly.

"Jason." She breathes my name and I stifle another groan.

"I am so fucking hard, I won't be able to leave the office without some assistance," I growl.

"Oh, you got the parcel," she squeals. "I was worried as soon as I sent it that it would get lost and someone else would get an eyeful." She giggles, but I grumble at the thought of anyone but me looking at that picture. Given her threesome fantasy, I happen to believe Sam would be fine with sharing as long as we are together, but at the moment, I honestly can't think past her being mine to even consider it an option for our playtime.

"I got it." My voice is deep and hoarse.

"So I thought maybe if you want, we could…well, you could…I thought you might like to try some rope work on me." Her voice is breathy and flustered. I can imagine her cheeks a beautiful shade of pink.

"I would like that very much, Sam. Do you think you are ready?" I swallow the dryness in my throat. We have come a long way with her submission in these past months, but Shibari can take that to a whole new level. For her to truly enjoy being bound, she will have to let go, give herself completely. I know she trusts me, but the restraints we have used are nothing compared to the restriction of intricate rope and suspension bindings.

"I trust you, Jason." I hear her swallow and breathe heavily out of her nose. The glow I feel from her words is like a pure surge of energy and fire in my veins.

"You have no idea what that means to me, Sam. I will never let any harm come to you." My tone is soft and commanding. She needs to believe every word.

"I know, Jason. I want to do this. I've seen it done before, and it looks very sexy. I just never could…you know, but with you…I can do anything." Her voice is a breathy plea.

"Thank you." Her faith and love blow me away, because if that isn't love I don't know what is. The silence is portent but her sudden, light laugh breaks the seriousness.

"Only if you're up to it. I mean the rumours could be wrong," she taunts.

"What rumours?"

"Oh, I heard you were the best Shibari Master in the club but maybe—" I growl my interruption.

"Oh, baby girl, I am the best. But let's not make this a punishment session. I'd much rather your first experience was all about pleasure."

"Your punishment is always a pleasure," she purrs.

"If you try and make me jealous, it won't be." My tone shifts to stern, and she falls silent and I remain quiet.

"I'm sorry, Jason." Her voice is soft, and I know she regrets her tease. My jealousy has eased since she hung up her whip, but we are both prone to shades of green colouring our vision from time to time.

"I know beautiful, I know. It's forgotten." My tone is gentler to assuage her remorse. "My hard-on from hell, however, is not so easy to forget or ignore." She lets out a loud laugh that turns into a gargled choke. She must have been drinking because she coughs and splutters nosily for a good few minutes. The hacking sound alone is enough to take the edge off any remaining erotic imagery.

"Sorry…went down the wrong way." She is still trying to clear her throat. "You need some help?"

"That wasn't the type of help I was hoping for; nevertheless, the net result is the same." My dry tone causes her laugh out snort. I shake my head and smile at her hysterical giggling.

"Oh, Jason, I'm sorry…tonight, I'll make it up to you tonight." She exhales a deep breath, trying to control herself. I don't care. I love it when she laughs so freely she can't control herself. I love it when she falls any which way, tears of laughter or screams of ecstasy. I'll take whatever I can get as long as I'm the one drawing those emotions from her body.

"Yes, you will." Her gasp is the last thing I hear when I end the call. A sound barely audible to the human ear. My cock, on the other hand, heard it loud and clear.

I text Sam her instructions for tonight this afternoon. When we play, I still get a nervousness I can't explain. It's probably no more complicated than realising how fucking lucky I am to have Sam switch for me. I have to admit it floors me every time I open the playroom door at the club and she is there, exactly as I requested. Any doubt is quickly replaced by a raw passion that surges through every fibre of my being, pure unadulterated desire and love for this amazing woman. We may not have started as slow as she thought she needed, but we have progressed at her speed, and her eagerness to push herself has brought us here. I lock the door behind me, and her head tilts to listen, but she doesn't raise her head. She is kneeling in the middle of the floor directly under a single spotlight. Her hair is loose and has fallen, covering her face, it almost reaches her waist and is as straight as a die. She is wearing tiny, white boy shorts and a white, fitted crop top as per my instructions but nothing else. Her dark tanned skin glows warmly in the single beam overhead. She radiates a luminescence almost like an angel—my beautiful angel.

I walk over and drop my own ten-foot jute rope on the floor in front of her knees. The heavy weight lands with a dull, loud thud, making her jump. The rope she sent to my office earlier was suitable and fit for purpose, but, this is our first time and I want my softest rope, one I have personally worked to perfection. I stroke her soft hair, and she leans into my touch, her deep steady breathing causing her chest to rise. Her perfect round breasts are barely contained by the Lycra and string straps of her top.

"Stand up, beautiful." I command. She is very agile and hops to her feet with a little jump and is instantly standing. She flicks her hair from her face. Her eyes sparkle. Dilated pupils replace any colour in her irises and transform her eyes into deep inky wells of wanton desire. She draws her bottom lip into her mouth, something she does when she is holding back. Her lips curl, because if we have learned anything in our short time together, it is that neither of us holds anything back.

"Something you want to say, beautiful?" I tilt her chin, my thumb lightly stroking her skin. I can't help it. I have to touch her.

"Do you want me naked?" She almost sighs the words and shifts her legs together, not her only display of her obvious arousal. She smells good enough to drown in, an intoxicating aroma better than any ambrosia.

"Oh, Sam, I always want you naked." I kiss her lightly on her nose and grin. Her reciprocating smile is adorable, bright and innocent, a stark contrast in a room designed for sin. "But no, I think this first time you will be more comfortable like this. Besides, with you naked, I couldn't promise not to fuck you when you are all tied in knots," I caution but my tone is playful. There is enough sexual tension in the room as it is.

"Would that be a bad thing?" She giggles.

"Shibari is deeply erotic but doesn't involve sex." I explain while holding her gaze, my tone more serious. "It can. I mean, let's face it, anything can involve sex, but that is not the point of this exercise. The knots and ropes will cross your body like brush strokes on a canvas. They will lie in places, over pressure points and erogenous zones that, if I'm doing it right, should cause you a great amount of pleasure. It's all about the pleasure, but no sex. Not this time. Understand?" She pushes her bottom lip out in a cute pout and nods. I run my hand down her cheek and hold her gaze. I want her to not only see my own desire but also the truth behind my words. This is extreme bondage, but it is so much more than mere sex. I think in the first instance it's important to distinguish the two. I want to give her maximum pleasure. "You ready?" She nods again, and I raise my brow.

"Sorry...Yes, Sir." I flash her a comforting smile, and she takes a deep breath. A tinge of nervousness clouds her eyes, but she shakes it away.

"Good girl." I quickly remove my shoes, shirt and socks so I only have on loose fitted pants for comfort, although they will do little to hide my massive erection that is just starting to make an angry appearance. We may both experience higher levels of pleasure tonight from this play, but I will also have a severe case of blue balls. I turn her away from me and scrape her hair into my hands, pulling any loose tendrils into one ponytail. I slowly braid it and can't help smiling when she moans and relaxes back into my chest when I'm done. She loves having her hair stroked, guaranteed to send her to sleep in under two minutes. I don't want her asleep, though, but relaxed and pliant works, too. I run my hand down the length of the braid. It's still very long.

"Can you twist that up into a bun? I don't want it getting tangled." I give a gentle tug.

"Oh, sure. I definitely don't want to get scalped." She snickers and deftly secures a neat bun with the single tie already in her hair.

"No, darling, scalping is next week." She snorts out a big laugh and is about to turn when a low grumble emits from my chest. She checks herself and quickly stands, awaiting instruction. I pull my hardening cock free from its awkward position in my pants and give my balls a little squeeze, which does nothing to ease my growing ache. It's going to be a long session.

From behind, I take her both of her hands in mine and help her fold her arms behind her back, crossed and at waist height. I walk around to her front and pick up the rope, taking my time threading the length through my hands into large but manageable loops. I hold her gaze and the only noise is our breathing and the rope moving in my palm. The only smell is the oil on the rope warming from the friction in my hand and her increasing arousal. I stand very close. My breath kisses her skin. My hands touch and stroke as I place the rope around her body. Around her chest above and below her breasts, then thread it between them to separate and confine. Multiple knots, loops and ties create an exotic looking exoskeleton of intricate, intertwining rope on her body. I take my time and frequently check her eyes to see her slowly drift closer to the head space I want her to be in. Her face is completely relaxed, her breathing soft and deep, and her eyes are a mix of glaze and shine.

I stroke her cheek to gain her attention, my voice deep and firm, breaking through her haze. "Hey beautiful, are you okay?" Her smile creeps across her face at a glacial pace but lights up the room.

"Yes, Sir."

"Okay, beautiful. You ready to try some suspension?" Her eyes widen with worry, but I really want to take her here. "I wouldn't ask if I didn't think you were ready, Sam. Trust me?"

"I do, and yes, I'd like to try that." I swoop in to steal a kiss because my whole body is aching for more, and the way her lips part when she exhales a sweet breath are an invitation I can't deny myself. I secure the tie around her waist and loop the rope through that and the three-point pulley that distributes the weight at her chest, her hips, and eventually her thighs once I have finished tying them. I pull her so she is floating at my waist height. Her head drops back, and she closes her eyes. I hold her close to stop her swinging and start to bind her lower legs to her thighs.

By the time I have finished with each leg, she is completely out of it. I know she's okay. I have checked repeatedly, and the soft smile on her face is all the evidence I need to know she is somewhere between earth and deep subspace. She looks absolutely amazing. Suspended horizontally with her legs wide, secured, bent and bound. She couldn't be more vulnerable, and I am fucking blown away that this strong, captivating woman gives herself to me like this, that she belongs to me. If she would just wear my damn collar, I would die a happy man but that's for another day. Now, I will just bask in the image before me for a moment longer before I start the equally important and possibly even more sensual untying and release.

I loosen her hair and drag my fingers through the long silken strands, pulling and massaging her scalp. Her hair hangs almost to the floor, and she rocks gently with just the depth of her breathing moving her suspended body. She lets out little sweet moans every time my fingers skim her body. Although in an almost dream state, her senses are highly reactive and sensitive to my touch. She glows and glistens, alive and on fire, tiny hairs dance over her skin in waves. I trace my fingers along her body, along the ropes that bind her. Her skin is so damn soft. The rope presses hard with a suspension, and I know there will be an array of indents and ridges. But no burns, no pain or soreness from being bound tight. Just a euphoric feeling of release as I untie each knot.

I carefully lower her to the floor and thread the ropes to loosen her legs, her thighs, and the ropes that thread between her legs. I help her into a seated position cradled between my legs as I kneel. She lets out a deep sigh, her lips form a lazy smile, and she meets my gaze with eyes that are dazed and glazed with moisture. I hold her for a moment, stroking her hair and kissing her head as she starts to draw in some ragged breaths. I tip her chin and kiss her full, soft lips as the first tear falls and the salty wetness coats our joined lips.

I take my time to release the remaining ropes and hold her securely when she crumples with each release. The torso ropes, then the chest and arms, each seem to create a surge inside her, and she visibly trembles but instantly calms in my arms. Fucking perfect.

I hold her wrapped in a cashmere blanket, cradled in my arms. She tips her head to look at me, her brow crinkled with confusion and her eyes pool with too many tears for her lashes to hold. Fat drops fall freely down her cheeks, and she starts to sob. I rock her and pull her even tighter to my body. She pushes her arms free of the blanket and slinks them around my waist, holding on for dear life. I hum a soft tune and kiss her hair. My fingers have carefully traced every indentation created by the ropes when I untied her, and I know there is no damage. But I don't think that is why she is crying. Her body trembles and I just hold her until she's ready. Long minutes pass; it could be hours for all I care. She's in my arms, holding me as much as I'm holding her, and I couldn't be happier.

After a while longer, she shifts and looks up as I'm looking down. Her cheeks flush with colour but are dry since she stopped crying a while ago. I smile and she flashes a tentative one back at me.

"I'm sorry," she whispers, and I actually want to growl in frustration that she could even think she has a single thing to feel sorry for. Nevertheless, I know she must be feeling raw to have reacted the way she did.

"Hey, beautiful, I can't imagine what you think you have to apologise for, but I'd rather you didn't," I lightly admonish.

"I cried." Her voice is barely above a whisper.

"You did, and you were amazing. I am so proud." She softens at my praise, and her smile spreads a little wider.

"Why did I cry? I enjoyed it." She seems confused. "I've never felt anything like that, and you were pretty amazing yourself." She rushes her words and praise. I chuckle, and she nestles against my chest. A searing heat penetrates my heart, clenching it tight like a molten vise. It kills me that she doesn't seem to grasp what she does to me.

"Why, thank you." I kiss her on her forehead, then her nose, and then her waiting lips. "It was intense, I won't argue that, but your reaction is not uncommon." She arches a brow.

"You've had women cry like that before?"

"No, not personally, but then I have never practised on someone that I have such a connection with, either. Believe me, that takes this experience to a whole different level."

"Really?" Her smile would outshine a supernova.

"No fucking comparison, beautiful…no fucking comparison."

FIFTEEN

Sam

I can't explain the emotions coursing through me right now. Warm, euphoric, confused, are a few words that float in my mind, but I know they don't do the feelings justice. I'm an emotional mess but happy. I'm so fucking happy. Jason holds me. No, that's not right; he cocoons me in a blanket of himself, like a shield. I feel utterly protected, but more than that, I feel treasured and cherished. He's told me he loves me. Hell, he tells me all the time and shows me every day with his kindness and thoughtful acts. But this, he seems to have infused every nerve in my body with that feeling.

Intense, fuck yes, that was intense.

He stands, carries me to the door, and places me on unsteady feet before he opens it. We both chuckle at my slight wobble.

"Are you okay to stand? I can carry you if you'd like." His large hand cups my face, his eyes soft with concern.

"I'm good. I'll just nip upstairs to your flat and change into something a little more…" We both look down at my underwear. Not that wearing this would raise even a brow in the Club, but my plane Jane ensemble would look out of place. He pulls the large blanket closed around me, effectively covering any bare skin. His possessiveness makes me glow with a pure, warm heat from my chest to my toes but also makes me chuckle. "I think that I'm covered now, Jason." I remark playfully. He grumbles something unrecognisable but probably very cute.

"We could stay here tonight if you would prefer?" He opens the door and takes my hand to lead me through.

"Oh…um…no, I need to…I mean, I would rather stay at mine tonight. I have a busy day and Leon said he would help me prep in the morning." I can't hide my smile.

"Your second interview?" Jason beams down at me, pulling me against his hard chest in a tight hug. "I'm sure it's just a formality. You have got this in the bag, beautiful, and if they don't offer you the job, we have a legal department at

Stone that would snap you up."

"Miss being my boss that much, hmm?"

"Oh, baby, I am still your boss."

We start to walk along the corridor, and I nudge him hard in his side at his comment. "Hey, I have soft places, too, you know."

"Not many, but I at least know where they are," I tease and poke my finger at one of those places, causing him to curse.

"Thank you for the kind offer, but if I don't get this job, I'll just keep looking. I'm not in a hurry, and I really like the idea of working at the Mission. The first interview went really well, and the letter said they would tell me tomorrow either way. I like that they won't keep me waiting. I hate the anticipation; it's a killer." I admit.

"The anticipation is the best bit." His tone drops and is thick with sensual intent as he flips the conversation from real life to desire on a dime. I shiver and melt from his gaze. "That's not true. It's one of the best bits, but with you, there are too many best bits to count." His grin morphs from salacious to nefarious. "But in an ever-changing top ten, I would have to say number one goes to coming in your arse as you nearly pass out from my choke hold."

"Jinx." I hold his gaze and watch his eyes darken before me, causing a delicious melting heat to pool between my legs. He grabs my chin, his touch a mix of rough and forceful.

"Get changed and meet me in the bar. Don't take long, because I need to fuck you so hard the first question they will ask you tomorrow is would you would like a cushion to sit on," he growls.

"Ah, Jason, you say the sweetest things." I purr, running my finger down his chest.

"Don't I, though?" He grins but it falters, and his breath catches when I drag my nail down the length of his torso. His button down shirt prevents me from scoring his skin, but it isn't tucked in at the bottom, and I hook my finger just under the waistband of his lounge pants. Skin touching skin. I can see his straining erection lying heavy and hard against the thin material, and if I dip just a little further inside, I would feel the velvety smooth head of his cock. My hand is now pressed flat on his tummy, fingertips aligned with the point of his delicious V, just poised to slide down and grab what is mine. The anticipation crackles between us like caged lightning; so much pleasure, but just out of reach. He sucks in a breath when I slowly drag my fingernails up and down his happy trail, a torturous touch I repeat twice before I snap my hand free. His jaw flexes and a deep, frustrated moan rumbles in his chest.

"You will pay for that," he groans.

"Oh, I hope so," I tease and turn to escape up the stairs to his flat. He manages to get the last retort with a sound slap to my arse before I am at safe distance.

I bounce down the stairs not five minutes later. I have a small drawer in his large chest of drawers and some hanging space in Jason's bedroom. I slip on a pair of skinny black jeans and a black chain link top that skims my boobs and is mostly backless with a crisscross of spaghetti straps. My wedges aren't the highest but are studded and sexy with an edge of BDSM glamour. I freeze when I hit the main room.

I don't fucking believe it.

I know I left him with a raging hard on, but he couldn't wait five fucking minutes before he is sticking his tongue down someone's throat? At the far end of the bar, Jason is entwined around a girl I don't recognise. I can't really see much of her face since he is devouring it. A gut wrenching pain is subdued at the moment by pure, unadulterated anger. He said we needed to make sure we talk if there's a problem and not run away. I know my fragile self is all about self-preservation and wants to do just that but I'm not a fucking damsel this time, and I will not run. In this club, I am still Selina, top Dominatrix, even if I no longer carry my whip. I take a deep breath and walk over to the happy couple. Without pausing, I lean around them, grab his beer and her sticky red cocktail, holding both glasses high I tip the contents over their joined heads.

I don't even slam the glasses down I merely place then on the bar and offer an apologetic smile to the wide-eyed bar girl. I turn to strut away, oblivious to the stream of profanity echoing behind me. I barely make it a single step when I hit the solid wall of a familiar chest. White button down shirt, narrow trim waist and a glimpse of soft hair where his shirt is not tucked in properly. I drag my eyes up the firm, toned chest, broad strong shoulder. Up and up, chiselled jaw that is pulsing nicely, deep, furrowed brow and piercing dark eyes that are currently boring through me with disbelief. *Shit.*

That can't be right. He was at the bar. I know it. I would recognise him anywhere. Hell, I would recognise him blindfolded. I spin around to see the man I assumed was Jason stand and attempt to pat himself dry with ridiculously small cocktail napkins. He is drenched. It was nearly a full pint, and he took the motherlode, his companion barely took a splash by the look of her. She scowls at me and mutters something. The man looks up. Those eyes, that brow, he straightens and towers even at this distance, and that jaw is also ticking. Jason, I step back and jump when the other Jason, *my* Jason, holds my forearms to prevent me from retreating any farther. Not that I could go anywhere, I am flush against him, my back to his front.

"I see you've met my twin." Jason can't hide his own amusement. I can feel his body shake with pent up laughter, but I am mortified, and Jason's brother looks really pissed.

"Oh, God, I'm sorry. Will is it?" I step forward and offer my hand. He looks at me, at my extended hand and smirks. He glances above me, over my shoulder at Jason, who has stopped trying to hold back his laughter and is now making a racket behind me. I cringe but Will pulls me into a hug. I'm not sure if it is meant as a forgiving gesture or to ensure I soak up my fair share of the beer that his shirt has absorbed. The latter works. He releases me, and I now carry the unmistakable aroma of hops and maybe malt, my skin is damp, and glistens with the residue the napkin had failed to dry.

"And you must be Sam." His voice has the same deep timbre, but he has a soft hint of an American drawl.

"I'm so sorry, Will." I rush again to apologise. His once white shit now resembles a strawberry coloured Rorschach test as the cocktail I deposited seeps across the fibres. My face heats uncomfortably, and I turn to deflect my embarrassment.

"Why didn't you tell me your brother was here?" I narrow my eyes.

"What, and miss this?" Jason snickers but backs away with his hands up in surrender. "Hey, hey stand down soldier. I didn't know. I swear." He grins and chuckles. "I'm not saying I would've told you if I'd thought for a moment I would get this kind of floor show, but I honestly didn't know." He pulls me into his own bear hug defusing any rising anger. I'm not angry; I'm just dying of embarrassment. Jason whispers, "I fucking love it when you go all possessive of me, beautiful." He kisses my hair, and I peek up through my lashes to see his brilliant, heart-stopping smile.

"Not sure your brother would share your view." I shake my head against his chest, still feeling shamefaced but also a little better.

"Oh, I think my brother would love to *share* my view." I snap my head up. His eyes darken, my mouth is instantly dry, and my core is immediately soaked. Jason chuckles at my wide eyes and hitched breath. He wiggles his brow mischievously and grabs my hand to lead me to the now vacant seat next to his brother.

"Will, I am really sorry I thought—" Will lets out a dirty laugh, interrupting me.

"I can imagine what you thought, but from what Jason tells me, there is zero chance of him playing away, darling." He winks and does this non-verbal code thing with Jason. A series of subtle—well, not so subtle—facial ticks and grins.

We take our fresh drinks over to a corner booth and sit, Jason on one side with his arm proprietarily over my shoulder, Will on my other side, his legs stretched so wide one thigh is touching mine. He has also discarded his shirt and is just as gloriously toned as Jason. I can't help but wonder if the mirror image is reflective all the way down. I take a sip of my drink, which does nothing to wet my parched throat; I doubt any liquid will. He is just as charming as his brother, and I am a little mesmerised.

"Is that okay with you, beautiful?" Jason's warm breath brushes my neck, and I shiver, but I have no idea what he asked. I actually have no idea what conversation has passed between him and his brother in the half hour we have been sitting here. Christ, it's like I've never sat between two attractive men before. I shake myself.

"Sorry, what was that?" I look up into Jason's smiling eyes.

"All right, beautiful, I think it's time I got you home. I think you've had enough excitement for one day, don't you?" His knowing tone makes my face flush and my legs clench. I'm shameless. Jason chuckles and taps my nose. "Will is going to be here *all* week, Sam, but you have an important day tomorrow, yes?"

"Oh, yes." I let out a breath I didn't realise I was holding, and shake my head. What the fuck has gotten into me? I can feel my face burn a little brighter. Jeeze could I be any more obvious? "You're right, I do." I push against Jason, moving us closer to the edge of the booth seat and nearer to my escape before I make more of an exhibition of my wantonness than I already have. Jason holds one hand but I offer the other awkwardly to Will when I say goodbye. He grabs it and pulls sharply. I slap my hand on his chest to stop me from head-butting him on the chin. He tips my chin up just like his brother does, and I swallow thickly. His smiles spreads like warm honey lighting his face as his eyes darken. I've seen those eyes; I know that look. I fight to hold in the whimper that is just itching to make itself known. He plants a tender kiss on my cheek and helps me to steady myself.

"It's really nice to meet you, Will, and again, I'm really sorry for earlier."

"Oh, I'm sure you'll make it up to me." He grins.

"Maybe." Jason's warning tone surprises me, given all the overt flirting that has been flying unchecked from all directions this evening.

"Your call, brother." Will shrugs; his smile is affable and wide.

"No, it's *our* call." Jason chuckles as my whole body gives a full-on involuntary shudder.

"What's with the ice pack on your pussy or is Jason really that hot?" Leon laughs out.

"Please don't call it that; you know I hate that word." I scrunch my nose up with distaste. Another throwback piece of baggage I have repugnant Richard to thank for. I get an actual taste of vomit in my mouth thinking about the vile way he would repeatedly insult me with that word. Leon rolls his eyes. He knows I hate it, but I doubt he'll pander to my sensitivity. He is happy to try and desensitise me with its use. It's just a word.

"What would you prefer? Foof, nuun, hooha, mini, whim wam or my personal favourite c—"

"Fine!" I screech my interruption. "Fine, pussy is fine." I bite my lips together at his shit-eating grin.

"Yes it is, mighty fine." He waggles his brows, his playful grin reaching far and wide, making me laugh. I wince at the sudden muscle movement and carefully move the pack as the ice has started to warm. I really need the numbing qualities of the freezing temperature.

"I treated myself to a full Hollywood wax yesterday but failed to adhere to the golden rule, maybe I am a masochist after all." I pout.

"Nah, your pussy is too much of a pussy for pain if you're nursing like that after a simple beauty treatment and a little heavy pounding from lover boy." He chuckles at my scowl.

"Simple? There is nothing simple about…never mind." I shake my head at the futility of explaining pain thresholds to a masochist.

He arches his brow and continues to snicker. "It's no different for a back, sack and crack, babe. No pain no gain." He waves off my discomfort. "You want a drink to aid the numbing?"

"It's a little early." I glance at my watch. It's mid-morning on a weekday but looking at Leon he looks like it might be hair of the dog time. "Late night or early morning?" I inquire.

"Week off." He flashes a wolfish smile.

I nod. I'm sure he must have told me but my head has been a little distracted.

"Ah, so hair of the dog then." He grins and pours himself a shot of whiskey in his espresso. "I'll have a camomile tea, though. It might help calm me." He pours some boiling water into a cup and fishes out a bag from one of the many jars lining the back wall of the kitchen. He saunters over and carefully slides to sit next to me.

"I'm sure your *foof* will recover, no need to get antsy." I take the cup with one hand and nudge him lightly with my shoulder. "Not that idiot. I find out today if I will be gainfully employed as junior solicitor at the Mission." I beam.

He slides his arm around my shoulder and pulls me in for a side hug. "You definitely don't need to be worried about that babe. They would be crazy not to bite your arm off, and if they don't I know my firm would snap you up."

"Thanks, but I really want to work somewhere that makes a difference."

"Hey, we do pro bono. It's not all fat cats and criminals." He scowls but his words hold no animosity.

"No, I know, honey, I didn't mean anything by that…It's just…This place is important to Jason, too. He told me about it on our first date, so it is just a little special that's all." I give a light shrug, and he squeezes my shoulder.

"Ah, my baby girl's fallen in love." He lightly teases, but his eyes are soft, his voice is full of happiness. I have no smart remark just an incredibly warm feeling radiating from my chest, consuming me from the inside out. "I'm happy for you, babe." He kisses me roughly on my head and we both let out sap-filled sighs. "So tell…why did you wax yesterday, when the probability of you not doing a round or two with marathon man was always going to be nil."

"It was our four-month anniversary." I smile sheepishly.

"And nothing says happy anniversary like a nice, bald pussy," Leon teases and knocks is liquor laced espresso back in one hit. I snort and nearly spill my own hot drink in my lap.

"Not exactly. I'm hardly pin-up for the nineteen seventies down there as it is. I just wanted to try hair free for our first rope session." Leon's smile widens. One hand has slipped down the front of his pants and he shifts his very obvious semihard cock around, a slow massage in the ample room of his loose fitted trousers. "You think you could maybe not masturbate while you are sitting right beside me." I huff.

"I'm not." He sounds affronted but his wicked grin is hardly serious. "Not yet,"—he draws in a slow breath holding the pregnant pause—"but please do go on." His tone drops from higher pitched insulted to low and deviant. I lift the ice pack and dump it hard in his lap. He sits bolt upright, throwing the pack down where it skids across the floor. "Fuck, Sam! I was kidding! Did the waxing rip out your sense of humour, too?" he grumbles, rubbing his injured pride and joy.

"My foof is raw. I'm a nervous wreck about my interview, and my best friend is jacking off at my discomfort. Tell me which bit of that is funny," I snap, and he has the decency to look a little contrite. He drapes his long arm once more over my shoulders and pulls me more against his chest. He plants a heavy, apologetic kiss on my hair.

"I'm sorry, babe." I relax into his hold. I didn't realise how much tension I was holding until I let it go. "Four months and an evening of Shibari," he muses. "Why it's almost like you've skipped the awkward dating phase and gone straight to white picket fence." He places his hand on his heart, sighs heavily and bats his long lashes. His light mocking tone makes me smile even as his reference to a happy ending makes my chest ache. These four months have been, without exception, the best of my life.

"So tell me about the ropes. Was playing Tarzan all you hoped?" He winks and I sit back up and shuffle to face him.

"It was more…Oh, God, it was…I cried." My voice holds a fraction of the wonder I felt yesterday, but he smiles with understanding.

"He hurt you?" His shock is misplaced.

"God no, not at all. But, after, I mean…the aftercare, I just burst out crying. I couldn't hold it in. I didn't want to. It felt—" I look to the heavens for inspiration to put words in my head fitting enough to describe the indescribable.

"Cathartic?" he offers with a warm smile.

"Yes." I grin as the word I had been struggling to articulate fits so perfectly. "Exactly that. I've never felt anything like it." I exhale a deep satisfying breath as a flood of memories wash like a warm wave of pleasure across my mind.

"It's addictive." His tone is a light warning.

"I can imagine." I exhale still holding on to the memory.

"No, seriously, it's addictive. You think I feel any different when we play?" He raises a good point I hadn't considered.

"I didn't think about it. I mean I know I've elicited tears before, from clients, but I assumed that was from the pain aspect." I chew my bottom lip as I mull over these thoughts.

"It can be but if their experience is anything like mine, it's from the pleasure…the release and yes, you are really *that* good." He shakes his head dismissively like I am an idiot for not comprehending this before now. "Surely you must've known this?"

"How would I?" My tone is a little defensive. "I've fucked other guys, but not many, and there was rarely any kink involved. Even my session with Daniel was more about understanding the Dom/sub role in a play situation. I have just never been brought to that level of…hmm…" I let out a huge sigh.

"Subspace." He grins.

"Yeah, that. I've obviously seen it but never felt it. It's nice." My smile is wide at my own understatement. He lets out a laugh and rolls his eyes. "Oh, I'll tell you what else is nice…Jason's identical twin. I met him last night." I wriggle my brows, and he sits to attention.

"Really?" Leon drawls and raises an inquiring brow, silently waiting for me to elaborate.

"Identical." I repeat and fan myself. His laugh is deep and throaty. I tell Leon about the brief encounter, the misunderstanding, the drinks and the secret codes.

"You think all that nodding and winking was some sort of tag team code for twins?" he asks.

"It wasn't so much nodding and winking. It was more subtle and much more intense. The sexual tension between us was like a physical thing sitting at the table. It might as well have been a fourth person it was so obvious."

"If you are accepting applications for a fourth person, baby girl, you better include me in the tag team of a lifetime." He fixes me with a stare that is perfect mix of playful and absolutely serious.

I cough and splutter, my tea spraying far and wide. "Leon, it's a fantasy!" I gasp and shake my head as the delicious images of such a fantasy bombard me. "I just got a little carried away last night. I think I was still high on endorphins from the rope play. It's just a fantasy...and fantasy is very different from reality."

"Not for people like us, baby girl." He winks.

"People like us?"

"Card carrying members of the Club." He waggles his brow conspiratorially. My phone buzzes in my back pocket interrupting my full on chuckle. "A fair point." My smile fades when I get a message flash up from a number I don't recognise. I swipe the screen to reveal the full text.

Hello Sam, It's Peitra please don't press delete, I want to apologise. It's my last day as an intern at Stone Enterprises. I haven't applied for a full-time position here. I doubt I would get offered a place if I did. I don't deserve to work here after the appalling way I behaved. I am utterly ashamed of how I spoke to you and how I went after Jason when I knew full well he had a girlfriend. I can't imagine what you think of me. Actually, I can, and I deserve it. But I wanted to say sorry and maybe take you for lunch today as way of apology. It isn't nearly enough, but since I am going away for a few months tomorrow it is the least I can do. Please let me do this. As one of Sofia's best friends it is likely we will see each other at some point in the future, and I would like this opportunity to clear the air. If you are free, there is a new place opened just off Piccadilly called The Alpha Bar. I've heard the food is good. I have made a reservation for one o'clock. If you don't come, I completely understand, and again, I am truly sorry. xP

I had read the message several times when in a huff of frustration Leon snatches the phone from my hand and reads it himself.

"Wow." Leon hands me my phone back.

"I know." I stare at the message like it has something else to reveal. "Should I go?"

"Do you think she's being sincere?"

"I don't know. I don't know her at all. She's nothing like her cousin, but the text certainly reads like she means it." I lift my shoulders and let them drop heavily. I'm stumped. "I did not see this coming."

"Could it be a trap?" He raises a cautious brow.

"A trap for what?" I shake my head at his dramatics.

"I don't know. She could spike your drink and stage some compromising scenario to photograph you in and blackmail."

"A little elaborate don't you think? It's not like Jason doesn't have compromising photographs of me already." I grin at his mock shocked face. "Besides, it's not like Jason is going to take her back. He was not happy, and I doubt she still thinks she has a chance with him." I mutter.

"But, hell hath no fury and all that." Leon raises a very good point.

"Oh, I'm sure she was furious, but that ship has sailed, and she says herself we are going to bump into one another. Maybe she is genuine."

"In my profession I tend to see the dark side more than the light. Except with you babe…you are all light." He nudges me and I wrinkle my nose at his compliment.

"Okay, I'll meet her but if photos do appear on the internet explain to Jason that we *did* have our doubts, and I didn't just bound over to meet her like a big, dumb dog."

"And don't accept any unsealed drinks," he warns me. I scoff and point an acknowledging salute at his retreating form.

"Right you are, Dad." He ruffles my hair and jumps up from the sofa.

"What time's your interview?"

"Three thirty, so I have plenty of time to kiss and make up and then head over. I'll just drop Jason a text to let him know."

"Call me when you're done." He waits until I acknowledge his request.

"The interview?" I clarify.

"Both…I want to know you're safe and I want to get the champagne on ice to celebrate." He flashes his bright smile, white teeth a sharp contrast against his permanently dark tanned skin.

"Thanks, Leon." He leans over the back of the sofa to plant a soft kiss on the top of my head.

"Love ya, babe, but I have to crash," he groans.

"You can sleep after a shot of whiskey and a double espresso?" I chuckle.

"Watch and learn, baby…watch and learn." He waves his hand, his back disappearing into the hallway without a backward glance.

The Alpha Bar is in the basement. There is a bijoux art gallery above selling an eclectic mix of mostly modern art. In the centre of the large display window is a striking piece. I find myself staring for some time at the impressive glass sculpture. It's an abstract piece, I think, but to me it looks like a deep wave folding in on itself. The aquamarine colour darkens to almost black as the depth of the glass deepens, just like the ocean. I look up to catch a pair of kind grey eyes staring back at me. I give a little wave, which makes the gentleman in the gallery smile, but he doesn't return my wave. He motions to the door, which has a typed sign indicating viewing by appointment only, and I quickly shake my head and point to the entrance of the club. He nods in understanding, and I wave again, this time turning away. I descend the steps and am greeted by a young, immaculately dressed young woman, whose platinum blonde hair is scrapped back into a neat bun. Her bright red lipstick matches my own, and I recognise the shade. Unless I'm mistaken, it's a Chanel ninety-seven Desinvolte Rouge. She smiles tightly and asks me to follow her when I politely decline to give her my coat. I think to myself I might need to make a speedy getaway if this all goes tits up.

The room is dimly lit with a small drop bulb hanging over each table but casting little in the way of actual light. The dark walls have black and white artwork and old cityscape photographs. The tables all have crisp white linen and gleaming silverware. The seats are covered in dark leather and the fittings are highly polished steel. Modern with no atmosphere, it may be different when filled with patrons, but at this time, it has a creepy, clinical feel to it. The room is empty but for a lone barman, and seated in the rear right corner of the room is Peitra. I get a rush of nervous knots in my tummy, but she smiles brightly and I am happy the feeling quickly dissipates. She stands and reaches for my hand, grabbing it tightly in both of hers.

"I am so glad you came, Sam. I can't tell you." She rushes her words, flustered, and an anxious expression settles on her features. She motions for me to sit beside her on the padded bench.

"I was a little surprised to get your message." I draw in a deep steadying breath as I feel my nerves begin to rise unbidden. This is stupid. I shake myself; it's probably the thought of my interview later playing in my subconscious.

The waiter arrives with two aperitifs. I think about my conversation with Leon and shake myself again. The nerves are not only making me a wreck, they are inducing paranoia, too.

"I hope you don't mind. I ordered some drinks for us. I'm so nervous and honestly if you hadn't shown up I would've drunk them both anyway." Her smile is brief but friendly, almost shy. I return her smile and try to push my own worries aside. Still something in the way her eyes flit around the empty room is unsettling, and I don't know what possesses me, but just as she reaches for her glass I switch, placing mine before her and taking her drink as my own. Her face is impassive, but her lips start to tip upward and she slowly picks her glass up. My eyes are fixed on her lips and I exhale a stupid breath when she takes a large sip. I feel ridiculous. I take a large unladylike chug of the prosecco, grateful for the little buzz, cooling liquid and bubble. The glass is almost empty when I place it on the table. Her smile, which has remained fixed, purses to life as she raises her glass and spits her very full mouthful back into the flute.

"I'm so sorry, Sam." Her saccharin voice is as sickening as the smile that distorts her face with cold cruelty. It doesn't reach her eyes.

"Peitra?" I blow out a breath. I feel hot and a little queasy. My arms slide from the table and drop heavily at my side. They feel all wrong, so heavy. Peitra lifts my hand, and in my mind I yank it out of her hold but nothing happens.

"No, Sam," she repeats slowly as if speaking to a small child. "I'm really sorry for *you*." She slips the cuff Jason gave me from my hand and I shout at her and pull free. Only I don't...I don't move, maybe I slip a little further down in my seat but that is all I manage.

I feel exhausted. Maybe if I have a nap now, when I wake, I will be able to slap that bitch up. It feels like someone has placed large, fuzzy muffs over my ears. I can't hear exactly what's being said. I don't recognise the words, and I am having trouble focusing on anything because everything is as fuzzy as the sounds I hear and everything is moving. The last image of hanging bulbs bright above me dissolves to blackness.

SIXTEEN

Jason

"Sandy, my brother is meeting me for a late lunch. Don't let him go walking around the other departments firing people like he did last time. Daniel didn't find that amusing, and I could do without the icy glares that took months to die down." Sandy grimaces and nods, fully appreciative of the chaos Will had created the last time he visited me at headquarters. He may be a respectable scientist on the other side of the pound, but here he tends to delight in causing carnage at my expense.

"Will do, Mr Sinclair. Would you like security to keep him downstairs?" She bites her lips to hide her smile. Will also managed to bypass security and reset my clearance with his own fingerprint. He was only in the building for ten minutes.

"No, I don't want him anywhere near security. Just let him come straight to my office. But make sure he takes the express lift. Get Eddie to accompany him to be safe." I pointedly raise a knowing brow, and she nods in agreement.

"Good idea. I will call down to the front desk to make sure they know to expect him." I turn and notice my office door is closed.

"Is there someone in my office, Sandy?"

"Not that I'm aware, but then I have been in a department meeting for the last half an hour. Would you like me to check?" She pushes back from her chair, but I wave my hand for her to remain seated.

"No, its fine." I flash her an easy smile that always causes her cheeks to pink. She is an attractive woman in her late fifties, still turning heads and fiercely protective of me. As gatekeepers go there is no one better. I bet that feisty attitude keeps her husband on his toes. I smile thinking of my own someone keeping me on my toes.

"Would you like a coffee?" She interrupts my wayward thoughts.

"That would be great, thank you." I turn and walk to my door. The handle squeaks, and I push the door wide. Peitra is standing by my desk and nearly jumps a clear foot in the air with shock. Her face is a flash of panic but settles into an awkward, fixed smile. It's her last day, and I can't say I'm *not* relieved at the notion that she will be leaving the company permanently.

"Mr Sinclair." She smiles quickly but still looks nervous. I glance around the room to check for something amiss. The room has minimal furniture as it is, and I have a clear desk policy, so there are no loose papers with confidential information I need to be concerned with. My laptop is on the desk but it is closed and has fingerprint security. My jacket is hanging over the back of my chair but my wallet is in my trouser pocket. I don't know why I feel the need to do this mini inventory. I don't believe she is a thief, but I also don't entirely trust her, either. I walk around my desk and sit down. I subtly check the weight of the pockets on my suit jacket. I lift my phone free from the inside pocket and flip it open. No missed calls, no messages and no dialled numbers. I snap it shut and fix Peitra with an impassive stare.

"Is there some specific reason you are in my office with the door closed?" She flashes a timid smile, and she won't hold eye contact. If I wasn't so suspicious, I might put that down to her being intimidated or uncomfortable that our last interaction wasn't pleasant. But I read people, and that's not it at all. She is really nervous.

"I tried to catch you before your morning meeting, but I must have just missed you anyway, Um…well, I wanted to thank you, and I wanted to apologise." She rushes her words, her hands are clasped in front of her, threaded together and twisting. Her feet shuffle like she can't physically keep still. She is clearly anxious to leave, but she *chose* to come here. She could've said what she wanted to say in an email, as if reading my inscrutable face and mind, she starts to talk.

"I realise I could've put this in a letter, but I wanted to say it to your face." She struggles to swallow, and I almost feel sorry for her obvious disquiet. "However awkward and painful it is, and believe me, this is really painful." She tries to laugh, but it falls flat. She shakes herself and straightens her back. "I behaved appallingly and I hope you can forgive me." She nods to punctate and finish her point.

"It's not my place to forgive you, Peitra." I narrow my glare.

"No, no, I know, and I hope in time Sam will be able to forgive me." Her eyes drop to her hands, but her lips start to curl. She is beginning to really piss me off.

"I wouldn't hold your breath." I snap. Her eyes widen with surprise, maybe she is genuine, but more than likely, she is looking for another opportunity. I won't make that mistake again. "Is there anything else?" I have already dismissed her in my mind as I open up my laptop and swipe my finger to unlock the screen.

"No, nothing at all. Just if in the future…" She pauses, her soft breathy statement hangs pungent in the air. I fix my incredulous glare, and she withers a little.

"What the fuck! Seriously?" I glower. She hurries for the door, but her parting remark is as snide as it is cryptic.

"Things change, Jason." The door slams and I actually sink back in my chair relieved that she's gone.

"Can I get you gentleman anything else?" The young waiter with the trimmed goatee and full sleeve tats has read back our lunch order but I am just checking my phone, leaving Will to confirm our selection.

"Just drinks, two beers and a vagina for my brother." He addresses the waiter with a level voice and a deadpan delivery. I look up at Will, who is looking in all seriousness at the waiter. The waiter has lifted his pen from his pad mid word. I can see from here he was well on his way to writing the word vag when it must have registered what he was writing.

"I'm sorry sir, what was it you wanted?" His face is a picture of confusion, poor guy.

"Oh, my mistake. You see my brother here has turned into a massive teenage girl and all that's missing is the actual vagina." The waiter grins, and I reach over and discreetly nut punch Will, wiping the grin from his face and bringing a slew of tears to his eyes. I turn to face the waiter while my brother coughs and curses, but he has made a hasty retreat.

"You're so fucking funny, Will. You know that waiter actually started writing that down. You're such an arse." I go to flick the cover on my phone for the hundredth time but stop myself when I catch a glance of his righteous and overtly smug face.

"Truth hurts, baby brother, but I can't say I blame you. She is smoking hot." Will takes the beer the waiter places in front of him and downs half in one go. I do the same and exhale. He is partially right; she probably hasn't even finished her interview yet. She promised she would call when she was done. I just don't want to miss her call in case she doesn't get the job and needs me. It's crazy to think she wouldn't get the position, but I still don't want to miss her call. I absently tap the closed phone cover. The volume is on high and vibrate so I won't miss her call.

"She's all that and more." I take another sip of the iced beer that is sliding down way too easy for this time of the day.

"Yeah, I'm getting that." Will flashes a brilliant wide smile. His tan is much darker than mine. All those hours in the Florida sun counting turtles or fish or whatever the fuck he does. "I'm happy for you man, but how long are you gonna last in a one on one relationship?" he challenges with a tilt of his head and a knowing smile. Apart from a few years Will spent in the wilderness, we are tight. I trust him with my life, and he knows me. He may not share my tastes to the same extent, but he is far from vanilla.

"Who says I am?" I counter his smugness with my own. He balks and barks out a deep laugh.

"Yeah, right…You are not the cheating type, so what gives?" He narrows his eyes at my silence. "I know she was at your club, but you can't be serious…she plays?" He shifts in his seat and turns to face me fully, his expression alight with surprise and disbelief.

"*We* play." I correct. "It's early days. I know she is game but honestly I'm not sure I am…not with her." I try to shrug off my statement but he splutters, making it much more of a deal than I wanted to discuss over a late lunch.

"What! You're kidding?" His eyes widen with surprise.

"I'm not. I saw the way she looked at you, and I could just about control my rage because it's you. The thought of anyone else touching her, and all I see is red mist. Hell, I am ready to do time for that woman." I laugh but I'm deadly serious.

"Fuck, you're totally screwed." Will chuckles and clinks his glass to mine.

"Yeah, I am." I grin and join him with a more relaxed, deep belly laugh.

"Damn, so no sharing, hmm?" Will muses playfully.

"Now, I didn't say that, did I?" I bite my lips to stop my own grin, but Will's is wide enough for the both of us.

"I think you did." He corrects but his brows are arched high with excited expectation.

"No, I said I didn't like the *idea* of sharing. But the whole threesome thing is a fantasy of hers. Something she's never done, and that is definitely something I want to give her." Will's grin spreads even wider, and I fight the tiny embers of jealousy that flicker inside. I check myself. This is my choice after all. I could do this for her with someone I trust…*maybe*. We finish our meal and catch up. I haven't seen him in months, but it's like I saw him yesterday. I promise to take Sam out to visit, and he promises to take us both out for a spin in one of the

Coast Guard high speed boats. He has been seconded to them to help with illegal trade in tropical fish. I knew he did something with fish. The food was good and the conversation has kept me distracted. I check my watch, the time approaches six o'clock, and I only now think to check my phone.

No messages.

I get a sinking feeling that this can't be good. She really wanted the job at the Mission. I *really* wanted her to get this job for purely selfish reasons. I hate to contemplate the consequences of not getting it and the possibility that she would doubt her choice and return to her career as a Dominatrix.

"Still no messages." I flick the phone shut at his observation. "She could be out celebrating." Will tries to comfort me.

"She would've called if that was the case. Look, do you mind if we swing by her place? If she hasn't called, it's probably not good news." I slide out from the curved bench and fish in my pocket for my wallet.

"Wouldn't she call you with that too though?" Will replaces his when I tip more than enough bills in to the centre of the table.

"No. She wouldn't want to ruin your night." I grab my jacket and pass him his from the hook on the edge of the booth.

"Why would it ruin my night?"

"Because I would bail on you, you fucking idiot!" I shake my head. "Christ, it's a good job you got some of my looks, because you sure struck out in the brains department."

"Cute and it's a good job I got the lion's share in the junk department, because your girl is going to need me now, since you've traded in your dick in for lady parts." His shoulders start to shake with amusement.

"Arsehole." I punch him in his shoulder, catching him hard but he laughs then curses and rubs the impact spot. His laughter is now uncontrollable, but he does get out one last comeback.

"Thundercunt."

I burst out laughing at his insult. "I like that…I might get a t-shirt." I join his laughter now as we leave the restaurant and head toward Sam's apartment.

I wait impatiently for Sam to buzz me in, checking my phone one more time. I can see Will shake his head in my periphery but I don't care. The buzzer sounds and I push through and immediately start pounding on her front door. The large shadow that appears on the other side of the split glass panelled door makes my heart sink. Leon swings it wide, half asleep and running his hand through his hair. I push past, not bothering with an introduction.

"Jesus man, don't you own a shirt?" I mutter.

"I just woke up." I hear him yawn.

Sam's room is empty. Several outfits are laid out on her bed where she'd obviously been choosing what to wear for her interview. I get a tight pinch in my chest thinking how my confident girl must have actually been quite nervous given the number of clothes strewn across the bed and hanging off the wardrobe doors. I can't actually see the covers underneath. Nothing else seems out of place though. I turn sharply and walk back to the front door where Leon is rubbing his eyes and staring blankly at Will.

"Leon, this is Will." My introduction is curt, and I nod to motion Will to follow me into the flat. Will shakes Leon's hand they chat about something or nothing but end up beside me in the living room.

"Where is she?" I snap. Leon looks at his watch, and his brows start to furrow. He looks up at me, and his face pales. It's not that late, I know. She could just as easily have met a friend and got caught up catching up. So why does Leon look ill?

"Leon, where the fuck is she?" He doesn't answer but strides off to his room. He returns instantly with his phone. He silently flicks through, and I can feel my bubbling anger begin to rise. "For fuck sake, Leon, where is she?"

"I don't know, man. I just wanted to check if she'd texted. The last one I got was her asking me to wish her luck."

"Before her interview, so that would be what, three twenty?" I rub the pressure that is building in my temples.

"No, one twenty five just before her lunch with Peitra." Leon's words are like a sucker punch, but they make no sense.

"What are you talking about?"

"She texted you, Jason. I saw her do it. She forwarded the message Peitra had sent her about wanting to apologise. She offered to take Sam to lunch, her way of saying sorry." Leon's tone would have irritated me if he didn't look so fucking worried.

"She never sent me a text. I haven't heard from her since this morning when I gave her a kiss goodbye. What the fuck are you talking about?" I yell.

"Okay, okay, why don't we all just take a breath and calm the fuck down." Will steps in, he places a calming hand on my shoulder, and as much as I want to shrug him off, losing it now will not help. I take the suggested deep breath and walk over to the kitchen. I perch on the edge of one of the stools. This makes no sense, but my gut starts twisting uncomfortably all the same. I open my phone and start scrolling. It's possible she may have emailed me the message and not texted. It's possible it could've gone into my junk folder, but even as I quickly scour the screen for her familiar username, I know that isn't the case.

"I didn't get her message." My flat voice holds none of the raging emotions surging through me. I need to hold this together. I need to find Sam.

"She sent it I swear—"

"I believe you, Leon," I interrupt. I can see Leon looks just as worried. "Peitra was in my office just before lunch. I checked my phone at the time and there was nothing, no missed calls but I didn't check the deleted folder." Leon peers over my shoulder.

"But your deleted folder is empty?" He points to the little waste bin icon with the content counter at zero.

"No, I didn't check the other deleted folder. Anything that gets deleted goes to a hidden folder." I tap Tax codes folder and my screen fills with hundreds of lines of data. "It's not really hidden just labelled Tax Codes no one would actually want to open that folder." I shrug when Leon adds his agreement. "Anyway the point is nothing is ever really deleted but only a few people know that. Daniel is a little OCD when it comes to security, and I can't tell you how fucking glad I am that he is…look." I tilt the screen, which now holds Sam's message along with her question that if I thought she shouldn't go, to text her right back. *Fuck.* I quickly search my phone for the tracker on her cuff and can see it's still active which unfortunately gives me little comfort. It doesn't necessarily mean she is safe. It does mean her cuff, at least is in one piece and is still at the address she was meeting Peitra. Like I say, not much comfort.

I march to the front door with Will at my heel.

"Wait!" Leon calls. "I'm coming with you!"

I nod my approval but don't break my stride. In the taxi, Leon is busy getting dressed. I didn't stop to wait but he bundled enough clothes together and came running from the building. Barefoot and sporting just his boxers but he was just in time to catch the taxi door as I went to slam it shut. I spend the time making some calls. I call my head of security, Patrick, to alert the authorities. Not sure what I am alerting them to but I insist some sort of call is made. I speak to the office manager at the Mission and confirm Sam never turned up for her interview and she didn't call to explain why. My last call is to Daniel. I don't even care if the guy is on extended paternity leave and has a new baby to contend with; all I care about is Sam.

The taxi slows enough for the red light on the door to change to green and I am out of the vehicle and taking the steps down to the bar two at a time. The door is wedged open and several men in paint splattered overalls are working in the room. Dust sheets cover the tables, chairs and the bar at the back of the room. The smell of wet paint is strong but the room looks nearly finished, other than the sheets. I check my phone again for the tracker signal. I'm definitely in the right place.

"Can I help you mate?" One of the painters, a big guy, more fat than fit, wanders over to us now that Will and Leon have joined me. They look just as confused as I feel.

"My girlfriend was here for lunch." I say. His expression is comical as he looks around at the empty room amused at my statement. The place is clearly not ready to start trading.

"I don't think so." He gives a hearty laugh and his colleagues join in. I stiffen because there is fuck-all humour in this situation. I feel Will's hand on my shoulder easing me back. I hadn't even noticed how tight my fist was clenched.

"Do you mind if we have a look around?" Will smiles with an easy charm that isn't remotely confrontational. I'm glad he's here.

"Sure, I don't see why not." He nods and backs away to allow us into the room. I quickly walk through the main room and spend the next fifteen minutes checking every door, cupboard and room. *Nothing.* I run my hands through my hair in agitation. This fucking stinks. Leon and Will have both conducted their own search will equal fruitless results. The man approaches again.

"Find what you're looking for?" He grins but it's more taunting than malicious. I shake my head and let out a heavy breath.

"Not exactly but maybe the police will have more luck." I reach for my phone.

"I'm sorry." A young lad blurts out behind the big man in front of me. We all turn to look.

"You're sorry about what Jay?" the big guy grumbles.

"It was on the floor I thought it was lost property." He fumbles in his overalls, his face a picture of guilt and apology. He holds his hand out as far from his body as humanly possible. The shine from the platinum reflects the overhead lights and glimmers when he opens his fingers. Sam's cuff rests in his flat palm. I close my eyes, and my body starts to shake. I feel Leon step around me and I open my eyes to see him take the cuff from the young lad.

"Did you see the girl…did you see the girl who wore this?" Leon holds the cuff up so everyone in the room could see. They all fall silent but slowly shake their heads. "It's really important guys. If you saw her, you need to tell us," he urges.

"Honestly, mate, we haven't. I thought you were yanking my chain about lunch. We got here at five this afternoon to work overnight. The bar is supposed to open this weekend, but they haven't even installed the kitchen that's why I thought you were joking." He gives out a light laugh but snaps his mouth shut when I fix him with my glare. "I'm sorry, man, no one was here when we got here and I didn't know the lad had found anything until a minute ago." I turn away and pinch the pressure that is knotting nicely at the bridge of my nose.

"Okay, we believe you." Leon's voice is firm and seems to ease the growing tension. No one likes to be accused of lying, even if one of them is technically a thief.

"Come on we're wasting time." I state flatly and leave the basement.

On the street, I draw in a deep breath that does nothing to calm my volatile emotions. I lean against the railings and open my phone to check for any news. There is nothing. Will is standing silently to one side, and Leon is staring at the window display of the gallery above the bar.

"She was here." Will confirms but all I can do is nod. My phone buzzes, and I swipe to take Daniel's call.

"Peitra boarded a flight to Auckland at six this evening. She is due to stop in Singapore, and I have contacted the local authorities to make sure she is put on the first flight back. But that is still thirteen hours until you will get to speak to her and double that before she lands back in the UK and you can see her face to face."

"It might not be the best idea if I see her face to face." I grit out through my locked jaw. "Thanks though."

"Don't mention it. I will have Patrick alert the airports. Can you send over your most recent picture?" I let out a bitter laugh that hurts like a bitch.

"Not the most recent no, but I do have one I can send. I'll ping it over now."

"Good." He pauses and the silence is heavy. "We'll find her, Jason." His confidence goes some way to alleviating my worry, but it crashes once more with our next exchange. "What about her phone do you have a tracker on that?"

"It's switched off or broken. Either way, it's not working." I look up to the sky and silently pray. Without any other information that is all I have.

"Ah…" His silence speaks volumes. It is a big ass haystack of a world and my little needle is out there somewhere. "We'll find her, Jason." His assertion is absolute as he ends the call.

I turn and lean on the railings next to Leon, his eyes are fixed on the intricate glass sculpture in the window. The door to the gallery jingles open with the sound of the bells hanging above in an old fashion cast iron loop. An elderly gentleman fumbles with his keys in the lock. He turns to face us and tips his felt hat.

"My display seems to be working well at least. If only that would lead to a sale or two." He chuckles to himself and stands for a moment next to Leon, gazing at the display as we all are. "I did try and tempt a beautiful young lady earlier, she seemed to be just as enamoured as you gentlemen. But sadly no luck, just another window shopper." He turns to walk away and Leon nudges me sharply in the ribs.

"Give me your phone." He doesn't wait but snatches it from my hand and pushes into the man's face. The older man stumbles back a little but straighten and adjusts his glasses.

"Did she look like this?" Leon urges impatiently. The old man raises a bushy silver brow and chuckles.

"Well she did when she entered the bar." He leans in to whisper. "But she looked rather the worse for wear when she left. If you know what I mean." He taps his nose conspiratorially

"What *do you* mean?" I snap, startling him. He looks shocked at my sudden change in demeanour.

"Oh, forgive me. I meant no offence." His cheeks pink beneath his thick, grey beard, and he looks embarrassed.

"None taken, but please explain what you meant." I soften my voice. The last thing I need is him thinking *I'm* the dangerous person in this scenario.

"She had to be helped into the taxi. Well she was more carried actually come to think of it. Her head was terribly floppy. I just assumed she's overindulged in the vino department." He is about to chuckle again but one look in my eye and he wisely closes his mouth.

"And you didn't think that strange…You didn't think she might be in some sort of trouble?" Each word is spoken through an ever tightening jaw.

"Oh, you don't need to worry, she was with the owner. A terribly nice man, very well spoken." The old man waves his hand dismissively.

"His name?" My fingers are curled so tight I can feel the trickle of something warm as my nails puncture the skin of my palm.

"Mr Brookes-Hamilton, Richard to his friends." The old man puffs his chest out with pride that he obviously considers himself in that honoured category.

"You didn't happen to hear where they were going, did you?" My chest is tight and winded at the same time.

"I believe he said St Pancreas to the driver." The old man's eyes widen when they notice the slow drops of blood from my clenched fist.

"Fuck!" I curse to myself.

"Is that a problem?" Will steps up to me.

"We contacted the airports and docks but I doubt Daniel thought about the train. St Pancreas is the international station. If he gets her on a train she could end up in any number of European countries. Fuck!" I shout out to anyone in a five mile radius.

"Really sir, language." The old man glowers at me. "Richard Brookes-Hamilton is a respectable gentleman. I am sure you are mistaken with your concern for the young lady." His tone drips with disdain at my reaction to his 'friend'.

"Language! There is not language to accurately do Richard Brookes whatever-his-name-is justice but let me try. He is the *worst* of men, *sir.*" I can feel myself lose my tentative grip on my manners. "Just because he can pronounce his vowels like Prince Charles doesn't negate the fact that he is an abusive rapist, low life piece of shit." I snarl. "And now that fucking cunt has my girlfriend."

SEVENTEEN

Sam

Ow, fuck my head, no my stomach…legs. I draw in a breath and cry out. No definitely my chest hurts the most because it is torture just to breathe. I squint to open my eyes, the room is painfully bright but I am just going to add that to my never ending list of agonies. The bright striplight overhead makes it hard to focus but it's been like that every time I have started to regain consciousness. This time a least I feel more cognisant, less *high* but more nauseous. I am lying flat on a hard surface a few feet from the floor by the look of it. I try to sit up, but I have absolutely no strength. I peer down my body and can see several thick leather straps securing me to the bed. I can see the edge of my panties but I can't make out that I am wearing much more. The bindings cross my body at my shoulders, breasts, hips, thighs and ankles. The surface I am lying on feels like a slab of glass encrusted concrete against my skin but I am going to assume it's supposed to be a bed. I have certainly used it as such but I don't know for how long.

I relax against the bindings, even at full adrenaline-induced anger I wouldn't be able to break free from these straps. I use the exact same thing to secure my clients to the St Andrew's Cross in the full knowledge that they are only freed when I *say* they are free.

I close my eyes when my lids start to sting. How can my eyes lids hurt? I feel the tears trickle down my cheek and slide to the back of my neck, soaking into my hairline. I guess that would be why. But I must have been crying for some time for them to hurt like they do. My head throbs trying to work out what the fuck happened. What is the last thing I remember?

Fighting. I remember fighting and falling to the ground. Blood pouring from my mouth and being dragged by my hair. I think I got a punch or two in before I felt the sharp prick of a needle. But that wasn't the first time. *Think, damn it!* My head is throbbing and it feels like my brain is physically wading through thick sludge, picking out snippets of reality from my nightmares. This all feels like one fucking nightmare. I remember not quite waking but hearing voices, being manhandled but my muscles not responding. I can't recall much of what was said and the moment I opened my eyes I felt a dull pinch in my arm and then oblivion. My stomach growls an angry protest but I don't share its enthusiasm. I feel really sick. My mouth is like a cotton fuzz ball and I could down a litre of water and still be parched I am so thirsty.

Where the fuck am I? *Think Sam, what was the last useful thing you can remember?* My eyelids are already closed, and I try to focus my drifting mind. My blood is obviously still swilling with whatever has been pumped in my veins to keep me catatonic. I can see a solid ocean in a shop window, beautiful sculptured glass, with smooth depths and swirling layers I wanted to touch. Why didn't I touch it, it was right there and the man with the kind eyes wanted me to come inside. No, I couldn't because I was meeting someone and I didn't have time. I had an important meeting. *My interview!* I sigh out a happy laugh. Disproportionately pleased with myself at remembering something, anything that isn't a drug-filled mess of images and sounds. I don't recall the interview. That's right I texted Jason to tell him I was meeting Peitra for lunch. *Peitra.*

I retch and heave, I turn my head so as not to choke because I can't sit up or turn fully on my side. Concentrated stomach acid and bile burns a violent path from my stomach up my throat and out of my mouth. The pressure is enough to coat most of my torso but not enough to clear my body and hit the floor. I am coated in a slick warm sticky residue, the smell alone keeps me heaving until I am dry and my throat is raw.

Why the fuck would Peitra do this? Jason told me she wasn't happy about how things had played out but this is a little over the top, even for a woman scorned.

I hear movement outside the door. The room is completely bare, the floor is covered with a type of rubber with those dimples you get in wet rooms and public swimming pools. The walls are all white and the door is rounded on each corner and has a circular window in the centre that is also painted out white. It looks like a blocked out porthole. Only when that observations sinks in do I also realise the room is moving. I think up until this moment I thought I was probably still high but no, the room is definitely moving. There are no windows but I can absolutely feel the rhythmic pitch and roll of a boat. Possibly a very large boat or a very gentle swell. The handle shakes and the deep and loud groan of protest from the hinges on the door make me wince. I didn't know ears could hurt but mine do, I sniff out a bitter laugh and internally reprimand myself, every fucking thing hurts.

A pretty blonde-haired girl pokes her head around, she smiles brightly and bounces into the room.

"Oh, good, you're awake." She skids to a stop and slaps her hand to her mouth. "Ew, gross." She shakes her legs and steps back out of the vomit that has dripped from my bed and onto the floor. "You've thrown up all over yourself." She cries out, shaking her hands up and down like it's the most disgusting thing she has ever encountered.

"I didn't have much of a choice." My voice is beyond gravely, more like my larynx lost its fight with a cheese grater, almost as rough as I feel. I cough and try to generate some moisture but my mouth is too dry. "Can you get me some water, or better still untie me and I'll get it myself. I wouldn't want to be any trouble." My tone is heavy with sarcasm, which might not be my best approach but she just smiles inanely and giggles.

"Oh, you're funny. He didn't say you were funny." Her perfect brow wrinkle with confusion. "He said you were a bitch," she states like that is a fact.

"Well, you've caught me on a good day." I smile tightly and she bursts into a fit of laughter she tries to hold back, both her hands against her pink glossy lips. I stare at her because she looks vaguely familiar. She has blonde almost white hair pulled high in a ponytail, she's wearing long false lashes but other than the pink lip gloss, no other makeup. She is wearing skimpy hot pants that are currently giving her a wicked camel toe and a tiny white string bikini. The minute triangle patches of white material barely cover her nipples, skimming her gravity defying tits that are far too large for her tiny frame.

"See, you're really funny." She points her finger at me, her tone is lightly teasing. "I think once you're trained we will be great friends."

"Trained? What the fuck are you talking about?" She jumps at the sharp volume of my voice and steps back. I take a calming breath through my nose and force a pained smile. "Sorry, what's your name?"

"Lolli," she gushes.

"Seriously?" Her face drops and I curse under my breath. She probably has a smart phone filled with vacuous selfies, which I will need if I am ever to get out of here. "Sorry Lolli." It aches to curl my lips into a reciprocal smile but with effort I manage. "Trained for what?"

"Oh, I'm not sure I'm allowed to say." She drops her head and her words are soft and barely audible.

"Okay, trained by whom?" I try and coax but she shakes her head.

"Oh, I'm not sure I'm allowed to say," she repeats, her eyes like saucers when she looks up. I draw in a deep and much needed steadying breath.

"Okay, Lolli, how about where am I?" She bites her lip flat like she is physically having to suppress her desire to respond. "Let me guess? You're not allowed to say." I puff out my frustration when I really want to scream. "So what are you allowed to do?" I fix my smile but with no life to it, it probably looks like rigor has set in.

"Only what my Master allows me to do." She sighs as she chants this eerie mantra.

"Your master?" I raise my brow in query.

"And yours too now." Her smile is tight and she gives a haughty little huff. "But I will always be his favourite."

"And you will have no competition from me, I can promise you that." I quip.

"Hmm, you say that now but wait." Her warning is lightly mocking like she is hiding a delicious secret.

"So you actually *want* to be here." I struggle not to sound horrified when she is either genuinely happy or blissfully delusional.

"Of course every girl wants to be here." She rolls her eyes like I have just said the silliest thing. I am going to go with delusional.

"I don't." Her brows pinch and furrow. She looks utterly confused so I repeat more slowly.

"I don't want to be here, Lolli. Not. At. All." She gives a slow, knowing nod, and I get a warm rush of hope. That this is just some fucked up case of mistaken identity and Lolli… the lovely, utterly vacant Lolli, now that she understands is about to help me out.

"Ah, my Master said you would lie to me. He told me not to trust a single word you said."

"I'm not lying, Lolli trust me. I really, really don't want to be here. Please help me get out. Then you can have your master all to yourself." Her eyes sparkle at that last part but cloud with something that looked a lot like fear. Do stupid people feel fear? Because she has to be the dumbest person ever if she doesn't believe what I am saying.

"He said you would say that too. That's why he is the Master." She tips her head acknowledging her misplaced wisdom. "But you are very convincing. I'll give you that." She waggles her finger at me like some naughty child. "I can see I am going to have to watch you, Sweetheart."

I get a sudden pool of liquid in the back of my throat, it's acrid and it burns. I swallow it down, I'm dangerously dehydrated because I must be hallucinating. "What did you call me?"

"Sweetheart. My Master said that is your name. That is your new name," she states.

"Oh, God." My voice catches, and I squeeze my eyes tight. If I could reach my temples I would rub the instant pain that is piercing my skull like an ice pick.

This can't be happening.

"Consider yourself lucky. The other girls don't get names, and if you don't get a name—" She looks at the closed door and steps back over to me, carefully avoiding the vomit on the floor. "You have a name. Trust me, that's a good thing." She opens her mouth to say more, but the noise from outside causes a flash of pure fear to distort her pretty face, and she rushes back across the room. The door opens and in steps a vision from my nightmares.

"Ah, Sweetheart, you're awake." Richard's sardonic grin crawls across his face. Lolli has dropped to her knees, and I can see her tremble. *Fucking bastard.*

"I have a name you piece of shit!" I snap. My eyes bore into his, Lolli is trying to disappear, curling in on herself, but I don't break my gaze. He laughs but there is no humour in his cold eyes, and he quickly falls silent. He takes two long strides, and is flush against my bed. He towers over me. His six foot one frame looks so much taller from down here. He traces his finger along my cheek, and I snap my head away. It's the only part of my body I can move, and he doesn't get to touch me without a fight. He grabs my chin and forces me to hold still. His nails digging in harder than necessary. His eyes darken as I try to stop mine from watering. He leans down so close I can see the individual perfectly trimmed hairs on his new beard.

"It's okay, Sweetheart, don't hold back. I've missed your tears." I grit my teeth and the tiny amount of liquid I have been savouring on my tongue I launch at his face.

"You fucking little bitch. You will pay for that!" He pulls a piece of silk from his top pocket and pats his face dry. I can't help the satisfied smile that beams across my face even if I know it will be short-lived. "You will fucking pay for that, Sweetheart." He snarls the last word like that is a cruel promise.

"My name is Sam." My glare, I pray, would by some timely gift of supernatural power, burn the flesh from his bones, but sadly no. His face is inscrutable until he chooses to simply widen his evil grin. He takes a moment, my skin crawls and my body is cooled by an ominous chill. Drawing his clenched fist back, he swings.

"Not anymore, Sweetheart."

An incredible cramping in my stomach wakes me, but I don't bother crying out. No one comes, but if I'm honest, I prefer it like that. I think it has been a few days since Richard graced me with his presence but I could be wrong. With no daylight and falling in and out of consciousness, time is a very abstract concept. But I have had twelve meals at somewhat regular intervals. Lolli brings my food, and I use the term loosely, undercooked rice and tuna so dry I wouldn't feed it to a cat. I was reluctant to eat at first but my hunger gnawed a painful knot in my tummy that kept me awake, and sleep is the only thing keeping me sane. Although she hasn't spoken since that first time, I don't mind Lolli so much. She always has a bright smile that looks wholly out of place in my living nightmare. I am not so keen on the big guy that accompanies each visit. He leers at me like I'm a piece of meat. But then I am laid out almost naked, on a slab so the simile is not wasted on me.

He stands guard as I eat and watches over me as I take care of business in the corner over the smallest bucket I have seen. I don't remark about the useless size of receptacle, because I know it will be deliberate. The fact that I can't use it without pissing on myself would amuse Richard. He always did love to humiliate me, but I'm not that girl anymore, and I won't give him the satisfaction. I do stink though, and would happily kill for a shower and a toothbrush.

The door opens, but Lolli isn't carrying a tray. She bounces over leaving the door wide and starts to unbuckle my straps. I get a momentary surge of adrenaline thinking she is alone and I could easily overpower her, but then the familiar dark shadow of the hulk fills the doorway.

"Up, up you get, lazy bones," she says in a sing song voice, smiling sweetly. Her hair is braided in two plaits, and she is wearing a short-short pleated skirt and a button-down blouse that is tied in a sexy knot at her midriff. I know the look she is going for but today she looks very young with no makeup and wide, bright blue eyes.

"How old are you, Lolli?" She helps me up. I am eager to make some sort of bond with her now that she's allowed to speak, at least for the time being. She may not be the sharpest tool on the box, but she has been kind. If I can get her to understand that I am being held against my will, then maybe she might help me. I don't hold much hope, if Richard is really her *master*. But I have to hope, it's all I have.

"Oh, I'm sixteen in three weeks." Her eyes light with excitement but my mouth suddenly fills with vomit that spills into my cupped hands. I rush over to the bucket and empty my hands and what's left in my mouth, hacking up to clear my throat. There is no toilet paper, another *mindfuck*, so I just rub my hands together until they are dry. I feel so ill. I turn to face this child. I keep my face impassive because she doesn't need to see my horror. My judgement is reserved for the monster she calls Master. I'll cut his bollocks off the first chance I get.

"How long have you been with Richard?" I swallow and steal myself for her answer. She looks confused and I realise she would never refer to him by his name. "Your *master*…"—I grit out the word—"how long have you been with him?"

"Oh, three years." She nods enthusiastically. "I'm very lucky; most girls don't last that long. That's why I know I am the favourite."

"Jesus Christ, Lolli, what about your family?" I gasp.

Her face falls and she drops her gaze. "I don't have one. I was in a foster home but ran away. I seemed to grow these big boobs overnight and that's when the dad started to touch me. My Master saved me, Sweetheart." Her voice softens, and I can hear her adoration. It chills my soul. *Out of the frying pan…*

She tips her head for me to follow, and I notice that the hulk has stepped away from the door. I reach over and grab her hand.

"Lolli, I can help you…Let me help you. We can escape together." I plead but her eyes widen with disbelief.

"Why would I want to escape?" She sniffs out an incredulous laugh. "The Master is wonderful." She leans in to whisper. "He wasn't in the beginning, so learn from my mistakes, Sweetheart, and just do everything he says…*immediately*." Her eyes are grave with warning.

"You enjoy the way he treats you?" I have to be careful because I can see how deeply she cares for Richard. I find it repugnant, but this is her reality, if not her free will, speaking.

"Not all the time." She shrugs lightly. "But if I'm good he doesn't need to punish me. He hates to punish me." She smiles again, and her face lights up. My heart breaks a little more. "I love him, Sweetheart, why would I ever leave him?" She shakes her head lightly. "Besides he'd kill me if I tried." She flashes me a look that is filled with truth and wisdom well beyond her young years. I swallow thickly.

We walk along a narrow corridor past a laundry room, boiler room and massive kitchen. We continue to walk, and by the time we have climbed several levels, each becoming more luxurious, I realise this is no ordinary boat. It's some sort of super-yacht. These things cost hundreds of millions. I had no idea Richard was this wealthy. Lolli opens the door to a grand suite. A super-super king sized bed dominates the room, raised as it is on a platform. Tinted windows stretch the length of the far wall and I suck in a sharp breath. *Sunlight!* I don't think, I just rush over and gaze, this is my first glimpse of daylight in days, and it's stunning. Crystal clear blue skies and an endless ocean in every direction this view affords. My heart both lifts and sinks at the sight. From this aspect I can see no land and on a boat this size we could literally be in the middle of nowhere.

"Fuck, what is that god awful smell?" Richard's voice drowns out the noise of Lolli hitting the floor with her sudden and expected display of supplication. I turn and walk over so I am as close to him as I can voluntarily stomach. He recoils from the odour that surrounds me like a force field but doesn't step back. I take a big sniff in his direction.

"That would be you." I state calmly even if my nerves are alert and poised for anticipated impact. But he doesn't strike me, he smiles that creepy slow grin that makes me more nauseous than any six foot swell.

"You smell like shit and you look disgusting." His perfect enunciation is dripping with disdain. I bark out a bitter laugh and pat his cheek.

"But after a shower I will be clean. *You* however, could wash for a thousand years and you'd still be a piece of shit. Ow." I cry out as his hand covers mine still on his cheek and crushes the fingers together until I think my bones will crack. I bite back the tears but my knees start to give way. He grabs my hair roughly, fisting a large clump and dragging me into the adjoining room. He throws me on the floor. I rub my scalp and notice the handful of long strands still in his curled fingers.

"Wash yourself." He spits at my face but I turn so the saliva hits my shoulder.

"Fuck you!" I shout back.

"If you don't wash, Sweetheart, I will have Frank come in and give you a hand. You'd like that wouldn't you, Frank?" Richard calls over his shoulder and the hulk steps into the small space making it that much more oppressive. Frank chuckles and quickly retreats but not before he gives me a spine-chilling smile.

"Fuck you!" I repeat but I can feel my fire start to die. Richard steps closer, stoops and painfully grips my chin.

"You are going to be begging for that to happen by the end of the week, Sweetheart. I promise you that." He pushes me away with enough force that I skid back across the marble floor. I can feel my tears burn behind my eyes as I try desperately to hold them in. Please don't cry…not in front of him.

"Watch her Lolli, and if anything happens *you* will pay dearly, understand, sweet girl?" Richards voice is deliberately loud, Lolli's I can just about hear.

"Yes, Master." The door slams, and I fold over, hugging myself, my whole body begins to tremble. I don't sob but tears fall like a river from my eyes. Silent tears that don't capture a fraction of the hopelessness I feel.

I notice a light touch on my knee, and I raise my head to see a pair of worried blue eyes and a tentative smile.

"Please take a shower, Sweetheart." She pleads but I am not going to fight. I know who would suffer if I did and she is too young to have suffered half of what she must have endured with Richard as her master. I nod and her face lightens with relief.

I stand in the opulent shower with its gilt fittings, travertine marble tiles and luxurious soaps and gels. The water falls like a tropical downpour, heavy and hot. Pummelling the dirt from my skin and easing my aching muscles. I use the noise of the water to let myself really cry, safe that my devastation is concealed. He doesn't get to know how much he has taken this time, and I will die before he sees me break. But god, my heart is dying. I close my eyes, and all I can see is Jason, his soft brown eyes smiling at me. I can feel his tender touch as he traces my curves in the morning when he thinks I am still sleeping. I hear the rumble from his chest when he is just about to come inside me. That sexy as hell moment when he can't hold back a moment longer, that moment he is undone. I live for that and I believe he feels the same. We were perfect together…*were*. I can't describe the pleasure he wrought from my helpless body again and again. I have never known anything like it. But more than that, he saw *me*, through my shields and barriers, my utter *fuckedupedness*, he loved me anyway. I think he loved me more. I certainly never felt so loved and now…now I have never felt so lost.

Peitra took my cuff in the bar that much of that day I do remember. She must have known it was the one that held a tracker to remove it like she did. My phone was in my bag, but I can't imagine Richard handing that back to me. I think any fragment of hope that I could be tracked by my phone or my cuff died in that basement bar. If I was blindly optimistic, I might think there must be some other way. But most people aren't tracked in the first place. So with those two items out of the equation, Jason has absolutely no way of finding me.

All I can hope is that he doesn't give up trying because I won't give up fighting. I dry myself and even indulge in some of the body lotion; my skin welcomes the moisture. I am kneeling at the end of the bed where I have been placed by Lolli as she binds my wrists together with some heavy duty steel cuffs.

"Do you like dogs?" She looks confused at my response, which is a silent blank expression. She repeats with a giggle. "Do you like dogs? It's not a trick question, Sweetheart." I want to vomit every time she calls me that and beg her to use my real name. But I know she won't call me anything else, not if her Master has told her Sweetheart is my name.

"Sure, I couldn't eat a whole one, but yeah, I like dogs." Her brows shoot up, then her face crumples with laughter.

"You're so funny, Sweetheart…here look." She reaches round into her back pocket and slips out the holy grail. An iPhone. I suck in a breath and have to calm myself. I feel my fingers twitch, wanting to snatch the beacon of hope from her bright pink acrylic nails. She swipes the screen and scrolls, her nose wrinkled with concentration. Smiling brightly, she holds the phone for me to see the screen but not close enough to touch. She continues to swipe right to left, each screen fills with a mix of pictures of a screwed up grey, black-eared pug puppy or her holding the screwed up grey, black-eared pug puppy. She sighs softly and her eyes glaze when she finishes. She drops the phone in her lap.

"Cute." I comment completely distracted by the nearness of her phone. She nods at me and then jumps up.

"Oh, I've got some more pictures." She dashes from the room, her phone sliding with a dull thud on to the thick carpet. Once she is out of the door I pitch forward and grab the phone. My fingers shake and start to feel clammy with sweat. I rub them on the carpet and swipe the screen. No password I let out an excited laugh but try and suck the noise back in with a sharp breath. I stare at the screen. My heart is pounding so hard it hurts my ribs. *Fuck!* I don't know Jason's number, I don't even know Leon's number, and he's been my best friend for ten years. I'm screwed, my one chance.

I can hear rapid, light footfalls getting closer. Wait, I remember in Rome, Jason said something about a code. *Tap in a code and he gets a signal and I get rescued.*

What was the code?

I don't remember. No, he didn't tell me the code, bastard. Why didn't he just tell me the fucking code? I stare at the numbers on the screen hoping they will speak to me, glow or swell in the order I need to select. Come on Sam, think… He said the code was a date. It was the day I stole his heart. *I'm going to die on this boat.* I tap four digits but drop the phone before I press send. Richard's booming voice makes me jump and scares the crap out of me. I stretch to retrieve the phone but he is too fast and kicks it out of my reach. I scramble after it, crawling awkwardly and throwing myself after the device. Richard's foot lands heavy in my side lifting me clear off the ground and sending me flying across the room. I land in a heap against the far wall.

"You fucking stupid bitch!" he yells.

Coughing and wheezing, I try and draw in some oxygen. I think I cracked a rib when I hit the wall. My eyes flick over to the doorway where Lolli is transfixed with absolute terror.

"You gave her your phone?" His voice drops low with pent up rage.

"No, Master, never!" She rushes over and falls to his feet curled over with her nose to his toes. "I didn't. She tricked me. I'm sorry, Master." She sobs but he kicks her off and walks over to me. The phone dangles lightly between his long fingers, teasingly close when he drops to his haunches.

"Oh, Sweetheart, I'm sorry, you didn't get to finish dialling that number." His lips pout with mock sympathy. "Not quite enough digits there or maybe one too many but this doesn't look anything like the emergency services number, now does it?" He eyes me carefully but I try to keep my face inscrutable. "Maybe it *was* a code? I understand your boyfriend's company is forefront with this spy crap. Is that it, Sweetheart? If I send this number would lover boy come sweeping in to rescue you?" he sneers.

"I don't know *Dick*, why don't you press and find out?" I goad him but his smile is bitter condescension.

"Hmm maybe I won't." He holds the screen and deletes the numbers I had managed to save but not send. My eyes pinch shut because I won't be able to hide my fear. I jump at the sound of smashing glass and plastic. I shield myself when I open my eyes to see Richard destroying the phone with a large chrome paperweight. He drags his arms across the surface of the side table sending shrapnel flying across the room. He towers over my prone form.

"No one is coming to rescue you... Your life is mine." His eyes widen with ominous intent. "Whether you live or die is down to me." His eyes are dead but hold all the evil of a power hungry sadist. I haven't seen that look in a long time. I hoped I never would. "Do I make myself clear? Do you understand, *Sweetheart*?" His movement is so quick I almost don't get my arms across my face in time to protect my head from one more vicious hit coming my way.

EIGHTEEN

Jason

"You should go home, Jason, you look like shit." Daniel walks into my office and closes the door behind him. I don't bother to look up; I just keep scouring images of faces at train stations trying to see where she ended up. I know it's fucking pointless but I feel so impotent I have to do something. Even if I did spot her, it wouldn't give me much more information than what train she took. It wouldn't tell me where she is now or her final destination. I hate that I know jack shit, and it's driving me insane.

"You're the one with a newborn, Daniel. You're probably getting less sleep than me." I try to smile but give up. Daniel's eyes hold enough concern that I can't look up any longer.

"I doubt that." Daniel walks around my desk and looks at the screen, which is just a blur to my tired eyes. I can't find her, yet I see her everywhere. I worry that I have been looking so hard I would miss her now if she showed up on my screen. I close my eyes, and she's there, stunning and perfect. In my dreams, her beautiful face has become my living nightmare. Why can't I find her? Why can't I find him?

"Has Patrick found out how Richard got back into the country?" Daniel's voice interrupts my inner turmoil.

"No, he didn't fly but given that they were heading to St Pancreas International it's not a massive leap to assume he used the train. He still shouldn't have been able to get through passport control but he's a slippery fucker so he probably didn't use his own name." I drag my hand through my hair, which is thick with dirt and grease. I have barely left my office in the ten days since she was drugged and taken from me. It's been ten fucking days and nothing. I draw in a deep breath and drop my head in my hands. I am utterly exhausted but I won't rest until I've found her. I won't find any peace until that piece of shit is in jail or better, six feet under.

"It's strange that he hasn't surfaced." Daniel picks up the photographs on my desk. CCTV footage of Sam leaving the bar and being carried into the taxi. Several other photographs of the same taxi working its way across London. And a series of closely timed pictures showing several people exiting the taxi: Sam, a man I assume is Richard by the cut of the suit, a small figure, possibly a female, and a large male. The last photo is of them entering the train station. "I think Peitra knows more than she let on when she got back last week. I didn't buy her story." Daniel's tone mirrors my scepticism and I scoff.

"You mean the one where she tearfully explained that she was only trying to reunite two lovers. That Richard had come to her for help. No, me either. Richard wouldn't have even known who Peitra was or her connection to Sam without Peitra making that connection from working for me. I just didn't realise she had that much access to my personal files. It's irrelevant though, she's said all she is going to say and until Sam is back to give her version of events there is no point bringing her in. Not unless you want to see your Chief Operating Officer go down for murder." I state as a matter of fact.

"I really don't." Daniel gives me a pointed stare, which I hold.

"I'm making no promises because I'm saving that honour for Richard."

"Jason, I know you're upset—"

"Bethany." I silence him with one word full of portent. He nods. He can make no case for me to feel anything other than murderous toward Richard, because I know he has felt the same and would *do* the same. The silence hangs heavy but I shake it off and fill my best friend in on what I do know.

"Will spoke to his flat mate," I say but stop at the look of confusion on Daniel's face. "Sorry, I didn't tell you. Will shares his flat with two CIA agents. It's how I was able to find out about Richard when I first started dating Sam. They have a file on him as long as your arm." I massage the constant pressure at my temples and squeeze my eyes tight.

I can't focus when I think what a man like that is capable of and my stomach turns with the knowledge of what he has gotten away with in the past. How he is a free man is unfathomable to me, but Will assures me the CIA is working hard to rectify that. I shake off the barrage of painful scenarios that haunt me, one minute with him is too long, and Sam has been at his mercy for ten fucking days. "Anyway, they seem to think he has one of his parties planned." My stomach turns.

Daniel gives a curt nod. I had shared all the details with Daniel about Richard's business activities last week. "Where is it this time?"

"That's the thing; they are always off shore on some luxury yacht. They never leave from the same port, and no one has any idea who's invited, so we can't even sneak on the guest list." I can't help that the tone of my voice sounds dejected. I am struggling to see any light.

"Surely tracing his boat shouldn't be difficult." Daniel's remark has my hackles rising.

"You know Daniel, if I wasn't bone tired, I might smack you one for thinking I'm a fucking idiot," I snap. "Of course his boat is easy to track but he doesn't use *his* boat. He has some very rich and unpleasant acquaintances, and because of the service Richard offers, they are more than happy to host these events. They get the pick of the girls...hosts privilege." I pinch the tingle at the bridge of my nose but let out a frustrated sigh.

"Sorry Jason, I didn't mean to insult your efforts. If I ever went missing, I would hope I had someone as determined as you looking for me." He squeezes my shoulder, and it barely registers I am so tense. "You'll find her."

"Girls go missing around him, Daniel." My voice catches.

"I know. I read Patrick's report." He stands and walks to the door but turns and holds my stare. "You'll find her, Jason." I wish I shared his confidence, but I am grateful for it all the same. "Now go home or I'll fire your arse."

"Thanks." I sniff out a very tired laugh.

"You're welcome." He nods, making sure I see his genuine concern. I slap my laptop shut, grab my jacket and follow him the lift. We are the only two people left on this floor. I check my watch for the first time in I don't know how long. When did it get so late? When did I stop noticing the time? I swallow past the lump in my throat. I know when, the moment she disappeared and every minute apart became my living nightmare.

I let myself in to Sam's flat. Leon gave me a spare key and I prefer staying here. Sleeping in her bed, surrounded by all her crap somehow feels better than being alone in my own place. The living room is dark, just the glow from the television with the sound off. Leon has fallen asleep on the sofa. Not the first time I have found him like this, and until we find her, it won't be the last. Neither of us is sleeping much. I try to keep quiet, let him catch a few zees while he's able. I slip into Sam's bedroom and inhale. I just close my eyes and absorb anything that will make me feel a little better, because I feel like shit. It's only the knowledge that I have to hold it together that is preventing me from free falling into the darkness. It's shocking, amazing and all those adjectives that fail to express how incredible it is that someone can become so important, so integral, so vital to a person's life in such a short time. *Insta-love*, love at first sight, whatever you call it, that day she stole my heart, it was like being hit by a fucking freight train.

I walk to her window, her curtains are wide open but the thin muslin drape covers the glass enough to yield some privacy. Her room overlooks a narrow garden that is mostly decked and has some low level seats and an area for al fresco eating when the British weather plays nice. No flower beds or shrubs but she has some potted herbs. Or rather, I suspect Leon has some potted herbs. Sam freely admits her skills are non-existent in the kitchen, something we were enjoying working on. I let out a heavy sigh.

"No news." Behind me Leon's voice is soft, and he walks into the room and stands beside me.

"Nothing new." I don't bother to look at him, I know his expression of devastation mirrors my own. I feel his hand on my shoulder.

"Come on, man. I'll fix you a drink." He pulls me away from the window, and I follow him to the kitchen. "You want me to fix you something to eat?" I shake my head and slide onto the kitchen stool while he starts opening cupboards and laying ingredients on the counter top. He pulls two beer bottles from the fridge, flips the caps and hands me one. "You need to eat, Jason. You look like I feel, but you won't be any good to her if you get sick." He starts cracking eggs into a bowl. "I know you don't feel like it, fuck it's the last thing I'm thinking about, but she needs you fully functioning so I am going to make you a fucking omelette, and you're going to eat it." His voice has steadily risen, and he finishes his culinary tirade with a stern look and a spatula in my face. I laugh and slap the weapon away.

"All right, *Mum*," I quip. "That would be good…thanks." He gives a bright smile, but it doesn't reach his eyes, which under the harsh kitchen light, hold an unfamiliar redness on the lids. "I'll find her, Leon." The knife he is using hovers midcut and he flashes a glance at me. He swallows thickly and nods slightly. He is just as frayed, and however unwarranted, I get a twinge of jealousy that he feels this strongly about *my* girlfriend, but Leon clearly loves her too. He continues to chop and whisk and stir. The smells make my stomach groan in protest at my neglect, and I am struggling to remember the last time I had something that wasn't black coffee. He slides the delicious, puffy, light-golden omelette onto a plate and hands it to me. I cut my first forkful and devour it, biting down on the searing heat and burning my tongue. It's really good. I nod silently but enthusiastic enough for Leon to cast a wide grin and start to make another for himself.

"You've known Sam a long time?" I take a long pull of my beer.

"I met her the first day she came to the big bad city, over ten years ago." He smiles, flicking a glance at me while he works the eggs in the frying pan. "We've never fucked." He states as calmly as if asking for the salt. I bark out a laugh.

"I know. Sam told me." I wipe my mouth dry on the back of my hand.

"Good, I just wanted to get that straight, because you looked at me just now like you wanted to kill me." He raises a questioning brow.

"No," I chuckle. "Not kill, maybe maim…a little."

"Oh, that's all right then." He lets out a stilted laugh.

"I never thought I was the jealous type, but being with her has brought out this whole other side." I shake my head lightly. "Just takes some getting used to you know. You've been her best friend a long time, you clearly love her, and I guess she feels the same."

"Damn right she does but she doesn't love *love* me. She loves you and that, my friend, I never thought would happen. So count yourself *very* lucky." His tone is light but drops and lends the weight of seriousness to his comment.

"I do." I meet his silent stare.

"Good…then we are on the same side…no need to maim." He pauses for my reply.

"No need to maim." I take another, much needed pull of my ice cold beer. "She said you saved her."

"Hmm… she has a penchant for the dramatic so she would say that. It was more a case of right place, right time." He takes his full plate and walks around the kitchen island to sit beside me, his forehead furrowed in thought. "She had a pretty low opinion of herself, but at best, I stopped her from making a stupid mistake."

"And helped her make a different one." My tone is low, and I say the words through an ever-tightening jaw.

"Ha!" He drops his fork and turns to face me. "Okay, Jason, spit it out."

"She became a Domme because of you, because *you* needed that. You didn't think she could be something else?" I snap.

"I'm going to let the attitude slide because I know you are strung out, *and* I will answer your accusations because you seem to know jack shit about the girl you claim to love." I stand abruptly sending my stool crashing to the floor. He remains seated but has straightened and is meeting my hostile glare with his own narrowed stare. "She could be anything she wanted to be. I made her go to University, but she *chose* to study law. I gave her a roof over her head, but she *chose* to buy this place, and I asked her to help a friend out, but she *chose* to become a Domme. Because, and if you don't know this you are dumber than… fuck, Jason!" I am instantly at his throat, my hand tight around his neck. He struggles but continues to choke out what he wants to say. "Damn it, Jason, you can't make Sam *do* anything she doesn't want to do." He stands, making me step back and pushes my hands free from his neck. Leaning around me he bends down to pick up the stool. He pushes me lightly to sit.

All my anger has seeped shamefully out of my body, misdirected as it was. "You really think you can *make* her submit to you?" He raises a brow, but I don't answer the bloody obvious. "She doesn't even submit because she loves you; she submits because she *wants* to. No one can make her do anything she doesn't want to do, period." He puffs out a frustrated breath.

"Richard did." We both fall silent with that unpleasant thought. Leon swallows loudly.

"Richard is an abusive arsehole, and abusers don't tend to follow the safe, sane and consensual code." He flops back down on his stool and pushes his half eaten meal away. "She's not the same person he knew; she's not fifteen anymore. She is much stronger now." He looks at me, his expression grave. "But she has always made her own choices. She thinks I saved her back then, but it was the other way round." He smiles crookedly, and I get that twinge again. She shares so much history with this man, a man I can't even hate because he cares as much as I do. Well, almost as much. "She never needed to be saved."

"She does now." Apparently, I do have to state the bloody obvious. "I'm going to find her, Leon." I stand and walk away. "Thanks for the meal and I'm sor—"

"*De nada.*" He waves off my gratitude but adds with a solemn tone that makes my chest bleed. "She's counting on it, Jason."

I prise my eyes open at the first rumble of the vibration of my phone on the bedside table. My hand automatically reaches for it and flips it open even if I can't focus on the screen to recognise who's calling me in the middle of the night. It might be her.

"Sam?" I croak, my voice thick from sleep and exhaustion.

"Um, no Jason, it's Patrick. You said to call if I had anything new. I have something new." I sit up and drag my hand down my face to try and wake up. I look up to see Leon stagger against the doorframe. I furrow my brows.

"Light sleeper. I heard the vibration." He shuffles into the room, and I nod for him the sit on the bed. He wraps his arms around his waist feeling the early morning chill in the room because I sleep with the window wide open.

"Okay Patrick, I'm awake what have you got?" Leon motions for me to share and I flip to speakerphone.

"Your code was activated by deletion. It wasn't sent by the standard route, but we got it. We tried to bounce a signal straight back, but whatever sent it must have been destroyed because there was nothing to receive what we sent." The line goes quiet while I take this in. It's not good. It's good that Sam has tried to contact me, that means she's alive at least, but if we couldn't keep a signal, I don't know what that means.

"Destroyed, what does that mean exactly? Can we trace where the code was sent from or not?" I hear Leon suck in a breath while we both wait for Patrick's response.

"We did but it's moving and we can't get a lock on it. Which means at the speed it is travelling it will be out of our range in thirty minutes."

"Fuck, where is it now?"

"Off the cost of Florida but in International waters."

"Send me all you have now." I cut the call and dial my brother.

Fifteen minutes later, I am packed and impatiently waiting on Leon to get his shit together.

"I'm leaving in one minute with or without you!" I shout back into the apartment as I hold the front door open. Not caring if I wake the whole damn building. I'm going to get my girl.

"I have to check everything's switched off. Sam will cut my bollocks off is she comes back and her precious pension is burned to the ground because her boyfriend left the coffee machine on." He pulls the door shut and deadlocks it. I swing my bag over my shoulder, and we both race to the waiting taxi.

"Your brother didn't actually say he could help though, did he?" Leon challenges once we are on our way through the thankfully deserted streets of London.

"He will, he was just being selective. He doesn't actually work for the CIA so he's not going to promise what he can't personally deliver, but I know my brother, and he will help." Leon nods, but his expression is sceptical. "This isn't news to him, and his flat mates said they have been after Richard for some time. I've just given him enough information for them to go after him. Kidnapping is a felony, and this would be Richard's third strike." My tone is impassive because I happen to think life in prison is too good for that lowlife.

"The signal, Jason?" Leon looks at his watch, our thirty minutes are almost up, and that is the one thing burning the lining of my stomach. Will they act fast enough on the information I gave to pick up the GPS location before we lose it altogether?

"I know Leon, fuck…I know!" I drag my hand through my hair and catch the worried glare from the driver in the rear view mirror. I let out a steady breath. "Look, I have to hope they can trace the signal, block the signal, whatever, but if they don't, we will at least be in the right part of the world. And if I have to hire every boat on the East Coast of the States to search the coastline for that piece of shit I will. It's not like we are looking for a row boat. This type of yacht blocks out the fucking horizon. We will find her."

The plane isn't ready when we reach Heathrow but I can't sit still in the lounge; it's bad enough I am going to be stuck on a plane for nine hours. I decide to buy some things for Sam. I didn't think to pack anything for her. I just wanted to be on my way but now I think I should've spared a few minutes. She's going to want her own clothes, her own smells, she going to want things that are familiar. Fuck, I'm such an idiot. I turn to Leon who is about to stretch out flat on one of the long sofas in the executive lounge.

"Leon, will you help me pick out some stuff for Sam? I didn't pack her anything and I want—" Fuck, my voice catches, and I turn away, closing my eyes at the sudden sting. I feel Leon's hand on my shoulder.

"Sure, man, that I can do." He nods for me to lead the way. One of the Customer Service managers is happy to open whatever shop we want; most are still closed, but it is a perk of flying under the Stone Enterprise flag. Nothing is too much trouble. Leon has helped me pick out perfumes, body lotions, makeup and something comfy to snuggle in if she doesn't want to get dressed. I have also bought jeans, jumpers, t-shirts, sunglasses and some Converse trainers but I hesitate outside the Louboutin store. Leon comes to stand beside me.

"What are you thinking?" He follows my gaze. The ankle boot is easily six inches and studded with hundreds of tiny silver spikes; very sexy, very BDSM, very Sam.

"I don't know. Normally, I wouldn't hesitate, but she uses this armour, and the last thing I want is for her to feel she needs her shields up." I rub my jaw and hate that I feel uncertain.

"Good point. Besides you don't know what she's been made to wear, so she might not like the association however well intended."

I cringe and my stomach turns. I hadn't thought of that.

"You can guarantee she hasn't been dressed up in fluffy pjs, so I'm sure you're safe with what you've bought her. I think this other stuff, you'll have to wait and see. Let her take the lead on this one, Jason." He pats my shoulder.

I look at him, and he offers a tight smile filled with concern and understanding. "This isn't the first time she's survived him."

"It will be the fucking last though."

Nine hours later, Leon and I make our way through the ice-chilled air-conditioned Miami International airport. Will is waiting at arrivals. With the flight and time difference, Leon and I are still on afternoon UK time, but for Will, it's first thing in the morning, and he looks like he has also been up all night.

"Well?" I ask before I even say hi. He grabs my bag and reaches to shake Leon's hand. They exchange greetings but I huff out and fix him with a glare that freezes the air around us to something sub-zero.

"Okay, well, there's good news and bad news."

NINETEEN

Sam

It hurts to breathe now. Everything hurts, but when I take anything more than a shallow inhale, it feels like is have an ice pick jabbing into my lungs. I think he cracked a rib with that last kick. I haven't seen Lolli since I woke up, but then I haven't seen anything. I have a blindfold on and I am tied spread eagled on a bed. The sheet below me is either rubber or plastic. Every time I move I tear my skin from the hot, slick surface. The room is warm, but I feel like I am burning up from the inside, too. I pull at my restraints, and I can feel the heavy duty cuffs and know I won't be breaking free anytime soon. I freeze when I hear movement. The door opens and there are footsteps. My stomach turns and my skin prickles with an icy chill despite the tropical humidity that swept in with my visitor.

The bright light pierces my lids that are screwed shut when the blindfold is ripped from my face. Richard's sardonic smile would make me heave, but I don't have the moisture to waste or the energy to expend. I flinch away from his touch, though. I hate that he gets to touch me.

"Why are you doing this, Richard? Why me?" I try in vain to keep my emotions out of my voice, but it catches and just makes his smile that much more cruel. I bite my cheek and dig my nails into my palms to give me a distraction, a pain I control and can focus on. That is the last weakness he will see from me. If my gaze could kill, I would happily die tied to this bed if it meant he died with me. His hand comes out of nowhere and strikes my cheek with the full force of a six foot, two hundred pound psychopathic male. My eye feels like it is going to explode and I swear I could feel it move in the socket. Gross, but I fix him again with my sweetest smile.

"That all you got, *Dick*?" I practically spit his name, but again, no moisture. "No wonder you cowered away from me in the club," I taunt.

"Oh, Sweetheart, that is *exactly* why you are here. By the time I am finished with you, everyone will know I'm the Master," he sneers.

"Really? Your ego is that fragile it can be wrecked because of our little interaction in front of what…thirty people? Narcissistic much?" I blurt out a bitter laugh and reel from the instant physical retaliation. My head is pulsing with pain, but I force myself to smile. He seems to really hate that, and it's all I have.

"It's a small community, and I have a reputation to uphold. My business depends on my image as the one true Master. I won't have *you* affecting that. Everyone will see you kneel before me." He announces to the room like he is orating in front of a grand audience.

"Wow, you give me way too much credit. If this is a willy waving contest, you've won. I don't have one so even your pathetic excuse for a dick will get you first place," I quip with more bravado than sense.

"Hmm." He strokes his finger down the side of my face, resting his middle finger on my lip. "I have such big plans for this mouth." He drops his hand and roughly grabs between my legs. "And this pussy." He snarls, his perfect white teeth flash when his lips pull back in an ugly grimace.

"It won't be the first time you've raped me, Richard, but after the first hundred times the threat loses some of its potency." I blink my eyes to hide the truth. I might be numb to him now, but the pain of his treatment is as raw and vivid as the very first time. He stands back and sneers down at me.

"I don't fuck whores." He spits in my face, hitting my cheek with warm saliva that drips slowly down my face.

"No, you just fuck children, you sick bastard. You're a fucking monster." The anger I feel courses through me, and I can't keep the emotion in my voice level. I would kill him with my bare hands if I were only free to do so.

"Something I can thank *you* for." He lets out a slow chuckle that sickens my soul. "Once you have virgin pussy there really is no comparison. It's hardly my fault the pool of virgins is diminishing and girls today are sluts. If they kept their legs together a little longer, I would not be forced to hunt in a younger pond."

"Wow, you really believe that? You are as deranged as you are twisted. There is a special place in hell for people like you, you know that?" My mouth pools with bile, but I choke it back. He makes my skin crawl.

"Hmm, I don't doubt, so I may as well have as much *deranged* fun as I can, don't you think? Starting with you. I intend to make the next few days so unpleasant, you will be begging me to fuck you, just to relieve the agony." He purses his lips in a sadistic smile and drags his beady eyes slowly up the length of my exposed and vulnerable body.

"I'll die before that day, Richard." I tip my chin with all the hatred I feel focused in my glare and into his soulless eyes.

"All in good time, Sweetheart, all in good time." Cruel amusement distorts his face. His eyes are devoid of any life. I can feel my body start to tremble, and I have to focus all my remaining strength to not let my terror show. "But for now, I need you a little less defiant. I have a client that has very specific tastes, and I don't have much time before he arrives. He requested you unmarked, untouched, but not *unharmed*. I can work with those parameters for now." He walks away, and I let out a breath I had been holding, but it's a deep breath, and I cry out at the sudden pain. He turns sharply and raises a brow. "Problem, Grace?" I don't know what is worse, my ribs, which are obviously broken, or the way he uses my birth name like he owns it. He can have it. I am Sam, and I am Selina, and I will die before I give him any more of me.

"You need to work on your drama, Dick. Often less is more. I would happily give you some lessons, but I have a strict no arsehole rule." I bite a thin smile and silently brace myself. He steps closer and leers over me.

"Lucky for me I have no such rule, but you will find that out very soon." He snickers but the sound holds no amusement.

"See that's what I mean…you give it *all* away." I see the fury in his eyes at my mocking tone, but it's not the last thing I see. The last thing I see is his fist before the searing pain flashes across my face and I feel the gush and warm trickle of blood, I pass out before I can taste the metal on my lips.

Oh, that feels nice, soft and warm against my face. I drift slowly back to consciousness, but I can feel the stiffness on my face from the dried blood so this feels like heaven. My eyelids are puffy and sore, but thankfully, not from tears. He doesn't deserve my tears. I open them as wide as the swelling will allow and see bright, piercing blue eyes staring kindly, inches away from my face. I smile but my lips feel awkward and hurt. Lolli rubs the damp cloth across my mouth and like magic they feel instantly more mobile. The blood must have fixed them almost closed. Her face is the picture of concentration as she very carefully wipes my face and neck clean, taking time to rinse and pat my skin dry. The bowl of water balanced on her lap is now crimson with my blood, but she looks happy with the result. I personally couldn't care what I look like, but I do feel a hundred times better from the mini bed bath.

"Thank you, Lolli." She looks surprised at my gratitude which confuses the hell out of me. "Did I say something wrong?"

"Oh, no, I just thought you'd be mad at me." Her voice is pitched with amazement.

"Why would I be mad?" My tone is light and curious.

"I told Master you had tricked me, but you never did. I was just stupid and…

and I blamed you." She drops her head and won't meet my eyes.

"Hey Lolli, I understand. Don't sweat it." I let go with a dry laugh and try for a reassuring smile. I try to flip my wrist to wave away her concern, but it is secured pretty tightly and only my fingers move. "You did nothing wrong, and I could never be mad at you."

"Really?" She is wide-eyed and disbelieving.

"Really." I confirm with a warm smile. She sags with relief. "Did he hurt you?" I ask a little more sharply than I had intended. Her eyes flit to me then over her shoulder. She looks back to me but, again, won't meet my eyes. She shakes her head. I draw in steadying breath. What I wouldn't give for my bullwhip and a pair of pliers.

"You make him mad." She mutters under her breath.

"He's a prick. He deserves more than my bad language," I bite out, my tone heavy with disdain. Her hand slips to her mouth to cover her smile. "Did he hurt you because he was mad at me?"

"No. I was punished for the phone, but he has forgiven me now." She rushes to explain. "I just know when he is angry, and he always looks really angry when he comes away from here. You need to be careful, Sweetheart." Her tone drops to gravely serious. "He won't damage you now, but once the clients have finished with you…well…" Her eyes widen and gloss with tears. The blue in her irises glistens like sunlight reflecting on the deepest ocean. "You need to be careful. You wouldn't like him when he is really angry," she warns. I snort.

"I wouldn't like him if he put on a red suit and pretended to be Father Christmas. Something that rotten has no redeeming features I could ever like." I let out a sigh and wait until she is looking at me. "He is a bad man, Lolli, and when I get out of here—and I *will* get out of here—I am taking you with me."

Her head snaps over her shoulder and her eyes fill with panic. She holds her fingers against my lips. "Please, please don't talk like that," she whispers. "I… it's not so bad, Sweetheart. I'm his favourite," she whispers but there is fear in her eyes.

"For how long, Lolli? What happens when he loses interest?" Her face pales and my chest aches. She knows exactly what happens when he loses interest.

"I won't go back into foster care." The tears in her eyes finally escape onto her cheeks, and I feel like a complete shit for making her so sad. I can't even hug her.

"I won't let that happen, I promise, Lolli." She nods but her face is impassive, and I feel I have lost her to a darker time. I shudder that anyone has a darker time than this.

"I'm sorry." She gives me the saddest smile.

"You have nothing to be sorry about, Lolli." I try to offer some comfort to ease her pained expression.

"I do." She slides off the bed, carrying the bowl of water she used to clean me up. She disappears into the bathroom and returns empty handed, but not for long. She lifts a box from one of the high glossed black chest of drawers. She drops the box and lifts the contents. My legs try to shut but the restraints cut my ankles at the futile attempt. I recognise the wand, an extremely effective external vibrator, powered by the mains. It can be relentless. She lays it between my legs and sets about arranging straps and pillows to adjust the round head precisely on my clit. I start to tremble before she even flicks the switch. She looks devastated, so I try to smile, to hide my horror.

"How long?" I swallow thickly.

"I'm sorry, Sweetheart." She shakes her head and bites her lip tight.

"I know. This isn't you, Lolli, but it might help if I know how long?" My voice sounds desperate to my own ears. My anxiety spikes at the unknown and skyrockets with the known.

"All night." I jolt as she switches the wand to full. I was wrong. Knowing didn't help at all.

I want to die but not as much as I want to come. Every muscle in my body is utterly exhausted from perpetual spasming, teetering on the edge as I have been for that last decade. I know it hasn't been that long but god its feels longer. Richard was right about one thing I do want to beg, I do want to fuck, it hurts my heart to think that at this moment I would probably beg *him* to fuck me I need release that badly. Twelve hours I have been strapped to this device, I haven't slept, I've tried to move, to dislodge it but the one time I did, Lolli appeared and fixed it tighter to my core. She motioned to the corner of the room where a smooth black sphere is positioned to the wall. A camera, no doubt recording my torture but certainly alerting anyone who's watching that I have managed to secure myself a moment of respite. Lolli returned at first light but just to offer me some water.

I think it is the same day but I am a little delirious. Richard enters the room with Lolli on his heels. She drops to her knees at the end of the bed and he glares down at my wracked body. Twisted, tense and covered in a slick sheen of perspiration. I bite my lips tight to keep from howling. I am so desperate for release. He flicks the wand off and I sag, my legs still shaking uncontrollably.

"Something you want, Sweetheart?" He croons.

I groan out with a heavy exhale. "Oh God, yes." His grin crawls across his face. "I could use a good fuck right about now."

"See I told you, you would be begging me before the week was through." He laughs out.

"I said *good* fuck, Dick…If I wanted a lousy fuck you would be my go-to guy…ahhh!!" He switches the device back on and with his clenched fist he pushes it hard against my raw clit. Oh God, that's unbearable… Tears spring to my eyes but I quickly close my lids to prevent them showing. He storms out of the room with Lolli, his silent shadow.

If one thing comes from this it's that I will never use orgasm denial as a form of torture again, or a wand, or restraints. In fact I think I will go cold turkey and come out the other side as vanilla as Mary Fucking Poppins. My wrists are raw from trying to manoeuvre away from the source of pain. I know I have cut the skin on my ankles as well as my wrists, and my poor clitoris is so swollen it's probably the size of a tennis ball not the cute little peanut it was before this marathon stimulation nightmare. I start to let out tiny panting breaths, it seems to help to focus on something else and it doesn't hurt my chest so much as a deep breath would. I count in blocks of ten and repeat. Similar to the breathing exercises I use in yoga, desperately trying to focus on my breathing not the excruciating agony going on between my legs.

I don't fall asleep, I can't, but I do zone out into some sort of delirious trance. So when Lolli appears beside me I jump. She is hold a glass up but is standing at the end of the bed with her back to the camera.

"Keep your legs tense and I'll turn it off, pretend it's still going okay? Pretend you are still in agony."

"That is not going to be hard." I gasp. She flicks the switch off and I sag but instantly tense again when her face flashes with worry.

"Good just like that and they won't know." She winks.

"They?"

"Oh, if Master isn't watching Frank will be. Someone is always watching, always recording," she warns. I tip my head as she hold the glass to my lips. My whole body trembles and not because I am trying to maintain a façade. My nerves are raw and have a mind of their own. God, what I wouldn't give for a little light manual relief.

"Would you like me to help? I can't uncuff you. I don't have the key but I could stand at the end and you know…help." Her cheeks flush with embarrassment and I feel mine heat too at her reference.

My eyes water with such sadness. The fact that this child knows what agony I am suffering breaks my fucking heart.

"No darling, that's quite all right. I'll manage, what's a little frustration between friends." My laugh is flat but it's the sentiment that counts. Lolli smiles.

"We're friends?" Her face lights up with innocent joy.

"Sure we are." I swallow a little easier now I have had some water but the lump is there for a whole different reason.

"But it's not a little is it…It's not a little frustrating, I mean?" Her gaze drops to the apex of my legs but quickly averts her eyes.

"No, it's not but I *will* manage. Some more water would be good please." She nods her head and rushes to refill the glass. She bounces on to the bed, and I wince. A small cry escapes the back of my throat, and she looks mortified.

"Oh God, Sweetheart, I'm so sorry." She runs her finger along the edge of my hairline. The hair is slick to my forehead but her soft touch feels nice.

"It's fine…really. Lolli." My voice is a whisper but as serious as I can muster. "I will get you out of here…I promise." I want to wrap my arms around her and use my body as a shield. She looks so young, too damn young to have lived the life she has. She flashes me a tentative smile, looking rapidly over her shoulder and then back.

"I'd like that." She screams out and throws herself on the floor as the door crashes wide. Lolli drops the glass of water, which hits my head and covers me with the remaining water.

"You stupid, fucking bitch! You let her have your phone and now I have the US Coast Guard all up my arse just hovering on the international border and placing a no fly zone so none of my clients can land," he snarls and walks over to a cowering Lolli. He picks her right off the ground by her high ponytails. She squeals with shock and tries to grab his hands to support her weight. Her legs dangle as he swings her like a rag doll, walking to the side of the bed.

"Let her go, you piece of shit. Pick on someone your own age, you fucking monster!" I cry out, struggling against my cuffs and causing a fresh river of blood to flow.

"Oh, I will." He regards me coolly, a sadistic smile distorts his face. "I have to deal with *this* first." He shakes his hand, and Lolli screams.

"Leave her alone, Richard, please…I sent the code. It's me you should be angry with. It's me that's ruined your plans." Even as I beg for mercy, my heart races with the knowledge that Jason is here. That this nightmare is nearly over.

Richard laughs. "My plans aren't ruined, Sweetheart. They are merely delayed, a couple of weeks max." He pauses and glares at me. "Do you know how long a vessel this size can remain at sea before we need to dock? Months, maybe a year if we start losing mouths to feed." His lips flatten into a thin, cruel smile. "And time is money, and your precious rescue party is most definitely on a government budget. They will maybe hang around for a day or two, but we are in international waters and there is fuck all they can do about it." He peers down at me then at Lolli who has stopped fighting but is now clinging for dear life to Richard's forearms. He drops her to her feet, and she instantly drops to the floor. He looks over to the bed and glares between my legs at the dormant wand. His eyes narrow and my heart stops.

"Stand up, Lolli." His voice is calm, impassive, and chills my soul. His eyes cloud but are vacant. His smile is evil. I've seen that look before.

"Richard," I cry out but he doesn't acknowledge me. Lolli's eyes dart to me, then back to the man towering above her, backing her against the wall. "Richard, please don't hurt her. She's just a child for fuck's sake." My voice breaks with the desperation I can feel impotently freezing through my veins.

"But she's not a child is she? Why, she's very nearly legal." His remark makes me sick, and I feel liquid pool in the back of my throat. I fight to swallow it down along with the thick lump.

"Please don't hurt her, Richard. I'm begging! Do anything to me, but please, don't hurt her." He sneers out a sardonic laugh that chills me to the bone.

"Oh, Grace, you really think you are in any position to negotiate?" He draws in a dramatic sigh and places his large hand around Lolli's slender neck. "Besides I have no intention of hurting her." He pauses, and I hold my breath. My heart stops beating, and it feels like time stands still. His voice punctures my bubble. "Is that dramatic enough for you?" His glare burns through me, but I don't hold it, Lolli has gasped and is trying to scream, her arms are flailing, legs kicking as Richard increases his grip. Such a strong man against a fragile child. My stomach clenches, and I turn to vomit, all water and bile, but I can't stop. Heave after heave, agony when the muscles clench and my cracked ribs move. I can't look but I can hear her struggle, her cry gets weaker.

"Richard please," I splutter in between heaving, fighting to get free but utterly useless. "Please don't…please." I close my eyes when I see her arms go limp. Tears stream, I can't hold them back, and when I hear her lifeless body slump to the floor, I break, I sob, I howl. "Jesus, no…please, no…please." My chest is cleaved in two, I can't breathe. My whole body convulses, and I lose it. I don't remember much more. Darkness maybe and pain. I remember pain, absolute pain.

I'm drenched and awake. I don't want to be awake. I don't want to remember. Richard stands at the end of the bed with an empty bucket. The ice cold water doesn't even register I am so numb. He calls out, and Frank appears at the door.

"Fetch me my bull whip and dispose of *that* will you." His eyes motion to the crumpled heap of little girl by my bed. I close my eyes and pray. *Make it stop, please make it stop.* If Jason is here, why isn't he here now? Why didn't he come and stop Richard from killing Lolli? Why didn't I stop Richard? This is my fault. If I hadn't taken her phone, she would still be alive. I sent the code, Jason is here, and it didn't make a goddamn bit of difference. She's still dead.

Frank walks into the room and scoops Lolli into his meaty arms like she weighs nothing at all. She somehow looks even smaller in his arms. I can't stop the tears from free falling, and I hate that I have no strength to hide them. Not anymore. He has broken me. I have nothing left. Frank returns with a looped, black woven bullwhip. Similar to the one I used on Richard in the club. Another wave of guilt consumes me. If I hadn't made a show of making him back down, none of this would've happened. Why didn't I just walk away? I close my eyes as I hear the leather unfurl and hit the thick carpet with a soft thud.

"There is one good thing that has come from your little irritation circling us outside on the ocean." I don't acknowledge him. I keep my eyes closed. I can't stop the tears, but he will get nothing else from me until Jason comes—if Jason comes. "I get you all to myself for two weeks until your guest arrives that is. I will have to allow a week for you to heal, but I think I can allow myself at least one week for my own pleasure." He hums with anticipation and swishes the end of the whip playfully in the air above my head. "I have to say, I was rather impressed when you cut me with such precision." He cracks the whip just by my ear. I can't help but flinch, the noise is so loud. He chuckles. "I imagine that takes hours and hours of practise." He cracks it again. "What? Shy all of a sudden …no smart remark?" He draws in a deep breath. "No matter, we will call this my own practise session. Hmm, I wonder if your boyfriend will still find you beautiful when I am finished. Peitra said he called you beautiful all the time. It must have been an important feature for him, don't you think? It was always the only thing that kept me remotely interested." He sighs absently, and my stomach knots in agony. "But don't worry, Sweetheart, I will spare you the humiliation of rejection. He won't get to see you the new you in the flesh. You will have joined your new friend when we are finished, but I will be sure to send him lots and lots of pictures." He laughs and groans with pleasure at the first strike.

"Mmm." I bite down as my skin is sliced open just above my right breast. It stings like a motherfucker, but I will crack my own teeth before I cry out for him. His rhythm is relentless, and every inch of my body burns and bleeds. My eyes are dry because I have no more tears, and I feel like I am being flayed alive. He has sliced and whipped my skin raw, my legs, my torso, breasts, my face, along my cheeks, and if I hadn't moved my face, I think he would've taken my eyes. The cuts may be deep enough to bleed to death; I'm not sure, but I kind of hope they are at this point. If I'm left long enough, I will either get an infection or bleed to death. Either way, it will be a blissful escape. One thing I do know: The cuts he has littered my body with will scar.

He has made his mark.

TWENTY

Jason

"This is bullshit, Will. He has her right there!" I point out the window on the main deck of the Coast Guard boat. "Do you know what he could be doing to her right now? Do you know what he is definitely doing to her now we've shown up?" I am exasperated at this state of limbo.

"We have no authority. The ship is in international waters and that is a Russian flag they are flying, Jason. You have to be patient." Will tries to placate me but that is never going to happen.

"That's' my girlfriend over there in the hands of a psychopath, so I'm gonna pass on the whole patient thing if you don't mind," I snap.

The guy in charge, Luke Harrison, looks over and offers a tight smile. He finishes his conversation with his men and walks over. "Jason, I understand this is frustrating, but unless they start moving, there is very little we can do other than let them know we are here. We have no jurisdiction. But the minute that boat starts to sail we can manoeuvre it into US territory. I promise we are just as anxious to get that asshole as you are." He dips his head, an apologetic expression fixed to his face. "Maybe not quite as keen but we want on that boat...trust me."

"Sir," the Coast Guard captain interrupts, "they have just started the engines." I suck in a sharp breath. This is it, not long now.

"Good. The GPS is jammed, yes?" Luke turns to one of his operatives.

"Yes, sir, and I have plotted a subtle trajectory that will bring them into our waters within forty-five minutes, maybe sooner depending on the speed they set."

"Okay, suit up men, and ready the launch. I want to be ready the instant they are on this side of the international line." There is a rush of bodies, and Leon and I turn to follow.

"Sorry, boys." Luke stops us in our tracks. "You know you can't come with us, right?"

"Wrong." My clipped response is all I can manage without losing it at the wrong guy. I know he is here to help.

"Look, I know you want to, but I can't risk more civilians, and I can't risk this getting thrown out of court on a technicality. Your brother can come because he is seconded to the Coast Guard and carries a badge, but for you two, it's a definite no." He has the decency to look sorry but he is also resolute.

"Fuck!" I can feel my temper rise proportionate to my impotence in this scenario. Will puts his hand on my shoulder, but I shuck it off. I hate that I can't be the one to find her, and I kind of hate my brother at this moment, too, which I know is selfish and irrational, but fuck it, I'm not feeling all that rational right now. Leon storms out feeling every bit as frustrated I'm sure.

"I'm sorry, man. Look, I won't go if you're gonna hate me for it. We can listen to what's happening from the bridge." Will holds his hands up in a defensive gesture, and I feel like a complete shit for acting up. I shake my head and try for a calming breath.

"No, you should go. Your face at least is familiar, and I would rather you carried her out of there than a stranger," I admit reluctantly. He gives a slight nod and again tries to squeeze some comfort into my shoulder.

The next forty-five minutes are the longest of my life. My heart is hammering so hard in my chest I would be surprised if everyone couldn't hear it. Leon is silent next to me and all the men are already situated in the launch boat. The boat starts, and I lean over to Will, shouting over the roar of the engine.

"Find her fast, Will. Understand? Find her fast!" He meets my gaze and gives a curt nod. Will is the only one not carrying a firearm but he still looks intimidating in his official uniform.

"It's the only thing on my mind, Jason." The small launch pulls away and fires up once it is clear of the main boat. Leon and I return to the bridge.

Sam

My skin is on fire, but the slicing has stopped. I open my eyes to see Richard glaring down at me. He is drawing in large puffs of air. His chest is heaving and his brow is peppered with sweat. It's hard work beating a woman to death. I close my eyes. Looking at him makes me feel worse. I laugh to myself. Like I could feel any worse. How long have I been here, how long has Jason been waiting on the edge. What is he waiting for? Is he waiting until it's too late? The door crashes open, and Frank fills the space with his immense frame.

"Boss we have a problem." He is breathless.

"What is it? Can't you see I'm busy?" Richard snaps, wiping his brow with the sleeve of his white shirt.

"Jesus...shit!" Frank's voice holds all the evidence I need as to my appearance. "Is she still alive?" His tone is incredulous.

"What business is that of yours exactly?" Richard growls, and Frank steps back, a wise move as Richard swishes the tail of the bullwhip.

"Not my business, sir. It's just that we have visitors, so you might want to hide her in the hold."

"What!? What visitors?" Richard throws the whip down, and I relax only to whimper at the slightest movement. He storms out the door, cursing. My mind is racing, but that could be due to the pain-induced delirium. I can't distinguish one pain from the next, but I can feel my heart start to beat a little faster, and the pain that comes with that makes me smile. Is that Jason, finally? God I hope so, because I don't think I will survive another hour at the hands of that madman.

I jump and cry at the sudden noise. Richard barges through the door and flies toward me. I flinch and fresh tears sting my face covering open wounds and causing more tears. A vicious cycle. Frank follows him.

"How the fuck did the Captain let this happen?" Richard growls at Frank, firing lethal looks his way as he fumbles to unlock my cuffs. "He had one fucking job, now I can't keep those interfering arseholes from inspecting the whole damn boat." He kneels on my chest to reach for my other cuff and I feel something snap. Excruciating pain fires from my chest like a red-hot spear piercing my lungs. I gasp but can't get in another breath. "Make sure the girls are locked in the freezer, they'll not check there and delay them until I can dispose of her." He snarls inches from my face. I can feel his toxic breath. "She's the one they are looking for." He yanks me upright and despite the pain, I manage to grab some vital air. Frank rushes from the room with his fresh orders.

Richard unlocks my ankles and pulls me to stand, but my legs have no strength, and I crumple to the floor. My feet and hands burn with the surge of blood, and my wounds start to seep profusely from my brief upright position. I feel lightheaded and bright spots dart across my closed lids, and when I open my eyes, the darkness seems to encroach more with each passing second.

I cry out in agony as Richard grabs my hair and hauls me to my feet. He curses when he drops his keys, and I sway unsteadily, unsupported as I am when he drops to his knees to pick them up.

"Jason." I cry out at the vision before me. Tall and handsome, in black combats and a slim black T-shit. I frown. I don't think I've ever seen him in this type of get up. He looks…he looks hot. His eyes fix on mine and flash from fierce to devastated. I can't look. I can't see *me* reflected in his eyes.

"Step away from her and put your motherfucking hands in the air, you piece of shit." His voice is scary, stern but it isn't Jason's. I look again and notice the darker tan, his hair is longer, and I don't think it could've grown that much in two weeks or however long I have been in this hell. His eyes soften when he notices me staring.

"Will?" My voice catches, my throat is so dry, and I struggle to make a sound. He nods but fires his hate-filled glare to my right. Richard grabs my arms and pulls me in front of him. My naked body offers little cover for his large frame, but the coward uses me as a shield nonetheless.

"I said, let her go," Will spits out through gritted teeth.

"And what did you bring to this gunfight to make me do that, exactly?" Richard's voice is eerily calm, and I start to shake when his arm stretches out in front of my body, his hand clasping tight around a small black handgun.

"Drop the gun and no one gets hurt," Will demands. His eyes flash to me and mine instantly fill with tears. I want to beg Richard to drop the gun. I can't bear to witness anyone else get hurt because of me, but I know begging is useless.

"Will, just leave please. He'll kill you. Please, just go." I stutter, my voice shaking almost as much as my body.

"You should listen to her." Richard's stiff voice is full of derision. "She is at least still smart…important since her looks are no longer an asset." I crumple with the hateful truth. I hate that even after all these years and attempts to rebuild my self-esteem he can so easily break my resolve back down to my worth, my value being inextricably linked to my appearance.

"Her scars will heal while you rot in jail," Will states with compassion.

"But you won't be alive to see." He pulls the trigger, and I scream and grab for his arm. The bang from the gun is so loud it knocks me to the ground. No, I'm pulled to the ground by Richard falling, his arms still tight around my waist. I fight and struggle to free myself.

"No, no!" I cry, violent sobs wrack my body as I scramble over to Will's feet. His feet that are standing still, but still standing. I look up and watch as he slowly crouches on his haunches. His hand strokes the hair from my face.

"It's over Sam; you're safe now." His lips are moving, and I hear the words, but they don't make sense. I heard the gun go off. I turn sharply to see Richard's body lying flat. A small black mark singes a precise hole in the centre of his forehead. His eyes are wide with shock. His gun is still cocked. He didn't get a shot off. He didn't hurt anyone else. Another man in black kneels beside Richard, and he is slowly replacing his gun in his holster. I collapse and hug myself, sobbing freely with relief and pain and utter devastation. I feel a cool sheet wrap around my body, and I am lifted into strong arms that feel so familiar and yet a little strange. I rest my head on Wills chest but cry out with every step he takes. Curled up like this I feel the pressure of the broken bones in my chest, and I panic, because suddenly, I can't breathe. Will stops at my gasp and lowers me to the floor. We have made it to the open deck but I can't bear any more pain.

"Medic!" Will calls out and gentle tentative hands are prodding and poking almost right away, causing me to scream. My breathing is shallow, but I need more air. I feel like I am suffocating. A mask is placed over my mouth, which helps.

"We need to get her airlifted. She lost a lot of blood and I think her lung is punctured." The medic calls to his commander who puts in the call for air assistance. I feel a sharp prick on my arm, but don't make a sound. I've had worse. Will continues to stroke my hair. I speak, but he shakes his head not understanding the slight sounds I am making hindered further with the mask. He lifts it free.

"Don't let Jason see me like this," I plead but he looks shocked at my request. "Please…I can't have him look at me like you just did. He always called me beautiful. Will I can't…please promise me." He shakes his head like my request is somehow hurting him. He fists his t-shirt in the centre of his chest. I know that pain. "Please." I beg, tears falling unbidden. He closes his eyes but gives me the nod I need. He replaces the mask and we wait for recovery.

The noise of the approaching helicopter wakes me. I didn't want to wake from the blissful sleep, where nothing hurts, and I'm not scarred and Jason loves me. It was heaven. But the thunderous sound shatters that fantasy sending it into the four winds with the force of the powerful blades.

"The paramedics are going to move you to the gurney. It might hurt, darling." Will speaks close to my ear so as not to shout. The other men are gathered, and I can just about make out their conversation. Something about a clean sweep, no one else…only staff. My chest tightens and I get a surge of panic. That's not right! I struggle against the straps that now secure me to the stretcher and start to shout. My voice doesn't sound like my own, heavy and slurred.

"Relax, Sam, you're safe now. We need to get you to hospital." Will tries to comfort me with his soothing voice, and his large hand on my shoulder, but I buck under his touch and let out a heart rending scream. He lifts my mask, and I try to speak.

"Freeze…freezer." Everything sounds wrong and he looks so confused. I draw in a deep steadying breath and try to concentrate on making my mouth respond to my brain enough to make myself understood. "The freezer, Will. The girls are in the freezer." I must sound insane. I exhale as the last bit of energy leaves my body, but before I close my eyes and succumb to the delicious mix of drugs and exhaustion, I notice some of the men running off to check my insane revelation.

Jason

"I want to see her." I state flatly

"I'm sorry, sir, next of kin only." The doctor straightens in response to my audible growl.

"Well, she doesn't have a next of kin so—"

"Actually, she does." Leon shrugs sheepishly, but silences me with his statement.

"Mr Castell?" The doctor looks at his chart and back up to Leon, who is standing awkwardly beside me. "You may go and see her now. She has just woken up and is still a little groggy. It is up to her *if* she wants to see anyone else." He flashes me the stink eye.

"What is that supposed to mean?" It takes all my effort not to shout or tear this obnoxious adolescent in a white coat a new arsehole, but he has just fixed up my girlfriend, so I am trying to be nice.

"She was very insistent that she wants no visitors except Mr Castell." He turns and walks away, leaving me bleeding from the verbal knife wound to my heart. What the fuck. She hates me. She hates me because I didn't save her sooner. *I* hate me because I didn't save her sooner, but I am gutted she feels the same. I feel hollow, sick, like my guts have been wrenched out and broken with my heart beating its last, trampled as it is on the floor. I stumble to take a seat, winded and useless. My reason to breathe wants nothing to do with me. Where do I even go from here?

"She hates me." I choke out. Will sits beside me.

"She doesn't hate you but…but she looks pretty bad and she told me on the boat…" He hesitates and looks over at Leon.

"What? What did she tell you?" I interrupt.

"She made me promise that you wouldn't see her like this." He lets out a deep breath.

"What the fuck, Will?" I am stunned.

"She said you always called her beautiful, and she couldn't bear for you to look at her, well…I guess like I did." He shrugs by way of explanation.

"This is bullshit. Of course I call her beautiful. She is…she is a beautiful person. I love her…everything about her, and I don't get the chance to prove that because she thinks I'm that shallow I can't see beyond a few scars." I drag my hands through my hair utterly exasperated.

"It's a lot of scars, Jason." Will's voice softens.

"It won't be that." Leon interrupts. "It won't be that at all. She might say that now because she's raw but she doesn't believe that of you. I'm positive." His words have an instant calming effect on me. "Her insecurities will come from Richard. They always came from him and her mother. She loves you but she is scared, that's all. She's defending her heart the only way she knows how."

"By blocking me out?" He nods and I stand abruptly. "Not fucking happening, and I'm coming with you, understand?" I stride off, and Leon is quick to catch me, but he wisely doesn't stop me. We are in the right place for the mood I'm in if anyone tries to stop me.

She croaks out Leon's name, and he rushes to her outstretched arm. She wraps him in a tight embrace and closes her eyes. She doesn't see me. My heart breaks that I'm not the first person she calls for but that's now, and it doesn't have to stay that way. I take a moment to compose myself because Will wasn't lying when he said she is cut to shreds. Angry lines trace a pattern down the cheek I can see she's pressed against Leon's head. I have no doubt the other side is the same. Her arms are a series of stripes of varying thickness but all a deep crimson. Some of her skin is covered with large patches of gauze I assume to prevent infection of the deepest cuts. I hear her gasp, and her eyes meet mine. I keep my face impassive. If any emotion shows at all, it is certainly not pity, anger or hurt maybe, but not pity. She doesn't want it and I don't feel it. I just feel relief and a fuck tonne of love.

I walk into the room and Leon moves back. I sweep in and surround her, my arms thread around the back of her head and around her waist. As carefully as I can, I bring her into my hold, avoiding the tubes that still connect her to machines and drips. Her eyes sparkle and shine with tears, and her lip trembles. She opens her mouth to speak but it's been too long. I cover her words with my urgent lips; my tongue slides in to taste her. Oh God, I've missed her sweet taste. She moans into my mouth, and I can't help the grin that starts to pull at the corners of my kiss. But I'm not finished. My fingers tease and entwine in her hair, gently massaging and eliciting more sensual sounds that I adore. My tongue swirls and twists with hers, and she is quick to engage, which fills me with utter joy. Both breathless, we part when Leon coughs and motions that he is going to wait outside. Her eyes fill with a flash of panic, and I let out a warning grumble that makes her look a little embarrassed.

"Jason, I didn't want you to see me like this," she whispers but won't meet my glare.

"So I understand, and how happy do you think that makes me?" My tone is stern but hides the hurt I feel. She has enough to deal with without more guilt.

"I couldn't bear the thought of …" She bites her lips shut.

"Of what, precious?" Her eyes glaze, and I stroke her cheeks, marred and ridged with the welts and swollen, broken tissue. "Of looking at the most beautiful woman in the world and hating myself that I didn't save you from all this?"

"Please don't call me beautiful, and it isn't your fault, Jason. I'm to blame." She tries to pull away, but I hold her firm.

"Okay, let's stop this right now shall we?" I tip her chin so she is looking directly into my eyes. She needs to see me as much as I need to see her. "Firstly, I will call you beautiful because you are, inside and out. I can't imagine what fucked up nonsense is going through your head to believe I would think any different, but we will deal with that together." She blinks rapidly as tears pool in the corner of her deep chocolate coloured eyes. "And secondly, it's no more your fault than it is mine. I hate that I couldn't get to you sooner but none of this is your fault."

"If I hadn't taunted him at the club." Her voice is heavy with guilt and desperation.

"If I hadn't snubbed Peitra. There are a thousand if's, Sam. The bottom line is he was a bad man, and at the risk of repeating myself none of it was your fault."

"Lolli was my fault." Her voice catches, and it is barely a whisper as it is. I lean in closer when she continues to speak. "If I hadn't taken her phone. She would still be alive."

"Who would? You saved those girls, Sam. There were fifteen of them in that freezer. They are all alive because of you." I take a tissue and dab the fresh wet streaks on her cheek, which must sting something fierce.

"I'm glad, but Lolli…" She swallows and shakes her head, her eyes cloud with unbearable pain. "He killed Lolli right in front of me because I used her phone when she was out of the room. She was just a child, Jason. I promised to save her, but he killed her because you guys showed up and he knew I had sent the message."

"So you think that is my fault?" My tone is soft. My heart aches for her obvious grief.

"God no… you came for me. You came…" She sobs, and I pull her closer.

"Sam, I am so sorry I wasn't able to save her, too, but you can't blame yourself. Even if we had had no part in this nightmare, do you really think she would've lived much longer?" She tilts her head to meet my stare, and I can see the sad truth in her deep brown, glassy eyes. "He was going to kill every girl on that ship. He had no intention of leaving witnesses, Sam. His clients are rich and powerful, but they are sick bastards, and they pay to keep their dirty secrets. He was a bad man, and now he is dead because of us." I pause to let that sink in. "And I am not going to feel a moment of guilt because of it." She looks into my eyes, and my heart clenches at the first sign of a smile. "And neither are you." She nods and relaxes into my hold, and for the first time, I relax because she holds me right back.

Christmas Day

It's been just over six months since Sam was discharged from the Miami Aesthetic Surgery Center. The speedy and excellent care she received means that she really has minimal scarring from her ordeal. She was perfect before, and she remains perfect in my eyes but I do catch her tracing some of the faint lines that remain. One across her hip, a long six-inch line on her left thigh, and the eclipse under her cheekbone that is completely invisible with minimal make up. She recovered quickly like the survivor she is, and if it wasn't for the odd nightmare you would struggle to see any difference, but I know it's there. She moved in with me after a few weeks, shortly after taking up the position as a junior in the legal aid department of the Mission. Her office is nearer to my place, and it made sense. Besides, as much as I like Leon, I really don't need to see a half-naked dude first thing every morning at breakfast.

We've visited the club a few times together but she is guaranteed to have a nightmare if we do. So we haven't been for a while. It wouldn't bother me if we never went again, but I know it bothers her. Her nightmares are all tied up with images of what Richard did to her, which come back thick and fast at the first sign of the club, or a whip. She braved it on the few occasions when we were there because she hates the fact as much as I do that he can still affect her like this. As strong as she is and her desire to forget and move on is impressive, but her subconscious won't let go.

Today is our anniversary. The day she stole my heart, and I am going to allow something that makes me a little uncomfortable but something I hope will erase Richard permanently and give my girl new memories. Real life fantasies to write over her dark dreams.

We spent the morning in bed opening presents and the afternoon at the Mission like last year, but this evening, I asked her to meet me here at the club. I gave her instructions of what to wear.

The curtain moves and she steps through. Shit! I nearly drop my glass. The spotlight at the entrance shines around her like a full body halo, but she looks like anything but an angel. She is *so* dressed for sin. Her hair is pinned up with long strands curling artfully around her face. Her shoulders are bare and her body is pinched in tight into the sexiest back velvet and lace corset. Her panties are tiny with a delicate frill that I can see from this distance, and her long, slim legs have the sexiest damn stockings known to man—silk with a thin line up the back. I can't see that from here, but I gave the orders, and she is a stickler about details.

She walks slowly along the runway toward me, and I have to shift because my cock is instantly and painfully hard. Her lips curl in a knowing smile that sears my heart, a burning heat that brands me as hers. She comes to stand between my legs and runs her fingernails along my jaw, the scratch I can feel in my balls; it feels so good.

"Are you ready?" I draw my tongue along my bottom lip and watch her eyes widen and follow the sensually slow movement.

"For what?" She bats her long lashes and peers up through them with faux innocence.

"I believe I promised to fulfil your fantasy." I stand and take her hand, and she grips my fingers. I hear her swallow, and I bite back a chuckle. I like that she is on edge. We reach the playroom door, which is closed. I push the handle down but hold it for a moment. Her eyes shine with anticipation.

"Jason?" Her voice is a breathy mix of excitement and uncertainty. I push the door wide and she gasps. I lean in and kiss the delicate curve of her neck.

"Happy Christmas."

TWENTY-ONE

Sam

I don't think I'm being overly dramatic when I say that night Jason gave me my life back because he really did. I tried so hard to put the trauma behind me, and for the most part, I succeeded. But there was this tiny, insidious grain inside that revealed its presence in my subconscious and blossomed in my nightmares. It felt like somewhere in my darkness, Richard still owned a part of me, and I hated that. Not that I would hide this from Jason, but I couldn't if I tried. The nightmares would leave me wracked with tears and gasping for breath each night. The fact they only happened after we had played at the Club broke my heart, because I fucking loved playing with Jason at the Club and Richard had taken that from me.

Jason gave it back.

"Would you stop looking at me like that?" I elbow Leon in the side as he takes my coat and hands it over to the girls behind the counter at the kiosk in the Club.

"Like what?" He drawls and draws his tongue slowly across his bottom lip. "Ow!" I retrieve my elbow from its second more effective jab. "Sorry babe, after that night, coming here… what you're asking, is going to be im-fucking-possible!" His grin is pure filth and I chuckle to hide the flush of colour in my cheeks.

"Fair point." I let out a deep breath and some of the heat that instantly builds at the delicious memory.

Christmas Day

"Oh!" I gasp as the door to the playroom swings wide and there in glorious Technicolor and super high definition is my living, breathing fantasy. Jason's twin brother lounges in the high back leather chair, his legs spread wide, his faded jeans ripped on one knee and nearly worn through on the other. The first few buttons are already open. His chest is bare and rises and falls with deep, steady breaths. The dark tan helps to define his firm, toned muscles, very much like Jason's own tan does. He lifts his glass to sip the amber liquid, but his eyes never leave me. He shares the same intensity as his twin, and I can feel the burn begin in my belly and below. I begin to melt.

"Oh." Jason kisses my cheek and whispers in my ear. "Only new memories, beautiful, starting tonight." His hot breath scorches my skin, but I shiver all the same. My skin prickles with a million tiny bumps. Jason's hands stroke my shoulders, down my bare arms, and he takes my hand. He squeezes it and leads me into the lions' den. His eyes are dark with desire, but are kind and so full of love I hesitate. This is my fantasy, and although I know he has done this in the past, that was before me…before us. We still play, but Jason no longer shares. He turns to face me, and I pull him close.

"Jason, are you sure?" My voice is barely a whisper but he hears me, and his lips spread wide into a brilliant, wide smile.

"My greatest pleasure is to make you smile, and trust me, it's not a hardship to make your fantasy a reality…Having said that, I want you to memorise every moment, every taste and every touch, because I have told these guys this is a one night only deal." His stiff tone brooks no misunderstanding on my part only a little confusion.

"These guys?" I challenge his math.

"Well since it's just one night, I thought I could go one better than a threesome." His most nefarious grin dances across his face, and I swallow against the instant dryness in my mouth.

"Damn right and I wouldn't miss being that extra for anything." Leon's voice is behind me, and I spin to see him push himself off the back wall, sporting the same deviant grin and general lack of clothes as Will.

"Holy fuck!" I exhale a breathy exclamation that makes them all laugh. "I said that out loud didn't I?" Jason steps in front of me and breaks my eye contact with Leon. He holds my chin gently in his fingers. His smile is warm, his eyes like liquid chocolate, he melts my heart.

"Mine." His lips cover mine so gently I barely feel the softness, but it is so unbelievably intimate I feel stripped raw and naked. "You are mine, always." One more tender kiss, and I am undone. "Tonight we make new memories, no more nightmares, only dreams come true." He kisses my lips and holds me tight in his arms.

"Gay," Leon snickers but shuts his mouth when Jason fires an evil glare at him. I snake my hand around his neck and tug him back to me. My smile is wide because I feel treasured, loved and above all, like the cat that got the fucking cream.

"Thank you." I suck my bottom lip into my mouth and hold it back with my teeth, trying to temper my mix of excitement and nerves at this fantasy come true.

"I know you want your life back, beautiful, and I want to be the one to give it to you." He nods over my head, and I hear the leather of the seat announce Will making to stand up. "And these arseholes want to help, too." I can feel Will and Leon close in around me, but rather than feeling oppressive with their collective immense frames I feel closeted, protected and safe. "Think you are up to that?" Jason raises a brow as I bite back a wanton moan that is strangled at the back of my throat. "I'll take that as a yes."

He swallows and his eyes are on fire with desire so potent I tremble under the intensity. His hand is around my neck, and his lips crush mine in a display so possessive my heart swells. His tongue dives, urgent and demanding. He steals my breath; he already has my heart and soul. When he releases me, I sway but I'm steadied by hands, many hands, strong and firm, on my waist, my hips and threaded in my hair.

My eyes fix on Jason, and he holds my gaze like we are the only two people in the world, but I am acutely aware that is not the case. Will's hands sweep up my back and down my sides, skimming my backside and slipping his fingers under the suspender straps of my belt, raking his nails lightly along my stocking tops at the back of my legs. Leon has one hand on my side, and the other drifts over the stiff boned corset, tentatively inching up to the swell of my breasts. He pauses when my breath hitches. I haven't broken my gaze from Jason, and I watch him to check for any flash of jealously. He should see in my eyes he has no reason to feel anything but my love; however, I still haven't told him, and he needs to know I really do. His eyes flick to Leon and then drop to Leon's hand as he reaches over the top of my corset and strokes the round flesh of my breasts. Leon groans and steps a little closer. I can feel his rock-hard length on my thigh. Will follows Leon's lead and pushes his erection against my arse.

I let out a stuttered breath and watch Jason's smile creep wider across his handsome face.

"You okay, Beautiful?" I nod my response. Not surprised the power of speech has deserted me. He chuckles. "Good." He reaches behind him and draws something out of his back pocket. He holds up the long black tie and I frown and pull back.

"Why?" I shake my head. I haven't worn the blindfold since my ordeal.

"When you go to the dark place, I want you to feel us…to only feel us understand?" His voice is heavy with concern.

"Jason, I don't think I can." My voice waivers and the hands on my body that had been gently stroking hold still, firm and comforting.

"Trust me?" he asks, and I don't hesitate.

"I do…I just—"

"Sam." He swallows slowly, and his brows pinch together with worry. "I'm not sure I can risk you looking at one of these guys the way you look at me. I honestly think I'd lose it if—"

"Jason," I interrupt and place my hand on his chest. I can feel his heart beating just as fiercely as my own. "Not possible."

"Sam" His tone is a light reprimand but still a warning.

"Trust me?" I flip his own question.

"Damn it…of course. I still think—" He tries to argue but I interrupt and silence him.

"I love you." I declare and hold his gaze, which is stunned.

"What?"

"I love you." I repeat with a shy smile.

"And this is where you choose to tell me?" he growls playfully.

"Apart from the erections digging into me, I kind of think it's perfect. Perfect for us at least." I wiggle my brows and fix my lips with a mischievous grin. He shakes his head lightly, and I relax, my hand stroking the space above his heart. "If you think I need the blindfold to forget, then I will wear it, but you need to know I could never look at another person the way I look at you, because I have never loved anyone the way I love you."

"Gay…Ow!" Leon slaps his hand over mine as with lightning reflexes I now hold his prize possession in my vise grip.

"You want to play Leon, or do want the ball gag?" I narrow my eyes, and he motions to lock his lips and throw away the key. "Good." I turn back to Jason.

"Very well, beautiful." He drops the tie. "I think that's enough talking, we have a much better use for that smart mouth of yours." He pushes lightly on my shoulders, and I sink to my knees with no resistance and delicious anticipation making my mouth water. I stroke my hands up Jason and Leon's legs, just to the edge of the bulge in the material in their jeans. Close enough to feel the heat but not get burned. I shift around and do the same to Leon and Will while turning my head and looking up to Jason's lust-filled gaze.

"As this is a one-time thing, I am going to suggest we also make it a no regrets night. No waking up tomorrow saying I wished I'd…" Jason adds, his voice deep, gravelly and just holding on to his control by the look in his eyes.

"Agreed." Leon and Will almost groan out together. Their enthusiasm makes me ache.

"No safe words, beautiful. Tonight is all about your pleasure...your fantasy, but if you want us to stop just say no...okay?" Jason touches my cheek lightly with his finger to get my attention, and I turn to face him.

"I won't say no." My tongue darts out to dry my parched lips, and I notice Jason's eyes widen as Leon moans, and Will mutters something that sounded like 'fuck yeah'. But Jason has cupped my head covering my ears and has dropped to his haunches. His lips cover mine, but he is smiling wide, which makes me smile, too. He stands abruptly and starts to unbuckle his belt. I kneel up, eager to assist. In my peripheral vision I can see Leon do the same, and I don't doubt Will is either already naked or very closely behind the others. I tug Jason's jeans, and they fall to the floor. He kicks them free, his feet bare once he toes off his shoes. No socks. I smile to myself...so keen. His heavy, solid cock is reaching for his taut, flat tummy, and I wrap my right hand tightly around his thick girth. My lips hover, and I flick my tongue over the tip. His breath catches and his thighs tense, but I turn my head to where Leon is slowly fisting himself. My left hand reaches for Will and starts to work him up and down, mirroring the action I am using on his brother. I flash a look at Jason just to check that what I am about to do is okay. He pushes his hips into my tight grip and gives a slight nod—good because I don't want to stop—I am past that point. I know I am not going to say no, but there is no going back, not now.

I lick my tongue across the velvet tip of Leon's thick cock and he hisses then curses out loud when I quickly take him in my mouth and swallow him down as deep as I can. He threads his hands in my hair and grips and holds, aiding my movement. I work my tongue up and around, swirling until I let him fall from my lips, replacing my lips with my hand.

I shuffle around as do the men so I now have Will's beautiful cock poised on my bottom lip. My hands continue to work Jason and now Leon. I peek up through my lashes and can see three pairs of eyes gazing down with lust and adoration. Will throws his head back when I swallow him to the back of my throat, a deep groan rumbles from his chest and his hand is just as quick to guide me or keep me there. I can taste his excitement and I wonder if he would like to come down my throat as much as his brother always does. I pull back and barely draw breath when Jason is pushing his iron hard, extremely engorged cock between my lips. His hands wrap through and pull my hair, and he starts to fuck my face, the force and urgency an indication of his need to dominate this situation. I don't mind. Hell, I have never been so turned on by his obvious need for me.

I swallow and choke; his thrusts are deep and demanding. It takes all my concentration to time my breathing just right. I have lost my rhythm with the others and I am gripping Jason's thighs, my nails marking his skin. He is mine.

His thrusts become more urgent, and I am distracted enough that I jump and clench my jaw when I feel a hand dip between my legs. Jason curses out some garbled cry of momentary panic but barely breaks his stride. I don't know who is now between my legs; it doesn't matter. I was so engrossed in taking Jason deep and not choking that I had forgotten we had company.

"Holy shit, Sam!" Jason cries out but cups my jaw and strokes his thumb, his concern for me outweighing his near cock-ectomy.

"Sorry...just surprised that's...ahhh...oh Jesus..." I drop my head to my chest as two fingers slide inside my wetness, scissoring and working in and out. I tip my hips and grind back against the delicious movement.

"We good?" Jason holds my chin and meets my eyes, his question reaching beyond the recent and new activities.

"So good." I sigh. He makes the most of my lax jaw and slides his full length all the way back inside my mouth. I am just as eager to continue. Fingers are working inside me, hands are sweeping my body, pulling my breasts free and pinching my pert, aching nipples. I am so wet, the sounds fill the room, the aroma of lust and arousal permeates all of my senses, and I can feel my body start to climb.

"Jas, she's gonna come?" Will's voice is hoarse, but holds an unanswered question. "You sure you want that now?" I tense at the implication but relax when Jason responds.

"Don't stop...don't deny her. It won't be the only time she comes tonight, and that's a promise." Jason groans and pushes until he hits the back of my throat. I take him and swallow, grabbing his balls and tugging just enough...just the way he likes to make him...

"Ah fuck!" He comes with such force I struggle to swallow, some of his essence spilling from my mouth, but the sounds he makes when he loses it like that are enough to set my own climax racing to follow his release. I buck and crumple back onto Will's hand. Jason collapses onto his knees and draws in some deep, steadying breaths. My face is flushed with colour and alive with pleasure. I take a moment to come back down but barely hit the earth when Leon demands my attention.

"Our turn." Leon coughs and holds his hand out for me to take. I bite my lip and draw in the last of Jason's taste, savouring the salty flavour. Leon pulls me into his arms, and I feel Will at my back, arms embracing me, hands exploring my skin, and eyes devouring my body. Leon climbs onto the bed, I follow, and Will follows me. I look back to see Jason stand and pull the chair to the end of the bed, slap bang in the centre.

"You have the director's chair, Jason...any special requests?" I ask as I pitch up on my elbows, my skin glistens and tingles. I am alive with deviant desires coursing through me like a wildfire. I can barely keep still.

"I like the sound of that." He sits down, his cock still hard and getting harder. "All fours, beautiful, suck Will while Leon fucks you from behind. No arse, Leon...not yet."

"The director's cut is always overrated." Leon moans, and I snicker, but quickly move into position. I notice Jason take himself in his hand and begin to languidly stroke up and down.

Fuck that looks hot.

I don't get to look for long. Will strokes the side of my cheek with his cock to get my attention, his fingers under my chin tilting my face to meet his gaze. His smile is almost as breathtaking as his brother's but it's the sharp pull on my hips that makes me gasp. Leon drags my panties over my bottom and works them off my legs with a little assistance. Grabbing my arse cheeks firmly he fists the flesh and pulls me back, pushing his own steely hard cock against my entrance. With the slickness from my recent climax he eases himself inside, and I sigh with the pleasure of that first thrust.

Will doesn't waste the invitation of my dropped jaw. His fingers move from my chin to my hair and he slides his long cock into my open mouth. I am so unbelievably turned on right now I can feel my body start to take over and begin its climb. I would be embarrassed at how easy I am, but right now, I don't care; this is too good to think about anything else other than how fucking amazing it feels. Leon is setting a comfortable pace and doing this erotic little grind that has me wanting to squeal. Will groans when I try to make any sound. The vibrations in my throat dance along my tongue and around his shaft. He seems to like that. The thrusts in my mouth become a little more frantic, and I can feel Leon's grip move from my arse cheeks to my hips for more leverage.

Will pulls himself free and helps me up as much as is possible with Leon still buried inside me. The heat our bodies create when flush together like this is borderline explosive, Will presses hard against my front, Leon still slowly working me from behind, hands gliding over my body leaving a blaze where they touch. Will threads his hand behind my neck and tilts my flushed face up to meet his. His lips curl and look so soft, so familiar I can't help but lean in to close the gap. I close my eyes and relish the anticipation of that touch but there is nothing.

"Not a fucking chance." Jason growls and is looming where Will was only a moment ago. I look to see Will sprawled on the bed with a wicked grin and a low laugh causing his chest to shudder. I turn back, a little breathless and a little confused. Jason soothes me with his tender touch; his hands cup my face, his lips cover mine, Oh, God, that kiss. Forget everything else, I would die if I ever lost this kiss. He pulls back, his eyes alive with fire and possession. "Mine," he declares.

"Yours," I exhale on a breathy sigh.

The bed shifts and Will is once more at my side, his irritation at being usurped an instant memory. "Ours tonight."

Will takes my neck and I tense for a second, thinking he is going to kiss me, but he dips past my mouth and kisses my neck and collar bone. Jason once again takes my mouth and Leon, who is still moving deep inside me, kisses down the top of my spine.

I feel so cherished, so adored…so damn lucky.

Leon pulls out when Will takes my hand and eases me his way, he leans back and helps me straddle his waist. Leon stands on the bed and walks to the head, perching on the padded rail, holding himself and watching my every move with a salacious grin. I thought when I first saw him in the room that I would feel awkward or just plain weird, but in here, all I see is a smoking hot someone I happen to trust with my life and love as a friend.

Will starts to unhook the clips on my corset and lets out a long slow breath that comes from deep in his chest when he discards the garment. My breasts fall free into his waiting hands. He cups and massages the soft, round flesh, and his fingers tease the tips with sensual light touches. He switches to pinch to the point of pain that makes me so damn wet I can feel myself melt onto Will's skin. Jason's hands dip between my legs, and he gathers some of the wetness. I start to tremble before his hand has ventured any further than my core. His lips are on my neck, and his soft words scorch like a liquid fire in my veins.

"You ready, beautiful?"

"Oh," I manage to mouth, but I'm not sure any sound escaped. Jason has spread my slick arousal over my other hole and dips his thumb through the tight ring of muscle. I push back against him, and he chuckles, a deep, throaty sound that is sexy as hell. He lifts my hips and supports my weight; Will drops one hand to position his cock at my entrance and Jason lets my weight go so I sink down at my own pace. I can feel Jason behind me, pulling my cheeks apart and pushing himself forward. I tense because I feel his size more keenly now that I am already full.

"Here." Leon hands Jason a small tube of lube and winks at me. "There's *always time for lubricant."*

My giggle turns into an erotic moan as Jason works the tip of his now well-lubed cock inside my arse. I drop my head to my chest and suck in some much needed oxygen as my body stretches to accommodate the intrusion of a lifetime.

"Ah fuck!" Will mutters beneath me, Jason's hot mouth is at my neck as he pushes himself to the hilt. My skin is on fire. I am breathless and soaring at the same time. I pant and force my body to relax and enjoy.

"How do you feel, beautiful?" I smile, but my head is bent so I know he can't see me. I lift my head and turn as much as I can. Jason's eyes are dark with lust, but their fierceness is softened by the warmth of his smile.

"Full." All adjectives have vanished from my vocabulary, but this fits. He flexes his hips at that, and I give a full body shudder that has Will cursing.

"Not quite," Leon takes my chin with one hand, and with his other, he parts my lips with his straining erection. I suck and draw him deep into my throat. He holds my head, and I close my eyes to absorb all the sensations bombarding me as each one of them begins to move inside me. I feel giddy, delirious, and drunk all at once. The pressure inside me with two large cocks alternately working me deep and deeper still is indescribably good. I am wound so tight when Jason snakes his arms around to stroke my clit, I explode at the slightest touch.

Hands, fingertips, lips, tongues and glorious cocks...Jesus, not an inch of my body is left untended. Jason's strong arms hold me as I am filled again and again. I am moved and manoeuvred this way and that, and every time, the constant I feel is in the safety of his hold. I lose count of the times I am driven to unbearable heights of ecstasy where I can't breathe and float on an ethereal plane until I am coaxed back down, soothed and sated, only to be driven once more by eager lips between my legs or urgent fingers teasing and coaxing my body for more...always more. My last conscious moment is of Jason pulling me up his body having swallowed his release, vaguely aware of Will fucking me from behind and Leon beside me helping my hand move up and down the length of his cock. Utter blissful exhaustion the final victor.

I wake in a tangle of too many limbs and gentle breathing. Jason has me tight against his chest, and I tip my head to see if he is awake. The gentle rise and fall of his chest would indicate he is either asleep or very relaxed. A wide smile creeps across his face when my eyes meet his.

"Hey, beautiful...how are you feeling?" His voice is a soft warm whisper and he pulls me tighter against his chest. I'm not sure who is flush against my back but he grumbles as I am pulled away from his contact. I draw in a satisfying deep breath and think about his question. How do I feel? Sore and stretched, aching and alive, adored and...

"Amazing." I settle for this but I feel so much more.

"You were amazing." He kisses my nose, and I offer a shy smile at his compliment.

"What time is it?"

"It's late." Jason yawns and it sets off a chain reaction that makes me giggle. I jump at the sound of the door but relax when Will enters carrying a large duvet and now wearing some snug fitting boxer shorts. He climbs onto the bed and manages to wedge himself between Leon and me, pulling the duvet over all our bodies.

"What the fuck, Will?" Leon pitches up on his elbows all disgruntled.

"Snooze you lose, Leon, and don't even think about spooning me unless you want to be on the wrong end of some serious blood play.'

"Tease." Leon drops his voice, and I splutter out a very unladylike laugh. Will looks a little unsettled by Leon's response, which makes me laugh harder.

"Come to this side, Leon, and I'll lay on top of Jason then I can hold you all. Well, until I crush the breath out of Jason and he kicks me off." I wriggle my body until I am curled over Jason's chest, my legs tucked and wrapped around his waist. Leon moves, and I stretch my arms out so they are draped across both Will and Leon's chests.

When I wake up much later, we are alone, Jason and I, and no hint of a nightmare to disturb my sleep. I give a sleepy sigh and stretch out some of the stiffness. Jason slides his arms around my body, and I feel like my heart has truly found its home. Perfect.

Present

"You think he'll change his mind?" Leon's words break me away from my red hot trip down memory lane.

"Does he strike you as the sort of person who would?" I raise a curious brow, and he returns my query with a pout.

"Shame." He huffs and I pat his cheek with affection. "He might think differently after tonight?" he offers, and I smile. I love that about him, ever the optimist.

"Or he might not. You think me doing this will make him less possessive?" I snicker.

"Um no." He frowns.

"The only way that night will ever get a rerun is in your dreams or if I begged." Leon pulls me into a hug and kisses me roughly on my head.

"Bless your heart." He grins.

I slap his chest. "Arse-wipe...I didn't say I would beg."

"But you didn't say you wouldn't," he teases and wiggles his dark brows playfully. I shake my head and wave my incorrigible friend to move ahead.

"Go...go. Make sure he's at the end of the bar then cue Marco with the music." My voice is pitched with excitement.

"You do love a show don't you, babe?" Leon grins.

"This is my stage, Leon, and tonight he gets to see the show of a lifetime." Leon flashes a quick smile and disappears through the thick velvet curtain.

I take a deep breath at the first bar of *Grace You Don't Own Me*. I step through the curtain, the spotlight falls on me, blinding me momentarily. But it means I can't see the eyes of the club that I know will be focused my way. Tonight I chose to wear my trademark Mistress Selina red leather basque with fishnet stockings that just peek above my thigh high boots. I have on red long sleeve gloves, and my hair is pinned high so nothing is going to obscure my visual display. I drop the string of diamonds from my hand, holding one end I pull it high. The sparkles reflect bright light across the room and I glance up to see a pair of intense eyes shine back so much brighter than the precious stones in my hand.

I slowly loop the diamonds around my neck and close the clip to secure it once it forms the high collar I wear for Jason in private.

This is very public.

My mouth feels dry and my tummy is doing somersaults, but it feels so right. I smile and meet his heat-filled gaze, which widens when I drop to my knees.

I keep my eyes forward as I slowly make my way across the runway at a sensual crawl. I can hear murmurs and gasps, but with every movement, I feel empowered with the knowledge that this is right.

I kneel up when I reach Jason, and his expression makes my heart ache. His eyes are wide but glassy, too. He softly skims my cheek with his knuckles, and I can't fight my own smile, which makes my cheeks hurts.

"Up," he commands, and I bounce to my feet. In my heels, I am almost nose to nose. "You look very beautiful in my collar, Sam." His tone is deep and heavy with heartfelt emotion that is just as tangible as the collar around my neck. His lips cover mine before I can utter a sound. My heart soars with the passion and love I feel for this man. I have never felt so free as I do belonging to him. He breaks the kiss but not his hold. "Mine," he whispers.

"Yours." I smile but bite the idiot grin that is just itching to embarrass me.

"You do know what this means." He takes my hand in his, and I gaze into the intensity with which he seals my soul to his.

"I do." His deft fingers slip something on my finger, and I gasp when it catches the light. "Jason?"

"You are wearing my collar, and you already said I do, beautiful. Now where's a damn priest when you need one?" He pulls me into his arms because I am too stunned to respond.

"He's in playroom three, but I can get him if you want." Leon winks at me, and I burst of in a nervous fit of giggles.

"No Leon, we're not getting married in a sex club, Sam deserves more. Sam deserves the dream wedding. Sam deserves the world, and I intend to give it to her."

Leon probably had a smart remark but I didn't hear it. All I hear is Jason promising me the world when it's too late for that.

He gave me the world when he gave me his heart.

The End

ACKNOWLEDGEMENTS

I completely understand why authors start this section with an apology for missing anyone. My list of thank you's has grown considerably since I first pressed the publish button and I am rightly worried I will forget someone. I'll start with a blanket THANK YOU EVERYONE...yeah because that should cover my arse...not.

So I am going to start with some key players: A huge thank you Shannon Boltin and Kris Ward who tirelessly promote and pimp me to all and sundry and I know Facebook doesn't make it easy.I am and will be forever in your debt because I literally would not be visible in the ocean of Indie authors if it wasn't for you ladies.

Joan Readsalot, pretty much there for me from day one. I am so grateful for your honesty and constant unwavering support. My other Beta readers, Melinda, Amy Adkins, and Heather Callahan...thank you so much for your invaluable input into making Disgrace all I'd hoped and more. My street team, especially, Susan, Kim , Gaynor, Chillie, Jenny and Melissa(s), Jenny, Lisa, Maxine, Charlotte, Vickie Charmaine and Lynne..But really all my street team...I love you ladies...you totally rock!

My Chosen One's and Disgraceful Diva's...That would be most of you listed above too but there are many many more and I am so grateful to have you in my life...making me smile daily. I love these groups and for a moment I thought I would lose them...and I was not a happy bunny...but with some tweaking we pulled through...Libby and Cleopatra et al ;)

Barbara Shane Hoover...words fail me...I am so grateful for your grammar ocd...I can't even...Saya at Redquille, Jane Kennedy...my extra extra pair of eyes. Stacey at Champagne formats and Judi for my glorious and totally on the edge of being reportable, cover...You ladies are the foundation. Neda my publicist, sorry for just being a little crap with dates....

Bloggers: Missy's Book Blog, Philomela (2 friends), Claire, Steph, Vicki and Vivienne at Fictional Mens Room, Kelly at Our Kindle Konfessions, Jesey at Schmexy Girl, Samantha at RedHotRomance, Afterdark Book lovers, Mel and Gayle Bloggers from Down Under...super grateful to you guys. Other authors... because this is a community in every sense and I have drawn inspiration and guidance from many many talented people but here's a few and in no particular order…Jodi Ellen Malpas, M Never, Stylo Fantome, JL Perry, Robin Lee, Kitty French, Donna Alam, LP Lovell, Stevie Cole, Audrey Carlan, Jana Aston and JA Huss…Don't get me wrong most of these people wouldn't know me if I sat on their face but they have affected me in a positive way and for that I am thankful.

I would also like to thank my bestie..Kymme because in all honestly there would be no books if it wasn't for her, for all the swag making for the signings…..and definitely above and beyond with that trip to the dungeon…and not drinking the water…you know just incase ;) I love you to the moon and back.

My family…again are quietly supportive…which is probably why I spend so much time on Facebook. Not just because of my books but there is a whole community of filthy minded lovelies happy to share this wonderful book world…you make each day a treat. I often get these utter bursts of happiness, either writing or reading and you guys are the ONLY ones that understand <3 Sorry back to my family…my husband and children (all grown up) I would like to thank you for not moaning (much)…it is your way of showing your support I know and I appreciate it…One day i'll write a story you can read…but not this day *and definitely not this story!*

But mostly, I'd like to thank you, for choosing to buy my book and taking the time to read it—a huge, I mean really huge, thank you, you will never know how incredibly grateful and honoured I am that you have and I would be even more so if you are kind enough to **leave a review** at your favorite ebook retailer or Goodreads.Please…please…oh and please :)

The People who make it all happen.

Dee Palmer—Author
Website—www.deepalmerwriter.com
Follow me here
Facebook
Facebook Chosen Ones Reading Group
Twitter

Editor—Ekatarine Sayanova at Red Quill Editing
Formatter—Champagne Formats
Cover Design—Judi Perkins at Concierge Literary Promotions

Disgrace Playlist

Numb—Linkin Park
Guilt—Neo
The Driver—Bastille
Wicked Game—Chris Issak
Linger—The Cranberries
You Don't Own Me—Grace
Devils Touch—Tiaan
Truly Madly Deeply—Savage Garden
Like I'm Gonna Lose You—Jasmine Thompson
No Air—Jordan Sparks
This Years Love—David Grey
Confident—Demi Lovato

DISGRACEFUL

The Disgrace Trilogy, Book Two

DEE PALMER

DEDICATION

Tess…
Yes, I am dedicating this book to my beautiful dog…
She was the heart of our family, she was loved, so very much, every single day.
and I will miss her
Every Single Day.

ONE

Sam

He proposed. I can't believe he proposed. I twist the ring that feels oddly comfortable on my engagement finger. As a new piece of jewelry to me, it shouldn't feel so good, but it does. It's perfect. I exhale a deep breath and stroke the smooth surface, mesmerised by the early morning light catching the stone, reflecting brilliant shards of light across the room. *He does like me in diamonds.* The largest Asscher cut stone I have seen outside of a Bond Street jeweler is surrounded by a halo of baguette diamonds and set in an Art Deco pattern on a platinum band. It's stunningly beautiful, and I can't imagine how much it must have cost. I lift my hand to the equally expensive collar that I haven't removed since I made a show of putting it on at the club last night. What did I do to deserve all this? What did I do to deserve Jason?

He is curled up on his side facing my empty space. The shadow that darkens one side of the room covers his face. I couldn't sleep but have been watching him from the chair at the end of his bed—our bed, I suppose, since I moved in a few months ago, and definitely our bed now that I am going to be his wife. The covers have dropped or more likely were pushed down to his hips, more shadow hiding more deliciousness. We both sleep naked, him because he gets so hot, and me because every night he peels off each attempt I have made at covering up. I tried to argue that I don't generate heat like he does, and I need my PJs to ward off the cold, but there really is no need. All the warmth I desire is afforded by his strong arms and firm body holding me each night, or at least until I wriggle free.

"Penny for them?" His deep voice makes me jump. His voice has an edge of sleep-induced gravelly roughness, and his stretch and groan are more reflective of his semiconscious state.

"I'm sorry. I didn't mean to wake you." I keep my voice quiet, which is ridiculous now that we are both awake.

"Your body isn't next to mine, and that always wakes me." He shifts so his torso is now bathed in the silvery glow of the moonlight through the gap in the curtains. His face is pale, but his eyes look sharp and clear. His gaze is searching.

"Not straight away, though. I've been sitting here for a while." I tuck my toes under the edge of the throw, which I have draped over my shoulders.

"And I've been awake for a while."

"Really?"

"Yes." His lips curl in a sexy grin.

"You've been watching me this whole time?" A pleasant ache starts to tingle between my legs at the thought.

"Yes." His tone is as flat as his answers are brief.

"Why?"

"Because I can." His smile spreads, and I feel a warm glow ignite deep in my chest. He curls his finger, and I move without hesitation, not from his silent command but from the innate draw I feel to him. I crawl onto the bed, and he sits up so I am kneeling beside him. He rests his back against the headboard. "Now tell me what has you a million miles away when you should only ever be right here." He takes my hand and places it on his firm chest. His skin is smooth and warm, and I can feel the strong, heavy beat of his heart beneath my fingertips.

"You proposed." My throat feels dry, and I swallow loudly in the quiet of the room.

"I did." His hand covers mine and holds it firmly. "And you said yes."

"I did." My voice waivers, and I try to avert my eyes, but he dips to maintain the contact.

"You did. Is that cold feet already, Sam?" His tone is light, but his expression is anything but jovial. His thick brows knit together with concern.

"Did you really mean it, Jason?" I meet his gaze and search for any signs of regret. There are none, and his words only confirm his feelings.

"You think for some reason I would ask the question if I didn't?"

"But marriage, Jason? That's a huge commitment. I believe marriage is for life," I tell him in all earnestness.

"I would hope you did." He laughs lightly, but my smile is tentative at best.

"But for us, Jason…is that even viable?" I can't hide the anxiousness in my voice. I didn't realize how much I had been holding in until I started to talk. Now all I can feel is a huge wave of uncertainty and a sense of my own doom. I don't deserve this.

"I don't understand." His voice is calm and filled with concern.

"Just four weeks ago we were having a four-way with your brother and my best friend, and you're going to be happy with a normal missionary marriage until death do us part?" I squeal at the sudden speed with which he has pushed me flat and pinned me to the bed with his full weight. His legs wedge between and ease mine wide. I can feel his instant heat and solid erection at my entrance. A gentle roll of my hips makes us both moan, but he clears his throat with a sharp cough.

"Sam, I want you as my wife. I have never wanted anyone the way I want you. I never saw myself getting married, but being with you, I can't see that there is any other life for me." His lips cover mine in a gentle, possessive kiss, sweet and soft. "We don't have to do this tomorrow. For now, I'll take you any way I can, but understand this…I want you as my wife. Our happy ever after is inevitable, and the marriage bit is probably the only normal thing about our relationship." Before I can utter a single word, his lips consume mine once more, this time with an unhindered urgency that steals my breath. His tongue traces the seam of my lips and dives inside, swirling and drawing my bottom lip into his mouth. He sucks hard, and I can feel the painful pull of blood into the full swollen tissue before he lets it pop from his mouth. "We have our own *normal,* beautiful, and our marriage will be everything we want it to be. And very much until death do us part." His smile is a perfect mix of striking and salacious. I find I am just as speechless at his perfect words as I am breathless from his weight. "And there is nothing wrong with missionary." He grinds his hips. I feel his thick cock spread my soaking silken folds, and I get that deep tingle of anticipation. With one deep, firm thrust, he sinks inside me—hard. He is so unbelievably solid and impressively large that he hits the very end of me and makes me gasp. He pulls back, a wicked grin etched at the corners of his smile. "It's a classic for a reason." He pitches up on his elbows, but the majority of his weight covers my body. I close my eyes and relish the feeling. My muscles start to twitch around his cock as he holds himself firm and immobile. I open my eyes to meet his intense, fiery gaze.

"You are having doubts." His voice is low and stern, but the gentle rotation of his hips is more than a little distracting to the seriousness of his statement.

"Mmm…that feels so good, Jason." I sigh.

"Yes, it does. You are having doubts." He repeats both his statement and his heavenly hip action. I swallow thickly and watch as his eyes darken, and the tiny muscles inside me begin rippling like crazy along his erection.

"Not about us…not about how I feel about you." The pitch in my voice is remarkably level, but the words are breathy and strained.

"Good." He pushes deeper, and I lose all cognisant thought until he draws back just a little. "That is all that matters, Sam. Everything else is detail…we will deal with the detail together as husband and wife." I had been gripping his taut shoulder muscles, and I slide my hands down his back and flex them wide to take a good grasp of his fine backside in each hand. The way his defined muscles contract under my hands with each thrust and drive is the sexiest fucking thing. I sink my nails into his skin to secure my hold.

"Some of those details are pretty fucking big, and we've not exactly sat down and discussed the future." This feels so good, why the fuck am I bringing up this subject now?

"What details?" Oh God, he just grinds with the perfect pressure that makes my clit pulse like a needy bundle of aching nerves and it drives me crazy.

"Please, Jason." I try to shift down and tilt to get a little bit more friction, just where I need him, but he sinks like a dead weight preventing any further movement on my part.

Stupid dumb ass, you deserved that, Sam. You couldn't just wait and have this conversation in the morning?

"What details, Sam? What specifically about our future do you wish to discuss?" I can see the muscles in his jaw clench with effort, controlling his temper or his libido, I can't quite tell. His face is stern and his voice is calm.

"I don't want to discuss any of it now. *Now*, I just want to come," I grind out through a fake and frustrated smile.

"And if you tell me what details, I might let you." His tone is a perfect mix of lightly mocking and threatening.

I let out a defeated puff of air. His face is impassive, and he has now frozen all orgasm-inducing movement. I can't exactly think straight, but I know him well enough to understand he is more than capable of keeping me hanging until he gets his answers.

"My house for one," I call out.

"What about your house?" He raises a curious brow.

"Do I sell it? Am I living here permanently?" He chuckles, a deep throaty rumble I can feel in my chest and much lower.

"You're getting riled over this? You're adorable. Yes, you are living with me permanently. That's what husbands and wives do; they live together. I couldn't care less where that is — here or at your place is not important. Sell your house, or don't; that's your decision, beautiful." He shifts a little, just enough to send a wave of tingles from my clit to every waiting nerve in my body. I stifle a whimper. "What else you got that's troubling you?"

"Babies," I blurt out, but my tone is more like an accusation.

"What about babies?" His words come out slower and with more caution. His brows pinch together to form a dark, almost-touching line.

"Well, we've never talked about them and that's a pretty big detail to leave unmentioned, don't you think?"

"I don't want children, so it honestly didn't cross my mind, but since it is a detail you have clearly considered, tell me, Sam, do you want children?" His tone is soft, but I feel like an ice blast has frozen my heart at his stark revelation.

"I…I don't know…maybe one day." I swallow the lump in my throat and try to push his heavy body away as I fight to take in my next breath.

"Hey, Sam, look at me." His stern tone draws my gaze. My nose tingles, and I feel stupid and exposed that this has upset so. Of course, he wouldn't want children. Too domesticated for someone like the kinky owner of London's elite sex club, and certainly not with someone like me.

"It's fine…I understand." I dig my nails into his biceps to get him to move, but he doesn't budge at all.

"You clearly don't." He arches a brow, and I can see his lips start to curl with amusement, which fires my blood with irritation, and I struggle like a wild animal to get free. He grabs my flailing arms and pins them high above my head. He pushes his hips harder onto mine, and I swear I can feel him swell inside me. "You're making me painfully hard, Sam. It is very distracting, and we need to clear this up before it gets silly."

"Silly?" I snap, my tone piqued. I'm incredulous at his flippancy. He narrows his eyes, and his dark stare makes me bite my tongue. He looks deadly serious.

"I have never wanted children, and that hasn't changed. What has changed is you. You are my world, and I will do anything in my power to make you happy. If that means having a dozen children, then I will *happily* be your baby daddy." All tension has left his face despite his serious tone. His smile is breathtakingly beautiful.

"Oh." I mouth the word, because he's once more rendered me speechless.

"Oh…happy now?" He nudges my nose with his.

"You won't get bored?" I hate that the doubts just keep bubbling up.

"What?" He shakes his head a little.

"There aren't many married members at the club, Jason. I don't think it's what normal couples do. I worry the whole domestic nature of marriage is going to be a huge turn off." I try to shrug, but my arms are still stretched taut.

"Actually, there are several married members. And what have I said about our 'normal'? We make our own rules, beautiful, and as long as you belong to me, nothing else matters." He gazes at me for endless seconds that feel like hours. I didn't realise I was holding so much tension, but his words wash over me and seep into my soul, making me a pliant, gooey mess.

He rolls his hips, and I can feel every inch of his considerable length slide in and out at a gloriously languid pace. His eyes darken and his brows crinkle with concentration.

"Any other details you want to discuss?" His deep voice drops an octave, and the roughness sends a tingle of shivers across my skin. I shake my head and tilt my hips at an inviting angle that makes him groan. "Words, Sam, I need to hear your words. I need to know you are happy."

"I am, and in about five short moves, I will be euphoric." He growls and drops his weight to stop me from moving against him.

"Sam." His tone is reprimanding, but the last thing I want to do is extend this conversation.

"I am very happy, Jason. I have no other details to discuss other than I would very much like to finish what you started." I try fruitlessly to grind a little pleasure from his body.

"You love me?" His question makes me stop. His deep chocolate eyes shine with flecks of gold, but there is hesitation in his voice that breaks my heart. I hope to god that I haven't made him doubt that I do.

"With all my heart, Jason. I'm sorry, but I struggle to believe I deserve this happy ending. I can't help looking for the catch." I rush to try and explain my destructive doubts.

"No catch, beautiful...our happy ending is just a little different. It's just you and me and our very own kinky ever after."

"I like the sound of that." I let out a sigh that is captured by his eager mouth over mine. His tongue takes possession, and we duel with sensual strokes and urgent kissing that leaves us both breathless. "Now, fuck me like you hate me." I cry out when I manage to catch my breath. His eyes light, and his smile turns from warm to wicked in a flash.

"With pleasure."

"Oh good god, Leon, what is that smell?" I instantly slap my hand to my nose when I step into the kitchen of my old apartment. The detritus on every surface looks days, possibly weeks old. Take out boxes and half-eaten meals congealed and decomposed on every plate I owned. Stacks of glasses...and is that a vase he has used for beer? "Jesus, Leon, I'm surprised someone hasn't called environmental health."

"Do you want a coffee?" Leon ignores my comment and runs his hand through his long dark hair. He does, at least, have the decency to look embarrassed.

"In what, Leon?" I wave my hand at the array of dirty cups.

"It's six in the morning, Sam. I wasn't expecting visitors." He picks up one of the fresher dirty cups and starts to rinse it under the tap. I push him to the side, flick the tap to boiling hot, and squeeze a large dollop of washing liquid in the bowl already crammed to bursting. Once the bowl is full and soaking the dried-on, stained crockery, I open the cupboard and pick out a large black sack. I hand it to Leon with a scowl.

"Maid's day off." He tries to joke but bites his lip shut at my thunderous glare.

Thirty minutes is all it takes to clear the surfaces, load the dishwasher, and clean up enough to make us both a fresh cup of coffee.

"Seriously, Leon, you can't live like this." My tone is sharp. It's not as if I used to clean up after him when we lived together. He had always been the tidy one. "Get a cleaner if you can't be arsed—"

"I miss you." His words stop me dead, and I soften inside and out. I step up to him and wrap my arms tight around his trim but naked waist. It's been four weeks since we became more than best friends, along with Jason's twin brother, Will. The most amazing night of my life not just because…well, it was my number one fantasy, but because I became *me* again. Richard had very nearly succeeded in destroying me, with kidnapping, torture, and murder. Even being saved wasn't enough to bring me back to my old self. The physical scars healed, but I didn't know how to heal the scars inside. Jason did…he saved me.

Leon and I have seen each other since then, and it's not been at all awkward, but I had no idea he felt like this about me moving out.

"Oh Leon, sweetie." I nestle against his chest and draw in a deep sniff of his manly overnight smell. "I miss you too, but you are always welcome to come over. There's a spare room, and I know Jason wouldn't mind."

"I think he would." His arms hold me a little tighter when I start to move away. "Besides, the last thing I need is to be listening to your marathon fuck-a-thons. Jason's like the fucking Energizer Bunny." He kisses the top of my head and releases his hold. I sniff out a laugh.

"He really is. But you and me…we're okay, right? You're not saying it's the last thing you need because you want something to happen between us, right?" My voice raises a touch high with worry.

"I definitely want something to happen with us…but I mean *all* of us. I can't get that night out of my head." He drags his hand roughly down his face, and I hear the sound of his morning stubble scratching his palm. "But no, we're cool, babe, you know that." He ruffles my hair in its already messy bun. "I just miss you being here, and seeing you with Jason. Damn." He lets out a heavy sigh. "I'm happy for you, babe. Your relationship just made me realise how lucky Jason is in finding someone like you. I mean you love that kinky shit; you both do, and I don't know if I'll ever find someone who gets me like that." He shrugs, but the genuine sadness in his eyes tugs at my heart.

"And to think just this morning I was worried that Jason would be bored once we got married and become all domesticated," I joke.

"Boring is not the word I would ever use to describe you two, and it's just a piece of paper, babe. It doesn't change who you are. It just changes your last name…if you want that. Besides that little display you did last night was more of a binding ceremony in our world."

"So why propose at all?"

"Maybe he doesn't think that way. Maybe for him, this lifestyle is just play. The fun and games are great, but now he's found the real deal, and under all that kink, he is Mr Traditional, after all, just like you." He bops me playfully on the nose, and I frown.

"What are you talking about? I love the kink." I balk at his accusation.

"I know you do, Sam, but I also know you hide behind it. It's easy to turn your back on an ideal if you think you'd never get the chance of experiencing it. But that is exactly what you have with Jason. You, my darling, have the whole fucking package."

"Maybe, but it doesn't stop the doubts," I murmur aloud.

"Doubts?"

"I struggle with happily ever afters, Leon, and he doesn't want kids." I throw that in like an unsubstantiated criminal charge.

"Um, not to state the bloody obvious, but you don't want kids, either. You have that three-year implant thingy because you're scared of forgetting pills, so I don't think you can hold that against the guy," he challenges me. "Did you change your mind?"

"No. Well, maybe, I don't know. I never thought I would be in a position to consider it. When Richard got me pregnant, I was terrified. When I lost the baby, I was devastated; that's why I have the implant. My experience of the whole thing was not something I would wish on my worst enemy. But I love Jason; I want a real life with him, and that might involve children." I shift under his soft but intense gaze.

"And you think he feels any different? Because I will bet my arse he doesn't. And as for not deserving a happily ever after, fuck that bullshit! That's your mother talking if ever I heard a put-down." He steps up to me and holds my chin firmly, his eyes searing right through me. "Don't let her ruin this for you, Sam. You deserve to be loved. You deserve him." Although he grits his teeth slightly with that last word, I get a warm feeling from the sentiment and sincerity of his words.

"Thank you, Leon. I've missed you, too." I lean up to kiss his cheek. "Do you have time for breakfast? If you have eggs, I could whisk up something scrambled?"

"You cook now?" His eyes widen with shock.

"Jason's been teaching me," I offer shyly.

"Maybe I will come for a sleepover if a cooked breakfast is on the menu. There are eggs in the cupboard, and I think there is a loaf in the bread bin, but don't quote me on that." He turns to leave. "I'll grab a quick shower," he shouts over his shoulder and disappears into the hallway.

Fifteen minutes later, Leon appears in a crisp white shirt, tie, and elegant three-piece navy suit. He scrubs up well even if his face is still unshaven, and his hair is damp. I plate up the glossy eggs and split the last slice of toast between us. I pour him a fresh black coffee and slide onto the stool beside him.

"No work today?" Leon's appraising glance at my casual skinny jeans, oversized scoop neck cable knit sweater, and some flashy five-inch suede ankle boots might be a giveaway.

"Day off. It's why I'm here. I am hoping I left my passport here." Leon raises a brow, waiting for me to elaborate, which I happily do. "We're going on a weekend break, but I don't know where. It's a surprise and very last minute." I can't hide the excitement in my voice, and it's clearly contagious as Leon returns my beaming smile.

"If you kept it in your room, it will be safe. Out here...not so much." He grimaces as his eyes take in the bombsight that used to resemble my living room. I jump off the stool and go to check if what he has said about my room is true. I have moved most of my stuff to Jason's over the last few months, but I had left a few things. I shake off the likely notion that this in itself is evidence of my reservations. This is stupid. I don't need to keep my room here. I don't live here anymore. I fish my passport out of my bedside drawer and return to the kitchen. Leon has washed the dishes and is just wiping the counter. He flashes a knowing smile.

"There are two bedrooms empty now, Leon, you should get a flatmate to share." His smile widens.

"You gonna move the rest of your stuff over to Jason's then?" He purses his lips, trying to suppress his grin.

"I am as soon as I get back." I nod my affirmation.

"Then perhaps I will. I could use some company. Maybe some twins would be fun, don't you think?" He bites his lip flat, and I feel my cheeks heat with instant fire. I throw the nearest thing at hand, which lucky for him is a cushion.

"Jackass." I narrow my eyes, but he catches the cushion and barks out a deep chuckle.

"So no repeat performance on the horizon…you know we have Valentine's Day in a few weeks, hmm?" He wriggles his dark brows suggestively.

"You're incorrigible."

"I really am. But I didn't hear a no," he teases.

"That's the thing with fantasies, Leon. They are like favourite places or moments in time. The shine and brilliance of the experience you can never recreate, and going back is always a disappointment."

"By that token, fucking Jason would lose its lustre, no?" He challenges my hypothesis.

"Ah…you have me there, my friend, because that just gets better and better." I pat Leon on his cheek. "And it is never a disappointment."

I return to Jason's place just as he is loading the boot of his car with our bags.

"Perfect timing, beautiful. Are you ready?" He sweeps his arms around my waist and covers my lips with his before I get the chance to answer. His soft lips taste of sweetness and bitter coffee. My body melds to his, and my hands fist the collar of his jacket, holding him tight to me. I can't get enough of the way he makes me crave him, every touch, every taste. He's addictive, and I'm a blissfully happy addict. He releases my lips but holds me steady as I sway, a little giddy from the kiss.

"I am." I wave my passport. "Where are we going?"

"Amsterdam."

Jason

I hit the accelerator just outside of Calais. The motorway is pretty clear, and at this time in the morning, we should make the journey through Belgium and up to the north of the Netherlands in less than four hours. Sam has kicked her fuck-me heels into the foot well and has her fluffy sock-clad feet resting on the dashboard. Her head is resting on her shoulder, and a mass of dark hair has fallen to partially obscure her face. My fingers twitch to stroke the hair away and reveal her flawless skin; even the tiny scar on her cheekbone is perfection. It's a permanent reminder that she is a survivor. She glows with strength that, every day, I am humbled to witness. With extra effort, I still my hand and let her sleep. Today was a surprise early start after an action-packed and seriously interrupted night's sleep. I guess I should be tired too, but I'm anything but. We fucked like we were both possessed, and that is exactly what she does. She possesses me when she comes apart in my hands and surrenders everything she is; at that moment, she is at her most vulnerable, most beautiful, and that's why she fucking owns me.

She's crazy if she thinks anything is going to change the way I feel about her, but she's right that marriage is a big deal. I love that she made the display at the club with my collar in front of everyone but, even if she hadn't, it would never be enough for me, not now. She changed all that. I only invited Will and Leon to join us at the club on Christmas Day because I thought it was the only way to bring her back to me. I am so fucking glad it did, but there is no way I could share her again, and for someone like me, that is a *massive* fucking deal. I sound more like Daniel than I do myself. But with Sam? I. Don't. Share.

I know she's mine, and there is no hurry to get married. I want her to have the perfect day, and that takes time, but I also want her to realise that nothing has to change. That's what this weekend is about. After she fell asleep, I went online and arranged this trip to the sex capital of Europe. The legalised drugs aren't of interest, but because of the liberal laws regarding the sex trade, some of the private clubs are...*special.*

"Mmm," she moans and arches her body into a decent stretch given the confines of the R8 interior. "Are we there yet?" She yawns and pulls her legs into her chest, wrapping her arms around her knees and shifting onto her side to face me.

"What are you...four?" I mock.

"I didn't say 'Are we there yet, Dad?'" She pouts and wrinkles her nose. She has soft pink lines on her face, crumpled skin from a heavy head against her shoulder. Her tongue darts out to wet her lips, and it's all I can do to keep from swerving off the road. She looks edible.

"Oh beautiful, you can call me *Daddy* if you want, but I'm always gonna prefer Sir." My voice drips with sensual meaning.

"I prefer Sir." Her sultry, soft tone feels like a direct hit in my balls. I push my head back into the headrest and straighten my arms; my fingers tighten on the wheel, a subtle, instant reaction that makes her giggle. I try to shift in my seat to ease the painful ache from my now rock-hard cock.

"Sorry." She sucks in her lips and fails to look even vaguely apologetic.

"No, you're not." I groan when her hand reaches over and rubs the material stretched taut over my shaft.

"Not remotely, but I am more than happy to help." She slips the seatbelt over her head so it is only wrapped across her waist, and she slinks across the center of the car, like a super sexy feline. I lift my left arm to make room. Christ, my balls feel like they are ready to explode, and she hasn't even loosened my buckle. Oh, now she has...shit!

"Sam, I really don't think this is a good idea." My voice catches, and I try to swallow the sudden dryness in my mouth.

"Really? I think this is a great idea. Besides..." Her warm breath sears the fibers on my pants; her head hovers as she deftly releases my erection into her waiting hand. "Breakfast is the most important meal of the day."

"Holy. Fucking shiiii...Ah! Oh yes that...do that again!" I swallow back a choking cough and let the most amazing feeling radiate through my body unchecked. She has her fist tight around the base, but her mouth covers the engorged end, and she swallows me down like I really am the best meal of the day. I can feel the muscles in her throat, and I fight the urge to jerk my hips forward. The back of her head keeps nudging the bottom of the steering wheel as it is. Her tongue does this thing where she slides and wraps it around my shaft, all the while drawing me deeper into her mouth, until I am touching the back of her throat. She pauses only to catch a breath before she swallows me deeper. *God, this feels fucking amazing.* I know I'm not all in; her hand is taking over where her mouth is physically unable…at least at this angle.

I am counting backward in Italian just to try and not think about losing control. But when she releases my cock, and her lips instantly wrap around one of my balls, I swerve the car onto the hard shoulder and into the police only waiting area. I'd rather get arrested than die, and she is fucking killing me here. Her head pops up, and I slip from her swollen lips.

"Problem?" Her devious smile is all faux innocence.

"No problem." I am impressed I can maintain a level voice and a steady exhale. "There will be though if you don't get your fucking jeans off and ride me till I come." Her pink cheeks flush a little redder, her eyes darken with pure passion, and her slim throat takes a deep, slow swallow.

Now I've changed my mind.

"Wait… No time, just finish what you started, beautiful." I thread my hand into what's left of her messy bun and pull her back into position. Her eyes meet mine and flash with mirrored desire before bending over millimeters from my aching erection.

"Yes, Sir." She exhales a breathy sigh with her words, scorching the wetness seeping from my tip. Her tongue is quick to take the moisture, and her lips quickly follow. She sinks quickly onto my length, and eager to please, she almost swallows me whole.

"Fuuuuuck!" Every muscle in my backside tenses, and I grip the steering wheel like it is my only anchor to Earth. One of her hands pumps the base of my cock, which makes my spine tingle from top to tip. She palms my balls with her other hand, and her magic tongue is driving me insane, tracing the pulsing vein from the very bottom of me to the sensitive top. She tilts her head to flash me a wicked grin and smiles wide, pulling her lips free and exposing her bright white, straight, and from memory, surprisingly sharp teeth. I suck in a sharp breath and brace myself. I fucking hate teeth.

But there are no teeth, and I don't know whether to sigh with relief or growl with irritation. I do neither, because her heavenly mouth takes me as far as her breathing will allow. She swallows repeatedly, and I explode down her eager throat. My stomach muscles spasm from the intensity of my release, and I take a few moments to draw in enough air to compose myself. She softly licks me clean, and even though I am not remotely soft, she expertly tucks my cock back into its cotton cage. Crawling back to her seat, she faces me. Her eyes never leave mine, even as she slowly wipes her wet lips with the back of her hand and proceeds to lick that clean like a kitty. Damn, that is the sexiest thing—next to what she has just done, that is.

I reach out and cup the back of her head, drawing her forcefully to my waiting kiss. I press hard, the taste of me fresh but faint on her lips. Her taste is intoxicating, and I can't get enough. I twist my body and try to drag her from her seat. The car fills with a sudden bright blue light, and a piercing siren screams a brief but effective interruption. We both freeze, Sam's eyes, wide at first, transform with her impossibly huge grin once the initial shock has faded.

"Uh-oh, someone's in trouble." She wiggles her brows playfully, and I fire a scowl with no anger intended at her. She starts to giggle.

"Oh, someone's in lots of trouble, but let's get out of this first, shall we?" My tone is lightly reprimanding.

"We? You're the one who pulled over into a police only wait zone." She bites her lips to stop full-blown hysterical laughter as a figure appears at my window.

"Because a ticket is better than death…although…" I muse and press the window to open. I greet the officer and catch a quick glance at Sam. Her mouth drops at my fluent French. I pulled the car over just south of Belgium's border with the Netherlands. This country is one of the few that are trilingual, speaking Dutch, German and, lucky for me, French. The officer is stern, and a series of explanations and questions later, he gives me a warning but not a ticket. I shut the window when he tries to take another peek inside at my flushed faced fiancée.

I pull smoothly back into the traffic but keep to a sensible speed as the police car has pulled out right behind and is currently tailing me.

"You speak French?" Her clipped tone makes her question sound more like an accusation.

"What can I say? I'm very good with my tongue." She scoffs out a loud laugh mixed with an uncontrolled snort that sends her into a fit of giggles. I adore that sound almost as much as the little moans and sighs.

Once she has calmed herself, she raises her brow with an unasked query and fixes me with her enquiring stare.

"I did French as an extracurricular at Uni, and you know the Italian I picked up when I lived there. I find languages very useful and easy." I shrug lightly, but her face lights with interest.

"I'm impressed. So, what did you say to the officer?"

"I told him I thought my fiancée was having an allergic reaction and, for safety, I pulled over." She frowns and looks dubious. "I explained that the swelling had gone down and was now really only visible in your lips." I answer, deadpan and serious.

"Oh, my God, you didn't?" she gasps, both her hands flying to her mouth.

"I did, and it worked…no ticket." He flashes a wicked grin.

"He didn't believe you, did he?" Mortification at my revelation colours her cheeks, and they turn an adorable shade of red right before my eyes.

"Nope. Might be why he's still on my tail…hoping for a sequel," I quip.

"He'll have a long wait." She sniffs derisively.

"What?" My head snaps round.

"Relax, Jason." Her hand pats my thigh, giving a reassuring little squeeze. "I didn't mean a long wait for another blow job." She snickers. "I mean a long wait before I put on a show for an audience."

"You had me worried for a moment." I let out an exaggerated breath that makes her laugh.

"And you have me still hungry." She pats her flat tummy, this time for actual food.

"We can stop in Bruges for breakfast if you like, but not for long." I flick the indicator for the next exit on the motorway.

"Yes, please. And why the sudden time frame? I thought this was a spontaneous trip?"

"It is…but I've still made plans." I flash my knowing grin.

"When we get to Amsterdam, you mean?"

"I do." I offer flatly. She narrows her eyes at my evasive responses.

"What kind of plans?" The tone of her voice is filled with suspicion. She's very perceptive. This may be last minute, but I want this weekend to be about our *normal.* I want her to understand we set our own rules.

"Just the usual tourist things people do in a city—sightseeing, museums, galleries," I muse playfully but drop the tone of my voice to a deeper timbre for portent, adding, "Dinner and a *show.*"

Sam pokes her head out of the roof top window. The view from the loft room reaches far over the entire city on a clear day like today, but it's January, and it's bitterly cold. She briskly rubs some warmth back into her arms after shutting the window. Turning my way, she flashes me the most excited smile imaginable. That look alone makes my chest clench. She rushes toward me and wraps her arms tight around my chest, and she delights in squeezing the breath from my lungs. For such a slight figure, she has some impressive upper body strength.

"Thank you! This place is stunning." She covers my lips with hers but breaks away before I can get my fill. She giggles at my audible frustration and walks across the room to explore the en suite. The room is spacious for a central city hotel, but then it is the best on the Grachtengordel or Canal ring. Most are converted town houses, which are compact at best and the loft rooms can be a challenge for someone of my height. This is perfect, though, white painted wood-panelled walls that slope to the ceiling, heavy beams span the room but are high enough that I won't knock myself out every time I stretch.

"Oh, wow, have you seen this bath, Jason?" Sam calls out as I finish unpacking. I laugh when I enter the adjoining room to see her fully clothed mock swimming in the very large claw footed bathtub. "You could fit a whole football team in here." She squeals and throws her arms around my neck when I stride over and scoop her into my arms.

"No football teams, beautiful…just me from now on." My gravelly tone is more forceful than jovial at her remark, and I am rewarded with a full body shiver.

"Perfect." She beams. "Only you." She purses her lips for a kiss that never happens.

"Damn right!" I dump her unceremoniously on the sumptuous bed, and she screams with surprise, but instantly relaxes in the luxurious comfort of an over-stuffed bed. She lets out a deep, satisfied sigh and pitches herself up on her elbows. Ever so slowly, she draws her bottom lip in between her teeth, and her eyes darken with wicked intention that transforms her innocent features into temptation personified.

"So what now?" Her voice is an overtly breathy whisper, and she wiggles her brows seductively. Only for a moment though, because she yelps when I throw her jacket for her to catch, her quick reflexes prevent a direct hit.

"Behave! We are going sightseeing. We have a personal guided tour booked." Her eyes light with excitement. Her salacious alternate plans forgotten, she instantly jumps and shuffles to the end of the bed ready to join me.

"It kills me to say this, but you will be much more comfortable in the walking boots I packed." I actually groan at the thought of her taking off those killer fuck-me heels and wearing the utility sturdy fur-lined footwear I bought her. She raises her perfect brow and purses her lips.

"Really, Jason, I could walk a marathon in these. I know they are high, but I've broken them in so they feel like slippers to me. I'm sure I'll manage walking a few city streets." She mocks my concern.

"On a bike?" I clarify and watch her jaw drop.

"Excuse me?"

"We're going to be riding bikes," I repeat. My smile stretches far and wide as I watch this information sink in. "It's a great way to cover a lot of the city. We've only got a few hours, but if you think you can manage in what you're wearing…" I teasingly wave the more practical boot in front of me at arm's length.

"I haven't ridden a bike in forever, Jason. I hope it's like they say it is…you know…just like riding a bike?" She sniffs out a nervous laugh and grabs the boots. The soft mattress and abundant covers envelop her tiny form when she perches on the end of the bed. Even doing something as ordinary as this, she looks too damn tempting. It takes all my restraint not to push her back flat, cover her body with kisses, and take what's mine.

"No need to worry yourself about that today, beautiful. I hired a tandem for us to share, and the personal guide will ensure we see the best bits. We don't have time to 'do' the museums, but I'd like you to get a feel for the city. You won't be in any danger." I pull her up and into my arms as soon as she stands. Her smile spreads wide across her flawless face, and all I can do is look. She is *everything*. Her hands snake around my waist, and she grabs my arse cheeks and pinches hard, pulling me flush against her.

"I think the danger will be that I get to stare at *this* all afternoon, and I won't be able to do a damn thing about it." Her breathy words make my cock twitch, and her brows shoot up in response. "Do we really have to go out?" She grinds her heat against my now very hard erection and gives a sassy little wiggle.

"Again with the killing me here, Sam." I groan but have to admit this feels like a much better option. After all, when in the sex capital of Europe… "Ladies' choice, beautiful, our guide is waiting downstairs with the bike." I nod over to the telephone on the bedside table. "If you want to call down and tell her you want to ride me instead, I am more than good to go right now." I grin because this is a win-win situation for me, and I'm enjoying every second.

"Hmm, damn it!" She huffs and a sexy little furrow creases her forehead. "After this morning in the car, and staring at your arse all afternoon, I am going to be so ready to blow by the time we get back. I swear you will only have to look my way." She squeezes her legs together as if to emphasise her plight, and I get just that little bit harder. This might just be hell for both of us. She clears her throat and places her hand on one cocked hip. "Just so you know, you will have a horny time bomb on your hands," she warns, playfully pushing me away and letting out some built up heat in a loudly exhaled puff of air.

"I'll bear that in mind." I snicker but also have to adjust myself. It's going to be a long afternoon. "You ready?" I grab my wallet while she puts on her puffy jacket. She pulls a black knit woolen hat with a large fluffy pompom down to just above her brow, framing her face perfectly. Her bright, glossy red lipstick is a vivid splash of colour that draws attention from more than my eyes.

We make our way down the stairs to meet our part-time tour guide, and full-time local artist, in the lobby. The elegant white marble entrance has a thin strip of royal blue carpet that leads from the double glass entrance doors to a circular antique table by the reception desk. A tatty brown leather satchel leans against the oversized vase and looks wholly out of place. Much like the lady currently leaning to get a closer look at a large, ornate oval mirror hanging low on the wall. She turns and smiles when she hears us approach, and she instantly offers her hand. Before we even get the chance to say one word, she has introduced herself as Elsa, our guide.

"How did you know it was us that you were meeting?" Sam asks what I was thinking.

"It's low season, and it is very cold. Not many tourists wanting a bike tour." She chuckles by way of an explanation. "I have your bike outside. Are you sure you want a tandem? They can be tricky?"

"We're sure," I confirm, and Sam is also nodding with a huge grin. This is going to be fun.

There is a light frost on the ground but nothing dangerous as we weave our tandem bicycle from the heart of the city where our hotel is to the outskirts of Amsterdam. Elsa steers us down narrow streets and over many of the bridges that cross some of the one hundred and sixty canals. The streets and waterways span out from the center of the city in the shape of a fan and make it easy to navigate. In all, ninety islands make up one of the most popular and picturesque cities in Europe. Throughout the ride, I can hear Sam gasp and coo at the sights Elsa is pointing out along with snippets of information that Sam seems eager to absorb. She tugs on my jacket if she thinks I've missed something. I regret that I can't see her face, but we stop occasionally and I get the feeling that she loves every minute.

The farthest point we reach is Vondel Park, acres of landscaped parkland, which would, no doubt, be heaving with visitors in the summer months. Today it is sprinkled with a few hardy dog walkers and, of course, cyclists. We make a complete loop of the outer path, past the lakes, and head back toward the hotel. The ever present flow of cyclists becomes heavier as we join what must be a shortcut through the under pass of the Rijksmuseum. We stop for a well-earned beer, and Elsa happily answers all Sam's questions that she was unable to ask while we rode through the town.

"So you will be visiting De Wallen later?" Elsa gives us both an easy smile. She has long grey hair that it neatly plaited down her back. Her thick glasses magnify the many lines crinkling at the corners of her eyes, and she is wrapped in several layers of shabby chic colourful clothing. However old she might be, after nearly two hours of constant cycling, she isn't remotely out of breath.

"De Wallen?" Sam frowns and looks at me.

"The Red Light district." I grin and watch as Sam's cheeks pink up more than they have all afternoon from the January chill.

"Oh, I don't know," Sam mutters shyly.

"You should definitely go. It is the oldest part of the city and very beautiful. Many interesting bars and museums. It comes alive at night. I think it is the best time to experience the atmosphere." She smooths out a map of the city and draws a big black circle around the rosse buurt, another name she called the famous area. "But take care, also." She laughs lightly. "You will be safe with this one I am sure." She leans over to pat my arm and smiles warmly at Sam. Her Dutch accent flavours her English, but her meaning is perfectly understood. Sam snorts out a laugh at the massive understatement. I have no problem that I am overt in my protectiveness of the woman I love. It is born out of the scariest time in my life. A time I never want to repeat, and if that means everyone knows Sam belongs to me, so be it.

"We have tickets for a show," Sam explains, her voice light with excitement.

"Oh really, which one?" Elsa turns to me when Sam shrugs and shakes her head.

"*Chez-moi*." I reply with a flat, impassive tone. It's Elsa's turn to blush.

"Oh." Elsa laughs nervously and quickly smiles at Sam. "That will be…that is…I'm sure you'll…" She gathers her satchel and mumbles something about needing the ladies but won't look directly at me. Sam turns to me with a curious pout to her lips.

"Oh?" Sam questions. "Should I be worried?"

"Do you trust me?" I gently take her chin and tip it so she meets my gaze. She always meets my gaze, and her eyes perfectly reflect the love I feel.

"Of course," she states without hesitation.

"Then no, you shouldn't be worried." My lips cover hers, and she returns my urgent kiss. It's been too long already.

THREE

Sam

Jason has laid out on the bed what he wants me to wear for this evening, and the thrill of the unknown just kicks my heart rate into overdrive. I've been on edge since the cryptic conversation with Elsa this afternoon. I'm tingly, excited, and more than a little aroused, entirely due to Jason's sensual massage and our bath together. The abstinence thing is becoming an issue and not just for me. He has been rock-hard and taunting me with his nakedness while we have been preparing to get ready. But he has plans.

"There are no panties?" I finish clipping the opaque soft wool stockings and stand with one hand on my hip and one just lifting the center of my skirt for a full on peep show. The short skirt is pleated soft leather that flares wide and skims my thighs just below the tops of the stockings. My bra is a type of mini corset that hugs my rib cage and makes my breasts look perilously close to spilling out with every breath I take. Jason turns from the wardrobe adjusting the cuffs of his shirt to sit just right. His eyes darken, and he bites back a growl that I can still hear rumble from his immaculate suit-clad chest.

"Jesus, what was I thinking?" he mutters, striding toward me. I hold my hand up to halt him, and although it presses flat against his chest, it does nothing to stop the momentum. I am stepped back hard and fast into the wall. His mouth is on my neck, searing my skin like a branding iron, the heat runs like a wildfire through my veins. My hands fist his shirt beneath his jacket, my knuckles pressing hard into his firm, unyielding chest. He bites down, and my whole body quakes.

"Ah!" My breath catches, and I finish my cry in a silent gasp of air. He stands tall, every inch of his firm body presses against mine. The sexual tension is tangible, and I want to rip through it—right now. I tip my head forward so my mouth is just a sleek film of lip gloss from his, but he collects himself, straightening out of my reach on a steady exhale of held breath.

"I have plans." His deep voice is thick with lust that he struggles to swallow back down.

"Your plans do involve fucking me at some point though, right? I just want to clarify, because I can promise you one thing; I will not make it through this night without a little relief." I visibly sag when he moves back, letting out a low throaty chuckle, which just makes me squirm a little more. God, that is a sexy sound.

"You have my word, beautiful, before the night is out you will be more than sated—" He wiggles his dark brow as I interrupt.

"Enough with the cryptic. Are you going to tell me what we're doing tonight?" I huff like a petulant child. Patience is not one of my virtues.

"Dinner and a—"

I snap my interruption.

"Show. Yes, I know that much. Fine, don't tell me." I pout and step around him to finish getting dressed. The black silk wrap blouse is elegant, the criss-cross back is sexy and the very low front exposes glimpses of my corset bra. It is all perfectly Amsterdam scandalous. Jason holds up a full-length cream cashmere coat with a fur-lined hood and helps me in, turning me and tying up the belt with an overly firm tug and an obnoxiously smug wink.

"Just tell me this: Is the whole teasing, touching, not actually fucking, all part of the plan?"

"It's a surprise, Sam. Where would be the surprise if I told you?"

"God, you're infuriatingly smug about this." I narrow my eyes, but he remains ever impassive.

"I am. I really am. Shall we?" He offers his elbow, the guise of the perfect gentleman harbouring the wicked sadist beneath.

"I am yours but to command, Sir," I say with a heavy dose of sarcasm and a slight curtsey before sliding my arm into his. He pats my hand and leans in to whisper, his nearness drenching me in his unique and intoxicating scent: a mix of mountains, mint, and pure manliness.

"I was really hoping you were going to say that," he replies with lethal sincerity and a grin that wouldn't look out of place on the devil himself.

The club is in the basement of a five-story town house, no different than the other hundreds of houses stacked and wedged on the narrow streets of the Old Town. This building is just off the main thoroughfare and the heart of the popular Red Light district. The small gold nameplate bearing the name Chez Moi is the only item on the glossy black door. The reception area is small with barely space for the reservations desk. Low-level lighting from candles creates a warm and inviting ambience. The walls are covered with a bold velvet pattern, and a large crystal chandelier hangs from the vaulted ceiling. The space might be small, but it is richly furnished and exudes luxury and wealth. I didn't think Jason would take me to a seedy club, but he had said it was a surprise, and that would've definitely been a shock.

The hostess greets us with a friendly smile. Her hair is pinned up in a sleek bun, and she has the most striking eyes, which are framed with dramatically long lashes. Her eyes are the only thing to notice though, because half of her face is concealed with a plain black mask. She hands Jason a slim, shiny, gift-wrapped box and proceeds to take my coat. I am left curious for only a moment. Jason loosens the elegant ribbon and opens the lid to reveal two similar black masks. He shucks his coat, handing it over, and takes the smaller mask from the box. He motions with a slow twirl of his finger and a salacious grin for me to turn. The mask is the softest leather imaginable and molds perfectly to the contours of my face. He secures it tightly, and I get the feeling there might be a reason for that. I turn back and watch him cover his own face. His piercing dark eyes look almost black, and sparkle with mischief. I can't stop my thighs pinching together at the liquid pooling inside me, and I am really missing my panties right about now. Long silent seconds pass as he holds me captive with that look. His lips, full and soft, give just the hint of a smile, and there is too much sexual tension to feel anything other than pure unadulterated lust.

Damn! The last thing I want is dinner and a show.

"If you would follow me, please." The light voice of the hostess interrupts our sexy silent standoff. Jason's lips curl into a heart-stopping smile, his hand slips to the base of my spine, and he guides me to follow through a darkened archway. The hostess holds open one side of a large double door, and we step into another darkened room. Ambient lighting is in the form of simulated flames from sconces on the walls above secluded booths. The center of the room is a large circular plinth encased in frosted glass. I try and glimpse inside what looks like an enormous empty display cabinet, but the glass merely reflects the darkness of the room. We are led around the narrow path that separates the center display cabinet and the booths. From the chatter and laughter it is obvious all the tables are occupied, but the clever curve of the high backed seating makes it impossible to see inside.

I slide into the cozy padded booth, and Jason slips in beside me.

The hostess leaves and is immediately replaced by a mask-wearing waitress. Jason orders the taster menu and some Champagne without bothering to look at the menu being offered. I don't think he has taken his eyes off me for a moment.

"Very good, Sir." The waitress clutches the superfluous menus. "The show will commence shortly. If you do not wish to view, you can simply press the privacy button here." She points to an indented panel with two buttons. "And if you require any assistance press the service button." I roll my eyes at the way she drawls the word assistance, and her mask does little to hide her desire for *my* man.

"We won't need any assistance." Jason's curt response makes her back stiffen and sends a warm tingle straight to my chest. She flashes a tight smile and disappears into the darkness.

"What's with the masks?" I lean over and whisper. I'm not sure why, but it feels a little underground and clandestine. He leans down to meet me.

"You'll find out," he whispers back conspiratorially. I huff out in frustration. Damn, that man can keep me on the edge like a pro…*and I should know.*

"Are you wet?" His deep voice is like a rough tongue along my sensitive core, and I am instantly sentient and alert, if a little taken by the blunt question.

"Excuse me?" I swallow, but my throat is too dry.

"Would you like me to repeat the question?" His tone I recognise and its deep commanding timbre sets my heart thumping hard in my corset restricted chest. Dominant Jason has come to play.

"No, Sir," I answer without hesitation but don't lower my gaze. When we play, he allows me to keep the eye contact unless he tells me otherwise, but that is rare. I need the connection. I need to see how much he wants me…needs me. "I'm very wet, Sir."

"Spread your legs wide." His hands are resting on the table, but his fingers twitch when my leg brushes his as I do exactly as he says. I suck in a breath when the waitress returns with the Champagne, but with effort, I keep my position. Jason's lips curl in an appreciative smile as he hands me my glass. We clink and both take a long sip. I like that his throat is obviously just as dry as mine. He dips his finger into his glass and wets it before dropping his hand below the table and between my legs. I jump at the contact, cool liquid on hot fingers. He drags his middle finger along the length of my intimate flesh, as much he can from the angle and my position. I shuffle to the edge of the seat to gain a little more.

God, I want more.

He chuckles a low throaty sound, and his scorching breath bursts across my collarbone when he turns his torso to face me. He is, oh, so close. I am going to combust or suffocate; I can't draw a deep enough breath.

"Jason," I gasp, but my cry sounds more like a plea. He sinks two fingers inside and curls them around, slow firm pressure, but nowhere near enough. He pumps a few more times and withdraws, causing the saddest little whimper to escape my throat. His fingers glisten with my arousal even in this dim light. He slowly sucks one finger clean, briefly closing his eyes with pleasure, before holding the other one at my lips. I open and suck his finger dry, causing his eyes to widen and a groan to rumble from his chest and his jaw to twitch with tension. Good, we're both in erotic hell.

"An amuse-bouche," he offers, drawing his full bottom lip between his teeth, savouring my flavour in his mouth.

"My bouche is anything *but* amused," I grumble, and he barks out a dirty laugh.

"No, from that pout I think you're right. Something you need, beautiful?" His eyes flick down to my deep cleavage, an enhancement caused by the tight pinch of the corset bra. The thick material hides my hard and aching nipples, but even without that, he must know I am off the charts horny and desperate for more than a few strokes of his talented fingers. I want to beg. He loves it when I beg, because it's a very rare occurrence.

"Sir, please." I exhale slowly, a sexy mix of sigh and moan. "I really, *really* need to come."

"Soon." He shifts back in the seat, failing to disguise his own arousal, but that at least gives me some comfort, certainly more than his frustrating response. My whole body sags but still trembles with anticipation. "Soon," he repeats and rests his firm hand on my thigh, holding rather than teasing.

The first course arrives, and I decide that I can't sit like a sexual time bomb all evening. I will be exhausted or just explode.

"When do I get my part of the deal?" My voice is tight but is surprisingly level.

"The deal?" His fork hovers at his lips, and he flashes me a look with, I assume, a raised curious brow under the mask.

"Our deal…I wear your collar and submit, and you let me tie you up and torture you. What? You don't remember that? I'm shocked!" I hold up my hands in mock horror.

"I don't believe I struck *that* deal. It was more of a statement of two unlikely events." He eats the food on his fork then waves it lightly at me. "Well, *one* unlikely event."

"Wearing your collar was just as unlikely," I scoff.

"Think that if it gives you comfort, beautiful, but wearing my collar was inevitable." His hand cups my jaw and is so big it nearly covers half of my head. I rest into his hold. His words are softly possessive and make me melt. "If it's important to you, I have no issue with it. I trust you; I just won't derive any pleasure from it so I don't see the point." He shrugs lightly.

"You wouldn't get turned on?" I can feel my brow furrow, but he won't be able to see the confusion on my incredulous face.

"Fuck, yes! I'm a man, and you're the sexiest fucking woman on the planet. Of course, I'd get turned on, but it's not the same. I don't get off on that. I'm not a switch. I get off on the control and your submission. But I'm a man of my word, and if it would make *you* happy…I said I would do anything to make you happy." His eyes fix me with nothing but the truth.

"Ah, you've taken the fun out of it now. How am I supposed to enjoy tying you up and torturing you if I know you take no pleasure in it? Damn, that sucks." I pout playfully.

"My brother, on the other hand, he is more like Leon than me," he goads.

"Now you are definitely teasing because you said no more sharing."

"I wouldn't share. I would let you torture Will while I watched you in action, and then I'd—" The waitress returns to clear our dessert plates.

"You'll what?" I rush out in a not so quiet whisper. He chuckles at the eagerness in my breathless voice.

"I can't tell you now."

"What?"

"It would be like unwrapping your birthday presents early." He taps me lightly on my nose.

"Oh my god, Jason, you are a sadist! I am dying here. None of the eating, drinking, and especially not the conversation—none of that has quelled that fact that I really, really need to…" The lights flicker interrupting my truculent tirade. The center of the room illuminates and the frosting to the glass clears to reveal an extremely well equipped dungeon. A man and a woman enter. He leads her into the middle and places her awkwardly against the St. Andrew's Cross. He is wearing some ill-fitting leather pants, and she is in a lacy white bra and stockings, but she isn't wearing panties. I suppress a snicker thinking maybe that is the Amsterdam dress code of choice. She is skinny, and he is fit but not toned and is quite pale. He starts to tie her up, and I turn to Jason.

"Is this the show? You've brought me to a live sex show?" I keep my voice low, but I doubt we would be heard through the thick glass. The performers on the other hand can be heard, surround sound, in the booth.

"Of sorts." Jason turns a dial by the service button and the heavy breaths from the speakers quieten.

"Still with the cryptic…It's clearly a show, but they look like it's their first night."

"It most likely is." He flashes a glance at the performance but mostly keeps his eyes on me.

"Jason?"

"They are patrons. It is quite possible this is their first time performing to an audience." My jaw just drops. He holds my gaze but doesn't elaborate. I turn and watch the scene unfold in front of me, feeling for the first time in my life like a voyeur. The man is tenderly stroking the skin of his partner, her arms, her cheek. He tentatively grasps her breasts and she arches into his hold. The movement encourages him, and you can see the remnants of stage fright being replaced with confidence and desire.

"Does everyone have the same view we do…I mean is everyone watching this?"

"Yes."

"Can they see us?"

"No."

"Why would they do that?"

"Why do you think?" His knowing grin is wide and wicked, and I don't bother to reply to the question. I know why people would want to do something like this, perform for others, experiment with any form of kink really. *The thrill.*

"The masks. In the ladies earlier, I was about to take it off, and the attendant stopped me. Is that the reason?" I nod toward the man now kneeling between the woman's legs. His back is to us but, by her clenched fists and gaping mouth, I think she's having fun. "So no one gets recognised before, during, or after."

"Precisely."

"Hmm," I muse and let my gaze follow his back to the show. I have never seen a live show before, porn yes, but nothing up close and very personal. These are not actors or prostitutes; these are ordinary people exploring their sexual desires safely in a private-public way. The woman's skin flushes with excitement. I fight the need to pull my legs together, but Jason feels them twitch. His grip on my thigh stills my involuntary movement. The unbearable ache that has been bubbling under the surface all evening is driving me insane. I drop my hand onto his thigh.

"Nuh-uh, hands where I can see them." His light reprimand is accompanied by a nefarious smile.

"It's only fair. You're killing me here," I whine.

"You like the show? You like to watch?" His question isn't flip. His tone demands a considered answer.

"Voyeurism isn't my thing. Watching someone have sex is for masturbation as far as I'm concerned, but this is different. This is a mix of the two, watching and being watched, and that is very erotic…seductive. I can't imagine what she is feeling." I draw in a deep steadying breath as my pulse rate rockets.

"Can't you?" His question is leading and hangs heavy in the air. I swallow the thick lump choking my next needy breath. I can't believe how turned on I am. I hated when Richard fucked me in front of his friends. How could I be aroused by the thought of this? How could I want to be her, in that room, on display, being worshipped, adored, and fucked raw. How could I want that? I do because this, this is very, very different.

Jason hasn't taken his eyes off me. I can see him in my periphery. I can feel him in the blood burning through me like lava. The lights on the stage dim with perfect timing, capturing the climax but not the come faces. No one wants to see that.

"Did you enjoy that?" His hand threads to the back of my neck, and his fingers dig in to grab a fistful of hair. He moves in close as I gasp, millimetres from his lips.

"I think we could do better." His back straightens, and he pulls back to meet my serious stare.

"You want to repeat that for me."

"I didn't think you liked repetition, *Sir*."

"I don't. But, I think in this instance I need you to be *very* specific as to your meaning." I shift round to face him, my knees coming together for the first time in a long time.

"I said I think we *will* do better."

"Fuck!" He groans as if in agony.

"Yes, please." His lips crush mine and his hand slams over the "Call for Service" button.

All the years I considered myself putting on a show, dressing the part and acting my arse off as Mistress Selina, I never once felt this excited or turned on. Oh, and nervous, don't forget nervous. Jason disappeared for about ten minutes, and we waited in a 'green room' for the performers whilst the stage was prepped for a further fifteen long arduous minutes. Plenty of time for me to change my mind and back out, but every time Jason looked at me with undiluted fire and lust, my smile got just that little bit bigger. After his last and final check, he takes my hand, pulling me from my seat. He strides purposefully through the display room door. What little light there is bounces off the mirrored walls, casting a softly, sinister glow. But this is a stage I am more than familiar with. A dungeon, fantasy, or playroom, they all serve one purpose for Jason and me… *pleasure*.

"First position, beautiful. Let's show them how it's done." He circles me as I drop to my knees. His fingers sweep along my jaw line, and he tilts my head right back. I struggle to swallow when he flashes a wicked grin. He takes his sweet time drawing his lip between his teeth as he peruses the array of implements at his disposal.

He unhooks a sturdy leather swing hanging from an even sturdier looking chain and bolt through the ceiling. He loosens all the straps and then curls his finger for me to come to him. I hop to my feet and walk to face him.

"Take off your blouse and skirt." I lick my dry lips and do as he asks. He sucks in a breath, and his eyes widen as they draw slowly from my high heeled ankle boot, up my stocking clad legs, to my corset bra, and finally resting with untamed desire on my wanton gaze. "So beautiful." He breathes out, and I can't help but smile. He calls me that all the time, but sometimes when he says it like that I actually believe him, inside and out. "Undress me, but don't touch my skin." I fight back a smart remark and a groan. Damn, he *is* a sadist.

"Yes, Sir." My fingers are deft at removing his tie, but his buttons prove a little tricky…so damn close to that soft taut skin over cut muscle. It's all I can think about. I use my fingernails, light and nimble to remove the shirt from his shoulders and get to work on his belt. I tug the material away from his body with more strength than he was expecting, and he chuckles then braces himself with a wider stance for balance. His trousers drop to his knees, and I am grateful he is commando because there is no way I could remove skin-tight boxers without touching him. I drop once more to my knees and help him out of his shoes and pants. I look up when I get to his socks. He can't keep them on, and I can't remove them and obey his wish. He flashes an easy grin and quickly removes each sock. He is gloriously naked, and I am rightly worshiping the heavenly image before me. How did I get so lucky?

I don't think I have ever seen him so hard. His cock is straining to touch his belly button and looks angry and desperate. I certainly get the latter. *I am the definition of desperate.* His fist grabs the base of his cock, and I bounce up from sitting on my heels. I'm pretty sure I would be panting if I didn't think I would look ridiculous—not that I care what I look like with him, but it's not just him. He places the velvet tip to my lips, and I open with a satisfied sigh.

Finally.

He pushes in and my tongue darts to take the glistening arousal dripping from the crown before swirling along the length. He pushes slowly farther down my throat. His hand sweeps the fallen hair from my face back around my ear and comes to rest on my throat. His fingers gently massage with a rhythm matching his gentle thrust. He hits the back of my throat, and with a gentle stroke of his fingers, I swallow a little bit more and take him deeper. He rolls his head back and makes the sexiest groan that makes me melt. He slips from my mouth and, because he hasn't said I can touch him, I have to let him, but I sag. He grins at my swollen, pouting lips. He lifts me high, and I wrap my legs around his firm, narrow waist, gripping him with my thighs like my life depended on it. Relishing the feel of his scorching hot skin on my inner thighs, I sink my weight to try and gain a little extra contact where I need it most. My fingers finally find freedom in his hair and I tug, grip, and pull with wanton abandon. His lips crush mine, his tongue diving in, demanding entrance and taking what is his. I parry his attack with my own desire until he finally breaks us apart, and we both gasp for much needed oxygen.

One of his hands leaves me and grabs for something behind me. The next moment he carefully lowers me onto a wide sheet of soft leather; my bottom is on the edge, but the natural sway and instability of the swing has me falling onto my back. The leather supports my body perfectly, but my legs are dangling, and my hands grip the chains for balance.

Jason scoops one leg into a padded loop, also secured to the bolt in the ceiling, and slides it to just above my knee. He repeats this with my other leg and makes sure the padded part of the strap is comfortable against my skin. He takes a moment standing between my wide spread legs, my body hoisted. His hand rests flat on my tummy, and he pushes me away with a slight sway of the swing. Swinging back I bump back against his thighs, his cock still straining at full attention.

"My turn to worship you, beautiful." His voice is a deep rumble that I feel like wave of electricity, a charge that prickles my skin, as every single tiny hair on my body jumps to stand. He drops to his knees and blows a blast of cool air on my molten center. I must be dripping; I know I am, and the sexy sucking sounds he makes are evidence of the fact. I buck and grip the chains trying to ease the intensity of this amazing feeling building. His tongue is firm and relentless, and when he circles my clit, I cry out. I really wasn't lying when I said I was ready to explode.

"Please, please may I come, Sir?" My voice is strained through gritted teeth. Every muscle in my tummy clenches hard with anxiety that he might deny me. I'm getting better at orgasm denial but I will die if he doesn't let me come.

"My tongue will be very disappointed if you don't." He takes the respite to wipe his glossy mouth on my thigh. I relax with obvious relief.

"Oh, I wouldn't want to disappoint your tongue, not when it's been so *very* good." My voice is a mix of excited anticipation and breathless relief. He grins, and I drop my head back with a heavenly sigh at the long firm sweep of his tongue. He slides two fingers as deep as he can and curls and twirls a blissful rhythm that sends me cresting so damn high I am blinded by the stars dancing behind my lids.

"Oh God…please…Oh…ahhhhh!" I scream and cry out when he sucks down on my clit, and I free-fall, weightless and drifting on wave after wave of absolute pleasure. His glorious mouth buffets the waves, and his tender lips kiss and rock me back to earth. My eyelids flutter open to see Jason towering dark and dominant, pressed at the apex of my thighs, his cock heavy in his hand. He sweeps the thick head along my slick folds, gently teasing until I am fully sentient once more. "Mmm," I moan and arch into the erotic movement that instantly has a deep ache building in the base of my spine. The anticipation is killing me, but it's obviously too much for him too, because with one hard thrust, he pushes deep inside me. The momentum instantly has the swing lifting me from his cock, but he grabs my thighs and pulls me roughly back.

Oh my fucking God!

I would cry out, but I have no breath to speak. He has pushed every bit from my body and filled it with his massive cock. He has *never* been so deep. I didn't know it was possible to go that deep. Unbelievable pleasure paired with pain that dances on the edge of just too much, but is divine nonetheless, a tantalising tortuous paradox. He pauses on his down stroke, and I lift my head to see concern and heat in his eyes.

"Are you okay?" I can feel his thighs tremble against me as he fights to restrain himself. If this feels half as good for him as it does for me, it is Herculean effort he is utilising, holding back like that.

"We have *got* to get one of these." I bite my shit-eating grin back but laugh when he drops his head and lets out an equally happy sound.

When he raises his head all humour has dissipated from his eyes, and his face is a picture of fiery feral passion. I clench and brace, suck in and hold a baited breath, waiting for him to unleash euphoric heights and erotic hell. He bucks his hips and pulls out, thrusts hard again and again and again. Each time he plunges deep, I swing away, and he grabs me, pulling me back, hard, back to where I belong, thoroughly impaled and loving every single inch.

One of his hands gripping the top of my thigh moves to a breast bursting out of the confines of the corset. The rough jerking movements is too much for the soft flesh. He squeezes, a rough, desperate grasp and pinches the nipple. He bends over to take it in his eager mouth. He never breaks his relentless pace. My hands rest on his sweat-covered shoulders, and I sweep them to his waist, holding firmly for some illusive stability. He moves his hand to my throat and starts to apply pressure. My body reacts like an instant detonation, no countdown, no steady build, just fucking nuclear explosion. I gasp for air and come, hard.

I don't remember much after that. His hand may have threaded around my neck. I think he might have told me he loved me, but he could've said *Kangaroos make him horny* for all I know. Because I am aware of nothing except him, deep inside me. Him holding me like I am his anchor to the earth, when the truth is he is mine.

FOUR

Jason

She's glowing under my fingertips as I help her dress. Giggling in fits when her fingers fumble with the tiny buttons on her skirt. Her arms flop listlessly to her side when I take over the simple, but seemingly impossible task. Her smile is soft, sleepy, and her eyes hold so much love, I know with a profound ache in my chest she would destroy me if she ever chose to take that away. She leans heavily into me when I put my arm around her tiny waist, making our way out of the club and on to the still busy street. She sways when we are hit with the late night winter breeze, and she snuggles deeper into my protective frame.

"Think you can manage the walk back, beautiful?" I hold her close and relish the full body shiver that makes her tight little body ripple against mine.

"My legs are like jelly; I think you broke me." She grins with a satisfied little laugh.

"Well, I can't have that." I scoop her into my arms and wince at her high pitched squeal that shatters the quiet of the street. Her subsequent deep throaty laugh, however, fits perfectly with the ever-present atmosphere of darkness and sin in the De Wallen. She wraps her arms around my neck, lets out a deep sigh that morphs into a yawn. Her head rests against my chest, and she is asleep before I even reach the short distance to the corner of the street.

She surprised me tonight. No, that's not right; she completely blew me away. The show I thought would be fun, something a little different, but knowing her history, I didn't dream she would want to perform like we did. I should've known better. My girl is strong and brave and fearless. She may be scarred by her past and the hell that Richard put her through, but she doesn't let that constrain her. It doesn't define her, and she will not let it stop her from doing exactly what she wants, what gives her pleasure. *Lucky me.*

I wake up with a muscle-aching stretch, not because the hazy winter morning sun is peeking through the heavy curtains, but because I am alone. I woke several times in the night and each time I am exactly where I want, my arms wrapped around my prize, entwined and perfect. I rise up on my elbows and listen for telltale sounds in the room and from the en suite. Nothing. I drag my hand roughly down my face, trying to rouse properly when the handle on the door to the room rattles. I leap from the bed, and in two long strides, I pull the handle and swing the door wide. Sam jumps back on a gasp, her eyes wide with surprise, quickly dropping from my face. Shit!

"And good morning to you," she drawls, biting her bottom lip to stop a full-on smirk.

"Oh, my goodness!" A shocked gasp and blur of elderly woman behind Sam in the corridor is confirmation that my naked state has not gone unnoticed. Since the corridor is now empty, I don't bother to retreat, but I do grab Sam's arm, dragging her into the room and my waiting arms.

"And where have you been?" I draw in a deep breath, my nose buried in her thick messy bun. She's intoxicating, and I'm now hard. I stretch my other arm out to slam the door, but Sam wiggles from my hold.

"Wait, wait." She steps into the corridor. "I'll show you." Her voice is a little muffled by the chinking and rattling of flatware and glasses. She pushes a trolley into the center of the room. The large serving tray is set with two ornate silver domes, Champagne chills in an ice bucket, and that smell... steaming hot, freshly-ground coffee.

I take an exaggerated sniff and pat my tummy when she lifts the domes to reveal a feast fit for an army.

"I so want to fucking marry you." I step up to her and lift her so she wraps her legs around my waist. She throws her head back and laughter bursts from her lips, filling the room with utter joy.

"That's lucky." Her smile is shy at first but blossoms and steals my heart with its purity. "Because you've got me. Ball. And. Chain." She punctuates each word with kisses on my waiting lips.

"Speaking of chains—" I wiggle my brows suggestively and drop her so she is just above the tip of my attention-seeking erection. She might not feel my heat through her jeans, but she understands my intention perfectly. She tenses her thighs to prevent the drop and lifts herself free, pushing me playfully out of the danger zone.

"Hold it right there, Mister! I hunted and gathered this morning." She waves her hand at the full Continental breakfast: pastries, meats, cheese, and fresh fruit on one plate. The other plate is definitely off menu, a full English breakfast. She grins sheepishly.

"I didn't see this on the menu." I take a crisp strip of bacon and bite down.

My stomach aches with anticipation of more bacon, juicy fat sausages, glossy scrambled eggs, tomatoes, mushrooms, fried bread no less, and baked beans.

"It wasn't. I said I hunted and gathered remember? After last night, I thought you might need the sustenance." She lifts the tray and places it on the bed. I crawl over and sit behind her, wrapping my legs on either side. I am starving but I am not interested in the food much anymore. She shuffles back into my hold and pours some coffee. Then she takes a pull of a croissant, the sweet flaky pastry crumples under the pressure, flattens and disintegrates. She offers me a bite over her shoulder, but I shake my head. She may want to eat, but I still want what I want…her.

"You're not hungry?" She shifts in my hold, and her face is crinkled with concern. She doesn't understand that she would make a starving man forget to eat. Her eyes flash with unexpected worry.

"I am, and this looks amazing. On point with the gathering, beautiful, but you are more appetising than any food and much, much more satisfying." I pepper kisses on her neck and along her t-shirt covered shoulder.

"Okay, but you're going to have to sit there watching me eat all this, because I am starving." She shrugs, dismissing my amorous little speech and pops the remaining pastry into her mouth, chewing down with a grin.

"You'd eat all that?" I chuckle.

"You know it." Her words are muffled as they fight with her half-eaten food.

"I do." I grab the full plate of steaming cooked food and slide back to lean against the headboard. I pull the sheet to cover my morning erection and lay the plate down.

"Hey, you said you weren't hungry. I was going to eat that." She pouts playfully but hands me a knife and fork, shuffling to sit beside me.

"I can't have you too full." I bite a piece of the fried bread, which is crisp, golden, and a heart attack away from nutritional food. God, it tastes good.

"Too full…why, what's on your to-do list today?"

"Just one thing on my *to-do* list, beautiful." My voice drops a sensual octave.

"Oh." Her skins dances with a slew of prickles, and she shivers. Her eyes fix on my lips; it is she who now struggles to swallow.

"Oh."

We spend the morning wandering the streets. Unlike the UK, many of the shops and boutiques close on Sundays so the city is relatively quiet. We take a canal boat tour that meanders through the waterways at a leisurely pace so you can really see the beauty of the buildings and see why this city is called Venice of the North. The tour stops several times at key tourist hot spots, but we are happy to sit back and lazily absorb audio feed culture from the comfort of the arse-numbing plastic bucket seats. Several couples leave the tour at the stop near the Anne Frank house, and Sam lets out a heavy breath and relaxes against my side.

"Are you okay?" She tilts her head up to meet my gaze, her face a light blush of colour.

"I just keep looking at every couple wondering if they were there last night, watching."

"That bothers you?"

"No, not bothers, it's just very different from anything I have ever felt before. When I'm Mistress Selena with a cli—" She hesitates when my whole body tenses. I fucking hate her talking about being with anyone else. "When I'm Mistress Selena, I know it is a performance, and I play my part. Last night was very different. It was very, very personal. I was your sub, but I was very much me." Her smile is tentative, and the rosy hue on her cheeks deepens. She lets out a light laugh trying to cover her misplaced embarrassment. "I totally get the masks, but looking at other couples, I can't help wonder."

"Your concerns are misplaced, but your blush is adorable." I tickle her cheek with the back of my fingertips. "I doubt there is anyone here who was there last night."

"You can't know that," she scoffs. "We don't exactly have 'Kinky as Fuck' tattooed on our foreheads, but we are. You can't make a sweeping statement like that, and if I've learnt anything in my time as a Domme, you definitely can't judge a book by its cover."

"I would agree, but in this instance I can." She shifts to face me, her flawless face a picture-perfect mix of confusion and suspicion. "You don't honestly think I would let a bunch of strangers watch you?"

"Hmm?"

"I may choose to share some of you…*may*…but those little sounds and your face when you fall are too precious to share with strangers. I cleared the restaurant. That's why it took a little longer for me to arrange our time slot."

"But I wanted to…I mean, I was happy to…perform."

"I know, beautiful, and that in itself is fucking amazing. You are amazing. I honestly wasn't expecting that reaction, but you asked, and there was no way I would deny you, when I know how brave you were to ask." I cup her delicate face with my large hands; she looks so small in my hold. Her dark chocolate eyes glisten with unshed tears at my words. "Before you, I wouldn't have dreamt of giving it a second thought, but you are just too precious to share with strangers. You are mine. My heart and my soul…Understand?"

"Wow." Her lips crush mine, and I can't help the smile that splits my face— making it difficult to maintain the delicious dance of demanding tongues. She climbs awkwardly onto my lap, her knees bent on either side of my thighs, and her long coat draping over us, creating a blanket of cover. She bounces perilously close to my now rock-hard cock. I groan at the instant unbearable ache in my balls. Jesus, this woman is going to kill me with pent-up lust. I hold her hips firmly to stop what she's about to do, which is drive me insane. She fights against my hold, but I am unyielding, and she pulls back with a resigned and playful pout.

"Spoilsport."

"This may be a liberal city, but we would still get arrested for fucking in a glass topped boat. But you keep wiggling that delectable arse and screw what I just said, the whole damn city can watch you come apart. I will spend the next ten years trying to erase all YouTube evidence when I change my mind because this—" I slip my hands to her tight round arse and grip harder than necessary, but it seems I need to clarify. "—this is mine."

"Yours." Her eyes, her smile, and her body soften, and she folds herself into my arms. *Perfect.*

After almost an hour, the boat glides to a stop next to the Bloemenmarkt, Amsterdam's famous floating flower market.

"Can we?" Sam first stretches to get a better look out of the window, but from this angle there is nothing to see except the backs of the numerous white tarp, framed, tented stalls.

"There aren't any flowers; it's more a bulb market."

"I know. I'd like to have a look all the same." She jumps from her seat and holds out her hand, which I take, eager to keep that smile exactly where it is, spread wide and glorious on her face. The market is a series of stalls knitted together and floating on large permanent barges on the Singel canal. It is home to thousands, maybe hundreds of thousands of tulip bulbs, and Sam is actually quite engrossed searching through the different varieties.

"Searching for The Black Tulip?" I call after her as she disappears into the interconnecting stalls. I find her bent over a large display. I wrap both arms around her as she leans over to read the descriptions of the flowers. There are over three thousand recognised varieties in the Netherlands, according to the tourist information leaflet. I wonder which one she is searching so intently for.

"Hmm?" She turns to kiss my cheek before turning away to carry on her quest.

"Dumas's *The Black Tulip.*" I recall the abbreviated story I just finished reading in the tour guide. "In the story a reward of a hundred thousand florins is offered to the person that can produce a truly black tulip. It was a huge reward at the time but remained unclaimed. To quote, 'Black tulip became a symbol for tolerance and justice but also divine love between two people'. So I'm cool with you looking, just know that you are looking for something that doesn't exist."

"I did know that actually…but not from the story. My mother grew tulips, prize winning flowers in every colour imaginable except my favourite: blue."

"Blue doesn't exist either, beautiful, unless it's been dyed. I think what you are looking for is also unattainable." She lets out a sharp bitter laugh.

"Oh, I know but that perfectly represents how I felt growing up. She demanded the impossible," she muses sadly, shaking her head, but there is only a trace of hurt in her deep brown eyes. Even that trace is too much. "Here, this is pretty close." She points to a picture of a vibrant blue purple flower above a bucket filled with small dry, flaky bulbs, waiting dormant for their moment to shine. "I know they aren't natural; these are a hybrid. They are a product of our environment, just like me." Her eyes shine bright, all sadness quashed with the strength of her smile, spreading wide across her adorable face and lifting her spirits. Happy with her purchase, we make our way back to the hotel and begin the journey home.

We hit the outskirts of London when Sam turns to me. She has drifted in and out of sleep for most of the journey.

"I had a wonderful time, Jason, thank you." Her soft smile spreads warm and wide, lighting her eyes, illuminating her face.

"My pleasure, really, my pleasure." I drop my hand to her knee and slide it firmly up her thigh. The sleepy noises and dream-filled sighs she has emitted over the last five hours have kept me in a painful state of semi-arousal the entire time. We are nearly home, and I am more than ready to finish what she started all those hours ago on the boat. "You never need to worry that marriage will change a single thing about who we are. The kink runs deep with our kind." I tap my fingers in a light rhythm, the tips teasing the apex of her legs. She scoots down, lifting her feet to the dashboard and pushing her core into my hand.

"It does. It really does." She giggles, and I join in her infectious joy. My laughter abruptly stops though when I pull my car around the end of my street and see two things: The lights blazing from almost every window in my townhouse and a badly parked motorcycle in my resident's space. Leon. I double park next to the bike and turn an accusatory glare at the sheepish looking figure beside me.

"Mind telling me how Leon gained access to my home." I arch an eyebrow.

"*Our* home," she rightly corrects, and her tone has an edge.

"*Our* home yes—yours and mine—not Leon's," I clarify, and my tone is less clipped but more plain irritated.

"I left a spare key at the flat just in case."

"Hmm," I mutter, but it comes out as a disgruntled sound.

"Don't be mad. He was lonely last time I went round. He misses me, and I said if he was ever lonely to just come on over." Her face is soft with concern.

"I'm not mad. I'm…" I continue to air my frustration, but she interrupts.

"Horny…I can see." She snickers but slaps her hand wisely over her mouth to stop a full explosion of laughter. "I'm sure he won't stay long."

"I'm sure he won't," I retort.

"Don't be like that. He's my best friend, and he is always welcome." Her brows knit together, and her eyes flash with sadness. I don't want that, but she's oblivious to my real concern.

"He's your best friend who now looks at you like you're next on the menu," I clarify.

"Ah." She sucks in a slow thoughtful breath, her lips pursed at this revelation.

"Ah," I repeat. The thoughtful silence only lasts a moment before she breaks it.

"But that is hardly his fault. Look, he is probably trying really hard to act like he was before Christmas, but the man thinks with his dick. He'll get over it. He just needs another toy." She pauses, her eyes taking in every inch of my face for tells that I am buying this explanation. I have my doubts, but he is her best friend. Her smile creeps tentatively across her face, and her tone is more a plea, which hits me hard. "He misses me, Jason. We lived together on and off for nearly ten years, and that is longer than most marriages."

"Not ours," I state as a matter of fact.

"No, not ours" She leans over to plant her soft full lips on the tight thin line of my mouth. "He's adjusting, and it would really help if you two got on."

"We get on," I scoff.

"Each other's nerves, maybe." She pats my thigh and opens the car door. "Come on, the sooner he gets his Sam fix, the sooner you can have yours." She bites down on her bottom lip and winks. She turns and bounds up the steps to the front door, swiping her finger before disappearing inside, leaving me with the bags and a tight, painful, jealous pinch of pain in my chest. Stupid, but it's still there, nonetheless. Her friendship with Leon is something I struggle with, one minute loving that she has someone else who clearly adores her to hating that she has someone else who does so.

I dump the bags by the front door and follow the delicious smell and laughter into the kitchen. Leon is stirring a pan on the cooker, his back to me but half facing the room. Sam is pouring chilled white wine into the third of three glasses. She walks over to hand me one, kissing me lightly on the cheek and tipping up to whisper in my ear.

"Play nice."

"He doesn't look like he will be leaving any time soon," I growl under my breath, and she rolls her eyes at my stubborn refusal to see past my own selfish needs.

"Play nice," she repeats with a sterner tone, which has lost a good deal of its playfulness.

"Fine." I kiss her forehead and do my best to shuck off my dour mood. I know he is important to her and that makes him important. Period. I drag my hand roughly down my face, acknowledging that my extreme tiredness and the long drive is probably a large contributing factor to my lack of empathy. I am certainly behaving more like a sex-starved petulant teenager than a mature adult and future husband.

"This is a nice surprise, Leon. You shouldn't have." Despite the undercurrent and glare from Sam, my words are level, and Leon grins, unfazed by my taunt.

"I bet." He shakes my offered hand. "Stupid to cook all this for one, and I thought you'd appreciate some home cooking. After all, you've been living together for a while. You must be sick of take out," he jokes, and I laugh at Sam's expense.

"Hey, no ganging up with the insults. I'm right here." She screws up a dishcloth and hurls it at Leon. He ducks, missing the missile, and blows her a kiss in return. I have a large table that fills the center of the kitchen, and I take a seat next to Sam. Places have been set, and Leon looks like he has everything under control. Despite my initial irritation, this is actually really nice. Sam is relaxed and smiling; Leon is certainly at ease in our house, and for the first time in forever, this place feels like a home.

Leon dishes up three large bowls of beef stew and creamy mashed potatoes. My tummy makes an audible approval that I don't try to hide. This looks so good, light fluffy mash drenched in rich gravy. If it tastes half as good as it looks, I might just ask him to move in, too.

"Tell me what you got up to, and don't spare the blushes." He grins and pointedly winks at my girl. Yeah, maybe I *won't* be asking him to move in.

"We took a boat tour and I bought some bulbs. Oh, and a chocolate vagina for you, but it's packed, so you'll have to wait."

"A chocolate vagina? Really? Not weed or a hooker? You suck as a best friend," he quips.

"I thought at least it would mean you'd get some—" Sam's cheeks pink right up when Leon blurts.

"Pussy." Leon grins and Sam cringes.

"Thank you, Leon. Yes, that," she snaps.

"What was that?" I ask around a mouthful of really good food.

"Sam doesn't like pussy," Leon teases.

"Oh, that's a shame," I offer with a knowing smile and a cheeky wink.

"I don't like the word," Sam states flatly, and my interest is piqued at her evasive answer.

"So you do like pussy, just not the word pussy?" I push, feeling the swell in my pants at the mere thought of my girl with another girl.

"Is there any chance we could stop using—actually, can we change the subject?" She takes a long slow sip of her wine, hoping the time delay is enough to have moved the topic along. Fat chance.

"After you answer the question." Leon and I state in unison.

"I don't know. There, answered. Now, move on boys." She takes another large gulp of her wine, and as much as I want to pursue this line of questioning, I don't want to make her uncomfortable, which she clearly is. I also don't want to encourage Leon, or to aggravate my raging hard-on any further; it's fucking painful enough as it is.

"Fine, what else did you do? Did you both get high and eat your body weight in waffles?" He wiggles his brow playfully at Sam, but her eyes flash nervously at me. My jaw is tense. I can't help it. I hate drugs. Even though I am aware of the pros and cons of Marijuana, and I'm all for choice, my own personal experience with Will has left me with a zero tolerance. No matter how legal or innocent the intention. Sam didn't express a desire to visit any of the Hash bars, but I wonder from the shy shared looks whether that was because of me. "Did you actually manage to get Missy here to smoke a joint? I mean it's legal there, Sam, you had no excuse," Leon taunts with a playful smirk.

"Had better things to do." Sam shakes her head at Leon, and a brief frown furrows his brow. Sam looks at me, and Leon follows her gaze with confusion.

"Sam's being sensitive, but it's fine." I draw in a deep breath. Part of me is thankful Sam has kept my past as secret as I'd hoped, and a much bigger part is warmed to my core that she didn't share this with her best friend. "My brother was a drug addict, and my view of 'harmless drugs' is a little tainted because of it."

"Ah, sorry man, I didn't know. I mean there is no way he is now, right?" Leon's genuine shock is confirmation that this is completely new information.

"No, he's been clean for years, but—"

"We're a product of our environment." Sam reaches across the table and takes my hand, squeezing comfort and love from her tiny fingers directly into my soul.

"This is code, isn't it?" Leon throws his fork down in a huff and a clatter. "This is what I hate about couples. They start to have these fucking shortcut codes and a secret language. All lovey dovey and deep meaningful stares, which pisses me off." He roughly crosses his arms over his chest, and a dark scowl shades is face.

"Jeez, you're sensitive or possibly stupid…maybe both." Sam snickers, retrieving her hand and reaching for her drink. "It's not code. Jason's view on drugs was shaped by what happened to his brother. Environmental, duh!" She pulls a cute dumb face that makes us both laugh. "Isn't that right, honey bunny?" She pushes her tongue into her cheek and fights back giggles with pursed lips. Leon slaps his hand to his mouth and pretends to hold back vomit while making muffled retching noises.

I stop drinking after my second glass, but Leon continues. Sam tries to keep him company, but her sips are getting more infrequent. He bought a lemon tart because he confessed he couldn't be arsed to cook a dessert too, but he knew very well Sam's preference for all things sweet. I clear everything but the coffee while they catch up. Sam includes me as best she can, but Leon monopolises her for most of the evening. When she yawns, I take that as my opportunity to reclaim what's mine.

"Thank you for the meal, Leon. It was really good, but it's been a long day, and as you can see…" Sam's face pinks up with embarrassment when she fails to hide another huge yawn.

"So when are you two getting married?" Sam's sleepy eyes snap open wide. Shit! I am never going to get her to bed.

"We're in no rush," she offers, but her eyes meet mine. Her voice is tentative, and her statement inflects like a question, for me. I walk over and crouch down on my haunches so we are eye to eye.

"True, but I would like you to start getting some ideas together. I want you as my wife, and I want you to have the perfect day, the latter I understand can take time. Sometimes, when people say there is no rush, it is because there is actually no real intention, and I want to make it very clear that that is not the case here. For me, the sooner the better, but for us there is no rush." Her hands cup my face, warm, soft, and possessive.

"Urgh," Leon grumbles, and that is also enough for tonight. I stand and scoop Sam into my arms.

"It's been a pleasure, Leon, but I'm taking my girl to bed. Feel free to stay, but don't expect a quiet night. Is that code enough for you?"

FIVE

Sam

Jason steps into the kitchen, and I nearly miss my mouth completely, my spoonful of cereal bumps my lips, dribbling milk down my chin. He winks at me and walks over to the coffee machine to fix his morning espresso. I have yet to see him in any garb in which he doesn't look drop dead gorgeous, but in a sharp three-piece suit, he is absolutely lethal. Crisp white cuffs peep from a midnight navy, Italian, hand-cut cloth; his tie is a burnt ochre with flecks of gold that match the specks in his eyes. His hair is still damp from the recent shower, and he looks fresh from his early morning jog. He must have Red Bull running through his veins after the tedious drive yesterday and his Olympic gold medal performance in the bedroom last night. Which left me shattered and limp, very much like I am this morning, hunched over my breakfast but greedily taking in the morning glory that is Jason.

"Keep looking at me like that, beautiful, and you won't be going in to work at all today." I shake my head to break my gaze, feeling heat in my cheeks at being caught drooling. I really had been staring *that* hard.

"How do you do that? I'm a wreck and you…you look like you you've stepped off the cover of GQ, and I bet you've just run a marathon." I wave my hand up and down his immaculate self as exhibit A.

"A half marathon, don't exaggerate and that wasn't the exercise I was thinking about." He grins and stalks over to me.

"I'm seriously thinking of joining a gym just to keep up. I thought I was fit, but you're like the frickin' Energizer Bunny." He perches on the edge of the table in lieu of taking a seat. He doesn't often eat breakfast, maybe a bite of toast from my plate, but I have nothing to share today. Besides, his preference is to start to the day with something hot, liquid, and highly caffeinated.

"I love your curves. Don't change a damn thing." His hand slides up my thigh and squeezes the flesh and muscle.

"Oh, you did not just say that." I drop my spoon to a dramatic crescendo that halts his hand mid-massage.

"What?" His face flashes with genuine surprise, his concern evident by the deep crease of his frown.

"Call me fat." I slap his hand away from my silky pj-covered leg.

"Obviously, I did." He sits back and meets my glare with a fixed expression, impassive. His tone is flat and without inflection or a hint of humour. "I find you repulsive, which is why I have a permanent hard-on. Jeez." He blows out a puff of frustrated air. "You hear what you want to hear, but for the record and the love of all that is holy...You. Are. Gorgeous." He leans down and punctuates each word with a soppy wet kiss. "I love the soft swell of your tits and the curve of your hips and your tight round arse, and I am not going to apologise for that ever." He kisses my lips once more, next my nose, my forehead, then my brows, cheeks, and continues to pepper my face with a million butterfly kisses, whispering as he does. "I love every single inch of you, beautiful. Inside and out." I squirm a little and, laughing, I playfully push him away.

"I just think since I've stopped whip-welding, there might be a few more inches." I rub my belly, which has a small round bump from breakfast, but I know is normally flat. I'm not over weight, just under-toned. "And I will need to start some sort of fitness thing to keep up with you," I challenge.

"Don't on my account. If you're ever too tired, I'll just roll you over and fuck you in your sleep." He shrugs, his wide wicked smile is a mix of pride and smug.

"Oh, my god, you would, wouldn't you?"

"No, beautiful." He chuckles, sipping the last drops of his coffee. "I want you sentient...sleepy sex is fine, but necrophilia is a kink too far." He rightly wrinkles his nose at that hard limit.

"Ya' think?" I mirror his distaste. I know we are both advocates of the 'no judgement' rule, but we are also proponents of Safe, Sane, and Consensual.

"Has our guest risen, or did he not stay after all?" Jason nods his head up toward to the guest room above us.

"Risen and retreated while you were pounding the streets. He told me to thank you for the hospitality." I smile sweetly.

"Was he being ironic?" He sniffs derisively.

"Jason," I warn.

"I'm not remotely sorry. I am selfish when it comes to you, but he is your friend, and for that, he is always welcome. Take it or leave it," he states flatly as a matter of non-negotiable fact.

I jump up, skidding my chair noisily back across the hardwood floor, and throw my arms around his neck, squishing my body with some force against his granite hard frame. He lifts me with ease as if the extra inches I've mumbled about haven't in the least affected my weight.

"I'll take it, thank you." His hands fist the silk of my pj bottoms and slide possessively over my arse. I mash my lips to his; his tongue is a luscious mix of bitter coffee and him. A heated sensual duel of lips and tongues and desperate breaths ensues before he regains control. Pulling back with a pained groan, he lets me slide slowly down his body, but he doesn't relinquish his hold when my feet hit the ground. Instead, he simply envelops me in his strong arms, a firm possessive embrace filled with lust and love.

"What's with the magazines?" My eyes follow his gaze to the table where I had been picking through a selection of the numerous publications spread all over the table.

"Oh, Sofs sent some over the other week. Thought I might like to start having a look." I shrug and step out of his hold. I scoop the magazines into a not so messy pile. Dropping them on an edge to align and straighten, I place them neatly on the table.

"Good idea." He squeezes my butt and slaps it when I bend to clear my breakfast bowl from the table. I give a playful scowl but shrug off the topic.

"Hmm, I guess," I mutter on my way to the dishwasher.

"Don't sound so excited." He forces a laugh, but his tone is tinged with hurt. I spin to catch the same feeling reflected in his eyes. Damn it, I'm an idiot.

"No, no, I didn't mean it like that, honestly, but…" I scurry back across the room to him and take both his hands in mine. I wait until his eyes are completely fixed on me. "I *am* excited, Jason, but I don't have a family or many friends so the whole idea of a big day is daunting. Not to mention shopping for a dress on my own." I shake our hands lightly, my words hold sincere concern, but I try to keep my tone light.

"Why the fuck would you be on your own? I will be with you." I chuckle at his indignant tone.

"You can't! It's tradition," I add and fight the desire to roll my eyes at his good intentions. "And I am guessing you don't want me to take Leon?" I raise a brow high with my query. He stiffens to his full and considerable height, making me shake my head on a light inevitable laugh. "No, I didn't think so. So, I'm going solo, and that is just not something to get excited about. Traditionally, this is a mother-daughter rite of passage with the odd best friend from nursery thrown in. I have neither, although I am not complaining about the former, but I am dreading all the sympathy remarks when I explain why my mother isn't sharing this moment. I'll get that pity look when all I'll want to do is shout 'ding-dong, the witch is dead'." I let out a deep breath and flash a sad smile.

"I don't want you going on your own." He pulls one hand from mine and strokes the hair from my face. His hand is comforting and warm as it cups my cheek. "What about Sofia?"

"She's probably busy. I'm a friend but not a *best* friend." I worry my bottom lip, feeling the pressure of forcing myself on an unwitting friend. This is a big deal.

"You won't know until you ask, and I bet she'd love to help. She sent the magazines, didn't she?"

"I guess," I repeat and move to turn away.

"Where's my lioness? I don't recognise this tentative cub," he teases, threading his arms around my waist from behind, pulling me close once more.

"You're right." I draw in a deep breath. I may not have the loving mother or the childhood friends, but I do have friends, and I do have a voice. "I'll call Sofia later, and if she's not free maybe Bets or Charlie."

"Charlie?"

"Leon's new Domme," I clarify the new name.

"Perfect, any or all of the above, just don't go on your own. Fuck tradition. If it comes to that, *I'll* take you." He kisses the side of my neck, and I shiver from tip to toe. "Or I'm sure my mum would help."

"No, no, it's fine. I'm not so pathetic I can't find a single female friend to go shopping with." I rush to halt his kind but terrifying offer. "It's no big deal."

"I think it's supposed to be a big deal." I turn in his arms to see his brow furrowed and a tight line where his soft lips are hiding.

"I didn't mean it like that. There's just no need to call in your mum, a woman I haven't even met." I shuffle nervously from one foot to the other, my voice drops to an uncharacteristic but understandable whisper. "She might hate me and my wicked ways for leading you astray." He barks out a dirty laugh.

"Oh, beautiful, that ship sailed long before you, and trust me, she knows it." He barely contains his laughter enough to speak. "She will be beside herself that I have been tamed. Believe me, she is going to adore you." He scoops me up his body, and I wrap my legs tight around his waist, giving a teasing little wiggle when I settle just below his belt.

"Tamed hmm? I'd like to see that." I roll my hips, my heat against his hardness.

"Oh, you would, would you?" His gravelly voice is a deep sensual rumble, but his grip stops my teasing maneuver.

"I know it would be a trial for you, but I'm sure I could make it fun. You do still owe me." I try to grind, but I am going nowhere unless he wants me to. He doesn't. He fixes his dark eyes on me, holding me in his arms, and my heart in his hands. Long intense seconds root us to each other, and I barely breathe. I don't want to be the one to break this moment where I feel bare, raw…owned. His slow, sexy smile splits his lips and transforms his face into the picture of sin and salvation.

"And I am a man of my word. Consider it your Valentine gift." His kiss is light, his tongue darts out to trace the seam of my lips, and I moan at its frustrating brevity. "Book a room at the club on Friday and I'm yours. One fucking night so make the most of it." I push out of his hold and, once on my feet, jump up and down, clapping my hands like a demented seal.

"Oh, my god! Really?" I can't contain my excitement. Not so much because I will be his Domme, but that he is willing to sub for me. I'm giddy.

"Don't get too excited, because I guarantee, it won't happen again," he grumbles playfully.

"I am excited. I can't help it. Ooooh, the possibilities." I bite my lip to stop my shit-eating grin.

"I'm regretting this already." He groans but pulls me into a tight hug, kissing my hair and breathing me in.

"One night, baby, and I promise you'll enjoy every single second." My breathy words have an instant effect. He adjusts himself, but his face remains impassive.

"We'll see, beautiful. Just bear in mind, we have an early start and a long drive to my parents on Saturday so—"

My wickedness interrupts him. "Take care where I stick—"

"Sam," he bites out his own interruption. His tone is gruff and holds no humour. I hold my hands up in surrender; enough teasing.

"Joke. It was a joke. I'm guessing pegging is a hard limit then?" I pull my lips into my mouth to hide my mirth, but I step back just in case I am taking the teasing a little too far.

"Damn fucking right! Jeez, what did I just agree to?" He lets out a heavy sigh that is all show and no substance. "I'm outta here while I still have a pair of balls. I have three days to get you to retract your request or for me to back out," he muses.

"Man of your word," I sing-song my response.

"Man of my word," he mutters begrudgingly. He grabs the back of my neck and plants a tender kiss on my lips, his face tight with tension and angst. I cup his smooth cheek.

"Thank you," I whisper, and his face softens, his eyes crinkling with a familiar smile. I wasn't going to pursue this deal, but in the back of my mind, I felt an imbalance. I trusted him with everything in me, and although I know he loves me, I couldn't help wondering if he really felt the same. I have my answer.

"Anything for you, beautiful, anything."

"Sam, your four o'clock appointment is here." Amanda, my co-worker, grins as she peeks around the corner of the resource room where I am nose-deep in journals.

"I don't have a four o'clock." I check my phone for scheduled meetings just in case I'm wrong, but I shake my head at Amanda as confirmation of the mistake. I do, however, take to opportune interruption as a chance to stretch my back out with a satisfying crunch over the back of my chair.

"I'll take it if you're too busy," she says with far too much enthusiasm for a Friday afternoon.

"They asked for me?" I pull my neck to each side too until I get that pop from my aching bones.

"He did. Oh wait, that's him." She points to the screen saver on my phone and every muscle in my body relaxes and then ignites. "Is that your fiancé?" She swallows thickly, and it's sweet the way her mouth just gapes open on an exhaled gasp. *He gets that a lot.*

"Yes, that's Jason, my fiancé." That word still feels so strange on my tongue. No, not the word, just the whole 'holy shit, I'm getting married' part of the situation. I shake myself and lightly shrug. Amanda lets out a heavy sigh when I add, "And my four o'clock, apparently." I don't bother to pack my stuff away because even if it is for a moment, I don't want to keep him waiting. He has never been to my office, and I'm excited to show him around. I briskly round the corner and stride down the long corridor. I can see him standing there, dominating the small reception area. My heart hammers excitedly in my chest then drops; it's not Jason. The recognition is almost instantaneous, and it's not the fact that he is no longer wearing the suit he had on this morning or that his tan is more South Florida than Southbank. It's the whole package. Will has same tall muscular build and strong stance, similar eyes with a piercing stare, and that smile—damn, I melt every time that is leveled in my direction. But the difference I know in my heart is what makes *all* the difference.

"Hey, darling." Will walks to meet me, and although there is clearly affection in his eyes and love too perhaps, it is a fraction of what I witness every single time Jason looks at me. *I haven't seen Will since Christmas day.*

"Will, what are you doing here?" I let him pull me into a big bear hug, even lifting me off my feet before he eventually sets me back down.

"Jason said he's been really busy, so he asked me to come and help out." His eyes dance with mischief, and I am thankful that I now know him a little better, since he calls all the time to chat with his brother, so I know he is yanking my chain.

"Of course he did," I reply with a dubious quirk of my lips and hand on my hip.

"Yeah, maybe not, hmm? He can be so selfish." His eyes darken at the same rate I feel my cheeks heat. It doesn't take much for me to have an instant high-definition flashback of our foursome at the best of times, but having Will in glorious Technicolor before me, it's difficult to picture anything other than my very own fantasy made reality. Not good. "I'm in between contracts at work and had to get some Visa stuff sorted." Will interrupts my very wayward thoughts, which I am also thankful for.

"Oh, right, good. That's good." *Smooth Sam, real smooth.* Will chuckles and I let out a puff of air and try to clear my throat.

"I've been at the American Embassy all morning, but they won't have my documents until Monday. So I thought I would visit my favourite soon to be sister-in-law." His easy grin instantly diffuses any awkwardness, and, yes, I am hugely grateful for that, too.

"Cool, does Jason know you're here?"

"I sent him a text and left a message with Sandy. I would've popped into his office, but they won't let me in the building." He bites back a wicked grin.

"I can't think why?" I mock. "Jason has told me of the havoc you create, so don't go trying the innocent act with me."

"Oh, I know you know I'm not innocent." He glances over my shoulder as he says this, and I hear a girlish gasp and giggle from whoever he is flashing that cocky grin at.

"Just came to create havoc here, I see," I quip and he barks out a dirty laugh but fixes his eyes back on me.

"Came to see what time you get off work, actually, and grab a key if it's going to be a while."

"Can't you get in? It's finger print. I would think Jason has you programmed in as an approved print."

"You would think wrong."

"And there was me thinking he trusted you."

"Only when he's there to keep guard." His voice drops to a low, sexy rumble filled with ominous intent. "I can't blame him for that."

"Afraid you'll have a house party or something?" I snicker.

"Or something." His tone makes me look up, but he closes his lids before I can see what devilishness danced there.

"I have a bit of work to finish up, but I won't be too long. Do you want to wait?"

"Could I have a tour?" His eager tone catches me off guard.

"Really?"

"Sure." He nods with genuine enthusiasm, and I get a thrill that I get to do this with at least one of the men in my life.

"Oh, I'd like that, not even Jason's had a look around where I work. He keeps meaning to, but he's been completely snowed at work. The big boss is out on paternity leave, so it's all fallen on him." I don't know why this needs an explanation, but I give it all the same.

"That's the price for the big bucks."

"Even so, he's worked every weekend since Christmas. Other than our weekend away, I've seen more of Leon these past few weeks, and I don't count the odd hour he's awake at home. Anyway, I miss him, that's all." I don't attempt to hide my tone, not so much frustrated as solemn.

"Then he's very lucky, but he knows this. We all know this," he grumbles, and his back stiffens so I have to tilt my head to keep eye contact now he is at his full height.

"Do I detect a touchy subject?"

"Not in the least. I'm happy for him. That he has you, I mean. He deserves to be happy. If you detect anything, it's a longing for the same that's all."

"Ah, Will, you're a sweetie. Who'd have thought there would be two sensitive souls in one family?" I place my hand over his heart and watch his eyes take in my every move. His hand covers mine, and his fingers interlock. A sweet smile flits across his face, but is quickly replaced with a wicked gleam in his eyes and a wolfish grin.

"Sensitive, kinky, with massive cocks, if you don't mind." He lifts my hand to his mouth, and his lips smile against the skin on the back of my hand.

"I don't mind, not one bit." I chuckle and wait for him to release my hand, which seems to take a little longer than normal.

I give Will the grand tour of my workplace, and to be fair, he tries to look interested. It's just an open plan office in a refurbished warehouse with bare brick walls and minimal furniture. Nothing remotely glamorous, but I love it. Everyone is friendly and my boss is the kindest man on the planet to be so accommodating and give me a second chance at the job when I failed to show up for the interview. At least *I* think he is. They also have very flexible office hours so I can work late, leave early, or even from home as long as I get the work done. I am still the lowest of the low in terms of the legal team, but I'm learning. I always feel that my work is valued and appreciated. Like I said, I love it.

"It's quite like my new place," Will says, when we finally stop back at my desk for me to finish up.

"Really?"

"The conservation charity spends all its money on the projects, not the buildings, so they tend to be a little run-down." I smile, but then I take a moment to look at my workspace through his eyes. I suppose the building does look a little tired; the furniture is dated but functional, so I never gave that a second thought. The decor is more artsy than neglected, the carpets are a little threadbare, but when it comes to this place, I will happily wear my rose tinted glasses. "But you seem happy here."

"I am." I beam.

"Doesn't your friend work in a legal firm, too? Why not work for his company. I bet the money is better."

"You mean Leon? He's a partner in his firm, so yeah, the money is better for him. Actually it would be for me too, but that's not what I was interested in. I don't need the money. I wanted to do something good. The Mission does really good work and holds a special place in my heart and Jason's," I add quietly. There are still people around even if they are getting ready to leave.

"And mine." Will captures my gaze; his eyes hold so much, swirling with turmoil and hurt, love and loss. If I didn't know his story from Jason, I would be begging to hear it from him now, just to ease his pain. "I like that you work here, Sam. It means a lot. I mean, I know you didn't do it for me, but I still love that you do." He shuffles, and I take his hands and give them a gentle, reassuring squeeze.

"Thank you, Will, that means a lot. " I smile at his sentiment and then shrug it off with a cheeky grin. "Besides, I loved my old job so much. It was important to find something that held just as much interest because I knew it was unlikely it would be quite as much fun."

"Your other job?" he asks. From his blank expression, he does this without thinking. My knowing silence draws a slow expression of understanding across his handsome face. "At the club," he says, and I nod, smiling my appreciation that he kept his voice soft, choosing not to announce to the whole office floor my stage name and previous occupation.

"You know what? I can call it a night now. I'm ahead with what I wanted to get done, so how about we grab a drink in one of the bars by the river and see if we can't tempt your brother to play hooky, too."

"Christ, if you can't tempt him, I'm not sure what throwing me into the mix will achieve."

"I'm not throwing you into the mix." I raise a brow, my tone pointed and serious. "That is not my call to make, just so you know." I hold his gaze, then my own wicked smile creeps across my face. "But I don't see the harm in a little light teasing."

"Bait, you mean I'm bait?" He fails to sound affronted, and his grin just widens when a voice blurts out.

"I'll happily take a bite." Amanda pokes her head up from behind her computer screen, and I jump. I didn't see her hiding, but I hear her now, that dirty laugh and lustful glare is burning a hole in Will's backside. "Sorry, I know he's your fiancé and all that, but I'm an old lady, so I'm allowed to be inappropriate."

"Oh, this isn't my fiancé, this is his brother. They're twins." Her jaw snaps shut, and I can see the strain in her cheek muscles as she fights back whatever she is too fearful to unleash. I grab Will's hand, because I fear for him, too.

"Something more inappropriate?" I ask her, suppressing my own laughter. She nods energetically but keeps her lips sealed tight and almost soundproof, just a sad squeak escapes as we wave our goodbyes. We reach the lift, and I let out my laugh.

"What was that about?"

"Be thankful you have no idea." I pat his cheek and press the button for the lift.

SIX

Sam

"You can go to the club. I'm fine staying in. It's been a long week, and Jason won't be too late…probably." We had a few drinks at the bar around the corner from Jason's home, but when it became clear he wasn't going to be joining us, I just wanted to come home. I dump my bag on the kitchen counter and open the drawer to look through the stack of take-out menus.

"Will you come with me?" Will peers over my shoulder at the selection I am flicking through.

"Let me think… go to the best sex club in London with my fiancé's sexy twin brother? Um, not if I want you to be sleeping in the spare room instead of intensive care." I nudge him in the side since he is standing very close.

"We don't have to play. It is possible to go there and just chat, have a few drinks."

"Possible, yes. Likely, hmm, not so much."

"Can't keep your hands off me, is that it?"

"Cute." I waggle a warning finger in his direction and ignore his loaded question. "I don't go to the club without Jason…ever. Besides I'm knackered and just want to order pizza in my PJs and fall into a carbohydrate coma on the sofa."

"Is this a preview of married bliss? Because you are not doing the campaign any favours." I flick the pen I had poised over my food selection at his head, but he ducks. I laugh, but it feels a little hollow, and I get a strange unsettling feeling that turns my insides, and it's an effort to swallow the thickness in my dry throat. "Did I touch a nerve?" He did, but I shake it off. Jason and he are tight but if I have doubts, or whatever this feeling is, it is Jason who needs to hear about them first hand, not via his brother.

"Are you staying in or not?" I snap with overt hostility.

"Hey, I didn't mean anything by it. I'm just jealous, that's all. Jason is a lucky son of a bitch, and I'm being an arsehole." He steps up to me, his hands offered up in surrender, and now I feel like the arsehole for overreacting. I let him wrap his arms around me, and it feels so good, that familiar strength and protective embrace. I look up as he looks down. "Forgive me," he asks, his eyes soft with a trace of uncertainty. The fleeting look is strange though. He is so filled with confidence and swagger, a borderline extrovert if he weren't so British, but maybe it isn't so strange that he tries to hide his vulnerabilities just as much as the rest of us.

"Nothing to forgive, Will. I'm sorry I snapped. It's been a long week, and I miss Jason like crazy, which makes me crazy." He squeezes me tighter before letting me breathe again and releasing his hold.

"Pizza and ice cream then?"

"PJs, pizza, and ice cream."

"Perfect."

We started to watch a movie but couldn't stop talking, so gave up and retreated back to the kitchen for experimental cocktail making. Even that didn't fare too well, and the kitchen now looks like a TGI's training bar. I have every single bottle of liquor on the side, various mixers, fruits, syrups, and an eclectic selection of glasses. The fancier the cocktail, the more disgusting it seemed to taste, and we both agreed that maybe less is more. I now have a line of six shot glasses with vodka and a dollop of ice cream on top, vodka floats, three each.

"This is like a drinking game for preschoolers. Where's the tequila?" Will grumbles, and I snicker then burst out laughing, because this is hysterical. I am shit-faced drunk and about to get a little drunker.

"No, no! No tequila. I get really drunk on tequila." I think I actually hiccup with that, but I am giggling too much to distinguish between the two sounds, neither of which I have control over.

"And this is you *not* really drunk?" he challenges, his face cracking a wide smile.

"I may be a little drunk." I press my finger to my lips to shush myself and make sure he understands he needs to keep this secret.

"Okay then, vodka floats…last one to finish has to clean up the kitchen," Will states, and I snatch up the first glass, slamming it down empty before he finishes his sentence. The race is on. I slam the last glass down and jump from my seat to do my victory dance. My arms stretch high in a whoop whoop, and my stomach rolls. Shit. I race to the hall and the downstairs toilet, crash through the door, and dive for the toilet bowl. Oh, my god, I'm going to die. The door softly closes behind me, and since I didn't put the light on, I am in darkness, which is nice. My arms are braced around the rim of the toilet to stop me from falling off the face of the earth and spinning out of control—much like the room is currently doing. Even in the darkness, I can feel it tumbling in on itself.

That was impressive, to go from happy drunk to stinking, 'this might be alcohol poisoning' drunk in one shot…*a one shot too many*.

My stomach retches, and I groan as, once more, the contents of the last few hours make their way back up my throat, burning acidic liquid and a vile aftertaste that ensures I keep heaving until I am raw and empty.

Several hours or maybe seconds later, a bright light splits my head in two, and I cry out, burying my face into the crook of my arm.

"Leave me in the dark. No, just leave me to die, please." I cough and spit the water pooling in my mouth. I must be empty; for the love of god, please let me be empty. I feel a firm heavy hand on my back, cool against my sweaty skin.

"Okay, beautiful, drink this." I can't see what he wants me to drink, but Jason's voice is so filled with love, I want to cry, and that would be ridiculous.

"I'm not beautiful," I sob, rolling back on to my heels and slouch to the side of the toilet. My hair is slick to my face, and my whole body has that nasty sticky film you get from relentlessly throwing up. My stomach is so tender I bet it's been hours.

"Okay, beautiful, if you say so." He chuckles and lifts me into his arms.

"Look at me, how can you think I'm beautiful? I look disgusting and I'm a whore. Grace, the whore." Fat ugly tears stream down my face, and I cling to him like he is the only good thing, and I am not worthy. I keep my eyes scrunched tight as he carries me through the house. The brightness of the lights is pure agony to my senses. He lays me gently in our bed and pulls the covers to tuck around my now chilled and trembling body.

"If you weren't drunk, I'd tan your backside for that last comment. Grace was never a whore—you were never a whore, and you are so very beautiful."

"Grace was so innocent." I fail to hold back the tiny tears that trickle down my cheeks at the unwanted memory.

"I didn't ask Grace to be my wife. I want you, Sam. Only you." His large hand feels hot against my cheek, both soft and strong. I lean heavily into his hold, his dark eyes searching mine. Concern etched on his face, his expression stern and serious, but his tender smile just makes him look all the more stunning to me. He breathes out slowly. "We make the perfect pair of non-innocents." He kisses the tip of my nose, and I let out a boozy laugh.

"Imperfect, I think you mean," I joke, but I definitely don't mean him, he is absolutely flawless.

"Perfectly imperfect." His soft lips touch mine, and he whispers the most perfect words to my ears as I sink into drunken oblivion. "I love you, Sam."

"What the fuck were you thinking, Will?" I wince and freeze at the kitchen door. The bellow of Jason's voice is like a frickin' foghorn to my delicate state.

"No, no, no! Shhh, no shouting. Fragile flower right here, no loud or sudden noises, please." I drag my sorry self across the wooden floor in my bare feet and crawl onto Jason's lap. I need the comfort, the warmth, and I need him to calm down. "Urgh, that was not my smartest idea, but it was *my* idea." My head rolls back so I can look up to try and catch Jason's eyes. He is scowling a death glare behind me, and I have to tap his chest to get his attention. "Hey, it was *my* idea. Will wanted to go to the club, but he decided to keep me company instead. He gave up a night of debauchery, Jason. He shouldn't be shouted at for that."

"It wasn't a hardship, Sam. It was fun."

"For you, maybe," Jason grumbles, but the fierceness has left his tone, and his arms just wrap a little tighter around me. I think he is taking as much comfort as he is giving.

"I had fun. Right up to that last bad shot, I was having a great time."

"Bad shot?"

"Yeah, all the others were fine, that last one was a wrong'un." I laugh but stop myself at the sound, which is like a jackhammer in my skull. "Ow," I simper and groan.

"Ah, poor baby. Do you want some breakfast or hair of the dog?" Jason chuckles, his mouth pressed to my head.

"No hairs ever again, and I'm not sure food is such a great idea." I brushed my teeth so my mouth doesn't feel quite like the floor of a taxi cab, but even so, the idea of anything solid makes my stomach roll, like that would just be a dare too far.

"What about a walk?" Will offers brightly.

"Hmm, maybe, yeah, some fresh air might work."

We walk along the Southbank, not really heading anywhere in particular. It's cold but dry, and after about an hour, I feel revived enough to stop for coffee. Looking at the boys, they are just about ready to devour anything that stands still long enough.

"Two mega full English breakfasts, coffee, juice, and…?" Jason pauses, looking at me for my selection, but I am going to play it safe.

"Poached egg, please." I hand my menu to the waiter. We stopped at a restaurant just off Piccadilly, which is richly decorated with gilt mirrors and swaths of velvet drapes, dark red carpets, and plush leather booths. I imagine it is quite a romantic place in the evening, although it feels a little over the top at this time of the day, I happen to know it also serves a kick-ass breakfast. The waiter returns with our drinks just as Jason's phone pings. I can't help my shoulders' slump when his face darkens as he reads the message.

"I'm sorry, beautiful. I have to go and deal with this." Jason slides out of the booth, but leans back to kiss me.

"No worries." I try to smile because I know he doesn't want to go any more than I don't want him to, and I don't need to add guilt to an already shitty situation. He strides off, his shoulders set, and he reaches the door before he makes a sharp U-turn and storms back to the table. He kneels on the curved bench and drags me up his body. It's awkward because of the table, but it's fantastic too. The irrepressible need and desire courses through him and straight into me. His hands secure me and caress my body. His touch is urgent; his kiss is the best, sweetly sensual and desperately possessive all in one glorious package. His tongue explores my mouth like it's the very first kiss on earth, reverent and glorious. I whimper and crumple against him, his strong arms holding me where my frame has lost all substance. He breaks the kiss, and I feel the loss like a vacuum in my soul.

"Just so you know, I fucking hate leaving you, and this situation is temporary. It will not always be like this, understand?" He growls out the words like it physically hurts him to go. *I feel exactly the same.* "I'll have my breakfast later."

"You want me to get them to put it in a doggy bag?" I wrinkle my nose at the thoughts of sloppy eggs and beans in a baggy.

"No, beautiful, that's not what I want." His tone drops, and I get that euphoric tingle in my sweet spot that makes me clench everywhere: my jaw, my thighs, and all the muscles inside.

"Oh," I sigh. His thumb traces a delicate line along my jaw, and then he backs away.

"And you take care of *my* girl." His words might be playful, but the tone of the delivery is anything but, and Will shifts beside me.

"Always," he replies, and Jason gives him a curt nod. Will turns to me. "Does he not know you at all? There was no fucking way I could've stopped you from drinking last night if that's what you wanted to do." He rolls his eyes, shaking his head with frustration.

"He knows me, and he knows that would be true for him, too. He's just cross he wasn't there, and you're an easy target—an *easier* target."

"Ha!" he huffs out a disgruntled puff of air. "It's not like he hasn't ever fucked up."

"Oh," I elongate that word, as I slowly lean toward him with intrigue in my tone. "Do tell?"

"I am almost pissed off enough to do just that, but since he's mad at me right now, I better not."

"Ah, you're no fun," I tease, nudging him in the side.

"That's not what you said at Christmas."

"Will." My drawn out use of his name is thick with warning.

"Sam," he mocks me and winks away the sexual tension with enough charm and a dash of blatant cheek.

The rest of the day is actually lots of fun. We take a couple of the street bicycles and ride around Hyde Park, the lake, and out across the road and into Green Park, up the Mall, and to Buckingham Palace. We make our way to the back of Knightsbridge and return the bicycles. I have decided to treat Will to lunch at Sofia's family restaurant, if we can get a table.

"This place must be good to have ridden over the whole damn city for." Will drapes his arm over my shoulder and ruffles my windswept hair.

"It is good. Well, I'm sure it's good. The new manager at the club and a friend of mine, Sofia, it's their family's restaurant." I try to tame my mane, but the bike ride, blustery weather, and Will's meaty hands means I am fighting a losing battle. I settle for scraping it back into a low messy ponytail.

"Marco? This is his family's place?"

"Yep, he's Sofia's twin, he worked here for years and was offered one of their other restaurants to manage but wanted to try something different."

"He certainly got different." Will chuckles and holds the door to the restaurant open for me, but as I step inside I can see this wasn't such a great idea. The place is heaving and there is a queue of customers at the bar. "You know I can cook," Will offers as he too clocks the fat chance of us getting a table.

"But you're a guest, shouldn't I be cooking?" My nose wrinkles involuntarily at the thought of me being in charge of an entire meal. *Carnage comes to mind.*

"I'm family, not a guest, and I don't know, should you? I don't think that's written anywhere in stone, and it certainly isn't written on that screwed-up face. Besides, I like cooking. I mean I would like to cook as a way of thanking you for letting me crash with you guys."

"You're family, you said that yourself. Do you always do that when you stay, then?" I narrow my eyes when he averts his.

"Um, no, not so much, but only because we're both usually out—" He snaps his mouth shut as his brain to mouth filter kicks in.

"Out trolling?" I place my hand on his chest and smile. "It's all right, Will." He is rigid under my palm. "You two are hardly the poster boys for abstinence."

"We didn't troll." He seems to stiffen a little more at my perceived character assassination.

"I don't suppose you ever needed to. The ladies would've flocked to your feet, I'm sure. I'm not judging, Will, seriously. I'm the last person to judge. I'm sorry. I didn't mean to upset you."

"I just don't like you thinking I'm some sort of manwhore. I like sex, but I'm —"

"I don't think that, Will," I state with absolute certainty, holding his gaze as I do. He gives me a slight nod, and I wrap my arms around his waist. "I'm sorry. I didn't mean anything by it, Will. Really I didn't." I am a little shocked by his reaction, but then I spent so many years not caring that people called me a whore because I knew different that I guess I have a thicker skin. He kisses my head, and I pull back. His wide bright smile is a picture of forgiveness.

"So I'm cooking then?"

"That would be great," I say, just as the headwaiter approaches us with some menus. I shake my head, and we turn to leave, bumping straight into Sofia.

"Sam!" She throws herself into my surprised embrace. I was holding the door open, and my arms were an open invitation, apparently. She holds me until I feel like if I don't hug her back, she is just going to remain stuck to me like a limpet. I pat her back and try to relax. Not that I am antiaffection, I am just not used to this from girl friends. *I don't really have friends who are girls.* "Did you get my magazines? I hope you didn't mind me sending them. I have stacks because I can't bring myself to cancel the subscriptions." She laughs, because her own wedding must have been easily two years ago.

"I did, thank you. It's all a bit daunting, if I'm being honest. I don't really know where to start." I shrug like the weight of the 'big day' is physically resting on my shoulders; they barely move at all.

"The dress. Start with the dress." She clasps her hands excitedly and does this little bounce on the balls of her feet. Her dark brown eyes sparkle, and her smile just lights her face. I am a little in awe of her reaction and not in a good way. I am definitely missing something—some wedding gene.

"Right, okay." I try to smile, but it catches, and I'm sure I actually bare my teeth in a strained grimace.

"I know some great places to shop for the perfect dress. If you want, I'd happily come with you. I mean only if you'd want. If you have someone else to —"

"I'd like that." My rushed acceptance interrupts her and takes us both by surprise. I let out a breath, and she seems to hold hers as if waiting for me to change my mind. I don't, and I let my own smile mirror hers. "Thank you." I can feel my cheeks heat, and my voice catches with a surge of emotion, which I swallow down, quickly adding. "We have to rush, but that is really kind of you, Sofia." I grab Will's arm and pull him away from the door, waving over my shoulder as we make our way down the street.

"I'll call you!" Sofia shouts after us, and I turn to see her enthusiastic wave and beaming smile, and now I feel like crap for bolting.

"What was that about?" Will asks after an uncomfortable silence deepens like a dark cloud, cloaking me.

"Um, nothing. Sofia was just being polite. I didn't want to hang around in case she felt obligated to offer all sorts of help she probably doesn't really want to give," I mumble.

"What?" He barks out an incredulous laugh. "Are you shitting me? That's what you got from that conversation? Wow!" He shakes his head, but I'm just staring at him with confusion plastered all over my face. "You know you are quite adorable when you're delusional."

"I'm not delusional," I challenge, letting go of his arm and stepping away as if the distance will help my rebuttal.

"Yeah, you are. That girl there was itching to help. So much so I think she had confetti in her veins. You didn't see that?" he scoffs.

"No, I didn't see that. Perhaps it's you that's delusional." My fake laugh falls flat, and his amused expression and knowing eyes just bore right through me. I shake my head at his misguided observation. "Look, she's an event planner, so, maybe she just likes weddings." He taps me hard on my forehead, and my instant reflex is to jab him in his stomach with a tight curled fist. He grunts but continues to laugh.

"No, darling, she wants to help you with yours. I doubt she does this for random strangers or people she doesn't really like. People aren't that nice, Sam. So when she offers something out of the blue like that, it's probably because she wants to. I mean *genuinely* wants to help."

"You think?"

"I know." He pulls me into a rough hug, and we continue to walk. "I wouldn't have believed that if I hadn't seen it with my own eyes." His tone is lightly mocking, but his reassuring squeeze helps to soften the judgement. I take a moment before letting out a heavy sigh.

"I've never had girl friends, Will, so I don't really know how it all works. I don't know the rules. If there is a sisterhood code of behaviour, I never got the memo."

"No school friends?"

"Nope. I wasn't allowed any friends. No, that's not strictly true. I just was never allowed outside of school. Friendships only grow with shared experiences and parties, after school clubs, even going round to a friends' place to study, and I wasn't permitted to do that. It didn't take long before I stopped getting invited, and then I just stopped being a part of a group." I let out a bitter laugh. "It actually got worse when Richard became my boyfriend, if you can believe that. Before him, I was invisible and after...Well, after, I was just outright hated." Will slips his hand into mine as we walk. His fingers thread and grip. "When I left home it got better because I had Leon, and that's all I ever needed: just one person who had my back."

"You have Jason and me." Will looks over at me; his warm eyes and tentative smile make my chest ache. I squeeze his hand and return his heart-warming smile.

"I do, and I mean I have work colleagues but no one close. Not close enough to ask about this sort of stuff. I just figured I'd be doing it on my own."

"Well, don't," he states and rolls his eyes with obvious frustration. "When Sofia calls you, bite her arm off okay?"

"If she calls." I hate that I sound so reticent, but this is uncharted territory for me.

"Jeez, I'm never going to get another erection if you keep this pussy act up. Where's the badass that blew three men's mind a few weeks back." I snuggle into his side and laugh out a dirty sound that matches the images playing in my head now that he's mentioned his last visit.

"She's getting wet just thinking about that night, thank you very much." He lets out a strained groan. "How's the erection now?" I challenge with a wide and wicked grin, pushing my hip out and into his side as we walk, knocking him off balance. He grabs my hand and pulls me back to his side.

"Hard and painful, so thank you very much."

SEVEN

Sam

"Can I do anything to help?" I ask loudly, with my best attempt at sincerity, but in my head I am secretly chanting, 'Please don't say yes. Please don't say yes'.

"I've got it all covered, darling, but thanks." Will flashes a cocky killer smile my way. "This is one of my mum's dishes. It's a one pot thing, so it's pretty easy to put together, but so damn good." He slams the oven door shut and dusts his hands off in a briskly dramatic clap. "It's just a waiting game now, a couple of hours and that lamb will just fall apart." He beams and rubs his flat taut tummy in anticipation. "So what shall we do in the meantime?" He wiggles his thick brows and I blurt out a predictable laugh, shaking my head with exasperation.

"How about you tell me what Jason was like as a tearaway teen?" I steer his relentless innuendoes down a safer path.

"I was the tearaway, remember? Jason was the good guy—*is* the good guy." He pinches out a tight smile, but the muscle in his jaw is set solid. It wasn't my intention to make him uncomfortable, and I rush my words to rectify this.

"Hey, you're a good guy." I reach across the kitchen table where he is now sitting opposite me and take his hand in mine. "You just lost your way, and I struggle to believe Jason was ever a Saint." He lets out a small laugh, and his eyes wrinkle with a genuine smile.

"He really wasn't. Did he tell you about the girl we shared in Sixth Form College?" He grins, and I sit up straight and lean forward, because this sounds more than a little interesting.

"Um, he might've. I don't remember." I try to shrug off the truth of my ignorance and add some disinterest to counter my overly eager tone when I am so obviously desperate for Will to tell all.

"Liar, there is no way he would've told you." He laughs and then purses his lips, biting back the juicy tale. "Actually, he'll probably kill me if I spill…Forget it." He waves his hand in a slicing motion across his neck, but I grab his hand

and turn his wrist back in a light, effective, and extremely painful twist. "Ahhh!" he grunts but doesn't fight it. If he did, I am just as likely to break his wrist at this angle and neither of us wants that. I just want him to carry on.

"Oh, no, no, *no*. No fucking way you can drop *that* and walk away. Spill the story, Will, or you'll get to see my nasty side." I put the smallest amount of pressure on his hand to make my point, but his groan is more erotic than pained.

"You know that's not a threat, right?" His wicked smile and heated gaze makes me remember Jason's comment about Will being more like Leon than himself when it comes to administered punishment and pain. I release my hold, and he lets out a deep and dirty belly laugh. I roll my eyes. *Relentless.*

"Tell me. You have to tell me. I promise I probably won't tell Jason that I know." It's not much of a plea, but I won't promise something if I'm not one hundred percent I can deliver.

"Oh, that's all right, then," he mocks in a heavily sarcastic tone.

"And I'll protect you if he does try and kill you. How about that?" I bat my lashes and clasp my hands together to add a little begging to my plea.

"It wasn't that bad, but, ah, fuck it. Okay, I sort of had a girlfriend, but we were never really exclusive, or I was a douche. Whatever. Jason and I would share her, but we never *actually* told her." He has the decency to grimace at this confession, but I let it slide even if I happen to agree that it was a douche move. "Anyway, she told me that she fantasised about having us both together and arranged to meet us after our classes in the gym store. The lock on the door was pretty loose, and it was common knowledge it was a good place to get some."

"And you both went?"

"Um, horny seventeen year olds? Hell, yes, we went." He rolls his eyes at my naïveté. "Anyway, she was all shy and asked us to strip first. Honestly, you didn't need to tell us twice, then she asked us to turn around while she took her clothes off."

"Hmm," I encourage, but my mind is racing ahead with this tale. He pauses, and this adorable pink hue flushes his stubble sprinkled cheek.

"We waited and didn't even peek, but after a few minutes of silence, Jason turned, cursed, and sprinted to where our clothes should've been. They were gone, the girl was gone, and the only things left on the floor was a pair of her frilly panties and a gym skirt. We searched that whole damn store room for something else, but she must've cleared it out because there was nothing in lost property, no other gym bags, no banners or random sheets we could use to wrap around ourselves. There was nothing but the skirt and panties she had left for us. You have to remember no one had phones back then, so we couldn't call for help. But I think that was a blessing because no cameras either. We had to walk

—well, sneak our way across town dressed in girls' underwear, and no one has any evidence, thankfully."

"Jason wore panties?" I snort a loud incredulous laugh, and my eyes water, as I can't stop laughing. "Oh, my god, I can't believe he did that!"

"He didn't." Will laughs, too, holding his hand over his face and shaking his head with embarrassment. "He ripped up the gym skirt and just wrapped the material, trying to cover as much as possible. He left me with the panties that didn't fit and were tiny enough to offer no fucking coverage at all. Christ, our mum was mortified."

"You told your mum about sharing a girl?" I drop my mouth wide with shock.

"Fuck, no, she'd have had a heart attack, after she killed us, that is. No, we told her it was a prank, but still, she was horrified that her boys had walked through town, nearly five miles home, damn near butt naked."

"Brilliant! I love this girl. If I had been allowed friends, I would've snapped her up."

"It taught us to be up front, that's for sure, and it turned out she was more than up for sharing. She just didn't want to be played. Lesson learnt: cards on the table from the get go."

"So girlfriends are told at the beginning what might be in store?"

"They would be, but I guess that's unlikely now, isn't it?" He raises a brow, and I just smile. I'm going to take the fifth. I would like to say, "Never say never", given that Jason is happy to share my fantasy. But I am not so sure I would be quite so happy to share him.

Will's eyes flash with a knowing spark, and his smile widens. "I like that you feel that possessive. It's sexy as fuck, by the way."

"It's the Domme in me, what can I say?" I lift and drop my shoulders. I'm not sure that's it, because Jason is the epitome of a Dom, but maybe it doesn't make me sound so crazy needy.

"But not with Jason? You're not Domme with him?"

"I have my moments, but no." I tip the remaining wine from the bottle into his glass and tap the bottom. "Oh, no, it's broken?" I stick my bottom lip out in an exaggerated pout.

"Is this wise? I got into trouble the last time you got drunk." He takes a large sip.

"But I'm not actually drinking this time," I point out, and he frowns, looking at his empty glass and my can of Coke.

"How did I not notice this?" He slaps his hand to his head like he is the world's biggest sucker. He's quite adorable.

"More wine?" I push back from the table and make my way to Jason's impressive wine fridge.

"No, I'll have a beer. This stuff seems to make me talk too much."

"I like you talking." I return with a chilled Corona, but we have no limes, so I slice a lemon and cram a wedge in the bottle before I place it in front of him. "So you have a girl back home who knows 'upfront'?" I slide into the seat next to him.

"I don't."

"Good." I shake my head when his eyes widen at my comment. "Sorry, that came out wrong. What I meant was I didn't picture you as a cheater, so I'm glad you don't have a girl back home. But then I guess if she was clued in, then that would be good, too, if she was cool with it, I mean." I let out a heavy awkward breath. "And to think I'm this articulate when I'm not drinking."

"It's okay, I understand. I'd never cheat. That's the fucking worst." He spits the words with shocking venom that makes us both sit up straight and look at each other in surprise. "Sorry," he mumbles and takes a long pull of his beer.

"It's okay."

"What's he done now?" Jason strides into the room cloaked with unwitting tension, breezes through it, and heads straight to me. His hand slides around the back of my neck, and he bends down to give me the sweetest kiss. His eyes would be filled with apology, if they weren't so damn tired.

"Will has cooked lamb hot pot." I lick my lips, and he would normally hone in on that movement like a shark does the scent of blood, but his head snaps to his brother.

"Mum's lamb hot pot?" Will nods, and the smuggest grin creeps across his face. All trace of whatever the hell that was is gone. Jason groans. "Fuck, yes!"

EIGHT

Jason

The amazing smell was wafting as I came in the front door, but Will confirming he has cooked my favourite meal has almost rescued this day from being a complete fucking nightmare...almost. We have good people at Stone, but when we have a delicate acquisition that Daniel would normally handle personally, and he is a little distracted, I have to go where I'm needed. I hate leaving Sam on a weekend; no, scrap that, I hate leaving Sam. Period. I steal another kiss because her head is just tipped ready and waiting. My lips are a little more forceful, and she rises to meet my mix of lust and needy aggression currently devouring her.

"Ahem, would you like a moment?" Will coughs his interruption, but it's Sam who pulls back. I couldn't give a fuck if he's here or not.

"Don't be silly. A moment is never going to be enough." She grins against my lips, but pushes me away playfully, stands, and moves to stand farther back. "Sit and I'll get you a beer. You look like you could use one." She sashays over to the refrigerator, and I slump into her vacant chair.

"I really could, although I would still prefer that 'moment'. I'm sure Will can manage on his own."

"You're incorrigible. Will has cooked for us," she states flatly, handing me the open bottle of iced beer. "I think you can keep it in your pants until after dinner, at least."

"Think again," I grumble, but she steps out of my reach and scurries around the kitchen table, using the large expanse of weathered oak as a successful barrier. *As if that would stop me.* She snickers, and her eyes dance with mischief and knowledge. I hold her gaze and delight in the flush of pink on her smooth, flawless cheeks. *She knows I will have my moment.* I take a long pull of my drink and turn to Will.

"So what have you two been up to?"

"Tourist shit. We took bikes for a ride around the parks, ran into Sam's friend, and then stopped at the market down the road to pick up supplies. Thought it's the least I could do as a thank you for all your hospitality." Will's brief summary is relayed with a warm smile, but his last comment is thick with sarcasm and pitched directly at me.

"When have I not been hospitable? When I let you crash here, or when I let you spend the day with my fiancée?" I counter.

"What do you mean let?" Sam butts in with an indignant tone.

"I could've taken you with me today." I stare her down.

"You could've tried." She holds my gaze, unblinking and hot as hell.

"You did verbally rip my bollocks off," Will adds and breaks my hold over Sam as we both look at him.

"You let Sam get completely smashed," I growl, and I can feel my temper rise.

"Again with the let—you get a brain transplant at work or something? Since when do you 'let' me do anything?" she snaps, and the anger dissolves, replaced with a wave of utter exhaustion. She's right; he's right. I drag a heavy hand through my hair and let out a heartfelt sigh.

"Fuck, I'm sorry. I'm just a bit on edge. I'm not sorry I laid into you for watching her get wasted, but I do know you would've been up against it trying to stop her." He narrows his eyes at me, then his face softens, and he twist his lips into a wide winning smile. I turn to face Sam. "The only thing I have or want control over with you, beautiful, is your safety, your heart, and when you come." My salacious grin and the fire in my eyes counter my stern tone.

"Forgiven." Sam leans over the table and places her hands on my face, staring with so much heat and love, it makes my chest pound with the strength of each heartbeat. "But you need to take some time off or you're going to give yourself a heart attack. No work tomorrow, understand?"

"You know it's not like that, Sam. This is just an exceptional situation that I have to handle."

"You're not going in, so think about ways you can 'handle' it over the phone, because that's all you're allowed, and that's only a maybe. It will all depend on if I'm in a giving mood," she states flatly, and I get the impression she is completely serious. *God, I love this woman.*

"Yes, ma'am." I purse my lips in a wry smile and lift my hand to my forehead in a Boy Scout salute.

"I'm going to hold you to that," she warns with a wicked wink.

"Don't tell Mum, but I think that was better than hers." Jason wipes his plate clean with the end of the crusty baguette before pushing the dish away. He leans back and pats his tummy, which despite the mammoth quantity of food, is disgustingly perfect and ripped.

"Oh, I am definitely telling her that!" Will puffs his chest out with pride, blows on his knuckles, and then polishes a pretend badge on his chest. I chuckle at his boastful stance, but it is completely justified. The lamb was melt in the mouth and the gravy was rich and to die for. "I'm going to get the train up tomorrow, just to show myself. Do you wanna' come? I know she's anxious to meet you." He holds Sam's startled bunny-in-the-headlights gaze, but then laughs. "Maybe not, then."

"Sorry." Sam lets out a shocked and nervous laugh. "I didn't mean to look so —"

"Horrified," Will offers as Sam struggles for the most appropriate word.

"I was going to say surprised," she corrects, but her expression is still this side of terrified. "Maybe just a bit more notice." She flashes a worried smile at me, but she doesn't need to be worried. The last thing I want to do is spend the day on a train.

"Mum doesn't like surprises, Will. Besides, I'm sorting out a proper visit."

"You are?" Sam's neck muscles strain to swallow that lump in her throat.

"I am. Don't panic. She doesn't bite, and my Dad is great." I wave off her concern.

"How could he not be? I'm sure the apples didn't fall far," she teases, but tension still edges her features.

"Who's Grace?" Will drastically changes the subject, but whereas I stiffen, Sam's brows furrow into intense lines of worry.

"The other night you said Grace's name, and Will must've heard you." I stand and walk around the table, pulling her up, and then sitting back with her curled up on my lap.

"Oh." She relaxes a little, but I think that is because of my embrace, not so much my clarification.

"Sorry, Sam, I didn't mean to pry. Jason's right, I heard you talking in between bouts of hurling, and you sounded upset. I just wondered if Grace was a friend or someone important. You don't tend to mention many people so…Look, I'm sorry." He shrugs and grimaces at my scowl, but it's too late to retract it; it's out there now and up to Sam what she is comfortable telling my fucking nosy brother.

"No, it's okay. I guess she just comes out to play when I'm completely shit-faced because I don't think about her at all." She lets out a heavy sigh, and my arms constrict like a snake, holding her just that little bit tighter. My lips press against her silky hair, and she leans into my hold, absorbing the comfort I know she needs when she thinks about her childhood.

"Grace is my birth name, but I changed it when I left home at eighteen. I have not so great memories associated with being Grace. I know she's part of me, but not a good part. I think she was strong in her own way to endure what she did, but I'm more than happy with being Sam."

"Sam fucking rocks!" Will states emphatically, and she lets out a tiny laugh.

"Sam rocks my world, that's for sure." She tilts her head back so she can look up as I gaze down. Her dark eyes swim with emotion, and her lashes are laden with moisture.

"Thank you." She closes her lids but when she opens them, all traces of sadness are gone. Just. Like. That. She absolutely floors me. She is so fucking strong. "Anyway, I chose the name Sam in the bar when I met Leon, the day I left home."

"Really, how so?"

"Well, like I said, I didn't want to be Grace, and I had to think quick. I saw the rows and rows of liquor bottles and just picked the first that could pass as a girl's name."

"Sam?"

"Sambuca,"

"It could've been worse, you could've been called Gordon, Tia, or Jack."

"Oh, so many, many much worse options." She giggles. "I like the name Sam, but more importantly, I *love* being Sam." Her tone is filled with justified pride.

"I love having Sam." My voice is low and husky against her skin, and she giggles.

"Because Sam is a kinky fucker who obeys your every command." Her perfect brow is arched high at the rhetorical question.

"Damn right she does, and speaking of commands. Bedroom, first position… now!" She shivers in my arms, and my cock strains to impossible proportions in my pants, beneath her cute little arse.

"Riiight," Will groans. "Maybe I will head off to the club, after all."

I stand with Sam in my arms, her attention is fixed on me, and I can see her eyes burn with pent-up lust. I set her on her feet, but before I can repeat my 'now' comment, she has skipped from the room only pausing to place a quick good-bye kiss on Will's cheek. I reach in my pocket and throw my keys high over the table to Will. He snatches them from the air.

"Take my car if you go and don't bring anyone home," I clip, my request not a request at all.

"Not an option." His expression is implacable, but his eyes flash with something I can't quite place, but it's gone, and so am I. "I'll see you later," he calls after me.

"Don't count on it."

Shit. I have this shooting pain across my shoulders, and the instant I try to move my arm, I realise I can't. I can't move either of my arms. The reason my shoulder is cramping like a motherfucker is because I am handcuffed to my headboard. I stretch my neck hard to the left then right to ease some of the muscle tension, but it is set like concrete. The fact that I am aching like this means I have been asleep in this position for some considerable time.

"Sam!" I yell out and wait. Nothing. Several more full-volume shouts and I get a twinge of unease that she has perhaps left me here and fucked off or worse. "Sam, get your fucking arse back here right now and uncuff me, or so help me, I swear—" I stop mid shout when the bedroom door opens, and Sam enters with a tray of sweet smelling food. Barefoot, she silently shuffles across the floor and places the tray on my bedside table. Her smile is timid, and my eyes bore into her, watching her every move. She steps back, slightly out of my reach, not that I could reach her but she's rightly cautious.

"Care to explain?" I rattle the cuffs roughly, and she sheepishly bites her lips together.

"They are pretty self-explanatory, wouldn't you say?" She looks sheepish because she knows leaving someone cuffed is a big fat no-no. "They've only been on for a bit and I watched the whole time, well, except to go and get breakfast. You were perfectly safe." She lifts the cover on the tray, and a warm waft of fresh baked pancakes hits me harder than the fresh cafetière of coffee beside the plate.

"Not the point." I reprimand. "Okay, beautiful, what's going on? You only ever get the pancakes out when you're worried." I pull hard against the cuffs and growl with frustration. I need her in my arms. This is unbearable and she will know that. "Talk to me, beautiful."

"I worry you work too hard. You looked so tired last night, and I needed to make sure you weren't going to take off in the middle of the night to go back to work."

"Why would I take off in the middle of the night?"

"Well, recently, every time your damn phone rings, you seem to have to go into the office." Her words are clipped with frustration, but I can see the genuine concern in her eyes. I breathe out a gentle puff and keep my voice calm. I know she has my best interests at heart, but tying me up was never going to be a great idea.

"This is exceptional. You know it's not always like this. Wait, my phone rang? I didn't hear it. Where is it?" I look toward the nightstand where I left my phone charging, but it's not there. "Sam?" I growl, fighting my rising anger.

"See, you were so tired, you didn't even hear it ring." Her hand drifts behind her, and I can only assume my phone is currently perched in the back pocket of her pyjama shorts.

"But I'm awake now, so how about you uncuff me and let me see who called." I grit out the words slowly through my clenched jaw.

"It was the office, someone named Greg. He didn't leave a message." Her hand is still tucked behind her back.

"Cuffs." I smile tightly, but my jaw is ticking nicely, and her eyes hone in on that little muscle as her head shakes slowly.

"How about you let me keep you cuffed and I make it worth your while to stay there all day." Her sensual tone does unfathomable things to my insides and my painfully hard cock, but...

"Tempting, but I still have to make that call to Greg. He won't have called me to shoot the breeze, Sam. It will be important."

"Hmm, a compromise then. I will let you make the call if you let me keep the cuffs on you."

"That's not a compromise, Sam. That is you getting your way."

"And that's bad because?" She fails at her attempt to look sheepish because her eyes shine with utter wickedness.

"It's not bad, baby, but it's definitely not a compromise." She holds my phone out and waves it in a teasing manner.

"Your call, Jason." She says my name in a singsong carefree tone that makes me flip.

"No." And there is no misunderstanding my resolute tone.

"No?"

"I'll happily play tie up, but I won't be manipulated. Even if it is done with the best intentions, beautiful." I add her nickname to try and soften the curtness and rage that is peeking through my veiled attempt at remaining calm and controlled.

"Shame." She places the phone next to the breakfast tray and sits beside me, the bed dips only slightly. Her fingers slide beneath the covers, and she pulls them down and off the side. I am naked, secured to the bedpost, and have the most enormous hard-on that springs to attention as soon as the sheet is dropped. Her hand wraps around the base, and she grips me tight. I hiss through my teeth because that pressure is fucking perfect. I can feel the blood surge under her hand, and I swell against her hold. She climbs onto the bed, her soft thighs encase mine, and her hair forms a curtain of loose hair partially covering her face when she dips to swipe her tongue over my sensitive tip. Her eyes never leave mine, predatory and scorching. Her tongue takes another swipe, and it's all I can do not to come right then. I suck in a sharp breath and let out an agonising groan when her lips cover the head of my cock and slide down as much as she can in one smooth beautiful move.

"Oh, fuck!" I would close my eyes, it feels so damn good when she does that, but her dark eyes are fixed on me as she works her way up and down my thick cock. And if that isn't the hottest thing, I don't know what is. Her hand moves over me in unison with her delicious mouth, and her tongue traces lines up my length and then sweeps and swirls over my tip, driving me fucking insane. My hips roll to encourage the rhythm she is setting, but I am under no illusion she is running this show. Her other hand cups my balls and tugs, her fingertips press the pressure point just behind my sack, and I feel the first surge of my climax. I choke out a gasp because her thumb presses firmly on my crown. It's like a fucking emergency stop. Shit! Before I can voice my objection, her hot wet lips are again taking me deep into her mouth and swallowing me down. The climax that had been denied starts to swell immediately in my balls and burns from the base of my spine through every single nerve ending.

My wrists burn with the strain I am putting on the cuffs. I so want to run my hands through her hair and just hold her right there, mostly to stop her from doing that again. I bite back a curse when she does exactly that. *Damn it.* Her smile is nefarious at best, but I think there might be a sadist lurking beneath the surface when she takes her sweet time dragging her tongue up the length of my throbbing erection after the third denied climax. Her breath is hot and feels like a flame on my raw, sensitive skin when she sighs and rolls back onto her heels.

"About that compromise." She smiles sweetly, and I know from the look in her eyes, she could do this for hours. I also know she won't top me, however delectable her bottom may be.

"Sorry, beautiful, what was that you said? I am a little out of it waiting for my next non-orgasm." Her eyes narrow, and she searches my face for any sign of the lie, but I am impassive, and I have never been so grateful she can't read the fucking torture that is on my face. She huffs and jumps from the bed. I let out a raucous laugh that sends her face into a furious reddening rage. She snatches up a pancake and forces into my laughing mouth. I continue to laugh while chewing down the food.

"Impossible." She turns and storms from the room.

I swallow the pancake, smiling to myself. It only takes a moment before I frown because I may have won that battle, but this victory hasn't actually improved my situation.

I shift and pull myself round to a kneeling position. The cuffs are sturdy, none of those hen party shit types you can get, unfortunately. The bedpost is also pretty heavy duty, solid steel frame. I rattle the bars, and it barely moves. Standing up, I try to pull up in a sharp jerking motion, which only cuts the cuff into my wrist. The pain is nothing, but the blood flows all the same. Shit.

"What the hell are you doing?" Sam gasps from the door and is instantly at my side, the edge of her cami-top pulled and screwed up against my wrist to stop the blood tricking onto the pillows.

"What does it look like?"

"Jesus, Jason, I was only gone a minute. I went to get the key."

"I didn't know that. For all I knew you had gone out for the day." My tone is flip and a little hostile.

"That doesn't even make sense. I want to spend the day with you, you idiot. That's why I cuffed you in the first place. You just don't play fair."

"I play very fair." I arch my brow and level a hard glare her way filled with as much irony as is possible. She has the decency to look a little sheepish.

"Okay, *I* don't play fair but I just—" She pulls in a deep breath, struggling for the right words. I help her out.

"I know, beautiful." I lean forward in lieu of being able to cup her face. She meets me half way and kisses my waiting lips. "How about we lose the cuffs and start again?" She fishes the key from her pocket and frees me. My wrists are raw, but I don't give them a second thought. I am instantly on her, pinning her to the bed and pressing my full weight on top of her body. "You are everything to me, beautiful. You know that? I will make this time up to you, but if I have to work, I have to work, and if I decide to let you tie me up, it's because I have made that choice. Understand?"

"I do now."

"Good." I cover her mouth and push my tongue roughly between her lips, sweeping in, and she fights me, fights my every push and pull. It's fantastic duelling for the next gasp and sigh. "By rights, I should make you pay for that little stunt, but I know you thought you were doing a good thing, so I will let it slide, just this once."

"You can punish me. I don't mind." She wiggles her sexy little body beneath me.

"Then it wouldn't be a punishment, would it?" I shake my head and sit back against the headboard, pulling her into my lap. "How about you feed me, and we work out what we are going to do in bed all day."

"Really?" Her smile is utterly breathtaking.

"Really." God, that smile just breaks my heart. She fucking glows with that simple concession. She leans over and puts the plate of pancakes on my stomach between us.

"They're a bit cold." She takes a nibble and offers me a bite.

"Hmm, they are, but still taste good. Besides, I don't mind, because the only thing I want on my tongue that's hot is you."

"Hot?" She wiggles her brows, sexy and suggestive, with eyes that dance with fire in them.

"And dripping." My voice drops to a low growl that rumbles from my chest.

"Always." She swallows back a whimper and sucks in her bottom lip. I can feel her heat and dampness against my skin. I groan when I hear my phone vibrate. Her shoulders drop, but she reaches over and hands me the mobile. I flick the screen and take the call.

"Guy, what do you need?" I keep my tone level, despite Sam arching back and pulling her camisole top clean off her body. She cups her perfect breasts and rolls the hard peaked nipples languidly between her fingers. *Oh, shit.* "You can handle that yourself." I choke back a cough when she pushes her middle fingers in her mouth, sucking them loudly and drops that hand into her shorts, hitching up a little so I know exactly where her fingers are heading. I have no idea what Guy is telling me, and there is no way I can contribute anything remotely constructive with this little show playing out in front of me in high definition "You need to handle this, Guy." I repeat a little more strained this time. "I won't be in today. If you can't sort it yourself, email me what you want me to check along with your notice." Sam raises a brow at my clipped tone, but dammit, there is a reason The Stone Corporation pays well. *Although it isn't necessarily so the Chief Operating Officer can eat his fiancée for breakfast.* I end the call and drop my phone on the floor with a thud and focus my glare on a startled looking Sam.

"Scoot up here, beautiful." I cup my fingers, encouraging her to climb farther up my body. She jumps to her feet, wobbling on the mattress as she pulls her pyjama shorts down and balances to get them completely off, kicking them across the room. She carefully steps on either side of my torso and lowers herself so her thighs slide on each side of my head. Now, that's what I call a breakfast of champions. My hands, thankfully free, grab her arse cheeks and pull her core flush to my eager mouth. God, she smells amazing. My balls ache like a motherfucker, and my cock strains against my stomach, *utterly intoxicating*. I drag my tongue along the soaking wet folds, lapping and sucking, my lips pulling her most intimate parts into my mouth. The tip of my tongue searches and dips inside. She is so damn wet I drink her down as she greedily rocks her hips against my face.

My fingertips grip harder, not to control her pleasure, but because I can't get enough, and the need to mark is so primal, I feel it in my soul. She cries out, and her hands fly to my hair, fingers pulling and gripping, as if I am her only anchor to Earth. My tongue sweeps long strokes and flicks lightly over her clit several times before I draw that needy nub of nerves into my mouth and suck down hard. It's an almighty detonation that I would have heard fall from her lips if her thighs hadn't clamped so hard around my ears, effectively cutting off any sound. Her legs tremble, and she shudders under my fingertips. Her essence pools onto my tongue, and I drink her down, every last drop.

After a few more full body shudders, she crawls back down my body and falls—no, collapses onto my chest.

Only after a few excruciating minutes of my hard-on brushing the curve of her backside every time I take a deep breath does she tip her head to look at me, a wry, cheeky smile curling her gorgeous mouth. *Oh God, that mouth.*

"Need a little help there, buddy?" Her eyes flash to between us.

"If you wouldn't mind, that would be perfect," I reply deadpan. She barks out a dirty laugh, and lifts up onto her knees and shuffles back to hover over my very angry-looking erection. She shivers as she slides down to the hilt, and her whole body grips and shudders as she holds me like a vice, sweet, hot, and sexy as fuck. Her head rolls back on a sigh, and when she looks at me through heavy long lashes, it is with the most heat outside of a supernova and just as spellbinding. She starts to rock, and with little encouragement, she is setting a perfect, punishing pace, and judging by the rapid breaths, flushes of colour on her cheeks, and the subtle sheen to her skin, she is just as close to a climax as I am.

"Jason…I'm close…sorry. I…I can't hold—" She moans out with a sexy catch of breath.

"Come for me, beautiful, I'm right with you," I groan.

"Oh God, thank you, thank you." Her head drops to her chest, and she pumps her little arse faster, chasing that release for both of us. I get the fire and shooting spike of pleasure at the base of my cock. My hands fist the flesh of her curves, and I grind her down onto me as I thrust hard and fast once, twice, and roar out a cry from deep in my belly, when every single muscle inside her grips my cock and squeezes me dry. She flops onto me, and I sweep my arms around her heaving frame. Her desperate breaths match mine, but we quickly fall in sync and calm to a less frantic breathing pattern.

"I think I'll need the day in bed to recover." I can feel her lips smile against my chest at my words.

"Me, too." She slides to my side, one sexy leg wrapped around my body, locking me to her.

"I said I wasn't going anywhere, there's no need for the vice grip, beautiful." I chuckle when she just flexes a tighter grip.

"I know, but I am happy with the vice grip. I feel safe with my legs coiled around you." I roll her on to her back and drop my weight heavily on to her.

"And I am happy when I have you like this, with me on top."

"Hmm, is that so?" Her eyelids are already closed, and she follows those words with an adorable stifled yawn.

"Damn right, but mostly, I am happy when you are with me because then I know without a doubt that you are safe."

"Are you coming back here tonight?" I ask Will, as he is packing his rucksack in the kitchen. Sam fell asleep, and I took the opportunity to make some fresh coffee and get supplies to last the day. If she wants a day in bed, she's going to get a whole day in bed.

"No, probably not. I'll stay over at Mum's and catch the early train in the morning. The embassy should have my documents ready by lunch time, and my flight is tomorrow night." He pulls the straps tight and clips all the loose buckles and zips shut.

"It really was a flying visit?"

"Yep." He rakes his hand through his hair and looks nervous. "I thought maybe you two could come and stay with me for a bit before I start my new job. I still have some time off and thought it might be nice to hang out."

"Yeah, sure, that sounds great." It really does, with the hours I've been working, but I have no idea why he'd be nervous about that. "You look like you were going to ask for my first born there, what gives?"

"Sorry, I just wanted to ask something else." There goes his hand again, and I know that's not good, because I do exactly the same when I'm on edge.

"Go on."

"Sam…is she…I mean, she seems okay after what happened, and I just wondered if she's just really good at hiding?" He looks strangely uncomfortable, which is even weirder because we have talked about this. He is pretty much the only one I can talk to about this, outside of Sam, so why he is having trouble bringing it up is just odd.

"She is really good at that, but I'm better at making sure she doesn't. So, yeah, she's good, really good actually. I've never known anyone so strong."

"Me, either, and she's really okay with the sharing?"

"That's two questions. It's me you should be asking, because I'm the one sharing, and no. But also yes, because that was for her. Her fantasy, and she needed that more than my jealousy. Besides, I can control the jealousy because I know for her, it is just that…fantasy."

"So it was just a one-time thing?"

"That's three questions, and that's between us, but you'll be the first or second to know. Do you mind telling me why you're acting so fucking weird all of a sudden? It's not like we haven't talked about this before. This is not new information, Will."

"Sorry, man. You're right, we have. It's just I guess the more I get to know her, it feels different, and I didn't mean to pry."

"Yes, you did. I know you care about her, and it means a lot that you do." I punch him on the shoulder. "I trust you, Will."

"Well, that just makes you an idiot." He laughs and punches me back on the top of my arm.

"Arsehole." My arm throbs because he hit it just right, fucker. He swings his bag over his shoulder, and I follow him to the front door. He stops on the threshold and pulls me in for a hug.

"When she got all bossy yesterday, man, that is seriously fucking sexy. I can't believe you've never let that side out to play." He lets out a low breath and a deep chuckle, pulling his collar wide at the neck of his t-shirt to supposedly let out some steam.

"It's sexy as fuck when she gets all possessive and caring, I agree, but I don't have a submissive bone in my body, so I just don't see the point." He nods in understanding, and I ponder for a second before feeling the need to clarify, since he hasn't walked away. "The only point would be if it was important to her, but she knows how I feel, so I don't think it would be *that* important." I absently rub the welt on my wrist. His eyes flick to my hand, and he grins when I add. "Well, if she didn't know how I feel, she does now."

NINE

Sam

Charing Cross train station is heaving, and I am a minnow swimming against the tsunami of commuters trying to get to work. I live in a city that boasts top designers and world famous shops, but Sofia insisted on taking me out into the sticks to hunt down my wedding dress. She dismissed my suggestion of Harvey Nichols, Browns, or even Harrods in favour of what, she promised, was unique and perfect for me. I edge my way along the perimeter of the station to the spot we had arranged to meet. It's after nine, but the throngs of people keep coming in relentless waves as each train pulls in busting at the doors with crumpled and disgruntled passengers. I can't see what the lure of the countryside is that would induce me to endure that daily hell, no matter how green the grass or fresh the air.

I spot Sofia, hard not to, in her bright red three-quarter length wool coat, nipped at the waist with a thick buckle belt and a matching woolen hat with a huge fluffy pompom. She waves like a crazy person when she sees me, pushing through the crowd to close the distance. She squeals and wraps her arms around me, hugging with the strength of a bear, not the petite and immaculate Italian princess she resembles. She doesn't act like a Princess; at least I have never witnessed any behaviour that is remotely precocious. Although Marco, her twin and manager of the club, has informed me she is more than capable of tossing a tantrum or two, but she is hardworking and has only ever been kind, genuine, and sweet to me. Today is a perfect example. She jumps us both up and down, excitedly displaying hidden strengths in those tiny arms.

"I'm so excited. I can't believe you asked me!" She beams at me, dark eyes sparkling with sincerity and joy. "I'm so honoured, Sam. I won't let you down." Her breathless excitement is replaced with a seriousness that takes me by surprise. It's just a dress.

"Um, I think it's me that is honoured, Sofs. You taking time off work just to buy a dress." She steps back, her hands flying to hold her gasp in. She shakes her head dramatically, her eyes wide with horror.

"Just a dress—you sound just like Bets. What is wrong with you two? It's not *a* dress. It's *the* dress." She threads her arms through mine and leads me head-on into the opposing wall of walking commuters. "It's like we're not even the same species," she mutters, tutting and shaking her head.

"Just a little out of my comfort zone, Sofs." I shrug and offer an apologetic smile.

"Well, you are slap-bang in the center of mine, and if you'll let me, I'll happily lend a hand." The pitch and tone of Sofia's declaration is filled with hope, and her eyes sparkle with anticipation, which honestly takes me by surprise. Something I fail to hide in my voice.

"Really?"

"Are you kidding me? I'm an event planner, Sam, I live for this shit. Although at work I don't get to do weddings. I have done one wedding, and even if I do say so myself, it wasn't too dusty." She puffs out her coat-clad chest with justified pride

"Sofia, it was perfect." She lets me go so we can file through the ticket turnstile. "Did you really do all that yourself?" I raise a sceptical brow.

"Pretty much." She nods and holds my gaze. "I know that's difficult to believe. You've met my family, after-all, but I had to take charge or my mum and aunts would've taken over, and there wouldn't have been a venue outside of Buckingham Palace that would've been big enough or grand enough." She smiles but rolls her eyes with humour. "Mums and their daughters." She snaps her mouth at her mistake, and before I can shake off her error, she has pulled me into another bear hug. "Oh, God, Sam, I'm sorry. I didn't mean anything." She squeezes harder, and I swear I feel a rib crack. "You're going to sack me before we even start, aren't you? Sorry, so, so sorry." She pulls back and holds my gaze, her face a picture of remorse.

"Sofs, stop. It's fine." I laugh, and I would be speechless but her face is still etched with heartfelt concern, so I continue. "I happen to agree." The soft edge to my response and sincere smile has a visible impact on her frame: her shoulders relax, she lets out a breath in a puff, but her eyes are still fixed on me. "Your mum dotes on you, Sofs, adores you, is your biggest cheerleader, and that is a beautiful thing. It is how it should be between parents and their children. Unconditional and unreserved, but just because I didn't have that type of relationship with my mother doesn't mean you can't talk freely about yours. That's just crazy." I pause to let my words sink in, and as they are quickly absorbed, Sofia is, once more, bright eyed and beaming at me. "And there is no way you're getting the sack. You're the only candidate, so you can pretty much say what you like, you're going nowhere." We walk the length of the platform to the middle of the train.

"Even so, I am sorry."

"Enough with the apologies," I clip but keep my tone light, holding my hand up to halt any further discussion.

"Okay." Sofia flashes a quick smile, finally accepting that topic is dead. "And I doubt I'm the only one, though, but I am super glad I am."

"How about the only permissible candidate?" Sofia's brows pinch with confusion, and she waits for enlightenment. "Jason wasn't a fan of me asking Leon, and he said he would come if you couldn't. He wasn't going to let me come on my own. Which is sweet, but—"

"Um, no, to both," Sofia snaps an interruption, wildly shaking her head in horror. "No way you would come on your own, and no way Jason could go with you."

"Sam, I would've understood if you'd told me to go to hell after what happened with Peitra." Sofia has been nothing but a brilliant friend, but still, Peitra is part of her family. "She's lucky she didn't get life, Sam, and she would've for kidnapping. It's only your statement that meant she got away with —"

"She's still your cousin, Sofs, and family is—"

"Family is everything, Sam, but it can also be fucked up and not who we would choose to have in our lives. What she did... You could've died... So, no, Sam, you are not the one I will be telling to go to hell."

"Families." I shrug off the heavy turn of the conversation with a puff of frosty air and an exhale of held breath. Since her arm is still threaded through mine, she squeezes it in the crook of hers, securing me to her side. The brief silence is broken when she turns to me,

"I can't imagine what you went through, but one thing you don't ever have to worry about is where my loyalty lies. You're a dear friend, Sam, and this is your day so, let's not dwell on events we can't change, and focus on making magical the events we can." Her bright smile and pure, kind words make my eyes tingle and my nose pinch. For fuck sake, when did I get so damn emotional? I swallow back the surge of raw feelings threatening to hijack this day before it even begins.

"Sounds good to me." I blink a few times, dispersing any residual liquid before it pools into big fat tears.

"Good." Sofia holds both my hands in hers and does a little excited bunny hop, unable to contain the pent-up joy in her body a moment longer. "And Jason is not allowed to see the dress you pick. That means no describing either. You have to promise," she warns with a sudden seriousness in her tone that is at odds with the bundle of bubbling excitement that is the woman before me.

"Lips are sealed." I motion to zip and lock my lips but leave a tiny gap to ask. "Although, since he's paying for it, shouldn't he have some say?"

"Absolutely not." She waves her hand, dismissing my silly notion with a flick of her wrist. The train doors open, and we step into the now-empty carriage and take seats next to the window, which has a table and four places to sit, two each facing each other. Sofia slides in next to me, still shaking her head. "Not a peek, it's tradition. Some traditions are flexible, but that one is set in stone," she warns, and I nod in agreement, failing miserably to hide my amusement.

"If you say so." I chuckle at her indignation.

"I do." The train pulls out, and we fall silent as the city vista slips away, replaced by frosted furrowed fields and winter-worn skeletal trees and hedgerows. "How much help do you want? I don't want to step on toes, so it's probably best if you lay out what you want me to do. Or is it just today?" Her dark brown eyes are so similar to Marco's, it's unnerving when her features otherwise are so delicately feminine. She holds my gaze, but I notice her gloved hands are clasped tightly together.

"Seriously, you don't mind helping?" Her eyes light up wide and incredulous. She beams at me, shaking her head.

"Was I not clear? Because I'm pretty sure I was over the bloody moon when you called." Her genuine pleasure about today is infectious, and I find I am enjoying the first flushes of excitement too.

"Not just being polite, then?" I tease.

"God, no, I don't have time for that shit. You're one of my best friends, Sam, and seeing you and Jason finally get it on, I'm really happy for you. So just take it I will do whatever you want me to. I don't need a title or anything." Her words may say one thing, her intonation and pleading eyes say something entirely different.

"You want a title?"

"I really do." She puts her hands together in a glove-muffled clap.

"What like Queen or something?" She snorts out a laugh.

"Maybe just Maid of Honour, although I quite like Queen." Her bright smile dances playfully across her face, but I am struck hard by the sentiment.

"Would you?" I hate that my voice has even a hint of insecurity, because that is not me, but this whole rite of passage, girl-bonding thing, is something I have never done. I have friends, but whenever I needed a little more, there was always Leon. I have never asked for anything; I have pretty much fended for myself for ten years. More than ten years when I consider the non-existent nurturing I received from my mother. But as foreign as this feels to me, Sofia makes it surprisingly easy.

"Abso-fucking-lutely, I thought you'd never ask." She grins a smile that would shame Alice's Cheshire cat.

She had arranged three appointments and saved the best until last. At the far end of the town is a long Victorian parade of shops with a paved pedestrian courtyard. One side has a canopied overhang that is supported by thin white columns stretching the length of the parade. We pass several boutiques, a teashop, and an Italian cafe where we stopped for lunch in-between fittings. Third from the end, Sofia stops and pulls the shop door open for me to enter. The ornate metal curled around a small bell above the door announces our arrival, and we step into a room so light it rivals the mid-morning sun in high summer. Sparkles and masses of cream, ivory, and white silks bounce and reflect the light off the many mirrored surfaces and are almost as bright as the smile of the young woman that greets us.

"Hello, hello, welcome, come in." She waves us in with both hands and bounces a little on the balls of her feet with obvious excitement. She steps up to me before hesitating; her hands twitch, and I wonder for a moment whether she is going to give me a hug. There is clearly an internal struggle with desire and propriety waging. Instead, she pulls one of my hands into both of hers and pumps them up and down vigorously. "I'm Katie. This is my shop, and all these dresses I designed and made myself—the veils too." There is that megawatt smile again, bursting with pride this time. I can't see all the dresses in detail because they are covered with a protective sleeve but the one in the window is stunning. Lace over silk, full skirt nips at the waist, and a high collar, not my personal taste, but I can appreciate the skill and detail.

"The dress in the window is very beautiful," I remark and she lets go of her hold and walks over to the dress in question.

"It was my first, so it's a little dated now. I keep if for show, but it wouldn't do for you." She shakes her head dismissively. She motions for us both to take a seat. "Would you like some champagne?"

"Do bears sh—" Sofia coughs out an embarrassed interruption, but I can see Katie is stifling a snicker or two.

"We'd love some, thank you." Sofia answers and rolls her eyes at my smirk. I can't help myself. The last two fittings were tortuous, enduring pompous snooty ladies with zero sales skills and even less manners. One visibly turned her nose up at my kitten panties, the photo image neatly covering my own *kitten*. The other, I swear, picked out the ugliest dresses for me to try, and when I asked if there was anything remotely sexy, she was horrified. When she said, 'A bride isn't supposed to be sexy, she is supposed to be virginal', it took all my effort not to retort, 'That ship sailed when we had a four-way with his brother and my best friend', but for Sofia, I held my tongue. If this fitting is the same, I am ordering my dress from eBay.

Katie returns with a chilled bottle in a silver iced bucket and three glasses. I like her already.

"Now, would you like to have a look through or would you like me to select some of my designs that I think will work best?" I take a large gulp of my drink.

"At this point, it doesn't seem to matter what I *would* like." Katie's brows pinch together above her pale blue eyes.

"Come on, Sam, don't be like that." Sofia nudges me, knocking my drink but not spilling it.

"I'm not ungrateful, Sofs, but you have to admit those last two places were awful."

"They really were. They weren't like that when I went, but then I had Mama, and you don't get away with that sort of attitude with her."

I scoff lightly. "No, nor me on a normal day, but this is not a normal day."

"It certainly isn't a normal day," Katie interrupts, picking up her glass and raising it toward us both. "This is a precursor to the best day of your life, so let's start it right. You get exactly what *you* want. So tell me what you asked for that was so impossible?"

"Sexy. I want a sexy wedding dress. Jason is hot and I want to make him groan when he sees me at the other end of the aisle because he knows he can't have me for a few hours." I clink my glass at her, waiting for the judgemental brow, but it doesn't come, not even when I add shamelessly. "I know Jason, it won't be hours. I'll be lucky if I make it to the vows."

"Oh my, that *is* hot." She sighs, downing her own drink and fanning herself. "I have the perfect dress." She puts her glass down and turns away, but instantly she turns back. "Look, I am happy to pull out several other dresses, but I know the perfect one. Do you want to go through the motions or do you trust a complete stranger?" Her face is light with excitement and for the first time today, I share that feeling.

I glance at Sofia who lifts her shoulders in a noncommittal shrug. My decision then. "In your hands, Katie, do your worst."

"I only ever do my best." She grins, and while I am expecting her to pick through the mysterious hanging gowns, she again disappears into the back of the shop. She is tiny, maybe five foot four and petite; her blonde bob is tied neatly in a ponytail. She is wearing a fitted black pencil skirt and tight back t-shirt with

Katie T embroidered on the back. None of this I can see when she returns, as her hands are held high above her head and she walks the covered dress in like a gothic headless bride. She reaches high on her tiptoes and hangs the dress on a hook next to a massive gilt mirror opposite where Sofia and I are seated. There is a cubicle, but she pulls the curtain closed and proceeds to move three oriental partitions to cover the main window to the street. She glances around the room with a finger tapping lightly on her lips like something isn't quite right. I take the time to pour another drink. Sofia starts to shake her head when I offer to refill her glass, her resistance half-hearted at best. Katie pulls out a large sheet from a drawer and throws it over the huge mirror and smiles, having prepped the room to her internal specifications.

"Right, Sam, up, up." She motions for me to stand while she starts to unzip the long protective sleeve.

"Kit off to undies?" I ask but I have already taken off my sweater and am undoing my jeans.

"Bra, too." She gives a playful smile at my wide eyes and panicked glance at the glass fronted shop window. "They won't be able to see in, I promise. Just make sure you stand in the center of the shop." She smiles mischievously, but my momentary disquiet is instantly replaced by wonder.

"Oh, wow!" I whisper, my fingers reaching to touch the delicate lace. Even though the hanger fails to do the gown justice, I can see it is a stunning dress. "Is that lace sheer?"

"Kind of. Let's get it on and you can see for yourself."

"But won't people be able to see...everything?"

"You said sexy, not slutty." She sounds mortified and places her hand on her heart like I have wounded her.

"Sorry, it's just..."

"Here." She ignores my concern and scoops the dress into her arms. "Can you drop so I can lift it over your head? You damn Amazonian goddesses and your height!" She snickers as I easily drop to my haunches in my bare feet and panties. "I'm just jealous. This dress really only works on someone of your height, build, gorgeousness, and confidence." She steps back, letting the surprisingly weighty material glide down my body, kissing my curves, and holding to me like a delicate second skin. Thin straps hold the unbelievably soft lace bodice and full-length mermaid tail dress up, but the scooped backless cut means they are the only things holding the dress up. The edging barely covers the curve of my backside, the material hugging me perfectly so there are no immodest gaps displaying more than is decent. This dress is decadently sinful. It's a paradox, and it is fucking perfect. Katie fusses and straightens, pulling and primping. I stand silent, just gazing down at my body. I have no idea what is looks like on with no reflection, but from Sofia's glazed expression and silence, I think it looks as good as it feels. Katie steps back and pulls the sheet from the mirror in a dramatic flourish, which isn't nearly as dramatic as my gasp. My hands fly to my mouth, and my damn eyes prickle. What. The. Fuck? I am not this emotional...ever. It's a dress, for fuck's sake. I draw in a deep, steadying breath. But it is a beautiful dress. No, it's more than that; it's my beautiful dress, and it's perfect.

"I know I am going to sound all sales womany, but this was made for you, sweetie." Katie crosses her arms, again fighting her desire to hug me, I think, but her face is beaming with pride. Rightly so—she created a masterpiece.

"You don't need to be a sales woman with this, Katie. I'd be crazy not to take this dress." My eyes flit to Sofia, who stands and positions herself beside me, slipping her hand into mine.

"I don't know about Jason, but I'm thinking of switching sides." She nudges me, and I snicker.

"God, Sofs, you're so disgusting, always making everything about sex," I tease and laugh when her cheeks flash bright red with instant mortification.

Katie helps me change, and we discuss cost and other fittings because apparently it's not that dress I'm buying; that was a sample, and granted, no one else had tried it on, still she wanted me to have something custom-made, and she wanted to tweak this design specifically for me. I wasn't going to argue. She was on-point with that selection, and I have absolute faith that she will make me feel like a Princess; a sexy-ass Princess, but still a Princess.

By the time we finish, I am starving and can't face the train journey home on an empty stomach.

"I need to eat." I pat my grumbling stomach, having only had a very light lunch, and with nearly a whole bottle of champagne between us, I am also a little light-headed. We huddle together, walking against the biting wind. Sofia nods, but her affirmation is muffled by the thick woolen scarf trying to strangle her. "What about here?" She nods, and we enter the first half decent looking bar that serves food. It turns out it serves very good food, but also wickedly good cocktails.

We flop into the seat on the train in a fit of giggles that started over what, I don't remember, and just continued throughout the meal, the many...far too many cocktails and the walk to the train station. I try to hush Sofia as I pick my vibrating phone from my purse. My fingers are gloved and my ability to focus is somewhat impaired: I miss the call. Turns out I missed several calls. I press the call return button and Jason picks up on the first ring.

"Hey, beautiful, are you okay?" His voice is deep and thick with concern. I need to not sound drunk.

"I am perfectly fine, thank you, Jason." Nailed it.

"Are you drunk?" His tone has switched from concerned to pissed. *Dammit.* I know he will have been worried, and if I had returned any of his calls this wouldn't be a problem. It needs to not be a problem.

"I bought a dress." I try for deflection.

"Are you drunk?" he repeats, his tone less impassive, more tempered fury, and it's got my back right up.

"I'm an adult, Jason, and if I want to get shit-faced, I can. You know exactly where I am and who I am with, so back off. You wanted me to do this, and after a shitty start, I managed to find the perfect dress and have some fun too. And, yes, I may well regret the two for one cocktails in the morning, but not now. You have no right to be pissed."

"I have every right. You didn't answer my calls, and I was fucking worried, so, yes, I have every right to be pissed, but I'm not pissed. I was just fucking worried." His tone is stern, but the undercurrent of concern far outweighs his irritation.

"I was perfectly safe, Jason." My voice softens because I can feel the tension in his voice. I know why he feels this way, and we both hate that any reminder of that dark time hurts us both. But him more so I think, because he felt so impotent. "I'm sorry I didn't call. I called as soon as I saw the missed calls, but I am sorry you were worrying. You have my tracker, Jason. You knew where I was. I am perfectly safe."

"Drunk on a train with Sofia isn't perfectly safe," he grumbles, but the fire has left his voice.

"A little drunk and the next stop is Charing Cross in thirty minutes. I'll be home before you know it. I will probably be home before you with the hours you're clocking." I risk a tentative laugh to try and lighten his mood.

"I just want you safe," he repeats almost to himself, and my heart aches that he hurts like this.

"I know."

"Call me if someone so much as looks at you, okay?" I bite my lip to stop from snickering at his ridiculously over-protective demand.

"See you at home, Jason. I love you, but I can still take care of myself."

"I know you can, beautiful, but that doesn't mean I will let you." He hangs up before I can retort, my drunken self a little slow with the witty comeback.

TEN

Jason

"Damn it!" I curse in the quiet of my office. I slip the phone into my jacket pocket and scoop my unfinished report into my briefcase. I know she's capable of taking care of herself, and I am stoked she's bought a wedding dress. But I am less than fucking pleased my beautiful girl is about to hit a central London train station this late at night, armed with little more than her sexy arse, her smart mouth, and Sofia. I check my watch. I have time if there is no traffic, but this is London, there is always fucking traffic.

I manage to park around the back of the station in a narrow dead-end street. I slam the car door and set off at a fast pace, clicking the lock behind me as I race to the main street and the side entrance of the station. Checking the arrivals board, I catch my breath when the train information indicates a delay. I open my phone and see I have a missed call from Sam. It rings again just as I am about to press the call return button.

"Hey beautiful." My tone has less urgency now I know she's near, but my heart is only going to stop the jack-hammering in my chest when I actually have her in my arms, safe.

"Hi, I called to let you know the train is delayed, but actually, it's pulling in now so that's good. I should be home soon. Are you still at work? Have you eaten?" She's rushing her words, and I don't know if it's the alcohol or whether she thinks I'm still pissed.

"I'm not at work and I have eaten, although I am still *hungry*." I deliberately drop my tone and lay a thick layer of salacious intent on that last word. I hear her breath catch. Oh good, it didn't go unnoticed.

"Um, I could probably help with that." Her voice is a breathy whisper.

"Oh, I know you could. Just so you know as soon as I see you, I am going to *devour you*" My tongue wets my bottom lip as I watch her train pull slowly to a complete stop, having reached the end if its line.

"Promise." She sighs, and that slow exhale makes my balls ache and my cock twitch to life.

"Promise," I state. My voice is softly hoarse, but my gravelly tone is more of a threat. I can hear the smile in her voice, but more importantly, I can see it too. Sofia has her arm threaded through my girl's, and they are hurrying to the ticket turnstiles.

"I will hold you to th—" She freezes when her eyes meet mine. Sofia turns to check her friend and slowly follows her line of sight to me. Sam bites her smile as her eyes search my face for some tell, and I keep my expression neutral. Now I can see her and know she is fine, I can relax and have some fun. I watch her slender throat contract and swallow; her chest rises under her warm winter jacket as she draws in a deep and steadying breath. She tips her chin and strides purposely toward me. Before she reaches me, I can't help myself; I close the distance and sweep her into my arms, across my body, and dip her low, swallowing her gasp with my kiss. Deep and urgent, breathless and sexy as fuck, she returns each swirl of my tongue, each moan and more, as if we are the only two people in this station. But we're not. Sofia coughs after an awkwardly long time, clearly gauging that we have no intention of stopping. I promised I would devour, and I keep my promises.

"Um, I'm going to grab a taxi," she mumbles. "So, thanks for today, and I'll see you around." I stand, pulling a dazed and pliant Sam with me. My arm is tight around her waist when she sways, not from the alcohol she has consumed, but from the desire evident in her heavy hooded lids.

"No need for a taxi, Sofia. We will drop you home," I inform her.

"No, don't worry; it's no bother. It's a ten minute taxi ride, and you look…" Her face turns bright red, and her eyes widen with embarrassment as she struggles to finish that sentence. Sam helps her out.

"Don't be silly. We practically drive past your place, and after all you've done, it's the very least. Really, Sofs, the very least. I am so happy you came today."

"It was my pleasure. If you're sure…" Sofia's eyes flit over to the long queue of people freezing in the wind whipping around the taxi rank and puts up no further polite objection.

"We're sure," I state and take Sam's hand and lead her to the exit. Sam stretches her other hand and makes sure Sofia is also in tow.

Sam slips into the back seat with Sofia, and now I feel like a fucking chauffeur as they continue to giggle about nothing. I feel Sam's hand at my neck and her fingers try to twist the hair at my nape. I like that, even as she is engrossed in conversation, she needs to touch me. No, I fucking love that, but she was right to sit in the back. My hands grip the steering wheel, knowing exactly where one of them would be if she had sat in the front, regardless of who was in the back. Sam's voice is at my ear as she breaks the train of thought that is causing a painful pressure in the base of my cock as it endeavours to expand in very cramped conditions.

"Jason, it's the most beautiful dress. You'll love it." She sighs and my heart swells more than my cock for once at the utter joy in her tone.

"I don't doubt that for a moment, beautiful. I'm glad you found something you liked."

"Oh, I loved it. It's made of—" Her words are muffled, and a struggle ensues as Sofia manhandles Sam into silence.

"Noooo!" I flinch at the volume of the screech that bounces in the confined space of my R8. "Sam, you can't…not a word," Sofia scolds.

"I just wanted to share a bit. I wasn't going to describe the low—" Her words are silenced once more with a light slap of a palm over her mouth, and her sentence is finished with in incoherent string of muffled nonsense.

"Nah-ah! Not. A. Single. Word. Understand?" Sofia's tone brooks no argument, and I chuckle when Sam muffles her acceptance and adds a promise to reveal nothing more. Not that she actually revealed anything other than she thought it was perfect. That in itself is not breaking news—anything on her would be perfect—but preferably nothing is better. Perfection needs no adornments.

I park the car and switch the engine off. Sam had switched to the front seat once we dropped Sofia home, but promptly fell asleep as soon as I started the short drive to our home. She is still sleeping even as the engine dies. I get out and walk around to her side, open the door, and still, she is dead to the world. Unfortunately, the car is too low to lift her straight into my arms without knocking her unconscious on the doorframe.

"Hey, you sleepy drunk, I can carry you to bed, but you need to get yourself out of the car." I tap her nose, which twitches under my fingertip. Her eyelashes flutter and open, her sleepy sexy smile spreads wide across her face before a cute frown forms, and she turns on her side away from the cold night breeze circling around the open door.

"It's cold, leave me be," she grumbles.

"It'll be much colder in about an hour when the heat has left the car. Come on, beautiful, let's get you to bed." I lean over and unclip her belt. She continues to grumble, but lets me ease her out of the car and puts up no fight at all when I lift her into my arms. I kick the car door shut and walk up the front steps with my arms blissfully full. I swipe the finger print entry and decide to take her straight up the stairs. I can finish my work later; she is going to need me.

I lay her on the bed where she wakes enough to help me undress her.

"I'm really sleepy." She crawls under the covers, all soft and gloriously naked, but she looks exhausted. So as much as I want to jump right in after her, jump on her, I tuck her in and go to fetch her some water. I kiss her forehead before I turn to leave; she is unconscious the moment her head hits that pillow. I still have work to do.

I didn't hear the footsteps on the stairs, but I hear the light padding across the kitchen floor. I rub the tiredness from my eyes, but before I can stretch the ache from my spine and tension in my muscles, her fingers are pressing a heavenly massage on my shoulders from behind. I groan when her knuckles dig into a tight knot of muscle.

"Have you been working this whole time?" Her voice is soft but filled with concern. It's almost three in the morning, and I tucked her into bed just after twelve.

"I have a lot on at work, and I wanted to clear my workload." I stretch out my neck to one side and feel the pop of pressure release. Her soft warm lips brand my skin, and I close my eyes and feel the burn. Her tender kisses trace a path to my ear when her warm breath whispers.

"Clear it for what? You have plans you're not telling me?" Her lips pull my lobe into her mouth, and her teeth bite gently to hold me captive. I feel the bite in the base of my spine and the pinch in my balls. I suck in a breath and hold back a groan.

"Keep teasing, beautiful, and I will bend you over this table," I grumble low and serious. I can feel her lips smile around my caught skin.

"Now who's teasing?" She sucks my lobe in and lets it go with a long drawn out release. "You *have* to be too tired—" She squeals as I swiftly take her across my body whilst standing up. I flip her mid-cry and push my palm flat and hard between her shoulder blades.

"Never too tired, beautiful," I interrupt, my lips against her ear, my voice hoarse with instant feral lust. I roll my hips against the flimsy silk shorts that offer absolutely no protection against my now raging hard-on. "Never too tired," I repeat. It's more like a possessive growl as I stand up but keep her pressed flat with one hand. My other hand deftly releases my cock and tugs her shorts down the curve of her perfect arse. I fist the base of my cock and slide it between her cheeks. She wriggles but tries to open wider for me. Her shorts though are trapped around her thighs when I kicked her legs wide as I pushed her flat; this is as wide as she can get. Not a problem. I push into her heat slowly, but she's so damn wet, and I am on the edge of exhaustion, so the gentleman part of me is taking a nap right now. I lunge, full force, slamming my cock balls deep and more. She grunts out a puff of air that I feel I have pushed from deep inside, filling her as I am. I pull back and do the same. This time her back arches, and she tilts her hips to take me deeper. God, I love this woman. I grab her hip and pull her back as I thrust forward, and I know from that particular pitch of cry, it hurt. I also know from that little moan that escapes the back of her throat that she fucking loves it. I thread my other hand into a fistful of her long mane and pull her back into a perfect bend, all stretched and taut.

"Harder," she gasps, her throat struggling to swallow at the angle I'm forcing. She turns her head to meet my gaze. Damn, she's on fire. Her eyes shine with such passion, liquid with wanton need and deep with desire for me.

"Fuck!" I growl out at as pure fucking ecstasy shoots through my body at her demand. I obey. I obey her because she fucking owns me. I thrust deeper, harder, and she holds her breath, eyes pinched tight, absorbing everything I'm giving her. I pump, relentlessly chasing the release that is crawling from the ache in my balls, poised on the edge, and I growl. "Come with me, Sam."

"Oh, God…I…I can't…You're so deep…feels so good…Ah, hmm…but…" She pants out the words, struggling to speak, but I know she can…she just needs a little help. My fingers on her clit would work or, in this instance, my thumb slipped into her tight arse. She drops her head, making me release her hair, her forehead thumps on the table as her whole body trembles and she takes me with her. Wave after wave of blissful, erotic, and sexy as hell contractions pulse around my impossibly hard cock. My fists grip her hips, anchoring me to her body as one. She sucks in long, deep breaths, as do I. But her body continues to shudder, ripple and ebb as her climax dissolves under my fingertips. I slip out of her and pull her into my embrace, sitting back into my chair. She snuggles into my hold, nestling into my chest and breathing me in as much as I do the same with her. My nose is in her hair, inhaling all her exotic scent: jasmine, ginger, and Sam. She is utterly intoxicating, addictive and lethal, my only drug.

"What plans?" she asks after our heartbeats have quietened and our breaths are not so frantic.

"This weekend, we're visiting my folks, but I thought at the end of the month, we could take a week out and visit Will, count some turtles or some shit." She sits up and swivels so her legs are draped over mine, her now dripping heat over my still-interested cock. Dammit, I need to sleep; she's gonna kill me with this insatiable desire. Her hands cup around my neck, and she looks up with sleepy eyes and the widest smile.

"I would love that." Her sweet lips cover mine, her tongue darting inside and dancing with mine. I pull her close and hold her there, still…immobile. She giggles into my mouth. "No need for that, you nearly killed me with that last orgasm. I need to sleep, too. I have no idea how you are still conscious." I stand, and she coils her long legs around my waist. I kick my trousers free so we don't fall when I start to walk and take us both back to bed.

"It helps I have the sexiest fucking woman in the world…whenever I want her…I'll sleep when I'm dead, beautiful." I thought she would giggle, but she holds me a little tighter and is quiet. "Hey, you okay?"

"I'm good," she says quietly, but I stop and wait for her to look up.

"Sam?" I prompt when she doesn't

"You work too hard." Her face tilts, and her eyes are deep, dark pools brimming with liquid. My chest feels tight and burns with the love I see reflected in her gaze. It's scary as hell, when you realise just how much another soul means to you. How vulnerable that makes you, weak, but it is also the *very* best thing in the world. It is the very reason to take that next breath because you get to share it with the one person that makes every day worth living.

"Hey, I'm not going anywhere." I brush my lips with hers and draw a smile at the slightest touch, instantly easing her troubles. "We just have a lot on, and Daniel is prepping for paternity leave, so it's unusually crazy. These last few weeks are not my typical, I promise." I tip my chin for her to kiss me, and she does, her hands moving from my neck to my face, cherishing me with her touch and the softness in her dark chocolate eyes.

"I'm not moaning. I just worry." She holds my gaze and my heart with her tender love and concern. "How about we skip tomorrow evening and have a night in just us?"

"Fuck, no, I made a promise. It's Valentine's Day, and I gave you my word. I may work hard, but I play hard too, and I am a man of my word. The Reaper himself is the only damn thing that will keep me from you tomorrow night, beautiful."

"Wow, I have never had anyone *that* eager to submit." Her grin is pure wickedness. I kick the bedroom door open and stride in, throwing her high onto the bed. Her shrill scream is drowned by hearty laughter.

"Eager to get it over and back to normal." I crawl up the bed as she edges away, slipping on the silky covers so I easily catch her beneath me.

"Normal?" She is breathless and biting that damn lip.

"Me on top of you," I state as a matter of fact.

"I like our normal." Her face beams and, just before I devour more of what is mine, I concur.

"Good."

There's a tentative knock on my office door, and my fingers pinch the pressure at the bridge of my nose, but my eyes are still closed. I asked Sandy, my PA, to field any interruptions so I could crash for an hour. I may have the sex drive of an eighteen-year-old, but after pulling a near all-nighter with my girl, I am painfully aware I don't have the reserves to keep me fully awake the next day. I draw in a deep breath that turns into a yawn and full-body stretch. I open my eyes and glance at my watch, four twenty. I've been asleep for over an hour, but I don't feel remotely refreshed. If anything, I feel groggier, but that is because I didn't wake up…I was woken.

"Come in," I call out, not hiding the irritation in my clipped tone. Sandy peeks her head around the door, and where I am expecting a half apologetic grimace, her face is pale. "What's wrong?" I am instantly on my feet and striding to the door. "Sam…is Sam all right?" I know it's been months since the kidnapping, but I can't help my first reaction is always her and her safety. I doubt that will ever change.

"Oh, I don't know. I hope so." Her face softens, and she averts her eyes. Her brow is knitted with concern, and she is now wringing her hands. "I'm sorry to disturb you, but…but." Her voice breaks, and her pale blue eyes pool with water. I wrap my arm around her shoulder and try to pull her into the privacy of my office, but she stiffens and shakes her head. "You need to see this." She dabs her eyes with a folded handkerchief and walks back around her desk and looks at me to follow, I do. I stand at her shoulder while she opens up an email from her spam folder and clicks on the attachment.

The grainy, pixelated video recording starts to play; the camera is hand held and moves wildly before settling on an image I never, never wanted to see. The video freezes before I can shut it off, the distorted image frozen on the screen is nowhere near distorted enough. A beautiful girl, arms held over her head by someone laughing, I can see the tension in her muscles as she fights against his hold. She is so small, the man holding her down and the many men circling the show, she doesn't stand a chance. Her legs are spread wide, again held that way by more than one man, two on each leg are still fighting to keep her still.

From what Sam has told me, I know about her past. I know it is Richard standing in between her legs with his back to the camera. But all I can focus on are the tears, so many fucking tears. I place my hand flat on the desk to steady myself. Must still be dreaming. This has to be a nightmare. Who the fuck is behind that camera?

"What...who sent this?" I click to close the screen and look at the email address I don't recognise.

"I don't know, Jason. I pressed reply but whatever I send just bounces back." She shrinks back in her chair. "I'm sorry, Jason, but I didn't realise what these were."

"These?"

"Yes, they started about a month ago. I just assumed they were spam and adjusted the filter to send them straight to the trash folder. I never opened them, but I know company policy is to delete all emails from unrecognised senders."

"So you deleted them all?"

"Yes." Sandy nods.

"But not this one?" I query.

"It came through with a false email address from our research department. I didn't spot it at first and clicked to open it, it linked straight to this email. I only noticed the difference in the sender email once it had taken me here. I didn't know. I'm so sorry." She sniffs and dabs eyes that are watery with tears.

"Sandy, it's not your fault." I place my hand on her shoulder for comfort, and she pats my hand to offer me the same. I can feel the tension radiating off me in waves, but she is obviously upset, too. "It is apparently very important to *someone* that I see this. I just need to know who that someone is and what they want," I mutter, still staring at the email address and icon for the attached document like it's a missing jigsaw piece.

"What they want?" Sandy looks up at me for answers I don't have yet.

"I don't think this is for my family album." I grit my teeth and close the screen down. "Someone wants something from me or Sam. I need to make sure they get whatever that is from me and don't go anywhere near Sam with this." I turn to face Sandy. "Forward all the files to me. Nobody is to know about this... no one and especially not Sam." My tone is firm and resolute.

"Of course, Jason." Sandy nods but looks shocked that I would suggest any different.

"Call James in IT and tell him I need a secure and private meeting set up."

"When?"

"Five minutes ago," I retort and walk off toward our IT department.

I don't fully understand the technical ins and outs of what our genius head of IT is telling me, but the nub is I can't trace the email, and the best chance of ever getting a lock is to 'catch' the email as it's hitting our mail system. He reliably informs me that with a bounce back, we might be able to attach a hidden code and blah-blah-blah.

"I need to know who is sending this, James," I snap, biting back the urge to hurl insults about not needing a fucking tutorial on the *how*, but I'm not an arsehole. I am just strung out, tired, and worried about my girl. I haven't shared the contents of the email, just expressed it as a matter of top priority. We've been at this for hours.

"This is strange," James mumbles but turns the screen to me. It's just a bouncing light hitting spots on the screen over a flattened map of the world. I raise a brow for him to enlighten me. "One of the emails had an IP address, and it's in the UK. It might not mean anything; other messages bounced all over the place when I tried to track them, but this one was the first and actually had a location, of sorts."

"Of sorts?" I raise a brow for him to elaborate.

"It's the arse end of London, mostly swamps and estuaries. There are no residential or commercial buildings there. Oh, wait, there might be a power station, but no homes, definitely no homes." He is scrolling on a split screen with a Google map of the location, zooming into a mass of green swamp and blue water.

"Grab that laptop, you're coming with me." I swipe my jacket from the back of my chair and stand to leave.

"Jason, I doubt there is anything there, and it's after nine." James taps his watch like that would make me reconsider.

"And?" I growl and fix my impatient and most deadly glare his way.

"I'll get my coat," he mutters as he quickly closes his laptop, packs away the cables, and grabs his phone.

"Good." I don't bother to wait but hear him run the length of the corridor to catch up to me at the main lifts.

"Fuck!" I slap the steering wheel in frustration as we hit slow moving traffic, but really I was hoping for a little luck on the roads. I reach for my jacket to try and dig my phone out but come up empty. "Fuck!"

"Problem?" James ventures, but his tone is rightly cautious. I am more than a little on edge. It's not his fault, and I take a calming breath before I reply.

"Possibly, but if I don't make this call *definitely*. May I borrow yours?"

"Sure." He hands me his phone and my face must register something strange because he just stares at me.

"I don't know her number. I don't know any of the numbers." I did know her number, but she got a new phone for work and couldn't see the point in having two devices. I never learned the new number.

"Oh." He retracts the phone with an apologetic curl of his lips. "Sorry."

"Shit," I mumble. This is not good. She'll be expecting me at the club any moment. Damn, she is going to be pissed. I shake my head. I can't think of that now—not when I have the chance to catch the utter scum who thinks it's okay to spread filth and hurt and devastate an innocent soul. "Talk to me," I snap, dragging my thoughts and focusing on the right now. "Where am I going?" James is sitting beside me with his small, state of the art laptop and tracker. He has pinpointed the static IP address, and we are currently forty miles away but the traffic has thinned and we are now speeding along toward the end of the motorway.

"Wait, give me your phone again. I do know the number of the club. I can get a message to her, at least." I mutter more to myself as James has already handed his phone back. I punch the numbers and wait for concierge to pick up.

"Stephanie," I interrupt her greeting. "It's Jason Sinclair. I need you to get a message to Sam."

"Of course, Mr. Sinclair. What is the message?" Her tone is polite and professional, and I can picture her pen hovering as I try to figure how best to tell Sam I might not make it tonight after all.

"Can you tell her I'm sorry, but something came up. Tell her, no wait, ask her to go home, and I'll make it up to her. Can you emphasise the sorry part," I add because that lame-ass message is going to land my bollocks in a vice, I just know it.

"Of course, Mr. Sinclair, I'm sure she'll understand. I'll go and find her right away."

"Thank you." I cut the call, feeling slightly better than the complete shit I felt moments ago for standing her up. I gave my word but this couldn't wait. I shake my wayward thoughts and focus on the dark road ahead.

We exit the last junction, but the motorway has already dwindled into a minor road. The junction feeds us onto an even smaller road still, and we speed along in darkness and near silence. The road is deserted, and there are no streetlights or houses to be seen. No light other than the one I cast with my full beams. The flashes of landscape reveal nothing but darkness, barren, bereft of bushes or trees, just emptiness, and I get a twist in my gut that this is a huge waste of time. But I have to try. If there is the slightest possibility that I can end this now, I am taking it.

"Next right is a dead end but leads almost to the coast. That's where the signal is." James points up ahead, and I see the sign for the turn but barely ease off the acceleration to take the tight corner. The tarmac gives way to an unmade road ending abruptly at a gate that looks like it hasn't been opened in decades. We exit the car, but I leave the beams on to give us some light. There is a small shed just the other side of the gate and I turn to James, who is squinting in the direction I am now pointing.

"Is that where it's coming from?"

James purses his lips and shrugs an apology. "The signal's accurate, Jason, to within fifty meters, but since there's fuck-all else around, I think it's that shed, yeah."

"Right, okay. Stay here and have the police on speed dial. If I'm not back in ten minutes, call them. Don't come after me, understand?" I state emphatically, my tone brooking no argument. He gives me a tight nod of acknowledgment and fishes his phone out of his pocket, holding it like a loaded gun carefully in his palm. I turn, and with one hand high on the top bar of the gate, I swing both legs over with ease and determination. The headlights behind me cast an eerie elongated shadow of my frame that stretches right to the shed. The abandoned building isn't a shed but a disused sub power station, obsolete with the new power plant, but probably still wired to the grid. The padlock to the door is missing, but my toe hits the chunk of metal as I push the door slowly open, bending to pick up the lock as I do. The loop metal of the lock has been cut with something heavy duty to slice the thickness so cleanly. I drop the useless lock and peer inside, confident it is empty. The red and green flashing light draw my attention to the corner where a small laptop is perched on an empty crate. I start to lift it up, but my heart stops and then beats so fast I feel like my chest is going to explode. I fall back at the flutter of what feels like a million wings in this tiny space. I nearly fucking shit myself at the ear piercing squeaks. I cover my head with one hand and reach down to grab the laptop before turning and getting the fuck out of there.

Once free from the flying rodents, I shake myself. I fucking hate bats. I continue to shiver and run my hand through my hair several times just to make sure. I jog back, hop over the gate, and go back to the car. The bats are now circling, not as many as I thought now that they are in the open, but enough. They flit across the beams of light like tiny birds, but I know better.

"You okay?" James asks still with his finger hovering over his screen. I nod and hold up the laptop.

"That was in there?" he asks.

"Yep. This and bats, lots of bats." I open the car door and slide inside, letting out a deep steady breath, even as my heart is firing on all cylinders.

"I don't like bats." James slams his car door and peers through the front window at the aerial display of night creatures.

"Me, either, but this I do like. This might help, no?" I drop the laptop onto his lap.

"Yes, it might. I will have a look on Monday." He slips the laptop onto the floor.

"You'll have a look tonight, tomorrow, and every waking hour there is, James," I correct. "This is my girl's safety at stake." His mouth drops for a moment at this information.

"Of course. Sorry, I didn't know this was about Sam." He picks the laptop back up and levels it in his lap.

"Well, you do now, but no one else needs to. The fewer people, the safer she'll be." Inside, the car is lit only from the soft glow on the cockpit display, but James can see the seriousness in my glare when I turn to face him.

"But you'll tell Sam?" he asks, but the question is moot.

"No, she doesn't need to live in fear when I'm taking care of it."

"You think that's wise? She'll be safer if she's prepared," he challenges but keeps his voice level and void of judgement.

"You're right, but after everything she went through last year, she doesn't need to know this shit," I state, and the car falls silent. I draw in a deep breath and let it out, slowly feeling the tension in the car creep into my bloodstream. "I'll make sure she is aware of a temporary security issue." I notice James nod his approval at my obvious compromise. In an attempt to lighten the mood, I offer up my next concern. "If she ever talks to me again, that is." It is only a half joke as I reverse up the single dirt track to the main road.

ELEVEN

Sam

I turn back from the curtained doorway for the umpteenth time. I take a long sip of my iced coffee. I never drink when I'm in charge of the playroom. My attention is diverted to Stephanie, one of the administration staff from the back office, hurriedly fumbling to thread her arms into her coat, her face is wet and she is rushing for the exit. Marco appears at the end of the bar where I am perched, waiting.

"Is everything okay?" He follows my gaze to where Stephanie has now left in the dramatic swish of the heavy velvet curtain.

"I hope so. Her husband just called. Her little boy has been rushed to hospital with a burst appendix." Marco's voice is filled with concern. His empathy for all his staff has quickly secured his place as the best manager this club has had in the five years I have been a member.

"Oh shit!" I get a flash of sickness in my stomach. That feeling of helplessness for a loved one, ill or in danger, has to be the worst. I shake the darkness from my thoughts and add quietly. "He's in the best place, at least."

Marco gives a brief nod but doesn't say anything; there really isn't anything to say, and it's obvious our thoughts are for the best possible outcome for Stephanie's little boy. Marco pours himself a finger of whiskey. He skips my glass but proceeds to top up that of the gentleman seated beside me. A former client, Harry has been keeping me company while I wait…and continue to wait.

Jason is late, and he hasn't called. I absently swirl my glass, the cubes clink and spin in the milky liquid. I'm not really listening to the conversation between Marco and Harry. I chance another furtive glance toward the door but the unchanged sight has my volatile mood dipping into darkly depraved thoughts of punishment for breaking his promise. One moment, I am clutching my chest at the tight pinch of anxiety where I fear the worst, and the next I'm wondering if I missed my true calling as a sadist. A deep voice with an American accent booms close to my ear and makes me jump.

"I thought it was about time I called your companion a cab." He places his arm on the bar, effectively separating me from Harry and completely oblivious to my precious personal space. My posture is perfectly straight, but the unwelcome intrusion makes me want to lean away. I don't, I tip forward, forcing him to take a step back. There, that's a little better.

"Excuse me?" I raise a curious brow and hear Marco cough whisper 'newb'. A not too subtle code for a new club member.

"Don't be shy, sugar. You've been trying to hide all those looks you're been firing my way all damn night. I just thought it was about time I let your guy here know you're gonna be playing with me tonight." He winks at Harry, who bites his lips tight. I can only assume from the crinkle in the corner of his eyes, the bite is to stop him from laughing.

"His name is Harry. Why would you call him Cab?" I respond with my best innocent and deadpan intonation.

"What? No, sugar, I want him to leave so...oh cute." He waggles his finger at me. "You're yanking my chain, aren't ya', darling?" He tilts his head like he is actually thinking about whether he is on the right track with his assessment.

"Little bit." I hold up my thumb and forefinger with an accurate measure of how little I am referring to, but he misses that reference and steamrollers on regardless.

"Can I buy you a drink? He waves the bar man over, but I interrupt before he can place an order.

"Got one. Got company, and I'm waiting on my date. Thanks, but no thanks." I flash a tight smile that is in no way an invitation to stay and chat, let alone play.

"Ah, sugar, do I look like I would give up that easy." He tries to lean in again but stops when he sees my eyes narrow to an inhospitable scowl.

"If you were smart, you would. So I guess that would be a no, you really don't." I carefully place my drink on the bar and wait until his eyes are fixed on me. "Look, how about I make it really easy for you. If you can turn me on, I'm yours." He sucks in a sharp breath, and his eyes widen as I pause for effect. "If not, you tuck that massive ego of yours between your legs and walk away. Deal?"

"You serious?" His voice catches, and he coughs roughly to hide the break.

"Absolutely." I can see Harry over this man's shoulder lightly shaking his head; his own shoulders are jiggling with laughter. I might as well have a little fun since my date is a no show.

"Oh boy," Harry mutters loud enough for me to hear.

"Damn right, oh boy." The man stretches his hand to my breast. Rookie.

"Nah, ah...no touching." I emphatically state my rule, and his hand halts, fingers stretching out in midair like a movie freeze frame. My words cause him to snap it back to his side, burnt but unharmed.

"What? How am I supposed to—"

"Please, don't finish that sentence. For the love of all the women in your future, *please* do not finish that sentence." I close my eyes and shake my head lightly.

"I'm going to need to touch you to tell if you're wet." His irritated tone would suggest I am the idiot in this exchange. I smile sweetly before mimicking retching into my own mouth, hand cupped for effect.

"Urgh, I think a little bit of vomit right there," Harry snickers. "Let's just say for the purpose of this exercise, we'll be looking for other signs?"

"Other signs?" he repeats, utter confusion on his handsome face, and he is handsome. Big, blond, beautiful blue eyes, and built, huge, wide shoulders and muscles pushing at the seams of his pale blue shirt. But it wouldn't matter if he was—well, it doesn't matter who he is, he's not Jason. I let out an exasperated breath.

"Yes, you know if my pupils dilate and my eyes darken. Of course, you'll have to stop looking at my tits for a second to notice that. Or if my breathing gets a little deeper, more rapid, perspiration might gather just here." I tap the indent in my collarbone and notice his throat struggle to swallow. "And if you're really lucky, I might get all perky in the nipple department." I give a sassy little wiggle that has my breasts once more the center of his attention.

"But no touching?" His voice has dropped an octave, and his knuckles whiten with the curl of his fists.

"Nope," I clarify with a curt nod.

He pauses for a moment, his brows furrow with deep concentration. "Fine." He chews his lips, carefully selecting the perfect prose for seduction, no doubt. He takes his time, but you can't rush these things, so I wait. I'm getting good at this waiting thing. He draws in a deep breath, and I sit up nice and straight, fully attentive and eager.

"I'm gonna' stick my dick so far up your ass—"

"Okay, let me stop you there," I quickly interrupt, holding my hand up, flat palm inches from his nose. "Back up, big guy, back up. You're really gonna' start with that? No hi there, my name is Chuck The Wonderfuck? No kiss on the cheek? No—"

"This ain't no date, sugar," he adds gruffly, stopping my 'to-do' before you 'do' list.

"It's *always* a date." I roll my eyes and shake my head at this poor specimen before me.

"But you said no touching, so I'm talking," he grumbles.

"And you're gonna go straight for the dick up my arse—no gentle caress— just two strides into the room and hand straight down my pants."

"It works for me." He shrugs.

"For you, maybe. Okay, look, why don't you start again?" I encourage with a smile because his shoulders are a little slumped, his chest not quite so puffed.

"Right." He draws in a deep breath. "I pinch your nipple—"

"I knee you in the crotch. Seriously?" I can't help myself, but I do manage not to laugh.

"Look, lady, I can do this if you'd just let me touch you," he pleads, his fingers tapping anxiously on his arms, which are still crossed over his chest all tight and defensive.

"That's my point, *darling*." I'm not great with accents, but I nailed that sweet endearment even if it was deeply sarcastic. "You shouldn't *need* to touch me. My man can turn me on with a glance. Hell, Harry here could turn me on with just one word." The man looks over at Harry for the first time since calling him a cab.

"Oh, really?" The man laughs out loud and sharp.

"Harry, if you wouldn't mind, would you give me just one word, please?" I ask as Harry grins and turns to face me. I click my fingers to get Chuck's attention. "And you, watch closely for those telltale signs. Because, even though I will be, you are not going to be sticking your hands down my pants to 'check if I'm wet'." I air quote from Chuck's previous declaration. "Harry?"

"Jason," Harry says quietly, and I let that single word work its magic. Several long seconds pass before I choose to address the man still looking at my tits, which granted now look a whole lot more interested.

"I'm going to share this with you because I'm in a giving mood. Not for you, but for woman kind: Seduce her here." I lightly tap my temple. "Make love to her mind before you even lay a finger on her body, and remember this as if it was carved along the length of your cock, in *really* tiny letters." I hold my thumb and finger barely apart to indicate exactly *how* tiny, before I continue. It's almost sweet how he seems to be waiting with bated breath for my proffered wisdom. "There is nothing sexier than a well-placed kiss on the neck. Start there, Chuck, because then, when she's crying out, 'oh, God', it won't be for Divine intervention to help her out, it will be because you've brought her there. And you're welcome." I wave my hand, dismissing the mildly dumbstruck but perfectly harmless newbie. He turns back after a few steps.

"My name isn't Chuck, it's—" I hold up my hand to stop him right there, and he nods, his eyes barely hold my gaze, and his face is a perfect picture of sheepish. He had his chance to tell me that, and he knows it.

Draining my glass, saving the ice, I place it on the bar and stand, checking my watch. Over an hour late and I swallow back the lump recalling his last playful threat. I hate the speed of my heart thumping in my chest, the tightness, and the hollow pit deep inside growing bigger with each passing minute. I am no longer pissed, now my thoughts are wading through darkness and struggling with the worst.

"Marco, can you call me if you get a message, or if he shows." My voice catches, but I swallow it down before it breaks.

"I'm sure he's just stuck in traffic, Sam. Stay. He will be here. There's no fucking way he wouldn't show," he offers lightly, but his words chill me to the core.

"I know." I don't meet his gaze because I can feel the tingle of tears. I need to find Jason. I bend to pick up my briefcase of tricks, which now feels like a dead weight, and turn to leave, pausing to clarify.

"Call me if you hear anything." I walk away before I crumble; the worry in Marco's eyes is more than I need to break my fragile façade. His curt nod is enough to know he completely understands my meaning.

I take my coat from the cloakroom and dip roughly into the pockets for my phone. My fleeting feeling that I was, perhaps, being overdramatic flatlines. There are no messages, no missed calls…nothing. Jason doesn't do that ever.

The night air is damp and freezing drops of ice fall from the pitch-black sky. I haven't put my coat on, and the sleet is no doubt slicing at my skin, but I can't quite feel it if it does. A cab pulls into the curb before me without my signal.

"Where to, love?" the thick East End London accent calls out. I open the door and sit back before I speak.

"Can you just drive for a bit?" I crumple over, my head in my hands, my insides in agony.

"Hey, if you're gonna hurl, you can get out!" the driver shouts in a panic.

"I'm not sick." I lift my head, and I can feel the first fat tear trickle down my cheek…that I feel. "I'm not sick," I repeat softly as the cab pulls away. *Not sick…I feel like I'm dying.*

My hand trembles, holding my phone, as I cut the answerphone message off for the millionth time on Jason's number. I press speed-dial number three and silently pray Leon isn't asleep.

"I wondered if you'd catch me before I boarded or whether you'd still be tied-up." His tone is playful and teasing.

"Leon, I—" My voice breaks, and his tone is instantly serious.

"Sam, where are you? What's wrong? Are you hurt?" he snaps.

"Jason…" is all I manage to say.

"Did he hurt you?" *No…God yes.* "Sam, talk to me baby?" he pleads.

"I can't get hold of him. Tonight, he didn't show for our *date*. He promised, Leon, and now I can't get hold of him…I'm…I don't know what to do." I'm a wreck, my tears are streaming down my cheeks, and I am only just containing the sobs that are bubbling under a very flimsy surface of restraint.

"Fuck." His tone is grave, and that is just what I didn't need. He is the only other person who knows me and understands how Jason feels about me. This isn't an overreaction. This is the only reaction. "When was the last time you heard from him?" His question makes me pause. It's almost midnight now. It's been hours.

"We spoke at lunch time. He said he'd text me before he left, but I went to the club early to set up and checked my phone at the cloakroom. I didn't think about it until…" I sniff and wipe my nose on the back of my hand. My face feels like it's melting; I'm a mess.

"Where are you, baby?"

"In a cab." I sniff, my voice barely audible above the dirty diesel engine.

"Where, baby?" Leon repeats with a much firmer tone that makes me narrow my eyes at the darkness through the window. The roads are empty, and I don't recognise the vista but the streetlights and shop fronts are bright enough for me to know we are still in the heart of the city. Just not an area I am familiar with.

"I don't know, just driving. Can I come to you? I don't want to go home." My fingertips press and rub the pressure point at my temple on the side not holding the phone. The sensitive spot throbs, and the pulse pounds without respite.

"Sam, I'm on the plane. I only took this call because the flight's delayed, and I hadn't switched my phone off. Shit!" I can hear the frustration in his tone, but I don't want him to feel bad. Especially when there is fuck all he can do about it sitting on a plane.

"It's fine. I'll be—"

"Shit!" he cuts in, but I couldn't finish the sentence. "I agree, don't go home. If he were there, he would've called. I think your best option is to go to his office. You never know? There might be a security lockdown or some such shit," he mutters. "You do that, Sam, and I'll check hosp—" He stops himself a little too late, and I squeeze my eyes tight as if that will make me un-hear what he just said. But I heard it loud and clear. "I'll check around," he continues, rushing his words. "I have to switch this off now, babe. If you don't hear from me, it will only be until we reach altitude, and I can call again, okay. I will call you back." His words offer little comfort because they sound awfully like a promise I heard only earlier today.

"Okay," I reply softly.

"Sam. I'll be on the next flight back. You're not alone, baby." His calm tone is filled with love and affection, but I can't feel a thing.

"Without Jason, I am." My voice is flat, numb, and I embrace that feeling like I embrace myself. My arms cross and hug my body but I feel nothing. Nothing is better than pain. I'll take numb please, because I've had enough pain to last a lifetime.

I can take it, but I know I won't survive.

The night security guard at the Stone building is reluctant to let me in. At his initial refusal, my sadness evaporated into pure fury, and the young man quickly backed down, fearing for more than his life. I take the lift to the basement first and check the garage. Jason's private reserved space is empty, crushing my last hope that he might be here. The ride to the twenty-fifth floor is silent, swift, and as ominous as the dark cloud cloaking my thoughts. Jason's office is at the end of the corridor; his door is ajar, but even from this distance, I can see there is no light inside the room. More darkness and disturbing quiet greet me when I enter, and my feet fail to move another step. My stomach churns, and I suck in a steadying breath that does little to calm my rocketing anxiety and, not for the first time, I wonder why I am even here.

But then I remember: I don't have anywhere else to go.

My call to Bethany goes to voice mail, and I don't have a direct number for Daniel to check if he is working somewhere with Jason. I can't phone Will, he is too far away, and with the time difference he will still understand that it's late here in the UK, and late calls always mean bad news.

I don't know for sure it's bad news.

It's this grain of hope I cling to as I curl up on the sofa in the corner of Jason's office, gripping my phone like it's my *precious*. I don't feel the tears saturate my face; I only know that they are, because the pale blue material of the sofa darkens beneath my cheek. I am numb, empty, and exhausted, but I don't sleep; I wait.

My heart stops at two thirty two. I know this is because my phone has those digits illuminated on the screen in my palm, and that is when Jason steps into his office, not noticing me in the darkness.

I don't move, I don't make a sound, but with my next breath, I leap and run flat out toward him. A missile of pure utter fucking joy and relief hurtles toward a shocked and startled looking Jason. His arms wrap around my body on impact. I hit him hard, and he takes a steadying step back with the momentum. I bury my head in his neck and let the tears flow unchecked, big, huge, ugly sobs. Too much liquid is pouring from my face, but I just don't care, and I grip him so tight I don't think I will ever let him go.

"Hmm, okay not the reaction I was anticipating and not *where* I was expecting to find you, that's for sure." He chuckles...*chuckles*. I died tonight, and he chuckles. Pushing from his arms, I jump down, draw my hand back, and slap him hard across his beautiful face. He reaches to stop the second strike, his hand gripped tight around my wrist. "Now, that *is* the reaction I was expecting, but you only get one, beautiful." His tone is stern with a gravelly edge.

"I thought you were dead." I struggle to pull my hand away, because I don't feel nearly done with my pent-up rage. We tussle, and he grabs my other fist with which I had managed to land a hefty punch on his rock hard pec. I am struggling hard to break free. My veins surge with adrenaline, frustration, relief, love, but also a shit-tonne of suppressed anger.

"What are you talking about?" he scoffs with a laugh, his face a picture of confusion, but his eyes are wide like I just said the craziest thing.

"You didn't call...nothing...no message." He deftly bends to the side as I snap my knee up to his crotch. He twists and spins us, slamming me hard against the wall and pressing his full body weight into mine. I can feel him hard against my thigh, and he rolls his hips and speaks with a low serious voice.

"Listen very carefully, and stop trying to kick me in the bollocks." He kicks my legs wide so my knees are no longer a concern. "I had an emergency. I had no choice but to deal with it. No choice, understand?" His voice softens, and his brows knit with concern, and I can see his eyes are pained at this clusterfuck. He shakes his head at the mess and continues to try and ease me down. "I left my phone on my desk, baby, look." He nods his head to the empty desk, but I take a second to glance and he's right. Some papers are piled in the corner and, just under one edge, the folded leather case of his phone. I didn't see that before. Stupid Sam, but it wouldn't make a difference, the net result is the same. His lips brush my forehead, and my eyes snap back to his. He draws in a deep, slow breath and exhales softly. The sickly sweet aroma of Red Bull is faint, but has obviously been effective at keeping him awake, when I needed no such artificial stimulant. "But I called the club and told Stephanie to tell you to go home...to tell you that I was sorry...that *I am* sorry, *Sam* ...because although it wasn't death that kept me from keeping my promise...it was important." He pauses, but my scowl is unchanged. "I left a fucking message, Sam." His tone is frustrated, but his words are pleading. He holds my gaze, searching my too-tired eyes for forgiveness. He can see firsthand what I have been through in these short but endless hours. "You didn't get the message." He sighs. It's not a question, but I shake my head all the same.

"Stephanie had her own emergency." I try to pull my arms free, but he keeps them high above my head. "I thought you were dead," I repeat, my throat raw from sobbing.

"A little dramatic, don't you think, beautiful?" His lips quirk, teasing me or waving the red flag. Yeah, the idiot waves a big fucking red flag. His grip loosens when I relax and exhale softly with a sweet smile. Instantly, I drop to my haunches and through his grip, I jab my sharp elbow in the back of his knees as I duck through the gap in between his legs and send him crumpling to the floor.

"Fuck!" he curses, hitting the ground hard with no time to brace. I scramble away, but he is on me, snatching my ankle before I can make a clean escape. He pins my foot to the floor and quickly immobilises the free, and more dangerous limb, flailing wildly, hoping to avoid capture…*inevitable capture*. With the stealth and speed of a seasoned predator, he crawls up my body, legs on either side of my torso, pinning my arms above my head but flush against the floor. He slides back down my frame, his full body weight crushing the air from my chest, his legs now wrapped like a vine around my own, constricting and effectively restricting any further movement and my ability to breathe.

"Calm the fuck down!" he growls, but I've lost it. His words have the exact opposite effect, and I buck and struggle with more strength than I thought I had left. He fights to keep control, and when I have no physical strength left, I scream with my last breath. An ear-piercing howl that fills the room and shocks him enough to let me go—completely. I scramble back and jump to my feet. My face is wet from a fresh slew of tears I didn't really feel.

"You don't get it!" I cry out, my arms hugging my waist as I watch him slowly unfold from the floor to his full height. His expression is wary, his eyes cautious and concerned.

"Don't get what, beautiful?" His softly spoken words try to soothe, but I can't feel their effect. All I feel is panic and sadness in huge waves, drowning me. I can't breathe; my chest is crushing my lungs. I fold over and crumple in on myself, sobbing. "Jesus, Sam." His voice catches, and I hear him step closer. I try to step back, but his hands pull me upright by my shoulders. "Talk to me, Sam…please, baby…talk to me." I curl my hand into a half-hearted fist and level a punch on his firm chest.

"You promised, Jason. I thought…you…you don't get to leave me," I sob, but my words are muffled into his hold, big strong arms capture me and lift me high. I slap his chest once more, but I've lost my fight. I cry out when he slams me against the wall.

"Never. I'm so fucking sorry, Sam." His mouth covers mine, swallowing the gasp he forced out with the impact. Hot urgent kisses then scorch my tears dry. "Sorry, baby," he murmurs against my neck, continuing to kiss and bite and mark my skin. I tilt away to give him more of me to claim. My fingers claw with wild abandon. His body covers me, consumes me, and I need him for my next breath and for my heart to take it's first proper beat. "I'll never leave—" he begins to say, but pulls back, his eyes wide with sudden and very real understanding, piercing mine, which glaze instantly. I am just too raw to brush this away even as I have him in my arms. "That's why you thought…"

"Jason, I'm not this crazy and unstable, but you promised tonight was supposed to be special. You said only death—" I suck back a sob, gritting my jaw tight to keep it in.

"Fuck. I know. I know! Shit, Sam, I'm—" I shake my head to interrupt his apology.

"You were gone, and I couldn't find you. You can always find me, but I couldn't find you! I feel the same way about you, Jason, dammit, and I couldn't —" His eyes meet mine, and I know he understands, he gets it—he gets me. I drop my head into his neck, pressing my lips to the soft skin that smells like a sweet sweaty mix of musk and my man. I draw the comfort I need from that scent before I have the strength to meet his stare. Stray tears still fall, but not so many now that I have him in my arms.

"Please, baby, no more tears. You're right, and I'll fix this. I'm so sorry you were worried." His tender lips press against mine…once…twice. "I'm sorry I ruined our evening." He sucks in my bottom lip and drags it between his teeth. A million tingles dance across my skin, and the deeply erotic swirling sensation in my tummy is doing an admirable job at erasing my sadness. "I'll do anything to make it up to you." His sensual tone and tempting words make my body shiver from tip to toe at that very thought.

"Anything?" I drop my head back with a light thud against the wall. My legs constrict around his trim waist, and he must be able to feel my heat, if not my melting core at the possibilities. "What if my *anything* involved your brother?" I bite my lip to hold back a whimper that is bubbling at the recall that is always just under the surface of my ultimate *anything.*

"Well, after what you've been through, I think I would owe you that anything." His thick brows furrow at my request, but his almost black eyes darken further with equal desire.

"Maybe not, if it's going to cause that brow of yours to look like that." I purse my lips and check his expression for any hint of reticence. This may still be my fantasy come true, but not at any expense…not at his expense. I'll happily relegate it to a one-time thing, if that is the case, but looking into his eyes now, I know that's not the case. It's just an exception, but not a rule, because he makes the rules.

"I said anything, beautiful, and I meant it. I live to fulfill your dreams. The jealously is inevitable, but I'll deal. Trust me, it's not a hardship to watch you. I enjoy you, enjoying yourself." His grin spreads wide and wicked. "Fuck, how did I get so lucky?" He grinds his hips hard and holds me firm against his erection.

"I'm the lucky one. But since Will isn't here to make good on that *anything*, how about you drop and give me twenty?" I raise a brow, maintain his gaze, and hold my breath to see how he responds to a direct challenge, Mistress to Dom.

"Is this a little of what I missed tonight?" His eyes narrow; his voice is low and gravelly.

"A soupçon…a little taste." My tongue darts to wet the dryness and his eyes follow the movement before flashing me his most brilliant smile and dropping to his knees.

"Don't mind if I do."

TWELVE

Jason

My heart pounds painfully in my chest from the broken expression on her face — heartbreakingly clear through her tear-soaked face. I had no fucking idea what was going on when she flew across the room and slammed into me...not a clue. But the instant that changed, I understood, and that fucking tore me up from the inside out. *I did that.* This may have been a simple case of miscommunication, but after what she's been through, I am not in the least surprised she had the mother of all meltdowns.

I never doubted how she felt about me, and I see it now, crystal fucking clear. If I have to put a fucking implant under my skin to ease her mind, I will, because I won't ever put her through that again. Ever. She needs to understand, I am never leaving, not while I still have a breath to give, because I will give it to her. But I guess that was the problem tonight. She knew that's how I felt, and she came to the only conclusion left.

I shudder internally as I drag my nails up her incredibly long legs, scouring her delicate skin until I get to the edge of her panties, under her sexy, skin-tight skirt. She trembles at my touch, and her breath catches when I yank the flimsy material to her feet. I tap her ankle, and she lifts for me to remove them completely.

I raise her leg and press it against the wall, my mouth waters at the sight and smell of her arousal—so fucking sweet. She's intoxicating. One of my hands supports her knee, while my other spreads her folds, wet and glossy on my fingertips. Her hands thread into my hair, and she grips for support; her whimper turns into a strangled scream when my tongue delves into her liquid heat. Her thigh muscles tremor as I take my sweet time devouring, sucking, and diving into her molten, soft center. Her little pants, and the tension in her grip, increases with every swirl of my tongue as I drive her incessantly toward her peak. The pad of my thumb rests on her clit, and I take the moment I hear her suck in a sharp breath to peek up through my lashes and watch her eyes squeeze shut and her tummy clench. She pushes out a steadying breath, and her head drops back against the wall. Her eyes fix on mine with such passion and fire, I know she's balancing on the edge. I drag my tongue flat and firm from her entrance to her clit where I rub in a steady rhythm…round and round…higher and higher. She cries out and comes so hard on my tongue, her essence pours over my lips; the muscles in her thighs contract and fight to snap around my head. I loosen my grip, and her legs do exactly that. They clamp tight around my neck. Scorching-hot, firm muscles in super soft silky skin engulf my head.

I stand and grab her arse cheeks, lifting her high, my mouth still glued to her core. I press her against the wall. Her legs constrict a little more, muffling any sound she might be emitting as I continue to devour. She tastes too good to stop.

The wall helps to support her, but she is gripping so tight I don't think she's in any danger of falling. *I'll never let her fall.* Her hips grind against my mouth, and her hands are trying to pull me this way and that. I growl low and scrape my teeth against her inner thigh. She tenses and gives this little squeal that I do hear, but her hands relax enough to let me do my job. She needs this, I know, but I do too, so fucking much. I need to take her there, my way. I will never get enough of her, and I will take whatever she is willing to give, because I know how damn lucky I am to have this precious gift in my hands.

"Oh, God, Jason, I can't…please, I need you…I really need you to…" She pants out a breathless urgent plea that nearly ends me. "Mark me, Jason. Make me yours. Make it hurt." I groan into her folds, sucking in the delicate flesh, as my cock feels fit to burst. *Holy fucking shit.* I want one more climax from her, then I'll gladly give her what she asks for, but she needs an overload of pleasure before pain. I understand her desire is an attempt to mask the hurt she felt tonight. I get that, and I am more than eager to mark what's mine, but first things first.

I swirl my tongue and suck my lips over her swollen, pulsing nub of nerves, and she screams. Not quite the howl that had me leaping from her a short while back, but a deep, sigh-filled, sensual cry that pierces the silence of the night and drowns the mere mortal sex noises that were prevalent just a few seconds ago. Her back arches, and her body jolts enough for me to lose my footing. I am seriously top heavy when I step back, so I swiftly let her drop from my shoulders into my waiting arms. The shock of the move obliterates any hope of coming down smoothly from that high, but it couldn't be helped. If I hadn't taken the evasive maneuver, we would both be sprawled on the floor and not necessarily in one piece.

I carry her over to the sofa and carefully place her on her feet. Her eyes are fixed on me, still a little dazed, but not for long. I sit on the arm of the seat, take her hand, and roughly pull her across my lap. Her feet skid on the carpet, and as they don't quite reach the floor, she is stretching both her hands and her toes to try and balance. Perfect.

"Hold still, beautiful, or this is going to be a very long night. You wanted me to mark you and since I only have my hand, and you have an exceptionally high tolerance for pain, I want to make sure you are absolutely satisfied with the result."

"I always am, Sir." She exhales, and her whole body relaxes under my caress. If I could bottle this feeling surging through me right now and sell it, I would give Daniel Stone and Bill Gates combined wealth a run for their money. Pure unadulterated power courses through me. She does this to me. Her unwavering trust and total submission give me that and so much more. I draw in a deep breath and stroke the curve of her backside once more before I peel the thin material up and fold it at her waist. Her skin glows in the fading moonlight, giving it a much paler pallor, ethereal and exquisite. My hand sweeps the skin, goose bumps dance under my touch, but I know she's not in the least bit cold. I lift my hand and hold it high, hovering. I love this bit the most—the anticipation —where her breath catches and her muscles tense and twitch expectantly. She forces herself to relax because she knows the pain isn't as bad when she does, but that first involuntary response gets me so hard I have to fight the urge to just spread her wide and sink balls deep for my own pleasure.

But this is all about her tonight; it's the very least I can do.

My first strike stings my palm but makes her sigh and sink a little heavier on my lap. The next makes her hips tilt, tipping her bottom higher, tantalising, teasing me for more. I'll oblige; I'm in a giving mood. Again and again, I bring my heavy palm down on her soft flesh. The bounce and ripple of her arse with each strike makes my cock pulse, and the deepening rosy hue to her skin is making my balls scream in agony. Her skin glistens with perspiration, and her panting breaths have ratcheted up to a level that matches my own erratic heartbeat. She pinches her legs together, and it takes all my effort to not drag my hands between them when I just know how wet she will be. But if I do, I know this ends right now; I won't be able to hold off burying myself inside of her. If this was a normal session with a normal sub, I would happily leave my sub wanting. After all, this is not just a marking session; she hit me, bit me, and very nearly kicked me in the balls. This should be punishment, too.

I know marking her as mine is one thing, giving her the pain she needs is another, but any punishment that would involve me denying myself, well, that is just not going to fucking happen. She's my submissive, yes, but our situation is unique, and this punishment lesson is in theory only, because this is Sam, and I can't deny her a single damn thing. The red patch on her bottom has spread across both cheeks, down her upper thighs, and at the edges are the telltale prints of individual fingers. A perfect representation of my erotic appreciation; my applause is literally all over her backside. The final strike ends with a tender stroke all over her inflamed skin. She barely makes a sound, but she exhales softly now that my hand is resting on the small of her back: The signal that I have finished.

I help her up, and we switch places so she is now lying over the edge of the sofa, her gloriously red arse a far too tempting sight.

I nudge her legs a little wider and position myself between them. My hand makes light work of the material barriers before it is holding my raging erection at her sodden entrance. She twists to look at me, and her brows crinkle with confusion.

"You're going to fuck me?" Her frown deepens.

"You thought I wouldn't?" I raise my own brow, my expression otherwise deadly serious.

"I thought—" She swallows thickly and bites her bottom lip in an adorable display of trying to suppress her evidence of pleasure. "I'm glad." She gives a sassy little wiggle, but yelps when I swipe my palm heavy across both cheeks. I might choose to be soft with her, but I'm still fucking hard, and, boy, she makes my palm twitch. I push forward and sink my full length in one forceful thrust that causes her mouth to drop open in a silent gasp. Her eyes are wide enough to register both her surprise and the painful depth. Her fingers grip the leather edge of the armrest with white-knuckle pressure.

"Good idea, beautiful, I'd hang on tight." My voice is hoarse and deep, my throat dry from tempered desire. My tone is heavy with a mix of sensual promise and erotic threat. Her hands fist a little tighter, and she tilts her hips to take me deeper. *God, I love this woman.* It's enough, I lose it…whatever it was…it's gone…sense…restraint…my fucking mind. I slam into her—relentlessly—hard and fast like a fucking jackhammer. I can't stop. One hand grips her arse, my nails biting into the raised pink flesh and my other fisting a large clump of her sweat-soaked mane, lifting her head back and pulling her up to meet my punishing drives. Perhaps this is a punishment, after all? No, that's not it. This isn't about punishment. This is just wild abandon, souls imprinting, and raw, feral fucking.

"Come," I growl in her ear. I don't recognise my voice; it comes from such a dark, desperate place, but she does. She takes that spark of recognition, and it ignites her body like a touch paper. Her muscles tighten inside and out, taut and tense. Ripple after ripple, her body succumbs to the explosion of a lifetime. I can only make that assumption, because that is exactly what it feels like for me. Shots of pure agony and ecstasy in equal measure fire from the base of my spine, electrifying every nerve ending until with one almighty explosion, I release, riding with her climax as we come together as one. Fucking perfect. I collapse onto her, even my bones ache, and I feel so spent, so drained, and yet overflowing at the same time.

I roll onto the sofa and pull her into my arms, wrapping my body around her limp form. She offers absolutely no resistance. Sticky and slick, we slide and mould together and fall into a deep and peaceful coma.

Her shiver wakes me, but the light in the office might've had something to do with that, too. I kiss her hair, and she tilts her head to meet my stare. Her eyes hold a little of the puffy redness from last night, and I get a twisting pain in my chest at that sight. Her warm, tender smile goes some way to ease that feeling but only some way.

"Hey." She leans up to cover my lips with her sweetness.

"Hey, you." I give her an extra kiss on her forehead when she pulls away. "How are you feeling?"

"Good." She nods, and I search for any hidden hurt in her eyes, but there is none. There is something though, some trace of sadness I don't want to see.

"How about we cancel my parents this weekend and just spend the weekend in bed, marking each other like crazy people?" My tone is light and playful.

"I'd love that." She giggles, and her face lights up like a kid on Christmas morning. Jackpot. "But won't your parents be cross? Will your Mum have gone to lots of trouble?" She worries her bottom lip. I pull it free with my thumb and forefinger.

"Probably, she would've made up the spare rooms already, but it won't be a problem. It's not a cancel, we're just postponing. I think we need this after—" She nods so I don't bother to go over exactly what that *after* is.

"If you're sure?" Her bright grin is wide and relaxed. "Wait, you said rooms, who else is staying?"

"Just us. My Mum is a little old-fashioned." I raise a brow and wait for that to dawn.

"Really?" She snickers. "Separate rooms? You have to be kidding. You're nearly thirty!"

"I'm still twenty-nine!" I grumble indignantly. "Honestly, it's never been an issue before, because I've never taken anyone home, but I am definitely not kidding."

"In that case, then, maybe it is a good idea to postpone. I don't want to sleep without you." Her voice softens, and her eyes fill with liquid. I pull her to my chest, my arms so tight I hope she can feel what she does to me. How much she means and how fucking sorry I am.

"Me, too, beautiful, and I'm so—"

"Don't, Jason. No more sorrys, okay? You're forgiven, and I don't want to think about it again." She lifts herself from my embrace and strides naked toward my office bathroom. "You made it up to me last night. Today, you have nothing to be sorry for."

"I think I do." I purse my lips and wiggle my brow; she frowns but follows my gaze to her backside. It is still tinged with red and mottled with tiny purple spots. My cock swells at the sight and gets so much bigger when she draws her hand back and loudly slaps one cheek.

"Not bad." Her tone is lightly mocking and deviously teasing. I stand and stalk toward her. Her gaze drops to my heavy, bobbing cock but snaps back to my eyes, which are on fire and ready to burn. She backs away, hands held up in a futile defensive gesture.

"Not bad?" I question, my sensual tone tinged with sexual menace. "Oh, beautiful, you haven't seen bad."

"I was so hoping you were going to say that." She spins on her toe and hightails it to the bathroom. Two strides and I am on her, and I have her in my arms. She didn't stand a chance, but looking into her eyes now, I know she didn't want one.

I wake to an empty bed and sunlight piercing the gaps in the heavy curtains. I rub the tiredness from my face and squint at my watch to try and gauge the time. We didn't get back home until the early hours. We narrowly avoided discovery by the night cleaners finishing their final polish of the reception area. We both looked fucked and dishevelled as we bundled into my car, but we escaped undetected. It's almost midday, and I can now smell something cooking. The sweet aroma wafting up through the house smells a lot like pancakes. My stomach grumbles with anticipation of the feast, but this isn't good. Despite some basic culinary tuition, Sam is a dreadful cook and never willingly cooks unless she's stressed—really stressed. Then out comes the ready-mix pancakes, comfort food enough to feed an army when she barely takes a bite herself.

I throw the bedcovers back and slip on my old, torn jeans, hopping from one foot to the other and running from the room as I do. I bound down the three flights of stairs and take a deep breath before striding into my very own International House of Pancakes.

I walk over as she pours more mixture into the ready pan, her concentration such that she hasn't heard me approach.

"Jesus Christ!" She jumps and jerks her arm, spilling a large dollop of mixture into the pan, drowning the smaller circles into one super-sized mutant pancake. She places the bowl of mixture down and tries to hurriedly fix the mess in the pan, but its too late. Her shoulders drop. "Oh, it's ruined." I step around and switch the heat off, taking the spatula from her hand and pulling her into my arms.

"That one maybe, but the other two hundred look perfect." I lift her chin so her eyes meet mine. Her nose and cheekbones have flour dusted in streaks, and she would look cute and adorable if her eyes weren't so damn worried. "Talk to me, beautiful." Her lips thin as she bites them together, holding back, but my mouth covers and coaxes with tender kisses. She's unyielding to begin with, but softens as the tension leaves her body, and she responds with more fervour than I had anticipated. I'm not complaining, but I also know her other method of coping is using this sexy little body as a distraction. I suck her bottom lip into my mouth and hold the soft flesh firmly hostage between my teeth. She whimpers and wriggles in my arms trying to climb up my body and take control. I bite down, and she freezes, her eyes widening, taking in my warning glare.

We need to talk, and the only time I'll accept her bottom to my top is when she's impaled on my cock. I narrow my eyes and emit a low grumbling noise from my chest. She pulls away, and I release her lip, tasting the trace of metal on my lip. She swipes her tongue and hums her approval, her eyes so fucking alive I have to check myself. Fucking temptress. "We need to talk." I state emphatically, more to myself and my raging hard-on than to Sam, who nods and now has the decency to look sheepish. Which is better than worried in my book, so I'll take it.

I lift her on to the counter and wedge myself between her thighs. We are almost nose to nose, but she has to tip her head slightly to maintain the all-important eye contact, and I wait. She holds my gaze, searching me as much as I am searching her. God, I love this woman, so much passion and fire dances in those deep brown eyes, so much hurt and hope and *love*. Yeah, there is a shit-tonne of love right there. My heart swells; I can feel it in my chest, beating just a little harder, a little faster, just for her.

"It was about me?" Her softly spoken words hit me like a sucker punch, because she's so fucking right. Everything is about her, but that's not what she means…not right now, at least.

"What was about you, beautiful?" I keep my intonation impassive, but she just slowly raises her perfect brow in query at my evasion. I concede a small nod of acknowledgement. "Yes."

She lets out her held breath, and her cheek dimples with a half smile. "Poisoned chalice that one—" She pauses, but she hasn't finished. "I'm glad it was about me that kept you from me, not something or someone else, I mean. But—" She hesitates for another long moment. "It's about me—" She leaves her statement hanging, and it's her turn to wait for me to fill in the blanks. But how much do I fill? She's smart, strong, and brave but she really shouldn't have to be all of those things. Not anymore, not with me in her life. *That is my job.*

"Did Richard have any siblings?" Her face pales, and her whole body becomes rigid under my fingertips.

"Shit!" She drops her head, but it snaps back with that familiar and welcome fire burning in her eyes. "What happened, Jason?"

I don't hesitate to answer. I don't want her to think I'm taking my time because I am censoring what she needs to know. I am, but she doesn't need to know that. Whether she would like that I am doing that is questionable, but protecting her is my job, and I take it very seriously. "I got an email, a threat of sorts, and it could only have come from someone close to Richard— a brother or —" She shakes her head, interrupting my suggestions.

"He didn't have any siblings. He had a younger cousin, but I never met him. He lived in the States. Richard's family went to live near them when they emigrated. What was in the email exactly?" I don't clench my jaw even though I feel the tension in every cell. She is watching me like a hawk, and I have no intention of sharing this little nasty nugget of information.

"It was vague. It regarded you and Richard, but there was an undertone I didn't like. Did you see anyone you recognised while on the boat?"

"You know I didn't, Jason. What did the email say?" She repeats it, but doesn't give me time to answer. "Did it say something about Richard and me as a couple or was it about what happened on the boat?" Her back straightens, and her eyes are suddenly wild with panic. "They watched…did they make a recording?" Her voice is pitched with terror. I shake my head.

"No, not that. I promise it wasn't that." She visibly relaxes at my words, and I curse that I am feeding her half-truths. But her reaction alone is justification that I am doing the right thing, being selective with the information. I will protect her from this at any cost, and I will find the fucker responsible. I will happily cleave his chest open, cut his dick off, and place it where his heart should be.

"I'll forward you a copy." *Well, I will send something that resembles a copy of the email I received.* "I'm sure you'll read it and probably think I'm overreacting." I shrug off my comment, trying to make light of the situation for her benefit. Her eyes are searching every tick and twitch on my impassive face. Once satisfied, she exhales a long slow breath. I cup her jaw with one hand, and she leans into it. "This is you, Sam, and you are mine. You are my *only* concern." Her smile is fragile, and she loops her arms over my shoulder and pulls me into her embrace.

"Thank you." Her lips purse for me to take, and I do. My hand slides into her messy bun, and I grip her hard against my mouth, forcefully, urgently, and utterly proprietary. When I release her, she is grinning widely and a little breathless.

"You are most welcome." I lean into her tummy and hitch her over my shoulder, slapping her cotton-covered arse soundly, the noise echoing in the hallway as I stride through the house. She grips my loose jeans to steady herself, giggling and gasping for air.

"What are you doing?"

"You really want me to answer that?" My tone is derisive. I take the stairs two at a time.

"Aren't you hungry?" She grunts as each step exerts more pressure on her tummy.

"Always," I growl, and I hear her swallow down a whimper.

THIRTEEN

Sam

I bounce back pretty quickly after my monumental meltdown and marathon baking session. I call Leon to fill him in, and Jason calls his parents to postpone our visit. In all honesty, I want to get that first visit out of the way, but I am not going to deny an entire weekend spent indulging in all things Jason. I happen to think a day trip is preferable to an overnighter in light of the separate bedroom disclosure. I still can't get my head around that, if Jason says his parents know about him, and I mean really know about him and it's not a religious requirement, I struggle to see what the problem would be. It's not like I'd leave the handcuffs still attached to the headboard or butt plugs in the sink...*hmm, well, I might.*

I lean back in Jason's mammoth bathtub; bubbles up to my ears and magical aroma oils infused in the water soothe my aching bones. My body is suffering on all levels of physical endurance, not just from trying to keep up with an iron/marathon man hybrid, but we played newbie tourists all day. I loved every minute, from riding the top of the sightseeing tour bus, to the London Eye and lunch at the top of the Shard. We have walked from our home on the Southbank over the bridge toward Covent Garden, Leicester Square, Bond Street, along Piccadilly to Westminster, and back along the embankment. Fucking miles and I didn't notice the pain in my feet until I stopped. My poor toes are throbbing but are currently in tootsie heaven, submerged in the searing hot, scented water, and I wriggle them to try and get the feeling back without the agony.

Jason returns with an ice bucket and two glasses, but that's not what makes my mouth water. It's his toned, muscled chest, cut abs narrowing down to that divine muscle that is like a homing beacon to my libido. His snug boxer shorts just exaggerate all the goodness that muscle is pointing to. My mouth is suddenly dry, and I hold out my hand for the glass. His wicked grin widens, catching me red-handed staring at his cookie jar.

"See something you like, beautiful?" His lips twist into a smug smile as he nonchalantly pours the Champagne.

I blurt out a short laugh and shake my head. "Oh, the last thing you need is a stroke to that massive ego of yours."

"You're right, that's not what I want stroked." His voice drops a level, to a delicious and deeply salacious tone. "I have something else that is massive, that definitely needs that attention—if you're offering?"

I groan at the truly tempting thought, but my whole body revolts, and I sink under the water for refuge from his relentless sexual demands. *His blood must run thick with an equal mix of Red Bull and Viagra.* When I surface, I am faced with an ice-cold glass of liquid heaven, golden bubbles race for the surface as condensation trickles down the outside of the slim flute. My taste buds tingle. I sweep the wet hair back off my face and take the glass, raising it to clink with the one Jason is holding.

"What are we toasting? This is a school night, you know? We both have work tomorrow." I shake my head with mock disapproval.

"That is never going to be a reason to not celebrate what we have." He clinks my glass and, with his free hand, drags his boxers down his thick thighs, kicking them to the corner for the laundry fairies. *I mean that.* I have yet to see a dirty pile of clothes or heap of damp towels like Leon used to leave wherever he dropped them. "As for a toast, how about to health and happiness?" He holds a wry, sardonic smile.

"Ah, you're so sweet, I think I had a little bit of vomit in my mouth," I tease. He carefully steps in the tub, lowering himself and sending a wave of surplus water over the edge.

"Cute. How about to too much sex and even more orgasms?" he retorts and hums a sexy laugh.

"Oh, I like that." I pull my legs up to give him room, but the water is so high only my kneecaps are exposed. "I would've said there could never be too much sex where you and I are concerned, but seriously, I can barely walk. I'm going to look like I've been fucked by—" He holds up a warning finger to interrupt and his face darkens.

"Please, don't finish that sentence, even as a joke. I do not like to picture you being fucked by anyone but me."

"You, then. I'm good with that." I smile sweetly and watch his features soften.

"Me and Will, you mean?" His brow raises, but his tone is playful. His eyes give nothing away, and that worries me.

"Only if you're happy with that, Jason. The fantasy doesn't go away. That's why I said what I said last night, but I'm cool if you don't want to. I get it, really

I do. This is not a deal breaker situation." My sheepish grin widens with his breathtaking smile. I add with a dismissive shrug. "Because I know for a fact I wouldn't be happy seeing you fuck another woman…a man on the other hand… Ow!" His fingers that had been trailing delicate patterns up my inner thigh reach forward and flick my nipple.

"Never going to happen, beautiful. So you can kill that thought right now." He holds my gaze and waits for me to acknowledge what he said. Even if I was joking, it is very clear he isn't. I nod and he gives me a wink, switching from stern to sexy so fast I get a little whiplash. "But I meant what I said, Sam. Christmas *was* a one-time thing, but the bottom line is, I make the rules, and my number one rule is to make you happy. I will do *anything* to make you happy. I'm happy when you're happy. It is that simple."

"You make me happy—very happy." I bite back the widest smile I feel begin to split my face, but it's pointless. Happiness is bursting from me because of him, and he deserves to see it. He really does.

"Good." He downs the rest of his drink and takes my foot in his hands, magically massaging the tiny tender muscles. "But not Leon," he states after a moment. I had let my head drop with the blissful feeling radiating from his touch and seeping through every cell in my body.

"Hmm?" I lift my head, but that champagne is working in tandem with his ministrations to send me to sleep.

"With Will, I know it's just sex. I mean he likes you, but it won't ever be more than sex. He's my brother, and I trust him, end of. With Leon, I'm not so sure. I won't pretend I don't hate that he has a connection with you, and I know there's nothing there on your end. But he loves you, and that line can get very blurred when sex is involved. Especially, phenomenal mind-blowing, out of this fucking world sex. So, I'm going to be selfish. Just thought I should make that clear." My heart beats a little harder at his words. I understand, completely, and the fact that he will share at all is massive for him. As much as I trust Leon, Jason isn't wrong. I know Leon loves me, and love complicates things even in the best of friendships.

"God, I love you." I pull my foot from his hand and slip my way up his body until I am wrapped and wedged around him, nose to nose, chest to chest, and heat to scorching heat.

"Good. Now, prove it." His cocky grin and hand on my shoulder makes me melt.

"Because nothing says 'I love you' like deep throating with champagne in the bath." I swipe my tongue enticingly along my bottom lip, fixing my gaze to his carnal glare.

"You got that right, beautiful." I sink down and wait for the sexiest sound known to woman—her man coming undone. I look up through my lashes as he drops his head back and lets out that gorgeous guttural sound as I take his length in my hand and squeeze. I swipe my tongue over the tip and feel him shudder. My lips hover just a breath away, and I relish his sharp intake of breath as I take him deep to the back of my throat, my fist making up the difference because he is just too damn big. *As if that's a thing.* I pump up and down, setting my own pace even as his hand threads under my hair and holds my neck with gentle pressure. I can feel every pulse of blood pushing through his thick veins with my tongue, and his salty taste is just as much an indication that he is close as is the constant twitch and tick of his taut thigh muscles. His fingers grip my neck, and I pull back and let him slide from my mouth.

I draw in a breath and look up to see two darkly dangerous eyes glaring back at me.

"You better have a good reason for stopping, beautiful."

"I do. I was thirsty." Before he can say, "State the obvious", I reach for the champagne glass and take a large sip. I hold it in my mouth, only to place my lips back at the tip of his steely solid erection. I can't speak, but really I don't need to. His eyes widen as I slowly push him into my mouth. Trying my best to draw his cock inside without losing too much of the bubbly liquid.

"Oh, shit, that's…that's…Mmm." His hips surge forward, and I have to quickly swallow. Some Champagne sprays from my lips, but the lustful look in his eyes has me reaching once more for my drink and repeating the process. I can't think of a better way to get drunk. The third time I do this, both his hands wrap around my neck, supporting but not pushing, and I relax and let him fuck my face. His gentle hip action and the swell of his cock fills my mouth and throat, and I swallow like crazy when he jerks and empties down the back of my throat with a final thrust and roar. My lips are still wrapped around him when he pulls me up his body and kisses me hard.

"You're amazing, you know that?" I don't get to answer; his lips are on me again, his tongue diving in and stealing the very words from my lips. His arms wrap tight, and he twists our bodies so I am on my back, and he is looming large and lethal. The warm silky water swirls around me as I scooch back and give him all the room he is going to need. My mouth dries, and I lick my lips to moisten them; I am suddenly parched.

He reaches over to grab his glass and the bottle from the ice bucket. He tips the glass to my lips and, none to carefully, he pours the remaining champagne into my mouth, most of it spilling down my chin and onto my chest.

"Oops." He grins a wicked wide and not remotely remorseful smile. He replaces the glass but holds the bottle poised over my breasts. "You spilt some."

"I did." My voice is hoarse and hushed. His eyes bore into me, so damn hot my skin sizzles until I jolt with the shock of ice cold champagne pouring onto my breasts.

"So did I." His mouth is on my skin, burning with wanton heat, searing where he touches from the sharp contrast of temperatures. I don't feel the bubbles, but my skin tingles as he drags his tongue and sucks on my body, licking it clean of the mess he made. His lips close around my aching nipple, and he sucks hard enough to make me cry out and arch into the draw of pressure.

"Oh, God," I pant out with fevered gasps of air. I hear the bottle thump to the floor and then his other hand is holding my other breast and pinching the nipple ready for his mouth. I am so damn needy, I fight to open my legs, but he has me pinned with his bent legs on either side of mine. I have absolutely no chance of getting off until *he* decides. I writhe beneath him. My hands pull his hair, and I moan for some sweet relief. "Please, Jason, please." He doesn't look up as I implore him, my eyes begging but to no avail. His focus is entirely on my breasts, and it feels so damn good, but fuck, I need to come. "Please, make me come. I need to come." I think I scream the last part, but the noise of swishing water and bodies sliding drowns me out.

He lifts me high into his arms and stands. I wrap my legs tight around his waist and cling for dear life as he steps from the bath and slams me up against the wall. His mouth is at my neck, his teeth scraping the soft skin and making me shiver. His breath cools the wet skin even though it feels scorching hot.

"You want to come, beautiful?" His deep tone is as rough as gravel, raw and sexy.

"Oh, God, yes, yes, please." I hold my breath, and the tension in my body is like a high wire when I feel his fingers between my legs, moving into position. I tremble and gasp when he thrusts his full and considerable length into me. So fucking hard and so very, very deep, my head drops to his shoulder, and I scream when he bites down on my exposed neck. I scream, and I explode. A million tiny sparks fire. Each and every nerve, and the individual hairs on my skin, peak with shots of electricity dancing across the surface of my skin. I cling to him as shudder after shudder wracks my body before they start to ebb, and I am able to breathe again. My heart is beating so hard, I see dark dots when I open my eyes. There is just not enough oxygen in my body to make me function like a normal human, but then that was far from normal. *I love our normal.*

"Wow," I manage to speak after some very deep and steadying breaths. I still haven't relinquished my hold, but Jason now has my bottom perched on the countertop with the sink, his forehead resting on mine. I get a warm, deep tingle of satisfaction that it is not just me who is affected by what we do together. He rocks my world, but together, we rock *us*.

"This isn't business, Jason. Are you sure Daniel is okay with it?" I take my seat in the Stone company jet. The large leather lounge chairs are absolute luxury, but I would've been fine flying commercial. Well, not fine exactly, I fucking hate flying, but I would survive.

"You don't like to fly, so I thought this would be better." He looks directly at me like I made the dumbest remark.

"It is, but I don't want you taking liberties and getting into trouble on my behalf." I try to argue, but his face just looks more confused until it changes and makes my core clench.

"Really, you don't want me taking liberties?" His lips turn up at the edges and carve a wicked smile.

"Oh, I definitely want—Shit!" The twin engines fire up, and the noise drowns out my thoughts and my curses. Jason's hand covers mine; I turn my hand up and return the hold, although mine is more like a death grip.

"I don't have to ask permission, if that's what you mean, and there is no way Daniel will be leaving the country anytime soon, not with the baby due." Jason's tone is calm, his hold a comfort, but it's not enough to quell my anxiety.

"Oh yes!" I mutter, but my mind isn't engaged with this conversation. I press my head back and feel the pull of gravity as we hurtle down the runway and lift off.

"Shall we play the rapid-fire question game again? That seemed to work at keeping your mind off flying. At least until I can *take your mind off flying*." His tone drops with sinful, sensual intent, and I get a deep tingle that starts at the base of my spine and makes me clench in all the right places.

"Okay." I flash a tight smile that barely crinkles my lips. "You go first."

"What's your earliest memory?" He fires at me without hesitation.

"Oh, um…" My fingers release the hold on the armrest to tap my lips, thinking.

"It's rapid fire, Sam. You do understand the concept?" he teases, his thumb softly stroking the wrist of the hand he is still holding with a firm grip.

"Right, sorry. I remember my Grandfather. It might not be my very earliest memory, but it's the first that springs to mind. I used to sit on his lap next to the open fire, and he would tell me stories. I don't remember what they were, but I liked them." I absently rub my leg with my free hand. "I can still feel the rough scratch of his tweed trousers against my bare legs. He had this big dent in his nose from his heavy glasses, and he always had butterscotch candy in his inside jacket pocket. He would secretly give me a piece or two. I wasn't allowed sweets." I turn to see Jason staring at me utterly absorbed, like I am telling the greatest story ever told. I can't help but smile at the memory. I adored my Grandfather, and that is a beloved memory I haven't thought about in forever. "You know, like the sweets from that television advert? He actually gave me those, just like the ad. They were forbidden and tasted all the better for it."

"I don't doubt that for a moment." Jason smirks.

"My turn. What's your most embarrassing memory?" I shift to face him, relaxed enough to move, which is an improvement from terror-induced rigor mortis.

"Hell, no, I will take the forfeit," he barks out, shaking his head.

"No fucking way! You have to tell me now," I challenge, my interest clearly piqued if the memory has this type of reaction on Mr. Shameless.

"Not a fucking chance am I revealing that, and if you ask Will to tell you, just know I will cut his balls off if he so much as utters one word," he states, but I shrug off his threat until he clarifies. "So he won't be able to *play*."

"That bad, eh?" I laugh as he hangs his head, shaking it lightly.

"You have no idea," he groans.

"But Will does. Good to know," I taunt, mischief etched in the turn of my smile.

"He won't tell you—on pain of death, he won't utter a word." His emphatic tone, I think, is more for his benefit, because I just smile ruefully.

"Hmm, I'm sure you're right. After all, who am I to get someone to tell me all their secrets? I wouldn't know where to begin…" I lightly tap my lips at the non-existent quandary. It wouldn't even be a challenge. "It can't be worse than walking through town in your girlfriend's underwear," I add with a wry smile, biting back the shit-eating grin as his eyes first narrow and then widen with disbelief.

"Oh, he did not tell you about that?" His jaw grits tight and a deep rumble growls low in his chest.

"Oh, he did, and I didn't even have to use my whip." I laugh and shake my shoulders with a certain amount of pride. Jason's lips flatten with a smidgen of smugness. It only takes me a moment to recognise that look. "Dammit, that wasn't it, was it? Tell me. I really need to know now." I clasp my hands together to aid my plea, but it falls on deaf ears and a wider smile.

"Dream on, beautiful, but that secret is going to our graves. Try another." He waves his hand, moving the conversation on to safer ground.

"Fine! What's your happiest memory?" I pout, but only for a second because I am more interested in his answer than pursuing a topic I know he won't reveal unless he wants to.

"I have two moments tied at first place. Seeing you alive in the hospital." He pauses to swallow, and his eyes flash with pain we both share, but he shakes it off just as quickly. "And then seeing you come apart in my hands on Christmas Day. *That* was pretty fucking spectacular…definitely my happiest moments."

"Wow! Mine, too. Although, you walking through your office door the other day when I imagined the worst comes a close second, but how about before me?" I love that we share a favourite happy moment, but I am eager to hear what else brings him joy besides me.

"That's two questions?" he counters.

"Technically, it's still one. I'd like to know something before me. Our shared stuff I know about. Give me something more." I wiggle my brows suggestively, a playful grin dancing on my lips.

"You want more." His deep voice drops a little to a rough sexy timbre that makes my whole body shiver.

"Jason." My tone is a warning, despite being deliciously distracted.

"Fine." He holds up his hands in surrender, his bright smile dazzling, and I find I am a little more distracted. "Okay, it has to be seeing my Mum's face when my brother came home, clean. She'd been through hell, and to see her so happy after so much heartbreak, that definitely made me happy. Will and I both vowed that she would never again suffer the way she did with Will, well, with both of us really. I wasn't the easiest son. She's an amazing woman and deserves all the happiness in the world. She smiled that day, and she hadn't for so long. Yeah, that's my happiest memory."

"That's really sweet, Jason, and I'm sure she's super proud of you both. She did good." I playfully fist bump his chin and he flashes a shy, adorable smile.

"Her happiness is important, so I try." The pilot announces we are free to roam and Jason takes the first opportunity to scoop me onto his lap. His lips brush my neck, and I feel the shock of a million prickles kiss my skin. His breath scorches as he exhales a low whisper. "Tell me a secret so dirty it turns you on just to tell it?"

I drop my head to the side to give him all the access and more, then sigh. "Jason, you know all my dirty secrets. You fulfill all my dirty desires, and you own this depraved body and soul, but that wasn't a question."

"Maybe not, but that was the perfect answer." His mouth covers mine, his urgent hands explore my body, and I relish in his undivided attention and distracting tactics for the entire eight-hour flight.

Getting through customs took a little longer than anticipated, due to my passport having a US stamp from leaving the country on my last visit but not one for entry. The officer looked highly sceptical at my explanation—and that actually gave me a disproportionate amount of comfort, that, thankfully, a kidnapping is still rare enough to raise an eyebrow or two. He did have to seek out his superior before I was allowed to re-join Jason, and we were both let through to the arrivals lounge, where Will was waiting.

Will leans against a column a few feet back from the welcoming crowd. His hair is perhaps a little longer, and he is wearing the scruffiest board shorts and faded T-shirt, which when he raises his arm in greeting, exposes his trim tanned stomach. His grin lights up the airport and having instantly clocked us, he is already striding forward to close the distance. Jason's arm, which was loosely draped across my shoulder, tightens, and I snicker and playfully jab my elbow in his side.

"What?" He just pulls me tighter so there is no room to poke him again. I raise a curious brow, but he holds my glare with impassive innocence. Before we take another step, I slip out of his hold and step in front of him, causing him to bump into me. His arms grab my shoulders to steady us both. His brows furrow with confusion, and I take that moment to reach up and softly kiss his lips, his cheek, and whisper in his ear.

"You own me…just you." I rock back on to my heels and watch his lips spread wide and deep into the most stunning smile, eclipsing his brother's grin, much like the sun outshines the moon.

"Damn right, I do." His gravelly tone is clipped, and he makes me squeal when he snaps to bend and lift me, caveman style onto his shoulder. I wriggle and reach, too late to grab my suitcase, as he strides away.

"Wait, wait, my case!" He slaps my arse, and I bite back a howl because, man, that stung like a bitch, but we are already making enough of an exhibition.

Regardless of my cries, he continues to walk away from my worldly goods.

"Hey, man." Jason greets his brother with a shoulder press—his other shoulder. "Grab Sam's case, would you, Will? I kinda got my hands full."

Will barks out a laugh. "I can see that." He continues to laugh as he finally comes into my line of sight. I have one hand gripping tight to the seat of Jason's pants, partly for balance and partly to yank hard if he gives me any trouble—any more trouble, that is. "Hey, Sam, good to see you." Will has my case and is following directly behind Jason, grinning like an idiot as I bob uncomfortably on his brother's shoulder, grunting with the impact of each long stride.

"Yeah, you, too. Did you bring your car, or is he going to carry me all the way to your apartment, do you think?" I tease, but Jason doesn't break his stride.

"You honestly think you're staying with me and my flat mates? He hasn't even let me shake your hand yet, Sam." Jason spins so I am facing the sea of cars in the airport parking.

"Where are you parked?" Jason asks, completely ignoring our banter. I take that break in momentum to wriggle and slide down his body. He lets it happen; I would still be impaled on his bony shoulder if that wasn't the case, but he keeps his arms protectively around my waist even as I turn to face Will. I offer my hand for Will to shake. He stretches out, dropping the handle of my case. He takes my hand and turns it, and leans down to kiss the back. He flashes me a wicked smile and yanks me from Jason's hold. I hit Will's chest with a gasp. Will leans in and presses his lips against mine. I wedge them tight, but even without his tongue, the kiss still feels nice. He releases me, and I step back a little dazed and a lot apprehensive. I glance at Jason, expecting to see a shit storm brewing, but he is just standing there with his arms crossed. Muscles flexed on his forearm, his back ramrod straight, and a stern thin line behind which his full soft lips are lurking.

"Remind me why the fuck I decided to visit you, exactly?" His calm delivery belies the tempered fury I see etched on his face. "Do we need to take this outside so I can lay the boundaries out clearly in the form of kicking your sorry arse and painting a purple palette of bruises all over your pretty face?" His eyes narrow, and although his tone is not quite deadly, it's not exactly light and fluffy, either. I step between them, my palm placed flat on both their sculpted chests. I draw in a breath and lightly tap my fingers.

"Now, now…let's play nice." My soothing voice has absolutely no impact on the raging testosterone, but I persevere. "I *know* you both know how to do that. So how about we put our swords away until later and go grab something to eat?" I bite back my smirk, because as funny as I thought my double entendre was, I don't think Jason is quite ready for my jokes.

Will hold his hands up in an open display of surrender and laughs, instantly easing the tension. "Stand down, Jason. You can't blame me for trying, besides I never thought this day would happen, so I'm allowed a little slack in trying to get a rise out of you," he blurts out another belly laugh at Jason's disgruntled growl.

"Laugh it up, brother, but one more stunt like that, and Sam and I will find another playdate." Jason snakes his arm territorially around my waist, and I watch as Will's eyes widen with understanding at what he has just heard. I have to bite back a whimper. I really don't need to add anything flammable to his powder keg of testosterone.

Will swallows slowly, his tongue darts out to wet his lips, mirroring my own, but he is looking above me and directly at Jason. I don't see it, but I feel the shift, an understanding and acknowledgement of the balance of power. All in a silent exchange that makes me shiver and melt.

"I'm parked over here." Will breaks the burgeoning sexual tension, and I let out an exaggerated breath and mockingly fan myself. That makes Jason smile. In truth, there is very little mocking; I am off the charts horny and burning up, sandwiched, as I am, between my man and his mirror image.

Jason sits beside me in the back of Will's beat-up Jeep. This time of year, the heat isn't too bad, which is a blessing because this thing pre-dates air-con. I think it might pre-date the Ark. Jason's arm is a weighty reminder along my shoulder that he has yet to fully relax. I lean into his hold and place my hand on the buckle of his belt, my fingertips creeping under his thin sweater. His tummy tightens at my touch, and I can feel more than hear the low rumble of pleasure travel from the back of his throat. I rest my palm flat on his taut abs; his skin feels like it's on fire, or maybe that's just me. I look up to see him looking down at me; carnal desire so raw, I know for a fact it isn't just me.

"So what are your plans exactly?" Will yells over his shoulder, his bright enthusiastic tone momentarily drowning out the noise of the car's ancient engine.

"A few days at the Four Seasons and then we're heading down to the Keys for some privacy." Jason's disclosure is a shutdown statement if ever I heard one. I pinch his skin. It has little give so it stings enough to warrant a warning glare.

"Play nice," I mouth. Will has fallen silent, and I can see in the rear view mirror his brows are set in a deep frown. Jason draws in a deep breath and reaches his arm to nudge Will's shoulder.

"You're gonna hang with us though while we're in town right?" I can see from the crinkle in Will's eyes that the question has caused a big ol' smile, and I squeeze my appreciation tight around Jason's waist. Apart from Will's surprise visit last month, they normally don't see each other very often, and I don't want to be the one to make that situation worse.

"Yeah, I'd like that," Will calls back, his light tone evidence of his lifted spirit.

"Good. I've booked us a table at the steak bar for tonight, but then I've got nothing planned, so I'm happy for you to take the lead." Jason offers the olive branch.

"Oh, really?" Will's highly suspicious mocking tone makes my heart sink. Jesus, you just can't help some people. I snap upright and shuffle to the corner of the car.

"Right, call a truce, boys, or so help me, I will book myself into the nearest spa and you won't see me for the next seven days…either of you!" I bite out these words with utter conviction and seriousness, but I add just in case there is any misunderstanding. "I won't come between you…not like this. I mean it." Jason laughs and purses his lips like I have just done something incredibly cute. Will just snickers.

"Stand down, soldier. This is just Will being an arse hat. This has nothing to do with you. This is how we are." I narrow my eyes, because I have my doubts. Jason slaps Will's shoulder. "Isn't that right, dickhead?"

"Yeah, buddy, that's right." Will shifts to the side, twisting so he can look directly at me while we are parked in the heavy lunchtime traffic. "Look, Jason loves you, Sam, and I couldn't be happier, but he's also my brother, so I just have to take my shots when I can. It's sort of like the law, but I respect the shit out of what you two have, and I will only *ever* come between you two *if* I'm invited." His warm smile is genuine and heartfelt. I particularly like the way he emphasised the word *if*, because the *whens* would be entirely at the discretion of Mr. Possessive sitting beside me.

Jason sweeps his arm out and scoops me back onto his lap and as if reading my mind he whispers, "You green light the *if*'s, beautiful, but I decide the *whens*, understand?"

"Yes, Sir." My whispered response is more breathless because he does that with his words and his actions; he steals the very air from my lungs.

"I heard that!" Will yells over the noise of the car now that we are moving again. "And now I have a killer boner trying to rip my shorts in two. Cheers, guys." He groans and then starts this weird disgusting mantra, mumbling, "Genital warts and Granddad bollocks, genital warts and blue waf—"

"Okay, okay, we get the picture—you need distracting. How's work?" I jump in with my interruption before his list becomes even more disturbing.

"Work might not help. I fucking love my job, but I don't officially start until next month." He chuckles and tries to discreetly fix his predicament. "I'm kind of on a sabbatical between contracts. It's why I was able to sneak in that extra visit to you guys. I don't normally get this much free time." He grins like the cat with a bucket of cream. "How about I tell you what we're doing tomorrow?" His voice is pitched with infectious joy.

"Oh, yes." I bounce a little and lean forward, my hand gripping either side of the headrest. My tone is eager for information, my expression a picture of excitement. I flash a wink at Jason, but quickly turn back when Will starts to talk.

"I thought you might like to come see the center where I am going to be working. We have a compound at the back for the rescue animals. I'm more on the conservation side, but we do get calls where people don't know what to do with whatever they've found. We don't keep them there for long. We try to find suitable homes straight away, but yesterday we got a call to pick up a white tiger cub that was in a crate on one of the boats that was impounded at the dock. "

"Really? That's awful." I mutter.

"It is, but I've seen worse, and this little fella is one of the lucky ones." Will shrugs, clearly not wanting to dwell on that aspect of his job. "He's pretty cute, but he gets picked up sometime tomorrow, so I thought we could drop by before we go to the lake."

"The lake?" I look back at Jason who shakes his head and shrugs, because this is news to him as well.

"Thought we could take the jets out for a race, if you're up for it?" Will's smile is as wide as his tone is challenging. *Bring it on…although…*

"Oh, I'm up to it, but I've never actually driven a Jet Ski, so—"

"Then that would be a *no*," Jason interrupts with a look of disbelief blazoned on his face.

"What?" I cry out.

"You just said you've never driven a Jet Ski, but you are happy to have a go at racing my brother!" He rolls his eyes, and his condescending tone has my hackles rising.

"And?" I snap and lean back as far as the back seat and sitting on his lap will allow, but I think he gets me.

"You must have lost your mind somewhere over the Atlantic if you think I'd let you do that." He chuckles. *Maybe he doesn't get me.*

"You don't get to tell me what I can and cannot drive. You are not the boss of me," I state flatly. My eyes fix him with my sternest stare, but he is unfazed. In fact, that spark and flash of heat I see means, if I'm not mistaken, that he is turned on.

"Wrong!" He grabs the back of my head and smashes my face to his, crushing the sass right from my lips and melding me to him. I twist and crawl so I am now straddling him because this kiss is all fire and lust, and I can't get enough. He breaks and fixes me with eyes burning with passion and love.

"We will race, but you will be wrapped around me when we do, okay?"

"Spoilsport." I playfully poke my tongue before I grab him right back, kissing him with a fever I feel in my soul and pray will never fade. Not even when I hear Will moan.

"Fucking brilliant!"

I barely notice the rest of the drive until we come to a complete stop under the shade of the large canopy overhang of the Four Seasons Hotel Miami. Arrangements to meet in the bar tonight are quickly made, but he has no intention of sitting around as third wheel for the afternoon. Will dumps our bags with the bellboy and waves us off.

FOURTEEN

Sam

"Will's waiting in the bar downstairs," Jason calls out from the bedroom. He opted for a quick shower that could've happened five minutes or five hours ago. I am in heaven, drifting in and out of a bubble-bath-induced daze, soaking aching muscles and soothing sun-kissed skin not used to exposure this early in the year.

"And I'm still in the bath," I yell back but make no movement to remedy the problem. My eyes are closed, the lids too heavy, or maybe I'm just too relaxed, but I feel him watching me. I peek through one eye and smile. He is dressed, but his stealthy approach meant even his shoes made no sound on the marble tiled floor. I open my eyes, and at the first sight, I find myself sitting taller, leaning toward him because he does that; he draws me in, and he knows it. I drag my stare so slowly up his immaculately suited form. I am not at all surprised by his knowing grin, spread wide and wicked across his handsome face.

"Keep looking at me like that, beautiful, and see what happens." He pulls his cuffs free from his jacket sleeve, adjusting the platinum links I bought him for Christmas—puzzle pieces to match my tattoo.

"You can't be serious? I can barely walk!"

"If it's only barely, then I think you know the answer to that one." He steps farther into the cavernous bathroom, which suddenly feels claustrophobic and a little too hot, but I hold his heated gaze. He towers over me, blocking the overhead soft lighting, all dark and dominant. So fucking hot, but I wasn't kidding about the sex. He may very well be half man, half machine, but this human needs to skip a service.

"Back up there, Tony." I hold my hand up and sink down into the deep water up to my neck; a mass of silky bubbles cloak my nakedness. But the way he holds my gaze, it doesn't matter, he sees me, *all of me.*

"Tony?" He queries with a wry smile.

"Stark, you know as in Iron Man, never mind—"

"Oh, I get the reference, but if you're going for Marvel superheroes, I think I prefer Thor." He smirks.

"You do have a very impressive hammer, but you're not the only one that can pick it up, are you?" He steps back away from my wet arm and dripping hand as I make a grab for his magic tool.

"Cute, but I meant demigod," he states without a hint of irony, and I shake my head. He's so full of himself, even if I do happen to agree. "And if you get me wet, beautiful, I'm joining you in that bath right now." His tone holds a light warning.

"Fine!" I snap my hand back and hide it under the blanket of bubbles. "Look, you go down to the bar. I'll follow in a bit. I am not quite recovered from this afternoon, or the flight."

"Really?" His sinful tone and the playful wiggle of his thick brow make me snort a short loud laugh.

"Really. Don't look so surprised. If I died tonight, they would have to bury me in a Y-shaped coffin. You're relentless." I roll my eyes at his salacious grin.

"You make me relentless. I can't take all the credit."

"Jeez, you're incorrigible."

"I really am." He steps back to bend closer, his hand cups my cheek and his fingers slide to pinch my chin. He swoops down to plant a tender kiss on my expectant lips and hovers just millimeters from me. The sexual charge between us fires like a lightning storm, and my skin prickles despite the heat. Endless erotic seconds tick slowly by until he breaks the hold, pulling back to speak. "If you're sure. I don't mind keeping him waiting." I puff out a breath I didn't realise I was holding and regain my senses enough to respond.

"I'm sure. Please go. It will give you a chance to catch up and maybe we can drop all the willy-waving and actually have a nice evening together." My comment is playful, but I am only half joking.

"I don't willy-wave. It would imply there is some sort of competition. There is no competition." He punctuates his matter-of-fact statement with a cocky wink.

"No, there isn't. None at all. So let's have some fun." I reiterate my feeling for the umpteenth time.

"Fun we can definitely do." He blows me a kiss from the doorway.

"Perfect." I close my eyes and lay my head back; the light curl of my lips spreads to rival the Cheshire cat when I hear his parting words.

"Yes, yes, you are."

"Reservation under the name Sinclair," I tell the pristinely groomed male host on the spotlit podium at the front of the restaurant. I don't think I have ever seen a goatee trimmed with such precision, and each hair on his head is sleek and styled to GQ cover perfection. The young man is Philippe, according to his gold-plated name badge. He swipes at the concealed screen, his haughty expression barely cracking a courteous acknowledgement of my presence. "I'm a little late. I was supposed to meet them at the bar, but they might've gone to their table by now," I offer to fill the awkward silence.

"The table would not be kept empty, I can assure you. Wait here while I check." He gracefully dismounts his stage and disappears behind an embossed, opaque glass screen. He returns almost instantly with a flush of colour to his cheeks.

"I am sorry to have kept you waiting, please follow me." He is quick to usher me inside, and I follow behind, only to freeze immediately after I enter the room. At the far end of the restaurant, a long sleek bar stretches the length of the room. Low level lighting and not an empty table means the room is alive with atmosphere, buzzing with animated chatter, and oozing glamour. All of which pales into insignificance at the sight ahead, in the center of the cocktail bar.

"Oh, my," I exhale quietly.

"I know." Philippe looks directly at me. His eyes twinkle with mischief, and, thanks to my six-inch heels, we are closer to eye-level so I can actually see the reaction up close. His prior implacable expression softens, and I snicker at the resurgence of that flush to his cheeks, as he, too, clocks my man—*men*. A cursory glance around the room and it is all too evident that the Jason and Will combination is attracting more than its fair share of attention. From furtive fluttered lashes to actual jaws dropping, it would be comical if it weren't wholly justified.

They are both perched on bar stools, facing each other, and at this moment, laughing. Each is dressed immaculately. Jason, I know, is in a navy tailor-made jacket and trousers. I like him in navy. He has a matching dark tie and crisp white shirt. Will looks to be wearing the same style, if not from the same tailor. The cut and quality of the cloth only serves to enhance the packages beneath. Fine Italian fabric shifts over broad shoulders as they both reach for their beers, mirrored and synchronised movements that are too fluid to be staged. Will drags his hand through his hair, which is longer and a shade lighter than Jason's. Even from this distance, I can see he is still sporting his five o'clock shadow from when he picked us up. Christ, they look hot. I swallow back an inaudible whimper and, as if sensing my presence, they both turn. Strike that, they don't look hot, they look absolutely lethal.

"Oh, shit." That exclamation wasn't quite so inaudible.

"What a waste." I turn to see Philippe holding his beating heart and playfully dropping his shoulders, his bottom lip protruding in a playful pout. I laugh and lightly pat his cheek.

"Oh, trust me, Philippe, there won't be any waste." I blow him a kiss, which is my only concession to waste this evening, and I make my way over to the bar.

The heat emanating from these two is palpable and my legs tremble from the effect, but I hold Jason's scorching gaze and draw in a steady, fortifying breath. With each step closer, I feel his burn like a brand on my fevered skin. Tonight, there is no doubt I will be playing with fire. Jason stands before I reach them and sweeps his arm around my waist, molding me to his body and claiming me for all to witness. Urgent powerful lips crush mine, and he doesn't stop until he is ready. I'm in no hurry. I relish the dance and duel of tongues, sweeping and demanding, taking and tasting each other as if we were starving. He releases my mouth, but holds me tight, which is a blessing, because my legs are no longer capable of supporting my weight. He lifts me onto the bar stool and removes his jacket, placing it over my shoulders.

"I'm not cold, Jason. You've just spent five minutes devouring me. I am off the charts turned on, but I'm not cold." I try to shuck the jacket, but he pulls it farther across my body. I slap his hand away when he tries to do the button up.

"I know." He still crosses the front panels as best he can.

"I'm not wearing this all evening." I scowl.

"We'll see." He flashes a self-satisfied smile, pleased with my modified appearance.

"I'm not." I straighten my back and raise a challenging brow. "This is a sexy dress, and the whole swamped in a suit jacket isn't the look I was going for," I quip.

"But giving everyone in the building an erection was?" he retorts.

"Well, duh!" I tease and wink at Will who has remained quietly amused by our exchange. "How about I wear this until I am a little less pointy, hmm?" I smile sweetly, offering my only compromise.

"Sam," Jason grumbles, and I respond with a teasing impression of his stern warning.

"Jason." My attempt to recreate his deep tone causes me to cough and splutter. He reaches over to offer me some water, and when I finish sipping, he nods his agreement to my suggestion.

"That dress is wicked sexy, Sam," Will adds, and I brace, waiting for Jason to pull out some sort of balaclava jumpsuit to hide me in, but he just steps to my side, sweeping my long hair over one shoulder. His featherlike touch makes my whole body shudder, maintaining a chill that ensures I remain covered, *sneaky*. He brushes his lip along the nape of my neck and rests his hand on the bottom of my spine, against my bare skin. The loop of the red silk backless dress barely hugs the curve of my bottom. Thin spaghetti straps hold the floaty material that skims and exposes tantalising amounts of skin. I have it secured discreetly in all the right places and it hangs a modest length just above my knee, but I don't kid myself…it's a fucking sexy dress. Even so, I still needed my killer heels, because looking at these two? They set *that* bar very high.

"Why, thank you, Will, you don't look too dusty yourself." I lean over to kiss his cheek as Jason orders more drinks.

"But it's not *me* giving everyone in the room a boner." He raises his glass like this statement was a toast. I clink my glass to his and take a large sip.

"Philippe, the maître d', would argue that point." I *call* his argument and *raise* since this feels like a high stakes games we are playing. "And judging by the death glares I'm getting, I think you will be responsible for a wet pair of panty or two."

"But there is only one wet panty that is of any interest." Will takes another draw from his beer and holds my gaze as I hold my breath.

"Oh, I forgot to say, Will, Sam can't come out to play today." Jason takes my empty glass for a refill and raises a brow at my dropped jaw. *He has to be kidding?* Dressed like they are, looking like they do, and knowing what I know…He can't possibly be serious. "You're over an hour late, Sam. I take it you fell asleep because you never take that long to get ready."

"I may have had a nap, but—"

"Nah-ah," he interrupts, placing his finger across my lips to silence me. I start to bare my teeth to take a bite of that digit when his words stop me. "You're clearly exhausted, beautiful." He traces his finger along my jaw. I might've thought for a moment he was teasing, but I can see the genuine concern in his eyes.

"Jason's right, Sam." Will adds his opinion with just as much thoughtfulness in his tone. "You need to be fit and healthy. There's no rush."

"I am fit and healthy," I grumble, leaning back into Jason's hold. I look directly up to his face, which is smirking down at me.

"And utterly shagged…you said so yourself. You need to take it easy for a day or two before we wreck you," he states calmly as a matter-of-fact.

"A day or two?" My indignant cry is cut short. "Wait, wreck me?" My breathless words transform Jason's smirk into the familiar nefarious curl of his soft lips.

"Hmm, hmm." He slowly nods, and I tingle from tip to toe, shiver, and melt all with one sharp intake of breath and clarity of understanding.

"Shall we?" A voice behind me speaks.

"Oh yes, please." My eager response makes Jason laugh out and shake his head.

"Your table is ready, Mr. Sinclair." That voice again…not Jason or Will, but our waiter. My heart drops, my cheeks flush with embarrassment, and my tummy rumbles.

"First things first, beautiful, food, then rest, then—"

"Wrecking?" I slide off the stool and thread my arm through Will's offered crook of his arm. Jason still has his arm wrapped around my waist.

"Yes, beautiful, then you get wrecked."

"If I was wearing any panties, they would be soaked right about now," I mutter low, but loud enough.

"Oh, fuck!" The brothers exhale together, and their whispered exclamation sounds a lot like a plea.

"You know where to find me when you think I've had enough rest." I smile sweetly as I take my seat in a semi-circular booth, flanked by the sexiest men on the planet. My tummy may rumble, but I am not in the slightest bit hungry for food.

The meal is amazing and delicious enough to take my mind off every woman's wet dream seated on either side of me. Even with Jason absently stroking my thigh, the only groans of satisfaction leaving my mouth are entirely due to the melt-in-the-mouth steaks and triple-cooked chips—sorry, fries. But I am also vocal with my disappointment at the size of the key lime pie. I thought everything was supposed to be super-sized in this country. The delicate biscuit disc in the center of the plate holds a petite tower of pale green mousse and an elaborate curl of chocolate filigree on top of that; it looks very much like a work of art, but it is tiny. I finish mine in fewer than three bites and can't help but covet Jason's untouched order of the same. He doesn't even glance my way, engrossed as he is, talking to Will, but he skilfully switches our plates, and that is why I love this man.

I clean that plate, too, and just wonder if requesting another would be *bad* when Jason excuses himself. I nod my understanding when he mentions the men's room, but I felt the vibration of his phone along the shared seat, and my heart sinks. If it were work, he would say so, and *that* is a worry.

"I'm sure it's nothing." Will covers my hand that is fisting the napkin into a tight ball. He picks my fingers free and threads them with his own.

"You felt that too, huh?" I take comfort from his offered hand and squeeze it in return.

"It was either that, or you're packing more than a killer body under that dress." He wiggles his brow playfully, and I bark out a dirty laugh.

"You think I'd need any more stimulation sitting between you two," I scoff, but my humour is short-lived.

"Did he tell you?" I ask quietly, searching Will's face for secrets shared.

"Tell me what?" Will's eyes narrow, and I answer his ridiculous question with my silently raised brow. He lets out a heavy sigh. "He told me what he told you, Sam." Will's dark brown eyes hold all the compassion and honesty of his brother, and I feel the warmth of that in my bones. "He worries about your safety, that's not surprising considering…Look, he told me he received an email. But cut him a little slack, he is trying to protect you. You're his life, and he nearly lost you. I know how deep that fear runs in him."

"I know, but protecting me can feel a lot like hiding stuff, and if it's about me, I need to know. I may not like it, but I deserve the chance to make up my own mind."

"I'm sure he knows how you feel." His claim feels very much like a brush off, and I get an uncomfortable feeling there is something more.

"Well, if he doesn't, you two are pretty tight. How about you remind him." I push my point, but he shakes his head before I even finish my sentence.

"Fuck, no, I am not getting in between you two…not like *that*." His grin is utterly wicked but softens to a smile filled with concern. "You're his world, Sam, and he is just protecting his world."

I puff out a deep frustrated breath. I get what Will is saying, but this trust thing goes both ways and sneaking off to take calls doesn't feel like trust.

"So dodged the bullet meeting the in-laws, I see. Really, Mum's not that bad." Will throws his head back in raucous laughter that completely stuns me.

"What?" My face crinkles with confusion. "What do you mean? I don't understand. Jason said your Mum was cool."

"Really? He said those exact words?" Will runs his hand through his hair front to back and repeats the move. His agitation is doing little to calm my rising anxiety.

"I don't know, now. Yeah, he definitely said I wouldn't need to worry. He said she would be thrilled he was settling down with someone." My words are a rush of nervousness. "He said she wouldn't care what I was, I mean." I pull my hand out of his hold and wrap my arms around my waist. I've never cared what people think about me, so why should I now? I know exactly why...because this is Jason, and this is his Mum, whom he adores. This is a big deal.

"Hmm." Will looks pensive but doesn't try to make light of the conversation, which sends me reeling into full on panic mode.

"Will, is she going to care what I do, what I *did* for a living?" I can feel my tummy roil, and I now challenge the wisdom of Miss Two Desserts.

"Kind of—" He grimaces out a tight smile. *Shit.*

"Why would he tell me different?" I almost screech, the panic rising in my voice but my gritted teeth manage to keep the volume to that of my indoor voice.

"Probably because he loves you and didn't want to freak you out. That's just a guess given that we are over four thousand miles away, and you are, in fact, freaking out." He passes me a glass of water that I snatch and down in one long unladylike glug. I let out a slow breath, but feel the prickle of tears behind my eyes. Will is silently focused on my every move.

"She's going to hate me, Will." I pinch the pressure at the bridge of my nose and squeeze my eyes tight.

"No, she won't." Will reaches for my hand and pulls it free from my waist. He clasps it between his and shakes his head, emphasising his resolve.

"This is not good. Jason adores her. He told me very recently that he would do anything to make sure she's happy."

"And?" Will's dark brow furrows like he is not following the problem...that *I* am the problem.

"Believe me, Will, her son marrying a sex-trade professional, albeit an *ex*-professional, is not going to make her happy."

"I haven't lived in the UK for years. She's probably lightened up a bit." Will has the decency to look embarrassed at his statement that, given his own admission that he hasn't actually spent much time in the same country, he has absolutely no foundation for.

"Really?" I splutter, my tone thick with sarcasm. "You're sure about that? Because isn't this the same woman that won't let her twenty-nine year old son share his bedroom with his fiancée for one night?"

"Ah, I see your point. You're totally fucked." He pinches his lips together in a shy grin, which morphs into a much larger smile. He's right, but it's hardly his fault, and that face looks far too much like the man I love to stay mad. I screw up the napkin and hurl at his adorable grin.

"Thanks." I let out a resigned sniff and join his smile.

"Who's totally fucked?" Jason slides in beside me.

"Me. Your Mum is going to hate me." Jason scowls at Will, who holds his hands up.

"I was trying to steer the conversation away from your not-so-suptle disappearing act."

"And that's what you came up with? Genius." Jason rolls his eyes at his brother, but quickly turns his full attention to me. His hands cup either side of my face, so we are almost nose to nose. "My Mother will love you because I love you, end of. And what she doesn't know won't hurt her. I won't hurt her any more than I would hurt you. She can be a little judgmental and protective of her boys, but what mother isn't?" I tense in his hands, but he looks mortified. "Ah shit, I didn't mean that. Look, beautiful, I just didn't want you getting all worried. It's not like you ever introduce yourself like 'Hello, my name is Sam, and I'm the best ex-dominatrix in London. Would you like to see my impressive whip collection'?" There is an awkward cough.

"Would you like some coffee or brandy perhaps?" Our waiter is trying desperately hard not to look at me and failing *magnificently*.

"I don't need to introduce myself when you do it *so* well." I flash a tight smile at Jason and address our poor waiter. "I'll have a peppermint tea please and a ball gag, if you have one." The waiter's wide eyes haven't left my face, but his cheeks flush with an adorable splash of dark red.

"I'm sorry, ma'am," he stutters.

"Two espressos and a mint tea will be all, thank you." Jason curtly dismisses the waiter before he starts to drool. "Behave," he grumbles at me.

"*Me* behave? After *that* introduction?" I retort with mock indignation, pulling away from his hold.

"I did say you were the best, and I did say ex. Now, play nice when our waiter gets back." His stern tone is tinged with humour, and his eyes crinkle with the wide smile spreading across his gorgeous face. He shakes his head lightly. "There is no way he will be getting our order right. He couldn't take his eyes off your lips."

"They're very nice lips," Will adds his two cents. I try to smile, but the spread of these 'very nice lips' barely makes a full curl.

"Hey, you have nothing to worry about." Jason threads his hand around the back of my neck, and his hot palm brands my skin. He holds me fixed; his eyes bore into me with a heart melting mix of love and concern. It takes the edge off my worry to some extent, but his mother isn't my only concern.

"And the phone call?" He stiffens and flashes a look at his brother. I can't see the exchange, but his eyes soften when they return their fix on me.

"It was an update, nothing to worry about." He drops his forehead to mine, but I nudge him back up so I can see his eyes.

"Okay, that's all right then, I won't worry…said not me!" I try to pull away, but his hold is strong; his tone is resolute.

"Tomorrow, I will tell you everything, which, by the way, is nothing, but I will tell you tomorrow. Let's have tonight." His voice drops to a sensual whisper that has every hair on the back of my neck dancing.

"But I won't be able to think about anything else," I mutter my objection like a brat.

"Oh, I think we can help with that." His voice is barely audible by every cell in my body heard it in Dolby HD.

"You said no playing." My voice cracks; my throat is suddenly parched.

"I changed my mind." Jason's dark glare is utterly carnal, and I absolutely melt from its intensity.

"Check, please!" Will shouts out, not sure if it was a twin thing, but he certainly read *my* mind.

I'm going to internally combust. Let me paint the picture that's causing this very real crisis inside me right now. We left the restaurant and took the lift to the Presidential suite. Jason and Will stood behind me, silent the whole way, but I could feel their eyes on my back, my legs, my neck, my hair, and definitely my butt. We entered the room, and Jason told me to stand in the lounge area, eyes forward, legs wide, and he warned me not to move while he fixed drinks for himself and Will. They took their sweet time coming back into my line of sight, but damn when they did. Will had lost his shirt completely, and Jason had his loose and open, neither of them had shoes or socks. They each take one of the armchairs facing me and relax, iced drink in hand. Gorgeous—no, that's a wholly inadequate adjective. I wrack my dazed brain, but I don't think there is a word in the English vocabulary to describe this picture of perfection. Two pairs of impossibly dark eyes smoulder and sear my body, from the painted toes of my feet to the tousled hair fallen around my face; carnal, raw and so damn intense. I ache to move my legs together; they twitch enough to make Jason pull his bottom lip through his teeth and raise a knowing brow. This anticipation is pure agony. I'm in heaven, and this—this is sweet hell. I am so ready to burn.

FIFTEEN

Jason

"Lose the dress." I'm impressed my voice sounds as calm as it does, because she looks so fucking beautiful. My throat is bone dry, and my lungs have all but seized up, fighting to get some much-needed oxygen inside. Her hands instantly, but, oh, so slowly, slip the thin straps from her slender shoulders. The weight of silk glides the dress to the floor, revealing the single most amazing view on this planet: My girl, almost naked, and in killer fuck-me heels. Her eyes dip to her thong and then meet mine. She bites her lips tight in an impish grin.

"Tsk, tsk, Sam, you lied about the panties." I shake my head lightly. "Teasing like that deserves its own punishment, don't you think?"

"I think making me stand here looking at you two, all hot as hell, is punishment enough," she grumbles, and I can see her thighs tremble with the effort to keep them parted. I can smell her from here, and my balls are in fucking agony; that aroma is sent from the gods to drive me crazy.

"Oh, I don't think it is." Her eyes widen as I loosen my belt and unzip my pants. Will follows my lead, and I release my straining erection into my waiting fist.

"Oh, shit," she gasps and drops her chin to her chest.

"Eyes on us, beautiful." A deep groan escapes her pursed lips, but she obeys. Her face is flushed, and her jaw is clenched, as her greedy eyes devour each languid stroke I administer to my rock-hard cock. Not for pleasure, mind, I just need to relieve some of the unbearable pressure building in my groin… and, perhaps, to return the favour. Her 'no panties' comment meant this evening I endured a hard-on from hell, at least until the main course was served. Now I think on it, this is definitely to return the tease. I continue to stroke my length, but I am far from getting the relief I crave, because what I crave is just a few tortuous steps away. For a moment, I wonder whom this is teasing exactly.

"Jason," Will mutters beside me, and I can hear the strain in his voice. It would match mine if I spoke. I stand abruptly and kick my loose pants to the side. I turn and nod for Will to do the same. He doesn't need to be told twice. Sam's breath catches when I face her, but she holds it with a pained expression and thin lips when Will and I step closer. She pants out some sexy little puffs of air when we stand on either side of her trembling body, close enough to feel the electricity fire between our bodies, but not touching, not yet.

"Jason, I can't breathe." Her soft voice breaks into a whimper that I feel in the base of my spine.

"Burning up, beautiful?"

"So hot," she gasps, and I don't know if she's referring to the situation we are in or her personal body temperature. It doesn't matter, because she's right. *She is fucking hot.*

"Shower," I state and watch her whole body shudder before she manages a heartfelt, ball-aching moan and replies.

"Oh, God, yes."

Will strides off and opens the door to the en suite, and I scoop Sam into my arms, my erection bobbing and stroking the curve of her arse with every step I take. I walk us both straight into the cavernous shower and wet area and hit the rainforest downpour dial on the control panel. The water is instant, heavy, and hot. The lighting in the room dims with spotlights of blue and green, and there is a soft background sound of a rumbling thunderstorm, which is apt. I am consumed with uncontrollable pent-up lust and tempered desire poised to unleash, just like a storm...a wild force of nature.

We are all instantly drenched, and despite the hot water, Sam's nipples are tight peaks begging for my attention. She cries out when my eager mouth covers and sucks, twirling my tongue around the stiff little pebble. My hands hold both breasts up for my pleasure, and I take turns teasing and squeezing, nibbling and grazing with my teeth. One of her hands fists my hair, and I look up through soaked lashes to see she is leaning back against Will, her other arm reaching high and back behind her, her hand cupping his neck. He is leaning forward, kissing along her shoulder and up to her ear; his other hand wrapped around her waist, holding her tight as she writhes and undulates between us. The moans and groans echo off the tiled walls, but they are soft and no competition for the Amazonian soundtrack playing through the hidden speakers.

I pull back and stand tall, pressing my body against hers. The water aids the glide of skin on skin, but I'm surprised it hasn't sizzled or turned to steam; her body is so damn hot, and we three are all on fucking fire. I tip her chin up, and her lashes flutter with heavy drops of water. Her lips part and are full and wet.

"Thirsty?" I ask, releasing her chin as she tips her head fully back and opens her mouth. The downpour quickly fills her, spilling over her lips. She lifts her head and her wide smile lets the water fall back out. She doesn't swallow…*yet*. I place my hand on her waist and twist until she is sideways between us; her palms are pressed firmly on our chests. I can feel Will's eyes on me, waiting, but mine are fixed on her. I raise a brow, and she instantly drops slowly to her knees. Dragging her nails down our torsos until her tight fists grab a cock in each hand. She looks up at me, then Will, but she always returns her gaze to me; those heavy lids and the utter raw desire alive in her eyes is the fucking sexiest thing ever. Oh, and she's on her knees with my dick in her hand, yeah, that too. She tilts her head like she is weighing her decision, the wicked curl of her lips almost makes me make that choice for her, but I keep my hands flat at my side. She might like to tease, but she's not stupid. I slam one palm hard against the wall to steady myself when her tongue flicks my essence clean off my sensitive crown. Her lips quickly follow, and her tongue works its magic as she eases me into her mouth. Her nimble fingers help to push me farther as she swallows more and more. *Fuck!*

My head drops, and I watch her work me with her lips, her hand; her whole fucking body moves with the rhythm she sets, and her other hand is just as attentive. She groans, and I have to fight not to come; the vibrations at the back of her throat are very nearly my undoing. She switches just in time, and I let out a stuttered breath filled with timely relief. Her smirk and raised brows makes me think she *owns* me. She literally has me by the balls, and I fucking love it.

I can't take my eyes off her. She presses the crown of Will's cock against her lips and looks up to his eyes and then to mine; her smile is short-lived as she sinks her mouth over his length, never breaking her heated glare with mine. *God, I love this woman.*

She repeats this once more and is about to switch again, but I have had enough and judging by the fierce expression on Will's face, he feels the same. We both reach a hand under her arm and lift her to her feet. She sways a little, but we have her.

"Head or tails?" I growl. Sexual tension is coiled so tight, I am one big fucking trigger, and she is the hairpin. Her cheeks are an adorable pink, flushed and wet, her lips are swollen, and her breath is short and rapid, but her perfect brow pitches with confusion.

"Hmm?" Her eyes flick between Will and me for clarification.

"Do you want my cock in your arse or your pussy?" I calmly state. Lady's choice, and I don't really care which, but I told Will he's not allowed anywhere near her pussy, so this decision could suck for him, literally.

"Shouldn't the question be cats or dogs? You know as in cats are pussies and doggy from behind. I think that would work better, don't you?" She snickers at her own joke, but there is way too much tension and testosterone to filter in any humour.

"Sam." My tone is thick with lust and warning.

"Heads," she blurts, and I spy Will's widening grin, his lucky night. Sam turns to face me, between my arms, bouncing on the spot. I make the most of the move and lift her high on to my hips. "I want your head." Her hands clasp my face, and her lips kiss a thousand kisses all over my face, playful at first, but like I said, too much sexual tension. I fist her sodden hair and yank it back. Her head tilts, she gasps, and I thrust my tongue into her open mouth. It's ferocious and wild like the storm brewing in the speakers, crashes of thunder as her hands grip and pull my hair. She parries each move of my possessive tongue with her own demanding moves. My cock nudges against her entrance, and I brace my legs. I feel some cool liquid and foreign fingers move skilfully around her entrance, barely touching me...barely. One tilt of my hips and I bury myself to the hilt. Her arms tighten around my shoulders, and her whole body tenses at the intrusion. I'm not surprised; I don't think I have ever been this big—well, maybe once, not so long ago.

"You're going to need to relax a little, darling," Will whispers in her ear, but my ear too, since we are all so close. Sam pulls back and breaks the kiss, her eyes wide and alive. She gives a little nod and lets out a deep and steady breath.

I feel the pressure first against my cock and see the recognition and wince of pain flash in her eyes.

"Relax, beautiful," I coax, and she nods. Her eyes glaze, but I can still feel the tension in her frame. "Look at me." She does, her bottom lip is gripped between her teeth. *So much for relaxing.* "Breathe with me, baby, feel me, hmm?" She nods, and her lips soften. "Feel how deep I am. How good does that feel?" My tone is deep and gravelly, but I keep it calm, like a soothing wave to wash her worries away.

"So good." She sighs, and I roll my hips once more, making her gasp when I hit that sweet spot. "Oh God, so good." Her voice catches and her mouth drops open on a silent cry.

"More?" I exhale and wait for her to nod, which she does. Her eyes are fixed on me, deep, dark pools of liquid lust.

"More...please." She lets out a deep breath and all that tension, and it's enough. It's more than enough, and Will pushes past her tight barrier; the thinnest of membranes separates us, and she doesn't flinch. She is floating; her lips part with something unspoken and an inaudible whimper. We all take a moment... a heavenly moment as one, arms locked tight, skin on skin on skin. So fucking erotic, but I want more. My hips start to move, and Will and I quickly find a perfect rhythm of push and pull, in and out, but always keeping her full.

Driving her higher and higher.

She does her bit, lifting her tight, little body and dropping down hard, but I'm setting the pace, and it's me that will take her there. My lips seek hers, and she is ravenous for the contact.

"Jason." Her cry is an urgent plea as her body starts to take over.

"Come for me, beautiful." My lips are pressed against hers, my words soft, but she hears them loud and clear. She throws her head back, every muscle in her body clamps down, constricts, and she comes like a fucking freight train all over my cock. I can't ease her down gently; I no longer have that level of control. My hips piston into her, and I don't stop until she is screaming once more, and I am coming with her second and equally impressive orgasm. I step back and am thankful for the seat, which stops my body sliding down the tiles from hitting the floor. Sam's head is resting on my chest, her heart hammering the same beat pattern as mine. It's only after a few long moments when the blood is no longer rushing in my ears that I look up to see Will standing with his back to the water and a very angry-looking erection.

I tap Sam's cheek; she's all floppy and pliant. She tilts her head to look up into my eyes. "You got a little feisty and slippery when you came," I add, but I don't think it really needed an explanation. She had two cocks inside her, and now she just has me. She looks over at Will and back to me for permission. I tip my chin, but before I can agree verbally, Will speaks.

"Only if you're up to it. I can finish myself; I just thought I'd ask." Will shrugs like this offer isn't killing him, and I appreciate his attempt at least to be gracious. Sam shifts in my lap and off my cock to face him, but she leans back in to my chest. I wrap my arms tight around her waist.

"Heads or tails?" Her words are breathy and sexy as all hell and I can't see it but I can feel the grin.

"Oh, definitely heads." Will's tone drops an octave as he drops to his knees and wedges himself between mine and Sam's legs. Hers are draped over mine. Will's hands sweep along her thighs but rest at her hips, part gripping her arse cheeks, part holding her thigh. He freezes when he catches my scowl. I don't need to have this fight here…now, he fucking knows.

"Sorry, man, heat of the moment." He stands up and takes a slow step back, cupping himself.

"Right," I drawl. My hands drift down Sam's stomach to the top of her thighs that have instinctively tried to close. I press my palms flat against the taut muscle and pull them wide again. "So now you're just going to have to watch."

Sam tenses in my arms but wisely remains quiet.

"Damn it, Jason." Will's jaw is clenched, but he's in no position to argue. He's my fucking guest.

"My rules, Will. There's the door, if you want it." Sam's back arches when I cup the apex of her legs possessively with a growl heard deep from my chest. She turns her head and has a flash of concern in her eyes. That's not what I want. This isn't a problem, but I won't let the heat of an encounter undermine my rules or me.

I take one hand and grab her jaw, pulling her open mouth to my lips. My tongue plunges into her softness and takes ownership, as if that was ever in question. Her arms thread around my neck, and my other hand grips and holds her steady, as her hips want to roll against my hold. She thrummed under my touch, and I want to take her there…just me. I spread my legs wide and as hers are over mine, hers are much wider. I guess Will has a great view, but I couldn't give a fuck. Sam is with me, her eyes never leaving mine.

I reach for the edge of the seat and hook the slim lightweight chrome showerhead. She shudders against my body and my cock strains against the small gap of her arse.

"Up you get, beautiful." I sit up straight so she lifts herself and pitches forward. Her hands rest on my knees, her arse lifts, and she positions herself just above my cock. I grab the base and push the tip firmly against her tight ring of muscles. "Ease back down, baby, but take all of me. Don't stop until I say." Her muscles clinch tight, and I catch a breath. Jeez, that is tight…shit! She relaxes and drops a little more. It's clearly taking effort on her part as short sharp breaths are being pushed out with equal force as her hands grip at my knees.

"Jason," she gasps, and I steady her with one hand on her hip, my other still has the showerhead that is pulsing a steady stream of water down my leg.

"Nearly there, beautiful, nearly there." I swallow the thick lump, my eyes fixed on her tight arse sliding slowly down my cock, perfect round swells of smooth skin, slick and shiny from the steam or sweat, it doesn't matter. It's fucking perfect. Her thighs tremble as she holds her weight, and she lets out a pained groan that filters out into a sensual sigh, finally sinking. All. The. Way. Down. We take a moment, and I let out a deep satisfying groan that I feel in my balls. *Damn.*

She starts to move her hips, rolling round, up and down, pressing her body to mine, using one arm around my neck for leverage. She tilts her head so our lips meet, frantic and urgent, and she squeals into my mouth when I press the fierce jet of water between her legs. The needles of the individual jets prickle the base of my shaft when she lifts her arse, but the bulk of the spray is directed right at her clit. The fingers from my other hand push into her entrance and pump gently to match the thrusts I am driving into her from behind. I am so fucking deep, and she is pounding hard, wanting more. My hands are wedged between her legs, one hand holding the shower head and the other with three fingers curled inside her, feeling the torrent of water rushing past my fingers and filling her as I pump and push the water back out. She's drenched.

Her own fingers grip my hair as her back arches away from me with the intensity of building pleasure.

"Touch yourself, beautiful," I groan against her lips, but I'm not sure she hears me; she takes a while to respond but then moves. Her hand drifts down her body, and she squeezes her pert, heavy breast, pinching the hard peak, before dropping it to join mine.

Our joined touch sends a jolt through her body that makes her arch and tense and cry out all at once. Her nails in my hair grip, and she holds so tight as my final thrusts take us both barreling, unstoppably, to the crest of a euphoric wave all our own, *mine*. She slumps against my body, dragging in frantic breaths and shivering despite the heat. I lift her off my cock and maneuver her until she is tucked up in my embrace, molding perfectly to my body. Her expression sated and satisfied, her heavy lids struggling to open, but they do, and the smile that spreads softly across her face is breathtaking. Happy in my favourite place, and I all too easily begin to drift off.

"Fuuuuuck." Will's distant voice breaks through the haze of my climax-induced daze. I drag my eyelids open and see that he is supporting himself on unsteady legs in the corner of the shower. *So he decided to stay after all.* "Fuck!" he repeats, dragging himself upright and hitting the button to stop the water. He rests his head against the wall and takes deep breaths, making his chest swell as he slowly recovers. I take my own moment to come back to Earth before I try to move.

I shift Sam into my arms and carry her out. Will already has a warm towel and wraps it around us both.

"Definitely wouldn't be doing *that* if we stayed at Mum's." Will grins, roughly dragging a towel through his hair.

"Ya' think?" Sam can barely keep her eyes open, but she still has a little sass in her tone and the snort-laugh.

"What she doesn't know won't hurt her and this...this would kill her," I quip and stride off to our bed. I lay Sam down and climb in beside her. Will is about to climb in the other side.

"Are you staying?" I ask, and he freezes mid-climb and rolls his eyes at my curt tone.

"Yes, because if I don't, I will end up feeling like a fuck toy. I have feelings, too." His mirth has a tinge to it, and he tries sliding a little closer to Sam.

"Now who has the vagina?" I laugh but stop him snaking one arm around my fiancée.

"You do, you lucky son of a bitch." He lightly kisses Sam's shoulder and closes his eyes. Sam sighs, she nuzzles close into my side, molding her body flush to mine. I kiss the top of her head.

"Yes, I am."

"Fuck off!" I whisper grumble. A sharp pain at the top of my ear is getting fucking irritating. I squint one eye open and see Will leaning up on his elbow with a finger bent and poised to flick me again. He tilts his head and motions with his agile brows that he wants me to move. I start to curse, but Sam shuffles in my embrace, and I fall silent. She is still dead to the world, so obviously whatever Will is so fucking desperate to discuss only involves me. I slide my arms free and roll her on to her side, swapping my body for the warm pillow I was sleeping on. It's no substitute, but she coils around it all the same.

Will eases himself off the bed. I drag my boxer shorts on and stumble after him. The breaking dawn might be peeking through the blinds, but I am nowhere near done sleeping. I fail to mask my grouchy tone, but then I'm not really trying.

"What the fuck, Will?" My clipped question is masked by an exaggerated yawn. He doesn't reply until we are near the bar area of the suite and he finished pulling the rest of his clothes on.

"I have to leave, get a change of clothes before I pick you guys up later." Will keeps his voice low in a hushed whisper so I do the same, but my tone is a little more irritated.

"I would've worked that out, arse-wipe. You did not need to wake me for that earth-shattering revelation."

"Jeez, you're grumpy, and it's not because you woke up on the wrong side of the bed because you had Sam all fucking night," he quips.

"Damn right I did, and I'm grumpy because for no fucking reason you've dragged me away from that," I retort.

"Not for no reason…What was that call about last night?" His voice is no longer whispering, but is quietly serious.

I drag my hand down my face, feeling the tiredness in my brows, cheeks, and jaw, but I am fully awake now. "Put some coffee on while I grab a T-shirt, would you?"

"Sure."

The coffee machine makes a hell of a noise, but Sam doesn't stir as I sneak back into the bedroom to grab my top. Will is seated in one of the two chairs in the corner of the room overlooking the ocean now that the blinds are open wide. I blink, adjusting to the bright Florida sunshine, the sun having fully risen above the glittering calm of the endless horizon. I take the offered espresso. Looks like I'm up for the day now.

"It was James, my IT guy. He, I mean, I got another email that he tried to trace." I puff out a breath, barely containing my own frustration.

"And?"

"And jack-shit!" I snap, but shake off my anger, or its misdirection at least. "Whoever is sending this is smart enough to stay hidden. But I don't get it, because if its money, why doesn't the fucker just ask? This isn't about Sam. It is, obviously, but they contacted *me*. They want something from me. I just wish they'd fucking ask instead of all this playing games bullshit." I rub my thumb in small circles against the instant pressure pulse in my temple. Will waits a while before speaking.

"What did the email say? The new one, I mean?"

"Nice try."

"I'm just asking—" He holds his hands up, offended at my brush-off, but I wave him down and interpret.

"No, idiot. The email. It said, 'nice-try'." He tips his head in understanding, and I continue to explain, my tone choked with doubt and impotence. "I can only assume whoever it is, now knows we've got the laptop he was bouncing the email from."

"Did you get anything off of it in the end?" Will leans forward, fingertips pressed together in contemplation or prayer maybe. It seems that's what is needed…Divine intervention.

"No, it was pretty much an empty shell. James is still checking, and he's going over the old emails to see if there was something, some code, or some shit that he missed."

"You want to send it to me and I'll get my FBI flatmates to have a look?" Will offers.

"James is the best," I snap, and my tone is too harsh for his best intentions, but I put that down to the lack of sleep.

"I don't doubt that, but a fresh pair of eyes can't hurt." He holds up his hands, palms out in a show to calm my open hostility. I let out a slow breath and give a light nod. I'm just damn tired.

"No, it can't. I hate the fucking waiting though, but until the fucker lifts their scumbag head above the parapet, I can't take a proper aim. When they do, I am damn sure going to be the one to take that motherfucker out."

"Take whom out?" The soft voice from the bedroom warms and chills me in equal measure. Shit, I flash a worried glance at Will, who winces with the same dread I feel in my gut. How much did she hear? Her feet pad softly across the floor, her hair is loose and wild—a little like her, and she looks *fuck-me* gorgeous in my dress shirt and nothing else. She slips onto my lap and snuggles into my protective hold. Her voice is sleepy, and her eyelids flutter closed when she yawns. "Are we going somewhere now?"

I release the breath I seem to have held since I heard her voice, and I notice Will do the same.

"No, beautiful, not right now. Will is going home to get changed, and then he's coming back to pick us up. Late morning though right?" Will stands and walks around the small coffee table and towers close to my seat.

"Yeah, late morning. I have to check with work that it's okay to drop by and load up the Jet Skis. Maybe pack a lunch if I get time." I'm not sure if his long list is trying to gain him favour or make me feel bad, but after last night, I feel neither.

"Are you trying to avoid the walk of shame, Will? It's okay to admit it," Sam teases, tugging his trousers in a playful manner.

"No fucking shame here, darling. I'd wear a T-shirt with pictures if Jason would let me." He winks mischievously at Sam, who giggles; her whole body jiggles in my arms with mirth. Will leans down and holds her chin. I suck in a breath through my teeth and hold it for the second time this morning. He pauses millimeters from her lips when she smirks. This is like an ultra-high definition torture scene playing out right in front of me.

"You have a death wish, Will?" Sam asks calmly, but her eyes flick to mine, and Will's follow. He turns her head to face me and gently kisses her cheek.

"Just dickin' with my brother, darling." He stands and swiftly steps out of reach as I swing my clenched fist to administer the rightly deserved nut punch.

"Hey, don't be doing that." Will grabs his precious package with one hand. "You might be needing these later." He wiggles both his brows and roughly shakes his handful.

"Don't fucking count on it," I grumble, sinking my face into Sam's sweet ginger and orange blossom scented hair, inhaling my fill. Everything about this woman calms my mind and fills my soul.

"Never do, brother, never do." His wide grin is as bright as the sunlight streaming through windows. He grabs his jacket and slips out of the door, calling out, "Later," before the suction seals the door closed and silences the room.

"I like your brother." Sam looks up as I look down, her dark brown eyes impossibly large and wide, her smile breathtaking. She is absolutely flawless, seriously sexy with a surprising mix of innocence that owns my fucking heart.

"Yeah?" I lift her into my arms and walk back to the bedroom. Her lids are heavy, and her face is still crinkled with sleepiness that seems reluctant to yield its hold just yet.

"Hmm, yeah." She sighs and conforms around my body so there is no distance—none at all—and it is perfect. I kiss her hair and climb into the bed, still holding her tight to my chest.

"Me, too, beautiful, me, too." I kick the bed sheet up enough to partially cover our entwined bodies and instantly fall into a heavy sleep. *Fucking perfect.*

SIXTEEN

Sam

I am so damn excited. Jason let me ride shotgun in Will's jeep, and we just pulled up to where Will is going to be working starting next month. A single story modern office block set back from the main road on the edge of town. Don't get me wrong; it's completely horrific and disgusting that people deal and trade these precious exotic animals. But today, I get an up close and personal visit with a two-month-old white Siberian tiger cub, and that is something that just doesn't happen, so I am off the charts giddy. Jason and I sign in, and Will gives us a brief tour of the fairly standard offices: one large open room with too many desks for the space, an old drink machine in the far corner, and a very sad looking potted palm tree by the main door. Very different from Jason's elegant office overlooking the Thames, but Will beams with pride, and there is certainly no hint of jealousy between the two on a professional level, or any level for that matter.

There is a small kitchen, a conference room, and two small private interview rooms, and we poke our heads in before Will leads us into a large open backyard with a variety of small caged pens.

Most are very basic, but some have dug-out pools. Will explains is mostly for the Crocs and Alligators, but today, they are empty of water and prehistoric man-eaters. The pen at the far end is much larger and has a cozy-looking kennel with several blankets scattered all around. There are colourful toys strewn, balls, chewed up rope pulls, and a sagging fluffy bear draped half in and half out of the kennel, effectively blocking the entrance. I gasp as we get close enough to see the saggy bear is actually the fluffy bundle of white and grey fur of the baby tiger, dead to the world in the midday heat. Will goes to open the door to the enclosure.

"No, don't wake him!" I grab Will's arm, and he turns back with a confused look on his face. "He's a baby. Don't wake him just for me. If he wakes while we're here, that's different, but if he doesn't, I'm happy just to be this close." I keep my urgent plea in a soft, hushed tone, but I fix my steely glare on Will so there is no misunderstanding.

"Really?" Will screws up his face, incredulous at my comment.

"Really!" I emphasize my commitment with a sharp nod of my head. "No one really likes being woken up, Will." I crouch down on my haunches to get a closer look.

"Ain't that the truth," Jason chides, punching Will in his arm. They both stand behind me chatting, but I am engrossed with the little fella asleep just inches away from me. Tiny round ears peek out of the mass of white fluff, twitching occasionally with unseen disturbances. The stripes on his head are closer together, dark and more defined than those on his body. His paws stretching out in front of him, on the end of his little legs, are disproportionately large, giving a telltale indication of how big he is going to get. I look back up at Will.

"He's got a proper home, right?" My voice is still soft, so Will leans in to hear me.

"Yeah, darling, he's off to a big cat reserve and rescue center." He smiles softly at me, and I notice his lips carve a bigger curve when they check out the cutest cub ever.

"Do you get many cases like this?" I can't hide the sadness in my voice. This little fella is just a baby.

"We get enough." His somber tone speaks volumes, and I turn back to stare at the adorable creature still napping. I sit there transfixed until my bum starts to get numb.

"Are you sure you don't want me to give him a prod? Kinda feels like a waste of time," Will mutters as Jason helps me to my feet.

"No, I do not want you to give him a prod." I roll my eyes, and he has the decency to look a little apologetic.

"Okay, if you have finished gawking and really don't want me to wake him, let's head out to the lake. I've packed some food, but it's nothing fancy. I made some rolls, got some fried chicken, brats, chips, and beer." He beams and pats his very flat, fit tummy. "Oh, and watermelon," he adds a little louder, making me jump. His grin widens as he mentally checks off his lunch list, satisfied he has remembered everything.

"Sounds perfect. I'm starving," I gush and slip my arm around Jason's waist and through Will's arm. "Is it far to the lake? I wasn't joking, I will need feeding ASAP."

"It's about an hour drive, but I suppose I could let you have a roll to tide you over," Will muses.

"You are too kind. Unlike your brother, who made me skip breakfast," I remark with a little attitude and a lot of sass.

"That's harsh," Will goads, his tone filled with mock sympathy.

"Isn't it though?" I sigh, wearing my wounded self in the full curl of my pushed out bottom lip, sad doe eyes, and clutching my aching heart, all very melodramatic. A low grumbling sound rumbles from Jason's chest.

"I believe I told you exactly how much time we had until we needed to leave, and I believe I even offered to order room service, which you declined." His tone is stern and reprimanding, but tinged with humour. "Care to tell Will why you declined?" I shake my head and bite my lips into a tight, thin line to stop from smirking. "No? Care to tell Will what you chose to have instead of breakfast?" He fixes me with his dark brown eyes that scorch a path straight to my memory bank and alight my blood like a wild fire, melting my core and leaving me a liquid mess of wantonness.

"I didn't think you were serious," I mutter, but my defense is very weak and the timbre of his voice drops to a deep and serious rumble.

"What on earth gave you the idea I *wouldn't* be serious about making you come...again?" His tone is light but holds that erotic undertone that makes me tingle in all the right places.

"Not a single thing and I'd happily forgo my morning muffin for my muff —" I am cut off mid *overshare.*

"Yeah, all right, guys, I get the picture. In fact, I'm getting the IMAX version and these shorts are not up to hiding the aftermath of this conversation, so zip it." Will jumps in with his rushed interruption. "And I still have to show my face here, and I'm kinda like Jason in mixing work and pleasure." He flashes me a scowl that darkens his features for a moment.

"Sorry." I beam my widest, most innocent smile, which makes his face crack with a loud belly laugh.

"Tell me another, why don't you, because that is not the face of contrition." His face tries to hold a modicum of seriousness, but it's tentative at best.

"Oh, Will, what big words you use! Someone else who is not afraid of a mouthful, hmm?" I drag my bottom lip in slowly, and he freezes for a second before he catches himself and shakes his head at the lost cause that is me and strides off in front.

"You can't help yourself, can you?" Jason leans down, snickering at his flustered brother, who is not so discretely adjusting his flimsy shorts.

"I really can't." I giggle as Jason pulls me tighter into his side now that his brother has stormed ahead, eager to leave his place of work and take refuge in his Jeep.

"Behave. You might want to cut back on the teasing, though, because I have no intention of sharing you again so soon," Jason states as a matter of fact. He looks into my eyes for something, maybe a reaction, I'm not sure, but I am more than fine with his statement. This thing we have, this thing we *do*, may be my ultimate fantasy, but it's only fun if it's fun for him, too. He has to be completely happy, so I am more than happy to follow his lead—on this, at least.

"I only do it when he's getting you all riled up. It seems only fair," I clarify my position with a light pitch and drop of my shoulders.

"Ah, beautiful, that's sweet, but I can handle my brother." He taps my nose, and I can't help myself; it's too damn easy.

"So can—" I snap my mouth shut mid-taunt at the instant cloud distorting his handsome face and the scary draw of his dark brows. I puff out a petulant breath of air. "Fine," I huff as we reach the car. Will is already seated in the front, and Jason opens the door for me. "You're no fun," I mutter but slide into the back seat on my own.

"That's not what you said this morning." He slams the door before I can retort or most likely agree.

The drive down to the lake seems to take no time at all, and I spend most of the journey with my head resting on my arm, hanging half out of the window. Letting the warm sun saturate my skin and the wind whip so hard, I have to close my eyes, even behind my sunglasses. We turn off the highway and head inland and then hit a dirt track that leads almost to the edge of a stunning lake. Will backs his Jeep and trailer onto the slipway next to the jetty, and Jason and I unpack the supplies. Gorgeous soft sand surrounds the lake, from the water's edge right to the trees that offer some much needed shade. But looking around, you could be forgiven for thinking you were at the ocean with the expanse of water and no sight of the opposite shore line. Kids off in the distance are squealing in the water, motorboats racing in the distance, and there is a waft of burgers cooking on portable barbecues. But there is no cooling salt-laden sea breeze licking my skin. The air here is hot, probably not for a local, but certainly for a Brit in February.

We unload and set up a cute mini camp, close to the water, but secluded enough from the throngs of families, almost private. By the time we have finished though, I am no longer hungry, but I am a ball of sweat and desperately need a dip in that nice cool lake. I peel my thin sweater over my head and shimmy out of my loose jeans, kicking my Vans off as I do. Jason and Will freeze and stare, jaws dropped so wide they look hysterical.

"Do I have something in my teeth?" I drop one hip and quirk my lips, hiding my knowing smile. The bikini I was hiding under my clothes is super cute, white crochet, with string ties and tiny crystal beads sewn in the material, which catch and reflect the sunlight. But it is teeny tiny, so I know it's not the sparkles that have caught their attention. Jason drops the case of beer, narrowly missing his brother's foot, and strides over to me, hauling his T-shirt over his head as he goes. I see the look of determination in his eye, so before he gets too close, I spin on my toes and dart into the water. Two ungainly hop-steps and I am deep enough to spring forward into a dive and submerge myself in the crystal clear and not surprisingly, cold water. I gasp when I surface—shit, that's freezing. I start to swim just to warm up and possibly to allow that mountain of furious male on the shore time to cool down.

I call out. "I'm not coming back in until you stop clenching your jaw and put your clothes back on."

"You better be a strong swimmer then because I was going to say the same," he yells back in a grouchy grumble and folds his arms over his naked chest, all hard lines and soft tan. His forearms are pumped with tension, and the muscles swell to that delicious taut roundness that I just want to sink my teeth into. He's so damn sexy when he's mad. I quite like him mad. I splash a wave toward him, blow him a cheeky kiss, and swim off.

My legs start to ache after my second large loop of this little area of the lake, and I head back into the shore. I have cooled down and warmed up. I near the edge of the lake and notice that Jason is still standing there with his T-shirt in his hand; he hasn't so much cooled down, as stewed. I find my footing on the sandy lakebed and stand; the excess water glides down my body, and the air chills my skin. Jason's eyes are pretty much the size of saucers as they drag slowly up my body. I peek down; my bikini is lined, so I know it's not translucent like white swimwear can be, but it is now slick to my rather perky body.

"Jesus Christ," Jason seems to say without moving his lips, but then I realise it's Will's voice. Jason's lips are fixed in a strained grimace. I smile my widest and lean up to kiss him as soon as I am close enough.

"Calm down, caveman, it's just a pair of tits." I chuckle.

"Wrong. It's *my* pair of tits." He reluctantly returns my kiss, his full but dry lips slide against my wet ones, and he releases a soft groan. With stealth like efficiency, he quickly dresses me in his T-shirt that swamps me and hangs to just below my knees. I roll my eyes, but accept his chivalrous offer to protect my modesty.

"And this is mine, but you don't see me hiding you away. Quite the opposite. Everyone can gawk all they want, because I love that it is *all* they can do. Because all *this*—" I crawl all my fingers up his torso and link my hands together once they are around his neck. "*This* is all mine."

"Damn right, beautiful. It's not that I don't understand where you're coming from, but we're gonna agree to disagree on this one." He grabs my arse cheeks roughly in each of his sizeable hands and lifts me high. I wrap my legs around his waist and he carries me back to our picnic spot. "And I'm not hiding you, I'm protecting."

"You know I'm quite capable—" My objection is interrupted by a low growl.

"I know you are, beautiful, but I wasn't talking about you." He nods over to the jetty where a group of young lads are hanging off the side of a speedboat. "I'd rather spend the week with you than in a cell explaining why I beat the crap out of some horny teenagers."

"Careful there, brother, I didn't pack enough plasters for your knuckle-dragging activities," Will teases, and I snicker.

"Laugh it up, Will, but you'll be exactly the same when you find someone like Sam." Jason's voice drops to a soft whisper, and his eyes fix on mine with absolute adoration that makes my chest ache.

"There *is* no one like Sam," Will states, but when I flash a glance his way, he turns away, and I miss his expression.

"Ah, guys, you'll make me blush," I mock sweetly, jumping down from Jason's hold.

"That makes you blush, never mind being all wet and naked," he scoffs.

"I'm not naked." I sigh, exasperated.

"Semantics. You *look* naked," Jason grumbles, stubbornly hanging on to his grouchy mood.

"Yeah, she does." Will grins.

"Fine, I look naked. I'm not naked though, and just as this conversation is now wearing on my last nerve, I am in fact wearing *your* T-shirt, so unless you want me to take it off, let's just eat." I flop down in an angry flounce, cross my legs, and fold my arms.

Jason lowers himself beside me and tentatively rolls to sit a little closer. He leans over, and with a hushed, calming tone, starts to speak.

"It's just—"

"Nah-ah!" I interrupt and hold my finger against his lips in case he feels inclined to continue to explain. With my other hand, I make the universal sign of lock your lips and throw that motherfucking key away. "Agree to disagree." He nods and opens his mouth wide capturing my finger in one swift grab. He holds it between his teeth and swirls his scorching tongue around the captured digit before slowly releasing it in a seductive reverse pull of his lips.

"Hungry?" That tone is temptation from the devil himself, and all I can manage in response is a strangled whimper and a lot more liquid pooling in my bikini bottoms.

I thought Will had packed enough food for an army when it was all finally laid out on the picnic table. But, after an hour of picking at the variety of dishes and drinking beer, we have collectively decimated the feast. All that is left is a few sad-looking watermelon slices and more beer, and until we've been out on the skis, I'm the only one drinking.

"You fancy a spin round the lake then?" Will sucks his fingers clean from the last of the fried chicken.

"Do I get to drive?" I ask excitedly but am shot down in stereo.

"No!"

"Well, unless you want a visual recap of my lunch, I would suggest giving me an hour. You two go get all that showboating shit out of the way." I wave them off.

"You sure?" Jason frowns, but Will is already walking to the jetty and Jason is half turned, clearly eager to ride.

"Very sure. If I go now, the first wave we hit, you'll be wearing that very lovely lunch I've just eaten, and believe me, it won't look quite so appetising all over your back." I stick my tongue out as if my explanation needed further clarification.

"Thanks for the visual." He wrinkles his nose and laughs.

"You're welcome." I swipe a blanket from the top of the cooler box and go to lie in the sun. My British body may be in shock at being exposed this time of year, but I am going to make the most of the Florida sunshine. I yank Jason's T-shirt over my head and watch his eyes narrow and his lips thin. Ignoring the rising levels of testosterone, which seems to correlate with my skin exposure, I screw the material up to fashion a makeshift pillow and lie down. I pull my shades from the top of my head over my eyes, sink into the soft fibres of the blanket, and bask. Bliss.

"Ahhh!" I scream and wildly flail my arms, but the damage is done.

Drenched, I jump bolt upright from utter shock that instantly turns to blind rage. "What the fuck! You fucking…fuckity, fucking arsehole!" I shake off the excess, freezing cold water and angrily snatch the towel that Will is holding out to me at arm's length. *Very smart.*

"I told you she wouldn't find it funny." Will wisely steps back.

"No, *she* doesn't find it fucking funny. I was asleep, you shithead." I roughly dry my stomach and legs. My head snaps up to Jason's uncontrollable belly laughs. He waves his hand slowly up and down, and I find my blood boiling. If he's going to say what I think he's going to say…

"It's just a bit of water, calm your tits." I notice Will wince and brace, but it isn't him that needs to brace. I push off like an Olympic sprinter on the start block and fly my full body weight and considerable momentum into Jason's middle. Utterly shocked and wholly unprepared for my surprise attack, Jason falls flat on his back and grunts as I knock the wind right out of him. I quickly try to fortify my position and as strong as I am, my attempt to pin him to the ground is laughable. And he does laugh, but only once. He instantly has me flipped, and our positions are reversed, then he continues to laugh and laugh and laugh. I am so fucking mad. I don't know why I was mad in the first place but, boy, that smug grin makes me pine so hard for my trusty bullwhip.

"Wishing you had your tool bag, beautiful?" His eyes sparkle with mischief, and he flicks his head to move the hairs of his damp fringe that are obscuring his view. Although why he needs a perfect view when he can so clearly read my mind, I'm not sure.

"Something like that," I grate out through gritted teeth, bucking wildly beneath his immovable frame.

"Would you just—"

"If you tell me to calm down one more time, I swear to fucking god—"

"Well, would you maybe stop wriggling, at least, you're making me hard." He snickers, and I lose it. I lift my hips with strength I didn't know I had and knock him off balance, enough to swipe my elbow wide and whack him in the side. I twist and scramble away, but he snatches my ankle and hauls me back. As I fight his capture, and we tumble and tussle together rolling, grabbing, and each struggling to gain the upper hand, something changes. We both feel it, because it's like a fucking tsunami of pure unadulterated lust. I've never actually fought anyone, not like this, and by the wild and wanton look in Jason's eyes, I'm not sure he has. He holds his face inches from mine, but his body covers mine, his weight and power absolute. I let out a stuttered breath, but not because of his heavy frame crushing me, because I can't breathe from want so raw…so primal.

"Sam?" Jason's voice is low and tentative. He must know this should have triggers flying left and right for me, but it doesn't…not at all…not with him.

"Can we do this again?" My voice a breathy plea, my mouth is bone dry, and my tongue has little success at moistening my lips, but I drag it along my lips all the same.

"Fuck, yes." He crushes his mouth to mine, owning my words, my thoughts, *owning me*.

"Ahem." I hear Will's exaggerated cough, but only after the third maybe fourth attempt does Jason relinquish my lips and slowly turn his head to his brother. "Um, public place, guys. I take it we are done for the day?"

"No!" I yell. Jason flinches because his head had turned but hadn't moved away and his ear was right where my mouth is. "No, I want to have a go on the Jet Ski," I repeat, but this time with my indoor voice. Jason lightly kisses my nose.

"Your wish is my command." He pulls himself to his feet with me in his arms and carefully places me on my feet, but keeps me wrapped in a tight embrace.

"Oh, I do hope so," I whisper back and feel him shudder at my words.

I know he can't hear my squeals of terror and joy over the roar of the engine and thump, thump of the ski as it drops against the endless waves that he and Will are creating and circling back on. But my throat is hoarse from yelling, and my fingers are numb from gripping so tight. *This is so much fun.*

We have raced the length of the lake several times and messed about for ages in the heat of the afternoon, but I don't want it to end. Every time Jason asks if I've had enough, I grin like a kid on Christmas morning and shake my head. I unclip the front of my life jacket because Jason did it a little tight, and I am seriously hot, but I keep it pulled close and press against Jason's back. Will is tucked in behind us, riding our wake, but I only chance the odd glance back over my shoulder because even the slightest movement tips the balance of the ski, and we wobble, or at least I feel that we do.

We hit a massive wave created by arsehole behaviour from the young guys in the speedboat racing too close. Jason yells *motherfuckers*, and we hit another crest, but this time it is on a sharp turn, and I lose my grip and am thrown high off the back. I know it probably happened in a split second, but the next few events seem to play in front of me like I am standing just outside of them, breath held, hoping it won't play out quite like it's going to.

I tumble in the air, spray and white angry water swirls below me, and my scream is sucked back as I snap my mouth shut preparing for the water. It doesn't come, not when I expect it. My head smashes against the hard yellow rim of Will's Jet Ski, but I feel the slice more than the impact. I hit the water before I can dwell on what that means. I think I gasp for air or cry out, but my lungs are burning to breathe, and the weight of the water is crushing me. My head feels heavy, my legs, arms…the hairs on my arms; everything is so very, very heavy. My eyelids are the worst; they must be bleeding from the weight because all I can see is red…so much red.

SEVENTEEN

Jason

The longest forty-eight hours of my life. No, wait, Sam was drugged and kidnapped, and I couldn't find her...that was the worst. But sitting beside her bed while she is in an induced coma because of the swelling on her brain comes a pretty fucking close second.

"Here, drink this." Will holds a grey liquid that I suppose is coffee by the aroma assaulting my nose. I shake my head, but he lifts it close to my face and holds it there until I take the damn cup.

"How's the wife?" Will raises a brow and sits in the chair beside me. His comment makes my lips twitch; I fail to form an actual smile, but the intention is there.

"Semantics, brother...she's gonna be my wife and the sooner the better." My eyelids close briefly. It hurts to see her like this, but it's agony to tear my eyes away. "I was not putting that fucker Leon's name down as next of kin one more time. She's mine," I grit out through a clenched jaw, my frustration and fear morphing into impotent rage.

"I get it." He places his heavy hand on my shoulder and rests it there. "So how's she doing?"

"They did a scan this morning, and the swelling's gone down. The doctors were pleased, and they stopped the drugs keeping her in the coma a few hours ago. It's now just a case of waiting until she wakes up." I let out a long slow breath, failing to hide the fear those words hold. His hand squeezes tight on my solid, tense shoulder muscle.

"Is there any damage? Will she be okay?" His voice catches, and that causes a pain through my chest that makes me double over. *Fuck, this is killing me.* "Shit, sorry, Jason. I didn't mean...shit." He lets out a stuttered breath, and the room falls silent. We are both silent; Sam is silent. Only the machines that monitor her life are screaming an unbearable sound to my ears. *Nails down a chalkboard.*

Will takes my full cup of cold coffee and mutters something about getting a fresh brew and something to eat. My stomach groans at the mention of food but churns with sickness at the thought of actually eating. Nurses and doctors come and go, kind words of comfort barely register, but I manage to nod my appreciation. I hold her warm hand and talk to her as if we are alone. I whisper, recalling our erotic playtime. I tease and make sinful threats, hoping my words will bring a flush of colour to her cheeks, as they do to the few nurses close enough to hear what I'm actually saying. "Dammit, Sam, it's been hours. Wake-up!" I drop my head and growl out in frustration. My angry tone fills the vacuum of desolation and hangs heavy in the air. *Nothing.*

"Jason." Will calls behind me, but I don't have the strength to lift my head.

"Hmm?" I stretch my neck to the side and wait for the pop, so much tension even my bones ache.

"Jason." His tone is urgent, and my nerves are that frayed that I snap my head round and shout.

"What?" I scowl at his wide eyes and open mouth. I take a moment to register his stare is fixed over my shoulder. My head twists back sharply to see what has him speechless. Those eyes…those beautiful, soul-stirring eyes are smiling at me. I stand and step close, still holding her hand. My other cups her face. I can't breathe.

"Hey." Her voice is croaky, but her lips spread wide. Her eyes are fixed on me, and I join her sweet smile. I let out a strange strangled sound that is a mix of utter relief and happiness, a laugh and gasp all in one. My lips fall to her forehead, and I close my eyes and breathe her in. The clinical covering of antiseptic masks her scent, but I can still find her essence in the breath I draw deep into my lungs. I pull back and cover her mouth. Her monitors instantly bleep a discord of their disapproval to my kiss, and I couldn't care less. This is fucking heaven because for the first time in nearly three days, my girl kisses me back.

"Mr. Sinclair, would you please step back." The nurse that has been mostly in charge tries to pry me away, but I won't be moved. She huffs and manages to squeeze in between the bed and me, but I am right at her side. I let her because she's checking shit, but I'm not letting go—not now—*not ever.*

"How are you feeling, honey?" The nurse asks Sam after taking a note of all her vitals.

"Tired." Sam gives a tentative smile that lights up my world.

"Well, you're in the best place. So get as much rest as you need." She steps away and walks around to the other side of the bed to fiddle with and take notes from the various machines still attached to Sam. She clutches the clipboard to her chest and starts to leave at the same time the doctor enters the room. I look over to see Will still standing in the doorway, but he is now sporting a wide grin filled with utter relief and joy. *Snap.*

"Mrs. Sinclair, good to have you back." The elderly Swedish doctor beams at Sam, and seems genuinely pleased and not at all surprised, which is a comfort.

"Mrs. what? I'm married?" Sam's face registers confusion, her voice piqued with shock. I cringe.

"Yes, Mrs. Sinclair, you are married. Your husband hasn't left your side for a moment, he has talked to you the whole time you've been asleep." The doctor takes the chart from the nurse and falls silent as he reads the new information.

"Boy, did he." The nurse behind me breathes out in a whisper that makes me chuckle. Sam tries to pull her hand free, but I squeeze a little tighter, not ready to relinquish my hold. Her brows knit together and she fidgets; she looks uncomfortable.

"What is it, beautiful? Are you in pain? Can I get you anything?" I ask softly.

"I...I don't know. I don't remember." Her eyes glaze with water, but before I can reassure her that this is an administrative issue, the doctor interrupts asking her name, and my whole world implodes with her reply.

"Grace," her voice waivers. "My name is Grace Cartwright." As much as I feel like I have been hit with a fucking anvil in my chest, *she* looks so much worse. Colour drains from her face and fat tears roll down her cheek. I squeeze her hand, and her eyes meet mine. That look nearly breaks me, so unbearably sad, vulnerable, lost. *My girl is lost.*

"Is that wrong?" She roughly dries her cheek; her tone flips from uncertain to sharp and irritated.

"No beautiful, that's not wrong." My voice is soothing, my thumb brushes her wrist, but even I can feel her pulse jump erratically beneath the skin. I turn to the doctor.

"Would you give us a moment?"

"We need to do more tests, Mr. Sinclair." He tries to argue, but I stand up to my full and not inconsiderable height. I am effectively blocking him from even seeing Sam, let alone getting close enough to administer more investigations.

"Just one moment," I state, brooking no other response. The doctor nods and leaves the room with the nurse. Will still hovers, and honestly, I don't mind that he is there, but Sam looks over to the door and back to me as if waiting for me to finish clearing the room. I turn, but Will has already taken the hint. The door closes, and it's just us. I should be elated, but I am suddenly terrified. The last time she was Grace was over ten years ago, before me, before The Club and Mistress Selina, before Leon even. I have no idea who Grace was, but I doubt she'd love a kinky fucker like me. *One step at a time.*

I sit on the edge of the bed, and she shuffles to face me but also moves a little further away, confusion etched on her face. *Fuck this.* I climb onto the space she's made, clearly aware that wasn't her intention when making it, but I settle back and pull her half onto my body. Tugging her arm to rest across my stomach, I gently press her head to rest on my chest. I finally tuck her limp hair away from her face and cup my hand around her jaw and hold her to look directly up at me, no escape.

"Hey, beautiful," I whisper, and my heart clenches when her lips carve the most amazing smile across her face. *Score one.* I don't care if she's remembered that is the name I call her all the time or not, it's made her smile, and I'll take that.

"Hey," her smile doesn't quite reach her eyes, and she lets out a sad stuttered breath.

"Hey, it's okay." I kiss her forehead and hold her close. I can feel her tremble and break with sobs. My shirt dampens under her head and I just hold her for endless minutes until she's ready. I soothe and hum, stroke her back and squeeze her as tight as her injuries will allow.

"I don't remember getting married." She lifts her head and her sad eyes almost break my heart.

"That's understandable since you aren't married." I keep my tone soothing but her brows shoot up with shock all the same.

"What?" Her face screws up with confusion and tension that I can feel radiate through her body.

"What do you remember?"

"Jason, I don't understand. What do you mean I'm not married? The doctor said Mrs. Sinclair, what—"

I cut any further questions as I instantly scoot down and cover her mouth with mine, my tongue forcing an easy path between her soft lips and diving in to taste her again, my Sam. Urgent kisses, tongues dancing, no…duelling as I feel her come back to me. She breaks the kiss, breathless and on fire. Her face glows, her eyes pierce mine, her hand fists my shirt, and she pulls me back for another kiss. *Fuck, yes.* She moans into my mouth, and her hand drifts from my waist to my pants. Her fingers curl over the waistband, and I can feel my cock strain behind the material to try and make contact with that light touch. My hand, the traitor that it is, rests over hers and prevents this situation from deteriorating out of my limited self-control.

"Sam," I warn, my voice a low, friendly grumble. Her eyes flick to mine, and I can see the cogs turning, processing, as her brow furrows, and she takes her time to pick through the fog that must be her memory.

"We are getting married, though?" She purses her lips in a playful pout, and I let out three days of anxiety and fear in a loud liberating laugh.

"Yes, beautiful, we're getting married." I plant an aggressive closed mouth kiss on her lips. "I told the hospital we were married because I am still not your next of kin, and when they brought you in, there was no fucking way I was going to give them the opportunity to deny me access."

"Oh." She nods slowly. "Leon is my next of kin."

"Yep, but not for long, and after the last three days, the sooner the fucking better," I grumble.

"Such a romantic...what happened to me having my dream wedding?" she teases.

"It will still be a dream wedding, but you will just have to step up the date that's all." I poke the end of her nose. A cute set of wrinkles appears on the bridge as she scrunches her face. "So what do you remember?"

"Red and water...we went to the lake with...is Will all right?" She looks over at the door as if he is still standing there.

"Will is fine—just worried, that's all. But he got the air ambulance to you in record time. You lost a lot of blood, your head was a fucking mess, but they patched you up quick and *that* definitely saved your life." I struggle to swallow the lump in my throat and watch her eyes register my nightmare. Her hand presses against my cheek, and I lean into her touch. *So damn grateful.* My eyelids close, and I savour her touch, her warmth. That time waiting for the ambulance, watching the life literally drain from her body I don't ever want to replay. The scar will heal, and she is back, but that nightmare will be forever etched in my brain.

"It was bad?" she asks when I open my eyes.

"The worst, beautiful. I thought I'd lost you when you went under like a fucking stone, and there was so much blood, you turned the lake red." I kiss the single tear tracking its way down her cheek. The salty water so sweet on my lips. *Mine.*

"Water and red," she repeats softly.

"But 'Grace' nearly gave me a heart attack." I'm deadly serious, but my face is a picture of relief and joy.

"Grace?" She sniffs and flashes a knowing grin. "Ah, yes, that *would* be a worry, not sure why I recalled that name, but having to teach her all of Sam and Selina's tricks would've at least been interesting."

"If she wanted to be taught. She might not like this kinky fucker as much as you do." I raise a perfectly valid point with a raised brow. She bites back a sensual smirk.

"Oh, she'd love this kinky fucker almost as much as I do." She tilts her head as an open invitation to kiss, consume, devour. R.S.V.P Abso-fucking-lutely

The next day Sam undergoes more test and endless questions, which establish she hasn't actually lost any memory, but the severity of the head injury and risk of repeat swelling on the brain means under medical advisement she shouldn't fly home for at least a fortnight.

"I can stay at the hotel, I will be fine," Sam argues for the umpteenth time. I hate that I will have to return to the UK without her. It's out of my hands with Daniel on paternity leave. This trip was only ever supposed to be a few days.

"I'll get a nurse to look after you." My angry tone is a reflection of my frustration. I have back-to-back meetings all week, or I would work from here dammit

"Oh, make sure he's really hot, would you." She grins, and that wicked smile is enough of a distraction.

"Cute." I narrow my eyes, and she sticks out her tongue. "If you're well enough to be waving that thing around, then I have just the place to put it to proper use." Her eyes sparkle, and I swear my cock groans.

"*I* never said I wasn't well enough." She licks her lips and kneels up on the bed almost as eager as I am but slouches back when the doctor enters the room, followed by Will.

"How are you feeling today, Sam?" Dr. Eriksson asks brightly.

"Well enough for anything, doctor." She swipes her lip wet with a flash of her tongue, winks at me, and bites her smirk back when I scowl. She'll pay for that.

"Good. Your tests are fine, and I understand you've agreed not to fly back to the UK just yet. I really think it is for the best." She nods but doesn't look happy. That makes two of us. "Do you know where you will be staying? Do you have family here?"

"She does," Will answers. "She can stay with me. I have some time owed from work, so I can take care of her too." The muscles in my neck tighten at this news. It might be perfect, but it's the first I've heard of it, and I don't like to be kept in the dark.

"She's not staying in your fuc— your shared apartment, Will." I correct myself, but he knows what I meant to say.

"She won't be. I'm house-sitting for my boss. He has a place just down the coast. It's a beautiful beach house, private, and perfect for resting. She'll be fine. I promise to take care of her," he adds, but I know he will, I just hate that he can when I can't.

"*She* would quite like a say in this," Sam huffs, and we all turn to face her and wait quietly for what she has to say. "That sounds lovely, Will, but you don't have to babysit. I will be fine reading and whatnot in the daytime. I'll most likely sleep all day."

"Yes, he does, or it's the nurse. I'll let you make that choice, but you are not staying home alone after a head injury," I answer for Will, who will soon share my frustration at herding cats—or getting Sam to do as she's told.

"Fine. There probably isn't a nurse as sexy as he is anyway." She snickers at my sudden frown.

"You're so funny this morning. Just remember it's your head that's injured, not your arse." Her face colours a fantastic shade of red and my palm twitches to match that colour on said arse cheek.

"I can't believe you just said that!" She slaps her hand over her mouth in shock, but the good doctor barely looks up from his clipboard. Will snickers, and I let out a deep belly laugh at her mortification.

"Okay, then." The doctor hands over his clipboard. "If you can sign these discharge papers, and wait for the nurse to bring you your meds, you are free to go." He holds out his hand and Sam shakes it, as do Will and I. They have all been amazing, and I happily tell them as much.

Sam is sitting on the bed with Will one side and me the other when a young nurse we haven't seen before bounds into the room with two large paper bags. She skids to a comical stop when her eyes flick wildly between Will and I. Sam groans and rolls her eyes. I shrug and flash a killer smile at the nurse that makes her jaw go slack.

"Jeez," Sam mutters with justified exasperation. Sometimes, I can't help myself. "Are those for me?" Sam holds out her hand, and the nurse snaps her mouth shut and offers a shy smile.

"Oh, yes, sorry. These are for pain, but only if you need them, and they are obviously safe to take in your condition." I take the bag from Sam's hand and pass it straight to Will to carry. "And these are your antenatal vitamins." I reach to do the same with the next bag, but my hands freezes mid-air and all air leaves my lungs in a puff.

"What?" Three voices of varying pitch and panic have the poor nurse looking like a deer in the headlights.

Not quite…The End

THE DISGRACE TRILOGY, BOOK THREE

DEE PALMER

DEDICATION

My Diva's
You know who you are and hopefully, by now, you know how important you are
to me.
You Rock My World

ONE

Jason

The nurse hesitates, only to hurriedly repeat her statement to the three dumbstruck faces gawping at her. "I...um...prenatal vitamins... Congratulations!" The perkiness in her voice disintegrates when she takes in the utter shock on all our faces. "Maybe I should get the doctor?" she mutters with a forced, tight smile.

"Yeah, maybe you should?" I snap, and Sam turns to look at me. My face must match hers for confusion, but I have too much shit swirling in my head to give her anything other than a dismissive shrug. Moments later, the doctor hurries into the room, red-faced, and looking anxious. I know that feeling.

"I'm so sorry, Ms Bonfleur. I thought someone had gone over the results with you." The doctor keeps flicking through his folder of notes, as if by some fucking miracle that will stop this free fall.

"The results for my head injury, yes. The result that means I need to be leaving here with prenatal vitamins, no!" Her voice rises with each word and I place a calming hand on her thigh even if it does nothing to sooth either one of us, her face softens with the gesture.

"Yes, sorry...I'm really sorry that no one told you. However, you are pregnant. The baby is fine. We did tests and scans. Oh I am so, so—"

"Please don't say you're sorry again." I grit out with a tight jaw. "How pregnant?" My curt tone seems to shock him and Sam. She flinches beside me, a puzzled look fixed on her face.

"Excuse me?" The doctors stutters, so I clarify for him, Sam and Will.

"Are we talking days?" *Will and I could both be the father.* "Weeks?" *Would make it just me.* "Or months?" *Would be my worst fucking nightmare.* My clinical cold delivery is heard loud and clear.

"Oh I see, weeks. We only picked it up on the further tests we ran. It's very early days." The doctor beams for a full second before his face falls blank when no one reciprocates his enthusiasm.

"All right. Everyone out." Sam stands abruptly and pushes the doctor and nurse from the room. "And you." She points to Will who looks to me for guidance. "I said out!" I don't get the chance to agree with Sam, but I would've. We need to talk. Alone.

She shuts the door and folds her arms, closes herself off, as hostility seeps from every pore. I hold up my hands in a defenceless gesture.

"What?" I ask.

"What do you mean *what*?" she practically snarls, her jaw tense. If her eyes could bore holes, I would be Swiss cheese right now.

"Hey beautiful, don't look at me like that. This has blindsided us both. We haven't exactly had the kids conversation, not seriously. If we had, I don't think I would've had to express that I'd want to know for sure the baby is mine. I wouldn't think I'd have to."

"So you wouldn't want me to keep the baby if it wasn't one hundred percent yours, is that what you're saying?" Her voice is quiet and tinged with menace. I can see the hurt and fury fighting for dominance in her piercing eyes. *This doesn't have to be a fight.* I let out a steady breath and try my best to explain and diffuse this ticking bomb in front of me.

"No, that's not what I'm saying, honestly. You have to know that I'm a possessive son of a bitch and having another man's kid would be a problem for me. I struggle with your relationship with Leon as it is, let alone you sharing an unbreakable bond with the father of your child who wasn't me." I can feel my own frustration rise with the pitch of my voice, and I drag in a steadying breath then run my hand through my hair to buy myself some much-needed, calming seconds before I continue. "I'm sorry if that makes me a selfish fucker, I make no apology for that. I'm a selfish fucker when it comes to you." Her arms drop to her sides, and she lets out a breath she was clearly holding. I step toward her. "All I'm saying is, with you being a few weeks pregnant, we dodged a bullet."

"Dodged a bullet? I'm pregnant, Jason." She shakes her head, dropping it to her chest.

"Yeah, you are…with *my* baby." I step up flush to her body and wrap her in my most protective embrace.

"I should tell you that…" Her voice catches, and I scoop her into my arms and sit on the bed. "After Richard… after I lost the baby from what he did, I mean…. It's just, there was a lot of internal scarring and trauma. I saw a specialist when I was twenty because I had some intermittent bleeding. Anyway, he said I could experience difficulty getting pregnant, and if I did manage it, I might never carry the baby to term. There is a really high risk I will miscarry, Jason. I just thought I should tell you, don't get your hopes up."

"So this little bundle of cells is a miracle then, hmm?" I place my hand on her tummy, and her breath catches for a much better reason: joy. It illuminates her face, and her smile lights my world.

"I guess." Her hand covers mine, and I lean in to steal the kiss that is yet to be offered. She smiles shyly when I release her lips.

"Now you're pregnant, I better make an honest woman of you sooner rather than later, or my mum will definitely kill me," I tease and kiss the tip of her nose.

"I'm not marrying you to please your mum, Jason." She purses her lips.

"No. You will marry me to please *me*." I correct.

"I will." A slow curve tips the edges of her lips into a soft smile.

"I think you mean 'I do'."

I watch her bite her lip and her brow furrow with irritation when I insist on carrying her into the hotel, through the grand lobby entrance and straight to the elevators. I hear people comment as we pass, sighing and cooing, with the word newlyweds being muttered. *I wish.*

"You know, I can walk, Jason." She wastes her breath with one more futile attempt to convince me she's fine. She may be feisty fit, but she's far from one hundred percent, and the fact that she has to stay Stateside until she gets the all clear to travel is only one reason I won't relinquish my hold.

"And you know I'm not going to let you, so hush." I kiss the tip of her nose that has a deep wrinkle creasing the bridge. "You know, you're adorable when you're being sassy."

"And you're a pain in the arse when you're being stubborn," she huffs.

"You had a serious head injury and were in a coma not so long ago, and you are now carrying my baby, so I'm not being stubborn. I'm being protective." I step into the lift and punch the top floor button. "Get used to it, beautiful."

"Gah, I'm not the first pregnant woman, Jason." She rolls her eyes dramatically.

"But you are mine, Sam, and believe me, that makes all the difference. Now I'm happy to carry on having this redundant conversation, or we can talk about something else." She purses her lips, and I can see her chewing on the inside of her cheek though her eyes are smiling.

"Fine, I guess." I know this must be hard for her; it's a shock for all of us, however it's done now, and I couldn't be happier." I carefully lay her on our bed.

"You gonna help me get undressed since I'm clearly incapable of doing anything myself." She raises her brow high and tips a wry and wicked smile my way. I pull the covers back as she shimmies out of her leggings.

"I'll help you, beautiful, but that's all I'm doing. You need to rest." Her eyes snap to mine, wide at first then narrow as her lips thin with distaste.

"You have to be shitting me."

"You tell me. Do I look like I'm anything other than serious?" My impassive, stony expression holds firm as her eyes search for any sign of weakness. She lets out a dramatic puff of air and crosses her arms with frustration.

"Damn it, Jason. The doctor didn't say anything about abstinence."

"Actually, he did. No strenuous exercise and no flying."

"For how long?" Her voice trails off to a whimper before I even get to answer.

"Two weeks."

"No sex for two weeks!" Her mouth drops open in a comical display of feigned outrage.

"No flying for two weeks," I clarify and watch her exhale a deep, much relieved sigh. "I think the sex we can play by ear, but will depend on how much you rest now. So how about you be a good girl and take a nap, and I will see if I'm in a giving mood a little later?" I flash a carnal grin that only pokes her frustration further.

"You better be in a giving mood. I still have my own hands remember?" She wiggles her fingers, and I grab the hand nearest and hold it still, kissing the tips to soften the move.

"Not if I handcuff you to the bedpost, you won't." My intonation might be teasing, but she can't mistake the resolution in my gaze.

"You wouldn't!" she gasps and pulls her hand free.

"Try me, beautiful. I'm deadly serious about your recovery. Now go to sleep."

"Why did I have to fall in love with a Dom?" She folds her arms over her chest only to scoot down the bed in readiness for a much needed, if not entirely wanted, nap.

"It doesn't matter why. All that matters is that you do." I lean down and search her dark eyes, so rich and deep, swirling chocolate colour with flecks of light. She holds my gaze, and I wait for only a fraction of a second for complete supplication to register. Her eyes are first, and then her whole body, subtle but sure, open and totally mine.

"I do," she whispers. Her sweet breath warms my face as her heartfelt declaration and tender smile wrap me tight around her little finger.

"Good. Now sleep." I cover her lips with mine, and despite her protestations, her eyelids are heavy and quickly drop closed on my gentle command. I kiss her once more, pretty sure she's actually asleep already, and leave the bedroom to check if Will has brought everything up from the car.

"How's she doing?" Will drops her overnight bag on the floor and strides over to the mini bar.

"Oh you know, loving being told what to do." I nod to his offer of a beer he has just taken from the cooler. The hiss and ice vapour puff of air released from the open bottle makes my mouth water. I tip it and drain the contents. *Damn, I needed that.*

"So what's next? The doctor said she shouldn't fly for at least two weeks, what are you going to do? Can you work from here? Have you let Sam's work know about the accident?" He bombards me with questions while my lips are still around the neck of the bottle.

"Thanks for letting me draw breath," I snark, wiping my mouth with the back of my hand. He holds up his hand and gives a light nod by way of backing off without actually doing it. I walk over to the sofa and slump down. None of the questions he has peppered me with are new, and unfortunately, I hate that I not only know the answers but can do fuck all about them.

"I called Sam's work so she is signed off sick. That's not the problem." I drag my hand down my face, the tension in my brow and jaw both working their way to giving me a killer headache.

"The baby?" Will blurts.

"What?" My face screws up with confusion.

"The baby. I take it the baby is the problem?"

I start to shake my head even before he speaks, when I see where his line of thinking took him. "No. No, not at all. I mean it's a shock, but we'll deal. I love her so that could never be a problem." My response is emphatic, even as he raises a curious brow and lets out a dry, flat laugh.

"Yeah, right. So that's why you gave the good doctor twenty questions about how far along she was, because you had no problem." His tone is thick with sarcasm.

"Lose the attitude, Will," I warn. Only he doesn't flinch. I draw in a deep and heavy breath. "Look, I'm not going to lie. If I had thought for one moment our little Christmas scene could have led to this, I would've had you and Leon double bagging your junk. We hadn't really talked about kids, but you can just take it that, sure as shit, I did not want Sam to be pregnant with another man's baby. That really shouldn't be a surprise, and yes, I'm fucking relieved that baby is mine. She knows this, and there is absolutely no point re-hashing that close call. That baby is mine, end of, so no, that isn't the problem. My problem is that I have to go back to London." I pull another cold beer from the cooler, open it, and only drain half the bottle this time.

"I'm guessing there's a good reason you have to leave?" he asks as I offer him another. He shakes his head, waiting for me to continue.

"If it was just work, I could manage from here, but I've had another email." I take a moment to let the soaring anger calm, and the recognition on Will's face means at least I don't have to go into further rage-inducing details. "He wants money, and I have to be there for the drop. I want to catch the bastard with my bare hands." My fingers grip the bottle, and I wish it was bone because the pressure would surely break that fucking arsehole's neck.

"Understandable, I would too." Will's voice brings me back from my wishful thinking. "Look, I have some time off, and I'm supposed to be house-sitting for the rest of the month. It's a great little place on the coast. I'll take care of Sam, and if you can join us at any time, just fly back whenever."

"What place? I don't want her sharing with you and your horny housemates." I hate this, but I would hate that more.

"She won't. It's just me. The place is quiet. The steps from the back of the house lead right onto the beach. It's perfect for recovering. Perfect for Sam." His voice is wistful, but he gives a light shrug, so I give it no more thought. It's still a shitty situation.

"Hmm. I fucking hate that I have to leave," I grumble. I know I'm making the best of a bad situation and it's not like either of us have a choice.

"You'd hate it more if this scumbag got away." Will just confirms my predicament.

"True."

"So that's settled. I'll take care of Sam." Will's grin is a little too wide. I give a curt nod and no smile whatsoever, because I'm far from fucking happy.

Sam

This is so hard, and I take little comfort that, by the look in his deep brown eyes, Jason is finding it just as tough.

"Call me when you land." My voice breaks like a lovesick teenager, and I can feel my eyes well with tears, but I don't care. I love this man, and we've been through enough for me to not even try to pretend that spending any time at all apart, is too much. He cups the back of my neck and pulls me roughly against his solid frame. His lips crush mine, and my head is screaming, "Yes, mark me, devour me, make me yours." I can't wait to be his wife, forever and always. He breaks the kiss, and I stifle a whimper. Dropping his forehead to mine, his warm breath kisses my skin, and his eyes burn through me.

"I'll call you when I'm in the air, Sam. I'm not waiting nine hours." He flashes his heart-stopping smile, and I crumple against him and let out a sad sniffle-type laugh.

The only good thing about him leaving is that he's taking the company jet and I can hug him until the very last minute when he will have to pry my arms from his trim waist to climb the few steps to board the plane. "I've gotta go, beautiful." My arms constrict like a snake at those words, but with enormous effort, I give him one last squeeze and let him go. He hugs Will who is standing just behind me and climbs the steps.

"I'm gonna expect lots of phone sex!" I blurt, and he turns at the doorway. His glorious grin widens with wickedness, and I squirm under his heated gaze.

"I'm going to expect lots of *video* phone sex." I give an exaggerated body shudder to show my approval and blow him one last kiss. I stand back and reach for Will's hand as Jason's plane taxis out on to the runway.

"You really love him?" Will scrunches his face and rubs his chin as if he posed a puzzling question. I slap him hard on his taut tummy. He tenses but doesn't flinch.

"Well, duh!" I roll my eyes, only to freeze when I hear the thunder of the engines prepare for take-off. "More than anything," I say, but the words are drowned out but the roar of the Stone jet hurtling down the runway. Will tugs me and I follow him back into the airport.

"Come on, let's get you back to bed," Will says, and I quirk my brow at his comment and bite my lips together.

"Don't look at me like that. I am under pain of death to make sure you rest." He cups his package between his legs as an afterthought. "And I value my bollocks too much to try anything else. Even if Jason is three thousand miles away."

"It's not Jason you need to worry about if you tried something. Trust me. And it's definitely your bollocks that would be in danger," I remark with a sly and sinister smile

"Tease." He grins, and I snort out a laugh. "I know my place, don't worry. Only when invited. However, this week and the next, please consider me your personal slave. Because I happen to agree with my brother on this. You are very precious and need to rest." His playful tone switches to sweetly sincere half-way though, and I squeeze the hand he is still holding.

"Jason never said you were a sweetheart," I gush, fan myself and dip in a mock swoon.

"I can imagine. What did he say I was?" He ignores my attempt to mock.

"Mostly a pain in the arse."

"Yeah, well that makes two of us."

"But you're both a nice pain in my arse." I wiggle my brows playfully.

"Really? You're going there?" He shakes his head and groans. I giggle, not remotely sorry that he has to shove his other hand down the front of his board shorts to make a quick adjustment. "This is going to be torture isn't it?"

"It *is* what I'm good at." I snicker.

The place Will has been asked to house-sit is amazing, not big, but it's quaint and homey. Bare, wooden floors and white-washed walls, one large open-plan room that looks out across an almost deserted beach and a crystal clear, calm ocean. I spend the days lounging on the terrace, maybe take a stroll along the beach with Will. The evenings we chat, watch a movie or I kick his arse at Halo on the Xbox—much to his irritation. But it shouldn't be a surprise since my best friend is a guy, and it was either learn or lose complete control over the television. Whatever I end up doing though, I make sure I'm back in my bedroom by six in the evening. Because, with the time difference, that is when Jason is also in his bed. Each night since he left over a week ago, he's called at that exact time and now, just nearing that hour is like ringing the bell for Pavlov's dogs but in my panties. I close my book and swing my legs to stand, a mix of excitement and sexual frustration keeps my nerves tingling and definitely gives me a spring to my step.

"Is it that time already?" Will looks at his watch but he knows from my grin that it is; it really is. "Mind if I join you?" His voice drops and I stop short in the doorway. I lift my sunglasses off my eyes to check if he is joking. The searing heat in his eyes is deadly serious, and suddenly, my mouth is very dry.

"I can ask." He looks so much like his brother, although they are poles apart in personality. No, that's not right. They are both passionate, kind, loving, and sexy as all hell, but Will is less intense, more carefree maybe, certainly less dominant. He is still a dominant, just nowhere near the end of the spectrum where you would find the likes of Jason, or Daniel for that matter.

"I'd like that." He clears his throat, and I nod my head for him to follow me inside. I hear his feet pad on the floorboards behind me and fall silent when they cross onto the rug in my room. He sits in the large wicker chair in the corner of the room, and I climb on my bed. I sit cross-legged in my loose shorts, bikini top and nothing else. I pull the arm of the television stand across and fix it to just in front and above me. Will took the TV off and helped me to adjust it to hold my iPad for my video calls with Jason and for a better 'hands-free' experience. On the dot, my iPad chimes with the Skype ring tone, and I shift to get comfortable. Jason's face fills the screen, and my heart aches and warms.

"Hey, beautiful." His voice is like rich chocolate and raw with pent-up lust.

"Hey." My mouth is instantly dry, and I drag my tongue over my parched lips. His eyes zero in on the movement and he waits until I have finished before he speaks.

"How's my baby?" He beams, and my hand instantly covers my abdomen.

"All good. Fuck, I miss you." I touch the screen, and he closes his eyes when my palm presses the screen over his face. Silly, yet I can almost feel his stubble on my fingertips.

"Me too, beautiful...me too. Not long now though. Tell me about your day. I miss your voice." He is unashamed of how sappy he might sound, and I fucking love him for that.

"Is that all you miss?" I'm always turned-on before the call even goes through. Just the thought, the anticipation, but tonight, with Will staring at me, I am more than a little eager.

"Oh baby, we'll get to that, I promise." His lids look heavy, and his sensual tone makes my toes curl.

"About that…I have company."

"You do, hmm? Do you want to play?" He sounds cautious, and his brows furrow with unease.

"Do you want me to?" I'm not second-guessing this; it's important that he is okay with it.

"No, but if it's what you need," he clarifies, and his expression relaxes.

"I need *you*." I state as an absolute, irrefutable fact. I think his chest might've puffed with pride at that, just a little. He's adorable.

"He can watch, but no touching." Jason states loudly—not for my benefit—and Will mutters something not so complimentary. Luckily for him, Jason doesn't hear, or I am pretty sure that offer would be off the table too. "Not negotiable, and only if that's okay with you, beautiful?"

"That's pretty fucking hot, so yeah I'm cool with that. Will?" I tilt my head away from the screen to check.

"I take it the no touching just refers to me touching Sam?" His voice travels loud and clear, and I smirk just after Jason does.

"Yeah, Will, that's exactly what I'm referring to." I watch Jason's face for any sign of unease, but his mouth is slicing his handsome face with a flashy wide smile and his eyes seem to sparkle with latent lust. "Okay, beautiful, tell me about your day."

"Seriously?" Will grumbles.

"You can always fuck right off, Will," Jason snaps. "This isn't about you getting off. If that's all you want, go call a sex line. I want to talk with my girl." Will lets out an exasperated breath, but doesn't make to move. In fact, he slouches down and pops the first button of his jeans. I sit up and start to tell Jason about everything and nothing. Nothing much happened today that was any different from the other days, but he asks me lots of questions all the same. He makes me laugh and tells me a little of what he's doing. I look over to Will who looks like he has dozed off.

"We might have a barbecue tonight. The weather is warm enough, and Will bought some steaks at the market earlier," I ramble on.

"Take off your top," he asks in such a level tone it takes a moment to register the words. I swallow thickly when I do. I loosen the bow around my neck and reach behind me and do the same to the back strap. The string bikini top falls into my lap.

"Lose the shorts." His voice drops to a deeper, rougher timbre that makes the hairs on my neck stand to attention. They are not alone. Jason tilts his screen so I have a full view of his naked body, his fist pumping slowly up and down the length of his achingly impressive erection. A small whimper escapes my throat, and I bite my lips, holding the sound captive. "Sam?" he growls, and I jump to my knees and quickly shimmy out of my shorts and sit back in just my bikini bottoms. My eyes are fixed on his slow moving hand and my tongue darts out to wet my lips when I see the first drop of moisture on his thick crown. *Damn.*

"Hold your tits and pinch your nipples. Lift them high for me, baby. Yes, just like that. You know when you push them together like that the only thing I want to do is slide my cock between them and hold your head so you can kiss my tip every time I thrust." His voice drops low and husky.

"Oh God, I'd love that." I pinch my nipples hard and a spark of pain and electricity shoots straight to my clit. I'm still kneeling, but I have to squeeze my thighs together to try and ease the searing heat and ache that is building.

"You'd let me fuck your tits?" His words may sound like a question, yet the intonation is all statement. I answer anyway.

"I'd let you do anything, Sir." My breathy response makes his jaw tense, and his Adam's apple bulges with the rise and fall in his throat.

"Fuck! Lose the bottoms. I want to see how wet you are." The gravelly timbre in his voice is so low, he coughs to clear his throat before he orders. "Sit back and pull your knees up, spread them wide for me, beautiful." I'm mesmerized by his languid strokes, and in my peripheral vision, I can see Will mirroring the moment I see on screen. It's like a high definition 4D experience. Sight, sound, and smell all bombard my body, and I sizzle with anticipation and desire. I tug the ties of my bikini bottoms and push them away. Sitting back I slowly draw my knees to my chest. I watch Jason's chest rise and fall then halt on a sharp inhale. I hear Will's breath catch at the same time I place my hands on my knees and push my legs wide open. I am dripping.

"Use just one finger and take a taste for me," he commands, and I visibly shiver. I lick the pad of my thumb and draw it down the centre of my body then switch to my middle finger when I reach the top of my folds. It slides easily along my slick core, down the centre, feather-light and very, *very* wet. I pull my hand away and up to my face. I hold his gaze as he holds his breath. Searing heat and electricity crackle between us all and through the screen as if there was no screen at all, no barrier. I open my mouth and push my finger in, wrap my lips tight and slowly bring it back out.

"Holy shit!" Will groans, and my eyes flick to see his cock straining in his white-knuckle grip. A deep pull inside me grows to an unbearable ache, and the muscles in my thighs twitch, eager for some relief.

"How do you taste?" Jason's voice rakes over my body like his nails would my sensitive skin. I am on fire.

"Like I really want you." I gasp and writhe, unable to keep my body still.

"Show me…show me how much you want me…Touch yourself, now." His tone is stern, and I don't hesitate to do exactly what he wants. I'm so desperate and needy, already teetering on the edge. My fingers sweep between my legs, and I arch into the contact, a few soft circles of my clit before I put a little more pressure and rub up and down in a rhythmic curl of my fingers.

"Open your lips, slide a finger right in, tell me how that feels, Sam." I do as he says and force myself to hold his intense gaze, because all I want to do is roll my eyes back, close my lids, and enjoy being fucked by his unbelievably sexy voice. I bite back a whimper, and my tummy muscles clamp down at the first erotic wave of my climax.

"Stop," he calls out, and I freeze, my eyes wide with surprise. I pant out a breath to fight the build-up that had begun. It's not necessary; on his order, my burgeoning wave disintegrated in my hand. I close my lips over my teeth in a growl but hold my position, unmoving. "Did I stutter?" he asks with astonishing calm while I'm a stunned and aching mess.

"What? I have stopped." My voice is pitched and a little whiny. I can't help it, he makes me whine.

"I asked you a question, Sam. I expect an answer," he states flatly, and I have to bite my tongue. This may be playtime, but still when we play, I know my place.

"I'm wet." I sigh and grind a little into my hand. "I'm very, very wet, Sir, and—" I swipe my middle finger over the soft sensitive tissue just inside of me and let out a deep satisfied moan. *If he tells me to stop again I'm not listening.*

"Good…go on," he encourages with a deep groan.

"I ache. My fingers aren't enough. I want you." I tilt my hips to get more friction, my frustration evident in my voice.

"Where?"

"I want you inside me. Your big cock pushing inside, right here." I arch and pump my fingers in and out, thrusting two as deep as I can. It's not enough; it will never be enough. "I miss you." I sigh and am hit with a wave of sadness that threatens this erotic little tableaux.

"I know, beautiful. Me too. Stay with me." His sensual plea brings me back, and his demands secure me there…right there with him. "Squeeze your breast, tease your nipple…you know that's what my mouth would be doing right now… do it for me."

"Yes." I gasp, my hips rolling onto my hand. "Jason I-I …please?" I cry out, breathless, my body on fire, tingling, sizzling, scorching heat peppering my skin with a sheen of moisture.

"Please what?" *How can he be so fucking calm?*

"Please, I need to come." I beg.

"Then you need to ask nicely," he states, his hand is flying at a rapid pace on his shaft, and I can feel the heat and want, radiating in tidal waves. It's enough… just enough.

"Please may I come, Sir? Please? I can feel my muscle twitch on my fingers…just one word from you and you will send me spiralling…crashing… coming. Please?" I plead.

"Come for me, beautiful. Come now," he demands, and I obey. I curl my finger round and press just where I need, riding the crest and nurturing the high with the heel of my hand, prolonging the pleasure. A fraction of what I need and get from him in the flesh. But needs must…and my need is softly simmering as my climax ebbs and I come back to Earth. I had closed my eyes, when I open them, the vision before me is enough to set me off again. Jason sprawled back on the bed in all his naked glory, his still-hard cock in his hand and a slick spray of his mess on his stomach. I lick my lips at the sight.

"If only, beautiful…if only. Fuck, when are you coming home?" He squeezes the base of his cock and a tiny river of his own climax dribbles over his knuckles. *Damn.*

"Soon. I have a doctor's appointment in a couple of days. I feel fine so I think—"

"Ahem!" Will coughs an interruption, and my mouth drops open and possibly waters. His cock looks painfully hard in his fist, and from where I am, I can see every other muscle is also just as tense: clenched jaw, pinched brow, and the muscles in his forearm taut and bulging.

"Oh." I scrape my teeth over my bottom lip, before biting down.

"What?" Jason's voice is suddenly filled with concern.

"Um, Will didn't…he's…um… He might need a little more help." I snicker and arch a brow in lieu of an actual question.

"Tough," Jason states as coldly and effectively as an ice bucket challenge.

"Jason, that's just mean." I try to mediate between two raging mountains of testosterone "This was super hot with him watching, and it's only fair I help him out."

"You think so, beautiful, but you mistake me for someone who cares about that," he clips, and I wince at his resolute words. "I don't give a fuck that my brother has a hard-on from hell. He heard, just as well as I did, that you were about to come." His tone brooks no argument, and I know better than to try. I can't imagine how much just having Will this close must be killing him when he is so far away. I pull my legs together and offer a slight shrug and an apologetic smile at Will's scowling face.

Will stands abruptly and drags his jeans awkwardly over his steely erection. I wince when he roughly pulls the zip shut. He walks over and pulls the screen to face him.

"You are a motherfucking sadist." He snarls at the screen.

"And you are an idiot," Jason retorts, his clipped voice not at all playful. Will storms out of the room, and I snatch the screen back.

"Well, that escalated quickly." I grimace, and once I'm sure Will is out of earshot, ask, "What the hell was that?" I'm completely stunned.

"That was my brother overstepping the line." Jason looks unfazed, but I'm rocked at the monumental switch in atmosphere.

"What do you mean? He just didn't finish when we did. That's hardly worth falling out over." I check to see if Will is going to reappear, but there is no movement outside my room, no sound at all.

"No, he had plenty of time, the same warning I did. He had a blow-by-fucking-blow countdown. He chose not to come," Jason states through gritted teeth, anger evident in his ticking jaw and curt tone.

"Why would he do that?" I shake my head in disbelief.

"Sam…" His soft smile is accompanied with a wry tilt of his head. He waits for me to catch up with his line of thinking. It takes moment but I get there.

"Oh…no. I don't think you're right." I shake my head more emphatically. He can't be right, Will doesn't think of me like that.

"I hope I'm not." He mutters and doesn't look remotely convinced.

"It was a timing thing." I wave my hand in a dismissive brush off.

"Maybe, but he completely mistimed if he thought I would be okay with you two playing when I'm thousands of fucking miles away." He makes a very valid point, and I slowly nod in agreement. I let out a heavy breath.

"Perhaps this wasn't such a great idea." I quirk my mouth in a tight pinch.

"It was a great fucking idea until he ruined it," he sniffs out, his words derisive and his whole demeanour heavy with accusation.

"He hasn't ruined it," I counter. "You're wrong…I'm sure. He's been nothing but helpful and brotherly to me all week. Nothing 'inappropriate'. He hasn't even flirted, and it's not like I don't know he finds me attractive." I think really hard about any incident that might contradict my disclosure, only I'm drawing a blank. Will has been the perfect gentleman. "No, I'm sure you're mistaken." My mind is comforted with this memory; my heart, on the other hand, is a riotous mess of emotion. God, I hope Jason isn't right.

"You think that, if it gives you comfort, beautiful, but I know my brother, and I want you on the first plane after the all-clear from the doctor, understand?" he states flatly.

"Is that an order?" I challenge with a wry twist to my lips.

"Yes…yes, it is," he confirms with a rumble I can feel in my core.

"Then, yes, Sir, I completely understand."

THREE

Sam

Will was quiet the next day, and I thought it was best to leave him to it, whatever 'it' was. The day after that, however, he was back to being his charming and easy-going self. I completely relaxed back into our comfortable routine and shook my head with exasperation when Jason continued to worry about my virtue at the hands of his brother. I dismissed his concern but didn't tease him, because jealousy is no joking matter. It can be corrosive when left unchecked and we both have little green monsters just perching in the background, waiting to consume and destroy.

Talking of destroying....

Will throws his Xbox controllers down with barely contained rage, and I puff out my chest and hold my hands up in a whoop-whoop celebration.

"Undefeated! Will, you may now kiss the ground I walk on and call me Mrs Master Chief." I laugh out, as I once again, kick his arse at Halo.

"I'd rather call you, Mrs Sinclair." My heart clenches because I can't wait for that too, when I turn my eager and beaming face toward him, his looks so serious, I get a nasty twist in my gut. His eyes search mine, and I pretend to not recognize what his gaze is so desperately trying to convey. I choose to misinterpret and ignore.

"I'm looking forward to that too, so how about the sooner you take me to my doctor's appointment, the sooner I can get back to my fiancé." I hold out my hand for him to help me up. His face drops with disappointment. I just can't go there, and I pray, for the love of all that is holy, he doesn't either.

"Sure." I let his hand go before he can pull me any closer, and I skip off to my room. I make a quick change of clothes into a long, floaty summer dress and cardigan, because the temperature is warm but not hot, and I grab my over-the-shoulder handbag. Will waits by the door with his keys, which he is swinging nervously from one hand to the next.

"You're making me nervous, Will, what with the key jangling and serious face. It's just a check-up not the firing squad. Any luck and I'll be out of your hair by nightfall." I pat his cheek lightly.

"Nightfall?" His voice is pitched and panic flashes across his handsome face.

"I promised Jason I would try to get the first standby flight once I get the all-clear. It might be tomorrow realistically, but I have my bag packed just in case." I explain with uninhibited enthusiasm.

"You've packed already. Can't wait to get away, eh?" His voice is quiet and he tries for a playful tone.

"Well, you are seriously crap at Halo," I tease and nudge his side as I pass through the door, trying to lighten the mood that has descended like a dark cloud across his features.

I sign in at the clinic and am called straight through. Will stands to accompany me, slipping his hand through mine. I don't see the harm, and if I'm honest, I'm a little nervous and welcome the comfort.

"So how have you been?" The doctor scans his notes, and I wait for him to look up. It isn't the doctor from the hospital, but I have seen him before. He has kind, grey eyes and is much younger than the other one.

"I have been good. Lots of rest and I feel great." I tuck my hands beneath my thighs and bounce with agitation. The doctor smiles but he doesn't comment.

"Other than the dizziness you mean," Will adds and I snap my head and comically drop my mouth wide open. Only there is nothing funny about his comment.

"What?" I splutter.

"You have had several dizzy spells." He tilts his head with sympathy and looks seriously at the doctor.

"I haven't had any dizzy spells." My head whips between the two men.

"That you remember," Will adds with such condescension I want to slap that warm and fake compassion right off his face; however, I don't want to add hysterics to my misdiagnosis.

"Doctor, I haven't had *any* dizzy spells." I scowl at Will, who is sporting the best poker face this side of Vegas. "I am perfectly fit to travel."

"I never said you weren't," Will answers for the doctors only he continues to distort the truth. "I just worry who would be liable if you were to travel and something terrible happened." I see the doctor's eyes widen and his pale colour fade to translucent at the mention of liability.

"I would like you to come back for a scan, Ms Bonfleur. I don't think such a long plane ride would be appropriate. Not until I'm satisfied there will be no other dizzy spells." He smiles at me but it doesn't reach his eyes. I think he's still pondering Will's worst-case scenario.

"There weren't any dizzy spells." I force the words out through my clench jaw and notice Will slide a little further away. Not fucking far enough.

"I can book you in on Friday." The doctor glances at his screen and pulls up a calendar.

"You mean today, Friday?" I look at the screen which is covered with big red 'booked' comments in each of the blocks on every time slot.

"No, sorry. Next Friday. I would like to make sure you have no other spells this week. So, if you could keep an extra close eye and if anything unusual happens, don't hesitate to come back in or call 911." The doctor hands me an envelope with my appointment. I snatch it from his hand and don't bother to say a single word as I storm out. I fear nothing but Anglo-Saxon profanity would pass my lips and there are children nearby.

I lean up against Will's car, seething. I feel rage, anger, and fucking astonishment in every pore in my body, seeping out of my cells. He approaches with a wide casual gait and a triumphant grin on his face.

"What the fuck was that?" I snarl, hands on my hips, fingertips gripping my flesh to stop them curling into fists and lashing out.

"What? You did get dizzy the other day remember, when you stubbed your toe?" He frowns, and his face is the picture of innocence. *Man, I would never like to play cards with him.*

"No, I wobbled and sat on a stool because Lucifer himself had stuck his poker under my toenail. I was in agony. I wasn't dizzy!" I scream at him—howl more like—having lost my tentative hold on decorum now that we were in a half empty car park.

"Oh I'm sorry. Only I thought you were going to black out." He maintains this charade, and my hands do find themselves in balled up angry fists.

"Well, I was, from the pain, you arsehole, not from my head injury!" I punch him full in the shoulder, and he stumbles back, not anticipating the strength of the impact. He saw it coming but didn't brace.

"The doctor only did what he thought was for the best." He holds his hands up, and I actually do a double take. *Really? He said that?* I step forward, and this time he straightens his back and draws in a deep breath. I poke my finger into his chest to punctuate each of my next words.

"You told him spells, plural, and then laid the liability card at his nervous feet. There was no fucking way he was going to sign me off after that, and you know it! Why?" I drill the tip of my finger right into the hard muscle of his pec on my question. His hand wraps around my digit. I know that will bruise. I try to pull my hand free, he lifts it to his lips and his eyes soften. His face changes and —*oh fuck*—I have seen that look before. I love that look, I crave that look like my next breath, just not from him. "Don't." My voice breaks, and I try again to pull my hand back.

"What are you afraid of?" His voice is deep and coaxing, but it feels all wrong, so wrong.

"Not what you think I'm afraid of, that's for sure." I quip and he lightly shakes his head.

"Really?" The cocky quirk of his brow is misplaced.

"I'm afraid if Jason finds out what you've done. The first time I meet your parents won't be at my wedding, it will be at your funeral." I manage to pull my hand free this time and climb into the car. I slam the door and fix my eyes on the road ahead. If I didn't feel dizzy before, I certainly do now. My heart is hammering and breaking all at once. *This isn't happening. Please don't let this be happening.*

The drive home is excruciating, the silence deafening, and the tension is like a fucking powder keg between us. He pulls up the sandy drive and kills the engine. He draws in a breath to say something, and I rush to speak. I need to get this in first.

"Don't. Please for the love of *everything*, don't." I hold his gaze for a second too long, and the pain and hurt buried deep flash to the front and I swallow back a choked sob. *Shit.* This is happening. I need to not be here. I leap from the car and take the porch steps two at a time, slamming through the screen door and unlocking the main one. I run to my bedroom and start to fling the last of my clothes into my case. Moments later, Will appears at my door and silently takes in the carnage of flying clothes and hastily thrown shoes and toiletries. There's no careful folding, no double bagging of creams and gels. If it fits, it's coming with me; if it doesn't, I don't care. I'm leaving today.

"Please don't go." His voice is so soft, I barely hear it yet it pulls me up cold all the same.

"I can't stay, Will." He steps into the room and grabs my elbows, holding me, just that look on his face has me transfixed. He's so handsome, and he looks absolutely heartbroken. This is killing me. How the fuck did this shit-storm happen without me seeing it? There was no cloud or even the slightest drop of rain to indicate to me that the look he is unashamedly levelling at me is justified. The other night… I get the other night; I should've seen it for what it was then. Jason did. *Fuck!*

"Sam, I—" He breaks momentarily, only to then steady himself.

"Don't say it!" I blurt and shake my head. Like that will stop him; the determination on his face is almost as fixed as that look of…

"I love you." Powerful words, so wholly out of place.

"And you said it." I exhale with utter sadness.

"I love you. I've wanted to say it for a long time, and I'll say it again. I love you, Sam." His lips twitch sadly, failing to break into even the slightest of smiles. The situation is too damn tragic for that.

"Please stop. Will, you don't love me. You don't know me. I love Jason… your brother. I love him more than anything, more than my next breath, more than my life. He is my everything." I rush to explain. I don't want to hurt him, although I can see as clear as day every word slices him raw. But he has to understand.

"I know. Still you can't help who you fall in love with, and I had to tell you. I'd regret it for the rest of my life if I didn't" His hand moves to my cheek. Warm strong hands hold me and I close my eyes and sigh.

"You might regret it for the rest of your life now that you have," I point out and he shrugs.

"I'll never be sorry I told you, but I'm sorry about today. I panicked when you said you would be leaving. I just wanted more time with you to…to…" He frowns like he is struggling for the right words. There are no right words.

"To what?" I take his hand from my face and hold it in both of mine.

"More time for you to fall in love with me," he states simply, his eyes still hold hope in the unasked question.

"Jesus." I drop my head to his chest, and the rapid beat of his heart matches mine, thump after heartbreaking thump. "I do love you, Will. It's just, I will never love you the way you want me to, the way I love Jason. That's not possible. He's my lobster." I shake his hand and try desperately to make this better.

"He doesn't even like shellfish. I'm the one that likes lobster," he mutters, offering a resigned shrug and an empty smile. *I'll take it.* "What are you going to do?"

"I'm going to go home." I confirm, soft but firm.

"And?"

"And I'm going to tell Jason I got the all clear."

"And?" he pushes.

"If he asks, I will tell him, Will. I won't lie to him. However, if I can at all help it, I won't tell him the whole truth either. Because I wasn't joking about your funeral." His sad smile barely moves his mouth, but his face softens.

"I know…I'd be the same. He's a very lucky man." He drags his hand through his shaggy hair and puffs out a slow breath.

"And I'm a very lucky woman. I have three amazing men in my life and you all own a piece of my heart." I hold his hand to my heart for a moment before letting it fall away. "You have to understand, my soul will only ever belong to Jason."

I feel like shit for the entire nine-hour flight. I have felt sick and so fucking tired. I can't sleep. I keep playing every minute of the last weeks over and over, wondering if I led him on. Made him think there was ever a chance. I asked him as I hugged him at the departures gate, and he looked shocked that I would suggest such a thing. I fucking hate that he is hurting like he is because of me, when I didn't have a clue. Not until it was too late.

I spot Jason instantly when I emerge through the arrival doors, and I leave my trolley, and in full-on *Love Actually* mode, I fling myself into his waiting arms. His mouth captures mine, and I die happy. His arms feel like home, his smell is intoxicating, and he tastes like heaven on my lips. I'm emotional enough to blame the stupid baby hormones, but honestly, I'm just overwhelmed, and the tears trickle unchecked down my flight puffy cheeks. He slides me down his body and takes my hand, walking back to retrieve my abandoned trolley.

"Glad to be home?" he teases, just as breathless from kissing as I am.

"Understatement of the fucking century."

"Did Will not take good care of you? Because if he neglected you—"

"Will was perfect. Still, I couldn't be happier than I am now… right here." My voice softens and I let out a huge relieved sigh.

"What happened?" I jolt to a stop, and he turns me to look directly into his searching eyes. He cups either side of my face; there is no escaping the scrutiny. I pause, holding the intensity of his gaze, and try to think of something to say. Something that will explain this utter clusterfuck, but I know from trying to come up with something for the last nine hours another few minutes will also leave me mute on the subject. Lucky for me, Jason speaks before I have to.

"He fell in love with you." It sounded like a statement even as he waits silently for an answer. *How does he do that?*

"Yes." I try and offer a light shrug as I feel a dark cloud descend.

"Motherfucker!" he growls, only for his lips turn up in a half smile, when he adds with a flippant tone, "I can't really blame him for that."

"You're not mad?" I tilt my head and frown, utterly unconvinced at his casual attitude.

"I'm fucking furious. I said I couldn't blame him. I didn't say I wouldn't rip his bollocks off next time I see him." *Ah yes, that's more what I was expecting.*

"That won't be necessary. We're cool, I made my position perfectly clear."

"What position is that exactly?" His voice drops an octave, heavy with sensual undertones. I smile sweetly.

"I have several actually, and you on top of me would be my first position of choice." His lips crush mine and he moans into the kiss, but pulls away before we get carried away.

"So, that is another one off our playmates list," he quips, and I lift my head and shrug.

"It would seem so." Our extracurricular playtime is hot as hell. Don't get me wrong, but it's not everything; he…*he* is my everything.

"Well, there will be no need to rip his bollocks off then, because that is punishment enough in my book."

FOUR

Jason

"Scooch up, beautiful." After dinner, I ran a deep and bubbly bath, and left her to soak and relax after a long flight and an even longer welcome home. I cleared the debris in the kitchen, but that is more than enough time of not touching her. The last two weeks have been an ultimate test of my endurance. If I wasn't weighed down at work with Daniel on paternity leave, or still getting daily cryptic emails from who-the-fuck-knows about Sam's video, I would've flown straight back the day after I landed. She's my life, and I won't pretend I found the separation frequently unbearable. The video calls and texts throughout the day helped. I also thought that Will was taking good care of her and that was a huge comfort…*was* being the operative word because that certainly bit me in the arse. Still, she's home now, and soon, she's going to be Mrs Sinclair. Very soon as it happens. I need to mention that. I tug my shirt over my head and kick my pants down, having gone commando, and with no socks, I am good to go. Her eyes widen, then her lids droop, and she drags her tongue over her lips, and my cock thickening with a surge of heat and blood.

She pouts, and an adorable wrinkle settles on the bridge of her nose when I cup myself and step in behind her, shaking my head. We made love for fucking hours when we got home. We had to; I was literally dying, and she was insatiable. Nevertheless, it was me who stopped because I remembered she needs to eat and keep her strength since it's not just her anymore. She's taking care of herself and my baby.

"How're you feeling?" I slide my arms around her tummy where her skin is silky soft from the bubbles, and my hands swoop up to cup her full breasts and pull her back to lean against me. Her fine arse nestles neatly against my growing cock, and she gives a tortuous wiggle. I pinch her nipple, and she bucks under the pain.

"Ow." She slips to the side and looks over her shoulder at me. I'm pretty sure it didn't hurt, but she definitely looks ticked-off. "Don't start something you have no intention of finishing." Her tone is full of sass, and her brow arches high.

"Who said I have no intention of finishing?" I release her puckered pebble and massage her breasts instead.

"You were cupping your cock like you feared for his life just moments ago, and you stopped earlier when I know you weren't finished," she challenges and pushes her full breasts into my firm hands.

"You needed food, and I was cupping myself because I want to relax a little with you before…"

"Before?" She hums.

"Before I resume fucking your brains out." I move my hands from her gorgeous breasts, which do feel a little bigger in my palm. They also feel fantastic, and that is not helping with my hard-on and the need to talk first.

"Oh…well, that's okay then. I thought for a minute you were going to go all 'you're carrying my baby, I can't possibly fuck the mother when she is with child' or some shit." Her voice drops an octave in a mock attempt at a man's voice…not mine, just some croaky Neanderthal.

"Nine months without fucking? Do people really do that?" I can't hide the horror in my voice, and she snickers.

"I don't know. I have heard it freaks some men out, the whole 'there's a baby in there'." She rubs her flat tummy, and I know for a fact only a medical certificate prohibiting intercourse would keep me from fucking her at every possible opportunity.

"Hmm." I mull what she's said, and it spins in my head but gains no purchase. "Nope…I'm fine with fucking your brains out, but we do need to talk."

"Oh that sounds ominous." She tilts her head to look at me and grimaces. Her eyes are as large as saucers. I tap the end of her nose playfully, and she relaxes with a soft smile.

"You have an appointment at the Porchester Maternity Hospital on Tuesday. I booked it for after work, not for my convenience you understand, I'm happy to take time out. I just thought you'd want to show your face at your work first and maybe talk to them about flexible hours." I entwine my fingers with hers and rest our joined hands where they gently rise and fall with each breath she takes.

"Flexible hours?" She twists again to look into my eyes. God she's utterly stunning.

"Sam, I want you to take it really easy…zero stress. You said yourself—" Her finger presses my lips, and I fall silent at her touch.

"I know and that's really sweet. I was thinking the same thing." She removes her finger and slips back around. "I know most women breathe a sigh of relief at twelve weeks, however, I'm going to be holding my breath until this little fella is in my arms." Our joined hands pat her tummy with a small splash of bathwater.

"Fella?" Back 'round she twists; she's like a spinning top.

"Or Fella-ess." She crinkles her nose and beams so brightly her face lights up the whole damn room. I don't know about pregnant women glowing, Sam is like this supernova.

"Twelve weeks, eh? So this is really early days then? Have you told anyone?" My other hand is drawing absent patterns in the thin film of bubbles on her bent knee.

"No, I'm still processing. I mean *we've* not really talked about it, have we?" She shivers when I draw my nail in a line from her knee and along the inside of her thigh.

"I don't think we should tell anyone just yet," I say. Only it comes out a little harsh and perhaps too eager judging by her reaction. She stiffens in my arms. "Did someone just stick an iron pole up your arse? Because you have just gone rigid in my arms." She slips all the way around and rests her delectable body on mine once more; it's very distracting and I still have one more tricky subject to discuss.

"You don't want to tell anyone?" Her eyes are heavy with hurt.

"Is that what I said? Or did I say it's early days and maybe we *shouldn't* tell anyone. We can, of course we can. I am surprised you would want to, that's all." I cup her face, and she sighs and leans into my comfort.

"I don't want to tell anyone yet…I just…I just need to be sure you're okay with this." Her voice breaks, and I fucking hate that uncertainty. But I know just the cure for that.

"I'm more than okay. There is only one thing that could make me happier." I hold her gaze and watch her expression change from anxious to adoring, her eyes soften and her smile eclipses any concern, wide and wicked.

"One thing, hmm? Do tell?" She rolls her whole body slowly up and down, aided by the soapy water. *Damn that feels good.* Her eyes sparkle with mischief.

"Marry me?" I ask confident in the outcome to the question.

"I have already said yes to that one." She rolls her eyes and puffs out a little breath.

"This weekend," I state, because I'm less certain of this outcome.

"What?" She gasps and chokes on a loud laugh that stutters to an awkward gulp and then silence. "You're serious?"

"Do I look like I'm joking?"

"Not at all. Shit!" She shuffles to her knees, and I bend and widen my legs to accommodate. Large swaths of bubbles glide down her perfect body, and I struggle to remember what we were talking about. "Shit!" she repeats, and I remember.

"You don't want to?" It's an option I hadn't really considered, and it churns my stomach that she could *not* want to. I steel my face and keep my emotions in check.

"Now who's putting words into my mouth? I didn't say that, it's just…fast." She runs her wet hands through her long glossy hair, scrapping it clear of her face. She's absolutely flawless. She's going to say *yes*.

"We both want it. Today, tomorrow, one month, nine months, five years. We are forever, beautiful, this is just timing." I sit up so we are nose-to-nose. "Personally, I don't want to go another night without you as my wife, though I will compromise and wait the six days."

"Wow, that's some compromise," she quips.

"Is that a yes?" She smiles and gives a short nod. "I need to hear the words, Sam."

"Yes, that's a yes." I slap my hands on her arse cheeks through the water and haul her onto my lap, she manages to wrap her legs around my waist, and now, her lips are a breath from mine.

"You make me so damn happy, soon-to-be Mrs Sinclair," I whisper. My words kiss her lips.

"And you are completely crazy, Mr Sinclair. A wedding in less than a week." She shakes her head at the madness, but she doesn't know about my secret weapon.

"Pfft…It's done. Trust me, all you have to do is turn up." Her eyes narrow and hold my gaze for only a moment when her brows shoot up with enlightenment.

"Sofia," she exclaims.

"Sofia." I confirm then cover her mouth with mine and consume.

FIVE

Sam

"Are you sure about this?" Charlie, my permanent replacement for Leon is perched on my old bed in my apartment nimbly twirling the small, curved silver *penis sound* in her fingers. She snatches the end between her thumb and forefinger, points it at me, and draws tight little circles in the air, waving it like a kinky wand.

"Oh I am sure. Jason took one look at my tool box, and I swear it was the first time he was speechless." I bite back a smirk. I know he has this reputation as a king of kink, but some of the stuff I have was clearly a little too close to his hard limits to stomach.

"So you've never—" She forces the *sound* through the tiniest hole her clenched fist can simulate, and I sniff out humourless laugh.

"—stuck anything into Jason's cock?" I finish. "That would be a big no." I lean forward and take the slim Dittle and replace in my kit of graduating sizes. I clip the velvet case shut and place it in the much larger cardboard box with the rest of the toys I will no longer need. I'm not having a thorough clear out, not by a long way. It's just I happen to know these tools of torture I will definitely never get to use again.

"So this is really it. No more Mistress Selina?" Charlie is peering into the stuffed box that I'm gifting to her. She smiles at the contents, but her face drops with an exaggerated downturn of her lips when her eyes meet mine. I beam my brightest smile back at her and chuckle.

"It's why you're here. So you can give the fake remorse a miss, Charlie. Besides, I couldn't be happier."

"That I'm taking over?" she offers brightly and nods.

"That I'm hanging up my whip."

"Won't you miss the kink?" Her perfectly pencilled brows draw close together and utter confusion fills her face.

"No."

"Really?" She practically gasps in horror.

"I won't miss it, because I'm not giving it up." I let out a loud laugh and shake my head at her misunderstanding. I clarify. "I am only giving up the job."

"Phew, hate to think we'd lost you to the vanilla brigade."

"Unlikely," I scoff. "You do know whom I'm marrying, don't you?"

"Yes…yes I do, you lucky bitch." She draws in a deep, slow breath, and I watch her closely as her eyelids flutter shut and she flattens her lips with her teeth. She lets out a breath and a huge sloppy smile spreads across her face.

"Did you just have a *moment*?"

"I did." She sighs unashamedly.

"For my Jason?"

"Hmm." She nods slowly.

"I'm not sure what to even do with that." I drop my mouth wide as a token of my mock outrage.

"Don't do anything. Look at you." She waves her hand up the length of my body, pointing with her extra-long, black acrylic nails. "He struck gold with you. Just allow a girl to mourn the loss of one more hot guy to the ranks of the wedded wastelands."

"You have a problem with marriage?" I drop my hip and raise my brow.

"Not at all. I would love to take a man as my wife. I'm just not sure where I'd find such a sucker," she replies with a completely serious, flat tone and a twitch of her lips.

"You're funny," I snark.

"I know. I'm hilarious." She grins and wrinkles her nose playfully. "Really, I just don't think it would be for me. I'm happy you're happy though. You deserve it, Sam. And I'm over the fucking moon I get all your kit. This shit would cost me a fortune." She goes to lift the box, but from her sitting position, it's actually too heavy. She turns and casts her eye around my room, hovering a little too long on my closed wardrobe doors. "I don't suppose you're dumping any of the outfits or this perhaps?" She stretches over my bed, to pick up my favourite handmade red bullwhip and strokes it seductively with her long fingers.

"Not a chance." I hold out my hand, and she pouts, quickly placing the whip in my palm. "I never said I was a saint. I do have one more thing for you that is much, much better." Charlie sits up straight and almost bounces with anticipation. I walk over to my bedside table and open the top drawer.

My contact book. I pick it up and wipe the thin layer of dust from its rough silk cover. Walking back around my bed, I sit next to Charlie and hand her my old life in a neat and meticulously kept record of all my clients.

"I never save contact details on my phone, and every night, I wiped the emails clean once I had transferred the appointments to my diary. This is the only hard copy of my clients' details, and I would recommend, if you don't already, do the same. Anonymity and privacy are extremely valuable commodities, and I'm only handing this to you because I have spoken to every person in this book and they agreed. Just so you know, you come highly recommended by me." I nudge her lightly because I can see from her expression she completely understands the significance of what I am doing.

"Thank you. I won't let you down, Sam. You can trust me." Her gaze is sincere, and her voice unwavering.

"I already do. I would never have given you Leon if I didn't." Charlie flashes a wide smile and slips the contact book into her satchel, patting it once the straps are buckled securely. "Speaking of...how is it going with him?"

"You know I can't tell you that." She raises a knowing brow, and I shrug my apology. I had to give her one last test; after all, my reputation is on the line.

"Honey, I'm home...Oh wait, she doesn't fucking live here anymore." I hear Leon mutter, supposedly to himself as I sip my tea, flicking through the newspaper while sitting on a stool at the kitchen island, waiting for him. Charlie left about an hour ago, and I decided to stay and spend a little time with Leon. *Maybe break the news that I'm getting married this weekend.*

"I think you need a cat, Leon." I snicker as he freezes in the doorway with a comical, albeit momentary, look of scared shitless on his face.

"Babe!" He beams and strides toward me, wrapping his strong arms tight around my waist and lifting me clear off the stool. I struggle to breathe, letting him have his fix. "I don't need a fucking cat. I need you to come 'round more often. I get that you're not gonna dump the guy, but do you have to be surgically attached to the fucker all the damn time? I was here first, you know." His tirade started off with a jokey undercurrent, but his tone sounded thoroughly pissed by the time he finished. "You're not married yet." My face screws up in a breath-holding grimace as he releases me and falls silent. I can feel his heated glare. "You're not married? Are you?"

"No, no." I shake my head, and he lets me slip to the floor. I plant my bottom back onto the stool and nervously spin my teacup, deliberately not meeting that searching look he's throwing my way. "That's this weekend." I hunch my shoulders, waiting for the booming reprimand. What I get is much worse. I get silence.

I open my screwed up eyes, and my shoulders drop from the weight of sadness I see in his eyes.

"Leon, don't look like that. I need you to be happy for me. You're my best friend. Please." My voice catches, and before I can say another word, my face is squished hard into his chest muffling any sound.

"I am happy for you Sam...I just wasn't expecting the rush. Why the rush? I thought you were going to take your time and plan the big day. You deserve a big day, babe." He releases some of the pressure in his hold, and I tilt my head back. He is trying to smile, but it's so far from reaching his eyes, it breaks my heart.

"I'm getting a big day, Leon. It's just after my accident Jason was really spooked, and what with the baby, it just didn't seem so important to wait anymore. It's not like I'm going to change my mind."

"I know. I just didn't think it would be so soon. It sort of seems really final...the whole marriage thing."

"It is final. It doesn't mean you aren't still my best friend. It doesn't mean you're not important to me, Leon. You're the first and only person I called about the baby for one thing. We had agreed not to let *anyone* know but I told Jason that didn't mean you." I reach up and hold his face. "You are *so* important."

"I was only just getting used to you not living here."

"It's just a piece of paper, Leon. It doesn't really change anything."

"Then why do it?" I let out a heavy sigh. I wasn't really expecting such a philosophical discussion, yet the question deserves more than a flip response.

"I love Jason. I'm going to have his baby, and he wants me to be his wife. It's not rocket science and as much as I don't need the piece of paper, I kind of want it too. Jason wants to claim me publicly as his wife...just his, and I love that he does. Whatever we do privately, he wants the world to know I belong to him and *he* belongs to *me*."

"Hmm." He leans in and kisses my forehead, his tone thick with doubt. "I still don't get the rush."

"It's not a rush. Well, it is, but for no reason other than...why wait any longer, when it's what we both want? I've never been a fan of delayed gratification." I wink, and that gets a small burst of laughter.

"Lucky you. I can vouch you don't feel the same for your clients. You are a fucking sadist when it comes to that shit.'

"You loved it." I slap his flat tummy, which tenses on impact, anticipating my strike.

"I did...I do." He grabs my hand and holds it in his, his eyes searching mine, but there is peace there now. Maybe not total happiness, somewhere in-between, and it's all I can hope for, for now. I pull my hand and break the intensity of his gaze and our conversation.

"How is Charlie working out?" My attempt to not so much change the subject, as to divert it away from me, doesn't go unnoticed. Leon's wry smile carves a slight curl in his lips.

"Good. Not as good as you but she'll get there. She has a real mean streak that I fucking love." He wiggles his brow salaciously, and I chuckle.

"I'm glad. That makes me really happy, Leon."

"She's not you, but she'll do."

"You want me to tell her that? She's just picked up my tool box, I—"

"She's here?" he blurts his interruption, and I snicker at the sheer panic in his voice. *Wow, she must have a mean streak.*

"No, she left an hour ago, and has all my torture toys now."

"Like she didn't have enough of her own… Shit. You nearly gave me a heart attack." He places his hand on his chest over his heart that must actually be thumping a strong beat by the heave of his deep breaths.

"That bad, eh?" I tease.

"That good, babe." He releases his hold on me and walks to the fridge, pulling out two beers then replacing one on seeing my dropped jaw.

"Sorry. My bad." He shrugs off his mistake. "It's not like you look like you've swallowed a beach ball or anything. When I look at you, pregnant woman is not the first thing I see." He pauses, and I raise a brow for him to continue his musing. "What I do see is a great rack." He takes a pull of his ice cold beer, his lips smirking around the neck of the bottle.

"Charming." I roll my eyes before casting a quick glance down. Since he isn't the only one to remark this, I have to wonder if I've got a Dolly Parton thing going on, but I can't see it. "I've checked your cupboards and you have zero food, so are we getting takeout or are you taking me out?"

"You're not leaving?"

"Did I stutter?"

"Cute." He narrows his eyes, his mouth is sporting a wide smile. "Takeout… I'm knackered. You choose what to eat, while I grab a shower…or you could join me." He waggles his brow playfully, and I laugh out loud.

"Tease."

"I don't tease," he states, but before any awkwardness descends, he shrugs off his comment and continues. "I look forward to you making my ears bleed with tales of the wedding and your sprog." He points an accusatory finger at my tummy, and my arm flies across my midsection in a protective gesture.

"Take that back! I am not carrying a sprog." I can't hide my disgust, and he chuckles.

"It's a girl then, is it? Okay then sprogette."

"Gah!" I screw up the newspaper and throw it at his departing body. It barely touches his shoulder but he does stop and casts a grin my way.

"Losing your touch already, Mistress," he goads.

"I still have my whip, Leon."

"Glad to hear it."

"We don't know the sex. What I do know though, is if you insult my baby again, you won't be glad...I promise you that." I grit out, adding my own lioness growl after my words.

"You're retired remember, so now who's teasing?" He steps quickly through to his bedroom before I can retaliate. *Incorrigible.*

Jason

Sam makes a mad dash across the narrow cobbled alleyway to where I'm parked. The rain is torrential and her thick wool coat has no hood, so she has it perched over her head for temporary cover. Squealing, she throws herself into the car along with a wave of London's finest winter weather. She shucks her coat from her head and launches across the centre console to kiss me.

"Hmm… missed you." Sighing, she collapses back into the seat. She gives a whole body shiver which I don't believe is a result of our kiss. Even with that short distance, her face was like ice pressed to mine. I blast the heaters and switch on her seat to gently toast her sexy arse.

"Is that so?" I waggle my brow, my chest warming with the sentiment I happily reciprocate tenfold. I flick the indicator and nudge the car out into the dense traffic, pulling out onto the main street to start our crawl across central London.

"God, yes. Stupid work stopping us from lying in bed and fucking all day." She grins and grumbles.

"Preaching to the choir, beautiful." I tap my cheek for another kiss, she wrestles with her seat belt and happily obliges, adding a few light kisses along my jaw for good measure. *Yeah, I missed her too.* "Did you talk to them about your hours?"

"I did, but we still can't stay home all day fucking…unless you're quitting too?" She sighs with mock sadness and pouts.

"You quit?" I blurt out, my intonation more hopeful than shocked.

"No…not exactly." She shifts on her side to face me, kicking her boots to the footwell and tucking her feet beneath her. "We agreed to switch my contract to pro rata, so I get paid hourly now. It's not like I have any cases of my own. I'm still pretty much the nerd research girl. Anyway, I spent the morning with my boss going over how it would work exactly, and they have set me up so I have remote access. I can now work from anywhere, whatever hours I choose. I think I'll still be full-time for a few months yet, but I can cut back whenever without it being a headache for them. I'm stoked they went for it, and if I'm honest, more than a little relieved." Her face beams with a bright, wide smile, even so, I can still see her eyes hold a wealth of concern. Her features are etched with the deep-seated worry I share, but have no intention of letting her carry the burden alone.

"That's amazing, although I'm not surprised they would try and accommodate you. You're an asset, and finding good workers is like the Holy Grail for any business. It's all about the employees, and now, for the sake of a little compromise, they have one sexy, intelligent, and hugely loyal staff member." I tell her as a matter of fact because it is the truth.

"My boss did mention the sexy thing was *really* important," she teases with a playful roll of her eyes.

"Cute." I reach over and squeeze her knee, sliding my hand aggressively to the top of her thigh and increasing my firm grip. Her breath catches, and she shivers, only this time, I know it's not from the cold. I pause a moment, my fingertips pressing her soft flesh, but all too soon, I have to return my hand to the wheel and try to focus on the rush hour traffic. "Did you manage to speak to Sofia?"

"I managed to have lunch" She bounces her knees with excitement. "She's like a wedding planner *force majeure*. You weren't far off, saying all I had to do was turn up."

"Are you happy with what she's arranged?" I can see she is, it's just with so much going on, I need to make sure.

"It's perfect actually." Her smile is shy, and her voice is a soft whisper. She can't contain that amazing smile, though. Straight, white teeth dazzle behind her slick, red lipstick, which slashes a perfect curve across her flawless face. "It's exactly what I would've picked, a small country hotel with close friends and family. She showed me a schedule, the flowers, photographer, and she's even sorted the cake!" she exclaims and clasps her hands together, her whole body bubbles with joy, and now, my own smile matches hers, her happiness is infectious and addictive. She rambles on, and I take in every word. "The wedding dress won't need altering because it's still too early for any significant change, and I know I haven't gained any weight. She's even sorted a little pampering in the morning for me…hair, make-up…a princess package, if you will."

"You don't need a princess package to look like royalty, but as long as you're happy?" I repeat my question.

"I'm very, *very* happy," she states emphatically and nods her head as extra clarification, her whole demeanour resolute, and I relax. I love it when a plan comes together.

"You might want to check the dress, though, because your tits are definitely bigger." My eyes dip to her chest. She gasps and slaps her hand on my shoulder, only I wasn't joking, and her brows furrow.

"Really?" She tips her chin right down and pulls the turtleneck of her sweater as far down as possible to have a peak. "Hmm." She lets the material snap back and traces a path down the front of her sweater with her hands, her fingers circling her nipples, which are tiny bumps beneath the ribbed material. Her hands grip and squeeze, lift and mould as she fondles herself. I nearly swerve the car off the road when she drops her head back and moans. *Fuck!* Her lips part and a soft sigh escapes. I grip the steering wheel with white-knuckle force, a second away from parking the damn car and pulling her onto my lap, regardless of the thousands of commuters pounding the pavement just outside the car. Just as suddenly, she snickers and drops her hands to her lap, folding them neatly and batting her lashes innocently at me. She can't maintain that façade for long because her eyes are drawn to the aching bulge in my trousers. I shift but gain no relief.

"Happy?" My voice is hoarse because my throat is dry.

"Lil' bit." She pinches her thumb and forefinger to indicate no distance at all then wiggles her brows.

"Oh you are going to pay for that." My voice is deep, and my tone is crystal clear with absolute certainty.

"Now I'm definitely happy." Her breathy response does fuck-all to help my hellish hard-on.

We sit in the spacious waiting room of the antenatal department of the private maternity hospital. It feels more like a hotel lounge, with sumptuous sofas, a large flat-screen television, serving tea and tiny cakes laid out on the low table. I'm surprisingly nervous. No, it's not surprising. Sam has had more than her fair share of trauma in her life, and what Richard did all those years ago has come back to haunt us both. I pull her hand into my lap and cover my other hand over the top of hers

"It's going to be fine." I state calmly.

"It might not be, Jason." Her voice is agitated and a little high-pitched. "I know you want to fix things and make everything right, just don't put so much pressure on yourself or me," she pleads, and I hate the uncertainty that is consuming all her confidence. She draws in a deep breath and lets it out slowly. "Whatever happens, we will deal, together." The next breath she draws is shaky. I hear the brave words yet her face is anything but. She's really worried about this.

"We will, Sam, together—you, me and my baby." I spear one of my hands into her hair and hold a firm fistful of her locks, so she's looking directly in my eyes. I hold her gaze for long seconds, hoping she can feel every ounce of sincerity in my words.

"*Our* baby," she corrects me with a grin.

"Our baby...but mostly mine." I nudge her, and she falls against my chest with a soft laugh.

"I love you, Jason, just in case you didn't know," she mutters into the material of my shirt. I am stroking her hair with one hand, and the other is still holding her hand.

"Well, you haven't told me since this morning, so I was beginning to worry."

"Mr and Mrs Sinclair." The nurse pokes her head around the doorway, and Sam tilts her head up to see me looking down, her perfectly shaped brow arches high.

"Thought it would save on the paperwork." I tap the end of her nose.

"Oh you did, did you?" She stands and straightens her skirt, her tight expression not the least affronted at my presumption. She offers her hand for me to take, which I do, only to pull her into my embrace as soon as I stand.

"Certificate or not, beautiful, you're already mine and always will be." I don't whisper, I proclaim, and I'd happily shout it to the world, although that isn't necessary because the only person that counts can hear me perfectly clear.

"You say the sweetest things." She fails to bite back her smile, and her cheeks flash an adorable pink.

"Don't I though?" I tug her to my side as I stride out the door and follow the nurse into a consulting room.

The baby and the scanner were both acting up and the doctor was unable to get a satisfactory reading, which was not what either of us really needed to hear, but the physician was very comforting. There was a strong heartbeat, and Sam is fit and healthy. Sam discussed her concerns, and I voiced mine, which were mostly regarding her need to take it easy. Sam's were more explicit and even I got a little hot when, after a very detailed, lengthy list, that wouldn't look out of place on a Dom/sub list of preferences, Sam asked if rough anal would be a problem. I was impressed the doctor didn't bat an eyelid at her question even if he did cast me a curious look. Yes, I was the insatiable monster in this relationship.

"It's not him." She rushes to defend my honour, catching just a glimpse of the doctor's expression before it reverted to blankly professional. "It's me…well both of us. We are both extremely…" She pauses as if she's now choosing to censor herself. I bite back a throaty laugh. A little late for that. "Active." She beams at me, I keep my lips tight, smiling as much as I can. God, she's adorable, and she seems pleased that her brain-to-mouth filter is kicking in. "I just want to be sure." She turns back to me, her expression more serious.

"I know, beautiful, me too." I pull her hand to my lips and kiss her fingertips. The doctor voices his understanding.

"And you are quite right to ask, if you have any uncertainty. I can assure you, very little shocks me."

"Oh please don't tempt her," I groan out and the doctor laughs, a hearty sound. I see the gleam in Sam's eyes, and I really wasn't joking.

The doctor shuffles his papers and closes Sam's thin patient folder that we have spent the last thirty minutes filling in. "I'm sorry about the scanner not working properly. If you can come back tomorrow after ten in the morning we will be able to give you another one and—"

"I'm not available tomorrow." My tone is clipped and irritated even though I know it's no one's fault. I just wanted to be there.

"I can wait." She squeezes my hand.

"No. I want you to have it done sooner rather than later." I shake my head at her offer. "I will make sure I'm there for the next one just get a picture okay?"

"You sure?" She checks again but I can see the relief in her face. She doesn't want to wait and I don't blame her.

"There will be other scans?" I turn to the doctor, but my question comes out more like an accusation and he looks startled.

"Of course, at least two. If you want more, we can surely accommodate you." He seems eager to appease but I'm feeling all kinds of unreasonable. "I understand this is an especially anxious time for you both, so anything we can do to make the pregnancy stress-free, we will." He really is trying now, and I shrug off my petty irritation and focus on the bigger picture, Sam.

"Okay then." I capitulate with a slight nod and turn my gaze to Sam. "I want you to come tomorrow, it's important."

"It is." She lets out a sigh that doesn't really ease her tension, but then, I wonder if anything will until, like she said, our baby is in our arms.

"Right, make the appointment, and when do we see you next? Is it next week or in a few days?" I address the doctor who just looks confused. I really wasn't asking a difficult question.

"Oh no…next month is fine." He waves his hand in a dismissive gesture.

"Really? Are you sure?" Now it's my turn to look confused.

"Perfectly." The doctor smiles warmly at Sam. "Mrs Sinclair will be sick to death of us if we see her more than she needs, trust me. If there are any problems, call us straight away, other than that, your next appointment will be next month." He hands Sam a card with the date of the appointment and a list of emergency numbers, including his.

"Oh, very well." My brow furrows because this doesn't sound right. Doesn't he realize how precious they both are? A month feels like a really long time.

"It will be fine." Sam's sweet voice and the teasing shake of her head bring me out of my worry. "I'm fine. We're fine. And a month will fly by." She stands and shakes the doctor's hand, thanking him, and I do the same. I don't feel nearly as grateful, bloody machine not working and then abandoning my wife and child for a month.

We leave the consulting room, walk the length of the corridor, and back out through the waiting room when she speaks.

"You know you're super sexy and adorable when you go all alpha papa on me." She lifts my arm and drapes it over her shoulder, snuggling against my side, and I cloak her body with mine.

"I'm not happy with the month thing. Do you think that's normal?" I grumble.

"I have no idea." She giggles and wraps her arms a little tighter around my waist. "I'll buy a book tomorrow. Needless to say though, I do feel much better having talked to the doctor."

"You do?" Her face twists to look up at me.

"Oh yeah." Her voice dips low with delicious intent, and my mind and cock are instantly recalling that list she recited in the doctor's office.

"About that list…" I growl.

"What about that list?" Her lips begin to tip and crawl into a devious smile.

"Which part of it do you think would be sufficient punishment for your behaviour in the car?" My voice is thick with latent lust, and my breath kisses her lips. She parts them a little, just enough to let her tongue dampen and tease.

"Oh…that was very bad." She feigns her sternest voice. "I think that warrants skipping the list and going straight to the rough anal."

"Now who says the sweetest things?" I crush the wicked smile right off her lips with my own urgent, demanding mouth.

I have been locked in sensitive meetings all morning and left a strict do-not-disturb instruction with Sandy unless it was Sam, but I didn't need to say that. We are at a critical stage in negotiations, and I know Daniel is keen for me to secure the sale, and I am pretty incentivized too. The bonus attached to such a lucrative deal should be just enough to pay for my wedding gift for Sam.

Sandy's raised voice from outside causes a wave of unease in the room, and all eyes dart to the door as it crashes open. James bursts through with Sandy tugging on his arm to try and pull him back. He straightens and fixes me with a knowing stare that makes my heart freeze, his face cracks with a triumphant smile. "I've got him!"

SEVEN

Sam

"You didn't have to come. It's so fucking early, Sofs. Really, the only time anyone should be up at this hour is because they are going on holiday." Sofia stifles a second yawn, waving her hand, dismissing my comment.

"Don't be silly. I'm an early bird, I just yawn a lot for the first hour or so." She laughs and starts another face stretching yawn that sets me off too. It's just after 5:30, and I have borrowed Jason's car because we have a lot of miles to cover. We are heading down south to pick up my wedding dress and then doing a quick U-turn and driving the three hundred miles north to Derbyshire, our wedding venue and hotel for the weekend. Jason's parents live nearby, and we have a small family meal planned tonight so I can at least meet them before the big day tomorrow. I understand Will flew over yesterday and is already staying with them.

"Is Paul coming up tonight?" I ask for the third time, turning the radio down this time. The heaters are still blasting the morning chill from the interior of the car, and I don't want to have to keep repeating myself.

"No, he's snowed at work, and he knows I'll be busy with the last minute bits. I told him that we are both at the spa in the morning, so he's just going to catch a ride with Daniel and Bethany. It's better that way or he'll just sulk that I'm ignoring him. And they say we're the needy ones," she scoffs, and we both laugh.

"Thank you for everything, Sofs." My voice softens and I reach over to grab her hand. I hope she can hear the shit-ton of gratitude in those few words because I'm so unbelievably grateful. As rushed as this is, she has gone above and beyond to make it completely magical and perfect.

"My pleasure honey, and anytime you want to share why the big rush, I am all ears." Her tone is leading, and her expression is piqued with eager interest at my response.

"Jason didn't tell you?" My eyes briefly meet hers before returning to the empty road.

"Nope. He just said he was done waiting, and could I sort it for this weekend. I spat my drink out at the time when I realized he wasn't joking. Man, he looks sexy as hell when he's serious—lethal." Her breath escapes, and she places her hand on her chest.

"You can say that again," I mutter, and I can almost feel the increase in her heartbeat because it mirrors mine.

"He said if I couldn't do it, he'd just take you to the town hall as soon as you landed. That was pretty much like laying down the gauntlet for a romantic like me." She sniffs derisively.

"And you don't think he knew this?" I quirk a curious brow and bite my smirk flat between my teeth.

"Hmm? Ooooh, he's good. I didn't consider that." Her eyes widen and she shakes off any irritation at being played by my beloved, not that I honestly think there was any real irritation to begin with. "No matter. I love a challenge, and if I do say so myself, I have excelled." She sits up as best she can in the racing bucket seat and puffs out with rightly deserved pride. "But I'm not going to toot my horn until you have given it the all clear."

"Oh toot away, Sofs. I couldn't and wouldn't have chosen anything different. It's perfect, like you read my mind, which is a little creepy."

"Jason was *very* specific." She gives me a knowing smile.

"Of course he was," I mutter as a smile spreads wide across my sleepy face. Sofia turns in her seat, and it takes me a moment to realize she is waiting for an answer to her passive question. I snort out a laugh. It's early and my brain isn't really awake.

"I'm pregnant." I flinch and shrink down at the shrill cry that fills the car.

"Oh my God! Oh my God!" Her excitement is like a physical friendly slap on the back, her bright smile and clasped hands barely contain her joy. I'm completely blown away. I don't think I have allowed myself to feel a fraction of this, not even at the scan. She claps her hands rapidly unable to contain her enthusiasm a moment longer. "Oh my God, Sam, that's fantastic. Congratulations! Oh my God, you are going to have the most gorgeous baby." I laugh, letting some of the pent up tension I permanently seem to carry ease. But the respite is brief because it's there, under the surface, lurking. I return her smile even if mine is tempered. "Do you have a picture?"

"Sore point, but no is the short answer. The scanner wasn't working properly the first time, and they couldn't get an accurate image. When I went the next day, the printer wasn't working. They were very apologetic and were going to send the pictures as soon as the machine was fixed. I sort of hoped I would have them by now." I hate that something as genuine as a technical problem makes me anxious. I draw in a steadying breath. "It's really early days, Sofs, just a couple of weeks, and I have history which—" My voice catches and she instantly reaches across the car to press her hand firmly against my knee. "We're not telling anyone yet." I manage to give her a fraction of my story, and her eyes fill with understanding and more.

"I get it, I do. I'm sure you'll be fine, and the pregnancy will be fine." She conveys genuine comfort with her tiny grip and flashes a wide, confident smile. "You're like this Amazonian goddess. I've never known anyone stronger than you, Sam. You've got this." She nods, stating her declaration with absolute certainty. I hope so.

The remainder of the journey is wedding talk and a little more wedding talk. When we arrive at Katie's bridal boutique I'm bubbling with excitement even if it is just after seven in the morning. Katie unlocks the door and is bouncing on her toes when we enter the shop. Her genuine, sweet smile gives me comfort that she is not in the least pissed to be opening up at this unGodly hour.

"I have coffee and croissants but let's get you fitted first." Katie's voice is elevated with excitement as she ushers us inside. We are hit with a wave of warm air, a welcome reprieve from the bitter morning breeze that whips around the courtyard of the shops like a mini tornado. I stand under the blast from the heater until my shivers have subsided and only then lose my coat.

"Sounds good." Sofia rubs her arms to get some warmth as I'm hogging the heat and jumps in my place the instant I step away.

"No coffee for me though. Maybe a mint tea if you have it." My head may crave the caffeine hit but my stomach rolls with disapproval.

"Or hot chocolate?" Katie offers.

"Hmm, yes one of those." I start to strip, eager to try on my dress and more excited for the chocolate. Now my tummy is rumbling at the very thought of sweet, liquid sustenance and buttery goodness of the aforementioned croissant.

"Okay, just so you know though, I'm not so much letting the steam from a cup in this room until the dress is packed back away," Katie warns whilst reaching up to unzip the protective plastic from the gown hanging on a high hook by the large, gilt mirror. Sofia has positioned the modesty panel across the doorway, although there isn't a soul around, but I'm in my boy-shorts and cupping my boobs, so it's probably for the best.

"Hmm, you might need to lose the shorts too." Katie's brow wrinkles with thought. "Drop to a squat, and I'll slip it over the top first. I happen to think those will ruin the line though." She holds the delicate material open for me to thread my arms through, and I stand and shimmy to let the silky lace material glide down my body. I squeeze and pull my boobs through the narrow waist but where the bodice should kiss the swell of my breasts, it's stuck in an angry stretch that if I take a deep breath will definitely rip. I don't need to take a shocked breath because Katie and Sofia do it for me.

"Oh!" Katie gasps in horror, and I stand transfixed and only puffing in tiny amounts of air, conscious of the tension in the lace and silk across my chest. I try to move when Katie's worried voice halts me. "No, don't move, honey! Let me ease this off." Her fingers slide against my skin and I let out more air to shrink enough for her to slip the material free. I don't know whether it's the early start, the hormones, and every other little thing, but this…this is the one that breaks me. I crumple into a sad heap and fold over, crossed legged and head in my hands, stupid tears soaking my hands and running down my arms. Sofia is at my side, her arm over my shoulders.

"It's all right, honey, we'll find another dress." She tries to comfort me. I feel like the most spoilt brat on the planet and that just makes me sob harder. *I don't want another dress…that was* my *dress.* Long minutes drag and the silence is filled with sporadic hiccups and soggy sniffles. I'm still mostly naked on the carpeted shop floor, and however warm the room is, it's not that warm, and I start to shiver. Katie drapes a large soft blanket over me and half over Sofia. She drops to her haunches in front of me.

"I can try to fix this, Sam." Her hand brushes my hair from my face, damp tendrils slick with tears resist. She manages to scrape enough back to see my sorry-looking face. Her smile is tentative at best.

"How?" I swallow the lump in my sore throat and wipe my cheeks dry.

"Get dressed and let's have that chocolate. Everything feels better with chocolate." She and Sofia help me up and manhandle me back into my clothes. I feel sick and numb when I'm fully dressed and sit down on the small love seat. I take the steaming mug that Katie offers. "The lace is imported but there is another designer in London that shares my supplier, so I will call her at nine and see if she has any in stock. If she does, I will get it couriered here, and I will add two discrete panels at the side which should accommodate the…" She hesitates and her eyes dip to my bust.

"Massive boobs." I help her out, and she quirks her lips to give a sympathetic smile. I let out a deep breath. "This can't be happening. I haven't gained any weight. How are my boobs suddenly wanting their own area code?"

"They're not that big, Sam." Sofia still has her arms across my shoulders, and she nudges me, her face now happily hopeful after Katie's contingency plan.

"There are a lot of ifs in that sentence." I don't share her optimism, which is understandable, I have just had the arse kicked out of my fairy tale, so am tinged with more than a little doom and gloom.

"Yes, there are, but if I can, I will." Katie states sternly, and I try for the first smile since I was hit with this couture crisis. "But," she adds with equal emphasis, "in the meantime why don't we try on some of my other designs. If worst comes to the worst there are five bridal shops in this town. I can promise you will be leaving today with one wedding dress that fits," she assures me, but my heart sinks.

"I want one of yours," I add like a sullen, petulant child. This is supposed to be *my* big day, and I feel a little upset is justified.

"I want that to. Let's eat and then I'll make the call." She pushes a fat, flaky croissant onto a small plate and hands it to me. I take it, and even though I'm hungry, I hesitate. Will this go straight to my boobs too? Sofia takes the plate Katie offers her and nudges my arm.

"Moment on the lips…nine months on the boobs," she leans in to whisper, and I let out a final breath of exasperation. It's just a dress. The sexiest, most stunning dress I'm ever likely to wear, but it's still just a dress. I rest my hand on my tummy, letting the hysteria dissolve and appreciate I have something much more precious, that apparently requires bigger boobs.

The sun had sunk low in the winter sky by the time the courier arrived, and Katie has been working flat out for three hours to make the adjustments. She was a fucking miracle worker because when I stood before the mirror hours later, I could see no difference. The dress hung low and sensually clung to my curves, the delicate material fitted perfectly, and I wasn't the only one weeping when I did my final twirl.

"Thank you so much for this, Katie. I can't believe you did this." The dress is packed away, and Katie hands the sheathed dress over to Sofia's waiting arms.

"Felt like I was on that television show *The Sewing Bee* for a moment with the minutes ticking. I'm so glad you're happy. I would've been gutted if I'd had to send you off to someone else. This design was made for you, even with the little adjustment. Congratulations, by the way." She holds my gaze, and I feel the heat in my cheeks.

"How did— " I stutter, and she snorts and waves her hand as if I'm being ridiculous.

"Oh please. You are not the first pregnant bride, and you won't be the last, but I can say this: You will be the most stunning."

"Ah I bet you say that to all your brides."

She zips her lips and winks. "I'll want pictures for my website!" She calls out as we go to leave and then rushes over to give me a slightly awkward hug.

"Oh yeah, sure, of course." My hands are full with bags, but I'm not a hugger, so I do this lean and pat thing that seems to placate her and makes Sofia laugh. She waves us off and continues to wave until we have walked the length of the courtyard and turned the corner.

"She's seen you naked yet personal space is an issue for you?" Sofia quips as we make our way back to the car.

"Many people have seen me naked. Intimacy is not the same as nudity. As sweet as she is, she's still a stranger and I don't go round hugging strangers." I clarify and Sofia shrugs lightly.

"I'm a hugger, even so, I can count on one hand the number of people that have seen me in my birthday suit and that includes my mum and dad." She grins, and as if to prove a point, she wraps her arms around my waist and pulls me into a sideways hug as we continue to walk. I don't mind; she's far from a stranger, and much more like a best friend.

EIGHT

Sam

We pull up the winding gravel drive just before midnight. It's difficult to see the place because there's absolutely no street lighting or neighbouring buildings illuminating the surrounding area. The front of the hotel has a warm, welcoming glow on the porch. We are both utterly exhausted, and I believe for us, this place looks like a mirage. I called Jason when we left Katie's shop, but the traffic has been one long never-ending snake of red taillights. A journey that should've taken just over three hours has taken close to six. I have missed the dinner with the in-laws and a chance to unwind, and I'm even too tired to be tense about it. All I want to do is cuddle up in the arms of someone who really isn't going to care if I look like shit, because I know he's seen me look much worse. The night manager checks us in and informs us that the wedding party all retired to their rooms some time ago. Lucky bastards.

I am tempted to wake Jason, but since Sofia scowled and gave me the 'bad luck' lecture, I posted a note under his door. Too tired to be eloquent, the note simply read, 'I love you'. I skulked off to my own room, the Honeymoon Suite, at the far end of the corridor, away from the other guests, and in record time, I have climbed between the heavenly sheets. Bliss.

Oh God that feels good. I stretch out on my back and unashamedly spread my legs wide. It's a dream and I have no shame. This is the best bit, I claw my fingers into his thick hair and pull him to just where I need him. Grinding my hips and moaning loudly…absolutely no shame. "Make me come." He growls that sexy, throaty sound tinged with menace, he's not a fan of being told what to do, lucky for me, this will help. "Please, Sir." I pull his hair, and my back arches high off the bed when his tongue drags hard and heavy over my most sensitive centre, again and again. Strong hands push the tops of my thighs so wide I feel the painful stretch in my muscles. Oh lord that tongue is relentless and perfectly distracting. Waves of pleasure start to ripple from my toes, tiny at first but building and creeping up my body, gaining momentum with every swipe and swirl. His breath is like a burst of flames at my core yet it's me that's on fire. My skin tingles with heat. My blood sizzles, and I dissolve with molten ecstasy at his skillful touch. He slides two fingers inside, and I scream with shock as my orgasm rips through me. *Holy shit!* He didn't even curl and pump those fellas. I tremble and smile to myself, even in my dreams he's just that good.

I jolt when a heavy hand covers my mouth and every muscle in my body contracts in panic as I buck, struggle, and fight to break free.

"Hey, hey, calm down." His deep, soft timbre does calm me instantly, and I shudder with the speed at which my body goes from utter terror to safely pliant at his voice.

"Mmmason," I mumble under his hefty palm. He lifts it free, and I squint up in the darkness as he hovers half over my body, his torso wedged between my spread thighs. "Jason?" I repeat the question, which sounds stupid now that I have.

"Who did you think it was licking you into oblivion exactly?" His eyes narrow, gleaming with wickedness. The room is still dark, although the light from the en suite casts enough of a glow for me to see him clearly, all dark and devilish, sexy as all hell with piercing eyes and soft full lips that are now very, very wet.

"I thought I was dreaming. Kiss me." I sigh and thread my hand around his neck to pull him closer.

"Was it me in your dreams, beautiful?" His husky voice is clipped, and his face flashes with something dark, uncertain. I don't hesitate, sitting up as much as I can I clasp both hands around his neck.

"Only ever you." I crush my lips to his, and I hope he can feel the truth. *Only ever him.* He takes my offering and returns it with passion tenfold, urgent and ravenous. His tongue dives and invades my mouth, my tastes coats him as he consumes me. We duel and tussle, claw and grab at each other like we're starved creatures, barely human, with raw animal desire, and just like that time on the beach, something switches in me, and that burn for more becomes too tempting to ignore…too delicious…too dangerous.

"You shouldn't be here. You need to leave." I break the kiss and push away as much as his weight will allow. I try to scissor my legs closed. He pauses for a moment, searching my eyes. My voice is serious and my face even more so, but if he looks hard enough he will see the fire in my gaze. This is a very fine line I'm leading him along, and it's only that I trust him with my soul that I feel safe enough to play with that fire, a fire his eyes now recognize.

"Make me."

It's like a touch paper being lit, and I explode beneath him. The force of the move and sharp twist in my body takes him by surprise, and I manage to scramble out from under his body and slip to the edge of the bed. He wraps a hand around my ankle and swiftly drags me back across the sheet, planting a sound slap on my arse cheek and laughing at my futile attempt to escape. *Oh I'm mad now.* I kick my legs, and once again, I'm free. This time, I'm quick and leap from the bed and race toward the bathroom. I only make it two strides across the room. He's like my shadow, instantly at my back. He grabs my arm and spins me against his chest, stepping me hard and fast against the wall. I grunt, breathless at the impact, and he steps back and freezes, his hands held up in surrender.

Not what I was expecting in the cat and mouse game of rough resistance play.

"I can't, Sam." His broken tone and soft words slice me. He shakes his head and steps up to me softening the rejection that must be plastered on my face. "Not because I don't want to…fuck look how much I want to." His eyes dip and mine follow his line of sight to the most painful looking erection straining against his abdomen. "You are the fucking sexiest woman alive but I can't play this game…not right now. What if I hurt you?" His question feels rhetorical and sounds like a plea.

"You hurt me all the time Jason. I like it, remember?" I can't hide the hurt and humiliation. My words are fired with a snarl, my tone harsh and hateful. He doesn't flinch and steps flush against my heaving body, adrenalin and desire still coursing through me despite his shut down.

"This is different, and you know it." He speaks calmly. His position resolute. "I want to try this. I get it, I do, but this could get very rough, and I'm not prepared to risk my baby." Shit now I feel worse. I deflate in his arms. *What's wrong with me?* He pulls me into his warm embrace, and I crumple in his arms.

"I didn't think…I just…" I falter, my guilt wrestling with my shame, rendering me speechless.

"That's what I'm here for. We're in this together, Sam, and I wasn't thinking either, or I wouldn't have started. This wasn't exactly covered on your 'list' at the doctor's, nevertheless I'm pretty sure he would've said no." He brushes the fallen hair from my face. His fingers sweep my cheek, and he holds my face so he is gazing unobstructed into my eyes. "You're strong, Sam, but really, you don't stand a chance against me."

"Oh is that so? We'll see about that." I let out a light laugh at his wry smile. His teasing tone is enough to bring me back to my senses without a shred of blame.

"In about nine months." He waggles his brows playfully, and I let my head drop onto his chest and smile against his warm skin.

"In seven months and a bit," I mutter. My breath catches at the depth of love in his gaze. He bends and scoops me into his arms, turns and walks back across the room, and unceremoniously dumps me onto the bed.

"We will rain check that new game, but for now, I'm going to go old school and just fuck your brains out." His voice is low and sensual. The bed dips as he stalks up my body. His eyes are filled with such desire and adoration, any trace of rejection is obliterated with that completely covetous look scorching my skin as it travels the length of my reclining body.

"I like the sound of that." I sigh, letting my eyelids flutter close at his filthy promise.

"Not sure all the other guests will share your view though Sam, so maybe keep the screaming down."

"I thought you liked it when I screamed your name." I suck my bottom lip in and let my most wicked grin plaster my face.

"I do." He hesitates and his expression is troubled; it takes a moment to sink in.

"Your mum…don't tell me she's a light sleeper?" I get a nervous knot in my stomach, and I wonder if his mother is actually the queen of bloody England. I really wish I had met her before because this pedestal her boys have placed her on makes my neck strain.

"She wouldn't have to be a light sleeper, Sam, you scream like a banshee." He settles, kneeling between my legs. His heavy cock in his hand, resting the tip at the apex of my thighs, before tapping a hypnotic rhythm.

"Fine, I won't scream." My mouth waters at the sight.

"I could gag you."

I smile sweetly. "You could try," I purr.

"Sam." He punctuates his stern address with a firm tweak of my nipple. I gasp when he gives me no warning then slams his full length inside me. *Shit!* I cry out in my head and mumble behind tight pinched lips. He pulls right out and slams back in, harder. He groans and closes his eyes briefly, only to sear through me when he opens them. Oh God, I'm in trouble. I swallow back a strangled squeak at the utter pleasure that saturates my body with each thrust. He angles himself to gain maximum traction and hits the very end of me with the next thrust. The agony is pure ecstasy, and he is far from going easy.

"I thought you said something about not hurting me." I gasp again on his unchecked downstroke.

"Resistance fucking and rough fucking are completely different, and I do believe we got the all clear from the good doctor regarding a little of the rough fucking." His hips drive forward pushing deeper and moving us both up the bed.

He pulls out again, this slow steady pace is driving me insane. Fuck, it feels oh so good. "Hmm wait…that's not exactly true is it?'" He ponders whilst giving me a delicious deep roll and grind of his hips. I think I should've opted for the gag. He pulls completely out, and with stealth and strength, flips me on to my front, hauling my hips up and back. One hand strikes my bottom cheek and the other olds his cock against my slickness, ominously moving slowly up and down, up and down, gathering moisture. I shudder. "Oh good, you remember what else the good doctor gave the all clear for."

He pushes hard against my tight entrance and I push back, because as much as it hurts—my muscles fight the intrusion—it hurts far fucking less if I relax and enjoy. And I *really* do enjoy. A deep throaty groan rumbles from his chest, and he hisses when I force myself back as he surges forward.

"Holy fucking shit, you're tight," he grunts.

"Holy fucking shit, you're enormous," I pant. A flush of heat prickles my skin, and I see dark dots when I open my eyes. His hands leave my hips, and he reaches to hold my shoulders, he leans over and presses a tender kiss between my shoulder blades.

"You ready, beautiful?" Sweet kisses trail my spine with each word.

"Would it matter if I wasn't?" I twist my head to look over my shoulder. He lifts his head at the movement, and a sexy, nefarious smile lights his face.

"Since this is rough anal, I'm going to say no, it really wouldn't." His tone is light and casual. He resumes planting tender kisses, and I can feel his lips curve in a smile against my skin. Then they are gone.

"Ah!" I cry out then snap my mouth tight at the noise. His sudden pounding has pushed the sound right from my lungs before I can stop it. I brace myself for the next time, because he wasn't lying, this is rough, brutal, and glorious. His hips slap furiously against my bottom as he all but tears through me, so fucking deep I struggle to breathe. The wild passion I felt briefly from our halted play earlier, returns with equal fervour, and my whole body thrums to his relentless rhythm. My breaths are rapid, and my skin is slick under his firm grip, as he uses my own body for leverage to thrust and pound, chasing his own pleasure and mine. He drags one hand down my spine and sweeps it around the front of my body. Eager fingers hunt for my tingling nub of nerves, and I buck in his hand when he strikes gold.

"I'm going to come, Jason. Please." My body starts to tremble, and my chest aches from panting so hard.

"Wait for me." I whimper at his words and grit my teeth because I don't think I have that kind of strength of will. His fingers slide along my folds, up and around my clit in time with his pounding from behind, the pressure perfect, and I rock against his hand. It's too much, my muscles clamp down, and I shake my head at the futility of trying to hold the floodgates.

"Sorry," I cry out, the flash of guilt replaced by hungry muscles contracting and squeezing every bit of pleasure from this immense orgasm wracking my body. My arms give out, and my head drops to the pillow. I'm a hot, sweaty mess, and now I'm being crushed to death by the sexiest man alive as Jason collapses on top of me.

"Mmm." My breathy moan is released when he quickly rolls to my side and pulls me against his hot, heaving body. "I'm sorry."

"What for?" His body moves so it perfectly aligns with mine. *Big spoon.*

"I couldn't hold on for you." I pant trying to regain my breath, and he lets out a raspy laugh like he's struggling for breath too.

"I noticed, don't sweat it, I caught up just fine." He kisses my hair, and his hot breath warms my face.

"You did?"

"You were a little out of it so you might've missed me."

"Oh good." I yawn and snuggle back into his hold, relishing his warmth and love. We lie like that for long blissful minutes when I turn in his arms. "You really shouldn't be here. It's supposed to be bad luck."

"Think we've had our share of bad luck for a lifetime, don't you?"

"I really do, so let's no tempt fate." I pinch his nipple and shove him playfully. He takes the hint and rolls out of the bed. He looks at his watch. It is still very much night-time.

"You will be my wife in less than twelve hours, I think fate's had its chance." I close my eyes as if that will make me not hear his boastful comment.

"Oh wow, you just had to say it!" I roll my eyes and drop my head in my hands with disbelief.

"Since when did you become superstitious?" He chuckles, slipping his boxer briefs back on.

"Since you started saying stupid things. Now go…go and pray, or find a black cat, or something to undo your taunt." He flashes me a wide smile and leans down to kiss my forehead, ruffling my hair as he does,

"You're adorable when you fret. Talking of fretting, did you open the letter from the clinic?"

"What letter?" I sit upright and suddenly very awake for the late hour.

"The one I left…" He looks around the darkened room and then turns and walks over to the dresser. He picks up something flat and walks back to me. "This letter." He hands me the envelope I hadn't noticed last night and switches on the bedside lamp.

I sit up and carefully tear the envelope. I don't bother to read the letter, more apologies no doubt. The slippery shiny photo I hold in my hand is the most precious prize. The grainy image is rubbish if I'm honest. It does, however reveal, the semicircle curve of a tiny spine is as clear as day.

"This is my baby?" Jason sits beside me, staring at the image. He takes the picture and squints.

"Our baby." I correct, my face beaming.

"I know, all the same I'm pretty fucking relieved it's mine." He nudges me, and I can see the truth in his eyes. That makes two of us.

I wait for him to hand the picture back and smile to myself that he seems to take in every line and dot in with such interest. He hands it back and traces my jawline, then tips my chin, kissing me so softly. It takes my breath away and makes my heart ache.

"I love you, Sam. No matter what fate decides, I will *always* love you." He places the picture on the bedside table and makes it to the door when I stop him.

"Jason, are we good?" I hate the sudden twist in my stomach but his words, which should warm my heart, do little to ease my rising anxiety.

"We're perfect, beautiful. See you at the altar. Don't be late." His heart-stopping smile spreads wide across his face, then his eyes warm and crinkle with joy. It should ease my mind yet, I find all the disquiet I felt, if only for a moment —yeah that's all still right there, festering in my stomach—waiting for the fates to come and play.

NINE

Sam

"Nooo…" I groan and quickly pull the covers over my head to soften the glare from the sudden burst of bright sunlight.

"What do you mean no?" I can hear Sofia pull more curtains open. "I hardly slept a wink the night before my wedding. I had to sneak in with Bethany just to get some sort of rest." She stomps around the room, and from the brightness filtering through my tightly squeezed lids, she must have already opened all the damn curtains and possibly erected a search and rescue spotlight and aimed it directly at me for good measure. "I left you as long as possible, but we've got the spa appointments in twenty minutes." She paces heavily across the room, her singsong voice irritatingly cheerful. Even on my wedding day, I'm not a morning person, and I grip the sheet a little tighter. She sounds like a bloody elephant not a young woman barely filling a size ten, and she is puffing like she's run a marathon. I still haven't surfaced.

Huffing loudly, she then falls silent. My curiosity has me peeking over the edge of the covers, squinting at the light. She has her arms folded and is trying to look stern. Her smile, however, is too wide to hide the abundant excitement, which radiates from her and hits me full force like the sunlight beaming through the full bay window. *She's got me.*

I grin and throw the cover back in a dramatic billow of material. I need to push the nerves aside and enjoy today. I get to marry the most amazing man, carry his baby, and I'll be surrounded by the very *best* of friends. *How fucking lucky am I?* I shiver at the morning chill and quickly slip on Jason's t-shirt that he must have left last night, physical evidence that last night wasn't a dream. *It so felt like a dream.*

"Okay, give me five minutes to grab a quick shower," I call to Sofia as I scurry to the en suite.

"I'll make us some coffee. We'll grab something to eat at the spa. They have an amazing restaurant," she shouts after me.

"Oh okay. Just mint tea for me, please." I poke my head round the bathroom door and she gives a kind, knowing smile and salutes her finger in understanding.

Ten minutes later, I emerge clean, fresh, and unbelievably excited. Sofia is sitting on the bed with the scan photo of my baby in her hand. The two cups of tea are untouched on the side. She turns to me with a strange frown and a flash of worry in her eyes. I'm instantly at her side, looking for what she sees that I must have missed.

"What?" I snap in a panic. "What is it? What's wrong?'" I take the photo. It's exactly the same grainy picture I saw for the first time late last night.

"Nothing, sweetie." Her voice is rushed but calm. "Nothing is wrong. Sorry, I just wondered something because you said you were only a few weeks pregnant."

"Yes, that's right. Why?"

"Well, there's no date on this picture. They usually have dates and weeks on the bottom here." She points to the blurred line of print at the bottom.

"They had trouble with the printer, maybe it still wasn't working properly. But the baby…the baby looks all right? I've never really seen one of these pictures I—" My voice breaks and she interrupts.

"No, sweetie, the picture is fine. I've seen a few, and this is a good one. A very good one, I mean, for a month or so. I was surprised because this is very detailed. Look, you can see the head, nose, round tummy." She sweeps her finger and it's like a great unveiling as the grainy image comes to life before me as she points things out that look so obvious now that she has. "Even the legs have little toes." The curl of her lips stops before her full smile covers her face once her eyes meet mine.

I feel my stomach drop and a cold sweat instantly coats my body.

I grab the letter from the bedside table.

The one I didn't bother to read last night. I silently take in the information that is slowly confirming my worst nightmare. I drop the letter and rush to the bathroom, slamming the door wide. I crash down on to the toilet just in time to empty the pitiful contents of my stomach. I can't move. I'm frozen to the cold tile floor, shaking. This can't be happening. I feel the gentle warm hands sweep sweat soaked hair from my face. After a several painful, endless minutes, I pull myself up only to collapse back against the bath with my head in my hands.

"So you're more like twelve weeks. You look bloody amazing for twelve weeks." Sofia shuffles to sit beside me. She nudges me, and her voice is light and holds no real concern…*yet*. "The clinic letter said you gave them the wrong dates that's why there was some confusion." She moves again to crouch on her haunches in front of me, her sweet face assessing the state before her. She stands and runs some water before dropping once more to the floor and tries to hand me a cool cloth. When I make no move to take it, she starts to pat my face, the soft coolness is a balm for my skin which seems to alternate between the extremes of an icy chill and spiked heat prickles with every passing minute.

"I gave them the dates I was given when I found out. The dates they gave me when I was in hospital after my accident." My voice doesn't sound like my own, lifeless, hollow and in total shock.

"It explains the boobs." She tries to make light, and I feel the first tear.

"What am I going to do?" I mouth the words, and they can only be heard because Sofia leans in at the first hushed croak of my voice.

"I don't understand, sweetie? You're a little more pregnant that you thought. It's not really that much of a big deal. Jason knows you're pregnant. You're still getting married."

"I can't." I shake my head yet she heard that whisper loud and clear, judging by her stunned tone.

"What, now?"

I look up into her eyes and hold her gaze. "Sofia, I don't know who the father is?"

"What the what now?" Her laugh is forced and has a touch of hysteria. I close my eyes but the tears fall anyway, soaking my cheeks. I pull my knees up and drop my head, the large bath towel absorbing the tears as quickly as they fall.

"Oh God, he doesn't want this." I mumble and sob, the tears won't stop and the pain ripping through me is unbearable. "He doesn't want a baby like this. I know he doesn't. I have to tell him. He has to know the truth."

"Sam, you're not making any sense. Darling, please, I don't understand." Her calm voice is trying to soothe, but her next words hold an edge of accusation. "You cheated on Jason?"

"No! God, no." My eyes snap wide with the horror of that suggestion, and I slap my hand to my mouth, shaking my head and that thought from my mind. Never.

"So Jason is the father?"

"He might be." I draw in a deep breath and watch as Sofia does the same. She waits, and I swallow thickly before I slowly exhale and clarify. "But then so might be his brother Will, …and Leon."

"Oh." I hear her gasp and gulp before silence descends like a bomb blanket, only this one has failed to shield me from the blast, this one has me contained underneath, surrounded by the debris and devastation.

A loud clap echoes off the poor acoustics in the white tiled room, and I look over to Sofia who has her hands clasped.

"He's still going to marry you," she states as a matter of fact. "He loves you and this is obviously something you did together, so he isn't going to shy away from it, Sam. He's not that kind of guy, is he?"

"He...I..." I clutch at my chest as the breath to speak catches. The pain is unbelievable. I hold it tight; it's the only thing that feels real. "I know just how much he wants this baby to be his...everything else...I ...I don't know." I squeeze my eyes shut as the pain from my chest sears through me and implodes with the uncertainty. I have to know. I jolt upright. "I have to tell him before the ceremony. He has to know the truth." I scramble to my feet and rush for the door like a woman possessed. I hear Sofia shrieking at me, but I am already down the hall banging on doors, and calling his name. My voice is hoarse from the tears and catches each time I utter his name.

"Jason?" I drop my head against the last door when not one has opened.

"Sam, sweetie, they've all gone out. Then they are doing the clay shoot activity. Jason gave me your room key this morning before he left." Sofia approaches me with a soothing voice and a tentative smile. "Come on back to the room, crazy lady." She gives a light laugh only her eyes are not quite smiling. I let out a shaky breath and take her hand, because right now, I have no idea what to do, and I need this guidance like a lifeline. She makes me sit on the bed and hands me my tea, which is now cool enough to drink down in gulps but I sip.

"What am I going to do?"

"Right." Her voice is so filled with authority it makes me sit up. "You're going to get dressed. We are going to go to the spa and relax. You will get your makeup and hair done, and then we will come back." Her list sounds so simple and... "You can speak to Jason then." I feel more stupid tears trickle down my face.

"What if he doesn't want to go through with it? I will be all dressed up and looking like a fool." I sniffle. I hope this is the hormones and I'm not actually this pathetic.

"You will look stunning, and he *will* want to go through with it, Sam. He loves you, and loves transcends everything. Trust me. I only speak the truth." She flashes her brightest smile that even causes my lips to twitch in an upward motion.

"You're a romantic, Sofia. You have such faith in what you're saying, I doubt you've encountered this type of situation." I hate to highlight this sordid scenario, yet I do. Even if I personally don't feel it's remotely scandalous, to an outsider, this can—at best—look irresponsible. Much more likely, the reaction will be a mix of horror and disgust.

"Maybe, but I've seen him with you, and I just know you have absolutely nothing to worry about." She takes the cup from my hands and holds out a neatly folded pile of clothes, which I numbly take. In lieu of a better plan, I agree to do exactly what Sofia has suggested.

My heart is aching and my head is a mess. I can't think of anything except talking to Jason, because as fucked up as this is, I won't walk down that aisle with an ounce of uncertainty. I won't let my baby grow up with a father that isn't all-in, not one-third. He has to be one hundred percent all-in.

TEN

Jason

"Sofia!" I call out, a muted shout. Sofia's hand is poised to knock on Sam's door only to turn at the sound of my voice. I wave my hand for her to come to me rather than shout out again, which would defeat the purpose of my interruption in the first place.

"Morning. Jason. You're up bright and early. I was just about to wake Sam. Is there something you need?" She doesn't draw breath, and I fight a grin because her excitement is infectious.

"Morning, sweetheart." She leans up to greet me with a kiss on my cheek and then wraps her arms around my waist and hugs the life out of me, making me chuckle. "Yeah, I'm excited too."

"I know right! I love weddings, and in that dress, Sam is going to be stunning." She beams.

"I have to argue that clothing just hinders. Her beauty is fucking soul deep." I'm not given to sappy shit, but if I can't express how I feel on my wedding day, then when can I? Besides, I have to test a little of this speech material out before I declare it openly to everyone later. Sofia's face crumples and she whimpers.

"Oh, Jason." Her fingers press against her lips, but I can see that bottom one start to wobble. *Result.* "You're going to make me cry." She shakes herself and pulls back to give me a playful punch on my arm, her eyes are already welling.

"Can't have that, well not yet. Maybe save it for the actual speeches."

"Oh God, I'll be a mess by then. The romance runs deep with this one." She places her hand over her heart and sighs.

"So I've heard. You've been fantastic, Sofia, and we're both really grateful. This place is perfect. Today is going to be just *perfect.*"

"Well, it will be if you let me wake sleeping beauty—"

I stop her mid-sentence. "Actually, that's why I caught you. She had a really late night. Maybe you could leave her for another hour?"

"Really?" Her brows furrow with confusion. "It was only just after midn— oh!" She quickly bites her lip at my knowing look, her brows now shooting high on her forehead and her cheeks flashing pink with understanding. "Oh. You know you're not supposed to see the bride before the wedding. I mean, you know that's a thing right?" Her air is almost reprimanding but she's fighting a smile, and it's a losing battle.

"And I won't see her before the wedding." She lets out an exasperated breath. I wrap my arm around her shoulder and steer her away from Sam's room and back down the corridor. "How about joining me for breakfast?"

"Oh, um no. If I can't wake Sam, I still have to check the kitchen and that the ceremony room is decorated." She pauses, counting on her fingers, obviously mentally scrolling down her internal to-do list, and not for the last time, I'm sure, I congratulate myself that I struck gold when I enlisted Sofia's assistance. "I'll give her forty-five minutes tops." She offers.

"Perfect, and you're sure I can't tempt you to some breakfast?" She shakes her head, gives me a frantic wave goodbye, and scurries off down the main stairs. I cast a glance at Sam's door and pat myself on the back for having incomparable strength of will in not doing exactly what I just asked Sofia not too —well not *exactly* what Sofia was going to do. I would certainly do more than merely wake sleeping beauty. Jogging down the stairs, I head for the breakfast room. It's no longer that early, my father and Will are still sitting in the bay window, picking over the last of the cold toast, having finished their full English breakfasts.

"Morning, Jason. Sleep well? How are the nerves?" Dad pushes back and stands to give me a hug. Will tips his head but won't meet my eye. We didn't get to speak much yesterday, and I still need to rip him a new one for making a play for my girl, but not today. Today is going to be drama free and fucking perfect, because today Sam will be all mine.

"You want some breakfast?" Dad signals to the waiter.

"Just an espresso will be fine." I take the seat next to Will.

"Did you have a good flight?" I ask since he has yet to acknowledge my presence.

"Fine," he clips. *Great.*

"So no nerves?" Dad repeats with a wide grin.

"I have nothing to be nervous about, Dad." I state emphatically, even though I know, coming from my dad, it was just a light-hearted question.

"You sure about that?" Will mumbles. I stand abruptly, my chair crashing to the floor, and I don't give a fuck who is now staring at us and the awkward silence that now cloaks our little table. "Outside, right now!" I storm off, leaving my Dad with a gaping mouth and a look of utter astonishment on his face. I hear Will's chair move and his heavy footsteps hot on my heels. Once outside, I walk around the side of the hotel where there is a little privacy before I turn sharply.

"I wasn't going to do this now, Will, given that it's my fucking wedding day and all, but since you're being a total fucking arsehole…" I push him with both palms on his shoulders, and he slams into the garden wall. He steadies himself and straightens, though he doesn't retaliate. My hands are shaking I'm so fucking mad. Adrenaline has my blood running at a temperature just below boiling. "If you so much as cough during the ceremony, I will rip your fucking bollocks off."

"I won't cough. I won't say a damn thing…I…I…" His tight, angry face changes, and I feel the hurt in his expression like a fist around my heart. I blow out a long, steady breath.

"Will, I don't even blame you for falling in love with her. It's what you did…You actually made a play for her?"

"I know…I had to Jason, but I'm sorry. Really… It was low, and I'm really sorry man, truly. You think she'll forgive me?" His features darken with genuine worry, and I take a moment before I answer. He did fuck up, and for that, he can stew for a few tortuous seconds before I give him some comfort.

"She already has, arsehole. It's me you have to worry about." His shoulders lose all their tension and drop a good few inches. Heaving a huge sigh of relief, he straightens to his full height and pushes my shoulder back with a playful punch.

"Nah, I don't have to worry about you. You're a good guy. You're my brother, you'll forgive me."

"Hmmph!" I snort.

"Might take a while, but you will." His confidence isn't misplaced, but I don't have to tell him right away; he doesn't get off that quickly.

"Yeah, just don't go holding your breath." I pull him into my hold and hug him. My tight embrace is already filled with forgiveness, because honestly, I don't blame him for trying. We break apart, and an easy peace settles and is sealed with his next statement.

"I'm happy for you, man. You deserve her. I would've fought harder if it was anyone else."

"There *is* no one else." I happily emphasize this point with my abruptness.

"Yeah, that's what she said."

"Are you two ready? The taxi is here." Our dad calls over to us, a strange, guarded expression on his face. Will slips his arm over my shoulder, roughs my hair and lightly punches me in the stomach.

"You need to get anything, or can we leave now?" Dad has the door to the taxi open and already has one foot inside. "I'm keen to show you two how to shoot properly."

"Yeah right, Dad, if the clay happens to fall at your feet maybe or the end of your nose…" Will jokes, laughing at Dad patting himself down in search of his glasses.

"We're good to go," I interrupt. "Should we say goodbye to Mum?"

"She left about half an hour ago with Aunt Sue to get her hair done. We have a good few hours before she's back and fussing."

"Okay then, let's go." Dad sit's in the front, and Will and I slide in the back. I chance a worried glance over my shoulder as we pull away. "I feel I should be there in case something needs doing."

"You think that young lady hasn't got everything sorted and double-checked? Because I met her this morning, and I can tell you getting out from under her feet is the only thing you can do to help." I grin at my father's wise words.

We reach the range and meet up with others from the wedding party, relatives and friends I haven't seen in forever. Sofia really has gone above and beyond.

"How did she find these guys?" I ask Will as I round the car and I slowly begin to put names to faces that have changed so much with the years.

"She might've had a little help."

"You?" He nods and flashes a wide smile. His shoulders straighten with pride at my obvious pleasure. "So you weren't *so* against the wedding then?"

"Never against the wedding, just the choice of groom." He jokes and wisely steps out of reach of my clenched fist. I won't mark his face because of the photos needed later, but he is not so safe from a nut punch.

"This is definitely a Kodak moment." I reach in my pocket to take some photos of this surprise reunion. "Fuck!"

"What?"

"I left my phone at the hotel." I pat all my pockets. I just know I left it on the bedside table when I came down for breakfast.

"Use mine." Will hands me his iPhone. I take it, still that doesn't help the tightness and uncomfortable drop in my stomach.

"I need my phone, Will." I run my hand through my hair, and Will grabs my jacket sleeve and pulls me away from the crowd.

"What's going on?" He sounds anxious, which must match my expression.

"We found the guy who's sending the emails. James got his name now. It's only a matter of time, and this arsehole's time is running out."

"But not on your wedding day." He lightly moves my shoulder back and forth, as if shaking some sense into me. I let out a humourless laugh.

"No, obviously, I still want to know what he finds out though, *when* he finds it out. I have to be able to act, and without my phone—shit!" I look over to the crowd, my father's worried eyes glancing my way.

"Calm down for fuck's sake. It's a few hours, max."

"A few!" My hand grips the back of my neck because, despite his calming tone, Will's information has done nothing to ease my tension.

"Look, we'll cut back after the shoot, not hang for the drinks, if that makes you feel better?"

"Not really."

"Jason, I know this is tearing you up, but you can't do shit about it right now. If you turn tail and leave, everyone will think there's a problem. So just give yourself an hour and then I'll take you back, okay?"

"Okay." He's right. For the next sixty minutes, I just have to keep telling myself there's no problem, until I know for sure there *is* no problem.

"Good. Right. Let's go and shoot some shit up." He drops his heavy arm on my shoulder and moves us both to the gathered guns.

ELEVEN

Sam

"How you feeling, sweetie?" Sofia's hand reaches over the centre console of the car for the umpteenth time in the short drive from the spa to the hotel. She covers my clasped hands with hers and gives a comforting squeeze.

"I'll be better when I speak to Jason." It's all I've said for the last two hours. The lady giving my massage gave up trying to ease the knots from my shoulders in the end. She joked lightly about the tension, but after a good twenty minutes trying to pummel the tight muscle into submission, she conceded defeat and moved on. Sofia answered all the questions thrown my way by both the make-up lady and hair stylist. The most I could manage was a slight smile when offered something to drink. I'm numb, and I can't focus on anything. I moved when I was physically maneuvered. I stared blankly because the words weren't registering, and in the end, we all just sat in an awkward silence.

This has to be the least celebratory wedding day preparation ever. The girls at the spa must think I'm set to marry a monster. That couldn't be further from the truth. He is a good man; he saved me. The car pulls up the drive, and the trees that line the winding road have large white silk ribbons tied around the trunks. The pillars around the porch have the same, and large bouquets of flowers I can't quite distinguish are placed in every window. The country house hotel looks more and more amazing and magical as we approach. Fairy lights in the trees, more freestanding floral displays, so many flowers, the heady scent filters into the car as we drive closer to the front of the house. I glance up at the window and wonder if he's up there. I feel dread surge through me like an ice storm in my veins. This might just be the last straw.

I know he loves me, it's just, I also know how he really feels, in his heart, about sharing me in the very real sense that having a child with another man would entail. I'm honestly terrified that this is too much for even the very best of men.

Sofia nods again at my reply and parks her car at the back of the hotel. The front car park has started to fill with guests, and I let out a deep, shaky breath as saliva starts to pool in my mouth. I pant to try and stop the urge to hurl. Sofia has her door open and dashes around the front of the car, quickly opening my door. Concern fills her face when she crouches in front of me.

"Slow breaths, sweetie, throwing up is not an option. It will ruin your make-up." I sniff and laugh at her panicked voice. Least of my fucking worries. I take a moment and stand once the sickness has passed. We take the staff stairs to avoid bumping into anyone. I have no time for small talk and pleasantries. There is only one person I want to see and need to speak to. I open the honeymoon suite bedroom door, walk in, and dump my bag just inside the room. I need to take the letter from the clinic with me, but it's gone. The surfaces are all clear, and I check the waste bin, nothing. *Shit.* The room has been cleaned and the rubbish taken away.

Never mind I'm sure he'll take my word for it. *Why the fuck would I lie about something like this?* Sofia hovers at the door.

"I'm okay, Sofs. Go and get ready." I tip my head in the direction of her room and add a flash of a smile.

"Really?"

"Yep. You said so yourself, love transcends all. So go." I shoo her out of the room, desperately trying to sound confident and convincing. She rushes forward and wraps her arms around me so tightly she takes my breath away. She's surprisingly strong.

"I'll only be a bit, then I'll be back to help you into that gorgeous dress." She smiles brightly and squeezes me once more before turning to leave.

I wait a moment and then follow her out and pause, hoping for some much needed strength to find me and praying quietly that I'm not about to crush the man I love with this news.

I knock and the door swings wide before my hand makes contact with the glossy wood a second time. Will roughly pulls the door open and looks as shocked at seeing me as I am to see him.

"What are you doing here?" He's looking over my shoulder as he speaks. I look back to see what I'm missing, only the corridor is empty. "Where's Jason?"

"What do you mean, where's Jason?" My voice is a little loud with confusion at his question.

"Yes, what do you mean, where is Jason?" I hear a woman's voice behind me, and I turn to see an older lady in a royal blue, satin twin set, a neatly trimmed dark brown bob, and exactly the same eyes as her sons.

"Mum." Will forces a smile, but I can see the tension in his jaw. This is not good.

"Will, where's Jason?" I ask again, trying to keep my voice level even as my anxiety spikes.

"Why don't you both come in?" He steps back, and I walk through the gap, followed by Will and Jason's mum, Mrs Sinclair. There is a surreal moment of hesitation when we all look to one another. We all know *who* the other is, and it feels a little late for introductions even though I haven't actually met Mrs Sinclair.

"Hello, Mrs Sinclair, I'm Sam. I'm sorry I haven't met you before today. This rush was very much a surprise." I swallow the lumps rising in my throat, and she steps forward with the sweetest smile, apparently mistaking my dread for nerves.

"Oh I don't doubt that for a moment. Honestly, these boys will be the death of me with all their shenanigans." She steps up to me and gives me a hug before holding me at arm's length and casting an appraising eye. "It's lovely to meet you, Sam, and I can see why Jason…Wait! Oh, my dear, you shouldn't see him before the ceremony!" She shakes her head and holds her hands to her mouth like seeing him is the worst thing in the world. Will steps up and puts a protective arm across her shoulder and helps her sit down.

"Will, I need to speak to Jason. I'm sorry, only this is really important." I add a tight smile to try and ease the building tension.

"He's not here. He left." His eyes are wide with panic and flit between his mother and me, gauging which one of us will break. His words hit hard and direct. Sill, I only crumble on the inside. Mrs Sinclair folds over in a gasp of shock. Will crouches instantly at her side and looks so worried I don't know what to do, but I still need answers.

"When…when did he go?"

"We came back from the shoot and he went to your room to drop his bag off and then just stormed back here and took off."

"Did he say anything?" I keep having to swallow the saliva filling my mouth and the rising lump in my throat. *This is really happening?*

"Not directly. He was cursing and said that he can't do this or believe this…I don't remember exactly. I tried to stop him but I could see in his eyes that wasn't an option. Sam, I'm so sorry." He makes to stand and step toward me, when his mother sobs out loud, and I have had a little more time with this news, so for the moment, I'm able to remain standing, even if it is like a statue. He leans around to wrap his long arm over the back of the chair, his mother looking more frail with each passing minute. I didn't think it was possible to feel worse.

My eyes glaze, and I feel the first tears fall onto my cheek. I turn and walk to the dressing table to grab a tissue, and there it is, crumpled in a tight ball. I recognize the colour of the paper and the clinic logo distorted with the crease of the paper. I grip the edge of the table for support and to steady the weakness in my legs.

"How could he do this to this poor girl?" Mrs Sinclair's voice wobbles almost as much as my legs. "I don't understand how he could be so cruel, Will?" Mrs Sinclair sobs, her broken words and deep unsteady breaths fill the room.

"I don't know, Mum. Please don't upset yourself. Please try and keep calm." Will crouches down, and I can hear the genuine concern and a touch of fear in his deep voice.

"How can I be calm? I lost a son today!" Her words come with a fresh slew of tears. "I will never forgive him for this." Her voice is as grave as her words are devastating.

"No!" I cry out. "No, you can't do that. He loves you so much, he…he…" I falter.

"I'm sorry Sam, you sweet, sweet girl, but this is unforgivable." Her kindness to me is heartbreaking.

"I'm pregnant." I choke out. The shit storm waters just keep rising, and I'm struggling to keep my footing. Drowning seems like a good alternative to the agony I'm witnessing in this room. Will's eyes widen to the size of serving plates.

"Oh Lord, no!" Mrs Sinclair presses her hand to her chest, and I can hear her laboured breathing. She takes a moment then lifts her head, eyes watery and cold. Her fierce glare strikes me, and I can feel all the warmth in my body freeze. "Then he's a coward…no son of mine would—" I can't let her finish, it's too much. He doesn't deserve this, he really doesn't.

"I don't know who the father is." I close my eyes tight at the confession, when I open them I see one pair of eyes deeply worried and one filled with utter hatred.

"You cheated on my son!" Mrs Sinclair screeches so loud I wince. I wouldn't have credited her slight frame and delicate demeanour the ability to make such a noise. Not when she looks so frail in the chair and guarded as she is by Will's large protective frame. The door bursts open and Leon rushes into the room, only to stand transfixed, as all eyes are on me.

"I…I…" I can't breathe. I look up, and the absolute agony on Will's stricken face and panicked eyes that flit between me and his mother is too much to bear. "Yes." I mutter.

"Yes!" She snarls and pulls herself to stand, but she wobbles, and Will is there, supporting her and continues to implore me with a light shake of his head. This must be killing him too but I understand where his priority is. Given his brother has hightailed it, I don't blame Will for standing by his mother's side. Family always comes first. "You are a slut and a whore to cheat on my son when he loves you so dearly. To try and trick Jason into marriage is utterly disgraceful. You should be ashamed of yourself." Not so fragile after all.

"Now wait a fuc—" Leon steps just in front of me and I quickly pull him to face me, and with one look, silence any further protestations on my behalf. He mouths a quick, 'What the fuck,' but my scowl silences even that. I'll take the hit. I've had worse. I do, however, need to take his hand regardless of the disgusted look Mrs Sinclair is now openly pitching at me.

"I am so very sorry, Mrs Sinclair. I love your son more than anything. I would never trick him. That's why I needed to speak to him, and it's clear he has made his decision and I have to live with that. I never meant to hurt anyone. I can promise your family one thing though, not one of you will ever see me again." I try to catch Will's eye, but he hasn't looked up since his mother called me a whore. I straighten my back and lift my chin. I used to have so much strength and yet now I'm clinging to the remaining fragments, hoping it's enough to hold my broken self together for a few moments more. I just need enough to leave the room.

TWELVE

Jason

"Do you want me to call the police?" James' voice holds a shit-tonne of concern over the speaker in my car, and rightly too. I have been cursing and plotting for the last hour how I plan to end this low life son of a bitch. Threatening me on my wedding day. That bastard sent me a personal message first thing this morning, but because of the early breakfast and clay shoot I'd left my phone in my room and didn't pick it up until later. Hopefully, it's not too late. My head's a fucking mess. He threatened to release that video on every social media platform from YouTube to fucking Facebook, today, on my fucking wedding day! I slam on my breaks to miss a rabbit on the narrow bend of this unbearably long and winding country road in the middle of fucking nowhere.

"No, I don't want you to call the police. I want you to tell me that fucking cunt is still at the address, because if I miss him one more time, I'm going to lose my shit. This is my wedding day for fuck's sake, and if I'm not back in time, Sam will very likely have my bollocks for dinner, and that is not how I prefer to have them served." It was a risk leaving, but the address James discovered was only thirty miles from our hotel, and that message this morning was the fucking limit.

I sent money the first time, against police advice, and the second time, they fucked up the rendezvous. So this time, it will be just me and him, and he has no idea I'm coming. It might be my wedding day, but this is too important to risk going viral. I have kept this from Sam, and if I'm back in time, it stays that way…If I'm not, then… I don't want to think about if I'm not.

"He's still there. He rented the place for six months and only moved in yesterday, according to the agent. He's still bouncing his emails from one of the city addresses, so I doubt he knows he's slipped up." James tries to hide the uncertainty in his voice. I tore him a new one after the last goose chase, although that was more from frustration than negligence on his part, and I apologized. It's just, now we have a name. I know it's only a matter of patience, and my tolerance has completely fucking run out. This ends…today.

"I fucking hope so." I swing the car up a single-track lane that is banked high on either side with thick hedgerows. The fresh spring leaves are such a vibrant green they don't look natural, more like a Photoshop filter has splashed the countryside with artificial life. The Sat Nav announces I've arrived, and I get a sick, excited turn in my stomach. I'm so ready for this to end so I can get back to my bride and we can start our life, without this cloud, this threat, hanging over our heads—well, my head. Sam is blissfully ignorant and I intend to keep it that way.

I crest the brow of the hill and ease off the gas. There is only one small building at the end of this road, which looks barely habitable. It is surrounded by rolling hills and open fields to the side and front. The house backs to a dense-looking woodland. The trees cast an eerie shadow over the single-story, stone building, despite there not being a cloud in the sky and the sun having risen as high as this time of year allows. I don't see another vehicle, and my hands grip the wheel with pent anger that this might be a wasted journey.

I swing the car to a skid on the gravel and dirt drive and jump from the car.

The slate roof is weathered and has gaps where the wind as taken bites and left ragged holes and crooked tiles. The windows are thick with dust and filth, and the door I'm about to pound on looks like it was made with wood from the Ark, it's so ancient. I half expect it to splinter with the first thump of my fist but it just creeks its disapproval and then swings open. The dark interior is filled with light, and I guess I should be looking at the two dark holes of the end of the shotgun inches from my face, yet I'm taken with the darker circles of the terrified man aiming the gun at my head.

It's not even a split second, but that fraction of time is all I need as the next moments play out in slow motion frame by frame.

The heel of my hand hits the barrel high and out of his lose grip. I snatch the weapon midair and flip it. Holding the barrel away from this arsehole, I jab the butt of the gun hard into his shocked face. Blood explodes from his nose as bone and cartilage splinter in his face. He stumbles back screaming, hands cupped to his face trying to stop the flow or maybe hold his face together. I don't care which. I jab him again, and he falls onto his back. His chest crunches beneath my boot and he gasps for the air that I have just stomped from his lungs. I'm now aiming the right end of the gun directly at his face.

"You broke my fucking nose!" His high pitched cry is muffled behind his hands and the squelching sound of the copious amounts of liquid pouring from his face.

"Trust me, I'm breaking more than that before I leave." I take my foot from his chest and step to his side. The shotgun in one hand, I bend low to grab a fistful of his blonde ponytail with the other and kick the front door shut behind me. He grabs for my hands at the first pull from my movement, only they are slippery with his blood and gain no purchase. His feet race comically on the flagstone floor, desperate to keep his body moving at my speed as I drag him further into the house. It's tiny; just two interior doors, and the first is open, so that's where I head with the piece of shit. We've been tracking him since James discovered his identity, but he's kept moving until now.

I don't need an introduction; I've stared at this face on my screen for hours, memorizing each line, making sure I would recognise him anywhere. The pale, lifeless eyes and sallow expression, praying I would get just five minutes alone. Stanford Johnson III, business partner to Sam's ex-boyfriend Richard. Well, ex-business partner. I haul him up only to drop him on the single chair in the kitchen, next to the table. This place is a hovel. I don't know what he spent the money I sent the first time on, but it wasn't interior decor. The walls are grey stone, damp, and each crevice, crumble, and crack in the surface houses a thick woven layer of cobwebs. The windows are bare, with no curtains or blinds; no pictures hang on the walls, no clocks or mirrors adorn the room, no rugs, no trace of home comforts.

There is only one freestanding unit in the kitchen, sturdy looking, stained, antique pine, and on the top, is a small travel kettle, a solitary cup with steam still rising from it, and the milk bottle cap on the floor, which makes me think I disturbed his morning brew. Even psychopaths need a tea break. I pull the drawers open in search of something suitable to tie him up. His head flops to the side and he lets out an agonizing groan. I don't think he poses much of a threat now, but I've watched enough movies not to take that risk.

I slam the last drawer closed, having found nothing, and Stanford jumps, crying out at the sudden noise. Pathetic. He's just a pathetic excuse for a human. Lank, thinning, greasy blond hair, tall but no build to speak of, and his pallid completion makes me wonder if he's nocturnal or maybe allergic to the sun. Even so, his eyes chill me. Even filled with terror when he opened the door, which made me think he'd never actually held a gun, let alone shot one, the vacant, soullessness was so much worse than the gun pointing at my head. I walk to the other closed door to continue my search for some rope or tape.

"No!" he shouts out in panic. "Don't go in there!" I take a step away from the door and turn to face him. His eyes widen with fear, his nose still pumps rivers of blood down his face and I can see his hands tremble as he tries to stem the flow. "Please don't go in there!" His urgent plea makes my lips curl with a cruel smile.

"Oh…okay." I take another step back and watch as he lets out a breath and his shoulders drop with relief. *Fucking idiot.* I pitch back on one leg and let the other fly forward and kick that motherfucking door wide open. The door swings hard against the wall and wedges itself open, the dust billows, and it takes a few seconds to swell and settle. When it does I don't believe what I'm seeing.

"What the fuck is this?" My feet won't move and I have to steady myself on the door frame. Movement brings me out of my trance, and I easily catch Stanford as he tries to make it to the back door of the house. His ponytail makes him an easy catch. *Idiot handle.* I grab it tight and slam his face once, then twice into the door before hauling him over to the bedroom and throwing him on to the floor. My stomach roils, and I have to swallow the bile that's leapt from my stomach because there is no way he's going to see how this disgusts me...how it affects me. A person would have to be a monster for this not to affect them.

The walls are covered with photos from various videos involving Sam: Sam and Richard, Sam, Richard, and an audience. I can't believe what I'm seeing, and when I turn around, my whole world implodes. This wall looks like a CSI incident room, only this is before the crime. There is a map of London, with pins of every place Sam has been in the last six months with corresponding photographs. There are lists of daily activities, foods she's eaten, where she's shopped. There are even photos of her in my fucking club! I kick Stanford as I walk over to the desk and he whimpers. Good. With any luck, he's going to bleed out, but not before I get some answers. The desk has three laptops, all the screens are blank, sleeping. Time to wake up. I touch the pads and they all flick on, bright and wide awake.

The desk is littered with junk, fake identity cards, credit cards, and a Stone Security employee swipe card.

"How did you get this?" I roll him over onto his back with my foot and crouch down to hold the card in front of his face. He squints mumbling something about pain. I'll give him motherfucking pain. I notice a packed black bag on one side of the bed and something in the top catches my eye, silver duct tape. Perfect. Reaching for the bag, I grab the roll of tape but tip the contents on the floor because who the fuck packs duct tape in their luggage? The contents litter the floor, a Stone security polo shirt and pants, rope, knife, plastic ties, and a brown medicine bottle with the label torn off. My hand grips the gun. I can feel my fingers shake and the sweat now coating my body makes the gun slip in my palm. One of Stanford's laptops pings, and I welcome the distraction as the macabre pieces of his evil plan fall into place.

I click to open the new email.

Dead Man Walking,

Transfer paid. I do this for my family. Enjoy my money and enjoy it quickly.

"My brother killed himself whilst at school not long after this video you sent to blackmail me with. I will not have my mother seeing this as the last memory of him. He told me about this video at the time, and I shared his shame, if you look later at the clip you will see he's no longer there. The fact that you have him at all is enough to pay this ransom."

If I ever find out who you are, you fucking coward, I will kill you myself.

Christov C

I turn and look at Stanford as he crawls and hoists himself more upright only to slump against the bed gasping for air. I hope I broke a rib, punctured a lung.

"Talk!" My voice is low, filled with hatred and menace.

"How did you find me?" He grumbles like a petulant child, and I walk back over to him so I tower above and he has to crane his neck to meet my glare. I hold the gun so the tip of the barrel stops his chin from dropping, maintaining our eye contact. I want to make sure he can see me, see what I am capable of.

"You don't get to ask the questions, you piece of fucking shit. What has Christov just paid for? And if you say Sam, take a deep breath because it will be your last."

"That was plan B!" He rushes to explain as if that will help his situation.

"Kidnapping and selling my wife was plan *fucking* B?" I roar, and he rightly cowers. The gun is shaking in my hand as blind rage consumes me.

"I wasn't going to…I mean I probably wasn't going to if everyone paid up… I needed the money. The Feds took everything from Richard's business, and half of that was mine!" His voice steadily rises in volume until it sounds more like a screeching girl than a thirty-something-year-old, weak excuse for a man. He gulps for air as he makes a piss poor case of defending himself. "I had to leave the States with nothing. I just want what's mine. I want my lifestyle back. I want my houses not a crappy apartment or this shit hole. I want nice clothes." I'm surprised he doesn't stamp his foot to punctuate his brat-like tirade.

"*Had* a lifestyle." I point out with utter contempt. "And the only clothes you need to worry about are ones that will fit snug, a tight wooden box."

"You're not going to kill me," he states with a misplaced degree of certainty. His voice waivers and his words are more like a plea, which I don't waste a breath to acknowledge, but he's persistent. "I know you…you're not a murderer." I respond with a bitter laugh, filled with derision.

"You threaten my wife. You have no idea what I am capable of." I grind my teeth as I spit the words with venom. "How many people have you tried to blackmail with this video?" He only pauses for a second before he wisely answers my question.

"Fifteen others and you." He tries to lower his head, avert his eyes. I jab the gun in his throat, and he struggles to swallow against the hard metal tip marking his skin.

"Has everyone paid?"

"Yes." He chokes out a cough, his voice is hoarse. I don't ease off the pressure. "There are some high profile people in that clip. Richard went to a good school."

"That produced arseholes," I reply flatly.

"I went to that school!" I ignore the chance to state the fucking obvious, because they clearly produced idiots too.

"Who else is going to come crawling out of the woodwork, Stanford? I'm having a tough time believing you're the mastermind behind all this." I glance at the table with the computer and over my shoulder at plan B.

"I'm a fucking genius, arsehole. I'm the brains, Richard was the charm." I burst out with a hollow laugh even though I know he's not being ironic. I arch my brow and quirk my lips in a condescending smile that seems to make his cheeks heat and his eyes flash with fury.

"Of course." I nod my head lightly. If I had a free hand, I would pat him on the head, but my hands are full, and my fingers are twitchy. "Is the video file just on these machines? Do you have an external drive?"

"I don't have to tell you shit. I have my money now that Chirstov has paid." He tempers his attitude when I nudge the gun against the underside of his chin. His tongue swipes his lips, and he forces a slow breath out through his pursed lips. "You can relax. I don't need plan B after all." His mouth slides into a grin, and I'm astounded he thinks it's that fucking simple. I level my eye along the barrel, the other eye closes as I pull it away from his throat. The blurred metal sight at the nib of the shotgun becomes crystal clear. I squeeze the trigger and fire at the gap between his legs. This close, the noise is like a bomb exploding in the room. My eardrums ache and my brain shakes in my head. There's a mass of wooden shrapnel and flying splinters, which I hope have pierced his bollocks and nailed his dick to the floor. He cries out in agony and his hands fly too late to protect is crown jewels.

"Sorry…you were saying?" He whimpers and is quick to answer me this time.

"It's on that one and I keep a copy in my case, that's it. You can take them both." His lips tremble and his whole body is shaking.

"How very kind." I spit my words with vitriol, my smile as cold as his eyes. I hate that I even have to look at him, but now I'm wondering what's my plan B.

THIRTEEN

Jason

I spend twenty minutes securing Stanford to the sturdiest oak chair outside of the ones I have in my London dungeon.

"One thing, Stanford, since you 'know me', you will also know I excel with ropes and knots. I would normally check your circulation, although in this instance I don't give a shit if you pass out or bleed out, and there is nothing normal about this situation. What I do care about, however, is that I know you won't escape…ever." I pat his cheek and start to pack away all the computers to take with me.

"What are you going to do?" Stanford splutters as I make one last sweep of the room. I have already spent way too much time here but I'm at least satisfied I have everything now. I'm just sad I don't have time to hide the body. Still that's what friends are for.

"I'm going to get married." It's my first real smile today, and it feels so damn good I hold it there.

"What about me? You know someone will find me here. It's not so rural that I don't get visitors." He tries to straighten himself only the ties don't allow for any movement when he boasts. "A postman comes here every day and then—"

"Let me stop you there before you think your threats will do anything other than make me laugh." I grab the back of his chair, tilt it and drag him into the kitchen. He squeals but stops when he realizes I'm not dropping him, just relocating him. I place the chair in the centre of the room and walk around to face him. "You were wrong about one thing, Stanford, when you said you knew me. Very wrong." I pause and take a long look at the motherfucker who threatened the woman I love and would have done so much worse if the scum he was trying to blackmail refused to pay. I draw in a breath at the sickening thought and exhale slowly before I speak. I can see from the tension in his jaw, he is holding his breath, waiting. "I wouldn't think twice about killing you, Stanford, but today is my wedding day, and I'm too tight on time." He lets out a puff of air that almost makes me smile.

"Oh thank you!" His words escape with a nervous laugh.

"Oh you shouldn't." My voice drops low. "You really shouldn't." He loses what faint colour he had to his sweat-smeared skin "I said I didn't have time, but you are going to die today. As the brains, this shouldn't come as a surprise." My tone is a mix of mock shock and caution. "You threatened some very unsavoury individuals Stanford. Christov, in particular, was more than happy to learn of your location."

"No...no, please. You don't have to do this." He shakes his head as I hold the rope up to his mouth to finish up and gag the motherfucker.

"I think you'll find I do...I really do." He turns his head this way and that, his voice pitched with panic and fear.

"You're a good man, Jason, don't leave me to die," he garbles as I thrust the rope roughly between his lips and tie it fast and tight, blood trickles at the corner of his mouth where the twine splits his lips. His words are now incomprehensible, not that anyone would need to be 'the brains' to get the gist of what he's begging for. I lean down so we are close, eye to eye, and I whisper.

"You threatened the woman I love. I *was* a good man, now...now I'm a very bad man."

These narrow lanes are the worst. I can't pass the slow car in front and I still can't get a fucking signal to call Will and let him know I'm running late. Not too late, and if I could get a decent stretch of road, I could probably make up the time. I texted a message before I left the cottage, which I hope will send as soon as that magical one bar appears, even if I am driving. I don't want Sam waiting at the altar when Will can just stall for fifteen minutes, maybe half an hour, so I can change. *Dammit!* I slam my brakes on as a tractor pulls out just in front of me and on a blind bend. *Not what I need.*

I can feel my blood pressure rising with every false rev of my engine and tease that there is enough of a safe gap to try and overtake. *How long is this fucking road exactly?* We reach the brow of the hill at a steady, exasperating 25 miles per hour when I catch a break. The tractor steers into a lay-by to let me pass, and I let my heavy foot hit the floor, naught-to-fucking-get-me-to-the-alter-on-time in three point two seconds.

In the distance, I can see a car on the verge with its hazard lights on. The road narrows and dips, it's possibly the worst place to break down, poor bugger. I slow down a little as I pass. The young woman has a baby in her arms and two children pressed flat against the hedgerow. There are no cars ahead and nothing in my rear-view. *Shit.*

I break and shift my car into reverse. Twisting round, I drive my car back to park it just in front of the woman's minivan.

I check my phone, my message is still in the draft folder waiting to send and the signal bars remain depressingly flat. The woman bursts into tears as soon as I round her car.

"Oh God, thank you for stopping. I haven't seen a single car in twenty minutes, and before that, only two, and neither of those fuckers stopped to help." She wipes the back of her hand over her cheek and continues to jiggle the crying baby in her arms.

"Mummy you said a bad word." The little boy tugs at her coat and shuffles closer to her side when he looks up at me.

"I know I did, sweetheart. Mummy's just upset." She smiles tightly at the child, but keeps her voice low and soothing. It's impressive because even I can see she is strung out, scared, and anxious.

"I won't tell." The child says, as if that is going to be a big comfort, and she smiles softly at him.

"Thank you, Billy. And I will try not to say another bad word. Hold your sister's hand like I told you, this is a very dangerous road." Billy instantly looks terrified and squishes himself and his sister flush against the hedgerow as they had been when I drove past.

"Nobody stopped, hmm?" I rub the back of my neck, which is tight and feels like concrete. I may well have shared the other drivers' unchivalrous behaviour, if only for a second. "Well, I stopped, so what's the problem?"

"No signal."

"You stopped here because you have no signal?"

"No, I have a flat tire, and I can't get help because I have no signal." She looks at me like I might not be quite right in the head, but it's been a long morning, so I'm going to cut myself some slack that I'm a little slow on the uptake.

"Oh right…of course. Me neither." I shrug and her shoulders drop like the weight of her child has increased tenfold. "However, I can change a tire. Give me a minute." I run back to my car and quickly set up the hazard triangle and then escort the woman and her kids along the road and into a field, a safe distance from any traffic.

There is no fucking way I'm getting to the hotel in time for the ceremony now. I just hope this is a good enough excuse to keep Sam from cutting my bollocks off…or worse.

The wheel is stubborn, and I slice my finger, knuckles, and back of my hand several times trying to remove it and mount the spare. I'm glad Billy is no longer in earshot because I have pretty much exhausted every *bad word* I know. I replace the jack in the back of her car and slam the boot shut.

"It's all done." I shout out and watch to see the young woman's head peek out from behind the hedge. She smiles but doesn't reply, only nodding her head for me to come to her. Sure, why not? It's not like I have to be anywhere.

"Sorry, my Elsie has fallen asleep, and I can't carry them both." Her thin smile mixes perfectly with her eyes to look deeply apologetic. She still has the baby in her arms, swaying her hips and lightly bouncing the bundle. Billy is dozing by the tilt of his head, but his sister is flat out on her back, on the grass. Her blonde curls partly cover her eyes, her cheeks pink and round, and her chubby toddler limbs are flopped wide like her little body just gave up and unconsciousness simply wiped her out. "Can you take the baby and I'll carry Elsie?"

"Oh um…maybe I should carry Elsie, she's probably heavier." I shift and freeze when she holds her arms out with her precious bundle.

"And will make the most noise if she wakes to a stranger carrying her. No, trust me, you'll be safer with this little one." She assertively hands me the baby, swaddled in a blanket and very much awake. Big watery blue eyes stare right through me. Do all babies do that? It's unnerving.

"Oh he's only two months old so focus is sort of new to him. There's lots of staring, some smiling and whole heap of screaming. You can relax; he won't puke or anything. Well, probably won't puke." She laughs lightly, and I flash a quick but petrified smile. I didn't even realize I asked that question out loud, and I feel anything other than relaxed. I do, however, feel tense, uncertain, and awkward…unbelievably awkward. We walk back to her car, and I'm holding this new baby like it's a ticking bomb. Every step I take is soft and carefully placed, no sudden movements, and I'm barely breathing.

"Not held many babies?" She grins and raises a brow with her query.

"That obvious?"

"You look just like my husband with our first. You get used it." She snickers and her smile is more relaxed now she is no longer stranded.

"I hope so." I swear this baby hasn't blinked once. *Is that normal?*

"Oh are you expecting?" Her interest pitches her voice sharp and loud.

"Yeah…our first…Kind of a surprise." I hand the baby over once she has secured her other children. She takes the little boy and flips and scoops him into her arms, and then manoeuvres him into his car seat. The whole time, I'm holding my breath as I expect him to slip, fall, or at least crack his head on the car door. *Parenthood is going to kill me.*

"They are always a surprise, even when they are planned." She chuckles. "Thank you so much…?" She pauses with an expectant smile, and I think it must be me with the baby brain since it takes long seconds to click on what she is waiting for,

"Jason. Sorry, I'm Jason." I hold out my hand and she grabs and shakes it warmly.

"Well, thank you, Jason. Thank you so much. Your wife is a very lucky woman."

"If she forgives me enough to say 'I do' that is." I'm only half joking, and she frowns at my quip so I enlighten her. "It's my wedding day today and…" I glance at my watch and get a painful hit to my chest that I would've been married for just under an hour…woulda…shoulda. *Fuck.*

"Oh no…you stopped to help me on your wedding day. Oh no!" She clasps her hand to her face, and the anguish I feel is reflected in her eyes. "If you need me to corroborate your story I will, if she doesn't believe you, I mean."

"I don't doubt she'll believe me, since trust is not an issue with us, but whether she forgives me? Now that I may need a little help with." I wave her off and run back to my car. Not that running will help me now. I need more than speed, I need divine intervention or a time travelling Tardis.

FOURTEEN

Jason

I swing the car around the sharp right-hand turn to the drive that leads to the hotel and instantly swerve to avoid the ambulance at my front bumper, narrowly avoiding a head-on collision. *What the fuck?* My heart clenches and my head pounds with possibilities, none of which are good. I am torn between following the blues and twos screeching off in the distance and racing to the hotel and hopefully getting some answers that aren't going to destroy me. I hope Sam's okay, Christ I hope the baby is…*Shit I just can't go there.* Being late for my own wedding has to rank pretty high in the spectrum of stress inducing situations. *What if Sam—No. I can't even think about that.* She has to be okay…*She just fucking has to be.* I can see Will on the steps of the hotel. He's alone and the car park that should be full, is empty. I pull up, blocking the entryway and leap from the car, only then does my phone spring to life with a chorus of rapid fire notifications that sound like a fistful of fire crackers has exploded in my jacket.

There's little point reading them now, Will's face says it all and it's not good, not good at all.

"Where's Sam?" I call to him over the noise of the car door slamming.

"What?" His face is pale and shifts from a tense worry to confused in a flash.

"Not a trick question, Will. Who's in the fucking ambulance? Is Sam all right? The baby?" I hurl my questions at him, barely drawing breath or giving him time to answer.

"What?"

"Say that one more time, I dare you." I snap now that I am eye-to-eye and brimming with anxious hostility. It might be misplaced, but right now, he is the only target and he hasn't answered a single Goddamn question.

"Sorry man, where the fuck do you think she is? She's gone." His dismissive tone is pitched at a level that makes me think I have asked something really stupid and my next question seems to compound his opinion that's exactly what I am.

"What do you mean gone?"

"We have to get to the hospital, Jason, come on I'll drive." He shakes off my question and tries to step around me. I block him with a side step and a firm hand on his chest.

"Will, answer the fucking question!"

"I don't know where Sam is…She left with Leon when you went AWOL and Mum…Mum is in the ambulance." He grates out with surprising calm but palpable tension. The worry in his eyes makes me back down despite my blood raging through my veins and curling my fingers into tight fists.

"Mum? Is she all right? What the fuck happened?"

"I'll explain on the way."

"I'll drop you at the hospital then I'm going after Sam. She can't possibly think I left her? What the fuck gave her that idea?" Will hands me the letter from the clinic. I drag my hand through my hair, my chest aches, and I feel so sick I can't think straight. I was reading this when I got the message from James but I was so damn angry I didn't give it another thought. Thought I threw that damn thing away. "Where did you find this?"

"It was in your bin. I noticed Sam look at it, just a glance really, then everything changed. She changed, and that's when she told Mum she was pregnant."

"Shit."

"No that's not half of it. Mum…" He hesitates and I can see the myriad of unpleasant emotions flash in his eyes and flit across his troubled features. "Mum said she'd never speak to you again for walking out. No one could get hold of you, Jason. Why the fuck would you leave on your wedding day?"

"The other half?" I ignore the snide accusatory tone and question.

"What?"

"You said that wasn't half of it. What happened after Mum said she'd disown me?" He lets out a sharp breath and runs his hand through his hair, a shared trait of open frustration or maybe hopelessness. I hope it's just the former.

"Sam said she didn't know who the father was. Did you know that?"

"I didn't…I mean I did, when I read the letter only something came up. So I really haven't had time to process." I shake my head and close my eyes trying to prevent these events as they start to play out in my head like a slow moving train wreck.

"Something more important than this? It better be fucking spectacular because your little stunt had Sam running for the hills. No not running, she left with grace, considering." He looks a little paler and I get a sick twisted knot and a deep sensation that my world is about to drop away.

"Considering?"

"Mum called her some pretty bad names."

"Mum? Why would she do that? If anything this is my fault, we're all responsible."

"I'm sorry…I'm really sorry."

"What…what are you sorry for? I'm just as much to blame, me, you, Leon and Sam. This is an all-for-one situation; don't beat yourself up." I try to ease his obvious burden but if it's a fraction of what I'm feeling, it's a futile gesture. "I don't see why Mum would call Sam names? What did she call her?"

"Slut…whore."

"Fuck, Will, and you let her?"

"I was worried about Mum she'd sort of collapsed, and look…I…I'm not fucking proud but I could see Mum wasn't coping. I panicked I didn't know what to do; it was like this fucking slow motion train wreck that I couldn't stop. Sam did all the talking, and I let her. I'm so fucking sorry Jason." He drags his hand over his face and the regret couldn't be plainer if it was tattooed onto his pallid complexion. "After Sam left, I told Mum it wasn't Sam's fault. I told her everything, but it was too late."

"Shit…you told her *everything*? Well no wonder she's in a fucking ambulance. What do you mean too late?"

"Mum was hating on you, but that all turned around when Sam said she didn't know who the father was and Mum asked her flat out if she cheated. She said yes."

"What? Why?"

"She looked at me just before she answered; I saw the plea in her eyes and did nothing, man. Mum was falling apart, Sam was breaking, and I did nothing. She took the fall for us, and I fucking hate myself right now!"

"I fucking hate you right now. Go on." I say the words, but they are half hearted because self-hatred is all I have at the moment.

"Sam took the whole blame, a direct fucking hit, and walked away."

"Why would she do that? I don't understand why she'd walk."

"She loves you, Jason, and maybe she also loved me a little to shoulder all the blame like she did. She wasn't going to stand in the way of family."

"She is my fucking family! How could you let her do that?" I pull back and punch him hard across his cheek. He falters only to strike back up under my chin snapping my head up with a bone crunching crack.

"You fucking left her at the altar, you piece of shit. I was trying to stop our mother from having a fucking heart attack." He staggers out of my range, and I spit the pooling blood from my mouth. My jaw snapped so sharply it sheared layers off the inside of my cheek.

"And how did that work out? She's still on her way to the fucking hospital because you told her anyway. Why bother when Sam already took the hit?"

"I felt like an arsehole all right. Mum was cursing her, and she was wrong. I couldn't stand it so I told her. I'm sorry I fucked up, but no more than you. If I was lucky enough to have Sam as my bride, there's not a fucking thing that would make me leave her on my wedding day." His righteous tirade hits hard, but I know he's wrong.

"Oh really?"

"Yes really." He swears and I silence him with more than enough evidence to justify my seemingly reckless behaviour.

"Well, it's lucky she isn't your bride or this would've gone viral On. Her. Wedding. Day." I throw my phone at his chest and his reflexes are such that he catches it instantly. "Open the last email." I draw in a steadying breath, which does little to calm my fury. His eyes widen and his jaw drops as does the remaining colour in his face.

"Shit."

By the time we arrive at the hospital, I have answered all the questions I intend to answer about Stanford, and Will is silently sulking beside me. It's for his own good and he really doesn't need to know more than that the situation is sorted and Sam is safe.

Mum has been moved from Accident and Emergency to the cardio unit, and Will and I find our Dad in the waiting room. He is pacing and his expression is, as always, impassive, but he stops and smiles brightly when he sees us round the corner.

"Never a dull moment with you two, that's for sure." His tone is lightly admonishing but his relaxed demeanour has both Will and I exhaling loudly with relief.

"How is she?" I ask first. We speak in forced whispers because the whole area has an unnatural quiet despite the numerous briskly moving staff.

"She's fine. Her blood pressure was a little high, they think the palpitations were just anxiety, nothing too serious. Well, that's what the doctor said after the exam in the Emergency room. They are doing some more tests now, and she's sent me out because I make it worse apparently." He rolls his eyes slightly.

"She's going to be all right?" Will's voice is thick with worry, desperate for more reassurance. He must feel like shit; I know I do.

"I'm so sorry, Dad," I say before he can reply to Will.

"She's going to be fine, son. She's a lot stronger than you two give her credit for." He pulls me in to a big hug and reaches his other arm to include Will in the embrace. I rest my head on his shoulder and take the comfort this big strong man always manages to give.

"Evidence to the contrary, Dad." I mumble into his shoulder and step back, my eyes flick to the door as I point out the very visible contradiction to his statement, the ominous Cardiac Surgery sign.

"I think we can at the very least say today was an exceptional circumstance." He pats both our shoulders with his meaty hands.

"She told you?" Will told me Dad was with the guests downstairs when this all went down.

"She told me." He tips his head with a slow, knowing nod.

"When?"

"I might have missed the show, but I got the critics' review in the ambulance." His wry tone makes me relax a little more because I know he wouldn't be making quips if Mum was in any real danger. "Jason, I think you need to explain yourself." He nods to the row of hard plastic bucket seats as an invitation for me sit and tell my tale, only I shake my head.

"I will, I promise just not right now. I have to find Sam." I squeeze the back of my neck, which is rigid with tension and barely gives at all when I try to press some relief along the spine.

"Do you?" He narrows his eyes but mine widen at his shocking insinuation.

"What?" My mouth actually drops open.

"Is it true you don't know who the father of this baby is?" He levels his sternest glare at me, and I feel transported back in time to wearing short pants, getting caught in the neighbour's garden stealing all their raspberries straight from the vine.

"Yes sir." I straighten at his tone, not judgmental but definitely reprimanding.

"And that's why you left?"

"No…no not that." I shake my head rapidly to dispel the very thought and draw in a deep steady breath. How to explain the unexplainable. "It's complicated, just know that I didn't leave because of that. I didn't leave, period. I was just late."

"To your own wedding?" His words hit hard.

"I'm not proud." I swallow the sickness that keeps pooling in the back of my mouth every time I picture Sam today…abandoned.

"So you're okay with not knowing if you're the father?" He pushes and I feel like he is throwing punches when I can barely stand.

"Um…I…I don't know. I haven't—" I stutter but check myself when he interrupts.

"Well, give it some thought now, son, because that girl just did an incredibly brave thing and is probably completely heartbroken. So don't you go getting back into her life if you have no intention of sticking and stepping up to be one hundred percent that baby's father regardless of the biology."

"I won't." I pull my shoulders back and stiffen to my full height.

"I mean it, Jason." My father does the same and I hold the challenge, because if I can't answer a few simple questions honestly, then I don't deserve to win this fight. "You think your mother was mad before? You go messing with that girl's head and you'll have us both to deal with."

"I have no intention of messing with her, Dad." I tip my chin and watch his stern face soften.

"Good to hear it son. So what is your intention?"

"I'm going to get my girl."

FIFTEEN

Sam

"Where will you go?" Leon has been silent most of the time I have been bundling my clothes into his rucksack. The selection is pretty slim, considering I had moved most of my stuff over to Jason's house however, I still need at least the basics. Just until I'm up to shopping for a replacement wardrobe, that is. I laugh bitterly to myself at that thought. I'm not going to hold my breath.

"I don't know." I pinch the bridge of my nose. Christ, I feel tired. I briefly wonder if that is the pregnancy and shake it off. I doubt it. After the last twenty-four hours, Hercules himself would need to take a nap. I roughly pull the straps tight and check my handbag for the essentials. Passport, iPod and credit card. I drop my phone on the bed, pull Jason's cuff from my wrist, and take off my engagement ring, I crumple when I hesitate at the clasp to my collar. Richard tore my body to shreds, that jet-ski accident nearly took my life but Jason... Jason, had my heart and soul and when he left he destroyed me. My useless fingers shake.

"Here, let me." Leon steps up and I am grateful. He unclips the necklace and wraps his arms around my trembling body, and not for the first time, holds me while I break. So many fucking tears. *I just need to get away.*

His shirt is soaked when I pull away. If his face is a reflection of a fraction of the sadness I feel, I must look like shit, utterly devastated, apt and accurate. I try to smile in an attempt at a brave face, only it hurts too damn much. "Don't try so hard babe; in fact, don't try at all...be sad. You have every fucking right to be, then get mad and move on. Take this time...whatever time you need. It's your honeymoon." He winces when I recoil like he's just dealt the sucker punch to end all sucker punches. "Sorry." His voice is gentle, and his face is so filled with love and concern, I have to turn away. "What are you going to do?"

"I'm keeping the baby," I state emphatically just in case for some bizarre reason he thought just because I was uncertain of the paternity that that might be an option. It isn't...It never was.

"Of course, I...I..." He stutters and I turn to see him struggling. This is a shock for him, and he is still here, being the best friend a girl could ever wish for. I reach for his hand and hold it in both of mine, hoping to pass a fragment of comfort his way. I only have fragments at the moment, and they are fleeting. Having a precious baby is definitely one of them.

"I'm not going to lie, I was thrilled and relieved when I thought Jason was the father, but you know what? Now…now I don't care. This is my baby. It wasn't an accident or a mistake, and I will never be ashamed of how it was conceived. That night brought me back to life and created this miracle, so I really don't give a fuck who the father is because I am the mother." I tip my chin and hold his gaze.

"Okay, feisty chick, I didn't mean anything by it." He holds up his hands in a surrender gesture, and I realize I may have let my vitriol fly at the wrong person.

"I'm sorry." I draw in a deep breath and close my eyes. I feel like I'm drowning. Although, even when I was literally drowning, it didn't hurt like it does now.

"Don't be, you have nothing to be sorry for." His voice is soft but his tone is matter of fact. "I would like to know why you didn't give that little speech to their mother when she called you a slut." He dips to maintain eye contact when I try to look away.

"It's complicated." I sigh and can't hold his gaze. I don't expect him to understand because I'm giving him nothing *to* understand.

"Bullshit it is. Will just stood there like a fucking mute and let you take all the blame. If you hadn't shot me the death glare and dragged me out of there, I would've told that prudish old witch just how 'wholesome' her precious boys are." He gestures with air quotes, mimicking a snippet of her outraged diatribe.

"I know, that's exactly why I pulled you out of there. Will had his chance to say something; it was only a pause, even so, I saw in his eyes he couldn't. I know why he didn't, and I respect that. He loves his mum, Leon. The truth would've hurt her more; they both made that more than clear on several occasions. He was protecting her, and I can't hold that against him." I try to shrug but the weight of my situation rests too heavy for light gestures. "It wasn't the first time I've been called that and I would rather that, than her disown Jason. He adores her, Leon, just like you do your mum, and I won't come between family. She doesn't really know me. I've been in her son's life for five minutes, and now she has to try and make sense of a clusterfuck of a situation. Which, from her perspective, is where her son was doing the right thing, and I betrayed him in the worst possible way. She is just protecting her baby, and I can't hold that against her either." I press my fingertips to the bulging pulse at my temples this time, but the spread of tension is all over my face.

"And what makes you so magnanimous?" His question sounds snide but I silence him with my next words.

"I'm going to be a mum."

"Simple as that, eh?" His frustrated tone softens and he squeezes my hand.

"Nothing simpler than protecting your own." I take one last look around.

"You'll get a test then, to see who the father is?" His voice is soft and tentative.

"No." I give a light shake of my head.

"What? Why?" His voice is more shocked than sharp.

"Because it doesn't matter. You didn't sign up for daddy-time, Leon, and I wouldn't hold you to any obligation."

"What if I want an obligation?"

"Do you?" I raise a wry brow because I know the answer, although the fact he has asked has amused me.

"No, but I'd like to be asked." He pouts and I almost laugh, there is no way I am going to respond to any form of happy emotion.

"Should I ask Will too?" I ask.

"Hell no, he lost his rights when he didn't have the bollocks to stand up for you, but I'm your best friend." His brow drops to a deep frown, and I step up to him and wrap my arms around his waist. His strong embrace is a tiny respite from my pain, and I cling to that small comfort, resting my head on his chest. I tip my head up to him looking down.

"You are and I know you'll be there for me as a friend whenever I need you, regardless of whether the child is yours. So again, it really doesn't matter." His eyes soften and his lips spread into an equally warm smile.

"I will." He kisses my forehead and releases his hold. "And Jason?"

"If Jason felt the same as you then the test is just as redundant." I let out an exhausted sigh. "He'll have a fight on his hands demanding a test. He walked away from us both." I place a protective hand over my tummy. My heart crumbles with my words and my attempt to hold myself together is slipping. I need to leave. I take one last look around and turn toward the door.

"Wait, why aren't you taking your phone?" He points at my abandoned device on my old bed.

"Off the grid...I'll call you when I get there." I shrug and sling my bag over my shoulder, then lift the rucksack over that.

"You know my number?" He looks doubtful.

"After Richard, last time... Yeah, I memorized a few important numbers." I sniff back the ever-present trickle of sadness.

"You think he'll try and contact you? You know, when he realizes what a massive fuck-up he is?"

I snort with an acrid laugh. "No Leon…he left me at the altar. I don't think he is going to be coming after me."

"So if he contacts me…?" His voice is hesitant. He isn't pushing, just clarifying.

"If you tell him where I am, you will be just like him," I state emphatically.

"What do you mean…just like him?"

"Dead to me." My icy response causes the colour to drain from his face.

I arrive at the main train station in Paris, the Gare du Nord, just before midnight with the time difference moving my body clock ahead an hour. Crossing that time zone from England into France seems more like it has moved me on a hundred years. I feel so utterly shattered. I checked into the nearest hotel opposite the station, not caring that the architecture was stunning or the entrance was old-world-grand. I just needed to sleep.

Despite the gentle, rhythmic rumble and hypnotic sway of the high speed train, sleep eluded me on the three-hour journey. I had closed my eyes, but all I saw were dark brown eyes with golden flecks and the most perfect smile, happy and easy, that once warmed my soul and made me feel safe. I make me safe.

I fight to keep my eyes open. They are sore from the effort and sting and burn from tears which fall unbidden all the damn time. I am broken, every cell in my body is raw and hurting, and I can't stop it.

"How long will madam be staying?" Bright blue eyes flick up from the screen and the smooth French accent brings me back momentarily from my suffocating agony.

"One night." I mutter.

"Just one? madam, it is such a beautiful city…the city of love…" The receptionist is trying to be charming, with a playful wiggle of his dark, bushy brows and his wide warm grin, but I just can't.

"One night," I repeat, my tone harsh, clipped, and an awkward silence falls, as he finishes the pre-payment transaction on my card. Well, it would be awkward if I cared. I don't. I just want a bed where I can collapse and sleep for a year…maybe two.

Springtime in Paris is the best time to visit. Trees blossom all over the city rivalling the evening lights for spectacle in the City of Lights, another name Paris is famous for. I have visited on many occasions and this is my favourite time of year. It's not too busy, and the evenings are sometimes warm enough to dine al fresco, perfect for strolling along the Seine, or up the Champs-Élysées and sitting for many hours watching the Eiffel Tower sparkle to life as the sunlight gives way to night-time. Breathtaking.

These are memories; I haven't left my room. My one night turned into three and counting. I have ordered room service and eaten just enough to keep from fainting. I haven't so much as looked out of the window to check if it is day or night.

I called Leon the morning after I arrived and told him I was safe, but that was all, and although I could hear the worry in his voice, I am in no state to deal with anyone else. In fact, as soon as he said 'Sam, I think…' I hung up. I don't want to know what he thinks; I just don't care. My heart is broken and I don't know how to fix it. For the first time in a very long time I don't know what to do. I don't know who I am and I need to figure it out…because it isn't just me anymore.

It's late when I ring the Club—Jason's Club—one of the few numbers I memorized, and the phone is answered on the second ring.

"Good evening, how may I direct your call?" asks the sultry voice of Stephanie from member services.

"Hello Stephanie it's Sam. Can you tell me if—"

"Oh Sam! How was the wedding? How's the honeymoon?" she gushes, and I just want to die. The pain is too fucking much, ripping my chest apart. I press my clenched fist hard into the bone between my breasts as if that will stop the pain. Stupid Sam. Nothing will ever stop this pain.

"Sorry Steph, I don't have long. Can you tell me if Charlie is in tonight?" I interrupt and she falls silent.

"Oh sorry, of course…let me check. Hold a moment." The line goes quiet, and I hold for a good five minutes before Stephanie returns. "I'll just transfer you." Transfer me? My heart actually stops beating when I think for one terror filled moment I am being transferred to Jason. I'm not ready for that call…one day, maybe, but not today.

"Sam are you okay?" Charlie's voice is damn music to my ears, and I let out a heavy sigh. "Sam?" Charlie's voice is tinged with panic.

"Been better." I manage to say, not sure if it's any reassurance, as understatements go, it fits the bill.

"Leon told me last night." She rushes to reassure me. "Not told me in a gossip way." That's sweet, however gossip is so far from my list of concerns, it doesn't even register. "He's been staying at my place, and we were in a session. I asked him to tell me something that could cause more pain than my cane. I'm sorry, Sam, really I am. What happened…well, it's fucking shitty. Never thought him a douche, but if this game teaches us anything, it's that you just can't judge. And you know, if he didn't own the Club I'd gladly tear him a new one for ya."

"I'm grateful you have my back, Charlie, but a girl's gotta eat, and the Club is still the best in the city, so don't go doing anything stupid on my account. I'm a big girl; I'll survive." The words are hollow, my voice holds a practiced calm, another trait mastered when playing our 'game'.

"You sure about that?"

"No. But I don't have a choice…Anyway, that's not why I called." I shake myself to try and regain focus.

"Damn, please don't tell me you want your client book back?"

"I don't…I'm still retired,,however, I do want Gabriel's contact number, if you have it to hand."

I hear her let out an exaggerated breath. "Whew…for a moment there, I was worried. I'm not saying the clients aren't happy with me, but one whiff of you back on the scene—"

"Retired… Gabe's number is all I need."

"Okay…do you want me to text it to you?"

"No, I have a pen." I tap it on the side of the phone, which won't mean anything without a visual. Thank heavens for landlines.

"A pen?" I can hear the confusion in her voice and it almost makes me smile…almost.

"Yes, you know 'mightier than the sword', the thing people used to communicate before phones…slim cylindrical—"

"Yes, yes, you're hilarious…okay I have it…happy?" she quips.

"Not remotely," I mutter and take the number. I thank Charlie and endure her heartfelt well wishes only I can't help feeling worse for hearing them. I then dial Gabriel Wexler's number and pray I am not making a bad situation worse.

SIXTEEN

Sam

The phone rings several times, and I know he must be looking at the number wondering who the hell this is calling in the middle of the night…from a Paris number if he even recognizes the international code. I will be lucky if he picks up at all.

"Who the fuck is this?" His gruff tone catches me off guard. I have never heard this Gabriel. Although, I know him as a super rich and a ruthlessly successful banker, he would be neither if he conducted himself the way he does with me.

"Sam." My voice catches, and I hate that I have so little inner strength that I am physically struggling to make the simplest call. I cough to clear my throat. "Selina…Hello Gabriel."

"Mistress," It's his turn for his voice to catch on a sudden and audible intake of breath.

"I'm retired, Gabriel…I am no one's Mistress." I close my eyes with a slow, sorrow-filled exhale.

"You will always be *my* Mistress…How may I serve you, Mistress Selina?" He slips effortlessly into his role.

"I need a place to stay, only I don't know for how long."

"Too easy." His tone is derisive and his words dismissive of my open ended request for a favour. "Anything Mistress, please let me do anything that would bring you pleasure." His voice drops and has a smooth, deep timbre with an edge of pleading I am more than familiar with. I let out a short, bitter laugh.

"Even I am not cruel enough to set you an impossible task, Gabriel, however, if you can offer me shelter it will be a great help." I am in no mood to even pretend to play.

"Of course." He is quick to appease. "I see you are in Paris. I have a penthouse apartment near the Louvre over looking the river or New York, if you prefer. Or maybe—"

"Somewhere quiet. Don't you have an island somewhere, with no internet and fabulous spa facilities?" I'm half teasing.

"I have just the thing. My yacht is docked in Barcelona. It has a full crew to cater to your every whim…or not…your choice." He offers heaven on a silver platter, and I almost smile. *Thank heavens for Gabriel.*

"That sounds really good, Gabriel." I look over to my unpacked bag and wonder how long it will take me to get ready to leave. Only moments.

"Good, I will tell the captain to expect you and not to leave until you arrive." His voice is light with misplaced excitement. This is not a holiday; this is a hibernation.

"Leave? Where is he taking your boat exactly?"

"He is taking my *yacht*…" He emphasizes his correction to my question with a groan of irritation. *Boat/yacht, potato/po-tah-to,* even if I knew the difference, at this moment in time, I couldn't care less. "…to Venice for the Gathering." His voice sounds a little incredulous at my question, and now I know why.

"The Gathering…of course." I hesitate. "But that's not for a few weeks?"

"I like to have her there with plenty of time… The preceding days' build-up is almost as much fun as the main event itself." He chuckles, a deep throaty sound. "That's a ridiculous statement; nothing is as much fun, I do like to spend a few days in the city though. The opera, the shopping and the *Ambrosia* is perfect for all the privacy I will need."

"Ambrosia?" I'm a little lost if this is code.

"My *boat,*" he mocks. "She's called *Ambrosia,* and she's stunning, a little like yourself, Mistress."

"So I will see you in Venice then?" I ignore his flattery and cast a cursory glance at the mirror opposite the bed where I am sitting cross-legged. The dark shadow of the room obscures my face. I know I don't look stunning…stunned maybe, shocked by the reflection of someone I no longer recognize…empty, hollow…alone.

"Never miss it." Gabriel's excited voice breaks through my morose musings. I hear him clap his hands together with glee.

"You're the host, Gabe; it's your party." I'm pointing out the bloody obvious.

"You could be my guest of honour." He tests the waters, and he is either feeling brave or reckless.

"Or I could not." I clip.

"Of course, excuse me Mistress." He is instantly contrite.

"Sam, please call me Sam, Gabe." I let out an exasperated sigh, which he must hear yet choses to ignore.

"Never. When do you think you will get to Barcelona?" Back to business.

"I'll leave here tomorrow, and I will be taking the train, so say sometime late evening." I yawn just thinking about a long day of travel. I have zero energy.

"I will inform the captain. I can send my plane for you, if you would prefer. It would be my pleasure, Mistress."

"No, no I prefer the train." I'm not a fan of flying and even less so now that I no longer have my own personal distraction.

"Until Venice then. If you need anything, anything at all, I am, as always, your servant." His voice drops an octave in supplication, and I hang up.

I close my eyes and force what I know is a sad smile even if he can't see it. I'm trying…I really am. He is being so kind. Even if he won't give me what I want—a *normal* friendship—he might just be giving me what I need—a distraction.

I have never actually visited Barcelona and if the taxi ride from the train station to the dock is an indication of its diversity, culture, and vibrancy, I feel I have really missed out and sadly, will continue to do so. I am in no mood to take in the tiny ancient streets of Las Ramblas or the numerous colourful markets that seem to pop up from nowhere, full of life, fiery smells and noise…so much noise. I shrink back into the cheap, slightly sweaty and well worn leather seat in the taxi. The half open window is a temporary barrier to the world outside, however, I know my soulless aura is much better equipped to physically repel the real world than a pane of glass. I'm counting on it.

The captain welcomes me with a charming wide smile and a curious brow when I hand him my rucksack. I am not sure what Gabriel might have told him about me, I know, in my current state, I am, as far removed from the notorious Mistress Selina as Selina is from a hapless stow-away. My jeans are a marginal improvement on sweat pants, and it is marginal. In just a few days, I have lost some weight, and they no longer hug my curves so much as hang limply from my hips as they would from a washing line. My T-shirt belongs to Leon and does a decent job of hiding most of my body. I keep my sunglasses on, and I've even bought a baseball cap that I could pull fully over my face if I need to. This isn't me; I know this, but it's me right now, and I am coping as best I can, just.

I forego the grand tour the captain kindly offers. Gabriel didn't exaggerate; it is a stunning luxury yacht, smaller than the one where Richard held me captive but only just. I am shown to a guest suite that would shame any five-star hotel. Stylish, highly polished teak, cream leather, and gold fittings drench the interior in gaudy opulence that seems to work and is totally in keeping with the owner.

Gabriel Wexler is the very personification of hedonist. He isn't gay, or bisexual or straight. He abhors labels but adores life. He indulges in the pursuit of pleasure and considers that in itself to be an extreme sport. If there were medals, he would easily be an Olympic champion. The Ambrosia is just one venue for such activity.

I throw my bag on the bed and wander over to the window. I release a slow, deep, pathetic sigh. *For fuck sake, Sam, there are worse places to tend a broken heart.*

SEVENTEEN

Jason

If he doesn't open this fucking door, I swear to God I'm going to kick the fucking thing right off its hinges. I know he's in. He's been away all fucking week, but his secretary said he was returning to work tomorrow, and I have been parked outside Sam's house for hours. I don't know how I missed him, but I did. One minute his bike wasn't there, and now it is. I haven't slept all fucking week so it's possible that I succumbed to my state of perpetual exhaustion and closed my eyes for a moment. It was obviously long enough. The living room light went on and I jumped in my seat like a shot of pure adrenaline had been stabbed directly into my heart. The first spark of life in over a week since Sam disappeared *on our fucking wedding day*! I have felt sick with a mix of rage and loss, but that ends now. I'm getting answers, if not from the horse's mouth, then I'm getting them from the next best thing, her best friend.

"Open the fucking door, Leon!" My fist pummels the frame, rattling the glass and echoing off the walls in the hall and ricocheting up the stairwell. It's not late, yet there won't be a soul in this building and the next, who can't hear my hammering. My knuckles start to seep with traces of blood, I only pause my relentless banging when the door swings wide. I draw in enough oxygen to curse and rip Leon's head clean off, the uppercut punch to the underside of my chin though, catches me way off-guard and knocks me back but not down. Oh good, I get to fight.

I steady myself and step into the next punch because I just know it's coming, I can see it in the flare of his wide angry eyes. I will match that and then some. I'm full of rage and hurt, but at this moment, undiluted fury is coursing though my veins. Sam might not thank me for beating the shit out of her best friend, only she's not here, and that's the fucking problem.

I duck his next swing and strike my fist hard into his side, catching him full in the ribs. He curses and lashes out, landing a punch on my shoulder. He throws his whole weight onto me, and we tumble back and crash into the wall. I get several hits to his stomach, and he does the same, punch for punch. It's an even match, although his breathing is more laboured than mine. I have a shit-tonne of adrenalin that will easily keep me going for hours. I feel like the fucking Energizer Bunny on crack.

A moment of hesitation and he catches my jaw, snapping my head to the side. My arm was already pulled back and strikes an instantaneous retaliation square in his face. My knuckles are numb from the fight, even so I feel the crunch of cartilage. Leon stumbles back, a dazed, glazed look in his eyes before the pain hits him and his hands fly to the blood pouring from his face.

"What the fuck, Jason?" His muffled words are angry and loud enough to be heard through his cupped hands. "You broke my fucking nose!"

"She broke my fucking heart." I rest my hands on my knees and draw in some deep calming breaths, still keeping one eye on Leon. I doubt he's up for a second round, but he struck first so I'm not taking any chances. He looks a bloody mess, although he doesn't look like he wants to keep fighting. He actually looks confused.

"She broke your heart?" He spits a mouthful of blood onto the floor beside his foot and holds his sleeve to the underside of his nose, which continues to spill a river of red. "She didn't leave you at the fucking altar. She took the fucking fall for all of us with your damn mother, not that I give a shit what your mother thinks of our little foursome but Sam did. She stood there...on her fucking wedding day...no groom in sight...and let your mother call her a whore! So tell me: Whose broken heart are we really talking about?" His voice started calm, quickly escalating to full volume, and he was now yelling in my face.

"I. Was. There!" I shout back, and the plea in my voice is clear because Leon's brows furrow with uncertainty. "I mean, I wasn't there in the morning but I hadn't left. I just had something to do." I stare at him, holding his uncertain gaze, my volume softened, but my tone is deadly serious.

"What was so fucking important you had to deal with on your own wedding day, hmm?" He swears under his breath and winces when his fingers lightly touch the bridge of his nose. He spits more blood onto the ground, only this time, I think it's for effect. It lands perilously close to my shoe. I slip my phone from my back pocket and swipe the screen. I select the email with the screenshot that left me with no choice but to leave that morning. His eyes take only a split second to register the image.

"Jason, what is that?" He snatches the phone from my hand, his brow furrows and the colour drains from his face. He looks sick, and I happen to know he feels it too...sick to his stomach because I felt exactly the same. "You better come in."

Leon steps aside to let me pass but doesn't return the phone. His grip is white knuckled, and I can see the tension and fury in his clenched jaw.

"I've dealt with it." I state as a cold matter of fact. His eyes flick from the image to mine, and he gives me a curt nod, his shoulders drop a little and he lets out an audible breath of air.

"Let's talk."

He turns, and I follow him through the hallway into the kitchen. His suitcase and travelling debris are dumped just inside the doorway, his wallet, keys, and passport on the kitchen worktop. I really hadn't given him five minutes to settle from his trip, and I don't really want to be 'talking' now, but I do want answers. He tears off a wad of kitchen paper and holds it to his streaming nose, then grabs two glasses and a fresh bottle of Jack. He uncaps the bottle and starts to pour when I hear it—running water. *The shower!*

I crash through the door. How did I miss this? She's been here all along. The train ticket and Paris hotel were all a hoax, she never took the train to Barcelona. She stayed here and got someone else to trade places. *Damn she's smart.*

The steam distorts her image. She's dyed her hair to a fiery red, and shit, she's cut it short, just below her neckline. I love her hair long. Oh fuck, it doesn't matter. She's here now. That's all that... What the fuck?

"You going to stare or join me, big boy?" The sweet, sexy voice has a West Country lilt, and the steam dissolves to reveal a not-so-shy and very naked Charlie. Sam's friend and replacement Dominatrix for Leon. *Fuck.*

"Neither." My reply is a little curt, shit, I so wanted her to be Sam. My mind is playing tricks. Even with the steam, I should've known it wasn't her. I did know, yet I still chased the dream all the same, and now, I'm even more pissed. I spin on my heel and out of the doorway, a cloud of steam swirls to escape the closing door. Leon, nursing his broken nose, is slumped in the only armchair, a small bag of frozen peas and more kitchen paper on his nose. He has three fingers of whiskey in the glass in his other hand. I doubt that's his first glass, judging by the near half-empty bottle on the counter. I take my drink and walk over to the window. It's getting dark. I drain my drink and turn to face Leon.

"Where is she?" I ask quietly, calm considering I'm still a riotous ball of anger and devastation.

"She's safe." He tilts his head this way and that to try and stem the bleeding.

"That's not what I asked." I force the words out through a jaw clenched so tight, I swear I will break a tooth any second.

"That's the only answer I can give you." He shrugs but doesn't sound remotely apologetic.

"Only answer you *can* give me or only answer you *want* to give me?" I hate that he has this hold over me, that he will always have a connection. On a good day, it's tolerable; on a bad day, it drives me fucking insane. Today is a very bad day.

"Both." He draws in a deep breath and lets it out slowly. I do the same as I feel my anger rise in parallel to my frustration. "Look man…I honestly don't know where she is, and I wouldn't tell you if I did." Blunt and honest I can at least respect that.

"I didn't leave her, Leon…I would never leave her. *Fuck!*" I drag my hand down my face feeling every second of tiredness from the last week of sleepless nights. "Richard's business partner had recordings. That screen shot was just a snippet of the shit he's been sending me for the last few months. He was a sneaky fucker though, and at first, I had no idea who was sending me this shit, and they seriously got off on fucking with me. Sending me all over the fucking country on a wild goose chase trying to get my hands on this. If Sam knew… I couldn't let her see this, Leon, it would destroy her." Leon looks over, and I catch a glimpse of empathy in his almost black eyes. "Anyway, with the last exchange, my tech guy found an IP address that wasn't a dead end. He found out who it was. I got vital information on my wedding day—his actual address—and I wasn't going to let that fucker get away." The timbre in my voice drops to deadly serious,

"You could've told someone where you were going." He purses his lips with all the smugness of hindsight.

"I didn't think okay. A red mist descended, and I just wanted to finally get that fucker." The accusatory expression fades for now, and he briefly nods with understanding.

"You got all the files?" His concern is still in line with mine for the time being.

"I did…he was at an isolated private address. He didn't know what hit him. Well, he did, but yeah, I got everything he had. I made sure of it."

"Where is he now?" Leon drops his voice to a whisper and leans forward, though his attempt at secrecy is moot.

"Where is Sam?" I ignore the question he really doesn't want answered. He pauses for a moment, and when he understands I have finished with that topic, he sits back with a sigh.

"She called me from Barcelona but I haven't heard from her for a few days. She can take care of herself, Jason." His tone is snide, which I also don't have time for.

"She's pregnant and should be my wife by now, so she shouldn't *have* to take care of herself." My retort sounds more like a snarl. "I just got back from Barcelona, and there's no trace of her. How can you be so calm? What makes you think she is safe after what happened last time?"

"*This* is nothing like last time. She left, she wasn't taken," he snaps.

"Fuck!" I walk over to the sofa and sit, slumping back heavily, and stare at the ceiling. I believe he's telling the truth, which makes this bad situation worse. It means with no phone, none of my gadgets on her person, and no further credit card trail, I'm fucked. I will only find her when she wants to be found. "Tell me what happened." I let out a resigned breath. I'm getting nothing useful that will help find her, so maybe getting the other side of this tale will shed some light on why she thought she had no choice other than to leave.

"You saw the letter. You do the math."

"The letter?" I'm still very much in the dark.

"The letter from the clinic… The one that means the baby might be any one of ours…that letter!" I flinch at his judgmental tone. He's not judging our actions but mine. Or at least what he perceived were my actions at the time. "Sam only opened it that morning and wanted to talk to you before the ceremony. She still had to get her hair and shit done or she would have to start explaining why she wasn't preparing for her big day. I think she probably felt she was safe to carry on getting ready…She probably thought you two were solid."

"Fuck off with the attitude, Leon. We are solid, and you know why I wasn't there. Why the fuck would she think that letter would make a—"

"Difference?" he butts in, his demeanour has switched from attitude to venomous. "Was that what you were going to say, because I'm pretty sure it was you who told Sam you would not want a baby if it wasn't yours."

"No, I said it wouldn't be my first choice at starting a family, but I wouldn't fucking give up on us on the strength of that. I can't believe she thought I would." I drop my head in my hands as all these imperfect pieces fall horrendously into place.

"When it came to it on the day, you weren't there, Jason. All evidence was to the contrary." He states this as a matter of plain, irrefutable fact.

"Shit." I shake my head at this almighty fuck-up and look over to him, for the first time this evening there is not anger or hatred in his eyes, there is something else I'm not sure is any better though: pity. "I really don't care who the father is, I just want her back."

"Really?" He scoffs and his voice is thick with judgment.

"Really. I mean, yes, I want to know if it's mine but not at the risk of not getting Sam back. If that's the proof she needs, I won't ever ask for a test. That's fucking irrelevant anyway. If I don't have her, none of this matters. And regardless of which of our swimmers got there first, I'm the motherfucking father, if she'll let me."

The silence stretches, and Leon breaks it by walking to the kitchen and bringing the bottle of whiskey back, refilling his glass and handing me the bottle. *Not a good sign.*

"Your brother just stood there, you know. I stepped forward to say something, only Sam gave me the death glare and your brother didn't say one word." He slumps back in the armchair.

"What are you talking about? He bloody did…he told mum everything. I walked into the fucking Sinclair apocalypse." I press two fingers against the pulsing headache that is shooting from my temple to deep inside my skull.

"Well, his timing was a little off, because he was a fucking mute when Sam told your mum she cheated on you. Why would he bother to say something, anything at all after…I mean, the damage was done, and he and you got away scot-free. I don't understand why he would do that."

"He loves her." I say this quietly, and Leon huffs out with clear derision. "No, he really loves her. He felt like shit for not stepping up when he had the chance, but he wouldn't let mum say a bad word against her, so he spilt the truth the moment Sam left. When I returned a few hours later, that war was still raging. I walked back in and didn't know what the fuck was going on. Will was like a fucking ghost, my mum had been taken to the hospital with a suspected heart attack, and my reason to fucking breathe was gone!" I keep my voice level. Still, I have to swallow the thick lump in my throat when I stop to draw breath.

"Does Sam know? That he loves her, I mean?"

I nod. "Yeah, she told me when she got back from Florida. She said she thought we might have to take Will off our plus one list too." I don't feel I need to elaborate.

"Too? You mean as well as me?" he quips, but there's an undertone of hurt, which is exactly why he is spot on.

"No offense, man, but love complicates things." I shrug, and he twists his lip into a half smile of understanding.

"It sure does. So your brother confessed to loving your 'wife' on your 'wedding' day. How did that go down exactly?" His air quotes are entirely unnecessary. I'm painfully aware that Sam isn't my *wife* because we had no *wedding*.

"Not well. Look, it doesn't matter. I can't blame him for falling in love with the best woman in the fucking world, and he did come clean eventually. But he's my brother, so I'm stuck with him. If he ever makes another play for her, though, I will cut his fucking bollocks off." I take a long slug straight from the bottle. "She shouldn't have run. We always promised to talk this shit through."

"You keep saying she ran like she had a choice," Leon snaps, his volume much louder than where our conversation had settled. "You weren't there, and Will left her hanging…literally. Two men who were supposed to love her hurt her more than Richard ever did. I'm not surprised she ran, though I will be fucking astonished if she ever comes back." His statement is like a blade, his words slicing my chest wide open. My agonized heart pumps and bleeds and will continue to do so until I'm empty or dead. Without her I'm both.

"I've heard they are debauched, but I don't think anyone's ever died." Charlie breezes into the room and goes straight to the fridge, grabbing a cold beer before jumping onto the sofa. She tucks her bare legs up and pulls her oversized sweater over her knees, so just her head is peeking out. Her hair is still damp from the shower and slicked back. Her pale face shimmers with moisture, and her deep blue eyes sparkle with mischief. She looks nothing like the fierce Dominatrix that replaced Sam as number one at the Club. I look between Leon and her for some clarification as to why she's here. I know he hasn't had time for a session. I was at the door the moment he got back…at least I thought I was.

"Sam told Charlie she could stay in her old room while her flat is being refurbished." Leon answers my unasked question, although that isn't really what I want clarified.

"What are debauched?" I ask Charlie.

"The Gathering…Sorry, I assumed you were talking about the Gathering in Venice?" She sucks on her beer, and I wait for the bottle to pop free.

"Why would we be?"

"You said something about not coming back. You meant Sam, right?" She scrunches her face like she suddenly remembers something bad and looks between Leon and me warily.

"Right…Go on." I reply. She hesitates for a moment, I narrow my eyes, and she notices my fist clench on the cushion beside her.

"Hmm…" She ponders a moment more. I think she's enjoying this. But then I have heard she's exceptional at torture. "I thought so. After your disappearing act at the altar, I wouldn't blame her for not coming back. Nevertheless, I'm sure she won't die." Her eyes narrow and she throws me a filthy look. I don't give a shit what look she levels at me if she knows where Sam is.

"Wait! What makes you think Sam is going to the Gathering?" I fight to retain any semblance of calm; this new information is not quite a 'gift horse', still, it's pretty damn close.

"She called me and asked for Gabriel's number. I just assumed—"

"That just makes you an ass." Leon is clearly unhappy with Charlie's disclosure. I get a cautious twist in my gut.

"Oh you are going to pay for that later, my love." Her voice drops, and I notice Leon catch his breath. So not the time for this.

"Charlie!" I snap, and she scowls some more. I can see the indecision flit across her face, what she knows against what she's prepared to tell me. I'm pretty confident if she didn't hold the esteemed position of Prima Domme at my club, it would be fuck all. But I have leverage, and she can see in my own determined expression, I'm not above using it.

"I gave her Gabriel's number a week ago. I don't know if she called him, but I do know that, if she did, he would do everything in his power to get her there. He's been trying for years. I'm also pretty sure that what Gabriel wants… Gabriel gets." She leaves that hanging in the air like a pungent door. My chest constricts painfully for Sam. Gabriel Wexler isn't a bad man. In fact, he's a very good man. Shit.

EIGHTEEN

Sam

I could get used to this, solitude and five…ten…no, more like 100-star service from the crew. Apart from one night of storms when my morning sickness was eclipsed by violent seasickness, the voyage from Barcelona across the Mediterranean Sea was wonderful. Waking every morning to endless blue skies and crystal clear azure waters, eating the most exquisite food prepared by Gabe's favourite chef and a daily massage. Oh yes, part of Gabriel's skeleton crew on this luxury yacht is a personal masseuse. If my heart wasn't broken into a million pieces, I would definitely be in heaven.

After a week cruising around the coast of Italy we are tugged in through the narrow channel of the Venice lagoon to dock just west of the main square, Piazza San Marco. I forgo the evening meal and decide to have a wander. It's been a while since I visited this very special city, and it'll be nice to walk on solid ground for a change. Ironic, considering Venice is hundreds of small islands, which make it seem like the stunning, crumbling buildings of the Renaissance rise directly from the sea bed and most of the roads are waterways.

Gabriel has a gorgeous Aquariva speedboat, which transports me not only from the main yacht to the shore but back in time to a decade of classic sophistication and elegance more befitting the continental 1950's and film stars of the silver screen. I feel I should be wearing a head scarf and dark glasses as I sit back in the semicircular, soft leather seating, surrounded by exquisite inlays of highly polished maple wood and chrome. Dressed in his crisp white uniform, Oliver, the first hand, navigates the busy waterway, cruising up the Canal Grande and depositing me safety and in style at Piazza San Marco.

"Call the *Ambrosia* bridge when you need picking up, madam." Oliver offers his hand as I step from the boat to the jetty, an easy task given my choice of flat footwear though I still appreciate the assistance.

"I don't have a phone," I reply with a wide smile. *And I haven't missed that one bit.*

"Oh really? Um, right, madam. In that case…" He frowns and I speak before he can think of a solution.

"Don't worry, I will get a taxi back to the boat." I turn to walk away.

"No, madam, I will return in an hour or so and just wait here." He flashes a worried smile, and I look at the queue of boats waiting to take his spot. I doubt that's really an option.

"It's no bother, Oliver. I will be fine." I offer and wave my hand in a limp wristed brush off.

"Please, madam, I must insist." His manner is pleading, so his words don't irritate me like they would otherwise.

"Fine, but give me at least two hours. I might want to eat, and I will definitely want to drink." Even if I won't, my desire for the numbing capabilities of alcohol, is battling with a daily dose of my very pregnant reality.

"Very good, madam." He steps back onto the Riva and starts to untie the ropes. "Hope you have a good evening."

"I will do my best." That is more than I can hope for. I wave him off. He doesn't return my gesture, he only gives a slight smile and a professional, curt nod.

There are hundreds of canals in Venice but there are also hundreds of streets, narrow and interconnected by many bridges. I wander with the crowds. The labyrinth of paved streets is spread out in a sort of grid pattern, and every so often, the narrow path I walk opens onto a square with some stunning basilica, palace, or grand hotel. Historical buildings cling to the majesty of the era in which they were built, many are worn and weathered in the fading light of the day. They are utterly charming, and on any other occasion, I'd have been completely awestruck. This evening, on the other hand, I'm in a daze, numb and barely aware of which direction I'm heading. I hope it's a circle.

I'm only vaguely glancing in the shop windows of the expensive boutiques I pass. I look at the stylish shoes that would normally have me drooling, with their sky high heels, encrusted with gems and shining in the spotlights, but tonight they leave me cold. I find myself staring at a display of masks. Most tourist shops hold a selection, but there are several specialist shops that actually deserve more than a cursory glance, and this is one of them.

The whole window is crammed with all different types of masks and historical costumes. Grotesque distortions of the faces draw me in, repulsed and fascinated. I guess that is the point. Some have pointed, oversized hooked noses, a mix of ugly and vulgar, and then there are those with devil horns and evil grins, hand-painted in burnt reds and black which look overtly sinister and wicked.

There is nothing sinister yet everything wicked about the feature mask displayed in the centre of the window. Absolutely beautiful, dark red, with ruby-encrusted filigree extensions and an elaborate red and black feather headpiece that is easily two feet high. The mannequin has a cloak that hangs from a structured shoulder piece and collar, embellished with hundreds of jewels and gold embroidery, exquisitely intricate. The cloak matches the mask in colour and hangs too long to see the end in the display, it's a thick looking, rich velvet. I'm not sure if the collar and cloak are one piece. It is absolutely gorgeous. I find myself absently stroking my own bare neck. Never wanted a collar, but damn, I miss it now that it's gone.

I pass several restaurants that would be suitable, only suddenly I don't feel like eating. I thought I had done well keeping my mind off things. Seeing something as silly as a shop display and wanting to share that experience with him, but I can't.

I no longer feel hungry; I just feel alone. I wrap my arms tight around myself and lift my sweater hood over my head. I look like a hobo. I doubt I would get served anyway. I shuffle back into the crowd and refuse to look at another window. The street vendors don't bother to tout their fake designer bags. The gondoliers don't ask if I want to take a ride as they do the other tourists. I'm being judged. It's not the first time, and at least it's for my clothes not for what I am…or what someone thinks I am.

I find myself back at Piazza San Marco, and the place is thrumming with visitors. Flashing cameras act like continuous strobe lights as people capture this night, this adventure. Street vendors sell cheap gimmicks, glow-in-the-dark toys, quirky torches, and selfie sticks to capture that special moment when you have no friends. *Perfect.*

I sit in a chair on the edge of a cafe where there is a mini orchestra playing Vivaldi to a small seated gathering and a much larger crowd standing around the edge of the tables. A waiter approaches and speaks abruptly in Italian. Other than his rather aggressive tone, I don't understand a word. He switches seamlessly to English, though his voice is just as harsh.

"There is a cover charge for the music, and you have to order a drink at the very least." He slaps the drink menu down, and I would normally rise to such attitude, only that part of me has long since ceased to care. I do, however, pull out my very real Prada purse and a wad of fifty Euro notes. He stiffens at the crumpled pile I place on the table, and his eyes widen. What I really want is a bottle of their famous Belini, but I'm being good. Maybe I could have just one glass. I'm trying for good, but I'm never going to be a saint.

"I'll have a mint tea and a smile if you want that twelve percent tip you are going to put on my bill." I hand the menu back with a wide, sweet smile that seems to confuse the waiter. He holds the menu while my words take time to register.

"Very good, signora." He forces a tight smile. *Maybe I do care after all.* He returns before I have the chance to slip my purse in my back pocket. He even lays out a small selection of antipasto that I didn't order. I thank him and settle back to enjoy the nightfall in Venice's main square. The acoustics of the piazza with impressive stone buildings on three sides means the sound is captured and held within the square. It feels timeless and beautiful, charming. I close my eyes and just listen. When the musicians take a small break, I shiver with a chill from sitting outside for so long; I don't know how long, though.

I'm just about to take the opportunity to make my way back to the dock when a tall, chilled flute of Champagne appears on the table in front of me, then another.

"I didn't order this." I state the obvious by the roll of the waiter's eyes.

"No, signora. The gentleman ordered," he answers and walks away, as if that was explanation enough. I sit up and look around but don't recognize anyone. I don't feel anyone, feel him I mean, yet my heartbeat quickens at the notion that he might…just maybe…

"Mistress…" Gabriel's deep timber slashes my hopes, and I sag in my seat. Why the fuck am I so disappointed? I didn't really expect it to be him, did I? He left me. He won't be coming to get me…ever. Fuck, that hurts. "You should only ever be drinking Champagne." He slides into the seat beside me, all debonair and dashing. His paunch is perhaps a little more festive than the time of year warrants, but he is still very handsome.

"Gabriel." I smile and gently push the glass away. "I can't drink this." He slides it back and scoffs.

"Why ever not?" I repeat my move in our game of Champagne table tennis.

"Because I am pregnant." I hold the glass steady to prevent him moving it back.

"Fuck!" I flinch as his booming voice echoes off the old stone buildings around us. He leans in and lowers his voice, a little too late, as all eyes are on us. "Or fucked? Are we happy about this bundle of joy, or have you run away to make a difficult decision."

"What? No. Nothing like that. I'm thrilled." I rush to put him straight, my hand protectively cupping my still flat belly.

"So this is just some R and R?" He raises a suspicious brow.

"Not exactly…it's complicated." I reply quietly, lifting my hand to massage the tension in the back of my neck. His large hand covers mine, and he applies more pressure, which eases the ache.

"Then let me uncomplicate it. It's what I do. I'm a trouble-shooter *extraordinaire.*" He flashes a wide and wicked grin.

"I can't help thinking you would not make this situation *less* complicated." I let out a light laugh, acutely aware that that is the first time I have made that noise in nearly two weeks. My face feels strange with the sudden use of forgotten muscles.

"Try me?" he asks, all mischief gone. He tone is stern and serious, yet his face is filled with compassion, and I'm shocked that now I break. Shit.

"Drink this." Gabriel hands me a mug of something warm that smells suspiciously like it has alcohol in it. I wipe my nose on the arm of his very fluffy and large bathrobe and almost smile when he grimaces. He managed to get this blubbering mess back to the Ambrosia, ran me a deep and bubbly bath, and now has me tucked up in my bed. I couldn't stop shivering despite the searing hot water of the bath so he swaddled me in the thickest terrycloth robe he had, which happened to be his, and it's enormous. The bed covers and the robe seem to have done the trick as only the faintest of tremors ripple patches of goosebumps across my skin. I shake my head and hold my hand up to stop him encroaching any further.

"I can't drink that." I shrug my shoulders in a slow apology for the huge trouble I know I must be to a man like him.

"Nonsense, you're not the first pregnant woman to have a little alcohol and you won't be the last." He fixes me with a stubborn glare I have never seen on him before, and it makes me smirk. I reluctantly take the cup, which is filled with fortified liquid chocolate.

"When did my sub get to be the boss of me, exactly?" I blow softly on the chocolate and inhale the sweet steam that rises in a puff of white cloud.

"When you so repeatedly pointed out that you are no longer my Mistress." He sits on the bed, and I slide my knees up to give him a little more room.

"Ah, fair point." I sip the chocolate, and honestly, there is only the slightest hint of rum. It tastes delicious, and my tummy growls its approval loudly.

"So?" Gabriel waits patiently for me to finish my drink. He takes my cup from my lips when he is clearly done waiting.

"So…I'm having a baby." The first genuine smile splits my face and breaks my heart at the same time. So much joy and so much pain. "I don't know who the father is exactly, and that is a deal breaker for Jason. We thought it was his, but the clinic got the dates wrong and now…" I swallow the thick, choking lump clogging my throat. Gabriel's hand rests heavy and comforting on my knee. "I don't blame him. It's just…fuck, I miss him." Fat tears appear from nowhere and flow onto my cheek.

"I would blame him. No man in his right mind would walk away from you." His voice is derisive, and he shakes his head in disbelief.

"On our wedding day." I add a little salt to my wound even though, again, I don't blame him. The day was irrelevant to the impact of the truth. As hard as that is, it's still better to face that ugly truth before we actually married, rather than deal with a messy aftermath. Rip that Band-Aid clean off, quick, sharp, and briefly painful. *If only that was the case.*

"Fucking arsehole," Gabriel grumbles, his eyes searching and kind. He hands me back my unfinished drink before I even ask. This must be very strange for him. I know he's never married, never had a relationship, as far as I know, still he seems very good at this compassion and empathy thing, for a hard-arsed, ruthless finance guru, that is. His brow furrows with thought, and he falls silent. He's handsome, in his late fifties, and looks very good in spite of his lifestyle. I don't say good for his age because, although he does, I think his relentless pursuit of all things elicit and wanton would wear more heavily on the body than the passing of time. He has a permanent, exotic, deep tan and lines on his face that add to his character. Some are deep wrinkles, others are the twisted skin of scar tissue, evidence of a colourful or chequered past I couldn't begin to guess at. As open as he is about his desires, he's a very private man in all other respects. He has dark hair, which is streaked with silver, and the most brilliant blue eyes that convey a perfect mix of intelligence and wild recklessness. "You want me to ruin him?" he asks deadpan, and I nearly spit my chocolate all over his pristine white silk sheets, bedcovers, and robe.

"Excuse me?" I splutter.

"Mistress, it would be no bother. I quite fancy owning that club of his." His demeanour is completely serious, and I have to take a moment before I give a very unladylike snort.

"That's very sweet, Gabe, and totally unnecessary. Ruining him won't change a thing. No, that's not right. It would make me very sad. He works hard and deserves to do well, so leave him alone, okay?" Gabriel is silent, and I wait until he is looking directly at me before I raise an impatient and accusatory 'Mistress Selina' brow.

"Fine," he huffs. "You know you are much more fun when you are being a cruel bitch."

"But I'm not a cruel bitch. You paid me to be a cruel bitch, and I do believe you loved every minute." I remind him.

"I do indeed." His salacious smile widens, and he draws in a slow, steady breath.

"Past tense, Gabriel…past tense." I repeat because the fact that I quit as his Mistress some time ago seems to be taking some *forever* getting through. He briefly closes his eyes and switches the conversation.

"What will you do then, if you are really laying down your whip for good?"

"My work has been really great. I mean, I have taken so much time off and they haven't fired my arse. So I will continue with them until the baby comes and then see if I can work from home." I have given this lots of thought, and this seems to be the best solution if I am raising this baby on my own. *No not if; get it through your fucking head, Sam, you're on your own.*

"And you don't know who the father is?" His question brings me back from one hard reality to another.

"I know who it could be but out of the three, no." I hold his gaze and unsurprisingly I see not a flicker of judgment in his eyes.

"And not one of them wants to play happy families?" His sarcastic lilt is apparent, but I can see the depth of concern in his eyes.

"I don't need charity, Gabe." I reply with a sharp bite to my tone, and he grins. "I deserve someone who loves me enough not to care. My baby deserves that too, so until that person steps up, I'm on my own." I can feel my hackles rise with my temperature and the pitch in my voice. "And I don't care if that never happens. I'm enough, and I'm happy with that." My voice wobbles at the end of my tirade. Dammit.

"You sure about that, Sam?" I suck in a breath at his tender intonation and use of my name. I don't think he has ever called me anything other than Mistress.

"I have to be." I reply on a sad, soft exhale and close my eyes when he leans in to give me a fatherly kiss on my forehead. I won't deny I welcome the compassion and safety I feel under his care.

"Why did you never marry, Gabriel? You'd make an excellent husband." I hold my hand to his cheek, and he sighs, leaning into my touch.

"I made a terrible husband." He eyes fill with tears, which he quickly blinks away, and he turns from me but not quick enough that I don't notice the look of devastation that flashes across his handsome face. I sit up and reach for him.

"Gabriel, I'm sorry. I didn't know." I hold out my hand, and he steps back to hold it gently in both of his. He forces a smile and kisses the back of it.

"Sleep well, Mistress, we have a busy day tomorrow." His voice is now light and excited. Any trace of whatever brought that awful expression to his face is gone.

"We do?" I'm still leaning forward, and I'm sure my face is a picture of confusion.

"We most certainly do." The echo of his voice trails behind him as he exits my cabin and leaves me perilously curious. Curiosity is rarely a good thing with men like him. I have no idea what plans he is referring to, although I'm pretty confident I will not want any part of them. I sink back in to the mountain of pillows and slide down the silky sheets. I shuffle out of Gabriel's robe, now too hot, and push the covers free. I stare up at the twinkling lights that illuminate the mural of the night sky above me and let out a resigned breath. I also happen to know I will have no choice in the matter either, because whatever Gabriel wants…Gabriel gets.

NINETEEN

Jason

I slam the phone down and Stephanie jumps. She put the call through from Gabriel's personal assistant. The open plan office at the Club affords zero privacy. I rarely use it, but I do still have a desk next to Marco, who is currently managing the floor. Stephanie is the only admin staff up here, and judging by the hunch of her shoulders, she probably wishes she was elsewhere. But then so do I...I wish I was in Venice.

"Fucking piece of shit!" I stand abruptly, and my chair ricochets off the back wall. I grab my jacket and keys then head for the door.

"Is there anything I can do, Jason?" Stephanie's voice is tentative, her face scrunched in preparation for more venom. I check myself with a calming breath before I speak

"Thank you, Stephanie, but unless you can get me a ticket to the Gathering, I'm not sure you can." I slip my arm into my jacket as I continue on my way out. She's already shaking her head even though I knew her answer before I asked the damn question, unfortunately.

"Oh no, sorry Jason, they are always an instant sell out. Even getting another ticket, you still have to be verified, which I take from the abrupt end to that call, would be unlikely." Her lips curve into an apologetic smile.

"Something like that." I push out the word through my clenched jaw. "I was invited, but apparently, the invitation has been revoked."

"Revoked? No!" She gasps. "Surely Mr Wexler didn't—"

"Oh yes, Mr Wexler did," I confirm, justifiably bitter. "His PA just informed me, so draw up his termination contract would you? He can dream on if he thinks he's stepping one foot back inside my club," I snap, and she gives a curt nod. "Find out who else got an invite and offer them a lifetime membership free if I can have it."

"You'd still need to be verified." Her voice is softer, and she's rigid in her seat with tension. I'm a little tightly wound myself, so I make the effort to let out a calming breath. I'm not quite ready to flash a smile anytime soon, but my voice is considerably less hostile.

"I will cross that bridge when I have a ticket. First, I need a ticket." She gives me a short, worried smile and nods again.

"Right. Okay, I'm on it. If a club member has a ticket, Jason, I will get it for you," she declares, and I'm almost able to smile at her obvious determination —*almost.*

"Thank you, Stephanie. I appreciate it."

"Have you asked Leon?" she exclaims as if hit with a flash of genius. I'm way ahead of her.

"That's where I'm headed now."

"Good luck!"

I mutter, "I don't need luck. I need a fucking miracle."

It only takes a moment in the car driving toward Sam's old flat when I cut a U-turn in the road and head for the office. I've decided not to ask for Leon's help. I may have convinced him that the wedding day was just a huge motherfucking misunderstanding, but I'm under no illusion where his loyalties lie. If Sam asks him why he suddenly wants a ticket to the Gathering, I would bet my arse he wouldn't lie for me. I can't risk her taking flight again, not when I know exactly where she is going to be, the time, and the reason she's there.

I screech around the corner and drive into the basement of the Stone building car park. It's become my home since she left. I let my head drop to the steering wheel when I park and absorb the wave of exhaustion as it drags my heavy eyelids closed. God, I'm so fucking tired.

I jump with the thump on my windscreen only to snap my mouth shut before I curse the motherfucker out for waking me from the only sleep I've had in over a week. Daniel has a dark frown staring at me, but the cherub faced smile and waving arms of his son Lucas are a clear indication that at least one of them is pleased to see me. I stretch my neck out left and right until it pops then open the door.

"What the fu…dge are you doing here?" I censor my language, and Daniel cracks an uncharacteristic wide smile, while hugging his son and kissing his dark messy hair. Lucas stretches his arms out to me. He's at that age where it's still counted in months, and his sister Leia is just a few weeks old, which is why I'm more than a little curious why he is here, at work, after hours, with his firstborn.

"I could ask you the same thing," Daniel remarks and eases Lucas across the gap and into my arms. I've held Lucas a hundred times, yet for some reason today, I really look at him. His pudgy fingers grasp for me, and his wide toothy grin seems to hit me a little harder in my chest. I try to shake off the effect his crystal eyes are having on me as they seem to bore right through me without blinking. God, it feels like he's judging me. It's unnerving. Do all babies stare like that? Will my baby stare at me like this? Fuck, I hope I get to find out.

"I asked first." I hold Lucas for a quick hug, just as soon as he is in my arms, he twists and is pulling for his dad. He's so wriggly.

"This little man is being more demanding than me when it comes to Bethany, and she needed some time with Leia." Daniel playfully tosses Lucas up into a series of sky high lifts that have the toddler squealing with delight.

"Another one that doesn't like sharing." I chuckle and Daniel grins and shakes his head, not in the least bothered despite his protestations.

"Tell me about it, still you can't blame the little guy, besides at fifteen months he's still a baby himself." Daniel twists Lucas in his hands and settles him high on his shoulders, which seems to make Lucas more than happy.

"Hmm." I just take in the picture of blissful happiness and calm contentment on my best friend's face and hate the uncertainty now swilling in my stomach like a putrid poison. It's not quite seeping through my body, but it's there, dormant and ready to destroy me, if I don't get her back and make this right.

"So do you want to continue to talk babies, or are you going to tell me why you are living out of your office?" Daniel raises a dark brow high and knowingly.

"I have been home," I retort with an indignant and wholly unjustified edge of attitude.

"Barely, Jason." He pinches his lips tight like he's trying to hold something back. "Still no sign of Sam?" His voice is tinged with concern, and he really doesn't know the half of it. He probably assumed, along with everyone else, that I simply changed my mind.

"Not exactly," I offer with an exhausted sigh, and he places a comforting hand on my shoulder.

"My office." Daniel tips his head toward the lift. I drag my hand down my face. I may not feel much like talking, but if nothing else, I know he has some seriously good whisky in there.

"Talk." Daniel paces but not with agitation, his long strides are smooth and rhythmical as Lucas is now cradled in his arms and he attempts to lull him to sleep, planting intermittent kisses on his forehead, hair and cheek. I can't tell you how weird it is seeing him like this, and I get a mix of warmth and dread swirling in my stomach as I wonder if I will be the same. Will I even get the chance?

"It's complicated." I walk to the back wall behind his desk where the drink cabinet is concealed behind the slick panelling. I pour myself two fingers of whiskey and hold an empty glass up to offer Daniel the same.

"It always is. Continue." He shakes his head at the drink. His hard stare is penetrating and insistent for me to elaborate. I slump down into his chair and decide to fill in the blanks.

"The email threats I told you about. James found out the bastard's name and tracked him down with an actual address. I got that information along with another email that threatened to let the videos go viral on the morning of the wedding. I had no choice." My tone was emphatic. I still believe I did the only thing I could, but Daniel scoffs, and a flash of rage prickles and straightens my spine.

"You could've asked Patrick to deal with it, Jason. You didn't have to handle this by yourself. That is what our head of security is trained to do." His dismissive tone is so fucking out of order it's lucky he's cradling his sleeping son or I would have the fucker pinned to the wall. I remind myself this is Daniel and draw in a calming breath, forcing my curled fist to unclench.

"Right," I drawl, my voice thick with sarcasm. "Just to clarify, if it was Bethany at risk here, you'd just hand that all over to Patrick? Something as important as getting your actual hands on the arsehole that threatened the woman you love?" I narrow my eyes and his widen with the sudden change in my demeanour and the bitter edge to my tone.

"When you put it like that..." he concedes, then shakes his head and continues to question my course of action. "It was your wedding day, Jason. I might've—"

I forcefully whisper my response. "Bollocks! You'd have done the exact same thing, so stop busting my balls, Daniel. I know I fucked up, and I should've told her all along, but I did what I thought was best to keep her safe, and now I'm fucking paying the price. So cut me a bit of fucking slack. If you can't say anything helpful, maybe just shut the fuck up."

"Say fuck one more time in front of my son and—" Daniel whispers back in as aggressive a tone as a whisper can be. With his scowl, I can see he's pissed. Good, join the motherfucking club.

"He's asleep," I point out, thin lipped and snarky.

"Lucky for you," he retorts and any animosity I could muster in response dies with the puff of air that's been keeping me upright when I exhale.

"Yeah, I'm feeling all kinds of lucky at the moment." I drop my head into my hands and use the heels of my palms to press against the building pressure at my temples. I mutter the next words more to myself than to Daniel. "I had to deal with it, I didn't have a choice." I hear Daniel sigh, and his footsteps come a little closer. I don't raise my head until after he speaks.

"You're right. Look, I'm sorry." His voice is low and filled with concern. "I would've done the exact same thing, Jason." His dark brow is furrowed, and his expression is dead serious. I give a short nod, acknowledging his obvious empathy. I pick up the heavy crystal glass and drain the golden contents before pouring myself another two fingers. This is barely touching the sides of my throat, and I get none of the usual glow of warmth or welcomed numbness from the forty proof liquor.

"Sam thought I stood her up because of the baby." I take a large sip of whiskey and wince at the burn when it hits my throat.

"The baby?" His voice is a little louder, but he drops it back to a whisper halfway through the word when Lucas jumps. He doesn't wake, just wriggles a little in Daniel's protective hold.

"Yeah, she's pregnant, and she found out that day it might not be mine. She thought I saw the letter from with clinic with the dates confirming that she got pregnant at Christmas. She thought I just left." I can see his brow furrow with confusion, and my jaw clenches with anticipation of his next question.

"Why would she think that?"

"I may have been a bit of an arsehole about needing the baby to be mine, but none of that matters." I shake my head and the unbearable thoughts cloud in anyway. "I have to get her back. I have to explain everything and I have to believe she will forgive me."

"For being an arsehole?" he quips, and I manage to let out a humourless laugh.

"Yeah, for that."

"I don't think you were an arsehole, Jason. Still, I'm finding it difficult to believe she would cheat on you."

"She didn't." I hold is stare with an arched brow, just waiting for everything to click for him, but there's nothing. I can't help my eye roll when I prod him to come to his own conclusion without me spelling it out. "I didn't think I would need to explain that to you." He tips his head with instant understanding.

"Oh, sorry, man. Damn, that baby brain thing is catching." He lets out a light laugh then turns quickly serious again. "I get it. So how do you feel now, about the baby, I mean?"

"I'm all-in, if that's what you mean."

"Even if…" He shrugs slightly and leaves the unasked question hanging ominously in the air. I don't hesitate.

"Yeah, even if…" I brush the thought away because it really is of no fucking importance. She is the only thing that's important. I groan and drag my hands through my hair. "I just need that fucking ticket."

"Ticket?" Daniel is again confused, and I can see why taking paternity was such a good idea. He is usually, and irritatingly, one step ahead of me, but not right now. Although I don't think anyone could've predicted this scenario.

"Yeah, Charlie from the club said Sam had called asking for Gabriel Wexler's number over a week ago. I only just found this out, and today, the club gets an email from one of Sam's previous clients asking why he wasn't informed Sam was doing an exhibition piece for charity at the Gathering. He had declined his invitation and is blaming the club for keeping this a secret. I tried to use the Club's connection to get myself in, only Gabriel's PA said it's sold out. That's bullshit, Gabriel has blackballed me."

"She's doing what?" Daniel ignores my rant and focuses on the more salient part of my speech. His tone holds more surprise than mine did, but then I was mostly just fucking relieved to have found out where she is.

"This was on the email." I hand him the folded piece of paper from my wallet with a scan of the invitation.

"You can't be worried about this?" He hands the invitation back dismissively.

"Fuck yes, I'm worried. She thinks I abandoned her at the altar, and she's holed up with Gabriel." I thrust the paper into my back pocket and pour another glass, wondering when, if ever, this stuff is going to do its damn job.

"You have a point." I look up to see if his impassive tone is hiding an ironic expression. It isn't. Damn.

"Thanks."

"You're welcome." He's unapologetic and his voice stern. "What are you going to do?"

"I'm going to Venice tomorrow and hope that Stephanie can get me a ticket for the Gathering on Saturday."

"You can have mine." He offers so causally I don't think I heard him correctly.

"What?"

"Because I like repeating myself, Jason," he retorts, but I'm still in shock.

"You have a ticket?"

"I always have a ticket. I haven't been for years, but Gabriel always insists on including me…for life apparently." He shrugs lightly and shifts Lucas in his arms to the side now since he's starting to wake.

"Fuu…dge! I didn't know." I'm pleased to censor myself just as Lucas's eyes spring wide open.

"No reason why you would. Colin keeps any invitations I receive in the second drawer down in his desk." He nods toward the closed door. "It will be there, but you'll have to get it yourself, my hands are a little full." His eyes dip to the toddler in his arms and an automatic involuntary smile spreads across his face. I'm already out of my seat and the door before he finishes his sentence.

I return with a spring in my step. I know I'm not out of the woods, but I can feel the break in the heavy canopy for the first time in over a week, and I'm going to bask in the first few rays of light and hope that warm my face.

"Thank you." I wave the ticket, my voice is deeply and most sincerely grateful.

"You're welcome, but you'll need some identification too. Take my driver's license. The picture is sufficiently fuzzy that you might get away with it."

"It's a Masquerade ball, Daniel."

"I'm aware, but they will still check. Gabriel runs a very tight and secure ship. If he doesn't want you in, you will need all the help you can get."

I walk over to him with the glossy black invite, holding it like its more precious than any winning lottery ticket. *It is.* "You may have a point." I take his license and slip it in my wallet. "Thank you for this."

"Don't mention it," he replies, and by his tone I know he means it. Then he switches to a more playful lilt. "Now will you go home and get some sleep, or do you need to be rocked too."

"You're funny." I ruffle Lucas's hair. Although he is now awake, he is adorably floppy, resting his head against Daniels shoulder. I drag in a deep breath. "I can't sleep without her."

"Well, if you fail to win her over with your words, she might just fall for the sympathy card. You look like complete shit."

"Thank you."

"Again, you're very welcome, Jason. I'm not joking."

"Fine, I'll go home and rest. I won't sleep but—"

"Rest is good. Anything else you need help with? Because it's time I got this little one to bed." He kisses Lucas's hair for the umpteenth time.

"Just the jet tomorrow." I pick up my keys. I'll leave the car and grab a cab, the whiskey has just started to dull the edges.

"It's yours. You really don't need to ask." Daniel follows me out to the corridor and along to the lift.

"I wasn't. I was being polite," I snark as I punch the call button.

"Don't bother, it doesn't suit you," he quips.

"That makes two of us."

"Now who's being funny?" He counters my retort, but I didn't mean to enter into some playful banter. I sigh and lean back against the wall of the lift as it descends.

"Not me. I won't be cracking so much as a smile until I have her back," I add with heartfelt hope and seriousness.

"Then just take some friendly advice and get some rest. I know this was a misunderstanding of biblical proportions, still the bottom line is you broke her heart for her to leave like she did. Trust me when I say you will need your strength because this isn't Sam you're going after, this is Mistress Selina, and you are going to have one motherfucking fight on your hands."

"Tell me something I don't I know." My knees buckle when the lift hits the ground floor because I feel like I've just hit rock bottom.

TWENTY

Sam

I'm lounging on the sundeck with my nose in one of Gabriel's books. Trust him to have a selection of Victorian erotica, and trust me to love reading it. I place *The Pearl* on the table and watch Gabriel walk across the deck followed by Oliver and another one of the crew, carrying arms full of bags.

"Someone's been busy." I smile and sit up, tucking my legs inside my t-shirt —Leon's t-shirt. It would appear I mostly packed clothes I had borrowed from him in my rush to leave.

"Someone had to do something about that!" He points his accusatory finger at me and it takes a moment to realize his turned up nose and disgust-filled tone are aimed at my oversized, discoloured, and entirely unflattering choice of clothes.

"At least I'm decent." I offer with a dismissive shrug.

"That's debatable, and I prefer you when you are indecent." His comment isn't remotely salacious, but deadpan and matter of fact. He takes a seat beside me and instructs the bags to be laid out on the end of my lounger and on the deck as there are too many for the sunbed.

"Gabriel?" My voice is guarded as I eye the boxes, and my mouth drops when another crew member appears with what looks like a coffin sized glossy black box.

"We have the opera tonight and an art film premier on Thursday. I'm having a little soirée here on Friday, and the Gathering is on Saturday. You need to be dressed appropriately if you mean to accompany me." He takes the tall cocktail glass offered and lets out an exhausted sigh.

"I don't *mean* to accompany you." My brows pitch together in irritation. I think I prefer Gabriel on his knees licking my boot and bowing to my command rather than this obnoxious steam-roller version of him.

"You are my guest, Samantha, and a dear friend who needs cheering up, and I would consider it extremely rude for you not to accept my hospitality in all its forms. More than that, my Mistress, I would be hurt." His last comment takes me by surprise with the softer tone and sincerity.

"Damn it, Gabriel, you don't play fair."

His smile spreads wide with satisfaction. "I never said I did. Now, open the boxes." He leans back and stretches his long, tanned legs out, kicking his shoes free and crossing his ankles. He rests one arm bent back behind his head. I hold his glare with determination, though after several minutes of his impassive, unblinking face, I groan.

"Gah! How did I ever dominate you?" I pout.

"Because I let you. Now, open the damn boxes." I poke my tongue out and pull the ribbon on the first box.

"Oh my," I gasp. Nestled in swaths of cream silk is the most exquisite pair of Loriblu black gem and feather sling back stilettos. I lift one up, the spike is tiny and easily six inches, covered in minuscule black stones that reflect so much sparkle they make me blink. The ankle strap has a chain to secure it and the heel design is scalloped with feathers that are stitched into the seam. I have to admit they are so damn sexy I think I'm a little wet. "They are gorgeous, Gabe. You know I can't accept—"

"Shut the fuck up and open the next one. You know what it does to me to give you pleasure, so please, not another word. Next…" He points to the tower, and I roll my eyes, defeated.

The next box is Roberto Cavalli. Inside is an evening gown that might just do the shoes justice. It's difficult to see exactly, lifting it only half out of the box. It is long and made of silk, with a plunging neckline and multiple straps. The next three boxes are all Cavalli, each holding equally stunning dresses. I spend the next half hour adoring everything Gabriel has bought for me, feeling a mix of guilt and joy, but his obvious pleasure outweighed the guilt pretty quickly. I was surprised at how well he had chosen, given that he has really only ever seen me in my dominatrix attire.

"I have enough here to last a month, you know that, right?" I quip with a warm smile.

"And if you wish to stay longer I will go shopping again," he states flatly.

"I can't hide here forever," I point out with an exaggerated downward twist of my lips.

"You can, if you want to." His casual response makes me wonder if anything fazes him.

"I'm pregnant, Gabe," I remind him, and his nose wrinkles like I have just blown him a morning breath kiss.

"Oh yes…maybe not forever then." He screws his face up, and I laugh. Standing, he walks over to the last box, and since he struggles to lift it onto the lounger, I wonder if it does, in fact, hold a body. He lifts the lid and my mouth drops open.

"Gabriel…" I shouldn't be shocked, and my tone is more irked than surprised. "I'm not going," I state. Almost on its own, my hand finds its way to the rich velvet material of the gown. I stroke the soft material, and I'm captivated by the glorious shoulder piece and collar. "It's very beautiful," I whisper.

"And only you could look more so. Please, Mistress, one final performance."

My hand snaps back like I've been bitten. "I can't, Gabriel. Don't ask me to do that." I know I must sound offended because he's quick to place the box down and kneel beside me.

"I don't mean it like that. I'm sorry if I upset you. What I meant was, I thought for one night you could perhaps do an exhibition piece for my charity. One last chance to submit to Mistress Selina for the highest bidder. I would be honoured if you would consider it, at least." His eyes soften, and his tone is genuine and pleading. He signals to a crewmember who brings forward the pièce de résistance—the mask. Not just any mask. This is the one that caught my attention last night. Fiery red ostrich feathers with black tips act as the headpiece, rubies over a shimmery red silk, the whole face covered in jewels and swirling intricate patterns. In the shop window it was mesmerizing. Now, in the brightest Mediterranean spring sun, it is absolutely breathtaking.

"I will consider it." I glance over to Gabriel who does his best to not look too smug. His lips curve in a slight smile. I repeat my answer, more for my benefit. "I said *consider*, understand?"

"Of course, Mist—" He stops himself when I narrow my eyes. "Let me take some of these to your room. You might want to check I got your size right." He stands and takes one bag and motions for the waiting crew to take the rest.

"I imagine you got my size spot on."

"I imagine I did." He grins and disappears down the stairs.

I fold the tissue paper back over the gown and a postcard flutters to the floor. I pick it up and shake my head. One side is glossy black with The Gathering embossed in the same raised print. I run my fingers over the bumps. I can't believe he did this. *What Gabriel wants…Gabriel gets.* The other side is gold with thick scrolled type, a vague address, time, and in big bold script slap bang in the centre:

Guest of Honour for One Night Only–
The Auction
of
Mistress Selina

"Son of a bitch," I mutter, but I'm still strangely surprised by the warm rush of feelings burning hard in my chest. I may not be able to smile just yet, and I know I feel more than a little lost, but this…this is something I know. I swing my legs to the side and rush after him.

"Gabe!" I call once I hit the bottom of the curved stairway. His stateroom occupies one end of the massive boat and the main lounge the other, and I'm far too lazy to be sprinting the entire length to track him down. I catch Joshua, one of the crewmembers, as he is about to pass. "Excuse me, you didn't see where Mr Wexler went did you?"

"He's retired for his…" He pauses and blinks nervously. His cheeks flush with colour, which is cute. "…um… nap, signora."

"That's fine. I won't disturb his 'nap'." I use my fingers to air quote. There is no way Gabriel is the type to need a nap though I'm happy with the euphemism. "Is Oliver on duty?"

"You need to go somewhere, signora?"

"Yes, I'd like to visit Murano, if he's available. Or I can get a water taxi, if someone could call one for me. I really don't mind."

He looks horrified at the suggestion of public transport. "No, signora, I'm sure that won't be a problem. If Oliver is not available, someone will be able to take you wherever you need to go," he insists with an earnest expression that borders on deadly serious.

"Okay, that's great." He visibly relaxes, which almost makes me laugh. "I'm going to get changed and grab my purse. I won't be five minutes."

"Very good, signora." The young crewmember gives me a bright smile and curt nod before turning away. I do the same but in the opposite direction, skipping off toward my cabin.

There are several unpacked boxes stacked in the corner of my room along with the coffin containing my costume. The rest have been put away. I open up the double wardrobe to find all the beautiful clothing Gabriel bought for me has been hung up. *Gosh, they were quick.*

I pick out some white capri trousers and an off the shoulder, black, ribbed top. Most of the shoes Gabriel has selected are sky high and not built for comfort, though there is a cute pair of white ballet slippers with large crystal flowers sewn on the toe. I slip those on, tie a plain silk scarf around my neck, and take the sunglass case from the dressing table that wasn't there this morning. I open it to find a pair of classic Chanel shades that complete my homage to the 1950's Hepburn look Gabriel was obviously going for, judging by most of the clothes hanging in the wardrobe. I slip my purse in my pocket and, not for the first time, relish the absence of my phone. It's easier to keep from checking who's *not* calling when you don't have the damn thing with you.

The Riva is idling, the engine purring and waiting, as is Oliver in his crisp whites and smart, slicked-back hair.

"Joshua said you would like to go to Murano Island?" He holds his hand out for me to take as I step into the much smaller boat and quickly sit down.

"Yes, if it's no trouble." The most I can manage is a half-smile.

"No trouble at all and maybe to Burano as well. It's where the lace comes from." His smile, on the other hand, is dazzling, and his face alive with excitement at his suggestion.

"Oh yes, that would be lovely, thank you." I nod my approval, which thankfully, is enough for him to jump into action.

"My pleasure." He releases the boat from its moorings and steers us away from the *Ambrosia* and out into the lagoon and beyond.

I spent an hour or so on Burano wandering along the narrow streets with row after row of vibrant and pastel collared houses. The island is tiny and entirely dependent on the tourist trade. All the shops stock only products for the influx of visitors to this popular spot. As Oliver said, it's mostly lace, and some of it is exquisite. Although I'm really after a gift for Gabriel. I don't think a tablecloth will quite cut it.

I have more luck on Murano. The neighbouring island is slightly bigger and has some large glass factories, which it's world famous for. One I entered had a small showroom, and when I expressed an interest in one piece, the owner took me upstairs to an enormous warehouse filled with every type of glass sculpture one could image. The large space had been broken into smaller rooms, each with different styles, from classic to modern, mirrors and ornaments, some of the most stunning pieces I have ever seen, all hidden away.

I pick a sleek piece that is named after the gondolas. It is more abstract and stretches almost a full meter in length. *The Silver Dogaressa*. The proprietor insists on delivering it personally when I give him the name of the Gabriel's yacht. I think Oliver and I would struggle, not so much with the weight, just the fragility.

I pick at a tricolored salad for my late lunch in a small restaurant overlooking the harbour. The basil is so fresh the fragrance would normally have me drooling, yet all my senses are sedated. The waitress takes my nearly full plate away, and I can't apologize enough because it really did look amazing. She didn't look remotely convinced when I tried to explain I just wasn't hungry, so I place the Euros on the table and quietly slip away, heading back along the harbour wall to where I had arranged to meet Oliver.

"Did you find what you were looking for, signora?" Oliver offers his steady hand, and my grip makes him wince. Sorry, but I'm not falling in the lagoon.

"I did, thank you, Oliver. They are delivering it tomorrow."

"Prego, very good." He beams. "If there is anywhere else you would like to visit, it will have to be another day I'm afraid. Signore Wexler has tickets for the opera tonight." He grins and I groan.

"Oh I had forgotten about that." I purse my lips and wrack my brain for excuses that might get me out of it. I know I'm being ungrateful, it's just I couldn't feel less like an evening out if I was a hermit.

"So home is good?" He unhooks the rope and jumps into the boat, striding to the wheel.

"Home would be perfect." I feel the hit in my heart like an ice blast that instantly freezes the muscle mid-beat. I close my eyes, but the tears just trickle from the corners. I'm glad Oliver is facing forward and the wind is whipping the tears from my face, so he doesn't see my sorrow. "Only, I don't know where home is right now," I whisper into the sea breeze and spray sprinkling my face.

"You look...you know, Mistress, I have no words." Gabriel holds his arms wide as I enter the lounge in my full-length Cavalli gown and black Loriblu jewelled heels. I shake my head at the offered champagne flutes and take a sparkling water. I failed to come up with an excuse, but then, I'm not myself, and I don't have the energy to take on the force that is Gabriel either. So I simply decided to choose the path of least resistance for the time being. If nothing else, it's a distraction.

"You're very kind, Gabe, and you look very dashing. You always rock the tux." I clink my glass to his, and his nose curls at the contents of my flute.

"It's bad luck to toast with water," Gabriel mutters, obvious distaste in his tone.

"I'm not drinking any more alcohol, Gabe," I lightly admonish with a roll of my eyes.

"That must suck, being heartbroken and unable to numb the pain with drugs and alcohol." His smile is on the tender side.

"Being heartbroken sucks, period, and I'm okay with water." I allow him to pull me against his side as he threads his arm across my shoulder and plants a gentle kiss in my long, loosely curled hair.

"And that is why we must keep you entertained, perhaps some cordial in the water though." He clicks his fingers and one of the waiters is almost immediately at my side offering up a choice of pink grapefruit syrup or elderflower cordial.

"I didn't take you for the superstitious type," I remark with a note of surprise. To appease my host, I select the elderflower.

"I'm not. Water is so bland, and I don't do bland."

"That's for sure."

"Shall we? We have a table at the Gritti Palace so we will have to shake our arses." He downs his champagne, and I barely take a sip of my newly flavoured drink when he takes my hand and starts to lead me toward the bow of the boat. The waiter catches my glass from my hand as I'm pretty much dragged outside.

"Thank you Gabe." I offer a very small smile with my most heartfelt sentiment. He sits beside me, takes one of my hands, and clasps it between both of his, warm and secure.

"It is my mission to make that smile of yours a little bigger, Mistress." He squeezes my hand and raises it so the tips of my fingers touch his lips.

"Then you have your work cut out for you, Gabe," I whisper.

"Trust me, this isn't work. This is pure pleasure, and I will very much enjoy every second." He waggles his thick brows playfully. He is pure charisma and utter class on the surface and the kinkiest soul alive underneath that impeccable tux.

We have the most amazing meal overlooking the Canal Grande, and Gabe is effortlessly charming. The opera isn't the best choice and I am grateful we are in darkness and secluded in a box high above the stage. The tragedy of *La Bohème* and Mimi's heartbreak is just a little raw. I can appreciate the splendour and artistry. In happier times, I'm easily swept along with the dramatic music and tragedy as it unfolds. But, right now, all my emotions are consumed with trying to salvage the wreckage of my decimated heart, and this particular spectacle hasn't helped one bit. We leave before the final act as Gabriel lightly tries to joke that he's out of tissues and not prepared to offer his handmade suit to mop my snotty nose.

We sit at the same cafe in Saint Mark's Square where Gabriel found me only a few nights ago. He orders some port and a mint tea.

"Thank you for this, Gabe. I didn't want to come out tonight. Still, it has been…" I bite my lip as I ponder an accurate adjective.

"A distraction," he finishes with a knowing smile.

"Yes, of sorts. I guess it's been a distraction." I drop my head back and gaze at the clear sky and millions of stars. It's breathtaking and rightly humbling. It has the effect of putting my insignificant existent into perspective. I place a protective hand over my tummy. Not completely insignificant.

"You really think he left you?" Gabriel's question causes me to snort out a very unladylike laugh.

"Sorry, did you actually say that?"

"I'm serious. I can't get my head around Jason doing such a thing." He shrugs off his observation like it isn't a big fat slap in the face.

"Oh well, he did. He definitely did." I bristle with the implication, but just as quickly sag back in my seat when I recognise the expression on his face is truly earnest. I draw in a deep breath and fight the inevitable prickle of tears behind my eyes. "I would've liked the chance to talk it over. We always promised that's what we'd do, but the net result would've obviously been the same. He doesn't want to bring up some other man's child…No, that's not even true. He doesn't want to endure the connection I would have with another man, if they were the father." I've had some time to process and this is my conclusion. I don't know why, but it helps to soften the blow of abandonment somewhat, knowing it's not the baby that's the issue, it's me.

"He still might be the father." Gabriel is pushing, and I can feel the tension building. I stretch my neck out and power through the urge to push back. I know his intentions are coming from a good place.

"Yes." I sigh.

"And?" His intentions, however, are still irritating.

"And?" I parrott.

"And… I don't have to spell it out, Sam. Would you take him back?"

He lays it out like a big white elephant on the tiny table before us. I take a moment before I answer. The cafe quartet is playing Vivaldi, and the night couldn't feel more magical, with the clear skies sprinkled with too many stars and ancient buildings twinkling with lights in the windows overlooking the famous square. I absently stir my tea and manage to look into Gabriel's concerned eyes and hold his gaze.

"When I'm not completely heartbroken, I'm extremely pissed. He was a coward to walk like he did, and I never thought him a capable of hurting me like he has." I swallow the thick lump, but my voice waivers at the end.

"And what if you're right?" He dips to keep my gaze when I try to look away. *He's good at this interrogation thing.*

"Right? What do you mean if I'm right?" I can't hide the incredulity in my voice but it doesn't rattle him. If anything, his tone softens, and he reaches for my hand.

"What if he isn't a coward, and he didn't hurt you? What if this is just a misunderstanding?" His voice is soothing, and I'm drawing the comfort I need from his hold because his words are slicing through me. I almost choke on the words as they spill from my open mouth.

"A fucking big misunderstanding, don't you think?"

"Enormous. Still, that doesn't negate the fact that it might be, in fact, a huge misunderstanding." I try to pull my hand free but he maintains the firm and steady hold.

"Why are you saying this, Gabe?" My voice catches, and I fucking hate that fat tears fall from my eyes, and I can't do a damn thing to stop them. My jaw tightens, and I spit the next words through gritted teeth. "He left me on my wedding day. It doesn't get any clearer than that...not to me."

"Then why is he trying his damnedest to get a ticket for the Gathering?" Gabriel's statement completely knocks the air from my lungs, and I fold. My hand presses against the instant unbearable ache in my chest.

"He is?" I mouth the words but Gabriel hears the faint whisper.

"Yes." He uses his free hand to sip his port before he continues. "He called my personal assistant, and when he was told they were none available, he offered me a free lifetime membership to his club, for a single ticket." He arches a brow high and has a knowing grin on his lips, only I'm not following what he thinks he knows exactly.

"You didn't accept?" My eyes must widen comically because he laughs, a loud, throaty sound, and it echoes off the high walls and quiet night.

"Do I look like I need charity, darling?" He shakes his head at my silly notion.

"No, but you do like drama." I raise my own brow in mock judgement, the edge to my voice making my comment sound more like a statement of fact.

"True." His chuckle softens, and his expression flits from playful to serious in a blink. "However, I wouldn't risk you, Mistress, not at any cost. You have nothing to fear, he will not gain entry to the Gathering." I let out a breath I didn't realise I was holding and relax against the hard back of the chair. "But I wouldn't be so sure he isn't already in Venice and will try whatever means to see you while you're here." His throwaway comment undoes his previous declaration, and I'm again tense and on high alert.

"All the more reason for me to stay on the boat." I mumble.

"Yacht," Gabriel grits out, and I bite the inside of my cheek to stop myself from smirking. "You will not hide, Mistress."

"No, you're right." I straighten in my seat and pull my shoulders back. How I can switch from desolate to determined seemingly with the change of the wind, is as impressive as it is exhausting. "I just… What you just told me is a surprise, that's all." I worry my lip and cast a furtive glance over the now deserted square. "Why would he want to come to the Gathering?"

"Why do you think?" Gabriel swirls the remaining port slowly in his glass and tilts his head, looking directly at me through his long lashes. His knowing confidence is one more thing I could quickly find beyond irritating.

"To get his arse kicked," I snap.

"Ha!" A short, bold laugh. "He would have to pay handsomely for the privilege, although I can promise you he will not get into my party."

"It's not his style, Gabe. Trust me, Jason is not the type of man to pay to be on the receiving end of my whip." I drop any hint of humour. "You promise he won't be there, Gabe?"

"Cross my heart and hope to draw my last breath under your boot." He draws his finger in the pattern of the aforementioned cross on his impeccable black tux jacket.

"A little dramatic, Gabe, but thank you." He pulls my hand up and kisses the back.

"Anything for you, Mistress." His voice is sincere and I'm shocked how much comfort I take from the sentiment and from him.

I let out a heavy sigh. "I don't want to see him…not yet. I'm not ready." I'm trying to explain but it feels more like a confession. "Jason being here…I didn't think it would even be a thing. He left me, it's just after what you've just told me, I honestly don't know what to think. But I do know I'm not ready to face him so soon."

"Then your wish is my command, as always." Gabriel stands and I do too.

At the first prickle of a goosebumps from the chilled evening air, Gabriel removes his jacket to place over my shoulders, and we make our way back to the jetty.

"I would ask how I can ever repay you, Gabe, but since you already have me performing when I had no intention of doing any such thing, I dread to think what else your silver tongue could entice me to do." I muse with a wry grin.

"My list is very long, Mistress." He flashes a decadent, wicked smile.

"I don't doubt that for one second." I nudge my bony elbow into his side, and he lets out a deep groan that is filled with far too much pleasure for an innocent gesture. "Behave. Gabriel. You know, I think you'd even give the Marquis De Sade a run for his money."

"Amateur."

"You're incorrigible." I shake my head with exasperation. He simply chuckles and pulls me against his side for a hug. I rest my head against him.

"It's the only way to be, darling." His lips press against my hair. I relax into his hold and very nearly smile. *What a fucking mess.*

TWENTY-ONE

Jason

The scorching spray pummels my shoulders, only the tension in my muscles is set solid. Pounding the pavement for my five mile run this morning didn't ease my mind, any more than the copious quantity of alcohol I consumed the night before. The scalding shower is just another thing I can add to my list of failed attempts to reach a state where I don't feel this pain. I am consumed with just one thing and it's thrumming and pulling every fibre in my body so taut, I know I'm a walking hair trigger. I don't want to contemplate the aftermath of destruction, if I don't get her back, I can't...I won't entertain that as a remote possibility. I switch the water off and step from the shower. The wide mirror over the sink is steamed up and my reflection is completely obscured. Good. I can't bear to look at my face right now. How could I be so fucking stupid? All I had to do was tell her, tell her I had to deal with some shithead that wanted to hurt her. It's not like she wouldn't understand. Hell, she would've probably ridden shotgun, if I had let her.

I rake my hand across the mirror, and the steam forms bigger droplets of water and streaks across the surface that warp the image of my face. Hazy and oddly magnified in parts, I look distorted but mostly my face just looks utterly exhausted. Daniel was right; I do look like shit.

I don't bother to shave, just brush my teeth and dry off.

Since I'm no longer able to sleep, I packed for this trip last night. It kept my mind from Sam, for all of five fucking minutes. I dress quickly and grab my case, keys and passport. When I enter the kitchen Will is holding my phone.

"Sorry, it was an unknown number so I took the call." He rushes to explain. "It wasn't Sam, sorry." His face falls in sync with mine, and I bite back the sickness that rises from my stomach, a reaction I get every time my damn phone rings.

"It's okay." I try to convey the truth of my words in my tone, though I know he doesn't believe me. None of this is okay, but I've stopped blaming him. He was just an easy target. This fuck-up is all mine. "Who was it?"

"He didn't say. He just said the package didn't make it and that he didn't think that would be a problem." Will quirks his lips and shrugs off the cryptic message.

"Hmm?" I'm in the dark until he elaborates.

"That's all he said. He had a thick Russian accent, and he didn't give his name." His brow furrows, and from his expression, it's clear he's putting considerable effort into understanding as my face must register recognition.

"Oh, that's okay I know who that was, and he's spot on." My derisive tone is clear, but my smile seems to confuse Will. "At least I did one fucking thing right that day."

"The email guy." He's usually pretty quick to follow, and I give a sharp nod.

"Yes."

"So the package…."

He understands perfectly well, and I have no intention of discussing this further. That fucking arsehole cost me enough. I'm not wasting another second on him.

"Are you dropping me at the city airport or not?" He narrows his eyes, then pushes himself up from his chair.

"Sure." I throw him my keys, and he follows me out.

The journey to the airport takes no time at all, still the seconds still drag on. Will interrupts my ever-present darkness with a question I have been pondering almost every second since she left.

"What if she doesn't want you back?" The question is spoken softly, its effect like a bullhorn in this confined space. My jaw clamps shut, and I grit out my honest answer through clenched teeth.

"Not an option," I say emphatically. "Next question?"

"Okay," he drawls, apparently picking up on my hostility, not for him, but for the impossibility of his suggestion. "What are you going to do then? It's likely from what you said about this guy Wexler's PA, you are not going to be welcome if you show up. He's obviously protecting her."

"I did get that impression, yes." I barely refrain from biting his head off, yet he keeps pushing regardless of my clipped tone.

"So?"

"So I don't have a fucking clue!" I slam my head back again the headrest. The uneasy silence deepens. I take a moment to draw in a deep breath and let it out slowly before I speak. "All I know is who she's with and where she's going to be at a specific time. I can't get hold of her any other way, so I'm going to be where she is, whether Gabriel Wexler likes it or not." I state flatly.

"She doesn't have a thing for this guy, does she?" His flippancy makes me want to punch the question right off his face. I settle for fucking incredulity.

"Jesus, Will! For fuck's sake, are you trying to stomp on my fucking heart now? I'm bleeding out here. I just want to make sure, because please, keep on with the same fucking questions I've been torturing myself with since she left." I'm roaring by the time I finish. My fists are clenched, and my blood pressure must be through the damn roof.

"Sorry, Jason, I didn't mean—"

"I don't know, Will. I don't fucking know." I drag my hands across my face and sweep them to my neck to massage the ever-present tension. "I mean, I don't believe she does. He's an ex-client, and I know she never crossed that line in the past." I hear him drag in a breath as if to speak. My scowl stops him dead. I know that fucking line of thinking too, and I don't need it spelt out. I drop my head back and sigh heavily. "I also don't believe you can go from loving someone to loving someone else so quick."

"Yeah, I guess."

I speak before I have to grab the wheel and pull the car over to kill my brother. "Don't say what you're thinking, for the love of all that's holy. I will hurt you in ways you've only seen in horror movies and not think twice," I warn in all seriousness.

"Saying nothing, brother, nada." He seals his lips, and I'm thankful he listened, for once.

"Good." I have to believe she still loves me. My only hope of getting her back relies on that being an irrefutable truth. *She has to love me.*

Will pulls smoothly into the drop-off zone at the airport, and I turn to face him. His face is a picture of worry, reflecting only a fraction of my own concern. "So to answer your question, what am I going to do?" I pause and a smile begins at the corner of his mouth before I even start to speak. "I'm going to do everything and anything."

"Good." He takes my offered hand and pulls me across the console for a hug. "I'm not saying good luck because luck is for pussies. You got this, Jason. Don't let her go."

"Not a chance." I hug him back and grab my bag from the back seat. Waving him off, I stride with purpose and determination into the terminal, eager to get my flight and end this nightmare.

The flight is uneventful, and I land at Marco Polo airport midafternoon. It's a testament to how infamous and exclusive this event is that all the top hotels are fully booked. I had to call in a personal favour from the owner of Hotel Danielli in order to get a room. There isn't another vacant space within a fifty-mile radius of the venue. My suite should be perfect however. Not where I normally stay, though he assures me the view overlooks the lagoon.

The meet and greet service picks me up from the airport and drops me via the hotel's private water taxi directly to San Marco's main square.

"Signore, if there is anything else I can assist with, do not—"

I interrupt the very polite porter. "I need a costume. I have an event I'm attending tomorrow, a masquerade ball. If you could get me the address of the best quality costumier, please. I mean, not the type of masks for tourists. The costume has to be authentic."

"Certainly, signore. You will want to visit Canovàccio on the Ponte di Rialto. They are a very old family and have many masks that will suit. I believe it is the preferred place for others attending the ball." The porter hesitates on that last word, and I know from his wry grin that it's not from a language barrier issue. He knows, or more likely, has heard rumours about the Gathering. *I couldn't give a fuck what he's heard.*

"Excellent, Oh and some binoculars, please." I add just as he is about to leave.

"Pardon, signore?"

"Ho bisogno di un paio di binocoli si prega." I hold my hands up to mimic looking through some binoculars, and he nods enthusiastically with understanding.

"Certo, signore. Pronto." He gives me a curt nod and briskly exits the presidential suite. I slip my jacket over the back of one of the many ornate chairs placed around the room. This one is directly in front of the full-height French windows. I pull the curtains wide. Opening both doors, I step out onto the balcony. This suite is the only one on the top floor, reserved for dignitaries, royalty, and favour-claiming BDSM club owners. It's several stories above street or water level, but the noise from the heaving crowds is deafening. The afternoon temperature is warm for spring, though all year round this spot has thousands of tourists flocking from all over the world. With almost daily visits from international cruise ships, spewing hundreds of people onto this tiny stretch of land, filling it to capacity and making it both vibrant and hellish, depending on where you sit on the spectrum of enjoying crowds. I'm glad to be above the throngs.

I'm too tired to sort my costume, even though the shops will be open until late. At the moment, I just want to crash for an hour and hope that utter exhaustion is enough to drag me to sleep before I resort to raiding the mini bar to numb the pain.

"What are you going to do?" My voice is hoarse with want. My fingers twitch to touch her, and I don't feel the burn of the rope when I pull against the restraints, she has me so distracted. I know I couldn't break them, she has tied me very tight to bed frame. But why would I want to break them? She's here and I said I would do anything. Her tongue drags languidly along her bottom lip and my balls tighten in anticipation.

"Anything I want to." Her voice sounds strange, flat and hollow. She starts to crawl up the bed, hovering over my body, her sexy toned legs straddling mine. Damn, I want to touch her, mark her, make her mine. I can't believe she's here. This is fucking torture, but this is for her so at least one of us is enjoying it. She isn't smiling though; not even a flicker of wickedness curls her lips, and the blood in my veins chills when I look in her eyes. God she looks so sad.

"Sam, I'm so fucking so—" She slaps her hand over my mouth and shakes her head to stop me speaking.

"Yes, me too." From nowhere she pulls a large black rubber ball gag, and as much as I want to twist from her to stop this happening, my head won't seem to move. She pulls my jaw down and fills my mouth with the gag, and all my words of apology and regret are just a mix of incoherent mumblings from now on. I slam my head back with frustration when she finally fixes it tight, and still my temper is quelled when she kisses my neck. Soft and so damn sweet I'd sigh like girl if I could get the sound past this Godawful intrusion in my mouth.

She works her way down my body with gentle kisses, sensual licks and teasing bites. Her face is so damn close to my erection, I'm going to fucking burst if she doesn't touch me soon. She's doing everything but touch me where I need her to, and it's driving me insane. I guess that's the point. She glances up, and again, I'm just hit with the devastating sadness in her eyes where I would at least be expecting something more sinfully playful.

"Mmm…. Mmm… Mmm," I shout out a jumbled mess of another apology that goes undeciphered. I pull on my restraints with unbearable frustration only to freeze when her tongue drags slowly from the crease of my thigh to the base of my straining, angry cock. Time freezes, and I hold my breath. Oh. My. Fucking. God!

She wraps her scorching tongue around my flesh like a snake and swipes it round and up and down my length and then—yes, please God—her gorgeous soft lips purse to kiss the tip and tighten as they push over my crown. Smooth and the fucking sexiest thing ever, she swallows me down, all the motherfucking way down. Her throat constricts, and I feel that like I take a hit of lightning at the base of my spine. Her hands move to cup my balls as she starts to move like she's on a mission. Her other hand squeezes the base of my cock almost painfully, but it feels too damn good to register. She pumps, and sucks, and all the time, her tongue is massaging me to the point of no return. My hips start to rock even though I have no control over this, not the pace, the depth, nothing. This is all her, and as much as it feels fantastic, I hate it. I hate not being able to touch her; I hate not being in control.

Her hand that is working it's magic on my balls tugs lightly and I almost come. Her fingers massage that sensitive spot behind my sack and the slipperiness from her saliva eases her finger along the small gap and straight into my arsehole. She sucks down as she pushes inside me and every muscle in my body locks down and prepares for the mother of all explosions. I squeeze my eyes shut as the pleasure rockets through me, but before that spark can light that powder keg, she releases all contact, her mouth, her hand on the base of my cock, and her finger inside. She wraps her tight fist around my cock and slams her thumb over the slit, and like an ice pack to my balls, my imminent orgasm dies under the pad of her opposable digit. Motherfucking bitch!

When I open my eyes she's gone. I didn't hear a sound or feel the bed move, and bewildered, I look frantically around a room I don't recognise. The dark walls are glossy, like wet ink, and the only light is coming from expiring candles slowly melting to the floor. The flames cast faint shadows, and I can see when the flames flicker, moulds of faces hang from the walls, grotesque and eerie with hallow eyes. This has to be the creepiest fucking dungeon.

The bed is the only piece of furniture, and I'm still fucking tied to it. There are no windows and only one door, which opens with an ominous creak. I'm not going to yell and groan when she enters, as much as I want to. She clearly has a plan and that plan involves putting me through hell. I silently repeat what I promised I would do to win her back…anything. She glides into the room, and she looks absolutely stunning. Her hair is pulled up with only a few stray curls, softening around her face. She has strips of diamonds hanging from her ears but no collar. Fuck.

The tight leather corset squeezes her in and pushes her up in all the right places, and her breasts look like they could spill at any delicious moment. Silk stockings and sky high killer heels finish the vision. My impossibly hard cock seeps with unstated desire at the sight.

The door opens again, and this dream vision becomes my worst fucking nightmare—Leon, Will, and Gabriel. Although I haven't seen Gabriel in years, I would recognise that smug expression anywhere. He walks directly up to her and wraps his hand around her neck. His eyes flick to me and my jaw snaps with the tension. I want to wipe his fucking smile off his face with my fist, but I freeze and watch the show.

His mouth crashes to hers, and I'm winded from the hit when her arms wrap his body and her hands fly to grab his hair. She returns his kiss like her life depended on it. Will and Leon close around her, and she is twisted and turned and shared between them in a hedonistic tableau that is breaking my fucking heart.

I'm screaming when Will starts to peel her panties down, no one seems to give a fuck. They barely glance my way as my throat burns with the roar that is muffled by this fucking gag. I try to swallow the pooling saliva dripping from my mouth. Leon and Will start to undress, and instantly, they are naked. Leon lifts her high onto his hips, impaling her on his cock with one swift move. Her head drops back against Will who is at her back with his cock in his hand, nudging to gain entrance into her arse. Please stop…please stop. I close my eyes only I can't seem to keep them shut. The scene is spiralling into my own personal hell every time I open them, an unbearable strobe light flash of devastating images. Her body slammed between Will and Leon, her legs over Will's forearms as she rides them both, ecstasy emblazoned on their faces. All the time, her face is buried in Leon's chest until Gabriel pulls her chin up to kiss what's mine… Mine! She's motherfucking mine!

The next time I open my eyes, it's just her and Gabriel. I would look around for Will and Leon, but I don't care where they are. I don't want them here. I don't want any of them here except her. Gabriel turns her in his arms and positions her so her hands are resting on the bottom bed frame; her head is dropped, and she still hasn't looked into my eyes, not since she put this fucking gag in my mouth. Gabriel is looking at me, though. His dark eyes gleam with avarice and desire, and he lets out a deep, unGodly groan when he penetrates her from behind. He fists her hair and pulls her into an arch, and that's when I break. Her sorrow-filled eyes pierce me, and the tears that soak her face are my undoing.

"No!" I scream, and fight and pull at my motherfucking restraints until I feel my wrists snap from the pressure. So much pain yet nothing compared to the absolute heartbreak ripping me apart inside.

Eviscerated and desolate, I silently scream my heart out.

I sit bolt upright, terror gripping my heart so hard I can't breathe. I grab at the unGodly pain in my chest, and I swear my heart is going to explode. I'm dripping with sweat, and I get a cold chill as the breeze from the open window hits my shaking body. *What the hell?* Sucking in some deep, steadying breaths, I wait for my heart to calm the fuck down. My shirt and trousers are drenched, and I start to shiver.

Only a few minutes pass and my heart rate is no longer a jackhammer in my chest. I swing my long legs over the side of the bed and start to strip down. I hit the shower for a blast of much needed heat and take some time under the spray to collect myself. That was fucking horrible. The searing water does the trick, and I rid myself of not only the chill but the slick of the nightmare that seemed to coat my skin.

Wrapping a single towel around my waist, I grab a handful of mini bottles from the fridge. It doesn't really matter what they are, I'm not having another dream like that tonight, and if an alcoholic coma is required to ensure that happens, so be it. I shake the residual water from my hair when there is a knock on the door. The porter hands me some binoculars, and without checking the room service menu, I ask for a burger and a bottle of Jack. He nods and disappears down the corridor silently before the door closes. The doors to the balcony is still wide open, and the noise has ebbed to a bearable thrum with some occasional classical music drifting above the hubbub.

It's dark now, and looking below, a person would think it was still midday with the thick crowd. I only give them a cursory glance because my attention is fixed farther afield. The whole reason I'm staying here rather than the Aman Grande is because of that fucking yacht anchored where the main canal meets the open lagoon.

It takes a moment to focus the sight and zoom in to the back of the yacht. The deck is crowded with guests, smartly dressed in tuxedos and cocktail dresses. There's a quartet playing, and it's all very sedate for Gabriel, the quiet before the storm. The Gathering is anything but sedate. Debauched is a more apt description, I should know. I scan the upper and lower decks as much as is possible from this distance and even with the excellent zoom I'm having trouble picking out anyone remotely familiar. Then I spot her. Damn, she's beautiful. She's got her back turned but I would recognise the curve of her spine and long dark hair from a million miles. She's standing just on the edge of the crowd and the man next to her is offering his hand, which she shakes her head to decline. Good. She's holding a glass but has yet to take a sip, and she moves off to stand alone, leaning her forearms on the railing and gazing out into the darkness across the open sea.

Her hands move to her neck, and she looks around. Her back straightens and her head snaps in my direction. I drop the binoculars with a sharp intake of breath. Shit. I quickly replace them again and try to find her, but the spot where she stood only a second ago is empty. I search frantically, cursing my stupid reflex. *It's not like she could see you, idiot.* I finally see her near the staircase. She's leaning up to kiss a man's cheek, Gabriel's, and fuck if he doesn't pull her into an embrace. Motherfucker. He kisses her cheek, and she hurries away, down the stairs and out of my sight. Damn it all to hell. My phone rings at the exact time to stop me from storming out to get her.

"What?"

"Whoa, just calling to see how you are, brother."

I'm still reeling from my nightmare and fucking Gabriel. "Not fucking good. Does that answer your question?"

"I take it you've seen her."

"Yes, just now, and it's fucking killing me that I can't go and drag her off that damn yacht." My tone is openly irritated and curt.

"You can't?"

"No. Gabriel obviously doesn't want me near her, and I doubt I'd get a chance to set one foot on board without him knowing." I twist my neck as I speak to pop the tension in the bones, left and right. "I can't risk him telling her and her taking flight. He's just the sort of man to have the resources to keep her hidden from me if she asked."

"You think she would?" I hear the uncertainty I don't happen to share.

"I don't think it. I know it. That's exactly what she's done. I don't blame her, yet I have to see her. I have to explain face-to-face, and the only chance I'll have is at the Gathering. I'm not going to blow it now by jumping the gun, not when I'm so damn close I can almost taste her."

"She might just need a little time, Jason." If he's trying to comfort me, he's way off the mark. The only comfort I'll get is when she's in my damn arms.

"She's had a little time," I retort.

"She's had two weeks."

I let out a humourless laugh. "Yes she has, and I'm feeling generous. I'm going to give her one more night."

"I'd wish you luck, only you sound determined enough not to need it."

I repeat his earlier sentiment. "Luck is for pussies."

"Now where have I heard that before?"

TWENTY-TWO

Sam

I didn't sleep a wink last night. I felt him. I don't know how, but up on the deck last night, with the enchanting music playing for all the beautiful people Gabriel had gathered, I felt Jason. The hairs on my neck didn't just stand on end—they came to life. My stomach twisted, and I lost all the composure I thought I had gained these last two weeks. Damn him. I tossed and turned all damn night in a bed far too big for one person, reliving that feeling. As fleeting as it was, that spark of life felt so good, so very good. My feelings for Jason are undeniable; that has never been in doubt in my mind. Two weeks haven't changed that; I doubt a lifetime will. Nevertheless, my heartbreak is so much easier to compartmentalise with him out of the picture. It's just me, my baby, and my broken heart. It isn't pretty, but I'm getting by. What now? Fuck, my head is a mess, a constant confused loop of unanswered questions, doubts and dormant desire. Damn him.

I wrap the thick terrycloth dressing gown around me and make my way to the upper deck for breakfast.

The area is completely clear of any revellers. Every surface gleams, polished within an inch of its life, spotless. I take a seat at the corner table, which is laid out for breakfast. I'm not sure how many guests might've stayed, still I'm hoping they had such a late night, I will have a quiet, undisturbed morning to myself.

I'm served a fresh fruit platter with toast and jam. My cravings are for all things sweet and carb loaded at the moment. I have refrained from cooking pancakes because they remind me too much of Jason. Besides, Gabriel's chef has banned me from the galley. I burnt milk when I tried to heat some for late night hot chocolate. It stunk up the whole lower deck, and it took ages to clean the hob. I still can't stomach coffee; however, I can now drink normal tea, very weak. I sit back and sip my morning brew and try, once again, to process what I'm feeling, if Jason is really here. I know he's here. So the pertinent question, if I assume I know why he's here, is, what the hell am I going to do now?

I finish my breakfast alone and decide, as decadent as it is to lounge around in a robe on a luxury yacht all day, I'd better get dressed. I need to busy myself today or I will go crazy thinking about Jason and the Gathering. *Shit! The Gathering.*

I pad barefoot down toward Gabriel's suite. It's nearly midday now so I hope I'm not just waking him up as I tap quietly on the door. If he's asleep, he won't hear and I'll leave. If he's—

"Come." His deep throaty voice sounds strained. I open the door, and when invited, I step inside.

"Jesus, Gabriel!" I squeeze my lids shut but I can't unsee that shit. My hand flies to cover my eyes just in case any stray image might burn through my tightly closed eyelids. "Damn it, Gabriel, you said come in."

"I think you'll find I said *come*." His voice isn't remotely irritated that I have crashed his morning orgy; if anything, he sounds amused. I turn away because I can't trust myself not to drop my hand or to open my eyes out of curiosity. *Did I really just see that?*

"I'll come back when you're—"

He dismisses me with his interruption. "You may as well ask now. We've really only just started." I can almost see the salacious smile spreading wide over his face.

"Not saving yourself for the Gathering then?" I quip. I'm stalling to regain my composure. *It's too early for this shit.*

"I'm the host, darling, and from past experience, I find it better to be fully sated before the activities commence. That way, I'm able to fully enjoy the *whole* evening, not just the first hour." His voice is so calm if it wasn't for the accompanying sex sounds, I would think we were just having a chit chat over coffee.

"Good to know." I can feel my cheeks heat, and I silently puff out a cooling breath. It's not that this is shocking behaviour for Gabriel, it's just I wasn't entirely prepared. Totally my fault, I really should know better, this is Gabriel after all, *hedonist extraordinaire.*

"It's good advice, Mistress. You are most welcome to join us." His voice is smooth, inviting, and I snort along with a sharp laugh.

"Oh it looks like you have more than enough holes to keep you occupied."

"I'll pretend I didn't hear that because you would never find me referring to you as a hole." His tone isn't remotely amused.

"No," I scoff. "Not if you value your bollocks."

"Quite."

"Right. Well, I came to say I can't do tonight." I keep it brief and grimace, waiting for the fallout.

"What!" He's incredulous, and I hear some rather unsavoury squelching noises. "Do not move."

"I'm not moving." I say.

"Not you," he mutters with considerable frustration in his voice. There is some undetermined movement, some heavy footfalls, and then Gabriel is standing directly in front of me, stark naked with an impressive glossy erection. I don't flinch; it's not the first time I've seen him naked or this flustered.

"I'm sorry. You did say to tell you now. It could've waited." I shrug and offer an apologetic, thin-lipped smile.

"No, it couldn't." His harsh tone softens mid-sentence. "What is it, Mistress? Please, if there is anything I can do. I must have you there tonight. My reputation depends on it," he pleads, not quite holding his hands together in supplication. His eyes could melt a much harder heart than mine.

"Ah hell, Gabe. You do not play fair." I fist my hands on my hips with obvious agitation, letting out a heavy sigh of utter exasperation. I shake my head. "I can't, Gabe. I felt him last night." I hold his gaze, and he holds his tongue until I explain my change of heart. "Jason. He's here and I know he's going to try and get to me at the Gathering. I'm not ready to face him. It's still too fucking raw." I blink to stop the tears that are collecting.

"He won't. You have my word." Gabriel is adamant, earnest, and I owe it to him to believe his word.

"Gabe." I try one last futile plea.

"I promise, Sam. He won't get in," he states flatly, brooking no further argument, so I try a different and equally important tack.

"I don't have my whip." I know it's a flimsy line of defence. I can pretty much use any bullwhip with the same level of skill. My handmade red is just my favourite. His lips carve a wide, wicked smile.

"Wonderful." He claps his hands. Relief and joy saturate his handsome face.

"Why is that wonderful?" I scowl, though it seems even my fiery glare will not dampen his spirit. Smug bastard knows he's won somehow.

"Because you have just agreed." He flips his hand in a brush off of my last objection.

"I don't think I did." I counter.

"Your whip is in my office. I had it couriered here the moment you agreed." I arch a dubious brow. "Very well, I had it couriered the moment I decided you would be giving your grand finale at my Gathering," he declares with absolutely no shame.

"Do you ever not get your way?" I mutter.

"You are proof that I don't, Mistress, or I would have you somewhere between me and those other fine bodies on my bed."

I shake my head at his brazenness. "What time do you need me ready?"

I'm defeated but not totally despondent. He's happy, and I do trust his word. I know I will have to face Jason sometime soon. I didn't lie when I said I'm not ready, and tonight Gabriel wants Mistress Selina, London's incomparable dominatrix. Whoever wins will have paid good money to be on the receiving end of my whip. I couldn't guarantee that if I had to face Jason, I would be anything other than a blubbering mess, not quite the experience the winner would be expecting.

"We leave at nine. The banquet begins at ten this evening, auction at midnight." He interrupts my internal musing.

"Right, well don't let me keep you." Before I can turn away he takes my hand as if greeting me for the first time, lifting it slowly to his lips he kisses the back. *Utterly charming, even in his birthday suit.*

TWENTY-THREE

Jason

I lost count of the times I ran the length of the Riva degli Schiavoni just hoping the catch a glimpse of her this morning. Because, despite what I told Will, I think if I saw her right now, I would do my damnedest to steal her away and end this fucking nightmare. All I managed to achieve were muscles begging for me to stop and some curious comments from the waiters setting up for the day, yet there is no sight of Sam. I ignore the insidious seed that's burrowing inside my gut with the notion that she somehow knows I'm here. Maybe she saw me last night and has already fled. No, not possible, I feel her. It's like her essence is in the air, all around me, and for the first time in the longest fucking two weeks of my life I can breathe her in.

"Have you seen something you would like to try, signore? The elderly gentleman serving as the costumier must be about a hundred years old. Nevertheless, he's spritely, and I have watched him scale steep ladders and hook impossibly high masks from the wall with the agility of a much younger man.

"I need a costume for the Gathering." There's no point being coy. If this shop does, in fact, cater to most of the guests, he will know exactly where I'm going and, most probably, exactly what I'm looking for.

"Very good. I can recommend any of the Bauta masks." His hand sweeps across a row of white and gilded masks. The individual decorations may differ, but they all share the grotesque protruding nose and thick, prominent brow, long chin and no mouth. "Or the Medico della Peste, the plague doctor, are very ugly no?" He beams, and the myriad of wrinkles deepen on his face with the wide pull of his thin pale lips. His cheeks may hollow to resemble the skull beneath, however his eyes sparkle with life.

"Yes very, they are wonderful too, but yes, those are a little disgusting." I shrug as way of an apology, only his face seems to light with overt pride.

"That is the point, is it not? They do the job very well, and you wish to be hidden, of course?" He steps aside to let me further into the shop.

"Of course." I give him an absent nod as I continue to look at the hundreds of frozen faces, some so distorted they are practically demonic. I can feel the hairs on my neck rise with the chilling recall from my nightmare. I shake it off and point to a much simpler half mask. It is just as dramatic, with the extra-long nose turned up at the end, bulging eyebrows and low forehead. I touch the one nearest to me and feel that it's made of soft leather. I tap my finger to indicate my choice.

"The Zanni, are you sure, signore?" The intonation and curious smirk that pulls at his lips makes me question my choice.

"There's a reason I shouldn't pick this one? I kind of like that it's not all glitzy or too creepy." I argue at his quizzical expression.

"Zanni is from the stage, the low brow is a sign of stupidity, and the longer the nose, the more stupid." He chuckles and goes to take the mask from my hand, but I pull it back and place it on the counter.

"Then it's pretty perfect." I flash a tight smile, which seems to confuse him. The look I send his way is loaded with meaning. "Because I've been a fucking idiot."

"Very good, signore. Now we have the mask we can take you to get the clothes." He places the box in a large bag and clasps his hands with bubbling enthusiasm.

"Take me where? You don't keep the costumes here?" I frown and can see many garments hanging which would indicate otherwise.

"The cape and the tricorn hat, yes. Also you will need the Venetian trousers, silk shirt, waistcoat, gloves. All of it you will need and all of it we have. Come follow me." He motions briskly for me to follow, and I do, through the shop and up a narrow stepladder that is easily as old as the proprietor. The loft space is vast, airy, and has a hazy dust laden glow from the numerous skylights. I need a moment to take in the rows after rows of costumes and fully dressed mannequins. It's like Aladdin's cave of dressing-up treasures. I imagine the costume archive at the Victoria and Albert Museum would run a close second to the stunning array of clothes hidden in this little gem of a shop.

I have attended only one other Gathering, but that year, Gabriel held it in New York, and the masks were the only homage to anything remotely Venetian. I'm not sure about this. Signore Canovaccio stands back from the almost floor-to-ceiling, gilt-edged mirror in order to do the great reveal. I'm really not sure about this. The black velvet trousers are cut just below my knee, which just feels wrong, and the fact that I am wearing knee-high socks that he called tights, is never to be mentioned again. The silk shirt is more like a blouse, with billowing sleeves and lace cuffs which gather tightly at my wrists. A lace jabot ruffles at the front and apparently isn't supposed to be hidden with the three-quarter length black velvet dress coat. The thick black braiding finishes the design with elegant detailing. I tug and can't help shifting uncomfortably, even though the materials are very good quality and the fit feels as if it has been tailor made.

"Molto eletti." Signore Canovaccio compliments, still I'm not convinced. "Here, the finishing touches." He holds out the full-length cloak, tricorn hat and cane. Well, the cane I can at least use. I give a curt nod, because as much as I might think I look ridiculous, if I know one thing about Gabriel's Gatherings, I won't be the only one.

I arrange for the costume to be sent to the hotel, and since I have a few hours to kill, I decide to wander over to the Palazzo Cavalli among other places. My feet seem to know where they are going as I stride purposefully toward the civic building where civil wedding ceremonies are performed. I'm clearly feeling more optimistic since sorting my costume.

The Palazzo Cavalli is just one of the several stunning palaces in Venice. It's typical of the gothic architecture with its heavily framed ornate windows and decorative balconies, perfect for that once-in-a-lifetime photo opportunity on that special day. Perfect and popular. *Unfortunately.*

I couldn't believe I actually had all the information and documentation to pull off another last minute wedding, thanks to Sofia being ultra organised. I didn't factor in the notion that Venice is a top wedding destination, and this place is booked up years in advance. *Damn it.* I leave, having been cheeky enough to put my name down for any *really* last minute cancellations. The old lady gave me a scowl that could burn me to ash when I said, only partially serious, *fingers crossed for some cold feet.*

I can't deny that would be the ultimate outcome and definitely worth the price of dressing up like a complete ponce. Anything would be worth it, if I got to leave Venice with Sam by my side, as my wife.

I'm restless, wandering the streets and even when the narrow walkways open up into stunning squares and piazzas, it's still too crowded for me. I can't take in any of the splendour or unique and crumbling beauty of the buildings. I admit defeat at the pointless attempt to distract myself and make my way back to my hotel and the rooftop bar.

I nurse my beer and pick at my late lunch, a massive plate of fried seafood and no salad or greenery to speak of. A slice of lemon is the only concession to anything remotely healthy; it's fresh and tastes fabulous. The view is stunning. I have the same from my room, and on a clear day like today, it's easy to pick out most of the historical landmarks and even some of the larger hotels on the Lido across the lagoon. But that's not where my eyes are focused. I didn't bring the binoculars up with me, because honestly, I don't need them. I can see clearly that the crew of Gabriel's boat are preparing for an evening to remember.

I give up my prime position as the sun starts to dip into the Mediterranean Sea and decide I may as well get ready. I have to be unfashionably early if I'm to work my magic on the Master of Ceremonies—and by magic, I mean bribe. I need to be the winning bid on the auction of Mistress Selina, and I don't have to assume Gabriel wants the same, I just *know* he does.

I take one last look at my reflection. In this penthouse room, surrounded by sixteenth century art and opulence, dressed as I am, I could easily belong in another time. I tug the hat into place and button the cloak at my neck. I have my invitation, wallet, and mask. That's all I need and all that is allowed inside the Basilica venue for the Gathering. No phones, no cameras, no electronic devices whatsoever, except those provided in-house for sexual play and torture, that is.

Many of the gondolas have been reserved for this evening's private use, and I step into mine. We slip into an erotically charged and somewhat serene covey of floating theatre. The odd bemused tourist-laden gondola filters in along the voyage only to drift back out as we near the destination. The gondolier deftly manoeuvres the thirty-foot iconic Venetian boat into a narrow channel that seems to be a dead end. Nearing our final destination, I secure my mask, and as we approach the iron-barred archway beneath the ancient Basilica, the gates draw slowly open, allowing us to glide smoothly alongside the sunken steps and vaulted underbelly of the building.

Sconces with candles and lanterns holding large flames make shadows dance over the cavernous room, up a wide staircase and beyond. I alight from the gondola and cast a backward glance at the stream of guests waiting their turn to gain entrance, dressed for decadence in bygone finery. It may be a little overdramatic for my taste, even so, I can't deny the atmosphere sizzles with anticipation and excitement. I'm escorted by a woman wearing a full, plain, white mask and Domino cloak, I know she's female from the soft lilt of her voice not from the androgynous garb. She leads me up the flagstone stairway and to a second flight of stairs covered in a thick red carpet, which softens the sounds of footsteps and dulls the echo on the thick stone walls.

The greeting room is filled with similarly dressed assistants and others dressed as Arlecchino, with thick patchwork costumes and plain black half masks. From the size and build, I'm guessing these are the male assistants. There aren't many guests, but then, I'm on time, and only first-timers would be this keen or desperate, I freely admit I'm the latter.

I present my invitation to the large man dressed as Captain Fraccasa. I honestly don't know how I'm recalling all these names, they clearly sunk in from my fitting this afternoon. The shop owner busied himself gathering my garments all the while giving me a detailed account of all the varieties of costume that I might see tonight. The Captain is wearing red and yellow velveteen trousers and jacket, a large white ruff, bright, feathered hat and a mask similar in shape to mine, only black.

"Your identification, Mr Stone?" His thick Russian accent is sharp and stony, a stark contrast to the jovial Italian character he is dressed as.

"Really, is that necessary?" I hand him my invitation, my fingers twitch against my wallet and my borrowed identification for this evening.

"You will not proceed without it, so the decision as to whether it's necessary is entirely yours, Mr Stone." The female voice is clipped and obscured by the body mass of the Captain, until she swiftly steps aside to reveal herself. Those sharp emerald eyes and that commanding, yet sultry voice I would recognise blindfolded. My memory is so ingrained with my own final training session with Mistress Eve that I can't help the tug at my lips from the flash of recollection.

I may have trained under the finest Dom in London at the time, but the most memorable part of my education came under the expert tutelage of this Lady. I spent five days of hell at the wrong end of her little black crop in her Paris dungeon, where I learnt the very strength needed to become a submissive. She helped me to understand what it is to submit and why I will always be a Dom.

I don't speak; it's too risky to reveal myself until I know for sure she's here to work not play. She certainly looks the part, wearing a stunning creamy white and gold flared skirt with a tight-fitted bodice. Fine lace sleeves are gathered at the cuff, and her waistcoat nips to an impossibly trim waist. Her trademark fiery red hair is curled and piled high on her head, and in lieu of any hat, she seems to have hidden gems woven through the strands that sparkle whenever she moves. Her gold mask is simple but for the intricate metal filigree that extends from above the brow and around the corners, perfectly framing her penetrating eyes.

I pull Daniel's driving license from my wallet and silently thank the knowing bastard for always being right. The Captain inspects the invitation and license, scanning for authenticity, and I briefly wonder if there will be fingerprints and mug shots, but then that would kind of defeat the object of the masks.

"Very good, Mr Stone. You may leave your cloak here. Drinks are being served in the great room where you will be summoned to the banquet." He sweeps his meaty hand out toward a heavy, dark red curtain that is subsequently pulled apart by two strapping Arlecchino's characters. I start to walk and look down to see the slender arm, gloved in gold and belonging to Mistress Eve thread through mine.

"Allow me, Jason." Her voice is a whisper, yet my body snaps to attention. Fuck. "Any particular reason you are needing an extra disguise, or are you going for a method actor's approach to tonight's activities?" Her light laugh I'm sure is entirely at my expense. This could be very bad.

"Excuse me?" My voice is flat, even as I stifle a telltale cough in the back of my throat.

"Well, you have picked Zanni, not known for his smarts, and you are anything but stupid, Jason, so why Mr Stone tonight? Or does this have anything to do with why we are having to double-check every guest this evening?" She steps in front of me as soon as we reach the great room. I grab two glasses of champagne from a passing Domino waitress and hand one to Eve. Her lips tweak yet the upward curl is barely noticeable when she takes a sip.

"It's possible." I fail to keep my tone causal, and my jaw is twitching with tension.

"Oh please, Jason, Gabriel has me all but giving rectal exams for the guests this year. He's not going to be pleased you got in." She holds my gaze with a seriousness that makes my stomach drop.

"He told you?" I drop my voice to a low grumble and in lieu of an arched brow I wouldn't be able to detect she drops her hip and places her hand on the one jutting out.

"I'm Mistress of Ceremonies, Jason. Of course he told me." Her words are filled equally with sass and attitude.

"I thought you had retired?" I counter, effectively changing the subject of my gatecrashing.

"I am, but this is special, so I don't mind presiding over the festivities. It's hardly a chore." She sweeps her hand out dramatically, taking in the stunning room with its enormous gilt mirrors casting abundant light from the many chandeliers. Rich oil paintings portraying dramatic biblical events hang from the walls, and swaths of golden material hide enormous stained glass windows. The ancient building has been lovingly brought to life, if only for tonight. Looking up, there is a balcony edging the perimeter of the room, with numerous discreet doors leading to private and not so private rooms, for later.

"Good, I'm going to need your help." I take her elbow and lead her to the edge of the room. The guests are starting to fill the room now, and personal space and privacy aren't really considerations at these events.

"And why would I do that exactly?" She sniffs derisively, and I draw in a confident breath and let my best smile fill my face before I speak.

"How are Bianca and the baby?"

"Jason," she almost gasps in shock, only she is too restrained to let any emotion escape her lips unchecked. "That is a little underhanded for you, don't you think?" I happen to agree but shrug her comment off and offer a half-arsed apology.

"I apologise, still desperate times, Eve. Very desperate times."

"So it would seem." She purses her lips and draws the bottom one fully into her mouth, like she is actually contemplating her options, when I already *know* she's going to help me.

TWENTY-FOUR

Sam

It took a surprisingly long time to get ready, and I was grateful Gabriel had arranged for someone to help. Not that I needed help with the stockings, invisible bra and heels, however, the full-length dress weighed an absolute tonne, and the bodice part had a million tiny buttons up the back that I neither had the flexibility nor the patience for. I kept my makeup simple, plain even, with only my red lipstick visible. Wearing layers of eye shadow and blush under the mask seemed slightly fruitless. Having secured me into the dress, my helper, Bibiana, silently and diligently curled and pinned my hair so it would hang softly around the mask and not detract from the elaborate plumage fanning the headpiece. She is an elderly woman, dressed impeccably in black with her grey hair pulled tight into a severe bun. I pondered to myself that her stern exterior wouldn't be out of place at the Dommes' table tonight. She had no understanding of English so I simply moved and responded to her varying hand and eye gestures.

She was thorough and meticulous, and when I stood in front of the oversized mirror in my room, I was completely awestruck. *Wow.*

Predominantly black velvet with vibrant slashes of red lace and thick, gorgeous brocade stitched at the edges, the dress fit perfectly. The cape clips to the intricate shoulder piece, which fastens flush against the tall, stiff collar at my neck. I take little comfort from the fact that *I* don't recognise myself in all this opulent splendour because that's irrelevant. Arriving on Gabriel's arm with the auction of my final 'show' very much the main attraction, every single person attending will know I'm Mistress Selina.

"Oh my," Gabriel declares with breathless wonder when I step up on the lower deck. "Mistress, you look like royalty."

"I feel a little constricted." I peek down at my considerable bust, which is poised and ready to burst from the boned and velvety confines of the bodice Bibana trussed me into. "I'm not sure eating will be an option, and I have no idea how I'm supposed to perform. This dress is hardly conducive to whip wielding, Gabe." I move at a glacial pace toward him and have to hold on to the railing, backs of chairs, anything that will aid stability.

"You lose the waistcoat and the skirt. It all unclips." He points to the row of buttons at my hips and at the base of the bodice.

"You might've wanted to share that information." I look to where he indicates, and sure enough, I can see how the whole garment can be detached and easily removed.

"I am sharing it." His droll lilt is accompanied with a slow roll of his eyes.

"I meant before. I have to go back and put some panties on now." I mumble.

"Oh not on my account." He teases and it's my turn to roll my eyes.

"You're funny. My whipping skills are the only thing I intend on showcasing tonight. I'm funny about knowing the identity of anyone likely to catch a sneak peek of my tush, and that is not what's up for auction." I pull a deep frown as I contemplate the arduous trek back to my cabin to get my underwear. "If you would just give me a few minutes or hours I'll rectify the situation." I turn slowly, and he chuckles.

"It's not that bad." His rumbling laughter is low and he shakes his head with obvious amusement.

"Says you, in basically golf pants, a lady's fancy blouse, and a house coat. This dress is almost as wide as I am tall. I need one of those 'vehicle is reversing' warning beeps or a 'caution wide load' sign on my arse. That would work." I snort.

"Very amusing. And tonight, I'm simply the blank canvas for you to shine against. This is your night, my Mistress." He dips for a low bow, and when he stands, he opens his arms wide.

"Gabriel." I sigh and take his offered hand, and he pulls me into a protective hug, or as close to a hug as my dress will allow. "I'm only doing this because, for some reason, this pregnancy has affected my ability to assert myself, but honestly, I'd rather stay on your boat."

"Yacht," he corrects with a childish huffing sound, and I compress my lips to hide the smirk. "We can eat here if you would prefer. Just turn up for the auction; you can then beguile us mere mortals with your incomparable whipping skills, and then I can arrange for the gondolier to bring you back." His kind offer is music to my ears.

"You don't mind?" I'm so grateful for everything he's done, I want to make sure his offer is genuine.

"Why would I mind? I know you have no intention in indulging tonight, and this means I won't have to share you until the very last minute, and not even then." He flashes a wicked, knowing grin and his eyes seem to dance with mischief.

"Gabe, what have you done?" I lean back, but he still has a strong arm around my waist, and I have to tilt my head back so he can see my suspicious glare.

"Mistress, you didn't really think your very last performance would be for anyone other than myself. Surely you are not that naïve?" He chuckles, and I exhale dramatically.

"You're completely insane, Gabe." I push lightly out of his hold, still shaking my head with astonishment. I'm not naïve, still I didn't think he was that crazy.

"No, insanity would be to let this opportunity slip through my fingers." He says this without a hint of irony.

"So, you've rigged the auction, is that what you're telling me?" I cross my arms, but if I'm honest, I'm relieved. At least I know Gabe, and more than that, with my niggling concern that Jason will somehow get in tonight, at the very least I know he won't 'win' me either.

"I have ensured mine will be the winning bid, yes." He gives a curt, self-satisfied nod.

"If that's the case, we could just do a scene right here, and I can get out of going altogether." My voice sounds expectant and hopeful.

"Now where would be the fun if I didn't get to flaunt my prize." With a regal swipe of his hand, he dismisses my suggestions like a puff of smoke.

"You're impossible, you know that?"

"It has been mentioned." He sniffs derisively. "Now, shall we eat here or—"

"Here please, and nothing fancy. My stomach is in knots as it is." I grimace as it rolls loudly as if on cue.

"Your wish is my command, Mistress." He drops his gaze and peeks through long lashes. He deftly balances on the fine edge of adorable and hugely obnoxious.

"You know, I used to believe that." I let out a flat, humourless laugh. "I can't believe you had me fooled all these years."

"No pouting, my Queen, it's most unbecoming." He doesn't deny my assessment, and his smile spreads a little wider before his attention is once again diverted. "What would you like to eat?"

"Honestly, I feel a little queasy, and the only thing that isn't making me want to retch when I think about food is cheese on toast and a glass of milk." I give a tentative smile and lightly and apologetically shrug. "Don't wrinkle your nose, Gabe. I can't help it. My baby is clearly craving dairy." I pat the stiff bone of the bodice flattening my stomach, still I can feel the tiny rounded mound resisting the pressure, and that brings a wide and wonderful smile to my face. I haven't smiled like that in so long my face twitches with the unfamiliar stretch of muscles.

"Then allow me." He graciously escorts me to the al fresco dining deck, and once I'm seated and he has helped remove my mask and headpiece, he turns to leave.

"I shall inform the chef and fetch you some panties." He informs me as he pauses at the top of the stairs.

"No thongs, I don't want to be prancing about with a wedgie from hell." I call after him.

"Well, I may be some time selecting the most suitable garment then." He waggles his brow playful, and I pinch the pressure at the bridge of my nose.

"Pervert!" I yell. He's incorrigible.

"High praise indeed." His chest puffs with pride, and he gives a showy bow before disappearing below deck.

Our sleek gondola glides through the canals. It is one of the very few that has a small cabin, a *fieze*, and I find myself straining to peek through the louvered windows, keen and excited to experience the city from this unique and luxurious taxi. I think the quietness is what I find so appealing. No motor noise or harsh headlights on a road this late at night, just the tranquil lapping sounds of the sea against the shiny undercarriage of the gondola and gentle undulations as we are expertly steered to our destination.

My tummy might have settled with the food, but my heart feels like it's going to explode, the strong beat bruising my ribcage from the inside. Why the hell am I so nervous? Stupid fucking question and only one stupid answer.

Jason

"Why isn't she here?" I snap at Eve the instant she takes her seat next to mine.

We are just about to be served dessert and there is no fucking sign of either Sam or Gabriel. My stomach drops that this is a huge fucking waste of time, and I should've just stormed the yacht and dragged her home.

"They decided to skip the feast." She sips her Champagne, and I fight the growl of frustration that is bubbling in my chest.

"Why? Why would they do that?" My voice is openly tense.

"Well, obviously Gabriel went into extreme detail about his private life with me." Her flippant remark and tone aren't helping.

"Sarcasm Eve? Really?" I snap.

"I'm here tonight as Gabriel's employee, Jason, so contrary to what you may think, he doesn't have to tell me shit about the whys and wherefores of his decisions." I'm pretty sure she's scowling at me right now from her irritated intonation.

"But they are coming?" I hate how needy I sound right now, but I'm literally going out of my mind, waiting and wasting time like this.

"I believe they are just setting off. Sam was feeling unwell so they ate—"

"Unwell! What's wrong?" I blurt my question a little too sharply, and she recoils before she answers with a sigh of exasperation.

"Really Jason, did I not just—"

I don't let her finish. "Yes. However, you clearly did know, so stop with feeding me snippets of information, Eve. This is killing me here." Her eyes widen beneath the mask and her lips quirk with a sad little turn.

"You really are, aren't you? I'm sorry, Jason, I thought this was some sort of power play. I had no idea." She reaches for my hand, and I take a surpassing amount of comfort from her squeeze and heartfelt sentiment. "Look, Gabriel said that Sam was feeling a little poorly. She didn't want to have to sit through a fancy meal, so they ate on the *Ambrosia* and left a few minutes ago."

"So what? They'll be here in maybe half an hour?" I glance impatiently at my watch.

"They will be here in time for the auction and the exhibition piece of course, and after that, your guess is as good as mine." She casts a knowing glance around the richly decorated banqueting hall. The long tables have been set in a large square, seating around two hundred guests. Black tablecloths and wrought iron gothic candlesticks, with hundreds of flames, flicker aiding to the nefarious air of the evening to come. The arched and vaulted ceilings are typical of any church or basilica erected in that time, and several heavy iron chandeliers illuminate the windowless room with sensual promise and wickedness. In the centre of the tables is a chequered floor which has been laid out to resemble an elaborate yet erotic chess board with real life players. When knight takes pawn, there is no euphemism, just hard and fast fucking.

Throughout the meal, the game has played out as one continual live sex show. The pieces are barely dressed at all. Only the masks and original placing on the board give any indication which piece they are supposed to be. I have to admit, Gabriel outdid himself with the decadence and debauched theme of this evening.

Eve informed me that the 'activities' won't officially start until after Sam's display. Still, it seems that hasn't stopped several guests from reaching for their neighbour or slipping beneath the table to quell their appetites in the meantime. I don't care what others do—never have—but right now, I just don't want to be here. I don't want Sam here, and as the memory of my nightmare collides with my reality, I admit to myself for the first time with absolute certainty that I don't want to share…ever again.

"I take it Gabriel has instructed you to fix the bids?"

"You would be correct."

"That's fine, just make sure mine matches his." I've switched from Champagne to whiskey, and just as soon as I sit down, I tip the glass up and empty it.

"If you match him, Jason, he will claim the prize as his, organizer's privilege, I'm afraid."

"His bid will be in euros, make sure mine is in dollars." I clarify and she giggles.

"Sneaky, I like it, but why dollars? Why not pounds?"

"Using pounds might give me away. I don't want Sam to suspect it's me until it's too late."

"Too late?" She tips her head with curiosity. It's actually quite a challenge to gauge people when there are no visual cues from their faces. Any nonverbal confirmations can come only from intonation and body language, although Eve is not so difficult to read.

"Until I'm at the wrong end of her whip." I elaborate. "In a room full of people, I might just gain a few precious seconds of a stunned silence to speak to her without her running for the hills."

"A few seconds, that's not long." She sniffs, and her voice is thick with doubt.

"It's all I'll need to know if she's still mine." I state this as a true fact. *I will know*

"You might not survive a few seconds if she's mad at you. I've seen her skills with that whip. She's deadly."

"Oh I imagine she'll be more than mad, but she has every right to be. I will let her do what she needs to do until…" I pause mid thought.

"Until?"

"Until she has exorcised her demons."

"On your skin?"

"If that's what it takes." My response is impassive and also absolute truth.

"I hope you're right. You've gone to an awful lot of trouble."

"I'd go to a hell of a lot more to get her back, trust me," I retort, deadly serious.

"I understand. I may lose my job over this, but I feel the same way about Bianca so I do understand." Her voice softens and her smile widens.

"How is she?"

"Just perfect and our little boy Pierre. " She clasps her hands together, and even through the gold mask, I can see her eyes crinkle with unsuppressed joy. She reaches into the purse that is secured to her skirt, and I raise a brow, for a moment thinking she has a phone in there. Because if there is one thing that would get someone thrown in the Canal Grande it would be bringing a recording device to one of Gabriel's Gatherings. Instead she pulls a small strip photograph out, one from a photo booth with her face squished against Bianca, a former employee at my club, and their son, a chubby infant, all grinning like happy idiots.

"I'm happy for you, Eve." She tucks the picture safely back in her purse and beams at me.

"And I'm grateful to you for sending Bianca my way."

"I didn't think I would lose an employee. I was only hoping she'd pick up a bit of French while on secondment," I reply dryly. Still, I meant what I said, I am happy for them.

"Oh but she did." She giggles, the sound is so light and innocent it floats above the background of muffled moans and sighs as the guests fail miserably to wait their fucking turns. Anyone would think they are all hedonists bereft of rules and morals…Oh wait…

There is a loud groan of the doors that lead down to the entrance and the great hall. All eyes turn to see who is about to emerge, fashionably late. Thankfully, here at all as far as I'm concerned. A hushed silence blankets the room, and for the first time this evening, I can hear the string quartet playing from the gallery.

My back straightens and my breath freezes in my lungs when she reaches the top step. My beautiful.

There is a ripple of applause, and Gabriel waves a welcoming hand like the fucking King himself, and I can see Sam shift uncomfortably when he turns to her and kisses the back of her hand. That's strange. Why would she be uncomfortable unless she didn't want to be here? And that bastard is forcing her? I go to rise from my seat, when I feel a vice-like grip on my taut thigh and turn to see Eve shake her head, and her eyes darken with warning.

"Just wait," she hisses softly.

"She doesn't look like she wants to be here, Eve. I think something's wrong," I whisper back.

"You interrupt this, and there will mostly definitely be something wrong. Calm the fuck down and ask yourself, would Sam really do something she didn't want to do, for anyone?"

I bite my lips tight, because as much as I understand what she's saying and what she believes true of Selina, I know for a fact Sam did do something she didn't want to do, for me and my brother. She took the fall for us with our mother and there's no way she'd have *wanted* to do that.

"Fine." I spit the words out through clenched teeth and look back to where Gabriel and Sam have just taken their seats at the head of the table. The chess game climaxed a little while ago, and the floor is now empty. My eyes bore into Sam, I shouldn't, yet I can't help but stare. She looks utterly amazing, though there's definitely something off. Her shoulders are stiff, and although her mask covers most of her face, I can see her eyes scouring the room and her gorgeous red lips are pulled into a thin contemplative line. I look away just in time. Shit.

TWENTY-FIVE

Sam

He's here. I just know he's here. The disguises and masks are unbelievable, stunning, and fail at the only job they are designed for, anonymity. For me because, thanks to Gabriel, I'm the star attraction; for Gabriel, because every single person in this room knows who he is and loves him in one way or another, mostly because of this very evening; for Jason, because in that sea of faces I couldn't possibly recognise, I know he's here. I stiffen and find myself gripping the thick oak table with white-knuckle effort. The hairs on my neck are dancing like crazy, and my lungs labour to draw in more air, restricted as they are with this impossibly tight bodice.

"Gabriel," I hiss out a whisper through a fixed and awkward smile, and all eyes are still very much focused on us.

"Mistress?" He turns and I have to tip my head away from the protruding hooknose of his mask. He nearly took my eye out in the gondola when he turned to speak to me.

"Jason is here."

Gabriel waves off my nonsense with his gloved hand. "Impossible, Mistress. I checked the guest list as we came in. Everyone here has been checked and double-checked. I can promise you he is not here." He places a calming hand over my clawed fingers and pulls them away from the table. "Relax and enjoy, Mistress. Please, for me."

"I'm sorry. Just a little on edge. You know, I haven't actually done this for some time. And the hormones, well, let's just say, I wouldn't want to be on the receiving end of my whip this evening." I give a faint smile, and he squeezes my hands. His huge smile spreads wider, and he practically glows with joy at my statement.

"I will have the first aiders standing by." His lips twist with salacious intent, and his voice drops to a low grumble.

"I may be rusty, Gabe, but I will not be drawing blood tonight."

"Mistress…" he grumbles and pouts like a spoiled child. I snort at the ridiculous expression on a grown man.

"It's an exhibition piece, Gabe, lots of flashy moves, slicing off clothes and some loud cracks when I snap back, which will sound amazing in this place." I glance up as much as the headpiece and mask will allow. The arched vaulted ceilings will provide an impressive echo that will probably be heard in the Piazza San Marco.

"I suppose beggars can't be choosers." He continues to pout, and I pat the side of his face, which is half mask and half jaw.

"Oh babe, you know I adore the begging." I drop into character for the first time in forever. The words just drip from my lips like a forgotten favourite flavour. My skin tingles with the memory, and I welcome the familiar comfort my alter-ego never failed to deliver to my troubled heart. I may be lost and uncertain of my future but this? This I know.

The drink has been flowing and although the rooms aren't technically open until after my show, this is very much a free-for-all by the looks of what's occurring around the room. Around the tables, laid out as they are, I can see several guests kneeling on the floor, one lady is perched between two men and has a cock in each hand, while nimbly darting between the two to take each down her throat. The men have their legs stretched wide and are carrying on a conversation as if they weren't getting head. The only tell is a clenched fist every now and then. Some of the servers are drawn into amorous embraces, both male and female, and one of the female servers closest to us has been laid out on the table, her Domino robe pulled up to reveal her fully naked body. One of the female guests is kissing her and another is leaning over between her spread legs. She's slowly pushing her fingers inside the naked woman as her legs are held elevated by two male guests on either side. If I wasn't hot before, this debauched tableaux is making this costume unbearable. I can't quite believe I have gone from never witnessing a live sex show to being up close and personal with two in the space of a few months. *It's been an eventful year so far.*

"Remind you of anything?" Gabriel leans in to speak, keeping his 'nose' forward, and I follow his line of slight and nod. I tilt my head with a silent query. *La Rose D'Amour.* "I saw you were reading my copy of *The Pearl*."

"Ah yes, your Victorian porn. Man, those guys were adventurous." I sniff with a light laugh and glance back at the scene before me. "Is that what gave you the inspiration to host these Gatherings?"

"Actually yes. Such a civilised and decadent way to indulge. An orgy isn't an orgy unless you are playing dress-up, and what better place than Venice."

"Well, you're obviously doing something right, your PA said the tickets were twenty-five thousand a pop, and you are always sold out."

"They get fed," he retorts dryly, and I blurt out a deep, throaty laugh. I don't think I've done that in a while either, laughed. Maybe I should slip Selina back on more often. She seems to be able to handle my sorrow much better than I.

"Yes, Gabriel, they come for the food." My tone is thick with sarcasm. "Do the servers get paid extra? I mean are they professional?"

"Actually they are guests that don't make the list. They have the option to attend as servers but they are not allowed to refuse a guest's advances. That's the deal."

"Seriously, they aren't allowed to refuse anything?"

"Really, Sam? We're going to have the safe, sane, and consensual conversation here of all places."

"Sorry, my bad." I grimace with the apology. This is not the place for naïvety, newbies, or innocence by the look of it. "So they sign up for this then?"

"Actually some invited guests prefer to play the role of server so it's a mix." His voice drifts off, and as fascinating as I find this, he's obviously bored with my interrogation.

"You don't have to stay with me, Gabe. You can go and play. I'm a big girl, I can take care of myself. Besides, I have this." I pat the coil of my bullwhip.

"I have all night, Mistress. After my whipping, I shall indulge, have no fear, suffice it to say that until then I will not leave your side."

"I'm not going to argue. So when's the auction?"

"Eve will open the bids in about half an hour."

"Bids?"

"Sealed bids, Mistress, nothing as crass as an open auction."

"Frightened someone might outbid you, Gabe?" I tease.

"No. I just don't leave anything to chance when it's something I want."

"You know, with all you've done for me, Gabe, I could've been persuaded. I mean I know I said no, and still, all this effort. It's a little crazy."

"Mistress, please this is nothing. Besides, you know I like to win, and what is a greater prize than your final performance."

"If you say so. God, I wish I could have a drink."

"I have told you one glass will not hurt your little parasite."

"Gabriel, take that back right now!"

"My apologies." His head drops and his tone is seriously contrite. My clenched jaw relaxes as a flash of worry widens his eyes.

"I'm sure the baby would survive a glass of wine. Nevertheless, I don't drink when I'm planning on using the bullwhip. Too much can go wrong."

"Pfft, I have never seen skills like yours, Mistress."

"So tell me, do you know everyone here?"

"Hmm, let me see." He takes his time surveying the room, before slowly turning to me with a knowing glee in his eyes. "No, I don't know a single person."

"Liar," I scoff, but it doesn't matter to me, he can keep his secrets. I understand the need for discretion. Given the type of people Gabriel mixes with, there could be royalty and presidents about to get their kink on for all I know. Not that I'd tell….

The meal debris has been cleared, more drinks poured, and the music continues to drift. I can't help feeling eyes on me, and as much as I trust Gabriel has done everything since learning that Jason wanted to come, I can't help feeling….

A stunningly dressed woman in a cream white and gold gown and simple gold mask approaches. Her eyes I can see are a sharp green, and her gorgeous, glossy red hair sparkles with gems. She's holding an envelope, and Gabriel turns briefly to acknowledge her arrival before pushing his chair back. The heavy wood on the stone floor scrapes loud and is effective in silencing the room. *I guess that was the intention.*

"Ladies and Gentlemen, it seems Mistress Eve has the results of the auction," he booms with obvious excitement. There is a ripple of applause and a general rumble of anticipation. Gabriel waves his hand to quiet the guests and takes the envelope from Eve.

Gabriel straightens his shoulders and puffs his chest. I fight the urge to roll my eyes. It's not like he doesn't know the outcome. He opens the envelope and pulls out two cards, before he can query, Eve speaks.

"There were two winning bids, monsieur." Her thick French accent holds some trepidation. Gabriel looks at the two cards, and I can see his has his insignia with five hundred thousand Euros neatly written above his signature. What that actual hell? Seriously, the man is insane, throwing money around like it's confetti even if it is for charity. This is silly and what's even crazier is someone else just as mad.

"Fortunately though, there is only one winner, and as Host I will claim hosts privil—"

"I'm sorry, sir, I didn't see that on the back of the card." Eve points to the other card and Gabriel flips it, a deep angry rumble I can almost feel escapes past his clenched jaw.

"Eve." His warning tone is low, and I stand quickly to try and interrupt to ease the burgeoning tension. So it's in dollars and Gabriel has lost. I can see he's pissed. Still, it's for charity, and as long as it's not in pounds, I can breathe easy. I place a calming hand on Gabriel's arm.

"It's charity, Gabe. Come on now, this is hardly Eve's fault." I tip my head for Eve to maybe take a cautionary step back. Gabriel is radiating all the animosity of a raging bull. *Gosh, he really did want this last session, or more likely, he really doesn't like to lose.*

He turns to me, and I can see the fury in his eyes, but with everyone watching and Eve now holding the winning card, there is fuck-all he can do about it without losing face. He flashes a wide smile that doesn't remotely reach his eyes under the mask and addresses the room.

"The very lucky winner, it would seem, is a somewhat crafty American. I have been outbid by a not-so-favourable currency exchange. Let me see, the winner is…" He holds out his hand again for the card and reads the name. My breath catches if only for a second. "Zanni, not so stupid after all." He chuckle is strained, but the gathered guests all join in with a light smattering of laughter. "If you would all make your way back to the great room, I do believe we are all set. The gallery will provide a somewhat better view, and the rooms will all be opened when Mistress Selina drops her whip for the very last time." He turns to me, and my hand flies to my chest at the melodramatic sigh he expels and the sadness in his eyes.

"You old softy, Gabe," I whisper so only he can hear, and he responds with a tender smile. He steps up to me and takes my hand, bows low, and while maintaining eye contact, he kisses the back of it. He stands briskly and turns, but before we step away he growls at Eve.

"This isn't over, Mistress Eve." His threat and tone are deadly serious, and I'm not surprised Eve takes a step back. Gabriel is kind of scary when he's mad, and I'm thankful, he's not mad at me. Eve gives a curt nod and lowers her eyes, stepping back to let us pass. Gabriel leads me away from the room, and back down the stairs to the great room.

Most of the guests filter up to the gallery, although there's still a good crowd gathered at the edge of the room. There is a sturdy, ancient looking St Andrew 's cross at one end of the hall, and I still haven't seen the winning bidder. Even so, it's not like I will need to guess; they will show their face soon enough, or not, what with all the masks.

"Who is it that won?" Gabriel just shrugs, his eyes still searching the crowd. "Well, it doesn't matter. Look, can you help me with these damn buttons? I need this skirt off."

"Really?" His pitch elevates with the excitement in his voice.

"Consider it your conciliation prize, because yes, I need help here." I point to the tiny buttons securing my skirt to the bodice section of my costume.

"My pleasure." His voice drops, and his tone drips salacious promise.

I narrow my eyes, although he can't see, so I let out a low growl. "Don't make me regret this, Gabe."

He holds his hands up in mock surrender and all innocence. I doubt there is an innocent bone in his body.

I have my back to the cross, and Gabriel is working the buttons behind me while I unhook the ones at the front. Eve comes over and coughs to announce herself, I think I hear Gabriel hiss, and I choose to ignore his sulky demeanour. This was his fucking idea.

"Mistress, Zanni has requested not to be tied to the cross. He promises not to move unless instructed," Eve informs me.

"Very well, I just need to go over some things with him before we start." I give a curt nod.

"He has assured me that won't be necessary. He's happy to proceed. 'Let you do your thing', I believe he said." She shrugs lightly and offers a thin smile.

"He doesn't want to speak to me?" I may not have attended a Gathering before but I have performed and not speaking to someone before engaging in something like this is unheard of—crazy even.

"No, Mistress. He was quite insistent on that."

"Really?" I know this isn't right, even at one of these notorious Gatherings, there has to be some semblance of protocol. I would never do this with a client without discussing limits and boundaries, but this isn't a client I remind myself. This is just for show and the winner is happy. No, the winner is insistent and it's his money, then I guess I should be too. "I don't give a flying fuck if he insists. I will not raise my whip to anyone I haven't spoken to." I smile sweetly to counter the sardonic lilt to my sentiment.

"He doesn't speak English." Eve rushes, as if defending the idiocy of the winning bidder.

"He bid in dollars?" I quirk a dubious brow, which she can't see. Still, I'm sure she can hear the suspicion in my voice.

"He only speaks French." She shrugs again and I exhale a breath filled with exasperation.

"You know what, fine. I will ask my questions and you will translate." I turn on my heel before she can agree. She quickly catches up to my side.

"Of course, although he's already on the platform," she explains.

"So?"

"There isn't room for all of us up there." Her voice is hesitant when she clarifies. "It is only a small plinth."

"I don't need to be up there, Eve, and I can assure you my voice does carry. You will hear me perfectly well, wherever I chose to stand, even from the other end of the room." I point out but I really won't be that far away.

"Oh, yes, very good." Her smile is more like a nervous twitch. I walk over to the elevated cross. It's only raised by maybe a foot in height but Eve is right, there isn't much room up there. Zanni has his back to the crowd, his chest is pressed against the wood of the cross with his arms already stretched out, untethered and perfectly still. Eve manoeuvres herself so she is slightly in front of him but facing me.

Eve translates each question and I'm pleased I get visual confirmation in the form of a nod or a shake of Zanni's head, so that when I'm finished, I'm completely satisfied that he understands the purpose of this display, and I know his boundaries. He has none, apparently. Well, none that were evident from the list I briefly went through. I'm not concerned, because this is not the arena for exploring limits; tonight is just for show

My skirt drops to the floor and I step free. Gabriel draws in a sharp breath through his teeth and I think either curses or praises the lord. The latter is somewhat at odds with the whole evening, but whatever. My tight black bodice nips at my waist and skims my hips. I'm wearing black silk panties that are sexy yet cover quite a lot of skin with very little of my arse cheeks showing. My silk stockings match my underwear with a thin seam up the back. The thigh-highs are secured with a black lace garter belt, and my cute lace-up ankle boots are sky-high with a deadly spike to the heel. I keep the mask on but lose the elaborate feather headpiece and gloves. I need my grip to be sure, and I can't have the tail of the whip getting tangled in the feathers when I do an overhead crack.

I gather up my whip and uncoil it, and the heavy leather falls with a tump to the floor. I work it around, loosening up my wrist, stretching out my neck, and desperately trying to draw in some calming breaths. *Why am I so damn nervous?* Most of these people are three sheets to the wind already, and I'm sure they are more interested in gaining access to those rooms than watching some ex-Domme showing off. *Let's get this over with.*

I requested a small bucket of gasoline and a spare whip to dip the end for some slightly flashier whip wielding a little later. I have a routine in mind and a flaming cut back would be quite a spectacular finale in this dimly lit and cavernous room.

I wasn't lying when I told Gabriel there would be no blood tonight but that doesn't mean I won't slice every inch of clothing from Zanni, the winning bidder. By the time I'm finished, he will be breathless, desperate, and looking very much like he has lost a serious fight with a shredder. My smile is full, wide, and utterly fake, plastered on for the occasion.

After Gabriel's effusive introduction, I slowly turn and make a small curtsey to show my appreciation. My eyes dip for a second, and when I rise to my full height, I take my first look at the man standing at the cross. My heart does this stupid flutter thing because from the back, he's certainly built like Jason. So damn tall and broad in the shoulders, with defined muscles bulging due to the wide-stretched pose. He is holding on to the top of the horizontal bar of the cross and the silk shirt may be oversized and almost floaty. The fabric is so fine it moulds like a second skin where it touches. He has it tucked in at his trim waist and, oh wow, this man has an arse I could bounce quarters off of. The room is too damn dark to see the colour of his hair. Even though my breath is coming a little faster, I only have to take another cursory look around the room to see that the man on the cross is not so dissimilar in build to several in the audience. Any of whom could pass physically for Jason. But there is only one Jason.

I shake myself as the room falls silent with palpable anticipation so intense it sizzles. I slice the air with a cattleman crack, and the sound echoes off the high walls and fills the space with an ear splitting sound. The tip of my whip kills the flame of a candle placed just to the left of Zanni's boot. There is an audible gasp from the audience, but it's swallowed by the quick succession of the following crack, and a second candle flame is extinguished. The smoke from the candles drifts up in white looping tendrils. I take a step forward, flicking and cracking my whip in a succession of slow and rapid figure eights. I move carefully in a small circle. I watch Zanni out of the corner of my eye, for any sign of movement. I watch his fingers, his jaw perhaps, or the rise and fall of his breathing for any signs of change. *Interesting.*

He's either done this before, or perhaps his hearing is impaired, or just very, very controlled. The noise alone has every single person in the room jumping each time I strike out yet nothing from Zanni, no matter how close I flick the tip.

"Losing your touch, Mistress?" I hear Gabriel goad me from the shadows. I won't rise to the taunt. I'm absolutely calm. However, I do flash him a wry smile before I turn back to Zanni. It's time to spice things up.

I take a step back, raise my arm high and let the tail fly, the tip, slicing a clean line on Zanni's forearm. The skin is exposed; I cut only the delicate fabric of the shirt. I do it again and again. Long slashes appear across his back. His sleeves are in tatters and the crowd is going wild and baying for blood. I won't give them that, but it's time to mark that tantalisingly perfect skin I can now see more clearly.

"Remove the shirt." Two assistants instantly relieve the statuesque Zanni of his tattered clothing. He hasn't uttered a word, no cry out or even a flinch, but then I haven't really touched him…yet. The remaining candles artfully arranged at the base of the cross flicker and cause a series of shadows to dance across his back. As dark as the room is, there is no hiding the fact that this man has a very beautiful back, sculptured to perfection. He has paid a great deal of money for the privilege of being at the receiving end of my whip.

I tilt my head as I get a flash of recognition, but before it takes hold and drives me crazier, I curse my baby brain and riotous hormones for playing tricks on me. It's not surprising I'm seeing Jason everywhere. He's always in my damn head, always in my dreams, imprinted on my damn soul, despite my best efforts. I close my eyes and force the feeling to pass. When I open them, I pull my arm back and fire off one overhead crack followed by a single flick along his shoulder blade. He doesn't move, not a twitch, not a single muscle, and sure as shit, he doesn't cry out.

These strikes might be light but that's the thing with a single tail, it doesn't matter because each touch bites. It's true, a whip-master can slice skin like tissue paper with a single flick, but even a butterfly kiss will mark the skin and sting like a bee. Without fail, each strike I administer will still hurt like a motherfucker. I should know.

I place several light stripes across his shoulders and back, avoiding the kidneys, taking care to avoid wraparound. I find with each strike I'm getting more worked up, which isn't like me. There's something about Zanni that is starting to irritate me. It's like he's taunting all my efforts not to harm him, which is probably crazy. This might just be the way he enjoys his punishment, but since I didn't ask him that specific question, all I can assume is I'm having zero effect on this ice man.

"Turn," I command. My voice is hoarse, and I take a moment to grab a quick drink. My arm aches from my efforts, and the sheen of sweat makes my skin glisten in the low lighting. I have to swap whips for this. I pick up the one with the tip I had previously coated in gasoline and carefully light the end on a nearby candle. A large ice bucket filled with water is placed beside my feet by some servers for when I have finished this particular display. The flame licks along the Kevlar and ripples up to about half way. There is an awed hush and I spin on my heels and raise my arm in a swift and showy Tasmanian cut back. A burst of flame explodes with the crack and lights the whole room with a flash of brilliant light. The applause is enthusiastic, but in that moment my world drops away as the whip falls from my fingers. There is a hiss of steam as the flaming metal hits the water in the bucket beside me. My hands fly to my mouth, holding back the cries of agony at the sight that momentary light exposed.

That scar on his abdomen, the one Will gave him. *It is Jason.*

Of course it's fucking Jason. You're an idiot, Sam, and he's probably laughing his arse off under that mask.

I turn before I make eye contact that will not only end this, but very likely end me. Gabriel is instantly at my side.

"Is everything all right, Mistress? Are you injured?" His hands are on my shoulders and he looks me briefly up and down, concern evident in his voice. I shake my head lightly; if I tell him, this ends now.

"I am fine, Gabriel, just warming up." With extraordinary effort, I keep my tone impassive. I'm not done, I'm not nearly done. I smile, though I can feel it doesn't reach my cheeks and Gabriel's eyes crinkle with worry as he steps away. I bend to pick up my own trademark whip, handmade and coloured the same as the red mist that now clouds my vision.

I strike his thigh, high enough for him to know this is no longer a demonstration. His trousers protect his skin but only for the first strike. I pull back, and in a lightning-quick succession of volley moves I slice his skin on each thigh in turn, until it's a plethora of tiny slashes and without hesitating I move to his torso. I throw one long strike across his chest and pause, the stripe is instantly obvious; the blood takes a little time to spot and trickle. He still hasn't moved, and I can no longer stop myself. My body is shaking from the power of feelings and raw adrenaline coursing through me. I have to see his eyes. His mask is so ugly. The long nose and deep brow have certainly made for an admirable disguise, but none of that would've made a blind bit of difference if I had actually seen his eyes before now.

They bore right through me with so much...so much of what? I have no idea. *He left me.* I can't breathe. My head is spinning, and my heart is the only sound I can hear thumping and pounding in my ears. I can feel my skin tingle, and a wave of sadness surges from my guts to just behind my eyes. I hold his gaze because I can't do anything else. I'm rooted to the spot, an intangible force holding me there. My heart is breaking all over again with him being here, so very close, in front of me, in front of *everyone*. That thought is like a slap to my face, a sharp awakening, and suddenly I don't feel heartbroken. I feel ambushed, and I'm instantly pissed off. This is not how fucking adults behave. I'm carrying a baby! I pull my hand back and strike once more completing the pattern and watch to see the blood rise to fill in the cross I have cut across his heart. His jaw twitches and still nothing. I lose it.

I swing my arm out to the side and strike once more, only this time, he steps into the line of the whip. The momentum of the throw makes the whip coil around his outstretched arm, capturing the remaining leather in his hand. I stumble two steps with the jolt, right myself, and pull back on the handle so the whip is taut between us. Fuck that, there is more than just whip tension.

The whole room is silent as we stand facing each other in this surreal stand-off in a kinky game of tug-of-war. I don't need this shit. I'm about to drop my end of the whip when Jason pulls his mask off. Simultaneously, he gives a sharp tug, pulling me toward him. Shocked and caught off-guard with the move, I fall forward and he closes the gap, and I crash against his body. He winces when I slap the open cuts on his chest. He pulls the mask from my face, the tears are already streaming but the dam bursts when I see the devastation in his emotion-filled eyes, the hurt and anguish ingrained in every tired line on his face. He roughly grabs my hair and pulls my face to his. His lips are so very close and his breath sweet enough to taste.

"Enough." He growls and crashes his mouth to mine.

TWENTY-SIX

Jason

God, she tastes so fucking sweet on my lips. I can't get enough, my tongue dives and claims and devours. The salty wetness from her tears mixes with the passion that I unleashed with this kiss. So much tortured desire explodes between us it's shocking, breath-stealing and heartwarming all at once. She's mine, still.

I break the kiss; it's the last thing I want to do, but we both need to breathe. My chest is heaving, and by the look on her face, she is struggling just as much as I am to hold it together. She blinks away more tears and shakes her head. My hand that's threaded in her hair grips tighter. I don't want to hear it. Her body straightens and she tries to step away. I hold her firm against my body. The pressure against the cuts she made across my chest makes them hurt like a motherfucker. Still, I am *not* letting her go.

"You left me." The words tumble silent and broken from her lips, and they fucking kill me.

"Not here," I state with as much of a level tone as I can muster. I won't do this with a fucking audience. They have had their show, now I need privacy.

"No! You left me at the fucking altar, Jason, and this is hardly my choice, is it?" she snarls, and I straighten my shoulders and pull to my full height at the anger and accusation in her voice. I counter her venom with calm.

"Not here." I insist and quickly drop and scoop her over my shoulder before she gets any stupid idea about running. I slap her arse a little harder than necessary to punctuate my resolution. This is not happening here, and I turn to leave. The room has been deathly silent, waiting for what, I'm not sure. This show is officially over. Gabriel steps into my path, his mask in place, but I can see the scowl behind the cut-away eye holes.

"Back the fuck off, Gabriel. I will kick your bollocks into next week if you try and stop me and you didn't go to all this trouble to spend the night of the Gathering in hospital." My tone is deadly serious. He takes a moment and steps aside. Good. I don't doubt for a moment he cares for Sam, but above everything,

Gabriel is all about self-interest. I stride to the main doors and swipe a cloak from one of the attending Domino assistants, leaving her naked and a little stunned. I throw the cloak over my shoulder, probably covering Sam's head and certainly covering her glorious backside. I'm so done with anyone else seeing any part of what's mine.

This isn't the entrance where the gondolier dropped me off. This one leads directly onto the street and the back of Saint Marco square.

The solid basilica door takes some effort to open, and once I'm outside, I feel I can draw my first safe breath. I have her. She may be wiggling like a sexy ass worm on my shoulder but I don't care. I have her. I could cry I'm so damn happy, but the heavens are doing an admirable job of expressing my sentiment. The rain is falling down in sheets, not cold, and we are instantly drenched.

"Put me down!" she screams, her shrill voice bouncing off the walls in an eerily distorted echo.

"No."

She tenses at my response and is no doubt spitting feathers at my calm delivery. The rain is torrential, and I continue to power us through the deserted street, pausing when I hit the square. The whole area is under water; it's not deep, but definitely flooded. The lights from the buildings are reflected in the water, the splatters of rain creating bursts of light on the ground and illuminating the square with artificial brightness this late at night.

"You're hurting my belly."

I freeze. I curse myself and just once hope she's lying. Her knowing grin makes me realise she was, as I ease her carefully down my body. Still, I'm enjoying the familiar feel of her curves against my naked chest. *She takes the sting away.* I cup her face and hold her gaze.

"Sorry, beautiful. Are you okay?" I know she is, but I ask all the same. I search her face for any sign of pain. Her dark eyes sparkle and shine, though her lips are pursed, and she flashes a scowl that, on any other occasion, would make me step back. Her knee shoots up and crunches hard against my semi-hard cock and painfully unprotected balls.

"No, I'm not fucking okay!" she snaps and steps around my crumpled body. I hear the splash of water as she wades out from the protective overhang of the buildings and into the ankle deep water covering the open square. I grab a few stuttered breaths and also my nuts. A little too late, yet, I just need to check they are still there. Damn, she's got bony knees. I scramble to my feet and call after her.

"Sam, for fuck sake, you're getting soaked!" She spins at my words, and her borrowed cape swooshes out in a wide circle, spraying the excess water in an arc. Her eyes narrow, and she stares at me, tugs the cloak free, and drops it into the water at her feet. Defiant and gloriously sexy, she just stands there with her hands on her hips. Her skin shines with the water drenching it, glossy and slick. Her hair is sticking to her face, the only other sign that she's completely soaked. Her bodice, stockings and panties look no different than they did in the great hall. God, she looks amazing. Even with an injury, my cock twitches, causing me to wince.

"I'm broken, Jason. You think I give a shit about a bit of rain?" He voice catches, and for all her defiance, she looks so vulnerable. It's cutting me to the core.

"Baby please, you're pregnant. Don't do this." I take some careful steps toward her.

"Low fucking blow, Jason. I know I'm pregnant."

Even in the rain I can pick out the rivers of tears from the water falling from the sky soaking her face.

"With my child, Sam." My voice softens and I open my arms, closing the distance. I'm cautious; she's just as likely to bolt or level another lick to my nuts if I get too close.

"You don't know that." She shakes her head, drawing in deep breaths and letting out heartrending sobs that are fucking killing me.

"I don't care," I state emphatically.

She barks out a bitter flat laugh. "Pity you didn't think of that before our wedding day, hmm?" Her hands fly to her hips, although it looks more like she is attempting to hold herself together rather than display attitude and strength.

"I did. I wasn't the only one who left that day, Sam, and I had a really fucking good excuse." If she would just hold my gaze, she would see the truth.

"I doubt that."

"That's your prerogative, but I can prove it to you." She meets my eyes for a second, only it's too quick for her to see the sincerity. Even if she can hear it, she doesn't trust herself to look in my eyes. She knows I'm not lying.

"Go on then." She starts to sway a little.

Her resolve is fraying. I can see her fists are so tight, her knuckles are white; she's fighting every step of the way. She's so fucking strong yet fragile. It's fucking torture not taking her in my arms right now.

"Not now, not here." I step closer, and she shakes her head but doesn't move. My voice is deep and husky, determined. "It's been too long, Sam. I need to show you what you mean to me and fuck, you need to remember."

"Jason, I…" She falters and her eyes finally meet mine.

"Then, and only then, I will tell you everything." She is trembling, and her eyes glaze over, but she is nodding before I finish asking the only question that matters. "Do you trust me?"

"Yes," she whispers.

"Good. Then, Sam, we've got this." I scoop her into my arms just as her legs buckle. Her head rests against my chest, and she breaths deeply, relaxing into my hold. For the first time in a really fucking long time I feel whole.

The concierge raises a brow but utters not a word. Sam is nestled in my arms as I walk through the hotel lobby, half naked and leaving a trail of water in our wake. I kick the door to my en suite open and walk straight into the shower. She's shivering and my skin is covered with goosebumps, we both need some heat to warm us, some water to wash away the doubt, and some intimate contact to close the fucking distance. I pull the lever, turn the dial to hot and hold us both under the spray until she stops shivering. It takes a while, and I take that time to kiss her hair and repeat a mantra I have said a million times since our wedding day. I'm so fucking sorry.

I ease her to her feet and reverently unclip every hook on her bodice. I can feel her eyes on me as I peel her panties down her legs, her stockings too. I carefully unlace her ankle books and pull everything off before I stand. Her gorgeous body is a sight to make me weep but there have been enough tears from both of us for a fucking lifetime. I raise my head and meet her gaze. Searing heat collides with my own white hot desire.

"Mine." I exhale the word and watch her eyelids close. Her lips pull into an involuntary smile, and no matter the reservations she is no doubt wrestling with in her head, she takes obvious comfort in my declaration. It's all I need.

My lips meet hers, soft and tender, I want to taste every inch of her, starting right here. My tongue sweeps in and she lets out a sigh that I feel in my heart. It fucking beats with the power of that little sound, loud and fucking proud. I hold her face and tip her this way and that as I lavish kiss after kiss all over her neck and her collarbone before I turn her and kiss all along her shoulders, up her neck at the back and suck hard just below her ear. "Always mine," I breathe, and despite the heat and steam, she shudders. I work my way down her back and smile against her skin as her hips tilt and she pushes her arse up and toward me.

"I'm getting there, beautiful. Just savouring the moment." I nip playfully at the round flesh in my hands.

"What moment?" she moans.

"Our moment." I drop to my knees, my hands flat between her thighs, and I pull them apart, wide. I press my face right against her core and drag my tongue as far as I can, reaching her entrance and dipping just inside. *Fucking heaven.* I fist the muscles of her arse and massage her flesh as I work my tongue around her slick sweetness. My cock is in agony, throbbing and aching for release from its confined space. My balls are still sore, but have almost forgiven her for the knee action earlier and are keen to get reacquainted in a much more mutually pleasing way. I thread one hand through and up, cupping her at her apex before sliding my thumb back and over her pulsing nub. She jolts at my touch, then pushes back against my mouth. Her thighs start to quiver, and I can hear her desperate little pants. I slide two fingers inside and press just where she needs me. She explodes on my tongue and sinks almost completely back onto me, my hand on her cheek, my face wedged against her arse cheeks, and my fingers inside her are the only things keeping her upright. I lap her softness until her climax subsides and feel her begin to support her body weight once more. She twists out of my hold and kneels on the floor, her legs between mine.

"I've missed you so much." Her bottom lip wobbles with her soft words, and I rush to cover the vulnerable movement, pressing my mouth to hers. I only relinquish the kiss when I feel her lips curl in a tentative smile.

"I missed you more," I respond and her eyes widen.

"Jason, you don't want—" She tries to argue, but I won't let her finish.

"Yes," I snap, and I can feel my jaw pop with tension, so I let out a controlled breath. "I have what I want, *all* of what I want, right here." I place my hand deliberately on her tummy, which feels only slightly rounder.

"Really?" Her uncertainty slays me. I fucking hate myself for that. I did that, though I will make this right.

"Yes." I'm resolute and unwavering, and hold her gaze until I see her finally believe each word. Her eyes flood with tears that are quickly washed away with the downpour from the shower. "Mine, Sam. Both of you are mine, understand?" I hold her chin. Her lashes are heavy with tears and her eyes are boring right through me.

"I-I…" she stutters, and I shake my head.

"Do I look in any doubt to you?"

"No, but—" Her fight is gone, yet she's still reluctant to believe me, and I honestly don't blame her, but she will.

"No buts ever. I will explain absolutely everything. Just know this as fact: I love you. You are my life. Our baby is our future, and you will be my wife. Understand?"

"Yes." She flashes a genuine smile, and it's like a burst of sunshine in this marble cubicle, bright and blinding, illuminating the gloom.

"Good. Now come and ride me like you own me, because Sam, you *do* own me, heart and fucking soul." The words tumble from my lips, feral and demanding.

"Yes, Sir."

Her whole body shivers. She shimmies up and widens her legs hovering above my now closed thighs. I pull at the zip and release my straining erection, hard and fit to burst. I squeeze the base to ease some of the ache. I know I'm seeping with want. I let out a tortured hiss when she covers my entire length with her scorching, sweet heat. I could die a happy man now because nothing feels as good as this—my own private Nirvana. She drops her forehead to mine, and I take her in. Her eyes search mine, and I see such raw, undiluted love there, I know I'm in heaven.

She starts to move, and I place my hands on her hips and let her take this. Her lips seek mine, her tongue utterly desperate as it pushes into my mouth and swirls and duels with mine. She fists my hair, her grip tight as she takes full control. Bouncing and grinding with furious energy, she pounds onto my rock-hard cock, taking everything she needs. It's barely a few minutes, and I can feel her greedy muscles start to ripple and squeeze me for all they're worth.

"Wait for me, baby." I grind out through my clenched jaw.

"No."

She grins, wicked and wanton, and I respond with a barking, dirty laugh. I guess I had that coming. She throws her head back, and my mouth homes in on her soft breasts and perky pink nipples. I drag my tongue over one nub then clamp my mouth around the stiff peak. She squeals when my teeth graze the tip, only she doesn't break her rhythm. She's falling and I will be damned if I don't chase that climax with her. I pull her hips a little harder with each of her thrusts, getting myself just a little bit deeper and tilting my own hips to make sure I'm right with her. She screams my name like it's a curse—or perhaps a prayer. Either way, I'm gone with that cry. My balls tighten, and when her muscles clamp and seize around my shaft, a lightning bolt of pleasure shoots from the base of my spine, through me, and into her core.

My hands shift from her hips to her shoulders, and I secure her to me, pulling her down and holding her tight, breathless, sated, and now limp in my arms.

My body envelopes her, our skin slick and fused together with not a millimetre of distance between us. *It's fucking perfect.* We remain entwined, letting our synchronised ragged breathing calm and it's only when I feel the first shudder of a chill ripple through her body that I make to move us from the shower.

I dry her body and she dries mine. She takes so much care over the cuts, tender and reverent. She places kisses next to the torn tissue before carefully covering each mark with cream, and where one slice of skin has continued to seep, she secures a small bandage.

"I'm not sorry for these," she whispers against my skin when she's done. I stare down at her as she looks up, a small smile playing on her swollen pink lips. *Her second genuine smile and it dazzles.*

"Neither am I." I scoop her once more into my arms and carry her to the bed. Sliding in next to her, she settles her head on my chest, her slim arm and warm long leg entwines around my body. She holds me to her, until there is no space between us. We are one. *Perfect.*

TWENTY-SEVEN

Sam

I'm shell-shocked, and not because of the monumental orgasm Jason demanded from my exhausted body after an entire night of the same, the last of which was only an hour ago. But because he has just explained the complete and utter fuck-up that was my wedding day from his perspective.

"You're an idiot," I declare when he finally pauses after telling me about the roadside rescue.

"I tried to call." One arm is wrapped around my back, holding me tight to his side while the other hand is tracing light patterns on my arms, which are draped across his stomach.

I scoff, incredulous, and flick his nipple to highlight his stupidity. "Oh yes, that's why you're an idiot, because you stopped to help a stranded mother and her children. All of this could've been avoided if you'd been upfront with me, Jason. If you had just told me what was going on." My head rests on his chest, and I'm enjoying the rise and fall with his deep, hypnotic breathing all while he told me everything that had happened right up to the morning of the wedding. I push myself up to a sitting position and cross my legs, pulling the loose sheet to cover myself. I don't want to distract him. We have so much to get through, now we've finally stopping fucking, that is. Following the nipple flick, I also administer a sharp slap to his left pectoral, as a mix of pure frustration and love courses through me. My nose tingles with ever present tears and the very real knowledge that, however well intended, those good intentions nearly ended *us*.

He grabs my hand and lifts the fingertips to his mouth, kissing each one. There is not a millimetre of my skin he hasn't lavished with kisses, not a single part of me that hasn't been worshiped, owned, and reclaimed. I know my hormones are wreaking havoc with my emotional state, tears one minute and unbelievable joy the next, but I don't try to hide the enormous smile pulling at my mouth when I recall that there is also not a spec of his body to which I haven't returned the favour. "You should've told me about the threats, Jason." He lowers my hand from his lips and lets out such a sad sigh I almost don't want to talk about this. It's so fucking painful for both of us, when we both realise how close we came to… I pinch my eyes shut to stop that thought. When I open them and look at Jason, his lids are tightly closed, and I know his mind has just travelled the same unbearably heartbreaking path.

"I should've, yes. Sadly that's still not my biggest regret." His eyes drop from my gaze, and when he looks back at me, I can see that his words have manifested in the saddest eyes in the world. "I should never have said what I said —all that shit, about needing to be the father." He clenches his jaw with anger, and the words fall like they are just as disgusting to him on his tongue as they were to hear at the time.

"It's how you feel, Jason. You have to be truthful, or this will never work." My stomach turns that we are back to this, though having sorted the misunderstanding of his wedding day disappearance, this is the crux for us.

"I didn't know what the fuck I was talking about. I was a fucking idiot, and it wasn't until I thought I'd lost you, that I realised I didn't *feel* like that. *Not at all.*" He cups my face and holds my tear-laden gaze with his own glassy dark eyes. "I love you, Sam. No caveats, no provisos, and absolutely no limits." His mouth covers mine, chasing the air I need and swallowing the gasp that escapes the back of my throat. I am flushed and breathless when he breaks the kiss only to leave me winded all over again with his next words. "You are the only thing in my life worth waking up for, you and *our* baby."

"Our baby?" My eyes dip down to my tummy, to where he's looking. My heart swells with the warm, tender smile that now dominates his face.

"Yes, this little miracle here is our baby, and whether biology is on my side or not, I couldn't care less. I'm going to be the best damn father to this little bundle if you'll let me." He places his hand over mine now that it's resting on the tiny bump.

"I'm not having a paternity test," I blurt and hold my breath waiting for the explosion. He just gives a light shrug, lies back, and pulls me back into his protective hold. I snuggle into the crook of his arm and entwine my legs with his, hugging his waist and conforming my body around his.

"I meant what I said, Sam. This baby is ours, yours and mine." He kisses my hair; I can feel him smiling as his lips press against me.

"What if Will—"

"He won't." Jason snaps but softens the bite with a gentle squeeze and a strong hand, stroking hypnotic patterns up the length of my back. "Will didn't exactly cover himself in glory that day, letting you take the fall, so let's not worry about him, okay?"

"Don't be too hard on him, Jason. I understood why he didn't speak up. Your

Mum looked pretty poorly."

"Yeah," he scoffs with a hollow laugh. "So telling her everything after you left wasn't exactly the smartest thing, but it still didn't stop him." His words are tinged with anger.

"He did what?" I quickly look for any sign that he's teasing and see none.

"Yep, told her everything. Sent her to the damn hospital with a suspected heart attack. Like I said, he did not cover himself—"

I push myself up onto one elbow, my jaw slack at the casual delivery of this news. "Your Mum had a heart attack? Jason, what the hell?"

"Suspected. Calm down, Sam, she's fine. Completely fine."

I'm still stunned, but he shrugs and gives a wry smile when he continues. "Well, she's pretty angry at Will, and I'm not exactly flavour of the month either. Physically, she's fine, no thanks to Will."

"Fuck! So I did all that for nothing. God, she must hate me." I run my hand down my face and sink back down the bed, Jason tugging me close to his side once more. He chuckles at my audible groan.

"Quite the opposite, beautiful. Both Mum and Dad think you're pretty fucking amazing."

"I doubt that." I sniff and the laugh that follows is flat and humourless.

"They might not have used those words exactly, but you did nothing wrong, and they know that." I'm not entirely convinced, though I do believe he's telling the truth. Besides, future in-laws are the last thing I am concerned with at the moment.

"And Will?" This is the loaded question. I know Leon's position, but even with Jason's new perspective on paternity Will is still a potential issue.

"What about Will?"

I know he knows what I mean, but I spell it out. I'm sick of misunderstandings. "He could want to know for sure I mean."

"He won't. He told me he wouldn't get involved unless I bailed."

"But—" His index finger silences my retort and his sentiment bowls me over.

"But nothing, Sam. Even if he did demand a test, which he won't, it doesn't change a Goddamn thing. You are mine, and you are carrying our child, whatever happens down the road we will deal, together."

I hold his gaze, and I have the craziest bout of butterflies in my tummy that makes me jolt. It's not painful, I've never felt anything like that. I move my hand from his waist and settle it over the area and notice it's nowhere near my stomach, and the sensation is gone just as quickly as it came.

"Together." I tilt my head, smiling so damn wide for the umpteenth time since last night my face aches.

He pulls me up his body to take my offered kiss only I speak before his lips touch mine. "Just you remember that when you get another email." My tone is light yet serious all the same.

"There won't be another email, Sam. I dealt with it." He states as a matter of fact, and I sigh.

"Jason, there will always be someone trying to get something for nothing. I doubt Stanford worked alone, or that he actually kept all the copies of the videos on him, at all times. Trust me, if I know one thing, scum like him are always lurking, and I don't care. Just promise you'll tell me next time." I feel him stiffen, and sure enough, when I look back up, his jaw is clenched, and he has a deep scowl darkening his handsome features. "You know I'm right, that's why you've gone all stiff and not in a good way," I tease to try and lighten the mood, but a dark cloud has descended. I puff out a breath of frustration. I've had enough. "Did you bring your laptop?" His face looks puzzled at my question and his brow furrows with deep lines. I unwind myself and shuffle off the bed.

I take in the grandeur of the room for the first time, but only as I search for his messenger bag. The late morning sunlight is streaming through the double door of the adjoining sitting room. We were too preoccupied too close the drapes last night and unconscious when dawn broke. It's a beautiful suite though, furniture richly decorated with golden fabrics, silk wallpaper, gilt-framed original paintings, and the most stunning fresco on the ceiling. This must be the royal suite because I have never seen a room quite so stunning. My feet sink inches into the luxurious thickness of the carpet as I pad over to the wardrobe.

"I didn't but I have my iPad in the safe, why?" He quirks an eyebrow high with interest.

"Because I'd like to make my own video." I grin over my shoulder and pull the double doors wide in search of the safe.

"Really?" He rises slowly, pulling himself onto his hands and knees, and prowling across the bed. His remark is followed by a feral sounding grumble. I pick up a cushion from the chaise beside me and throw it in his general direction.

"You're insatiable."

He bats the soft missile away and continues to stalk forward. "For you, I make no apology for that, though if we're making a video, it's not going to be on a shitty tablet."

"*We're* not making a video, *I'm* making a video." I roll my eyes when his grin widens with wickedness. I punch a code I'm confident will open the safe— two, five, one, two—Christmas Day. A life changing day for us both, and I give myself a little rapid clap when it pings open. I take the tablet and swipe it open.

On my way back to the bed, I slip one of Jason's t-shirts on and snicker when he grumbles his disapproval. He'll be glad I've covered up once I start recording.

"What are you going to do?" He slides back beside me as I settle against the headboard.

"Watch." I open the Photo Booth app and press record.

"Hi, my name is Sam Bonfleur, and when I was sixteen I met a real life monster. I'm not sorry to say he died last year. Unfortunately, evil never really dies and monsters like him rarely act alone. Two weeks ago, my wedding day was ruined and my life very nearly broken beyond repair because some low life arsehole tried to blackmail my fiancé. He threatened to release video footage of my rape and humiliation, and my fiancé, being an adorable idiot, thought he could save me from this nasty piece of shit and protect my reputation. But here's the thing, it's not my reputation on the line here. It's his, it's theirs, all of those shameful excuses of men who stood by and watched a man I was forced into a relationship with destroy me. So I have nothing to hide here, but you do and if you ever dare to come after me and mine in the future, Liam Neeson will have nothing on my determination to end you."

"Sam, you don't have to do this." Jason soft coaxing tone instantly draws me back from the darkness before it takes me under. I swallow back the taste of bile any recollection of my time with Richard seems to generate and shake the cloud away before it can settle.

"Actually I do. I won't hide or run or have what's mine threatened. Had you shown me this to start with, I would've done this then. Yes, I would've been upset. Fuck, what that man did to me I will never forget. I also won't give them any more of me, and hiding or paying a ransom or whatever, to me at least, feels like them winning." I twist to face him so he can see not only my sincerity but my determination. This ends now.

"There is no them, I promise, baby." He sweeps away the hair that has fallen across my face, and I lean into his hand.

"I hope you're right, but this is how we deal with it if it isn't." I kiss his palm and take all the comfort I need from that slight connection.

"Okay, beautiful. Whatever you want." He leans up and kisses my forehead.

"What I want right now is food, I'm starving." I reply brightly, happy to change the subject, more than happy to move on, *together*.

"You did miss the meal last night. Still, I assumed Gabriel would've fed you on his yacht."

"Cheese on toast, which seems like a lifetime ago." I stretch and rub my tummy at its timely grumble of dissatisfaction.

"Cheese on toast?" Jason wrinkles his nose with distaste.

"Baby." I shrug as way of explanation, and his lips instantly form the most stunning smile. He reverently lifts the bottom of the t-shirt I'm wearing. I place the iPad on the mattress beside me and move my arms to the side to give him all the access he's seeking. My breath hitches when his lips graze my skin, just at the crest of my growing bump.

"You, little one, are so very precious, but do you think you could maybe crave something a little more nutritious? We have to keep your momma fit and healthy." He peppers light kisses and blows a puff of warm air just above my clit, and uses his nose to rub a little circle on my sensitive skin that curls my toes. I sink deeper into the mattress and sigh, wiggling and tilting my hips so I can get a little more than just hot air. He pulls right off me and chuckles.

"Food it is then," he quips.

"Really?" I drop my jaw, then snap it shut with a mock scowl.

"Oh yes, beautiful. Let me take care of that need first then I will take care of anything else your sweet little body desires." He waggles his brows playfully but I keep my glare fixed and firm.

"It desires you…just you." I state petulantly, a tiny moan escapes the back of my throat.

"Good because I need to say this." His voice drops and all playfulness vanishes. His eyes darken, and his expression would be scary if it wasn't so deadly serious.

"Sounds ominous." I shift and get a flutter of nerves.

"Not ominous but since we are getting everything out in the open, this is not negotiable either." He flashes a quick smile that does nothing to calm my concern.

"I'm listening." I exhale quietly, waiting a moment before I draw another breath. The look on his face, I can't imagine what is so serious, unless he's sick.

"No more sharing, ever." His stare is incendiary, and if I was wearing any panties they would be ash from the heat alone. "I don't mean no sharing because we are now having a baby, because that won't change the kink we both need and love. I'm saying this because I'm done sharing *you*. I can't and won't, and I don't even care if that's an issue for you. I'm not letting you go, so you're just gonna have to deal with this new rule."

"Wow." A small giggle escapes when I suck in the air I now need.

"Wow what?" His deep frown still stern.

"Wow, you're hot when you go all Alpha on me." I tease, even as my heart is just about to burst with this unexpected declaration.

"I'm serious." His entire demeanor conveys there will be no compromise, and I hold up my hands in supplication.

"I can see that, and if you just want to slip your cock inside me, you will be able to tell how much I fucking love that idea." I wiggle lower on the bed and start to spread my legs as an open invitation.

"Nice try. Sam. I'm feeding you first." He taps the end of my nose. The flash of a playful expression vanishes, and he's back to deadly serious. "Have I made myself perfectly clear on this?"

"No sharing?" My question is more for clarification because I completely understand where he is coming from.

"Yes."

"Jason, I thought you were going to say you were sick," I reply.

"Oh beautiful, I am sick… depraved and twisted, but just for you." He hovers above me, and I melt under his intense gaze raking every inch of my body with his wanton glare.

"Just for me," I whisper on a slow exhale. "Jason, I couldn't be happier with the no sharing rule." I beam, blushing and breathless. "I was going to say the same, you just beat me to it.

"You were?" He tilts his head in an uncharacteristic display of vulnerability.

"Just you, Jason. It's always been just *you*." His eyes brighten, and if it's possible his smile becomes a little bit more heart-stealing.

TWENTY-EIGHT

Jason

"You have no reason to look so grumpy." She straightens my tie and leans up to place a quick conciliatory kiss on my tightly pursed lips. I can't believe she made me wear a damn suit. It's not like we're having tea with the bloody Queen.

"I have every reason to be *grumpy*. You're making me wear a suit to go for lunch, and Gabriel tried his damnedest to stop me from seeing you." I squeeze my finger and loosen the chokehold she has managed to secure around my neck. I forgot she is just as good as I am with knots.

"At *my* request, Jason. He only did what *I* asked him to do. He was being a friend." Her nose wrinkles in this cute deep line just at the bridge when she's trying to be stern and earnest. I'm not convinced with her assessment of the good Mr Wexler.

"Ha! Gabriel doesn't have friends, Sam, he has employees. And trust me, his reasons for keeping me away were far from altruistic." I raise a curious brow at her uncharacteristic naïvety.

"Oh I'm not saying he didn't want to keep you away for his own reasons— I'm far from innocent when it comes to what Gabriel wants from me—but I have never given him any reason to think he would get it either. I told him I wasn't ready to see you just yet, so he did everything he could to prevent that, for *me*." She emphasises the last word, but my stony expression remains unchanged, and the fact that I now have confirmation that he wants my girl has far from helped the situation in my book. She narrows her eyes as if contemplating a different angle. She doesn't need to know at this moment in time that I'd do anything for her. A lunch isn't really a big deal. I just don't particularly like the guy and would much rather spend my time with her, only her. She pats her hands gently on my chest and drops her gaze, then looks up at me through those long dark lashes, her smile as sweet as her voice is soft and coaxing. "Look baby, Gabriel is being extremely magnanimous with the invitation. When I spoke to him the other day, he was more than a little pissed you fixed the auction. He had a big mess to clear up, apparently, so for me, please play nice." She brushes imaginary lint from my shoulders and places her hand once more over my heart. "Besides, it's irrelevant, now isn't it? You have me lock, stock and barrel, so how about you drop the pout and let's go and have a lovely lunch on his boat."

"Yacht." I correct and watch her roll her eyes.

"So I understand." She sniffs with a dry laugh. I quickly wrap my arms around her waist before she can step away.

"I'd rather eat you instead." I nuzzle her neck and she wriggles, melding into the grip, tilting her head to give me a clear expanse of silky soft skin to claim.

"Jason, we haven't stepped outside this room for five days," she moans, her hands fisting into my hair and her sweet body writhing against mine. My cock is instantly hard and barely contained behind the thin material of my pants.

"And?" I mumble, sucking down on her neck and relishing the full body shiver as my reward.

"And he's leaving tomorrow, and I promised I would see him before he goes, and I need some sunlight." Her words hold little conviction. Her less than enthusiastic tone is accompanied by a whimper that makes my balls ache.

"You got some sunlight this morning when we fucked on the balcony." I growl and pull her against my erection, she grinds shamelessly against my stiffness yet shakes her head as if trying to wake from this erotic trance we're both enjoying.

"Jason." She sighs my name as a heartfelt plea, even if my statement caused a flash of colour to her cheeks and a sweet sexy smile to tip her lips.

"Fine." I groan out through gritted teeth. Reluctantly releasing my hold, she spins on her toes away from me to gather her bag and slip her strappy sandals on. I take a moment to adjust myself and challenge the wisdom of going commando when I take her in. She turns to face me, flushed, gorgeous, and all mine.

She looks absolutely stunning in a floaty, pale pink summer dress that skims her body and hangs some way below her knees. When the sunlight catches the silky material there is just a tease of her tempting curves that lie beneath, fleeting glimpses before she moves and the shadows once again modestly hide her attributes.

"Ready." She beams and her voice has a sing-song lilt of pure joy that makes my chest damn near swell tenfold with the exact same feeling.

"As I'll ever be." I hold my hand out, and she slips hers into mine. For the first time in just under a week, we exit the room. *It was fucking heaven.*

The promenade bustles with bodies and we weave our way through the crowds of tourists and street vendors, selling a pastiche of all that Venice has to offer as souvenirs, replicas and miniatures, from masks to gondolas, t-shirts and totes. Gabriel is standing at the rear of the yacht on the mid-deck, and he raises his hand, acknowledging us as we approach the *Ambrosia*. I tip a nod, and Sam waves enthusiastically and leads me up the gangway with a bounce in her step. I take comfort that she's happy, and I know without a doubt I'm the cause, from that first kiss at the Gathering and reinforced every minute of the last five days. That is only a mild sop to having to endure this lunch meeting with Gabriel.

I wasn't lying when I said Gabriel doesn't have friends. He only has ulterior motives. My phone buzzes just as I step foot on board, and Sam freezes and turns to face me. Her eyes are wide and she's biting her bottom lip with worry.

Swiping the screen I can see it's a local number.

"You're going to have stop worrying every time my phone rings at some point, beautiful." I squeeze her hand before letting go.

"Maybe. Who is it?" I show her the screen and she shrugs it off, equally clueless.

"I don't know, it's a local number though." I press the call button and take the call. Sam surprises me by turning and skipping away, disappearing up the stairway. I thought she'd want to listen in, given the concern on her face, but then I have promised to tell her if I received another threat and there is no way I'm risking this shit again. That in itself tells me she trusts my word.

"*Ciao.* Signore Sinclair?" the female voice asks.

"*Sì.*" I know my Italian accent is pretty good but she still slips into faultless English.

"Ah good, Mr Sinclair. You said you wanted to be notified if we had a cancellation?"

"Cancellation?" I repeat even though I heard her perfectly. *Didn't I?*

"Yes, this is the Palazzo Cavalli. We have had a very unfortunate last minute situation with the planned ceremony for this afternoon. The bride's mother has taken quite ill and they have postponed. If you are able to come today—"

"What time?" I'm curt, though I can't even pretend to feel sorry, because this is a fucking dream come true.

"Three o'clock, signore. I understand this is very short notice, only you did say—"

I cut her off with an equally abrupt declaration. "We'll be there." I end the call and take the steps after Sam two at a time. I hear Sam's warning.

"Do not repeat that Gabe, unless you want to be eating this amazing lunch you've laid on through a straw." She speaks with a wasted whisper.

"Repeat what?" In a few long strides I'm standing behind a seated Sam and towering over both her and Gabriel seated at her side. He reaches for his wine and waves his hand dismissively.

"I was just saying, I have never seen the room clear so quick after your little display the other night. Most of the guests thought it was all part of the show and were so damn horny we couldn't open the rooms up quick enough," he chortles.

"Why should he not repeat that, Sam? I'm taking it as a compliment." I don't particularly care what people thought, that wasn't why I was there.

"He wasn't finished," Sam mutters and then groans into her hands as Gabriel continues with a broad and smug smile.

"I have had several very handsome offers for a turn on the cross with my Mistress here." He pats her knee, and I tug her chair away so he loses his hold. He narrows his eyes at me and continues, "I was just negotiating when you so rudely interrupted."

"Oh God." Sam's head popped up for an incredulous open-mouth gawp at Gabriel before dropping her head back into her hands.

"You're funny, Gabriel, I'll give you that." I let out a flat, humourless laugh and lower my voice to add the necessary impact to what I need to say. "However, if you ever refer to my wife as your anything, you won't need that straw she mentioned."

"Okay boys, now calm down, put your willies away. Jason, yours is by far the biggest." She states this as a matter of fact. Damn right. "Come and sit down, and I'm not your wife." She pats the empty seat on her other side, but I shake my head.

"Yet," I counter. "Come on, we're going to fix that, right now." Sam cocks her head and gives me a placatory smile. "He's only joking, Jason. There's no need to be like this. Let's just eat and play nice hmm?" She pats the seat lightly again to encourage me down.

"Oh I don't give a shit about Gabriel." I turn and give him a slight shrug. "No offence." Honestly, I have long since moved on from worrying about Gabriel's games.

"None taken." He raises his glass to me, then sips as if toasting my statement.

"But we have to leave. There's something I need to get from the hotel safe." I twist her chair and pull her up. Her face is a cute mix of utterly confused and slightly irritated. I press my lips to hers firmly and smile against our connection.

"Jason, you're making no sense." She pushes me away and breaks the connection.

"We're getting married at the Palazzo in an hour, so we have to hustle, baby." I look at my watch briefly and start to tug her to follow me.

"You are?" Gabriel coughs around his wine, wiping the splatter from his chin with the back of his hand. He looks almost as comical as Sam does with her mouth dropped open in shock.

"I am?"

"Yes, you are… I mean we are. They've had a last minute cancellation. Sofia had all the documents, which I gave them when I arrived. I just told them to let me know. I wasn't expecting this, but I'm not going to lie, it will make me the happiest fucking man alive if I get to leave this place with you as my wife." I use my index finger to tip her dropped jaw shut and slide my hand to cup her cheek.

"Don't, you'll make me cry." Gabriel mockingly dabs his eyes with a serviette, and Sam fires him a deathly scowl before I can tell him to fuck off.

"Really? We're doing this?" She snaps her head back to me, a tentative smile beginning to take hold.

"Yes, beautiful, we're doing this. We can do it all over again with everyone when we get back to the UK, if you want, but right now, the only thing I want is you. Just you and me, baby."

"You, me, and baby." She places her hand over her belly, and I get a hit in my chest that knocks the wind right from me. I nod slowly, taking in her gesture and draw in a deep breath.

"Yeah." I press my hand softly over hers that is resting on her bump, clenching my fist with the other when I hear Gabriel make some indiscrete retching sounds.

"One more noise from you, Gabe, and you won't be invited." Gabriel holds his hands up in surrender.

"Fine, fine. I am only teasing." He pushes his chair back and stands to face us both. "Why don't you go and get whatever you need from your hotel, Jason, and let Sam get ready here. I do believe there is something a little more bride appropriate in your room. I will escort her to the Palazzo and we will meet you there." He offers and I scoff in his face.

"You have to be kidding me if you think I'm going to trust you." He doesn't flinch at my insult. In fact, his impassive expression and cool glare seem to soften as he seems to search every inch of her face. He addresses me, but doesn't take his eyes off of her.

"You see, Jason, that's where you are very much mistaken about my intentions. I have only ever had Mis—" He wisely corrects himself mid-word, and Sam snickers at my low warning grumble "Sam's best interests at heart, and even I can see this is going to make her very, very happy. Look at her, she glows in your hands, Jason. You are the luckiest son of a bitch this side of *me*." For once, I find myself in totally fucking agreement with the man

"Yes, I am." I roughly pull her close and cover her mouth in a proprietary move, my tongue diving between her sweet lips when she gasps. She's breathless and flushed when I break the kiss, and I hold her a little longer until she has stopped swaying. "Okay, Sam. You have twenty minutes to get ready and get this sweet arse to the Palazzo, think you can do that?"

"Just try and stop me." She exhales, and the smile that dominates her flawless face, not only makes my day but is about to make my fucking life.

I race back to the hotel. I don't need to change since Sam made me wear a fucking suit for the lunch, so I know I look smart enough. I just need to pick up the wedding gift I bought for Sam and brought with me. In this instance, I wasn't being a cocky bastard, actually, I thought the opposite. Either way, if she didn't want anything to do with me, I still wanted her to have it. *It belongs to her.*

When I arrive at the Palazzo, there's about ten minutes to spare and still no sign of Sam and Gabriel. I'm not worried—well, I'm mostly not worried. The building has been transformed from the other day, with chairs set out in rows, each with thick white silk ribbons tied to the back. The columns are also draped with white ribbon and entwined with flowers and vines. Plinths and vases, bursting with blooms, line the room, and the aisle is edged with candles leading up to where the marriage officiant, a man called Fabio Romano, is waiting. Whosever wedding this was, they had ticked every box in my book at least,

The room looks stunning, oozing romantic elegance. There are even musicians posed in the corner of the room, and I just hope Sam doesn't mind the fact that there are no guests.

My breath catches when I turn at the first note from the quartet, the "Wedding March".

Gabriel puffs his chest out, pulls his shoulders back and stands tall before grinning down at Sam. I can see her beam in return. Her eyes are wide with wonder as she takes in the room. Then they settle on me, and my chest tightens so much I have to fight to draw my next breath. I catch Gabriel wink at me as he starts to lead her down the aisle. *Wow, just wow.* She's wearing a floor-length, white, silk dress, with thin lace straps and her hair is loose and long, cascading in dark curls and clipped at one side with a small spray of flowers and something sparkly which reflects the sunlight blazing in through the large French windows.

She reaches me, and I don't think I've ever felt more anxious in my life. Taking my hands in hers, we both exhale with the comfort that small contact brings. She lets out a second puff with a tense laugh, and I pull her to me, thread my hand into her hair, and kiss her, hard and quick. I tell myself it's to calm her nerves but it's just as much to ease mine.

"You look breathtaking, Sam. Stunning." My greedy gaze quickly rakes her silk-clad body.

"My dress back home was nicer, still this will do." She gives a light shrug, her tone and smile are so joyful I know she isn't really bothered.

"We can do it all again, beautiful, when we get back, with your dress, everything and anything else you need." I don't care if we do this a hundred times, as long as we do this right now.

"I have everything I need right here, Jason." Her eyes shine, her whole body seems to glow with life and love.

"Good."

"Besides, I wouldn't fit into it…again." She laughs and Signore Romano is about to interrupt when I raise my hand to halt him.

"Not yet, signore." He mutters a begrudging concession, and I shrug it off. Nothing is going to dampen my utter fucking joy today.

"Just one more thing before you start."

"Jason?"

I smile so wide my cheeks hurt even as Sam's worried glances flit between Signore Romano and me. Her question is not so much a warning but sounds more like a prayer.

"I have some restraint, Sam. Give me a little credit. I just had to kiss you." She visibly relaxes, and I shake my head at her obvious wayward thoughts. I continue before I too get distracted. "I also have to give you this." I slip the thin velvet box from my pocket and hand it to her. Her brow furrows and then shoots right up when she unclips the latch and opens the case.

"Jason!" she gasps. Her voice is trembling, and her hand flies to her neck as if touching the ghost of the necklace nestled in the silky casing. "Is this…?"

"Yes." I take the case from her as she slides the necklace free and into her hand.

"My grandfather's necklace," she whispers. Her fingers dance reverently over the Cartier natural pearl and diamond necklace that her mother held ransom over her head and which she sold to regain her life at eighteen.

"How?"

"I've been looking for it for some time, and I wanted you to have it."

"You were pretty sure I'd say yes, weren't you?" she quips with a soft smile.

"Actually, I've never been more terrified in my life, but either way, this is yours. I hoped it would be as my wedding gift, that's all."

"Thank you."

My thumb catches a tear from her cheek, and I suck the salt from the pad. She holds the necklace up, and I lean in to clip it round her neck, and slip the case back in my pocket. Her fingers trace along the shiny spheres and I nod to

Signore Romano to proceed. Let's do this.

I don't hear much of the ceremony, but I damn well hear the part when Signore Romano says man and wife. I will have to thank Gabriel for the loan of the rings. Sam's is way too big, and the one I borrowed fits just fine, and as symbols go, they did the trick. As I wrap my arms around my bride and kiss her for the first time as my wife, there is nothing symbolic about the feeling coursing through every cell in my body and making my heart beat so damn hard it hurts. Her lips can't contain the smile long enough to continue the kiss, and she bursts into laughter holding my face to hers as I hold her to me. My wife.

Gabriel and the first officer of the *Ambrosia* are our witnesses, and we take full advantage of the photographer on hand to capture the day. We pose on the balcony overlooking the Canal Grande and sip champagne in the banquet hall. It feels slightly surreal standing in a semi-circle at one end of the massive, empty room, given that there are only four of us, five including Signore Romano who seems to feel obliged to stay to make up the numbers. It doesn't matter. There could be a thousand people here and it wouldn't have made a toss of difference to just how damn happy I am, or how happy Sam seems to be for that matter. *Gabriel was right; she fucking glows.*

"Wife?" I hold my hand out, and her shy smile is adorable. She places her fingers in my palm just as I pull her briskly into my embrace.

"Husband." She exhales the words and it sounds as sweet as the breath that kisses my waiting lips. My mouth covers hers, both gentle and possessive.

I release her bottom lip from my own with a soft plop. "First dance?"

"I'd love to." She beams and allows me to lead her to the modest space in front of the quartet. I guess the other wedding party didn't intend on dancing much, but this is perfect. The music drifts and fills the opulent room as I glide my amazing bride across the parquet flooring. Effortless and elegant, she moves with me, my slightest touch has her following my lead as if, once again, we are one.

"I can't be sorry about today, but I'm serious, if you want to do this again—"

"Shh, it's perfect." Her laugh is light and carefree, followed by the most dazzling smile.

"Not an anticlimax?"

"Hardly. Look at this place! Look at you for that matter. If you're worried about my climax…" She waggles her perfect brow suggestively, and I press my hand firmly on the small of her back and grin as she shudders, feeling my rock solid erection press into her soft form. She giggles, and it's the sweetest sound mixed with the delicate classical rendition I recognise as "Thinking Out Loud". I spin her out and back into a final dip low enough for her locks to tumble to the floor. The music fades and the Master of Ceremonies calls us to be seated for the meal. We both laugh because he looks slightly awkward, given that his announcement could've been whispered for the quiet that settled in the great room once the musicians had finished.

We are ushered into another room that has lavishly decorated tables, chairs draped in silk, tall glass vases with taller floral arrangements and so much crystal the room actually sparkles with the sunlight pouring in through the wall of windows. They are about to seat us at the top table in a line, which is ridiculous. There are only five of us for fuck sake, since Signore Romano has had a few drinks he seems more amenable to staying for the meal. Gabriel steps forward, and there is a flurry of activity, and a smaller, more intimate and appropriate table is laid in the bay of the centre window, overlooking one of the smaller canals.

"Much better." Gabriel announces and we all take our seats.

Sam is happy to eat her meal one-handed because I'm reluctant to relinquish my hold. I would have seated her on my lap but we might as well take advantage of the extra seat. The food is delicious and the wine flows. Still, this isn't a traditional wedding, and I find my tolerance for sharing has worn thin. I'm about to drag my bride away when Gabriel interrupts my thoughts by tapping his glass as if he needs to silence a great audience.

"My wedding gift to you two, the sickeningly happy couple, is full and exclusive use of the *Ambrosia*. She will be at your complete disposal. As you know, I leave in the morning, but you are welcome to start your stay tonight. You can sail back to the UK or around the Mediterranean for your honeymoon. The choice is yours." He clinks his Champagne flute against mine and against Sam's glass of orange juice, to seal his generous offer.

"Really?" Sam looks to me for my reaction. Hell, cruising in that yacht anywhere would be fine by me, even better now that I know Gabriel will no longer be breathing down my neck.

"My pleasure, Sam." Gabriel takes her hand and kisses the back. I take note and a good deal of pleasure from the fact that he no longer needs to correct himself with his choice of words when addressing my wife.

"That is very kind, Gabriel. We'll get our things packed and bring them over tonight."

"Nonsense, my man will do that. The *Ambrosia* is yours. I have a prior engagement tonight and leave at dawn, so I will say my farewells now, if you don't mind." He places his glass on the table and grabs his jacket from the back of a chair.

"I don't." The smile on my face is meant to soften the clipped delivery. Gabriel laughs, so I know he didn't take offence.

"Thank you, Gabe, for everything." Sam swings her slim arms around Gabriel's neck, taking him by surprise, evinced by the arch of his brow and the rod-like stiffness in his back. His meaty arms quickly wrap around her waist, and he squeezes. I bite back the jealous wave rolling in my gut. She may have a great deal to thank him for, but I still don't trust the charming fucker. I tug her out of his hold and watch as his brows wriggle with mischief. I'm so right about him.

"Okay, beautiful, let's go and make the most of Gabriel's kind offer, shall we?" I shake Gabriel's hand and pull her away. She's waving and skipping along to keep up with my long strides. I have had enough sharing to last me a lifetime. Now she's truly mine, I just want to bury myself, consume and dive into her warm, silky body and not come up for air. I scoop her into my arms when I reach the entrance to the Palazzo.

"What are you doing?" She giggles and throws her head back with a bright, infectious smile.

"It's tradition to carry my bride over the threshold."

"Into our home, not out of the wedding venue." There's a hint of ridicule in her words, though she doesn't shift in my arms to break free.

"Can't be too careful." I hoist her into a firmer grip and step over the entrance doorway.

"You're an idiot." She shakes her head with affectionate exasperation.

"Yes, but I'm your idiot."

"Yes. Yes you are." I drop my head so she can kiss me, her soft smile making it almost impossible for her to pucker up. Almost.

I walk us the entire way from the Palazzo, through the narrow streets, across San Marco square—much to the delight of the crowd—all the way to the *Ambrosia*. My stride doesn't falter and my arms don't even tire. I feel like fucking Hercules now she's really mine.

Sam directs me to her suite and I kick the door wide and gently lay her on the bed. Something catches my eye in the crook of my arm, a dark spot on my white shirt. I left my jacket back at the Palazzo as it was too hot with the walk I had planned, but I don't remember catching myself on anything sharp.

Sam suddenly groans, a strained and ugly discord slicing the perfect moment. The blood on my sleeve seems to be dripping onto Sam. No that's not right, the blood is coming from Sam; large dark red, almost black spots start to appear just where Sam is cupping herself, doubled over in agony.

"Jason!" Her cry is almost silent as pain seems to rip through her, stealing the oxygen needed to make a sound.

"Sam, what's wrong?" Even as I say the words her eyes glaze over, tears fall freely, and I know the answer before she mouths the words.

"Our baby."

EPILOGUE

Four Years Later

"Jesus, you're a pussy…A little bit of pain and you're screaming like a big girl." He wipes my brow will a cool damp cloth.

"I swear to God, Leon, I will rip your bollocks off if you make one more reference to how I'm handling pain. Where the hell is Jason? This is all his fault!" I groan the last word, which ends in an excruciating plea for more relief. The nurse looks kindly but fails to deliver any such help.

"Miss Sinclair…" The nurse pauses to take in the details of my chart.

"Missus," I puff out through gritted teeth. "It's Mrs Sinclair, but put that in pencil because it will be motherfucking Miss if he doesn't show up soon." I pant with barely contained vitriol.

Leon dares to defend my absent husband. "You're early, Sam. He wouldn't have gone if he thought you would blow. He's not left your side since you found out you were pregnant again, not after last time, so cut the guy some slack."

"Traitor!" I snarl and shuffle to all fours to try and get some relief. Nothing helps. I want Jason. I just want Jason.

I bury my head in my hands and rock, bracing myself for another contraction. Jason had left to pick up Roman. Today was the dress rehearsal for his first nativity play at nursery school, and Jason had volunteered to help. The school has lousy mobile reception. I told him to go. I wasn't due for three weeks, and if this baby was anything like me, it was never going to be early. But oh no, it's going to be just like Jason, who's never late, except for now.

"Ahhh… Oh God, please, for the love of all that's holy, give me some drugs!" I groan out my garbled plea just as the door bursts open and tears fill my eyes.

"You fucking bastard! You did this!" I growl. His face flashes from relief to concern and settles on shock at my venomous attack. I grit my teeth. "Where's Roman? Please don't tell me he just heard his mum curse like a sailor when I haven't so much as whispered the f-word in three years." I can't believe this is worrying me with the pain that's literally tearing my body in two, yet it does.

Three years ago last month Jason and I finally breathed a huge fucking sigh of relief when Roman was born, fit and healthy, and bang on time.

"She's not handling the pain very well, and she's only six centimetres, so you're in for the long haul, buddy." Leon walks up to Jason and slaps him on the shoulder. "I'm tagging out. Gonna go wash my ears out," he quips. "Where's the little munchkin?"

"He's at the nurses' station with his nana and gramps. Couldn't get him past without all the hugging and cheek pinching. Kinda like his old man that way." Jason shakes Leon's hand and stands there like he's just shooting the breeze.

"I'll take him home with me, if you want. Charlie's cooking spaghetti. On second thought, we'll get take out." They both laugh at Leon's lame-ass joke.

"Oh please, carry on guys, don't mind me!" I growl, my tone bordering on feral with the slight snarl.

"Yeah, maybe take him back to our place and stay there, if that's okay? I think Mum and Dad will want to stay, and I don't want to have to wake him up to bring him home when I'm done here. Think you're right about a long night." He chances a glance at me, and if I could move, he would be in so much trouble for that flip remark.

"Okay, you got it. Catch you later, baby!" Leon salutes on his way out.

I grimace because it's all I can do right then; however, when I catch my breath, I yell, "Fucking coward!"

Leon steps back to me and kisses my sweat-covered brow. He offers a kind smile that I fail to acknowledge. "Good luck, babe. You can do this. You are strong like bull." He wipes my wet hair free from my face and turns to leave.

"Oh God!" I cry out and Jason is at my side. His hands hover. He doesn't know which bits are okay to touch. I meet his eyes, only my vision blurs with the tears.

"You're doing so well, beautiful." His voice is firm and calm. I feel instantly better with him beside me, but the pain is too much.

"It really hurts, Jason." I sniff with a sad sob when the contraction ebbs enough for me to speak.

"I know baby, but you are amazing. You are stronger than any woman I know. You are stronger than most men. You got this. Remember last time, you swallowed all that pain for another six long months and gave birth to the most amazing little boy out there. All the time you worried like crazy, and he's perfect, right? Just like you. Now focus on breathing through that pain and I'll massage any tension right out of you, okay?"

I nod at his words and love how his focus is so intense and sure. He exudes confidence, and right now, I need every bit as I feel the seed of panic start to swell.

"Okay." A wave of pain blankets me, and I let out a heartrending howl. I know this pain, and it doesn't come from contractions.

"Not again! Jason, I'm going to lose the baby!" I sob, grab his hand, and meet the horror in his eyes, which must reflect mine.

"You're not! I said it last time and I'll say it again, Sam, you are *not* losing this baby."

His words are firm, and just like last time, I believe him. I'm terrified, yet I look into his eyes and believe every word. I give a sharp nod, then crumple.

"The pain is different," I gasp. Jason stretches to hit the alarm, and I can't breathe from the agony tearing up my insides. The room is suddenly filled with people—too many people. Jason is pulled away, but I won't release his hand. "Don't leave me." I feel the icy cold liquid flow up my arm, then the instant soft blanket of sweet numbness covers me. I lose my vision before my hearing goes.

"I don't care. If you take her without me and she dies, you're next!" My lips are numb but I think they would be smiling with approval. My man…he won't leave me. He saved me, he saved Roman, and now, he will save this baby too.

My mouth is so dry, and my chest feels like it's been in a vice. I struggle to sit up and freeze with the pain. I no longer have my bump. I look over to see Jason asleep in the chair. My eyes quickly dart around the room and find there is no baby. *Oh my God! Please no.* I feel the tears instantly soak my face, so many tears I can't keep them silent. I don't want to wake Jason. I can't bear to look and see the loss in his dark brown eyes. I try to hold the sobs back with the bed sheet wedged at my mouth, but it doesn't work. Jason is at my side with the very first whimper.

"Shh, shh, Sam…Hey, beautiful, why are you crying? Are you in pain?" He strokes my hair and wipes my face dry with his palm but there are too many tears.

"Our baby?" I splutter, devastation in my voice.

"Is doing fine. The little lady is in NICU but she's fucking perfect, Sam, just like her brother. You were amazing." He wraps his arms around me and I fall. I can't hold anything back. I sob with relief. I sob with joy. I just sob. "Hey, hey, come on, beautiful. We'll go see her together, okay?" He kisses my head and I hold him a little tighter, as if my life depended on it, on him.

"I thought—" I swallow the dry lump, but can't speak.

"I know, baby, I know. And if you hadn't told me you felt something was wrong…" He shakes his head and pushes the dark thoughts away for both of us. "You did tell me, and that precious amount of time saved you both. I stayed with you the whole time. I held your hand and watched the doctor lift her from your body. I was too fucking scared to breathe until they told me you were going to be fine." He cups my face in his large, sure hands, and his soft lips kiss away the tears that are still falling. His gaze is so raw, intense, and pure it pierces my very core. I feel him in my soul. His minty breath whispers over my face. "I held her for a brief moment, and she's perfect, Sam. She's fucking perfect."

"She?" I sniff back the last of the fearful tears, swallowing them as Jason's words finally take a comforting hold. We had scans only we didn't want to know. I wanted to be surprised. I didn't realise my surprise would be that my baby was alive.

"Let's go see her, yeah?" Jason's face lights up with obvious pride and I feel overwhelmed and start to cry again. "Yes, I think you need to see her right now." He kisses my head and disappears, briefly retuning with a wheelchair. I feel like a hot mess, but I can still walk. I push myself up and wince at the tight pinch and pull across my lower abdomen.

"No arguments, Sam. I'd carry you myself but apparently that's frowned upon." He winks, and I reluctantly let him lift me into to chair. It hurts like a fresh hell just to sit upright. I'll save the agony of standing and walking for another day.

We pass through some double doors, and at the end of the long corridor, I recognise Leon with his nose pressed against the glass holding Roman, the other light of my life, in his arms. Jason leans down to whisper as he continues to push me forward.

"They have stayed there the whole time. They wanted to keep guard until you came." He kisses my cheek and I lean into his touch. Leon turns and flashes a wide, tired smile.

"Hey babe...you did good." He strides toward me and kisses my other cheek. Roman's little cheeky face beams with the cutest chubby smile and he flails his arms, wriggling in Leon's hold.

"Mummy, I have a baby!" he squeals and lunges for me, but Leon holds him high enough for Jason to swoop in and intercept my gorgeous little miracle before he lands in my tender lap. It kills me not to hold him, though he'd not like to see me howl in agony when he jumps around like he always does. That boy has permanent ants in his pants.

My wedding night was the stuff of nightmares, emergency helicopter rides, transfusions, and six months of bedrest, but despite the bleeding and the godawful pain I didn't lose him. He was born in late September and looks just like his daddy. I had a caesarean because the doctors were worried a natural birth would not go so well and because of the first pregnancy trauma I had another one booked this time. The doctors were right, only I didn't hold on long enough to avoid this particular emergency.

"So I've heard, baby boy." I ruffle his tousled locks and kiss him before Jason lifts him back into his arms. I turn my head, smiling at my boys. "Would kinda like to see for myself though." Jason winks and has spun me round and is backing us through the door to the neonatal unit. Roman's now balanced and giggling on his shoulders. Leon follows and falls into step beside me.

Jason parks me beside the incubator with the tiny pink baby with a thick shock of dark brown hair and a nappy that looks set to fall from her tiny body if she moves. She has just one wire with a pad on her chest but she looks perfect. A nurse appears and smiles kindly.

"Hello, my name is Angela, you must be Mum." She pauses, only I don't respond. I'm still dazed that the tiny bundle in front of me is our baby. "Would you like a cuddle?"

"Yes." Leon says at the same time I timidly answer.

"I don't want to hurt her. If she needs to be in there that's fine I can just watch. If that's okay?" I can feel my eyes fill with tears, but I'm not sad. If I have to wait a day, a month to hold her, I don't care. She's alive and she's ours, and that makes me the luckiest woman in the world.

"Oh she's a strong little one, and you won't hurt her. She's only in here for a little extra observation. I think you'll be able to take her back with you in a day or two," Angela explains, all the while unclipping the cable and wrapping my baby's little body tight in a blanket. She scoops her up and hands her to my waiting arms. I'm a riotous mix of nerves and terror. Is this normal? Yes, I remember the exact same feeling holding Roman for the first time and thinking the same thing. *She's so small.*

"I was terrified when I held her the first time too." Jason kisses my cheek again and runs his little finger against our daughter's tightly fisted hand.

"Me too," Leon confesses.

"When did you hold her?" Jason queries, his expression looks like thunder and I swear I feel the room temperature drop.

"I've been standing guard and they sort of assumed I was the dad." Leon shrugs lightly.

"Sort of assumed?" Jason narrows his eyes with suspicion and Leon has the grace to shift under his scrutiny.

"Well, they asked if I was the dad, and I didn't deny it. I just said that I'd love her like my own. Which, if this little guy is anything to go by, is the truth." He ruffles Roman's mop of dark hair, and I smile. My heart is fit to burst as it takes on a little more love for my friend. "It's okay, they probably think we're have some sort of weird polygamous thing going on," Leon quips, flashing me a playful wink. Jason growls but I shush him. Jason never asked for a paternity test even when it was very clear Roman wasn't Leon's, though after a year, I paid to have it done. I knew it no longer made a difference. Still, I was so confident Jason was Roman's father he deserved the certainty.

"Tell me this is real," I whisper.

"This is real, beautiful." He slides Roman off his shoulders and onto the ground. He crouches until his face is millimetres from mine.

"Kiss me." He instantly covers my lips with a kiss that is both tender and proprietary.

"Tell me again." My lips are swollen from his kiss, and my smile is spread wide across my face.

"This is very real, Mrs Sinclair. You are my wife, this is our adorable son, and this is our perfect baby girl." His clarification is absolute.

"What's her name? Unless you really do want me to keep calling her little Leona." Leon wisely steps back with his hands up.

"You haven't?" My words convey a warning. He shrugs and gives a wolfish grin. I narrow my eyes, then turn to Jason. "So what's her name?"

"I thought you liked Mads?" He looks from me to our daughter. Her tiny dark features and light olive skin are a carbon copy of her older brother, just a fraction more petite.

"When I thought it was a boy maybe. Feels a bit masculine for such a pretty face." I lift her higher in my arms to kiss the soft fluff of dark hair and sniff her perfect baby smell.

"Little Leona it is then." Leon winks at me, and I chuckle when he winks at Jason before turning and leaving us alone.

"Madeline isn't masculine, even as Mads or Maddie or whatever nickname she ends up with. She's an angel and beautiful just like her mum."

"Madeline. I like it. She's perfect, Jason." My eyes well.

"You all are. I'm a very lucky man." He wipes the fat tears that won't stop falling.

"I was thinking the exact same thing." I lean in, and Jason covers my mouth with his sweet, soft lips.

"I'm glad I was wrong." I sniff back the tears and flash my brightest smile at my husband.

"Wrong?" Jason sounds more incredulous than curious. I chuckle.

"I said people like us didn't get the happy ever after. I'm very glad I was very wrong," I whisper.

"People like us, get an extraordinary happy ending, beautiful." There is nothing PG about Jason's grin. This super warm room just got a little hotter.

THE END

Other Books by Dee

The Choices Trilogy

Never a Choice
Always a Choice
The Only Choice

Never 1.5 (A Valentine Novella)

Ethan's Fall
(Can be read as a stand-alone)

Wanted: Wife 4 Navy Seals

The Games Duet
Wicked Little Games
Twisted Little Games

ABOUT THE AUTHOR

I met my husband when I was sixteen and I feel for him because there is no way I am the same person he fell in love with but after twenty ahem... something years perhaps I'm not so bad. He now has a wife that can name her favourite porn star...research of course, never says no...and knows a thing or two about ...probably too much ;). He may not 'get' what I do but he is a little more tolerant of the voices in my head because now they appear on paper. I love, love writing and hope to be able to do this until I am very old and grey...growing old disgracefully..and dee-spicably, always...xdee

Stalk me On

Facebook
Twitter
Book + Main
Instagram

Join my reader group...it's not all books, I have giveaways on Fridays and never a day goes by without some sexy shenanigans
The Chosen Ones

If you haven't already signed up to my newsletter now is a good time. I don't spam but you are the first to learn of new releases, freebies and extras
Click here for my: Newsletter

Printed in Great Britain
by Amazon

58243577R00378